Crime
at
Christmas

SEXTON BLAKE INVESTIGATES...

Crime at Christmas

BY GWYN EVANS

HOWARD BAKER

London

CRIME AT CHRISTMAS

Gwyn Evans/Edwy Searles Brooks

ISBN: 0 7030 0058 6

*Greyfriars Press Books are published by
Howard Baker Press Ltd.,
27a Arterberry Road, London, S.W.20, England
Printed in Great Britain by
Per Fas Printers Ltd., of Croydon, Surrey.*

About the authors:

GWYN EVANS

Gwyn Evans (r.n. Gwynfil Arthur Evans) was born in Port Madoc, N. Wales, in 1899, the son of a Welsh Anglican clergyman. His great-aunt was the famous George Eliot. It was said by his Fleet Street contemporaries that 'a book about the colourful character Gwyn Evans is long overdue', but an expert on Blake lore summed it up admirably when he remarked that Evans never created in his stories anyone as remarkable as himself.

It was in April, 1924, that his first Sexton Blake story appeared in the *Union Jack.* It was followed quickly by many more, as his popularity grew by leaps and bounds. In December 1925, came the first of those delightful Christmas novels for which he became truly famous.

Indeed, a Christmas *Union Jack* without a Gwyn Evans story was not really Christmas to his devotees.

His tragically early death in 1938 deprived the Sexton Blake saga of one of its finest chroniclers.

EDWY SEARLES BROOKS

Edwy Searles Brooks was born in Hackney, London, in 1889, the son of a Congregational minister who was a well-known political writer for 'The Times' and leading magazines of the day.

He was one of the best-known contributors to the *Union Jack*, and wrote many Sexton Blake stories. One of his most famous characters was Waldo the Wonderman, but Brooks was also a well-known writer of school-story fiction for boys. During the 1930's, he was able to make the transition to detective fiction completely, with an ease which in itself was a tribute to the excellence of his writing. Among his pseudonyms was 'Berkeley Gray' and 'Victor Gunn', under which he won world readership. He died suddenly in December, 1965, but his work, containing suspense, humour and thrills, is still widely read.

SPECIAL XMAS NUMBER of the

UNION JACK 2ᴰ

THE MYSTERY OF
Mrs BARDELL'S XMAS
PUDDING

—a *real* Christmas Story and a *real* Detective Story, too!
featuring SEXTON BLAKE, Inspector COUTTS, and SPLASH PAGE. Complete in this issue.

The Xmas Round Table

GATHER round, everybody! It's a jolly party at the Round Table this week.

The old saying and the calendar are in perfect agreement on one point at least—Christmas comes but once a year. And now that that joyous feast is upon us, let's enter into the spirit of the season and begin to enjoy ourselves!

First and foremost, may this Christmastide for you and yours be overflowing with happiness, and by that same token serve but to herald the coming of a glad New Year. To all of my reader-friends, at home and abroad, young and old, I extend my greetings in this ineffectual type, and only wish I could do it personally.

I do, indeed feel that you are all my friends. Sexton Blake and the Old Paper which goes on from week to week are a bond of union between us. That is our common meeting-ground, the evidence of our mutual taste; and so long as you can find a pleasure in these pages, for so long is it my pleasure to serve you and to provide a weekly feast of fiction which, as so many of you tell me, makes Thursdays so long between.

So, in the immortal words of Tiny Tim, quoted by our own Sexton Blake in this week's story: "God bless us, every one!" May the Christmas of 1925 live in your memories as an outstanding Christmas amongst many such! And may the troubles of 1926, if any, refrain from casting their shadows before!

As regards the immediate present, I think I am justified in claiming that you will enjoy this week's Christmas fare. I have been at some pains to obtain for you what I believe is a really unique yarn. I feel certain that there cannot be another story of this kind now on sale—a perfect blend of the spirit of Christmas and —if I may coin the word—detectivity.

But I will refrain from enlarging on it; the yarn itself will be more convincing than I, and even a glimpse at the opposite page will show you what to expect. So get in a quiet place where you will not be distracted, and plunge into this treat that is now set before you.

When you turn to the Supplement you will find that the Christmas appeal has not been confined to Sexton Blake alone. "The Copper's Christmas" gives us a peep behind the scenes at the revelry of Robert, and "The Riddle of Oscar Slater" recalls a mystery of seventeen Christmases ago. Even our "Law Talk" article has burgeoned forth under the spell of the season, and reveals to us some very interesting stuff about the laws of old-time Yules.

All in all, I think you will agree that this Special Christmas Number is worthy of the "U. J.'s" high traditions. There is only one way, I must admit, in which it might have been better. The quality cannot be bettered. But, you may say, we might have had more quantity; we might have had a Christmas Double Number.

In order to forestall possible questions on this point, I will say now that this suggestion has not been overlooked. There were insurmountable obstacles, however, of various sorts, technical chiefly, which put the idea altogether out of the realm of possibilities.

Nevertheless, I know you will be pleased with what has been done within the limits of the normal size, and realise that, if quantity is impossible, quality goes a very long way to make up for it.

As it is, this week's issue is packed to capacity, which reminds me that the announcement of the 4d. Library books which was to have been repeated this week has been omitted to make room for story matter. That being so, I take the opportunity of reminding you that our companion books are still on sale, and that, when you want additional reading matter this month, make a point of remembering the existence of the "Sexton Blake 4d. Library," likewise the "Boys' Friend" and the "Schoolboys'" Libraries.

And now a word in conclusion. Mr. Reece next week (see page 26), and Nirvana the week after, in a really great Christmas-week yarn. You may confidently expect that these, together with this present magnificent yarn of "Mrs. Bardell's Pudding," will be the last perfect touch in the attainment of what we all wish ourselves—a very Happy Christmas!

Your Editor

ONE THOUSAND POUNDS *FOR TWELVE RESULTS* FREE!

SCOTTISH AND IRISH READERS MAY ENTER.

👉 **YOU CAN USE THIS COUPON WITHOUT CUTTING INTO STORY-MATTER.**

One Thousand Pounds will be paid to the competitor whose forecast of the results of all the matches on this coupon is correct, or most nearly correct.

The coupon contains twelve matches to be played on **SATURDAY, DECEMBER** 19th, and

THE WAY TO WIN £1,000

is to strike out, **IN INK,** the names of those teams which you think will lose. If, in your opinion, any match or matches will be drawn, you should strike out the names of **BOTH** teams.

Coupons, which must not be enclosed with efforts in other competitions, must be addressed to:

UNION JACK, FOOTBALL No. 9,

7-9, Pilgrim Street, Ludgate Hill, London, E.C.4 (Comp.), and must reach that address not later than the first post on **FRIDAY, DECEMBER 18th, 1925.**

RULES WHICH MUST BE STRICTLY ADHERED TO.

1. All forecasts must be made on coupons taken from this journal, or from any of the issues of the journals which contain the competition offer.

2. Any alteration or mutilation of the coupon will disqualify the effort. When more than one effort is submitted, coupons must not be pinned or in any other way fastened together.

3. If any match or matches on the coupon should be abandoned, or full time is not played for any reason, such match or matches will not be considered in the adjudication.

4. In the event of ties the prize will be divided, but no competitor will be awarded more than one share of the prize.

5. No correspondence will be allowed, neither will interviews be granted.

6. It is a distinct condition of entry that the Editor's decision shall be accepted as final and legally binding in all matters concerning this competition.

7. All entries must be sent through the post, and any received after the first post on **FRIDAY, DECEMBER 18th,** will be disqualified. No responsibility can be accepted for efforts lost, mislaid, or delayed. Proof of posting will not be accepted as proof of delivery. Unstamped or insufficiently stamped efforts will be refused.

Coupons from "Family Journal," "Home Companion," "Woman's World," "Pictorial Magazine," "Boys' Realm," "Football and Sports Favourite," "Sports Budget," "Answers," and "All Sports Weekly," may also be used. Employees of the proprietors of these journals are not eligible to compete.

U.J.
FOOTBALL COMPETITION No. 9.

Matches played on **SATURDAY, DECEMBER** 19th.

Closing Date, **FRIDAY, DECEMBER** 18th, 1925.

CARDIFF CITY	v. BURNLEY
BURY	v. WEST HAM UTD.
SHEFFIELD UTD.	v. LIVERPOOL
SUNDERLAND	v. ASTON VILLA
W. BROMWICH A.	v. MANCHESTER U.
BRADFORD CITY	v. FULHAM
CLAPTON ORIENT	v. MIDDLESBROUGH
DARLINGTON	v. SWANSEA TOWN
HULL CITY	v. WOLVERHAMPTON W.
ABERDARE ATH.	v. BRISTOL RVRS.
CRYSTAL PALACE	v. BOURNEMOUTH & B.A.
WATFORD	v. EXETER CITY

I enter FOOTBALL COMPETITION No. 9 in accordance with the Rules and Conditions as announced, and agree to accept the Editor's decision as final and legally binding.

Name ....

Address ....

9

THE MYSTERY OF Mrs BARDELL'S XMAS PUDDING!

——or, to be quite precise, Mrs. Bardell's sister's Xmas Pudding.

A Yuletide Tragi-Comedy in Nine ∴ Chapters ∴

THE FIRST CHAPTER.
Santa Claus—Alias Sexton Blake.

"Good King Wenceslas looked out
On the feast of Stephen,
When the snow lay round about,
Deep and crisp and e-e—ven."

TINKER'S boyish, but not unmelodious, voice carolled gaily as he entered Sexton Blake's cosy consulting room in Baker Street. He grinned cheerfully at the famous detective, who was skimming through his extensive morning mail, in the intervals of doing justice to Mrs. Bardell's excellently grilled kidneys and bacon.

"Hooray, guv'nor! It's Christmas Day to-morrow, and to-night we're going to——"

"You amaze me, Tinker," interposed Blake, with a faint, satiric twinkle in his steel-grey eyes. "However did you deduce that fact?"

Tinker, not a whit abashed, chuckled, and in a passably good imitation of the celebrated detective's voice, he expounded slowly.

"By the calendar on the wall, which bears the mystic numerals two and four, with the cryptic letters D-E-C-, it is safe to assume that to-day is the twenty-fourth of December. This fact is supported by the date on the copy of the 'Daily Radio' propped up by the tea-pot.

"My well-known powers of observation, allied to my deductive ability, lead me to the conclusion that Christmas is in the air. By a curious coincidence, Christmas Day falls this year, as it did last year, on the twenty-fifth of December, and it is obvious——"

"Your glimpses into the obvious, my dear Tinker, are as refreshing as Mrs. Bardell's tea. Pray pour yourself out a cup while I attend to my importunate correspondents."

Blake's mild sarcasm was quite lost on Tinker, who was feeling particularly pleased with himself—and the world in general. He attacked his breakfast with gusto, and, pushing aside his plate with a contented sigh, he studied the pages of the "Daily Radio." If any proof were needed that Christmas was near, that go-ahead newspaper supplied it.

Right across the page, in the place usually occupied by scare headlines announcing a political crisis, or sudden death, was a message of goodwill, tastefully bordered with holly and mistletoe.

"A RIGHT MERRY CHRISTMAS TO ALL OUR READERS."

Most of the front page was devoted to descriptions, vividly written, of last-minute shopping in the Christmas bazaars. There were glowing accounts of festivities planned in the great London hotels, and announcements of pantomimes for Boxing Day.

"Oh, good egg!" ejaculated Tinker, as he studied the meteorological report. "I say, guv'nor, we're going to have a real old-fashioned Christmas. It says that, owing to a depression from the north, and the falling of a couple of isobars or something, the air currents will—— Anyway, it means we're going to have snow."

Blake smiled.

"Splendid, my boy! I'm glad to hear it. You have grown dreadfully lazy of late, and a really heavy snowstorm would provide you with some much-needed exercise."

"Why, what do you mean, guv'nor—exercise?" demanded Tinker, in some bewilderment.

"Keeping Mrs. Bardell's steps clear of snow," chuckled Sexton Blake. "A small shovel and some salt are admirable substitutes for a Sandow's developer."

Tinker retired behind the pages of the "Daily Radio."

Somehow the thought of snow was not so attractive as it had been. He turned over the pages and smiled a little at a vividly written two-column article bearing the well-known initials of Derek Page, the star crime reporter of the "Daily Radio."

"I say, guv'nor," he ejaculated at length, "Comrade Splash has let himself go. There doesn't seem to be any crime about, so he's written a descriptive article on 'Christmas with the Down-and-Outs.'"

"H'm!" commented Sexton Blake, thoughtfully filling his briar. "That's rather tame work for our cyclonic friend Splash. It's almost too much to hope that the Christmas spirit of peace and goodwill has permeated the underworld."

He sighed half regretfully.

"This Christmas seems to be a unique one in our history, my boy," he said quietly. "For the first time for many years we are care-free.

"Apart from the slight affair of Henry Murgatroyd's missing buhl cabinet, which can easily stand over, there is nothing to interfere with a thoroughly cheery Yule."

Tinker laughed.

"By Jove, we deserve it, guv'nor," he said heartily. "I think it's a great idea of yours to stay at home for Christmas. Mrs. Bardell is as happy at the thought of being able to cook us a real, old-fashioned Christmas dinner, and I bet Splash and poor old Coutts are bucked!"

Blake smiled whimsically and shuffled a small pile of envelopes. "More invitations, Tinker," he said. "Declined with thanks. Lord Oakleigh wants us to spend a week at Oakleigh Manor with him, Sir Anthony Trent has a jolly house-party at Garth Towers, and sends a most pressing invitation. Remember Professor Anstruther?"

Tinker nodded.

"A good sort, the professor. We had a lark solving the Great Waxwork Mystery at his place. Does he want us to go to Normouth?"

Sexton Blake nodded.

"I'm afraid they must all be disappointed. Home is the best place at Christmas-time, my lad, and I doubt if in all England there is a better cook than our excellent Mrs. Bardell."

Tinker nodded cordially.

He was looking forward to Christmas at home. Originally it had been Blake's intention to spend the holiday quietly at Baker Street, but somehow he had learned that Splash Page of the "Radio" was at a loose end, and had invited the newspaperman as his guest over the festival.

Then unexpectedly Detective-

Inspector Coutts, of Scotland Yard, lugubriously reported that his wife had been compelled to leave for the Midlands to nurse her mother through a bad bout of pneumonia, and the C.I.D. man was faced with a dreary bachelor Christmas at his Streatham home.

"Let's make a foursome!" Tinker had suggested, and thus it transpired that Mrs. Bardell had sallied forth to Farringdon Market to buy a turkey large enough to satisfy the healthy appetites of four people. The good soul was in her element. Her one abiding regret in life was that, owing to the exigencies of Blake's profession, she had seldom an opportunity to show him what she could really do in the culinary line.

But now Mrs. Bardell had come into her own.

"What time are they coming, guv'nor?" demanded Tinker. "I'd better hike to Covent Garden for some holly and mistletoe to make the place look festive."

"An excellent idea, Tinker. I expect them between five and six this evening. There are no newspapers to-morrow, so Splash, for once, can have an evening free."

Tinker skimmed through the remaining portion of the article, and then whistled.

"See this, guv'nor? Splash has been doing Limehouse, Poplar, and Pennyfields. He's discovered an anonymous old boy who seems to have been a giddy philanthropist—a sort of incognito Santa Claus. Listen to this!"

He read out the paragraph in his clear young voice:

"'No, the Christmas spirit is not dead, despite the cynicism and materialism of the present century, with its machine-made hotel revels and artificial gaieties.

"'Here, in the slums of the East End, are a thousand families as poor as Bob Cratchit's, but as truly happy. Christmas, to them, is what it was to the great master of Christmas, Charles Dickens—a good time, a kind, loving, merry time, when people think more charitably of each other, when the cares of the grey years are swept aside for a brief two days, and there is peace on earth to men of good-will.

"'In the poorest homes the magic of Christmas has transformed the drabness into something bright and wonderful; the kiddies know that, this year, at least, Santa Claus will not pass them by.

"'Limehouse, Pennyfields, and the poorer district of the East End are full of rumours about the identity of the generous donor who has presented lavish gifts of coal and food—and not forgotten the kiddies' toys. Many a harassed housewife blesses the unknown Santa Claus who mysteriously sent her the necessaries for a 'Merry Christmas.'

"'None are forgotten. I interviewed many poor women, many of them, alas, wives of criminal husbands, left to fend for themselves with large families, while the husband languished behind prison bars. To them the gifts of the mysterious benefactor were Heaven-sent. They had abandoned all hope, innocent victims of the just but relentless law of Society, until a day ago——'"

"Splash Page is an interfering old busybody!" interrupted Sexton Blake. "If the donor wished to remain anonymous why on earth should the papers try to discover his identity?"

There was a touch of asperity in the criminologist's tone, and Tinker glanced up in some surprise.

"Why, guv'nor! I think he's a deuced sporting old boy, this philanthropist.

It's dashed hard luck on a crook's wife and kids, guv'nor. That's why I think this chap's different to the ordinary run of charity-mongers. He seems to have given where it was most needed, and I——"

"We need some evergreens," cut in Blake quietly.

Tinker grinned, and reached for his cap. "Right you are, guv'nor! And, by gum, I'll make Mrs. B. kiss old Coutts under the mistletoe!"

Whistling cheerily, he donned his overcoat, and faced the crisp morning air.

After his departure Blake sat smoking thoughtfully for a while. Then, as if on a sudden impulse, he crossed over to the telephone.

"Hallo!" he called at length. "Is that the Poplar branch of the East End Charitable Association? Sexton Blake speaking."

A voice at the other end of the wire replied in the affirmative.

"Ah, Mr. Hukson," went on Blake. "I have instructed Harridges to send the—er—necessary additional parcels for distribution in Poplar. They should reach you this morning. Please add Mrs. Larson, No. 4, Lych Street, to your list. Her husband, Flash Harry Larson, was sent down for two years last sessions, and——"

"Thank you ever so much, Mr. Blake! Your generous gifts are——"

"And please take the greatest precautions to respect my anonymity," interposed the detective swiftly. "Especially as the Press seems interested. Good-morning, Mr. Hukson, and a very merry Christmas to you!"

He replaced the receiver, cutting off the secretary's profuse thanks. From the street below came the sound of childish voices singing the old, old carol:

"God rest you, merry gentlemen,
    Let nothing you dismay——"

Sexton Blake smiled and reached for a slim, leather-bound volume on his bookshelf. It was Dickens' "Christmas Carol."

Outside, there came a sudden light flurry of snowflakes, that seemed to thicken swiftly, turning the dingy grey roofs of Baker Street into dazzling parallelograms of white. The fire crackled cheerfully in the grate.

Blake gave one glance at the now thickly-falling snow. It was as if some genial giant up aloft was pouring a sauce-cup over this great plum-pudding of an earth.

Then, with a little sigh, the detective snuggled back into his saddle-bag chair and plunged into the ghostly adventures of Ebenezer Scrooge.

**THE SECOND CHAPTER.
The Curious Conduct of Roaring Bill.**

"BY Jove! Festive——what?"

Splash Page, his face aglow, his blue eyes a-sparkle as vividly as the icicles that formed beneath the snow-covered window-sills, entered Bloke's consulting-room promptly at five o'clock.

Tinker, who was perched on a ricketty step-ladder, deftly adjusting a festoon of holly over the mantelpiece, grinned cheerfully.

"'Lo, Splash, me lad! Hang on to this ladder. It wobbles like a jelly, and——"

He broke off with some alarm, as, with a prodigious effort, he recovered his balance.

Splash Page leapt to the rescue, and the holly was duly arranged in the interstices of the woodwork above the fireplace.

"Where's Blake?" queried the newspaperman, when Tinker had descended from his perilous perch.

The lad jerked his thumb in the direction of the laboratory.

"In there with his beloved stinks," he said inelegantly. "He's having a real holiday. Reading the 'Christmas Carol' all morning, then suddenly took it in his head to work out some messy chemical experiment to——"

"My Heaven!" gasped Splash Page, in mock dismay. "You don't think he's inventing a synthetic Christmas dinner, do you, Tinker? If so, I'm off! These giddy scientists, with their tabloid turkeys and plum pudding pilules—they'll be the death of me!"

Tinker laughed.

"Not on your life. I've just taken a peep at Mrs. Bardell's larder. Some turkey, my boy—a whopper. She made the Christmas pudding a week ago, and the mince-pies——" He rolled his eyes eloquently.

Splash Page flopped into a chair.

"Great idea this, Tinker. Mrs. B.'s taken my suit-case into the spare room. Is old Coutts staying, too?"

Tinker nodded.

"Yes. He's a grass-widower. His missus won't be back for a week, so we'll be a cheery crew."

"I wonder if he'll hang his stocking up?" chuckled Splash Page. "It'd be a lark to present him with a new pair of handcuffs, and a nice pocket finger-print outfit.

"Hallo, Blake, dear old sleuth," he added suddenly, as the tall, spare figure of the criminologist entered soundlessly from the laboratory.

Sexton Blake smiled.

"Welcome, Splash! How's the 'Radio'?"

"'Pon my soul," ejaculated the newspaperman, "he's still wearing that foul garment!" He pointed to Blake's beloved red dressing-gown, a woeful affair, patched, and discoloured with the acid stains of countless chemical experiments.

"I'm hanged if I don't get you a new one as a Christmas present!" ejaculated Splash. "It's not too late to change——" He broke off in some confusion.

"Thank you, my dear fellow, but I don't really need one. There are still years of wear in this," said Blake, with an affectionate glance at the sleeve of his gown.

Tinker chuckled.

"'Sno use, Splash. He won't part with his glad rags. It's his mascot, you know. Hallo, there's a ring at the bell! Sounds like Coutts. Mrs. Bardell's got a visitor, so I'd better let him up."

He crossed over to the door, and returned a few minutes later, followed by the burly figure of Detective-Inspector Coutts, of Scotland Yard. The C.I.D. man was dressed in his neatly cut reefer of Navy blue, and though he had abandoned his overcoat to the hall-stand, he still clung like grim death to his hard bowler-hat.

"Hallo, Coutts!" called Splash cheerfully. "How d'you like being a temporary bachelor again?"

The Yard man grunted.

"Pretty dull at home," he grumbled.

"What precisely did you want to see me about, Mrs. Bardell?" "The pudden—the Christmas plumpudden!" she replied in a sepulchral whisper.

(See overleaf.)

"Jolly decent of you, Blake, to take pity on me. Careful of that hat, Tinker, my boy," he added, as the lad finally succeeded in impounding the headgear. "It's a new bowler. Missus gave it me for Christmas."

Blake crossed over to the sideboard, and made pleasant, tinkling music with a decanter and glasses. Outside, the soft winter twilight changed to darkness; the lamps from the street standards sprang into yellow light that gilded the slushy snow underfoot in Baker Street into bars of gold.

"Draw the curtains, Tinker!" commanded Blake. "Throw another log on the fire, Splash. Coutts, there's your favourite chair."

An atmosphere of cosiness and festivity crept almost insensibly into the famous consulting-room, the walls of which had echoed so often to many strange and bizarre stories since Blake first took residence in Baker Street.

The firelight rose and fell, throwing strange, fantastic shadows on the ceiling, and tinting the dark-green holly leaves with gold.

"Touching picture of famous manhunters at home," bantered Splash Page, as he sipped Blake's excellent pre-war whisky with keen appreciation. "It is really most considerate of our crook friends to declare an armistice over Christmas. Don't you think so, Coutts?"

The Scotland Yard man laughed shortly.

"Don't you believe it, Splash! There's plenty of light-fingered gentry at work in the big stores, making sure of their Merry Christmas all right. The big criminals, I admit, seem to be lying low, but the small fry are still active. I'll have a crop of shop-lifting cases to deal with after the holidays," he murmured pessimistically.

"Don't," pleaded the newspaperman, with a groan—"don't, I beg of you, speak of work! We're on holiday, and no power on earth will shift me from this luxurious chair and excellent whisky. Tell me, Blake, while we're on the subject. What's your experience of Christmas crimes? D'you think they are fewer round about this time?"

Blake chuckled.

"Are you interviewing me for the 'rag,' Splash?" he bantered. "It sounds very like work to me."

Inspector Coutts guffawed.

"One to you, Blake! I never saw the like of these newspaper fellows. They talk shop, shop, nothing but beastly shop all the time. They can never forget their horrible profession. I'm willing to bet that the one thing Splash regrets about his own funeral is that he won't be in a position to write it up. I remember, when I was a sergeant down in Battersea, a crook of the name of Soho Sam ran foul of a nark. This chap——"

"Who's talking shop now?" interposed Tinker blandly.

Blake and the newspaperman chuckled, and the detective added:

"Personally, I'm all in favour of a man talking shop, whatever his profession, Coutts. It's the one thing he really knows well, and the one thing he is interested and interesting in. With us, each in our several ways, crime is the all-absorbing topic, and——"

He broke off suddenly, as a tap sounded at the door.

"Come in!" called Sexton Blake quietly, and a moment later the short, rather podgy figure of Mrs. Bardell stood blinking on the threshold.

"Yes, Mrs. Bardell?" asked the detective courteously. "What's the matter?"

His housekeeper smiled at Inspector Coutts, for whom she had an affectionate regard, and bowed in a dignified fashion to Splash Page, of whom she was secretly terrified. Her mental opinion of the lark-loving newspaperman was "a young limb, like Master Tinker, only older—and worse!"

"If you please, Mr. Blake, and I 'opes as you don't mind me troubling you, but seeing you 'ad Inspector Coutts 'ere, and knowin' your fondness for problems, I made so bold as to ask your advice."

Blake rose courteously to his feet.

"Pray be seated Mrs. Bardell. I trust there's nothing wrong?" he added, drawing out a chair.

Mrs. Bardell flopped down with a sigh, and drew a deep breath.

"Which I told Mary Ann Cluppins the week before she married Cluppins, who was a water-rate collector, and very well thought of in Bermondsey on account of his whippet-racing. Which I said to 'er, 'Mark my works, no good ever came out of lettin' lodgin's to single gen'l'men,' I says, 'even with an 'usband in the 'ouse.'"

"Er—quite," Blake interposed soothingly. Mrs. Bardell was inclined to ramble a good deal before coming to the point, and it was necessary to deal firmly with her, unless one wished to be hopelessly involved in some obscure genealogical tree and the philosophies of a thrice-widowed lady.

"What, precisely, did you want to consult me about, Mrs. Bardell?"

Mrs. Bardell flushed a little. She lowered her voice, and said, in a sepulchral whisper:

"The pudden! The Christmas plumpudden!"

"The pudding?" queried Blake, with a glint of amusement in his eyes. "Surely a mere man cannot presume to advise an excellent cook like yourself on the ingredients of a Christmas pudding?"

"No, sir. Which I sees as shouldn't, there's precious few people can advise me about the ingreedgience of a pudden, be it plain, fancy, or roly-poly. I wishes on be'alf of Mary Ann Cluppins —'er being my youngest sister—to insult you perfeshionally, Mr. Blake."

With great difficulty Tinker kept a straight face.

Mrs. Bardell's cooking was impeccable, but her English was weird and wonderful.

"Dear me! What has happened to the pudding?" asked Blake, with a twinkle.

Mrs. Bardell fixed Inspector Coutts with a gaze of such intensity that the C.I.D. man shifted uneasily.

"Mr. Blake, I regret to hinform you that the Christmas pudden 'as been stolen—pinched, in a manner of speakin'."

"What!" gasped Tinker. "Somebody's purloined our pud? I say, Mrs. B., that's a bit thick! I mean, I was looking forward to that pudding!"

Mrs. Bardell beamed graciously at him.

"No, Master Tinker. I'm happy to inform you that the pudden for your Christmas dinner is safe in the larder, but in view of what 'as 'appened to my sister, I 'ave double locked the pantry to keep it from the graspin' 'ands of criminologists."

Poor Mrs. Bardell was a bit mixed. She really meant criminals, and she gazed in bewilderment as Splash Page and Coutts gave a shout of laughter.

"I am afraid I still don't understand," murmured Sexton Blake soothingly. "You say that your sister, Mrs. Cluppins, has had her Christmas-pudding stolen? It is very unfortunate, but surely——"

"I'll tell you, sir," said Mrs. Bardell hurriedly. "I was making the Christmas-puddens last week, an' I 'ad a good deal of duff left over.

"So, just as a Christmas present like, I filled a basin with wot I 'ad to spare and gave it to my sister, 'er bein' a widow this last seven year, an' dependent only on 'er lodgin'-'ouse in Rice Street, Pimlico—which I 'opes as you don't think it was wrong of me to do so."

"Certainly not, Mrs. Bardell. You are the sole arbitrator of the larder, and it was a very kindly thought on your part," said Blake quietly.

"Well," continued Mrs. Bardell, beaming a little at the compliment, "Mrs. Cluppins came to me this afternoon in a terrible state. She went to the larder as usual this mornin'. The pudden wot 'ad been lyin' on the shelf was gone. Hutterly varnished into thin hair, as the sayin' goes.

"Nacherally she was a bit cut up about it, but she didn't bargain for Cap'n Barnes. 'Roarin' Bill Barnes' 'e is called in Pimlico. She 'appened to mention the fac' that the pudden 'ad disappeared to 'im. ('E's been a lodger there on the third floor back this past twelve munce). Would you believe that he used sich langwidge as I wouldn't dare to repeat? He stormed an' raved like a madman at my sister."

"Remarkable," interjected Sexton Blake. "Captain Barnes must have been disappointed—it is obviously a very high tribute to your culinary skill, Mrs. Bardell."

The housekeeper coughed, and glanced coyly at Sexton Blake. "Well, it is, in a manner of speakin', Mr. Blake. My sister, Mrs. Cluppins, did mention as 'ow I 'ad made the pudden, but that's no occasion why 'e should shout an' rave at the pore soul. 'E 'as a dreadful voice when in a temper, and though she offered to make another pudden, 'e wouldn't listen. 'E said 'e must 'ave the missin' pudden or nothink.

"'E went on at 'er like a maniac, and the pore soul came to me to ask my advice. I offered to give 'er another pudden, but she says as 'ow the captain wouldn't look at nothin' but the fust pudden, wot ain't there, nor likely to be there.

"''Oo took the pudden, an' why, I dunno. Not knowin', can't tell, as the sayin' goes, but my sister's that terrified o' going 'ome without a pudden that I decided to ask your adwice."

Sexton Blake puffed thoughtfully at his briar.

"This Captain Barnes seems to be a remarkably opinionated person, Mrs. Bardell," he said at length. "He should be the pride of every advertising man, for he evidently knows what he wants and will not accept substitutes or imitations."

"Ask gently, but firmly, for Mrs. B.'s Christmas-pudding!" quoted Tinker, with a chuckle.

"I am afraid the only advice I can offer you, Mrs. Bardell, is to tell your sister to mollify the irascible captain with another pudding. If you have another to spare, give it to her by all means; if not, perhaps you and she could drink each other's health in a bottle of port, and provide the wherewithal for a new pudding out of this."

With a deft gesture, Sexton Blake extracted a five-pound note from his wallet and handed it to his beaming housekeeper.

"Let me know how the captain gets on, Mrs. Bardell," he added, as the housekeeper rose to go. "These old sea dogs are very fond of plum duff, you know—probably his fit of ill-temper will pass when your sister returns."

"I 'ope so, reely," said Mrs. Bardell. "I wonder 'oo could 'ave pinched that pudden? Per'aps the old willain et it 'isself. Anyway, Mr. Blake, I thank you for your adwice. Mrs. Cluppins and myself will be pleased to drink your 'ealth. If you don't mind my seein' my sister 'ome, I'll be back about seven-thirty to serve dinner, Mr. Blake."

"Certainly. That will suit admirably," responded the detective. "Convey my best wishes to your sister, and the compliments of the season."

"Thank you, sir. And 'ere's success to your criminal insinuations," said Mrs. Bardell, with dignity.

"Hold me, somebody," said Tinker, spluttering with mirth, as the door closed behind the worthy housekeeper. "Oh, my hat, guv'nor! We've been moaning that there's no Christmas crimes. Who's the master crook that pinched Mrs. Bardell's pudden?"

"Aha!" chimed in Splash Page. "I see Comrade Coutts' mighty brain at work. Is he planning a deadly campaign against the villain? Prepare to tremble, for the whole massive machinery of Scotland Yard is at his back. Think of the headlines, Coutts, old bean!

"'PERNICIOUS PUDDING PURLOINER AT PIMLICO. POLICE AND PANTRY PERIL.'"

"Stow it, Splash," said Coutts, with a grin. "Mrs. B. may be a little rambling in her English, but she's an excellent cook."

"It's very odd, you know," Sexton Blake cut in quietly. "Purely as a little mental exercise, the little problem is worth studying."

Coutts snorted.

"Great Scott! I believe Blake is taking the matter seriously!"

"Splendid!" agreed Splash Page. The subject appealed to his impish sense of humour.

"As Blake has no aversion to talking shop, let's see what we can make of the Great Pudding Problem."

"If you think I'm going to traipse to Pimlico, and leave this cheery hearth for a fool stunt, you're mistaken, my lad," said the indignant Coutts.

"Ah, no, dear old C.I.D. man," drawled the journalist. "This is an entirely armchair case, to be solved at a sitting, like a cross-word puzzle. What do you make of it, Blake? Let's all propound a theory."

Sexton Blake chuckled quietly. The great criminologist was on holiday, but he entered freely into the spirit of the thing.

"It strikes me as odd," he began. "In the first place, the theft of a pudding, though singular, is not remarkable, especially at this season of the year. What strikes me as peculiar is the conduct of this retired sea captain who rejoices in the patronymic of 'Roaring Bill Barnes.' No pudding will satisfy him but the missing one. He refuses to be cajoled or comforted. Either he is an extraordinarily obstinate man, or he has some ulterior motive."

"By Jove, guv'nor! Supposing he's after the sixpences in the pudding! He may be an Aberdeen Scotsman, and——"

A general laugh greeted this sally, and Blake's eyes twinkled.

"That is certainly an original theory, my lad. Let us proceed, then, on the assumption that the captain wanted Mrs. Bardell's pudding because of its contents, either edible or otherwise.

"Somebody must have forestalled him, hence his anger. The fact that he 'mourns, and will not be comforted,' as the Scripture has it, by any other pudding, however good, inclines me to the belief that something of value was hidden in it."

"By Jove, Blake! That's a startling theory," commented Splash Page. "I wonder if there is anything in it?"

"How can there be? Mrs. Bardell isn't likely to hide her family jewels in a pudding-basin!" retorted Coutts, a trifle testily.

Tinker laughed.

"Well, so long as our pudding isn't pinched, I don't care what happens to Roaring Bill Barnes," he said. "Gee! What a name," he added. "It sounds like one of the old-time pirates."

"Pirates! Hooray! Here's your story for you," said Splash Page. His blue eyes gleamed, as his vivid imagination set to work to weave a fantastic story about the prosaic plum-pudding. Sexton Blake leaned back in his saddle-bag chair and took a sip at his whisky-and-soda.

When Splash began to weave stories he was worth listening to. None had a greater admiration for the journalistic genius of the newspaperman than Sexton Blake; between them existed a firm friendship, forged by the links of adventure and perils shared together in odd parts of the world.

Splash Page himself was essentially a newspaper man; he worked by intuition, and a sort of uncanny sixth sense—a "nose for news," with which every journalist worthy of his name is endowed. None knew better than he how immeasurably superior in crime matters was the keen deductive ability and cold relentless logic of Sexton Blake—yet, oddly enough, each arrived at the same goal in spite of widely diverging methods.

"Pirates," repeated Splash Page. "Mind you, this is only a theory, Coutts, but it'd make a corking front-page story." He cleared his throat impressively.

"Roaring Bill Barnes was the greatest cutthroat of the Seven Seas. A swash-buckling, black-hearted, and bearded buccaneer." He paused, and Tinker murmured, with a wink:

"Go ahead, Splash."

"His name was a terror on the Spanish Main. Men called him the 'Tiger of Tobasco.' He was real hot stuff! Hundreds of innocent victims were made to walk the plank, and the treasure-chest on his pirate ship, Hellfire Helen, was filled to bursting point.

"Then, one day, even his cutthroat crew sickened of Roaring Bill's blood-thirsty infamies. They mutinied, and he was forced to flee. From his treasure-chest he took a dozen priceless rubies—loot from a rajah's crown.

"He swam through a shark-infested sea, and landed on the shore of California, where the famous sun-kissed raisins grow."

"Twopence a packet—build bonny babies!" interrupted the irrepressible Tinker. Again the newspaper man paused—this time to replenish his glass. His face was preternaturally solemn, as he continued:

"Arrived safely with his booty, Roaring Bill determined to safeguard his treasure, and a diabolical scheme entered his mind. He bought a pound of raisins, carefully removed the pips and contents, and inserted in each skin a ruby as large as a pigeon's egg.

"These he stitched up so that he could smuggle the jewels past the customs.

"Judge of his horror when he was arrested that night in trying to jump a freight train, and sentenced to thirty days without the option. Worse was to follow. His bunch of raisins was taken away from him by a warder, who gave them to his kiddie.

"The kid swapped the raisins with an Italian peanut seller for a bag of nuts, and the dago presented the raisins to his cousin, who was leaving for Europe. The cousin was too seasick to eat them, and flung them down the hold, where they landed in a crate of sultanas.

"Think of Roaring Bill's agony on being released—of his world-wide quest for his missing raisins—until finally he traced them to the wholesale grocers, and learned that Mrs. Bardell had bought them for a Christmas pudding—a pudding of rajah's rubies!"

"Incredible as the story may seem," added Splash blandly, "it is nevertheless true. Somewhere in Pimlico——"

"You ghastly old spoofer, Splash!" yelled Tinker, hurling a cushion at the newspaper man, which effectually stopped further utterance.

"Shall we scrag him, Coutts?" he demanded. The C.I.D. man grunted. "It's as true as most of his previous yarns in the 'Radio,' anyway," he grumbled.

Spluttering with laughter, Splash Page rose to his feet.

"Well, anyway, if it's not true, it ought to be!" he cried, unabashed.

Suddenly the telephone bell tinkled, and Blake crossed over to the receiver. He listened intently for a moment or two, then his face became rigidly impassive, and his eyes set in a firm, straight line.

"What's that? No. 14, Rice Street? Right. I'll be along at once, Mrs. Bardell," he said quietly.

He replaced the receiver gently, and when he turned to face the others his face was very grim.

"The time for fooling is over," he said gravely. "Mrs. Bardell has just rung me up from the Pimlico Post Office. Captain Barnes has been murdered—stabbed in the back. Our comedy has turned to tragedy."

"What!" ejaculated three voices simultaneously.

The ominous word "murder" shattered the cosy, care-free atmosphere of a moment ago, and the room seemed suddenly very chill.

The joyous revellers were now jerked back to realities—the jesters were again the calm, efficient, deadly experts of criminology.

"Go and get the Grey Panther out of the garage, Tinker, my lad!" snapped Blake. He turned to the others. "I suppose you'd like to stop here until ——"

"Not on your life," replied Splash Page and Coutts decisively. "We're coming with you, Blake. We wouldn't miss it for worlds."

THE THIRD CHAPTER.
Mrs. Cluppins Tells the Story of the Pudding.

RICE STREET is ordinarily one of the dullest and most drab streets in that dreary region of faded gentility—Pimlico.

But as Sexton Blake dexterously steered the Grey Panther past Victoria Station and Ebury Bridge, the landscape took on an aspect as cheery as a Christmas card.

The drab houses of Rice Street looked almost beautiful; their yellow-bricked ugliness was softened by the powdery snow, and from the once grey roofs icicles glinted with a myriad facets like enormous diamonds.

No. 14 proved to be the end house of the row, and Blake parked his car near the kerb. A dozen window curtains were drawn back in Rice Street, and a dozen pairs of curious eyes peered out into the gloom to find out who Mrs. Cluppins' motoring visitor could be, for thousand-guinea automobiles are as rare in Rice Street as snowballs in the Sahara.

The door opened immediately as Blake mounted the steps, and Mrs. Bardell, her face a blend of alarm and a certain pompous importance, placed a podgy finger on her lips.

"If you please, sir, will you come into the drorin'-room? My sister is——"

"Now, Mrs. Bardell," cut in Blake decisively, "I want you to answer my questions as simply and as promptly as you can. In the first place, where is the—er—body?"

"Upstairs," said the worthy dame, in a sepulchral whisper. She led the way through a gloomy hallway and up a short flight of stairs. At the door of a back room on the third floor she paused impressively.

"'E's in there, Mr. Blake—and it ain't a pretty sight. If—if you don't mind, I don't want to see it again, and——"

Sexton Blake nodded understandingly, and entered the room with a certain brisk alertness, followed by Inspector Coutts, Splash Page, and Tinker. Pedro, the great bloodhound, was left in the tonneau of the car.

In one swift, comprehensive glance, the detective took in the scene. It was only too evident that tragedy, sudden and swift, had fallen on Roaring Bill Barnes in the little third-floor bed-room in Pimlico.

Stark on the bed, with his arms flung outward, was the body of a grey-haired man clad in a blue reefer suit. From between his shoulder-blades the haft of a Swedish knife protruded, and blood welled sluggishly from the wound.

At once Blake stooped over the figure, then gasped.

"Quick, Tinker! Fetch the Divisional Surgeon. There's a slim chance for the poor fellow—there's a spark of life still left."

Tenderly as a woman Blake withdrew the knife from the wound, handling the haft gingerly with his silk handkerchief so as not to obliterate possible finger-prints.

"Hot water, Coutts—and you, Splash, find out from Mrs. Cluppins and Mrs. Bardell what happened. Hustle to it!"

It was characteristic of Blake that his orders were obeyed at once and without question. While he removed the injured man's coat and vest, Coutts hurried into the bath-room, lit the geyser, and returned in the space of five minutes with a bowl of hot water, some improvised bandages, and a towel.

Blake deftly dressed the wound, with hands as skilful as a surgeon's. He then turned the limp figure gently over on his side.

A moment later a convulsive shudder shook the burly frame—his eyelids flickered and opened, and he groaned hollowly.

"Gently does it, Captain Barnes," Blake soothed. "Don't move about. You'll be all right soon. Try not to worry, and——"

"Curse you, let me get at him! What are you doing to me?" babbled the wounded man. His gnarled hands clutched at the bedclothes, little beads of perspiration trickled through the pores of his skin, and his voice sounded hoarse and cracked.

"He—he—stabbed me, the dirty Mex!" he gasped painfully. "And the pudding, it's gone—gone!" His voice rose into a scream. "Get the pudding! Don't let 'em find it! The secret's there—it belongs to May——"

The man's voice trailed away into babbling incoherencies, as he tossed restlessly about on the bed.

"He's delirious," muttered Coutts. "What the deuce is he rambling about puddings for? Who's this woman, May——"

He broke off abruptly, as the door opened, and Tinker entered, accompanied by a short, grey-haired little man with general practitioner written all over him—from his lined, kindly face to the bulge of the stethoscope in his pocket.

"I was lucky to find Dr. Williams, guv'nor. He was at the station doing a drunks' parade," Tinker explained.

The little doctor nodded.

"A bad business, this, Mr. Blake—— Why, hallo! There doesn't seem to be much work left for me." He surveyed Blake's skilful bandage and dressing with professional interest.

"A nasty wound, but clean. Just scraped the scapula. Another half-inch, and it would have been fatal, I imagine," he said.

The doctor nodded, and felt the injured man's pulse.

"Racing badly, Mr. Blake. I'm afraid he'll be unconscious for a considerable time. I've instructed the ambulance to call. From what I can gather the blade must have penetrated the cartilage past the left clavicle——" He droned off into technicalities.

A tap on the door interrupted his explanations, and Splash Page entered.

"Well?" queried Sexton Blake.

"Lor', what a business!" ejaculated the newspaperman. "The hardest interview I've ever had. How's the patient?" He jerked his head towards the bed.

"Unconscious. It'll be touch and go, but careful nursing might pull him through," replied the detective.

"It's a rum go," commented Splash. "As far as I can make out from those semi-hysterical females downstairs, they returned here about three-quarters of an hour ago. Mrs. Cluppins, having impounded another pudding from Mrs. Bardell, ascended the stairs to make her peace with the irascible skipper.

"She knocked at the door—got no reply. Becoming alarmed, she turned the handle, and saw the poor devil lying face downward on the bed—with a knife-blade between his shoulders. She gave one shriek and flopped down in a dead faint.

"Mrs. Bardell rushed upstairs, realised in a glance what had happened, and, after reviving her sister, dashed out to the telephone at the grocer's shop at the corner, and rang you up. That's all either of them know."

"H'm!" muttered Coutts, pursing his lips thoughtfully. "That's not much to go on." He squared his shoulders and crossed over to the window and peered out to the snow-covered backyard. He shivered a little. "This chap, Barnes, seems dashed fond of fresh air," he ejaculated. "Look at that—window half open."

From somewhere down below a bell shrilled. "The ambulance," murmured Tinker, and a moment after there came the tramp of feet on the stairs, and two blue-uniformed ambulance men entered.

It took only a few moments to lift the wounded man on to the stretcher, and as the little medico turned to leave, he smiled a trifle wistfully at Sexton Blake.

"You'll excuse me, I'm sure, Mr. Blake. Festive season, and all that—my services are in great demand at the station. This poor fellow will be in good hands at St. Luke's, and, of course, anything I can do to help—please let me know."

"Right, doctor!" Coutts replied briskly. "I'll drop in later, when we've completed the preliminary investigation. I see there's a constable outside—tell him to keep the crowd back. I'll report to Sergeant Green later on."

When the door had closed behind the medical man and the inanimate burden, a little silence fell on the four. Splash Page was the first to break it.

"Well, Blake, any theories?" he demanded. "What's all this about the pudding, and a girl called May?"

Sexton Blake ignored the question. He rose to his feet and crossed over to the half-open window with a curious alertness of expression, which in any other man would have been called excitement. But the great criminologist was not prone to show emotion. His keen, analytical brain merely functioned with lightning rapidity, leaping from analysis to synthesis, from clue to theory with a swift accuracy that never betrayed in his clean-cut, impassive features.

Inspector Coutts moved about the room, heavy and solidly as a bull. He stared at the neat dressing-table, absently handled the silver-backed military brushes, fiddled with the hasp of the drawer. He was evidently at a loose end, and awaited Blake's first move.

The detective glanced thoughtfully at the bed, a single, simple affair of iron and brass. It was placed midway between the window and the door.

The room itself was small and compact, and there was a neat, sailor-like tidiness about the arrangement of the plain furniture and Spartan necessities.

"How the deuce did anyone get into the place?" ejaculated Coutts. "See Blake, nobody could possibly have come in through the window. There's a sheer drop of fifty feet to the backyard—and look, the snow on the sill is as smooth as sugar icing."

"That's true enough," added Splash Page. "Mrs. Cluppins says he was alone in the house—her other lodgers, a young dressmaker and a young insurance clerk, went home for the holidays this morning. She states that Captain Barnes lately had a mortal dread of going out, and would sit in his room reading. He never had visitors."

"What's that?" demanded Sexton Blake. "You say the man seemed to be afraid of going out? That's significant. Tinker, my boy, please ask Mrs. Bardell and her sister to come up. I have one or two questions to ask them."

When Tinker had departed Blake thoughtfully withdrew the knife from his silken handkerchief and studied it intently through a powerful lens.

"What do you make of it, Coutts?" he asked. "It seems an ordinary sort of Swedish barrel-handled knife, such as sailors often carry. Take a look at it." Still handling the weapon with his silken guard, he passed it over to Coutts, who examined the knife with careful scrutiny.

"Anything strike you as peculiar about it?" asked Blake.

The Scotland Yard man coughed.

"As far as I can see, there isn't a single print on the handle. Hang on a minute." He took a pencil from his pocket, and with the aid of a penknife he scraped a few grains of graphite powder from the lead on to the dagger handle and lightly dusted it away.

"Jove, there's not a smear or a single greasy pore spot on it, Blake," he ejaculated.

"Precisely, Coutts. And what does that indicate?"

"Blowed if I know," replied the bewildered inspector. "Looks like a phantom assassin to me—unless the blighter wore gloves—but even then, there'd be some indication."

"The blade, man—examine the blade!" said Sexton Blake.

Coutts studied the sinister-looking knife with its ominous crimson smear.

"Jove, yes! A distinct print, half-way down," he ejaculated. "How the deuce did it get there?"

Sexton Blake did not reply, for at that juncture Mrs. Bardell entered. The good soul's face bore distinct traces of recent tears, and she gave a watery sort of smile as Blake courteously offered her a chair.

"Come in, Mary Ann!" she called. "Mr. Blake won't 'urt you. 'E's a kindly gen'l'man, though 'e is a detective."

"I'm so sorry to trouble you, Mrs. Cluppins," said Blake kindly to the little grey-haired woman, who was sniffing dolorously in the passage outside. "Pray come in. I shall not detain you long."

A little reassured, Mrs. Cluppins entered. She was a thin, anæmic little woman, and her face was red with recent weeping.

"Mr. Page has already informed me of your discovery of this sad affair, so I will not bother you to repeat it," said Sexton Blake quietly. "In the first place, how long has Captain Barnes been your lodger?"

"A year come next Febu-werry, Mr. Blake, sir."

"You mentioned, I think, that he recently altered in his habits—seemed frightened of something."

"Yessir. When 'e fust came 'ere, sir,

'e was a cheery conwivial chap—'e used to take me to pickshers every Thursday night regler.

"'E was a 'earty man, a good lodger, an' if 'e kep' clear of the drink, a perfec' gent. When 'e 'ad one over the eight though, 'e was a fair demon. Many an' many a time 'e's said to me: 'Mrs. Cluppins,' 'e said, 'I'm as gentle as a suckin' dove, if I 'ain't crossed, but if anyone crosses me, 'Eaven 'elp 'im! Roaring Bill Barnes, they call me—ask anyone from 'Frisco to the China Seas if they don't agree as 'ow Roaring Bill 'ain't a perfec' lamb—until 'e's crossed.'"

"H'm!" said Blake thoughtfully. "Then, apart from an occasional spree, you have little fault to find with your lodger?"

"No, sir! 'E always treated me just an' generous. I've only seen 'im drunk twice since 'e's bin with me, but I won't never forget it. 'Is langwidge! If 'e 'adn't bin so repentant the mornin' after, I'd 'ave sent 'im packin'—but 'e was that remorseful I didn't 'ave the 'eart to turn 'im out."

"Ah, when then, did this change in his nature occur, Mrs. Cluppins? He doesn't seem to me to be the sort of man to be afraid unless there was good cause for it."

"No sir. It was last week, Mr. Blake. I was takin' up 'is dinner as usual, last Thursday I think it was, the day 's usually treated me to the pickshers. 'E seemed to be strange in 'is manner—'is face looked gashly, and I asked 'im if anythink was wrong wiv 'im.

"'Wrong,' says 'e, with a funny kind o' laugh. 'Wrong—by the left hoof of Satan'—'e 'ad a queer outlandish way o' talkin' sometimes, Mr. Blake—'they've got me! They've traced me at last,' 'e said. ''Oo?' said I. 'The Income Tax people?' I know'd a lodger I 'ad once, a journalist 'e was, an' 'e' ad the same gashly look on 'is face wen 'e received a henvelope: 'On 'Is Majesty's Surface.'"

Splash Page winked slyly at Tinker, and a twinkle appeared momentarily in Sexton Blake's eyes.

"And what did he say to that, Mrs. Cluppins?"

The little woman rolled her eyes expressively. "I wouldn't repeat 'is langwidge, Mr. Blake. He roared and raved —used a lot of furrin soundin' words, and then 'e said, 'Mrs. Cluppins, remember, if any dodgasted son of a sea-cook of heither sect calls to see me, I'm out —dead—sloped without payin' me rent. Tell 'em anythink you like, but don't let anyone in, or I'll——' 'E didn't say what 'e'd do, Mr. Blake, but 'e almost bust with rage.

"Well, 'e kep' 'isself indoors that day, an' the nex' day, an' I thought mebbe 'e was 'iding from the perlice or somebody. It was arter 'e 'ad got a letter with a furrin sort o' stamp on it that 'e seemed to 'ave gone all to pieces like."

"Ah!" said Blake. "He received that on Thursday, did he?"

Mrs. Cluppins nodded.

"'E 'ardly ever 'ad any letters, that's what made me think on it now."

Sexton Blake raised his eyebrows, and drummed a light tattoo on the bed-rail.

"Now, Mrs. Cluppins, what's all this about the pudding Mrs. Bardell gave you?"

"Oh, sir. The Christmas pudden. It was orful——"

"Wotcher mean, Mary Ann Cluppins?" broke in Mrs. Bardell, greatly incensed at the slur on her culinary art.

"No offence, Martha. No offence," added her sister heartily. "I mean Cap'n Barnes' langwidge was orful. You see, I told 'im as you'd bin kind enough

to give me a pudden—just to cheer 'im up, like, for 'e was terrible down in the dumps and drinkin' more'n was good for 'im. A bottle o' whisky a day I brought into 'im from the orf-licence, Mr. Blake.

"Any'ow, this mornin' I went into the larder to 'ang up the goose, when I saw as 'ow the pudden 'ad vanished. I'd left it on the shelf as usual—nicely tied up in its little chiney basin, but there was no sign of it.

"I went into the kitchen, searched the pantry, searched everywhere for it. By and by the cap'n comes into the kitchen for some 'ot water.

"'Cap'n,' I ses, 'somebody's pinched the pudden!'

"'Wot,' he screamed, an' 'is face went almost green. 'What d'ye mean, you 'ard-'earted 'arridan?' or some such name, 'e called me.

"'Cap'n,' I ses, very dignified. 'That 'ain't no way to talk to the widder of a water "ate collecter wot was 'ighly respected in Bermondsey which the same testimonial as 'angs above the fireplace proves.'

"'Water rate widows be blowed,' ses the cap'n. 'Where's that plum pudden, woman? By the red eyes of Budda if that pudden's gone I'll—I'll——'

"But I won't demean myself to repeat 'is langwidge, Mr. Blake. 'E went on like a mad thing an' nearly 'ad a fit on the 'earthrug. Nothing would please 'im. 'E 'ad to 'ave that pudden or none at all. Nothin' else would do—an' now the pore feller's dyin' and——"

Mrs. Cluppins' lips began to quiver tremulously, and her fingers clutched spasmodically at her apron.

"Now, don't give way, Mrs. Cluppins," soothed Blake. "I'm happy to tell you that there is every chance of Captain Barnes' recovery. He's had a very bad wound, and the inordinate amount of whisky he has been drinking recently may retard his recovery for some time, but I have every hope that he'll pull through.

"It's our job to find the cowardly assassin that stabbed him, and your help may be very valuable. Just one more question please, Mrs. Cluppins: Have you had any visitor lately—one that asked you anything about the captain?"

Mrs. Cluppins shook her head.

"No, Mr. Blake, not a single person, an' thankful I am, too, that I weren't forced to tell lies to anyone 'as would come."

"Thank you, Mrs. Cluppins," said Blake courteously. "Later on, I shall ask you to be good enough to show me the larder from which the pudding was so mysteriously abstracted."

Mrs. Cluppins sniffed audibly, and rose to her feet, and was followed by Mrs. Bardell, who smiled at her master. "I'll look after 'er, Mr. Blake, if you don't mind, but what with the dinner at 'ome, an' all this upset, I——"

"Never mind the dinner, Mrs. Bardell," said Blake cheerily. "On this occasion I think that for the first time the whole of our Baker Street staff are engaged on a case—you are a most capable lieutenant."

Mrs. Bardell coloured at the compliment. "Lawks, Mr. Blake, fancy me a defective at my time o' life!" she gasped, and her eyes gleamed brightly with importance.

THE FOURTH CHAPTER.
The Proof of the Pudding.

"WELL, I'm blowed!"

Detective - Inspector Coutts, who had listened with ill-concealed impatience to Mrs. Cluppins' story, mopped his forehead with his handkerchief, more from affectation than any feeling of warmth.

"Of all the idiotic cases I've ever heard, this one takes the—er ——"

"Pudding!" interposed Splash Page, with a grin.

"Here's a retired Mercantile Marine skiupper," continued the inspector, with a withering glance at the journalist. "Goes off at the deep end about a Christmas pudding—acts like a lunatic and gets himself stabbed. He recovers consciousness—squeaks out something about a girl named May—yells that the secret's in the pudding, and goes off again. Stark, staring lunacy, I call it."

Sexton Blake lit a cigarette. There was an abstracted look in his eyes as he gazed reflectively at the half-open window. Suddenly he turned to Tinker and Splash.

"Look here, if we're not going to be done out of our Christmas dinner tomorrow," he said, "we shall have to hustle. The time element is essential if we're going to enjoy our holiday.

"Tinker, you go and see what you can find in the larder below, and don't help yourself to the mince pies. Coutts and I will concentrate on this room. I have a feeling that, far from being extraneous and absurd, Mrs. Bardell's pudding has a distinct bearing on the attempted murder of Captain Barnes."

"Good egg, Blake," said Splash. "Come on, Tinker, let us hunt the elusive pud. Bet you ten bob, Coutts. Tinker and I will solve this mystery from our end before you and Blake."

"Done!" snapped Coutts. And then growled something below his breath about cocksure newspapermen.

Sexton Blake, however, seemed oblivious to his companion's presence. When the door closed behind Tinker and Splash he dropped on his knees and carefully scrutinised every square inch of the threadbare carpet. A few cakes of muddy snow from the boots of the ambulance attendants, and a couple of trodden Navy Cut cigarette-ends were the sole trophies of his search, however.

Suddenly he straightened.

"Got the contents of the man's pockets?" he asked.

Coutts nodded.

"Just listing 'em, Blake. Here they are."

He pointed to a pile of miscellaneous articles which he had extracted from the captain's pockets, and which would be sent on to the hospital after examination.

There was a bunch of keys, a card-case containing a few stamps, and some faded cards with various shipping addresses, a worn wallet containing receipted bills, and five pounds in Treasury notes. Thrust at the back of the money was a thin envelope, and Blake pounced on it eagerly.

It was addressed in a peculiarly crabbed handwriting, and bore a French stamp, with a Marseilles postmark. Blake noted the date on the obliteration. It was the fifteenth of December.

"H'm!" he murmured softly. "This seems to have been the letter that caused the captain such inward perturbation, Coutts. Let's see what it says."

He carefully extracted the contents—a flimsy sheet of paper, and studied the brief message intently. It ran as follows:

"Lady Lou,
"Marseilles.

"Dere Roring Bill,—Just a line hoping this finds you as it leaves me in the pink. This is jest to tell you as them Mexes is after you. I see Jose in Marseilles he's got it in bad for you so lookout. He's coming home today. I never give him your address nowing your orders.

"Cheero from
"BEN BOLT."

"That's pretty explicit, Coutts," commented Sexton Blake. "Now, let me see——" He sat down on the bed and puffed steadily at his cigarette. "This clarifies matters considerably. Captain Barnes' reference to Mex seems to indicate—— By Jove," he added suddenly, and rose to his feet.

"I see the connection now."

His eyes gleamed as he stepped over to the window and gazed out into the snow-covered backyard.

The chill winter wind blew in freshly from the half-open window, and Blake shivered a little. He strained his eyes into the gloom beyond, then, as if making a mental calculation, he turned and studied the bed intently.

"Come on, Coutts," he said excitedly—"there's just a chance! Call in the constable, and tell him to mount guard over this room. We may, or may not, have a visitor to-night."

With sudden decision, he closed the window, and, seizing his grey Homburg hat, led the way below.

Coutts gave curt instructions to the police-officer at the door, who frowned majestically at a little knot of curious sightseers who had assembled at the door with the morbid interest of their kind.

Sexton Blake did not wait, however; he pushed into the kitchen, and found Mrs. Cluppins and Mrs Bardell holding a tearful tete-a-tete over a bottle of port.

"How can I get to your backyard, Mrs. Cluppins?" demanded the detective.

Mrs. Bardell pointed towards a small door just beyond the scullery.

"That way, Mr. Blake. The door's barred and locked, but the key is in the lock."

The detective nodded his thanks, and crossed over to the door. The key squeaked protestingly as it was turned and, after shooting back the rusty bolts, Blake stepped into the yard. By this time Coutts had arrived, and he flashed his electric torch inquiringly around. There was a peculiar calmness about the little squared enclosure, dazzlingly white under its mantle of fallen snow.

"What's the idea, Blake?" demanded the C.I.D. man. "Footprints?"

Blake nodded.

"Maybe. It is only a theory. Throw a gleam on this dark patch here, Coutts, just below the window."

The powerful electric torch cut through the darkness like a golden sword, and Coutts drew in his breath with a little hissing sound.

"Not a footprint! There hasn't been a soul here, Blake. The snowfall ceased at about four this afternoon, and look—it's as unsullied as a new table-cloth!"

Sexton Blake bit his lip with some vexation, and glanced up at the window, some fifty feet above them, where the comical shadow of a policeman's helmet loomed black against the oblong of yellow light.

"That's pretty evident, Coutts. Come, we'll have to try another tack."

He gave a single swift glance at the wall which divided Mrs. Cluppins' abode from that of the back of the house opposite. It was topped with an ugly arrangement of broken bottles set in cement—a barricade against predatory cats.

With the snow glistening on their sharp edges, the deadly things glinted like diamonds in the rays of the torch.

"Pretty well barricaded there," was Coutts' comment. "Where's Tinker and Splash?"

Blake smiled.

"On the trail of the elusive pudding. I guess," he said. "Come, Coutts, we've drawn a blank here, but there's still another avenue unexplored."

"But, hang it all, Blake," grumbled the C.I.D. man, "what are you looking for? My theory is that the skipper was alone in the house, there came a ring at the bell, and this chap, Mex, or Jose, or somebody, forced his way in and stabbed him. He couldn't have come in by the window; you see, yourself, there's no trace. The chimney's too narrow, even if he was Santa Claus. The only way he could possibly come in is through the front door."

"That's where you are in error, my dear Coutts," Blake explained patiently. "Captain Barnes had no visitor in his room to-night."

"What!" ejaculated Coutts in astonishment.

"Precisely what I say," replied Sexton Blake. "No living person entered Captain Barnes' room to-night prior to Mrs. Cluppins—and she merely peeped in."

"But that's preposterous," Coutts persisted. "How the deuce was he stabbed on his bed if no living person was there? You're not insinuating that a ghost tried to kill him, or that he stabbed himself in the back?"

"Not at all, my dear fellow," replied Blake suavely. "I merely reiterate that no one entered the room prior to Mrs. Cluppins."

"Great Scott!" gasped Coutts. "I see it now. May—sometimes used as short for Mary. D'ye mean to tell me, Blake, that Mrs. Cluppins stabbed the captain?"

"Well, I'm jiggered! I never thought of that. After all, we've only got her word for it. She admits that the captain took her to the pictures, and she might quite easily have some grudge against him. 'Hell holds no fury like a woman scorned,' as the poet says."

"My dear Coutts," said Sexton Blake "you excel yourself! I would hardly have credited you with such imagination. Upon my soul, you are coming on!"

The raillery in Blake's tone escaped Coutts' notice.

He flushed.

"Well, 'a nod's as good as a wink to a blind horse,'" he replied somewhat cryptically. "I'll admit I didn't get you at first, but now there's a difference. I'll examine that Cluppins woman myself this time. Come to think of it, her story sounded a bit thin."

"Coutts, don't be a fool!" snapped Sexton Blake suddenly. "Your idea is utterly preposterous! If you knew anything of psychology, you'd realise that Mrs. Cluppins is constitutionally incapable of murder, and if you worry the poor soul with any third degree questions, dash it, I'll—I'll put arsenic in your Christmas dinner!"

The worthy inspector spluttered.

"Then, in Heaven's name, what do you mean?" he demanded. "First you say that nobody entered the captain's room—yet he was found stabbed. Then you say that Mrs. Cluppins didn't do it—yet the man himself mentioned a woman named May. Then there's all this pudding nonsense; hanged if I don't think we're dealing with a pack of lunatics," he added vehemently.

"My dear Coutts, it is always unsafe to jump to wild conclusions, unsupported by facts. I say, quite calmly, that Captain Barnes had no visitor to-night. I will make you a present of three clues, and then we can then start level, but for goodness' sake don't argue from false premises."

"Well," demanded Coutts, somewhat mollified. "What are the clues?"

"Three words—snow, Mex, and pudding," replied Blake blandly, "and don't forget the significance of that fingerprint on the blade of the knife, and not, as one would expect, on the handle.

"Come, we will now try to explore a new avenue, as our politicians so quaintly express it."

THE FIFTH CHAPTER.
Tact.

IN the meantime, while Blake had been investigating the contents of the captain's wallet, and indulging in mental measurements in the room on the third-floor back, Tinker and Splash had embarked rather hilariously on what the journalist called the "Trail of the Purloined Pudding."

Mrs. Bardell had proudly pointed out the larder to the pair. It was a small cubby-hole, next to the coal-cellar, in the front basement of the house.

Mrs. Cluppins, in a hushed voice, pointed to the carcase of a fine goose, hanging from a hook in the ceiling.

"I brought that there goose in 'ere, Master Tinker," she explained. "That was this morning, about 'arf-past eleven. I'd put the pudden 'ere, on this shelf." She indicated a wooden shelf that extended round the whole larder.

It was a tiny place, not much larger than a wardrobe. Tinker noticed a small window, placed fairly high up on a level with the shelf about five feet from the ground.

The window was about a foot square, with a vertical iron bar on the outside, and it overlooked the area steps.

"Too small for a thief to get in by," murmured the lad. "Give us a leg up, Splash, while I look at that shelf."

The newspaperman obligingly made a back for Tinker, and the youngster examined the shelf carefully. A circular mark in the dust indicated where the pudding basin had rested, and he glanced up again at the window.

"By Jove!" he ejaculated. "Hold steady, Splash. I believe I've got it!"

He leant over and pulled the window open on its hinge.

"See, Mrs. Cluppins! The hasp's broken and rusty; a good hard push from the outside by anyone standing on the area steps would open the window.

(Continued on page 19.)

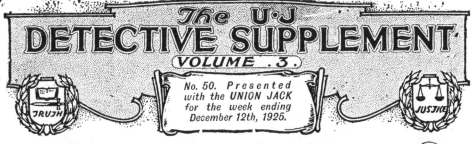

The U·J DETECTIVE SUPPLEMENT
VOLUME 3

No. 50. Presented
with the UNION JACK
for the week ending
December 12th, 1925.

TRUTH

JUSTICE

The Riddle of OSCAR SLATER

Of all the Christmas riddles that have ever been propounded, that of
the unfortunate Oscar Slater is surely the most tragic. Does his case
really form "a serious blot on the administration of justice," or ——?
The reader must judge for himself.

"I SUPPOSE I must reconcile myself to dying within prison walls, but it is hard! I have lived in the hope that, even if my innocence were never established there would come an end to my imprisonment, and I should be able to see the outer world again. But there is no relief now but death."

So spoke Oscar Slater recently when told that an appeal for his release from prison had been refused. For seventeen years Slater has been incarcerated in a Scottish gaol, suffering for a crime committed at Christmastime, and suffering for a crime of which many people think he was innocent.

The crime of which he was found guilty is one that presents many interesting problems to the crime student, and readers of the "Supplement" will find considerable mental exercise in weighing the facts for themselves, and in forming their opinion.

MISS MARION GILCHRIST was an old maiden lady, aged eighty-two, and for thirty years she had resided in a first floor flat at 15, Queen's Terrace, Glasgow. In fairly affluent circumstances, she lived a quiet, uneventful life, and was retiring by nature.

Like many other maiden ladies, she had developed a passion for collecting, but in her case, being comfortably off, she was enabled to collect jewellery, and during her lifetime had amassed a quantity of brooches, pendants, rings, and other valuable articles to the value of, perhaps, £3,000.

The possession of this hoard aroused in the old lady the thought that one day she might be attacked and robbed.

With the idea of preventing such an occurrence, two patent locks had been fixed to the outer door, and special fasteners on the windows. A further precaution was the arrangement made with the Adams family, who occupied the flat immediately below, that, in the event of anything untoward happening, she would notify them by knocking on the floor of her flat.

Miss Gilchrist was attended by a servant named Helen Lambie, a girl of about twenty-one, who had served her for about four years. There were not many visitors to the quiet flat. Occasionally a gentleman came on business, the most frequent visitor being a Mrs. Ferguson, an old servant of Miss Gilchrist.

Before passing to the night of the tragedy, it is essential for the reader to know a little of the lay-out of the flat. The ground floor of the building was occupied by the Adams, and they had a separate front door to their flat. The flat over Miss Gilchrist was empty.

Miss Gilchrist's flat had five rooms and kitchen, the outer door being on a stair-landing and fastened by three locks— an ordinary lock, a Chubb lock, and a patent lock. The outer door from the lower hall on to the pavement also had a lock; but, as is common in Scottish houses, this could be opened by the tenant in the flat upstairs raising a handle.

Thus the scene is set and the characters introduced.

THE evening of December 21st, 1908, found Miss Gilchrist sitting by the fire in her dining-room reading a magazine. It was a comfortably furnished room with an oval table in the centre, a long sideboard against the wall, a sofa and chairs occupying other parts of the floor. On the wall were a number of pictures, and an incandescent gas-bracket with a number of lights lit the room.

Helen Lambie, servant to Miss Gilchrist, for whose murder Oscar Slater is still officially held responsible.

It was the custom of Helen Lambie, the servant, to go out each evening for a newspaper, and on this evening she entered and was told by Miss Gilchrist to carry out some errands as well, being given a penny for the newspaper, and ten shillings for the other commissions.

Helen Lambie laid the half-sovereign on the dining-room table, intending, as she afterwards said in her evidence, to go for the newspaper first, and afterwards for the other things. Leaving Miss Gilchrist reading, she went out, closing the door of the flat on two locks and taking two keys with her. The outer door on to the pavement she also closed.

The newspaper-shop was in St. George's Road, some three minutes away, and straight there Lambie went, stopping for a moment to speak to a plain-clothes policeman whom she met at the corner of St. George's Road and West Prince's Street.

Having purchased the newspaper she retraced her steps to the flat, having been away about ten minutes. On her arrival back at the flat she found that the outer door was open, and that there were wet footmarks—for it had been raining- inside the hall.

To her astonishment, when she got up to the landing she found Mr. Adams there from the downstairs flat. He told her that there had been a noise in Miss Gilchrist's flat, and that the ceiling sounded as though it was going to crack.

The flat door was still locked, and, taking the two keys from her pocket, Lambie unlocked the door.

As Helen Lambie went to enter she saw a man coming from the direction of the spare bed-room, in which she noticed a light was lit. He passed her and went downstairs, walking with deliberation, and not hurrying.

The girl entered the kitchen and then the bed-room, but both presented nothing unusual. In the dining-room she found Miss Gilchrist lying on the rug in front of the fire. She thereupon rushed out, calling to Mr. Adams.

Miss Gilchrist had been murdered. Brutal blows had been struck repeatedly and with great force, and the neighbourhood of the fireplace presented a gruesome sight.

Mr. Adams had seen the man go downstairs, and had heard him bang the house door, but though he almost at once went down and into the road he failed to see anyone there.

Both the servant and Mr. Adams had

U.J. No. 1,157.
Page 12.

a good view of the man, and thus the police were enabled to circulate the following description:

"The man wanted is about 28 or 30 years of age, tall and thin, with his face shaved clean of all hair, whilst a distinctive feature is that his nose is slightly twisted to one side. The witness thinks the twist is to the right side. He wore one of the popular tweed hats known as Donegal hats, and a fawn-coloured overcoat that might have been a raincoat, also dark trousers and brown boots."

Helen Lambie examined the flat after finding her mistress dead, and in the spare bed-room found that papers had been taken from a box and scattered on the floor. Later she missed a brooch which had belonged to Miss Gilchrist, and which had lain with a gold and diamond ring in a small dish on the bed-room dressing-table. The brooch had been taken and the ring left untouched.

And now for Adams' story.

He said that on the night of the murder, while sitting in his own dining-room, he heard a thud on the ceiling above his head, and then three distinct knocks, as though someone were signalling by knocking on the floor. On going up he found that the house door was open, but that the door of the flat was locked.

He rang the bell three times—hard, rude rings, he described them—and, looking through the glass panel of the door saw that the lobby gas was lit. Listening, he heard what he thought was the breaking of sticks in the kitchen, for he did not know that Helen Lambie had gone out.

After waiting a few moments, he returned to his own flat, and told his sister that he did not think anything was amiss. She, however, with perhaps a woman's intuition, persisted in her belief that something was wrong, and insisted that her brother return upstairs.

Again Mr. Adams pulled at the bell, and still had his hand on the bell-pull when Helen Lambie appeared on her return from fetching the newspaper, and opened the door.

THE witness mentioned in the police-description given above was a young girl named Mary Barrowman. She was delivering a parcel, and when opposite the flats was knocked into by a man who came running out of the house. She saw him run toward, and turn down, West Cumberland Street.

There was a street-lamp where they touched each other, and Mary Barrowman said in her evidence that she had a good look at the man, both when he was approaching her and when he had knocked against her.

It was four days later, on Christmas Day, that the police heard that a German Jew, of the name of Oscar Slater, had attempted to sell the pawnticket of a crescent diamond brooch. In a vague way his description tallied with the circulated description, and the police were at once on his track.

In Slater's lodging they found evidence which showed that, with a woman, the wanted man had left Glasgow only a few hours previously; and on the 28th it was found that under the name of Mr. and Mrs. Otto Sando the pair had sailed on the Lusitania for New York.

A cable to the other side of the Atlantic resulted in Slater being arrested on arrival in New York. He voluntarily consented to return, and arrived back in Glasgow on February 21st. The trial commenced on May 3rd in the High Court, Edinburgh. Lord Guthrie was the judge, and Mr.

Alexander Ure, Advocate-General of Scotland, prosecuted.

The trial occupied four days, and created a great deal of public interest.

At the very outset the prosecution received a serious setback. They had based their connection between Slater and the crime on the fact that he had pawned a diamond crescent brooch, and that such a brooch had been taken from the murdered woman's flat.

In Slater's possession after the arrest was found the pawnticket, and the brooch was redeemed from the pawnbroker. Then came the discovery which might have suggested to the police that they were on the wrong track.

The pawned brooch was one that for many years had belonged to Slater; he had often pawned it before, and it was not the one missing from the flat!

Over the question of identification the

Oscar Slater, who was arrested in New York for the alleged murder of Miss Gilchrist one fateful Christmas-time. Convicted, and nearly hanged, he owes his conviction to circumstantial evidence.

prosecution nearly blundered. Mr. Adams, Helen Lambie, and Mary Barrowman had travelled to New York to identify Slater, and in New York Court said he was exceedingly like the man they had seen in Glasgow. Mr. Adams and Mary Barrowman, however, had previously been shown photographs of Slater. This method of influencing witnesses has, by the way, since been condemned in the recent Sheppard case.

Other witnesses gave evidence of seeing a man hanging about the streets near where Miss Gilchrist had lived, and identified—with varying degrees of certainty—Slater as that man.

In Slater's luggage was found a hammer, and this, the prosecution said, was the weapon with which the crime was committed. This was a matter for the expert witness, and, as is usual when such are called upon to give evidence,

there was a wide divergence of opinion between the experts of the prosecution and the defence.

One medical man said the hammer could have produced the injuries that killed Miss Gilchrist, and that the instrument looked as if it had been washed, scrubbed, and sandpapered, and his opinion was supported by another doctor.

For the defence, however, two doctors considered the hammer a very unlikely weapon; did not see how the wounds could have been caused by it; and said it had no appearance of being washed or scraped.

WHERE experts disagree, what is the jury to decide?

Reading the case to-day, the present writer is of opinion that the expert evidence cancels itself out, and that Slater's guilt or innocence could have been decided on other facts available.

The defence put up the best show possible, but they did not have legal big guns of the calibre of the prosecution, and the result was that, after an absence of eighty minutes the jury, by a majority, found Slater guilty.

It is significant to note that out of the fifteen jurors nine were for conviction, five for "not proven," and one for not guilty. In England such a difference of opinion would have meant a fresh trial.

The decision of the jury was not expected, and the final scene at the trial was vividly described by a writer present. He said:

"It is not too much to say that the verdict came with a shock of surprise to most of the auditors in the crowded courtroom. Upon none, however, did the blow fall with such fearful effect as on the man in the dock. He had been, it appears, throughout the trial confident of acquittal, and had borne himself from day to day with inflexible composure.

"The recording of the verdict and sentence which followed upon the jury's finding, occupied an actual seven minutes; but the tense stillness, broken only by the sound of the official pen, seemed interminable. It proved too much for the prisoner's iron nerve.

"He arose in the dock, and, labouring under strong emotion, made an incoherent effort to address the judge. Lord Guthrie informed Mr. M'Clure that he should advise the prisoner to withhold anything he had to say for the Crown authorities; but Slater commenced another hysterical appeal, which his lordship mercifully terminated by announcing the inevitable sentence, adjudging the prisoner to be hanged in Glasgow on May 27th.

"A scene more painful it is, fortunately, the lot of few to witness, and none who did so on this occasion is likely to forget it."

Slater was not hanged, however, for two days before the sentence was to have been carried out it was commuted to one of penal servitude for life.

SUCH is the bare outline of the case which caused a Christmas sensation in 1908, and the following facts may help the reader to come to an opinion as to whether Slater was guilty or not.

In the early days of the case the police undoubtedly argued that Slater's sudden flight to America was a sign of guilt. As a matter of fact, for several weeks before he actually sailed arrangements were being made for his departure. It was the receipt of two letters which caused him to quicken his preparations and book his passage.

The woman with whom he travelled to New York and a servant-girl he employed were able to prove an alibi for Slater on the fatal evening, but their evidence was not admitted. Lambie and Barrowman had both sworn that the man they had seen leave Miss Gilchrist's flat was clean shaven, while, in fact, Slater wore a short moustache.

The evidence of the pawned diamond crescent brooch showed that Slater had only pawned his own property; and, indeed, no effort was made by the prosecution to show that Slater had ever known of Miss Gilchrist's hoard, or was ever known to the occupants of the flat.

To sum up, the facts show that the evidence is strongly in favour of the defence. On practically every point the case for the prosecution was weak. The police, however, expected a conviction; they employed the best counsel money could procure, and the jury's verdict brought the anticipated result.

Slater was convicted and nearly hanged; but he was convicted on

Marion Gilchrist, for whose alleged murder Oscar Slater is now serving a life-sentence.

[Photos: Illustrations Bureau.]

circumstantial evidence. A gambler and an adventurer, a wanderer and a Bohemian, his mode of life shocked the rigid puritanical notions of the Scottish populace.

One writer said publicly in the Press: "Even if he did not do it, he deserved to be condemned, anyhow."

Such a statement shows how biassed public opinion was against a man who was friendless and alone.

The case aroused the interest of Sir Arthur Conan Doyle, the famous creator of Sherlock Holmes. A newspaper agitation was started, and three years after the trial a commission to examine

the case was appointed by the Government. Nothing resulted.

There the case remains. The mystery of Christmas, 1908, is a mystery still. Slater has declared his innocence; an unbiassed review of the evidence exonerates him of the crime.

As to what actually happened during those ten minutes that Helen Lambie was gone, we can only theorise.

The murderer was in the flat when the servant returned. Did he pick that time to enter, knowing her regular habit of going out to get a paper? How did he get in? Surely only by being admitted by Miss Gilchrist herself. She could have opened the street door from above and then admitted the visitor through the hall door. The whole evidence points to that as the only way the murderer entered the flat.

Motive? On the face of it the crime seems a motiveless one. Beyond the diamond crescent brooch that never was found nothing was missing, and crude robbery hardly seems the motive for the crime.

Possibly the solution lay in the papers which had been scattered over the floor from the broken-open box. Their nature has never been revealed, but it seems to the writer that the murderer was actually examining them in the spare bed-room when he heard Helen Lambie's keys in the locks, and had to make a dash for safety.

The only thing that seems certain about the case is that Slater did not murder Miss Gilchrist. Never was there a case which more needed the tactful work of real detectives, and never was there a more obvious case in which an apparently innocent man was found guilty.

It has been stated by Sir Arthur Conan Doyle that the Slater case is "a serious blot upon the administration of justice in Scotland," and possibly readers of the Supplement will have already come to that conclusion.

Prison Gate Dramas

No. 3.

PARTING OF THE WAYS.

THE dull clang of the prison bell is heard echoing from the clock tower of London's largest prison — Wormwood Scrubs.

A dull November day, and the sky is dark, sheets of rain sweeping the bare road running in front of the prison. It is eight o'clock in the morning; within a few yards of the ponderous iron gates figures pace up and down their cells.

They differ from the ordinary prisoner insomuch as they are clad in ordinary civilian garb, and as they prowl round their cells a certain awkwardness as regards their movements indicates that it is many months since they have worn civilian clothes— and enjoyed the luxury of pockets.

Soon after the clanging of the prison bell the cells of these unfortunates are unlocked with a jangle of keys. A warder gruffly orders them to follow him.

They file across the bare stone yard to the office of the chief warder. As they are ushered in one by one, they are given the money they had when they entered the prison, plus a square

ticket which entitles them to a free breakfast at a certain hostel.

As they see these tickets a look of scorn fills their faces; for on the back is the picture of a convict in a suit of broad arrows, his head bowed on his arms signifying despair, and below is inscribed that well-known phrase: "Honesty is the best policy."

Some of the men about to be released are given official-looking blue papers embossed with the Royal Arms, and marked, "Prevention of Crimes Act, 1907"—enough, for this paper conveys to the unfortunate holder that he is "Under the Act," and as such is liable to be arrested as a suspected person, and given twelve months' imprisonment without trial by jury—by a magistrate alone, providing a prima facie case of "loitering with intent" is proved.

Let us now glance at this motley collection of individuals who are about to step once more into freedom.

OUR eyes are attracted first of all to an immaculate young man in a lounge suit, with the unmistakable stamp of Savile Row on it. We glance askance at his patent leather shoes, which have lost none of their brilliance in the prison clothing store, and at his white spats. Obviously a bit of a dog!

Could we but glance at his dossier at the Criminal Record Office at Scotland Yard, we would learn that he is a clever hotel and jewel thief.

Even now he has his "stock-in-

trade" by his side should he desire to continue his "profession"—an expensive-looking leather portmanteau, carefully plastered with hotel and steamship labels, conspicuous amongst which is one: "Paris—by air."

Glancing closer, we notice that these labels have a peculiar shiny surface which is foreign to them—a coating of some varnish has been placed over them to prevent their rubbing off and thus spoiling the travelled look of the piece of luggage. This is but one of the many dodges of our white-spatted young jewel thief.

Let us now glance at the next man. What a contrast to the immaculate!

No well-cut suit here, but a garment of many colours, well perforated, and allowing the winds of heaven to penetrate. A tramp obviously—as can be seen by his odd shoes and bundle of "property" which he clutches so securely.

Passing down the line, we see an assortment of beggars, labourers, artisans, and nondescripts. One only deserves further mention.

A tall, thin man, with a heavy moustache, and dressed in neat black clothes. He looks "City"—and he is —for he is a solicitor, or, rather, I should say, ex-solicitor, since he is now struck from the Rolls. He has served a long sentence for misappropriation of funds.

Having all been interviewed by the chief warder, the prisoners are marched to the gate; for the last time

(Continued on page 384.)

The COPPERS' XMAS

When the "limb of the law" relaxes, he knows how to enjoy himself in the real old Christmas style. His official sternness unbends even where lawbreakers—the milder type—are concerned.

YOU have all read of Yuletide in the fighting Services. But have you not wondered how Robert spends his? Is he eating plum-pudding while burglars are a-burgling? Or does he lay down the drumsticks of a turkey in order to go and deal with gangsters?

Hardly! In fact, he sees to it that he has all the traditional concomitants of Christmas.

Among a fairly large circle of police acquaintances—no, there have been no warrants out against me—I have noticed that they invariably seem to get the largest turkeys. Is there some occult reason for this, or are poulterers fascinated by that charm of manner for which the Metropolitan, City of London, and other municipal police are noted?

There is, of course, a perfectly true story of a very pompous detective-sergeant whose lack of humour was the joy of his colleagues. He was actually refused a fat turkey by a merchant in Farringdon Road.

The sleuth was indignant—highly in-

". . . Offered surreptitious refreshment."

dignant—but he did not get the turkey, for it had just been bespoken by the wife of a younger member of the Force; but there was quite a scandal about it, and many small boys gathered round to

bear the argument and to cherish the memory of some of the expressions used.

Now, in London young bachelor policemen—incidentally some of the most eligible bachelors in the Metropolis—have their residence in the section house attached to each station.

They unite for Christmas, and provide their own feast, with the aid of the canteen.

There are the unfortunates who are on duty and have to wait until their relief arrives; but they have their dinner, nevertheless, and in most neighbourhoods Robert who is on duty round about one o'clock of a Christmas afternoon is offered surreptitious refreshment.

I do not hint that he takes it, but even a sergeant might turn a blind eye under the influence of the season.

Prisoners in the cells who have not been able to procure bail are not forgotten, either; and I know of one case particularly where a well-known business man from the Midlands, who was held and who could not prove his identity, was given a "feed" which he vowed was one of the best he has ever had.

When he comes to town nowadays he always visits the canteen of the particular station where he spent one Christmas not too unhappily, and on those occasions the canteen rule, which forbids visitors to purchase refreshments for members of the Force, is broken.

IN well-to-do neighbourhoods the policeman on duty is not forgotten by the householders.

Mary Ann is sent out to cheer him with a useful half-crown and something in a bottle; for there are most respectable citizens who remember being helped home after that convivial Old Boys' dinner, the annual meeting of the Ancient Order of Robots, or the supper of the Umpteenth Royal Musketeers.

In poorer neighbourhoods, where Christmas hospitality is wonderful, you will see the good wife poke her head out of the door as Robert saunters by, pretending not to smell the cooking.

"Oy?" she announces in a shrill whisper, which can be heard half-way down the street. Robert halts smartly, disappears in the doorway, and re-appears a few seconds later, a contented grin on his face, and perhaps a soupçon —as the Society novelists write—of foam on his upper lip.

On these occasions touring inspectors and sergeants are conveniently absent. Perhaps even they have succumbed to the Christmas spirit, too.

Christmas is usually a close season for burglars; but there are, unfortunately, abandoned wretches in our midst, who will not scruple to break the law on Christmas Day or on the night thereof.

I have heard the language in the detectives' office of a London station when a bright ornament of the sleuth branch

". . . May no gentle burglar upset his digestion."

has had to tear himself away from congenial company to go on the "crime-hunt."

Some low fellow, a Scandinavian fireman, had had the deplorable taste to assault another fireman with a bit of iron. Fortunately, the skull of the assaultee was thick.

Anyway, if you want to see good feeding, witness the police at their Christmas dinner. The chief-inspector makes a ceremonious call, just like the C.O. and company commanders in the Army. Then there is the divisional detective-inspector, and other high officials, just like the adjutant and the regimental sergeant-major in those days you and I remember.

To vary the old toast, "Here's to crime," let us say, "Here's to Robert, and may no gentle burglar upset his digestion!"

The Tragic History of Louis Danval

CONCLUDING PART.

The torments, both bodily and mental, through which Louis Danval, the Paris chemist, passed in consequence of being wrongfully condemned to the convict settlement at New Caledonia—on a false charge of poisoning his wife with arsenic—at last come to an end. He here describes his rehabilitation.

The medal which was struck in Danval's honour after his return to France, and presented to him by his supporters and admirers.

THE opinion of his judges had all along been contested by such distinguished experts as Professor Bouis, Member of the Academy of Medicine and Professor of Toxicology at the Higher College of Pharmacy, energetically supported by Dr. Gallard, the court expert, and Dr. Cornil, of the medical faculty. The former attacked the symptomatology, the latter the lacunas in the autopsy.

All, however, affirmed that there was no arsenic habitually present in the human body, and that, if found, its presence was either accidental or criminal.

Now, as the arsenic found in Mme. Danval's body was non-toxic, they attributed it to its presence in the dye of the curtains to the woman's bed, and it is well known to exist also in wallpapers. But the experts analysed two grammes of dust from the room, and got a negative result—hence there was no arsenic there.

This influenced the jury to find arsenic elsewhere. According to Gosio, arsenic can be inhaled in vapour. In other words, science has been completely revolutionised since 1878. It must be pointed out that M. and Mme. Danval slept in a room the window of which could not be opened. It was surmounted by a small ventilator obscured by an iron railing.

In 1901 M. Armand Gautier, a well-known French scientist, protested against the idea of curtains in a small room like that being able to contain thirty-nine milligrammes of arsenic. Curtains containing a great deal more would have constituted a real danger to Mme. Danval.

All the experts in 1878 were agreed that there was no arsenic naturally in the human body, and yet it was found in Mme. Danval. The jury heard this repeated on all sides. But were the men who condemned Danval to penal servitude living to-day they would hear just the opposite.

The Marsh test has scarcely been modified since, and Ogier, a leading expert, reckons it too sensitive for toxicological research; yet it has registered, according to M. Gabrielle Bertrand, the half-thousandth of a milligramme. This has brought about a revolution in science.

In 1900 M. Armand Gautier informed the Académie des Sciences that arsenic is constantly present in the human system, but he was contradicted by foreign scientists, who declared that this depended on the soil on which his subjects lived. M. Gautier proved that arsenic was present naturally even in such low forms of life as the sponge, and it existed in all forms of life, regardless of environment. The presence of the poison might be increased by permanent residence in a pharmacy.

The jury which condemned Danval were ignorant of those important facts. Moreover, revision of the Danval Case became more and more indispensible through suspicious deaths through arsenic poisoning at Hyères, Havre, and St. Denis—deaths which were manifestly due to accidental causes.

DANVAL'S appeal for a revision came before the Court of Cassation in 1906, but it was rejected. The judges of the great Appeal Court did not consider that a "new fact" of sufficient weight had been brought forward.

But Danval continued his struggle for rehabilitation.

He was determined to go on to the end protesting that he was innocent of the death of his wife; he placed his trust in the progress of science; was confident that the day would come before he died when his fellow-citizens would proclaim publicly that he had been wronged by Society.

That day did not come until seventeen years later.

In 1923 the Keeper of the Seals, on a demand for revision from Danval, appointed a commission of five experts, and on their recommendation sent the dossier to the Court of Cassation. This second appeal for rehabilitation came on before the Court in December, 1923. The audience was much larger than usual. Danval—now a man of over eighty years of age—stood there, striving to hear what was said. Was he to be disappointed once more?

Maître La Borde, quite unimpassioned, began to outline the case. It was necessary to go over the ground again, for who could remember the details of this drama of forty-five years ago?

He touched on the difficulties which had arisen after Danval's marriage, the bad feeling which had sprung up between husband and wife; he recalled her youth, her ill-health, and weak nerves; and then her mysterious death.

The autopsy had, as was now clearly shown, been made carelessly. There were important organs which had never been examined for traces of arsenic. The jury of 1878 had been influenced by

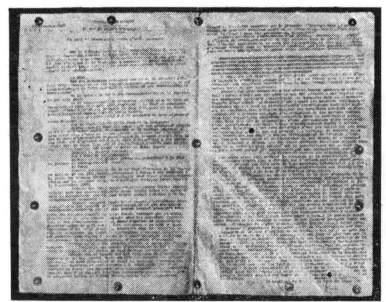

The document which was posted up by the French judicial authorities at the entrance to Danval's last place of residence in the suburbs of Paris. It is the official judgment of the Court of Cassation, rehabilitating Danval. By this means all who saw it were informed that an innocent man had been wrongfully condemned.

Maitre la Borde, who succeeded in establishing Danval's innocence.

circumstantial evidence and the defective testimony of the official experts.

In 1903 scientists had found that a certain amount of arsenic in the human body was quite normal.

Then Danval had been pardoned. But his appeal to the court had been rejected on the ground that there was no "new fact." Well, this second appeal was now being made on the ground that the desired "new fact" could be produced.

Counsel went on to say that quite recently three scientists, Kohn-Abrest, Sicard, and Paraf, had discovered that from one to three milligrammes of arsenic were quite normal in the human body; this quantity was no proof that the person had been poisoned. Hence his client's second appeal for rehabilitation.

But if Mme. Danval did not die of arsenic poisoning, what was the cause of her death? This was a question which modern science could answer without a shadow of a doubt.

Her death—inexplicable according to the decree of 1906, rendered by the court—was due to a malady unknown in 1878, but to-day recognised as acute suprarenal inefficiency. All the symptoms which had been taken for arsenical poisoning were those of this malady.

AFTER Maitre La Borde's stirring speech there was little doubt what the decision of the Court would be, yet the judges were in retirement for two hours.

On coming back into Court. the President announced that the appeal had been granted. Louis Danval was rehabilitated. The Count had decided that this poor man had been done a grave injustice by Society, and it was their duty to do what they could to lighten the burden of his declining years.

He would be granted an indemnity of 20,000 francs and an annuity of 12,000 francs.

That sounds a lot of money, but at the rate of exchange at that time works out to but £400 in English money for the indemnity, and £240 for the annuity..

A poor indemnity indeed for a man whose life had been wrecked!

The French Press and the League des Droits de l'Homme, which had done so much to bring Danval's case before the public, have been loud in their protests against the tardy justice done, and the smallness of the indemnity.

"Compare this with English justice!" they have exclaimed. The Court of King's Bench awards £25,000 to a Mr. Harnett after nine years' illegal detention in a lunatic asylum; but the Court of Cassation grants but four hundred pounds and a miserable yearly income to a man who has been treated as a convict for the greater part of his life.

But France's obligations to Louis Danval were never even fulfilled !

A few weeks after the details of the story of his dolorous life had been communicated to me, Danval passed away.

He had received a little money on account, but his indemnity, through administrative delays and formalities, never reached him. This was, naturally, a very sore point with the old man, who constantly commented on this last injustice that had been done him. But he never really lost courage.

Almost to within a few days of his death he was actively engaged in preparing these memoirs, and he had also entered into arrangements for the writing of the scenario of a film, which was to introduce the incidents I have related.

THE END.

Little Things the Law Forbids at Christmas - Time.

IT is no wonder that special laws, rules and regulations have had to be drawn up specially to cope with difficulties that arise because of the disorganisation of our normal, routined lives at Christmas-time.

The insurance companies especially have reason to look with distinct apprehension upon our festivities, and in nearly all cases they indemnify themselves against loss by fire and burglary, by inserting in agreements the clause by which they shall not be called upon to pay for loss "if the risk be increased without the knowledge of the company."

This means, of course—among other things—that stores of crackers shall not be kept, nor the Christmas-tree lighted with candles, nor inflammable balloons and lanterns given to the children, nor even paper decorations or highly-dangerous fireworks be indulged in without the written consent of the company—at the expense of an extra premium.

Often at Christmas-time the buyer of a big firm finds his breakfast-table loaded with gifts from traders he has favoured during the past year. This, of course, is little short of bribery and corruption with the object of securing better business in the coming year.

The Prevention of Corruption Act of 1906 was designed specially to stop this practice of giving Christmas boxes; but the fact remains unaltered that many are still in receipt of secret bribes and commissions in this form, from traders who have been markedly patronised.

Some few years ago a big London departmental store made such an attractive show in its windows before Christmas that the crowds of sightseers which collected entirely blocked the pavement. The firm was fined forty shillings, which was like a sprat which caught the mackerel. The firm cleared all its stock as a result of the unsought advertisement.

In connection with our evergreen decorations, it is a punishable offence to be caught affixing any kind of red berry on to branches of holly and passing the product off as a genuinely natural branch.

In the collecting of evergreens, too, it is a far more serious offence to be charged with trespass. Christmas shrub poachers in the past were so wantonly destructive of young trees that landowners had to seek protection from marauders who not only stole holly and ivy, but in doing so left gates open, allowing cattle to stray and generally causing trouble all round.

CHRISTMAS DAY is legally considered in the same light as Sunday, and in addition, there is a curious law—which seems to apply to London alone—forbidding demonstrations by gatherings and meetings of the unemployed, or other forces, on Christmas Day.

It is illegal to shoot game on Christmas Day, or to secure game with dogs, traps or nets; though fish may still be caught with rod and line. Bakers may not bake bread, nor may a theatre or any house or place of amusement be opened.

Louis Danval—seated in motor-car—surrounded by his admirers and supporters, consisting of doctors, journalists, and nurses, after his return to Paris from the convict settlement at New Caledonia.   [Photos: Paris and London Studio.]

PINCHED!

By . . Donald Campbell.

The humour (and otherwise) of being arrested—by one who has himself been "took up," but on unfounded suspicion.

I WISH to begin by saying that, although I contribute to this Supplement, I am not a hardened criminal, whatever the Editor may think.

The way of a quiet man who travels about is often hard in this cruel world, and it has happened to me to suffer temporary incarceration on various occasions. But it has happened even more to certain high-spirited friends of mine, and it is principally concerning them that I propose to tell.

One adventurous soul who had been running guns to Ulster before the War was arrested in Leicester Square for "creating a disturbance."

Some beggar had followed him and annoyed him. Said beggar was soundly shaken until his teeth rattled, and his howls were even as those of a lovesick hyena.

Our adventurer landed "inside."

The police were quite sympathetic, but explained that the Commissioner had given strict orders that Leicester Square and Piccadilly were to be kept severely disciplined.

Mr. Gun-runner was admitted to bail very shortly after his arrest, and described himself as John Smith, commercial traveller, because he did not wish for the least publicity at that particular time.

". . . Using unparliamentary language."

When he appeared before the "beak" next morning the magistrate beamed from his dais.

"Why, I'm sorry to see you here, So-and-so" (giving "John Smith's" right name). "Have you any money? Yes? Then I must fine you seven-and-sixpence."

There was a very amusing Box and Cox case concerning a festive young lord whose antics had excited the professional wrath of a C Division constable, who promptly ran him in.

The lordling gave the name of another peer for the purpose of obtaining bail; but, unfortunately, that nobleman had also transgressed and had given the address of lord Number One, also for the purposes of being admitted to bail. I did not hear how this tangle sorted itself out—if it ever did.

Being arrested by the English is a mild matter, however, in peace-time. In War-time it was different.

Being on leave in France during the War, I was waiting to sail from Boulogne to report back to a certain office in England before proceeding abroad again.

It so happens that I talk French as easily as English, and have served in the French Army. I struck up an acquaintanceship with a most amusing old French sergeant. We lunched together, and two French Red Cross girls came and talked to us. They were collecting for the hospital funds, and we did not talk of any military movements.

I had some money, wonderful to relate!

A quarter of an hour later four "red-caps," or English military policemen, invaded the hotel and arrested me at the revolver's point.

It turned out that an interfering Australian captain had hastened to the Intelligence Office with the information that he had run a German officer to earth!

Fortunately, I had reported at that same office on arriving from Paris; but, none the less, I was taken to the "nick," using unparliamentary language, to be released shortly after.

The reasons the "Aussie" had his misguided brain-wave were that I was in Royal Fusilier uniform, spoke French and Flemish, and had a wad of hundred-franc notes—then worth about three pounds each, as the exchange was then at about thirty-five francs to the pound sterling.

English Tommies never had money, he explained.

Anyway, I did not stand with my back to the wall; but I never heard the last of this adventure, nor did the Australian officer, so I understand. He was *not* given a staff appointment on the strength of his having discovered a German spy.

THE English civilian police are a pretty good-tempered lot, and it is amusing to be in a busy station on a Friday night when the "hardy annuals" are brought in.

"Hello! You again, Harry? What have you been doing now?" asks the desk sergeant.

"It's the malarier, sargint. Allus takes me queer on a Friday like," answers Harry, who is an honest hawker on other days of the week.

"Better go and have a little quiet sleep, Harry, and we will wake you in the morning and bring your breakfast in for you. Now, can we say fairer than that?"

Harry, slightly sobered up, goes slowly to the dungeon, scratching his head in an attempt to think of a dignified reply to the desk sergeant.

Being arrested on the Continent, on the contrary, is always a nuisance. No matter how innocent you may be, or who you know, you are always kept a long time before being released.

In the days of my extreme youth I was mixed up in a Royalist demonstration in the Latin Quarter of Paris, and called at the local "depot," or police-station to demand the release of other Royalist and youthful agitators.

I was hauled inside without apologies, and kept there until two o'clock the next afternoon, when I was taken before the commissaire—semi-detective, semi-magistrate.

This commissaire happened to be a Royalist himself, and he was quite sympathetic. He gave me a glass of cognac and a cigarette, and talked about everything under the sun except my "crime."

As I was leaving, a free man once again, he said:

"No notice will be taken of your little burst of enthusiasm, but do be more discreet."

". . . Come away from he e, young fellow!"

And I was saluted at the door of his office by the uniformed police orderly, who had signalled to a cab for me.

Military offences seem very terrible to many respectable fathers and mothers, and there is one ultra-dignified lady who still considers me a thorough-paced blackguard because of the following incident.

I happened to be up in London during the War, and was visiting at a relative's house, when this good soul asked me in low tones whether to be arrested was a serious affair in the Army.

I explained that it all depended what you were arrested for.

She then informed me that her "one and only," a distinctly knowledgeable youth of nineteen, had been "pinched" for abusing his company-sergeant-major.

"Madam, men of that stamp win V.C.'s," I assured her.

I believe she still refers to me as "that low scribbler."

One of the funniest scenes I have ever witnessed in connection with arrests was that of a notoriously hen-pecked little man who lives in my neighbourhood in London.

He had been violently assaulted by his Amazonian wife, and as these assaults occurred at regular intervals he was wending his way to the local police-station to procure advice.

He was actually mounting the steps, when his better half appeared.

"You come away from here, young feller, else you and I will have a war on!" said the wife. And she led him away with a firm grip on his wrist.

The policeman on the gate could not restrain a grin, nor could I.

THERE was a fiery old gentleman who lived in Bloomsbury who had led a very adventurous life, having, among other things, held a command in the French Foreign Legion.

One evening he was asked by a crony of his, who had just returned from West Africa, to purchase a bottle of liqueur rum, as the returned wanderer feared that he was due for a dose of fever.

The old gentleman wandered forth, procured the rum, and then saw a very young policeman, upon whom he advanced.

"Young man, can you tell me the way to Timbuctu?"

" . . Can you tell me the way to Timbuctu ?"

"Certainly, sir! Do you mind following me?" replied the constable, and led him to the Hunter Street police-station.

Next morning, after having given lectures on drill to a number of the Force, the old warrior duly appeared before the "beak." Although all the local police knew him and usually saluted him, he was charged under the name of "George Smith, pawnbroker's assistant."

It was explained to him beforehand that the officer who had arrested him was a new recruit, and did not know much; so the old gentleman's wrath was entirely modified.

The magistrate was in a good temper, and spoke as follows:—

"Good-morning, Major—I mean Mr. Smith! How comes it that you are charged with this offence?"

The gallant old major forgot his new personality.

"An old assegai wound, sir, from the Zulu War——"

A warning cough from a friendly inspector sounded through the court.

"I mean, sir, overwork adding up pawntickets—very delicate work, sir, I assure you. Makes one very absent-minded. I asked this young constable to direct me to—er—to some spot in the African desert, which I visited in 1889 with Fabre's flying column, when I was in the French Service—I mean to say I had been reading the book. You

will find it in the United Services' Institute library. Excellent work; I can warmly recommend it, sir.

"This young constable, doubtless fearing for my health, took me—took me—er—took me to his headquarters, where I was received with all courtesy, and released on parole, after being refreshed from the men's canteen.

"I wish to congratulate you, sir, upon the courtesy and fine physique of the Metropolitan Police. Fine body of men, begad! Remind me of the old Dublin Fusiliers when I was at the Curragh——"

The magistrate coughed gently.

"I am glad to hear you say this, Major—I mean Mr. Smith—but I am afraid that I shall have to ask you to pay five shillings as a contribution for the attention you received."

Now, could anything have been more courtly, more perfect in style? The old gentleman borrowed the five shillings and a little more from me, and then went out to refresh the policeman who had "taken him in" and to lecture him for the good of his soul.

But after that it was unsafe to mention pawnbrokers' assistants to the old major, who had the most sarcastic tongue in London when he was thoroughly aroused.

To conclude, I remember the late Mr. Plowden, when he was magistrate, hearing a case in which two enormous navvies were accused of fighting in the street.

They were both obviously decent fellows, and looked terribly ashamed of themselves as they stood in the dock.

Plowden wagged a finger at them.

"'All dogs delight to bark and bite,'" he quoted, in inimitable fashion, and no one in the court could keep a straight face.

"Go home and make friends," he advised; and those two budding Herculeses scrambled out of the court as if Old Nick himself had been at their heels with the traditional red-hot fork.

Prison-Gate Dramas

(Continued from page 379.)

(Continued from page 379.)

in charge of a warder, and here again they have to answer to their names, which the warder in charge of the gate reads out from a paper signed by the governor of the prison.

All being correct, the warder inserts his huge steel key in the lock, and swings the heavy iron gate open.

The prisoners are then allowed to leave at intervals of a minute—the reason being that they may not then continue their acquaintance in the outside world and thus indulge in concerted crime.

AS this queer collection of flotsam emerges from the grim gate—the good, the not-so-good, and the good-for-nothing — there awaits them an assortment of individuals as queer as themselves—mothers, fathers, wives, sweethearts, crook pals, crank reformers, journalists, and many others.

Many and strange are the dramas and comedies enacted at the gates of prisons. Many pathetic, many tragic and heart-rending, some laughter-provoking.

Here is the parting of the ways.

A return to the crooked path and the underworld—or, a clean start on the broad but uphill road of honest endeavour and clean living, which?

Old Christmas Laws.

CHRISTMAS has not always been the merry time which we endeavour to make of Yuletide now. Laws which were intended not only to repress but suppress entirely any attempt at observance of Christmas Day were once backed up by threat of all sorts of blood-curdling punishments, which did not stop at burning at the stake.

It is a long way to hark back, but the reign of one named Diocletis, who had his fling during the years A.D. 284-305, gives us instances that bear out the above statement to the bitter—and hot—end.

He was dead set against anyone keeping Christmas, and when he heard that a band of Christians in his city of Nicomedia had gathered in a church to celebrate Christmas Day, in calm defiance of his law, torch-bearers were marched to the church, the building was set on fire, and the occupants roasted alive.

About a century later, the pendulum swung to the opposite extreme in Rome. Christmas became a fixed date, a recognised Christian feast-day, to be celebrated on December 25th, instead of on alternative dates like January 6th and March 25th, thus straightening out the date-confusion which was rife. And an Imperial "rescript" was issued forbidding theatres to open on Christmas Day.

The law then eased up considerably on the slaves of ancient Rome. The slaves were seated for their Christmas dinner at their master's table, and were waited on by him and his friends. And gambling with dice, illegal at all other times, was permitted on Christmas Day. Usually the day really extended to a week, during which the Roman slaves were accorded by law the grand privilege of wearing the same sort of hat which during the remainder of the year only free men were entitled to wear—a painted affair, of which our present-day fool's cap, which we find in the Christmas crackers, is symbolical.

Coming nearer our own times, the kill-joy Roundhead Parliament absolutely forbade any Christmas celebrations, and likewise made a clean sweep of Easter and Whitsun. That dreadful prohibition lasted ten years. Then, when Charles II. became King of England, the kill-joys received a nasty smack, and Christmas Day came legally into its own again.

Nearer still to our own century—as recent as 1820, in fact—you would, had you lived then, have committed an offence against the law had you gone serenading in London with any body of waits not in the paid employ of the individual who legally held the office of "boss" of the waits.

In Westminster it was an appointment under the control of the High Constable and the Court of Burgesses. The legally appointed "boss" of the waits paid folk to do his serenading for him, whatever sum they "earned" going into his private pocket. In the year above mentioned, the holder of the appointment discovered several unofficial waits about, and put the matter in the hands of the police.

There was a rumpus, but nothing definite in the way of prosecutions seems to have resulted. Now anyone can "wait" in the street without fear of the law—providing he packs up and goes away if requested by any annoyed dweller of the thoroughfare to take his nocturnal warbling elsewhere!

The Mystery of MRS. BARDELL'S XMAS PUDDING

(Continued from page 10.)

A thief could push in his arm, and anything within reach on the shelf could be easily taken."

"Well, I never, Master Tinker!" said Mrs. Cluppins. "I never thought of that. Never 'aving no occasion to open the window; it's cool enough in 'ere in the winter, in a manner of speaking. Fancy that, now!"

Tinker did not reply. His eyes sparkled with excitement as he noticed a protruding spike, which was evidently once a transverse bar of iron across the upright.

The bar had rotted away, leaving merely a spike of about two inches long embedded in the mortar. Attached to the spike was a shred of cloth—a diagonal tear, about three inches long, of some chequered material. Very carefully Tinker detached it, and leapt lightly down from Splash's shoulders.

"How your pudding disappeared is solved, I fancy, Mrs. Cluppins," he said.

He held aloft the shred of cloth.

"The thief must have crept down the area steps, saw the pudding through the window, inserted his arm, and 'nicked' it. He was probably too excited to notice that he tore his sleeve on the rusty iron crossbar.

"Voila! Now our job is to find a man with a coat of grey checks, with a diagonal tear in the cuff of his sleeve. See, by the stitching, it comes from the cuff!"

"Now, ain't that wonderful, now, Mary Ann?" Mrs. Bardell beamed. "Shows you the wonders of criminal dessication."

Splash Page grinned.

"Bully for you, young 'un! There's a chance to win our bet from old Coutts. Let's have a look at that cloth, Tinker!"

He scrutinised it carefully.

"Seems too small a shred for Pedro to work on," he said quietly. "Let's have a try, anyway."

"May I see the cloo?" asked Mrs. Bardell eagerly.

Splash handed over the fragment of material, and Mrs. Bardell gazed on it with a mixture of awe and repugnance.

Suddenly Mrs. Cluppins gave a little shrill scream.

"O-oh, the young varmint! It's that himp of hiniquity, Ginger Brown! I reckernise the cloth."

"What's that, Mrs. Cluppins?" demanded Tinker and Splash simultaneously. "Are you certain?"

"Certain?" replied the landlady. "O' course I'm certain! Ain't that young imp and 'is gang been the plague o' my life, and the plague of every respectable 'ouse in Rice Street?

"An owdacious young willain, 'e is, which 'is father ain't no better than 'e should be, 'im bein' a tipster and a potman at the Cat and Fiddle.

"Young Ginger, now I reckerlect, was a-wearin' of 'is farver's coat, cut down fer 'im. I seen 'im only yesterday—'im an' 'is young scamps was a-singin' carols an' makin' 'emselves perfec' noosances abart the place."

"Aha!" chuckled Tinker. "That's useful, Mrs. Cluppins. And where does young Brown live?"

"I dunno exac'ly where, but I think it's the nex' turnin' but one, past the Cat and Fiddle, over Ebury Bridge. You'll find 'is father in the pub, an' believe me, if I 'adn't 'ad too many shocks to-day, I'd go there an' give 'im a piece o' my mind—the willain! Pinchin' a pore woman's pudden, and——"

"Don't you worry about that, Mrs. Cluppins," Tinker soothed her. "I'll go along and interview Master Ginger, and we'll get your pudding back, if they haven't devoured it."

Accompanied by Splash Page, he passed out to the area steps and halted opposite the larder window.

"See, Splash, it's quite simple. A kid could easily pretend to sing carols and pinch the pudding when no one was looking."

The newspaperman nodded.

"What beats me is—assuming Mrs. Cluppins is correct—what connection has a kid lifting a Christmas pudding with the person who stabbed Captain Bill Barnes?"

"Blowed if I know," ejaculated Tinker. "Come, we'll give Pedro a little run."

He halted before the Grey Panther. The great bloodhound was lying stretched on the floor of the tonneau, his head between his paws. His eyes blinked mournfully as Tinker opened the door, then he gave a sudden "Wuff!" of delight as the lad slipped the leash in his collar.

"Come on, old boy! A brisk stroll will do you good."

A curious crowd of people watched Tinker and Splash Page, accompanied by the dog, as they walked down Rice Street towards Ebury Bridge.

"Lumme! That's Sexton Blake's assistant. I reckernise the dawg," muttered one burly navvy to his neighbour. "Blimey, what a night! Amberlances, motor-cars, an' now p'leece an' blood-'ounds!"

At the Cat and Fiddle, a large public-house, aflame with scintillating electric light signs, Tinker and Splash halted.

"It's a delicate business, this, Splash," said the youngster, hesitantly. "Blowed if it isn't! Can't very well accuse the potman of pinching the pudding, point-blank, and yet——"

"Tact!" replied Splash Page. "Tact and a little diplomacy. What are potatoes without salt, my boy? Tasteless, unedifying, disgusting! What is life without tact? The same! Diplomacy is the salt in the potatoes of life."

"Go hon!" said Tinker mockingly.

They entered the swing doors of the four-ale bar, which was decorated with evergreens, in honour of Christmas. The air was thick with pungent tobacco smoke and redolent of beer.

A cheerful little man in a seedy suit of clothes and a battered bowler-hat was endeavouring, without much success, it must be admitted, to insert a penny into the slot of the electric piano.

"We must 'ave carols," he cried hoarsely. "Jolly ole carols! Christmas comes but once a year—but wen it comes it brings good——"

"Beer!"

Came a stentorian roar from the crowd of good-humoured persons at the bar.

"'S funny thing," said the seedy man. "I can't get this 'lectric piano to play carols! 'Ere y'are, Ikey, you try! Lesh 'ave 'Christians awake, shalute 'appy morn!'"

He turned to his companion, a dark, Hebraic-looking man.

"Vot! I ain't going to salute no 'appy morns!" said Ikey indignantly. "I ain't a Christian——"

"Lorbless me! No more you ain't!" said the seedy one, in sudden realisation. "Never mind—'ave a drink."

Splash Page and Tinker chuckled. The newspaperman's keen journalistic brain was registering impressions, taking mental notes, as was his wont on every and any occasion, to be embodied later in his writings.

"There'll be plenty of D. and I.'s for Doc Williams to certify," chuckled Tinker, as he sipped his beer.

"Your name Brown?" said Splash suddenly to a stockily-built potman behind the bar. The man had a horsey sort of face, and wore a loud check suit.

"Yes; wot about it?" ejaculated Mr. Brown.

"Simply that I want you to have a drink with me, old man," said Splash Page, with the suavity he knew so well how to use on occasion.

A few flattering remarks about Mr. Brown's success as a tipster, and his infallibility as a guide to the Turf, soon mollified the potman, and it was easy enough for Splash to glean his address, No. 14, Lych Street.

"Where's that young nipper of yours, Ginger?" demanded the journalist. "A young rascal, if ever there was one—but game, Mr. Brown! I like kids with a bit of go in them. He sang carols outside my room yesterday, and I had quite a chat with him. I suppose he'll be hanging his stocking up to-night, and I was wondering if you'd care to put something in it for me."

He slid a ten-shilling note across the bar, and the potman's fingers closed on it greedily.

"Thank you, sir. Merry Christmas to you!" said Brown pere, with a mental reservation that his young hopeful wouldn't see a penny of the money if he, Mr. Brown, had any say in the matter.

Splash nodded a cheery good-night to everybody, and, accompanied by Tinker, left the place.

"Well, what's the next move?" demanded the lad. "Suppose when we do get to Lych Street, they've eaten the pudding?"

"Don't cross your bridges till you come to them, laddie," replied the journalist. "We will try a little moral persuasion on the excellent Mrs. Brown. Tact again—your boyish brown eyes might help in vamping the good soul. This way, my lad. I'm getting hungry enough to eat the pudding when we get it!"

THE SIXTH CHAPTER.
The Pirates of Pimlico.

"'USH!"

A voice sounded in a warning whisper in a dismantled shed of corrugated-iron close to Bennett's Timber Yard, in Pimlico.

A figure emerged cautiously from the black shadow of a vast advertisement hoarding, and crept furtively towards a gaping hole in the fence which surrounded the snow-covered timber yard.

A light flashed, once, twice, like a goblin's eye in the gloom, red and malignant. The figure breathed heavily as it fell flat on its stomach and wriggled its way towards the ricketty shed, heedless alike of the mud and snowy slush that littered the forecourt of the timber-yard.

"'Alt! Oo comes there?" rasped a voice from the darkness.

"Blackbeard the Terrible!" hissed the figure, rising suddenly to his feet.

"Advance, Blackbeard, and give the countersign!" came the challenge from the door.

"Blood and bones!" The reply was sepulchral, and delivered with evident relish.

"Enter, Blackbeard the Terrible!" commanded the sentry. And the door of the dismantled shed swung creakily open. The newcomer blinked in the flickering light of two candles, which were stuck in the necks of two empty beer bottles. In his hand he carried a cheap bullseye lantern, and its red eye shone balefully on the weird scene.

Seated on a soap-box was an extraordinary figure clad in a sort of cape that looked suspiciously like an old Army blanket. His face was half-hidden by a black silk mask, and an enormous, black moustache, fully a foot long, wobbled pendulously on his upper lip.

To complete his bizarre appearance, he wore a belt of rope, in which was thrust a rusty carving-knife and a fearsome-looking pistol of incredible antiquity; and to crown his eccentricities, the top of his head bore a flaming aureole of red hair.

The majestic figure on the soap-box tugged thoughtfully at his gargantuan moustache, and turned to the other occupants of the shed, some six in all, each dressed in a weird assortment of garments, with black dominoes masking their eyes.

"What hast thou brought to our feast, Blackbeard the Terrible?" said the person on the soap-box, and, despite the solemnity of the tone, the voice was curiously boyish.

"These, captain. I nicked 'em when muvver was——"

"What!" roared the captain, in a terrible voice. He tugged at his moustache so violently that it came off, and had to be replaced hurriedly.

"I'm sorry! I—I mean, I captured 'em from the henemy—an' scuttled all the crew. 'Ere is the booty," said Blackbeard hastily.

With a flourish, he unearthed a jar of pickles.

"Excellent, Blackbeard! Soon will our feast commence! Orinoco Pete"—he turned to the figure on his left, who immediately saluted—"see that the pot is a-boiling, for to-night we shall carouse till dawn. Where's the rum, shipmates?"

"'Ere!" said a piping voice, holding aloft three bottles of lemonade.

"Pour out in the gobberlets!" commanded the captain sternly.

Orinoco Pete, known to his schoolmates as "Young Alf 'Uggins," unearthed a cracked cup and three empty cigarette-tins.

"The gobberlets await thee, Captain Kidd!" he said, with a deep obeisance.

Mr. Herbert Brown, potman to the Cat and Fiddle, would have been staggered to discover that his son and heir, young Ginger, was in reality the notorious leader of the Pirates of Pimlico—Captain Kidd—and many an innocent mother, thinking perhaps a little wearily of how to make a really good Christmas dinner on her slender allowance, would have been astonished to learn that her offspring intended to carouse till dawn on rum—with a password of "blood and bones"!

A fearsome crew, indeed, were the Pirates of Pimlico, the invincible gang who could lick all comers at footer, at conkers, and at japes. Pledged to the death to support their leader, the redoubtable Captain Kidd, known as

Ginger Brown to an unsympathetic and non-understanding world.

"Boil the duff, my hearties!" roared Captain Kidd, in his boyish treble. "This morning, with my own 'ands, I raided the sloop and took revenge on the henemy for preevous wrongs."

He laughed mirthlessly. The hurt inflicted on him weeks before still rankled.

It was a little matter, really—an affair of a cricket-ball that had smashed into Mrs. Cluppins's favourite aspidistra, which, being somewhat anæmic, had been placed out on the window-sill. Mrs. Cluppins had taken summary vengeance on the culprit. Fortunately, none of the gang had been there to see the indignity of their redoubtable leader being spanked—but Ginger never forgave nor forgot.

Life is dreadfully serious when one is a boy of twelve!

But now, Captain Kidd tasted to the full the sweetness of revenge.

At first he had planned to harass the enemy by warbling incessant carols at her door, but by chance he had noticed the broken hasp of the window, and, to use his own expressive idiom, he boarded the sloop and secured the treasure!

It had been a brilliant idea, this nocturnal feast of Ginger's. Long ago they had made their headquarters at Bennett's disused shed, but to-night was the first time they had arranged a banquet there.

The pudding started the idea; and, like a wise leader, Captain Kidd had instructed his trusty crew to forage for additional luxuries. These comprised a bottle of pickles, a pound of apples, a tin of sardines, three bottles of lemonade—which, by some mysterious magic known only to youth, took on all the awesome qualities of rum—and, to wind up with, there was the pudding, most gloriously captured from the enemy, and boiling now over a fire of wood in a disused fire-bucket.

Captain Kidd raised his "gobberlet" to his lips, and nearly swallowed his moustache as he quaffed deeply.

"Fifteen men on the dead man's chest! Yo, ho, ho!—an' a bottle o' rum!"

Six boyish voices took up the chorus. Then suddenly the song ceased as a deep, resonant bay sounded eerily in the night.

"W-w-what was that?" hissed Blackbeard the Terrible.

With a prodigious effort Captain Kidd kept his hand from trembling as he pulled out his trusty—and rusty—pistol.

"See to it, Spanish Joe! Thou art the sentry!" he commanded sternly.

"I d-d-don't think I—I—— You go an' 'ave a look, Ginger!" said Spanish Joe, in a panic.

"What, dog of a mutineer? I'll 'ave thee 'ung!" roared Captain Kidd, but somehow his voice did not sound very steady.

Again that deep, blood-curdling bay rang out, and the pirate horde looked anxiously at their chief for guidance.

Ginger stiffened; beneath his ridiculous moustache his lips tightened. Policemen, heavy-handed parents, and busybody school-inspectors he could deal with; but this horrid baying was different. With a mighty effort he descended majestically from his improvised throne on the soap-box.

His heart was hammering violently; but it would not do to show fear in the face of the enemy, especially as his crew was looking on.

Little Ginger Brown was a well-plucked 'un, but probably the bravest

act of his short young life occurred that Christmas Eve in Bennett's yard. With a voice that tried bravely to keep the tremble out of it he hissed:

"Bide 'ere! I will deal with the henemy!" and tottered towards the door.

For a moment or two he peered into the gloom of the yard. It looked an eerie, deserted place, with its great piles of wood throwing dark, purple shadows on the powdery snow.

With fingers that trembled on his triggerless gun, the pirate chief held his breath. A sudden wild longing for home, and a comfortable bed with a stocking on the rail, gripped him, but he thrust it aside as childish.

He was the leader; to him fell the task of saving the "gang" from annihilation at the hands of the enemy. But then he stiffened suddenly, and his heart was gripped by the icy clutch of fear.

A low, throaty bay sounded from somewhere near by, and he saw two figures, preceded by an enormous animal that seemed to his startled eyes to have two enormous horns and blazing eyes.

"Lumme!" said Ginger, in a panic. "It's a tiger, or a rhino-sosserus, or somefin!"

He closed his eyes in sudden fear. What if the tiger leapt at him and——

"'Alt! 'Oo c-c-comes there?" he managed to challenge.

A cheerful voice rang out of the darkness.

"Is that you, Ginger?"

A great gasp of relief rose from the kid as the "tiger" approached and resolved itself into a big dog, held on a leash by a sturdy, broad-shouldered lad of about seventeen, accompanied by a tall, loose-limbed young man.

"Yus, it's me!" said Ginger a little truculently now. "Whaddyou want?"

"Ginger, I would have speech with thee," said the pleasant voice of Splash Page. "I bear thee gifts and messages."

Ginger gasped. Who was this "torf" with a cheery voice who spoke so oddly and yet so understandingly?

"Quiet, Pedro!" said Tinker, as the great bloodhound gave a short, excited bark.

Ginger's little heart hammered fast with excitement; his brain was reeling.

"Didjer say Pedro, mister?" he demanded hoarsely, and a wild, almost incredible thought had entered his mind.

"Certainly!" replied Tinker. "Now, look here, laddie, I want to have a talk with you about a pudding. Your mother said you often played around Bennett's yard here, so we came here on the off-chance."

"Y-yes," said Ginger, and his lips quivered tremulously beneath his absurd moustache. It was all up now, he thought.

"The perlice, prison, an'—an'——"

The glory of seeing Sexton Blake's bloodhound faded.

"Cheer up, Ginger, my boy!" said Splash Page, with a whimsical smile at the oddly-clad, woebegone little figure. "We're not going to harm you. We just want to know what you've done with the pudding?"

Splash Page loved children, and his keen, newspaper mind had already gleaned that he had stumbled on a secret "gang" meeting so beloved of boyhood.

"Is there a place where we can talk in secret?" he hissed melodramatically.

Ginger brightened visibly.

"Ho, yus! But—but please is that Mr. Sexton Blake's blood'ound? An'—an' are you Mr. Tinker?"

"Sure!" laughed the young detective.

"But don't be so scared We're not after you, sonny."

"Scared!" echoed Ginger, half-lemented with excitement. "Oh, mister—mister, could you—could you let my gang see yer jus'—jus' for a minit?" he said.

Hero-worship shone in his eyes.

"We'll make you 'onorary members o' the Pimlico Pirates, an'—an'——"

Splash Page clapped the kid affectionately on the shoulders.

"Lead on, my hearty! We shall be honoured."

Ginger will never forget that Christmas Eve, which established once and for all his triumphant leadership of Pimlico boy gangdom. His little heart almost bursting with pride, he introduced Tinker and Splash Page to his petrified followers.

The newspaperman listened gravely as Ginger described his plans for a banquet. He and Tinker solemnly drank "rum" from the cracked "gobberlet." And then, with a little diffidence, Ginger described his theft of the "pudden."

"Where is it?" demanded Splash eagerly. "Don't tell me you've eaten it!"

"Naow!" said Ginger. "But we was just a-goin' to. It's in there, exac'ly as we captured it." He pointed to the fire-bucket sizzling slowly over the fire in the corner of the shed.

Tinker whistled softly.

"It's a near squeak. Now, Ginger, my lad, it was wrong of you to pinch that pudding. Real pirates don't rob poor women, you know—not really chivalrous pirates. However, we'll overlook that this time, on condition you give us the pudding."

Ginger nodded.

"I'm sorry, mister. But you see. I—I 'ad to 'ave revenge. She captured me, an'—an'——"

With downcast eyes he related the aspidistra episode.

Splash Page chuckled. He glanced at Tinker.

"Now, my bold, bad pirates, fetch the pudding, and ye shall feast till dawn," he said.

Blackbeard the Terrible promptly fished out the pudding-basin, the cloth of the basin tied around with string.

The newspaperman waited for it to cool, and then he whispered something to Tinker.

Pedro was enjoying himself thoroughly as the centre of an admiring crowd, who fed him with assorted tit-bits of sardines and pickles.

"Many thanks, Gin—er—Captain Kidd," said Tinker. "On behalf of Mr. Sexton Blake we would like to add to this banquet. Take this and divide it between you."

He took out a pound note from his wallet, and Page did likewise.

The astonished Ginger took them like one in a dream.

"But I—I say, mister——"

His eyes goggled. Never in his life had he seen such wealth. The future opened up vast—splendid—dazzling!

Pistols for the pirates—swords——

He gulped, then his shrill treble rang out.

"Orl togevver, shipmates! Three earty cheers for Mr. Sexton Blake, Mr. Tinker, and Mr. Pige!"

The old shed rang with lusty shouts as the pirate crew capered ecstatically. Tinker and the journalist quietly slipped out while the din was at its height.

Splash hugged the Christmas-pudding to his bosom, and he smiled in the darkness.

"Poor little kids! Remember when

"'Alt! 'Oo comes there?" rasped a voice from the darkness. "Blackbeard the Terrible!" hissed the figure with the wooden sword. (*See opposite page.*)

we used to play pirates, Tinker?" he asked.

Tinker nodded. The time was not very far distant when he had been a member of a gang in his boyhood. But that gang also was a really criminal one—somewhere in the East End. If Sexton Blake had not rescued him from that squalid slum——

He refused to consider the alternative, but in his heart was a great sympathy for little Ginger Brown. From the shed six treble voices chanted excitedly:

"Fifteen men on the dead man's chest! Yo, ho, ho!—an' a bottle o' rum!'"

"Happy days!" murmured Splash Page. "But, come, we've got the pudding. It's a darned good job we arrived in time. Let's get back to Rice Street and see what's happened."

THE SEVENTH CHAPTER.
The Man With the Beady Eyes.

INSPECTOR COUTTS was very much annoyed.

In the first place, he strongly objected to the interruption of a cheery, convivial Christmas Eve in Sexton Blake's home in Baker Street. Secondly, he was exasperated at the incredible amount of importance Sexton Blake attached to the missing Christmas-pudding; and, thirdly, he was disgusted with

his own obtuseness in not being able to see a single gleam of light amidst the encircling gloom that surrounded the attack on Roaring Bill Barnes.

"I say, Blake," he said plaintively, as he followed the detective out of No. 14, Rice Street, some ten minutes after Tinker and Splash Page's departure in quest of the pudding, "I can't make head or tail of those three clues you're talking about. What the deuce has snow to do with Mex, and Mex with pudding? The only Mex I know is a brand of petrol. Where are we going now?" he added.

Sexton Blake smiled. He had a genuine affection for the burly C.I.D. man, one of the most loyal friends he had in Scotland Yard. A dogged, brave, efficient police-officer, with a certain painstaking thoroughness, and a blind belief in the Yard machine—that was Coutts.

Imagination he had, in some directions, but he had none of those subtle flashes of intuition which are characteristic of the detective par excellence, and which were such a noteworthy feature of Blake's character.

"We are going to call at No. 8, Hengist Road, Coutts," explained Blake. "I have an idea that the mysterious Mex may be at home."

"What!" gasped the inspector. "Here, Blake, this is too much. I've seen what you've seen, examined everything in connection with the case, and yet you calmly tell me you know where the man who stabbed Captain Barnes lives!"

"There you go again, Coutts," said Blake, a trifle wearily. "I merely said that Mex may be at home. I did not make a definite statement."

"But how on earth——" persisted Coutts.

"Possess your soul in patience, my dear fellow," said Blake quietly. "Think of the millions of kiddies who are hanging up their stockings to-night, eagerly awaiting Santa Claus. Yet they've got to curb their impatience until to-morrow morning. Perhaps you may find the solution of the mystery in your stocking, if you hang it up."

"Bah!" ejaculated Coutts.

A clock chimed the hour of nine, and Blake whistled softly.

"Jove, Coutts, we'll have to hustle if we're going to have our holiday Christmas! Fortunately, Hengist Road is just round the corner."

To all intents and purposes Hengist Road might have been Rice Street. The same drab-coloured houses, with their air of faded gentility, composed its brief length.

At No. 8 Blake halted. He whispered to Coutts.

"I have no idea of what will happen," he said, "but there's just a chance that we're on the right track."

With a sudden gesture he gently removed Coutts' bowler hat and dented it with his fist.

"Here, hold on! What the—— Have you gone mad, Blake?" demanded the incensed inspector.

Blake grinned, and plucked out Coutts' neatly-tied cravat.

"Great jumping Jehosophat! I said I was dealing with a pack of lunatics!" gasped Coutts.

His eyes became alarmed. He glanced oddly at Blake's impassive countenance, and his voice became soft and soothing.

"I say, Blake, old man, you'd better come on. You're not well. The heat—I mean, the cold—it's been too much for you."

Blake chuckled, and promptly put his hat back to front, and, turning up his collar, began to sing in an execrable voice:

"Goo' ole pal,
Jolly ole pal,
You're the feller for me!"

Inspector Coutts became really alarmed. He glared round wildly, but Blake hissed out in a sibilant undertone.

"It's all right, Coutts, you ass! Pretend you're half-inebriated. That's the only way not to arouse suspicion."

Coutts sighed with relief. He was beginning to realise Blake's scheme. Blake ascended the steps unsteadily, accompanied by the slightly dishevelled figure of Coutts.

He rang the bell, and a moment after the door opened, to admit the odour of fried onions on the frosty atmosphere of Hengist Road. A tall, broad-shouldered, bullet-headed man looked at them shiftily with eyes as beady as black hatpin heads.

"Well, wodjer want, kickin' up orl this row?" he demanded.

Blake hiccoughed slightly.

"Ol' Jose, jolly ol' Jos'! Mex tole me and my pal 'e'd meet us at the Cat and Fiddle. We've waited hours, but 'e ain't come. Is 'e at 'ome?"

"I dunno oo yer mean—Mex. You're drunk, that's wot you are," replied the man with the beady eyes.

"Oh, no! Oh, no! 'Sonly a li'l Krissmus cheer," protested Blake indignantly. "I mean the dark, furrin chap. 'Im wot came 'ere this week."

"Ah!" said the man at the door. "Yer mean Face, Spanish bloke, name o' Fernandez or summat."

"That's 'im," said Blake, with a grin.

"Well, 'e ain't at 'ome. Gorn out a copla 'ours ago. 'E said somethink abart

meetin' a feller named Tosti or Costi at Dutch Joe's."

"That's me—Bill Costi," said Blake unblushingly. "But 'tweren't at Dutch Joe's; 'twas at the Cat and Fiddle. I dunno where Dutch Joe is."

"Um!" said the man doubtfully. "You're a pair, you are, you an' old Face. Dutch Joe's dahn by the river on Chelsea reach, back o' Lots Road."

"Thanks, mate!" said Blake. "An' a merry Chrissmuss t'you."

"Min' you don't get run in," said the beady-eyed man, with a grin.

The word Christmas had evoked a touch of cheeriness even in his melancholy visage.

"Excellent!" said Blake, as they reached the corner of Hengist Road, and resumed their ordinary respectable selves. "We now have another link. Mr. 'Face' Fernandez seems to be our man."

"Yes! but," began Coutts, still puzzled, "why pretend to be drunk? Why knock a dent into my bowler hat—my wife's Christmas present," he added aggrievedly.

Blake chuckled.

"The dent won't hurt it, my dear fellow. Besides, in this case we have to walk warily. Supposing we had announced ourselves as police-officers, do you think we could have got any information out of our bullet-headed friend?

"Then, again, if Fernandez had been in, and he didn't wish to see us, he would have been forewarned, and thus forearmed.

"But a couple of disreputable-looking, rather hilarious friends, calling round on Christmas Eve—who would suspect them? If Fernandez cut up rough, or turned out to be the wrong man, we could get out of it gracefully by acting disgracefully."

"Psychology, my dear Coutts. People like Mr. Bullet-head don't open up freely to representatives of the law, but they cast a lenient eyes on the convivial."

"Huh! I see that, all right, Blake. But what beats me is how you know Fernandez lived there."

"I didn't know," explained the detective. "Bullet-head supplied that information. I merely asked, vaguely, after Jose—or Mex—he kindly put me wise. You recall the letter which perturbed Roaring Bill so much mentioned that Jose was leaving Marseilles for England. Jose and Fernandez are evidently one and the same."

"Yes; but——" interjected Coutts. "How the deuce did you know he was staying at Hengist Road?"

"Because, if you will observe, my dear Coutts," replied Blake smoothly, "No. 8, Hengist Road is exactly parallel to No. 14, Rice Street—the backyards of both houses are separated merely by a bottle-encrusted wall. Does that make things any clearer to you?"

"Well, I'm blessed," said Coutts. "I never imagined that. But tell me, what's this Mex got to do with it?"

"Mex, I presume, is a contraction for Mexican," said Blake patiently. "Take that fact in conjunction with what I've just told you, together with the fingerprint on the blade instead of the handle of the knife, and you'll realise how Captain Barnes was stabbed—and why no visitor entered his room."

Coutts whistled.

"Jove, what an ass I've been! I'm just beginning to see it. But what's the pudding got to do with it? Why, hallo, here come Tinker and Splash," he added, as he saw two figures and a dog loom from the darkness.

"Hallo, guv'nor! We've got the pudding!" said Tinker cheerily. "Rescued it from a gang of bloodthirsty pirates."

It was Sexton Blake's turn to be startled.

"Splendid work, my boy. I really did not expect such a triumphant end to your quest."

"Ten bob, please, Coutts," chuckled Splash, holding out his palm.

"Hang on a bit, my lad. We haven't identified the pudding yet. Besides, we've—er—almost discovered the assassin who stabbed Roaring Bill."

"What!" gasped Splash. "By Jove, that's splendid! How——"

"Don't stand waiting here. We've attracted quite enough of a crowd as it is!" snapped Blake. He led the way to Mrs. Cluppins' house, and Mrs. Bardell, a little flushed of face after the port, ushered them into the front parlour.

"There, ladies and gentlemen," said Tinker, with a slight flourish, "is the purloined pudding!"

He placed on the table a pudding-basin about eight inches in diameter. Mrs. Bardell duly identified it.

"How on earth did you find it?" gasped Coutts. "Mrs. Cluppins, here, told us you discovered how it had been stolen, but when did you recover it?"

Very briefly Splash told the story of Master Ginger Brown, alias Captain Kidd of the Pimlico Pirates. Blake chuckled quietly as the narrative progressed, and Mrs. Cluppins muttered audibly: "The young villain—the ow'dacious young limb!"

"You are quite certain that the pudding is the same as the one you made, Mrs. Bardell?" demanded Blake, at length.

His housekeeper carefully scrutinised the basin, and lifted the pudding-cloth, which had been firmly tied down with string. "Perfec'ly certain, Mr. Blake. This is one of my own pudden-cloths; see the initial B in marking-hink."

She pointed to one corner of the damp cloth.

Blake nodded.

"Nothing like being methodical, Mrs. Bardell. And now to solve the pudding's secret."

He took a knife, and was about to cut the string, when he gave a low whistle of surprise. Tinker looked at him curiously.

"What's the matter, guv'nor?" he ejaculated.

Blake laughed shortly.

"I was—er—merely thinking how apt Splash's story was. You remember, he spoke of pirates at Baker Street?"

"By Jove, yes. But it was Roaring Bill he made a pirate—not Ginger Brown," Tinker agreed.

"Lawks! Supposin' as 'ow the old man 'as 'idden 'is treasure in the pudden!" gasped Mrs. Bardell excitedly, as Blake carefully untied the peculiarly knotted string.

The little group round the table watched with bated breath as the detective carefully removed the pudding-cloth—next the grease-paper, and, finally, turned over the basin on to a plate. Would Splash Page's fantastic theory turn out to be true, and a shower of crimson rubies fall out, or——

"Ah!"

The two women gave a gasp as Blake shook the basin and removed it, to disclose—a rich, brown plum-pudding.

"There's nothing there but a pudden," said Mrs. Cluppins, heartily disappointed.

"Wait a minute," said Coutts. "I vote we cut it up, and search the pieces; if there's nothing there, we can eat the pudding—that is, if Mrs. Cluppins doesn't object. I'm a bit peckish."

Plates and forks were produced, and the famous pudding was divided into six portions. Mrs. Bardell, aglow with pride, awaited the verdict.

"Scrumptious," said Tinker, smacking his lips. It really was an excellent pudding. Even Blake, who usually eschewed sweets, admitted that fact.

Suddenly Tinker's face crimsoned. He spluttered.

"B-by gum, I've bitten on something. I've got it!"

"What—a ruby?" demanded Coutts, excitedly.

Somehow he half expected to find a raisin-covered gem in the pudding, after the fantastic events of the past few hours.

"No," replied Tinker, removing something deftly from his mouth. "A threepenny-bit!"

He showed the gleaming little coin in the palm of his hand.

"Dash it!" grumbled Coutts. "That can't be what Captain Barnes was after. What is the secret of the pudding?"

Mrs. Bardell looked blank.

"I cert'nly didn't put anythink in the duff barring the raisins and flour and suet and the candied peel and the frippenny-bit," she protested.

"Then the pudding hasn't got a secret," murmured Splash Page, a trifle disconsolately. "In Heaven's name, what did Roaring Bill mean when he said that the secret was there? Why should he rave about that particular one, and refuse another made of the very same duff?"

Coutts tapped his forehead significantly.

"Bats! Bats in the belfry!" he said gruffly.

Tinker sighed. He was bitterly disappointed. On the face of it, excellent though the pudding tasted, 'twas a pudding, nothing more.

"Well, satisfied now, Blake?" demanded Coutts. "I told you that Barnes was mad, or drunk, or both."

"On the contrary," said Blake blandly, "the secret of the pudding is solved. Far from being a fool, Captain Bill Barnes had his wits about him. I can quite understand his dismay at the theft of this particular pudding."

"What on earth do you mean?" demanded Splash Page, in bewilderment. "Have you got a clue, or——"

Sexton Blake smiled inscrutably, and turned to Mrs. Cluppins.

"I suppose that, now your lodger is in hospital, and others are on holiday, you will find Christmas very lonely here. If you can manage to do so, I'm sure Mrs. Bardell would like to entertain you at Baker Street."

"Oh, thank you, sir!" said Mrs. Cluppins. "I couldn't a-bear the thought of bein' alone in the 'ouse. I'm glad you awsked the perliceman to watch upstairs while you was out."

"Very well, then," Blake replied crisply.

He glanced at his watch. It was twenty minutes past nine.

"Tinker, you take Mrs. Bardell and her sister to Baker Street in the Grey Panther. Please lay supper for us by eleven o'clock, Mrs. B., and you, Tinker, return to pick up Coutts, Splash and myself at 10 to 10.15 at a public-house known as Dutch Joe's in Lots Road, Chelsea."

Mrs. Cluppins and Mrs. Bardell beamed ecstatically at each other, and hurried away to don their outdoor garments. Sexton Blake's face was very grave.

"That woman ought not to stay here

alone an instant longer. It is very dangerous," he said.

"Coutts, I would like you to mount guard over the house until my return. Fernandez may, I am not perfectly certain, he may make an attempt at an entry. If so, collar him, never mind a warrant or charge, and hold him until my return from Dutch Joe's."

"Right you are," Coutts assented. "I'll have a chance of writing up the facts of the business and relieve Constable Johnson for a bit."

"You, Splash,"—Blake turned to the journalist—"you'd better come along with me to Dutch Joe's, and I'll explain as we go."

Tinker stared curiously at his beloved guv'nor. Who was Fernandez? What was the secret of Mrs. Bardell's pudding? What danger threatened Mrs. Cluppins?

His head whirled at the rapidity with which the case had developed, almost from nothing. The theft of a Christmas pudding by a small boy. It seemed a little thing, yet in its train had followed a murderous attack, and who knew what further bizarre adventures were to happen in the Chelsea saloon of Dutch Joe's?

THE EIGHTH CHAPTER.
At Dutch Joe's Joint.

SNOW began to fall thickly and heavily as Splash Page and Sexton Blake emerged from No. 14, Rice Street.

The newspaperman turned up his coat-collar and shivered a little.

"I didn't bargain for a murder hunt on Christmas Eve, Blake, old man," he chuckled. "Shows what a dog's life we've chosen. Now, if we'd been bank clerks or chartered accountants, with nice, placid little villas in Balham or Norbury, we'd be dressing up as Santa Claus and filling the kids' stockings; instead of which, we——"

"Instead of which, you old humbug," Blake interposed, "you're throughly enjoying yourself, and planning another front-page story out of Mrs. Bardell's Christmas pudding."

Splash Page laughed.

"I haven't quite worked it all out yet, Blake, and I'm not going to question you yet; but I take it Comrade Fernandez is the engaging gentleman who stabbed Roaring Bill?"

Blake nodded.

"It is not certain, of course; but I would rather like an interview with the gentleman."

At the corner of Ebury Street they hailed a taxi. By this time the snow fell thick and fast, a blinding scurry of white.

From neighbouring churches the Christmas chimes began to ring a merry clangour of sound that pealed the joyous message of Yule through the scurry of the snow-filled night.

Blake sighed a little, half-regretfully, as he settled back in the taxi. There was an unwontedly sombre look on his clear-cut face.

"A bit paradoxical—eh, Splash?" he said quietly. "Peace on earth—good will to men—and here we are on trail of a would-be murderer."

Splash Page nodded.

"Life is full of paradoxes, Blake. I

remember——" His eyes became abstracted. "Over in France I was war correspondent on the Mons salient just about Christmas time. There'd been a pretty hot 'strafe' on Fritz' side, then suddenly on Christmas Eve it ceased.

"It was weird, uncanny. Day and night for seven days the Germans had bombarded us; the din was terrific, and then, just for one brief half-hour, there was silence. We literally felt peace in the air. That was in '14.

"Our lads were exhausted with fatigue, almost dropping with weariness. Then suddenly from the German front line trenches came—what do you think?—the strains of a Boche gramophone, accompanied by a score of voices singing Christmas carols!

"Our lads joined in the choruses, and for half an hour friend and foe had forgotten the war, forgotten everything, save the old, old familiar tunes of Christmas. I remember one enthusiast wanted to go over the top and take a party of carol singers to entertain the Boche; then——

"Boom! The guns took a hand in the game, and it was war again. Rum business—war," added Splash thoughtfully.

Along King's Road, down Sidney Street towards the Thames Embankment the taxi bowled. Tugs hooted mournfully, nosing their way gingerly up the turgid Thames, white and mysterious 'neath the falling snow.

Chelsea old church, with its mantle of snow, and lighted windows, looked like some idyllic Christmas magazine cover as they passed through to Lots Road. Here Chelsea slums commenced, and they heard the high, piping voices of carol singers.

"Here we are!" cried Splash, as the taxi slowed down before a gaunt-looking restaurant at the corner of the Embankment side of World's End. Blake curtly told the driver to wait, and they passed into the gaily lighted place.

He took a keen, comprehensive glance around the room, which was crowded with a weird assortment of people. Chelsea artists in broad-brimmed black hats and floppy ties sat next to blowsy women from the World's End.

Here and there a sailorman sat eating fish and chips with gusto, but for the most part the customers seemed to be foreigners of various nationalities. In the corner a tired-looking orchestra played out-of-date fox-trots.

Blake glanced at his watch. It was a quarter to ten.

"Fortunately, this place has an eleven o'clock licence, Splash," he whispered. "I suppose the fat gentleman behind the counter is Dutch Joe."

An enormous man, with a greasy face and innumerable chins, was perched, like some porcine deity, behind a delicatessen counter. His face was as devoid of expression as a blancmange, when Splash Page inquired where they could obtain a drink.

"Trinks—oopstairs!" he nodded. "Ja. You to the left must turn."

Blake led the way up a flight of rickety stairs, and entered a long, garishly painted room, evidently used as a dance-hall. Little tables were perched at intervals round the wall. In the corner a peroxided barmaid with a shrill voice presided at the bar.

Another orchestra, that looked even more tired and torpid than the one downstairs, played on a little dais at the end of the room. The walls were weirdly and wonderfully decorated by cubist pictures, and paper streamers and Chinese lanterns were festooned from the ceiling. Over the bar holly and mistletoe hung.

one bunch of mistletoe resting coyly above the head of the peroxided damsel—a fact which seemed to have escaped the notice of most of the men present, much to her annoyance.

"Gosh! So this is Bohemia!" said Splash Page wearily. "How on earth these long-haired men and short-haired women manage to enjoy themselves in a foul hole like this, I don't know!"

He ordered two whiskys-and-sodas from a depressed-looking waiter, and the orchestra, probably out of sympathy with the lady beneath the mistletoe bough, played plaintively, "I Ain't Nobody's Darling."

"How the deuce are you going to recognise Fernandez?" whispered Splash to Sexton Blake. "You haven't got much to go on."

Blake shrugged.

"I have never had a description of the man, but I fancy that's the gentleman in the corner there, talking volubly to the bald-headed man."

Splash turned, and saw a tall, swarthy man, with liquid brown eyes, and short, aggressively waxed moustache beneath a beaky nose. A deep scar ran diagonally from his lower lip to the lobe of his left ear, giving his face a queer, lopsided grin that was ugly and sinister.

"What makes you think that's the fellow, Blake?" demanded Splash, who was always curious about Blake's uncanny deductions.

Blake smiled.

"The only hints I had to go on were what Mr. Bullet-head told me, and what I learned from Ben Bolt's letter. Bullet-head referred to him as 'Face'—a charming Cockney soubriquet to anyone with an unprepossessing physiognomy.

"I accordingly looked out for a man with features deserving of the epithet. That, alone, is, of course, not much to go on; but as Fernandez has only arrived in England a few days ago, and is a Mexican, that narrows the search.

"The gentleman with the twisted grin is a Mexican—note his tobacco-pouch, and his way of rolling a cigarette, the consummate ease of it. The high-heeled boots were never made in Europe; he speaks Spanish, with a mixture of Mexican patois."

"But, good heavens, Blake," said Splash, "you're too far away to hear what he's saying! He's right at the other end of the room."

"I strongly advise you to cultivate lip-reading, my dear fellow!" responded Blake, suavely. "It's a great asset to a pushful newspaperman."

"Kamerad!" laughed Splash. "What's the next move?"

Blake's answer was peculiar.

"Have you, by any chance, a piece of string in your pocket, Splash?" he inquired.

The newspaperman looked at him in astonishment.

"What on earth for? Are you going to tie him up?"

"No. I fancy a game of cats'-cradles," Blake bantered, with a whimsical gleam in his steel-grey eyes. Splash fumbled in his pocket, and produced a short length of twine. He watched Blake's slim, nervous fingers as the detective knotted it in a curious fashion, about a dozen times.

"Dotty!" said Splash, in an undertone. "Quite dotty!"

"Quite right. The principle is—er—dotty," replied the detective blandly. "Several dots, in fact."

He pointed to about a dozen knots in the string.

"Garcon!" With upraised finger he caught the waiter's eye, and as he shuffled towards him, Blake lowered his voice. "Get ready for action, Splash! Got a gun?"

The wondering newspaper man nodded. Things were getting beyond him.

"Garcon!" said Blake, in rapid French. "Voyez vous cet monsieur au coin?"

The waiter nodded.

"C'est une blague du Noel! It's a little joke for Christmas," Blake explained smoothly. "Take to him this piece of string, and say it is with the compliments of Captain Roaring Bill, please. And, waiter——" He slipped a silver coin into the waiter's palm with the dexterity of a conjurer.

The garcon gave a fleeting smile, and shuffled across the dance floor towards the man with the lopsided smile.

"Now watch!" hissed Blake.

His eyes gleamed with suppressed excitement, but the rest of his face was as impassive as granite.

Splash Page watched, fascinated, and then, like a flash, it happened. With a scream of fear the Mexican rose to his feet, his chair overturned with a crash. He stared stupidly at the piece of knotted string in his hand, and then his blazing eyes swept the dance-hall.

The waiter pointed towards Sexton Blake, evidently explaining. The Mexican's swarthy face became convulsed with fury.

"Madre Dios!" he screamed, and his hideous, twisted grin gave a fiendish expression to his face.

"Look out!" roared Sexton Blake.

Like a flash something bright whizzed through the air. Blake dragged the newspaperman downward.

Thud! The something buried itself in the wall, and stuck there, quivering, one inch above Splash Page's head. It was a barrel-hilted knife!

In an instant pandemonium broke loose in the crowded room. A woman's scream shattered through the babel of excited voices.

"Get the other chap, Splash!" roared Sexton Blake; and with a bound he hurled himself across the ball-room, fingers crooked, full at the Mexican's throat.

"Curse you!" snarled Fernandez sobbingly, as Blake bore him floorward with a reverberating crash. "I'll kill you, dog of a Gringo!"

The Mexican was a powerful brute; he squirmed and wriggled like an eel. His knee jerked and caught Blake a sharp blow in the plexus.

The detective grunted with the pain of it, his stranglehold relaxed, and, with a lightning gesture, Fernandez turned over and scrambled to his feet.

His hand flew to his hip-pocket, and, as if by magic, a nickelled automatic appeared between his muscular brown fingers. Blake was badly winded, but, even as the Mexican's finger trembled on the trigger, he leapt up and his foot caught the man's hand in a vicious kick.

Bang! Blake's boot caught Fernandez's wrist, the gun leapt upward, a tongue of flame spat out of the muzzle, and an instant later the hall was plunged into darkness. The electric light had been shattered by the deflected bullet.

Immediately the place became a shrieking chaos. Women screamed hysterically, men shouted as they struggled madly in the roaring dark. Sexton Blake, however, with uncanny accuracy, had "placed" Fernandez's position, just as the light was extinguished. He struck a violent short-arm jab upwards, and his knuckles barked against flesh and bone.

"Ouch!" A strangled cry of pain ripped through the darkness, and a body crashed to the floor.

Breathing heavily and painfully, Blake groped for his torch, and the yellow beam flashed through the darkness, to illumine the limp body of Fernandez asprawl on the floor.

Blake grinned ruefully amidst the pandemonium of noise, and from his hip pocket he withdrew a pair of hand-cuffs. Came a click, and Fernandez was pinioned.

"You all right?" roared the voice of Splash Page above the babel.

"Sure!" called Blake. "Got your man?"

"First go! Confound this darkness!" came the voice of the newspaperman.

Pheep, pheep! Police whistles shrilled through the night air, the stamp of heavy feet sounded on the stairs.

"Police, police!" cried a dozen hysterical voices.

"This way, officer!" snapped Blake, flashing his torch. "Let the others go. We've got our men!"

"Yes. 'Oo the perishin' blazes are you?" demanded a beefy constable, suspiciously flashing his bullseye on Blake's dishevelled figure.

"I—— My name is Sexton Blake," replied the detective blandly. "A very merry Christmas to you, constable! Sorry to disturb you, and all that, but here's something nice for your Christmas stocking!" And, with a laugh, Blake pointed to the unconscious Fernandez, of whom it might have been stated, "the subsequent proceedings interested him no more."

THE NINTH CHAPTER.
Sexton Blake's Treasure.

CHRISTMAS DAY in Baker Street. Outside, across the snowy roofs that gleamed white in the pale rays of a December sun, there floated the joyous carillon of Christmas bells.

"Good old Christmas!" yelled Tinker, dashing—late, as usual—into the breakfast-room.

He halted on the threshold, appalled at the frenzied din that greeted his entry—sounds that seemed almost sacrilegious in the usually calm and austere atmosphere of Sexton Blake's famous residence.

"What the deuce!" gasped Tinker, in amazement, as he opened the door. Then he grinned, unabashed. Sexton Blake, Splash Page, and Inspector Coutts were tapping incessantly with their forks on the sides of their tea-cups.

Ping! Pang! Ping!

The short, staccato notes were monotonous and deafening in their intensity, and Tinker flushed. He was being drummed out! He looked at the clock, which registered half-past ten.

"Hey, stop it, please—please!" he pleaded. "I'm sorry I'm late, but——"

"Late—on Christmas morning!" reproved Inspector Coutts, with an admonitory wag of his fat forefinger.

"All good children are up with the lark on this gladdest day of all the year!" added Splash Page, with a grin.

Tinker flung up his hand in mock surrender.

"Right-ho, kamarad! I plead guilty!" he said.

Immediately the tintinabulation ceased, and the lad sat down. By his plate was piled an assortment of brown-paper parcels, and Tinker gazed at them curiously.

"You don't deserve anything from Santa Claus, you lazy young rascal," said Sexton Blake, with a chuckle. "We're almost finished breakfast, and how you will find room for Mrs. Bardell's Christmas dinner I can't imagine."

Tinker laughed, and began to open his parcels with fingers that trembled slightly. He was yet boy enough to experience the thrill of unwrapping a Christmas present. He drew in his breath sharply, as he unfolded from its wrap of cotton-wool a beautiful gold cigarette-case, with a neat monogram of tiny emeralds. Inside was inscribed simply:

"To Tinker, from Sexton Blake, Christmas, 1925."

"Jove, guv'nor, what a beauty!" he said, his eyes glistening. "Thanks, ever so much!"

"It'll do to keep your woodbines in, young 'un," bantered Blake. "We all seem to have been in Santa Claus' good books this year." With a laugh, he indicated a pile of parcels on the sideboard.

Detective-Inspector Coutts pointed with pride to his box of Trichinopoli cigars, together with an amber-and-gold cigar-holder, a gift from Splash Page and Blake.

Blake himself glanced eagerly at a jade jar, filled with his favourite brand of tobacco—a present from Tinker, together with a pair of moccasin, fur-lined slippers from Splash Page.

"I'd have got you a dressing-gown—honest I would, Blake," said the newspaperman. "But——"

"No use offering the guv'nor a new one—he'll wear that atrocity till it drops off him," laughed Tinker.

It was a very merry breakfast-party. There were presents and good wishes for everybody. Splash Page was particularly pleased with a massive, big-barrelled fountain-pen—Blake's appropriate gift.

"Let the Government beware!" chuckled Splash, waving his present menacingly. "With this I shall assail the seats of the mighty. The pen is mightier than the sword. Stronger than——"

"Even my tobacco!" chimed in Blake.

From somewhere in the basement came the not unmelodious voice of Mrs. Bardell, singing a plaintive ballad popular in the days of her youth, about an unfortunate young lady who died on a Christmas morning, the burden of which seemed to be:

"'Er pore fice that once was so loverly in life
   Is as cold as the snow on the cem-e-tary;
An' the gallant young squire wot made 'er 'is wife
   Sits a-breakin' 'is 'eart for pore Bonny Mary."

Not that Mrs. Bardell was downhearted about the tragic fate of poor Bonny Mary. On the contrary, her buxom, good-humoured face beamed with placid contentment as, assisted by Mrs. Cluppins, she bustled about the kitchen, superintending the arrangement of the all-important Christmas dinner.

"Sounds of revelry heard 'off'!" chuckled Splash Page, as he rose to his feet. "Now, Blake, dear old sleuth, do

Even as the Mexican's finger trembled on the trigger, Blake's foot caught his hand in a vicious kick.

(See opposite page.)

for goodness' sake put us out of our misery! You are the darndest secretive old hoss I ever encountered. 'Pon my soul, you are!"

"We get into a rough house last night. Coutts gets his man safe under lock and key for attempted murder. We come home last night, burning with curiosity to know the why and the wherefore of it, and you calmly tell us to wait until to-day."

Sexton Blake laughed.

"Please curb your impatience, Splash. A good story, like good wine, mellows with keeping. You know my foibles. I have only to clear up one or two small matters this morning, and I promise faithfully that the secret of Mrs. Bardell's Christmas pudding shall be revealed in its entirety immediately after dinner.

"I have purposely asked Mrs. Bardell to alter our usual dinner-hour to seven o'clock to-day, so that we may have the evening free for the story, and to-night we shall abandon ourselves wholeheartedly to the Yuletide spirit."

———

THAT dinner! It would need the magic pen of the great master of Christmas, Charles Dickens himself, to describe it.

Splash Page, apt coiner of phrases, confessed himself that not even with his new fountain-pen could he do adequate justice to a description of the repast.

The turkey, a magnificent bird, had done its duty nobly on the altar of Christmas; and there came a solemn, dramatic moment before the entry of the Christmas pudding. Tinker fingered his collar a trifle ruefully, and grinned at Splash Page.

"Gee! I hope I find room for it, Splash," he murmured, and he patted his immaculate dress waistcoat rather doubtfully. Mrs. Bardell, flushed, triumphant, smiling, attired in a black silk dress in honour of the great occasion, entered at that moment, bearing the pudding—a noble, inspiring object, crowned with a branch of holly, and aflame with delicious Jamaica rum.

Mrs. Cluppins removed the sorely ravaged carcase of the turkey, and for a while there was silence, as Mrs. Bardell, in the reverential manner of some priestly acolyte, served the pudding.

Inspector Coutts, his red face gleaming and a rather glassy look in his eyes, gulped once or twice, and glanced in frank admiration at Mrs. Bardell.

"What a woman! What a cook!" he ejaculated below his breath.

There was a hint of envy in his tone as he glanced across at Sexton Blake at the head of the table—cool, handsome, and immaculate in his faultless dinner-jacket.

"Pray do not leave us, ladies! I have a toast to propose," said the criminologist a few moments later. Upon which Tinker drew up a couple of chairs to the table, and poured out two glasses of wine.

"Ladies and gentlemen, I can best echo the toast of Tiny Tim," said Blake, and there came an unwonted tenderness into his eyes. "A Merry Christmas to us all, and God bless us, every one!"

The toast was drunk with acclamation. Suddenly Splash Page sprang to his feet, a merry twinkle in his blue eyes.

"I give you another toast, gentlemen—Mrs. Bardell and her incomparable Christmas pudding!"

"Hear, hear!" echoed Coutts loudly. "Passed nem com."

Sexton Blake laughed softly as he caught an appealing glance from Tinker.

"I shall be delighted to pay my tribute to the excellence of Mrs. Bardell, first as a woman and then as a cook."

"La!" gasped the housekeeper, and she dabbed her eyes furtively with a handkerchief.

"I perceive you are all impatient for details of the very interesting case which Mrs. Bardell and her sister were kind enough to bring to our notice," began Sexton Blake, with a smile, when they were seated again.

"It has been an intriguing little problem, and I am happy to say that it has not developed into such a serious affair as it first appeared. This morning I visited Saint Luke's Hospital, and I am happy to tell you that Captain Barnes has recovered consciousness, and is now out of danger.

"He was able to clear up one or two minor points of interest, and confirmed my previous theories in almost every particular."

Blake paused, and the little concourse of listeners leant forward attentively.

"In the first place, when Mrs. Bardell mentioned the theft of the pudding to me," continued Blake quietly, "I did not think it important or significant, but the peculiar conduct of Captain Barnes gave it a different aspect.

"The brutal attack on poor Roaring Bill, and his half-frenzied words: 'Get the pudding, don't let 'em find it. The secret's there. It belongs to May——' gave me my first working hypothesis.

"A close examination of the room, and the fact that Captain Barnes was in mortal dread of some enemy, and would not, therefore, admit a soul in Mrs. Cluppins' absence, convinced me that the would-be assassin must have worked from outside.

"This was borne out by the weapon itself. It was a barrel knife, peculiarly-balanced, and of a sort used often by Mexican knife-throwers. The absence of a finger-print on the handle lent colour to this theory and was confirmed by an unmistakable thumb-print on the blade of the knife.

"Mexican knife-throwers almost invariably throw their knives holding the blade in their fingers and the hilt away from the body. The discovery of Ben Bolt's letter warning Captain Barnes to beware of 'Mex' made matters still more clear.

"What complicated matters, however, was the theft of the pudding by Master Ginger Brown. That was an unforeseen coincidence which is now rather laughable, but it might have had serious consequences."

"But how did you deduce Hengist Road, guv'nor?" Tinker broke in.

Blake smiled.

"The window was open, if you remember, when we entered the captain's room. My reconstruction of the crime, since confirmed by Roaring Bill himself, is that he was standing with his back to the window, affixing a loose knob on the bed rail.

"He remembers little, save a sharp stab in the back, and fell face forward on the bed.

"I searched the backyard for footprints, but found none. I then realised that the house in Hengist Road was right opposite the back of Mrs. Cluppins. It would not be difficult for an expert knife-thrower to hurl his knife from the window of the house opposite.

"The captain's passion for fresh air aided Fernandez, of course, and probably gave him the idea. It was a long shot, but I took it, and, as events have subsequently proved, my deductions were right."

"But the pudding, Blake—and this woman—May?" Coutts demanded. "We searched the whole thing and found—nothing!"

"On the contrary," said Sexton Blake. "I found this!" He searched in his pocket and brought to light a piece of string, peculiarly-knotted in several complicated tangles.

"What on earth's that?" gasped Tinker, in bewilderment.

"That, ladies and gentlemen, is what Captain Barnes was so anxious to guard. It is the secret code, relating to the hiding place of fabulous treasure buried somewhere in the Cordilleras, near to an Aztec tomb, on the borders of Mexico."

"What?" ejaculated half a dozen voices simultaneously.

"Precisely," replied Sexton Blake quietly. "This string of pampas grass is knotted in this manner for a definite reason. It is known as the Mayan string language, now extinct.

"The ancient Mayas used string tied into peculiar knots as messages—some of them very elaborate.

"I have some slight knowledge of this ancient knot language, and when Tinker recovered the pudding I at once saw the connection between Mexico and such an English object as a plum pudding.

"Captain Barnes' cryptic utterances were at once clarified. 'The secret belongs to Mayan language,' was what he was trying to say.

"I immediately realised that the Mexicans were out for possession of this ancient string, which is a rough key to a treasure buried in far-off Mexico. I traced Fernandez to Dutch Joe's, as you are aware, and frightened the truth out of him by tying a piece of string into the Mayan knot language to say: 'You have killed a man.'"

"Great Scott! And you said you were playing cats'-cradles," said Splash Page reproachfully.

Sexton Blake smiled. "There is little else to explain," he continued. "I managed to get a few details from Captain Barnes this morning. It seems that he did a good turn to an Indian peon, who was the descendant of the ancient Mayan and Aztec priests of Mexico.

"The peon gave Captain Barnes the string, and it was the skipper's intention, on his arrival in England, to submit it to the British Museum authorities and learn the treasure secret. Unfortunately a gang of Mexican bandits also learned of the existence of the string, and it was only by the skin of his teeth that the captain escaped.

"He determined to lie low until the hue and cry was over, for the Mexicans had sworn to follow him to the ends of the earth. When he received Ben Bolt's letter the captain grew terrified for the safety of the string, which he realised must be valuable.

"When Mrs. Cluppins proudly displayed Mrs. Bardell's pudding he was seized with the brilliant idea of removing the original string and substituting the Mayan cord.

"No one would dream of looking for it as an adjunct to a pudding basin. Unfortunately, Master Ginger Brown, of the Pimlico Pirates, took a hand in the game, and thus brought the case to our notice.

"When he recovers, I believe the skipper intends to present the string to the British Museum. He says he has grown too old for treasure-hunting. He offered it to me, but I do not propose to follow the clue of the Christmas pudding to find a probably non-existent treasure in the wilds of Mexico."

Inspector Coutts gave vent to an extraordinary sound, midway between a laugh and a choke.

"No, by golly, Blake!" he said. "You needn't go abroad for a treasure! You've got her right in Baker Street."

"La! Inspector Coutts, go along with you, do. I——"

"What better treasure can a man have than a perfect cook?" replied Coutts gallantly.

"You wait, Coutts!" hissed Splash Page, amidst a gale of good-humoured laughter. "I'll tell your missus when she gets home!"

"Tell away!" grinned Coutts. "It's Christmas-time!"

Outside, through the frosty night, came a mellow peal of bells, trilling their joyous message of "Peace on earth—goodwill to men!"

Into the festive scene the music sounded like a benison on a perfect Yuletide day—and a night that was yet young.

THE END.

Printed and published every Thursday by the Proprietors, The Amalgamated Press (1922), Ltd., The Fleetway House, Farringdon Street, London, E.C.4. Advertisement offices: The Fleetway House, Farringdon Street, London, E.C.4. Registered for transmission by Canadian Magazine Post. Subscription rates: Inland and Abroad, 11s. per annum; 5s. 6d. for six months. Sole agents for South Africa: The Central News Agency, Ltd. Sole agents for Australia and New Zealand: Messrs. Gordon & Gotch, Ltd; and for Canada, The Imperial News Co. Ltd. (Canada).—Saturday, December 12th, 1925.

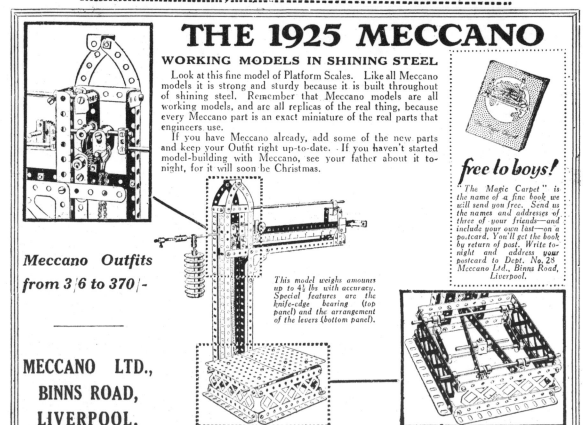

XMAS IS NOT XMAS *without this jolly detective story!*

UNION JACK 2ᵈ

THE XMAS WEEK

Mrs BARDELL'S XMAS EVE!

Sexton Blake's Jolly Xmas Detective Case, featuring Ruff HANSON, 'Splash' PAGE, TINKER and Inspector COUTTS.

No. 1,210.   EVERY THURSDAY.   December 25th, 1926.

Mrs BARDELL'S XMAS EVE

This is the story of the Great Baker Street Hoax; of the kidnapping of Mrs. Martha Bardell, Sexton Blake's housekeeper; of a real, old-time baronial . . . mansion and its Christmas ghost; and of the jolliest lark of a detective job that Sexton Blake ever handled. Read it and have a Merry Christmas!

When It's Yuletide in Baker Street.

"CHRISTMAS is coming," said Tinker, Mr. Sexton Blake's astute young assistant, as he neatly decapitated his second breakfast egg.

A grunt emerged from behind the voluminous pages of the "Times" on the other side of the table; that, and the emergence of a lean, sinewy hand groping absently for the tea-cup, were the only indications of Mr. Sexton Blake's presence in the dining-room.

"Christmas is coming—good egg!" repeated Tinker, with an infectious chuckle.

The pages of the newspaper were lowered, and the detective gazed solemnly at the lad.

"Your glimpses into the obvious are most refreshing, my dear Tinker. Am I to assume that the latter part of your sentence refers slangily to the approach of the festive season, or is merely an appreciation of the calcareous ovum you are sampling?"

"Eh, what's that, guv'nor?" gasped the startled Tinker. "I don't quite get the hang of the last bit."

Blake's shrewd grey eyes twinkled.

"My dear chap, that is about the twentieth time in the last few days you have announced the imminent arrival of Christmas. It is apt to become monotonous. Are you practising a variant of Coueism—hoping to hurry the advent of December the twenty-fifth? I would solemnly warn you against the peril of over suggestion. The case of that industrious scientist, Herr Offenbach, occurs to me——"

Blake paused, and toyed idly with his tea-spoon. His face was perfectly grave, but there was a mischievous twinkle in his eyes, as he continued.

"The unfortunate professor was afflicted by the deformity commonly known as knock-knees. A firm believer in auto-suggestion, he repeated daily the famous formula: 'Every day my legs grow straighter and straighter.'"

"Unfortunately his zeal overshot the mark, and he awoke one morning to find he was bow-legged."

Tinker choked into his tea-cup. It was rarely that Sexton Blake jested, and the lad realised that his leg had been successfully pulled.

"One up to you, guv'nor," he grinned. "You mean, if I keep on, Christmas will have gone before it's come?"

Blake smiled.

"The moral is obvious. But, seriously, my boy, it would not be a bad idea if we decided how, and where we spent the holiday. It is a fact that the crime curve tends to drop round about Christmas, and, with ordinary luck, we should have an uneventful and restful holiday."

The detective sighed, half unconsciously, and Tinker, who knew every phase of his guv'nor's restless, complex character, knew that it was not inaction, but action that he wanted.

For some weeks now, the two had had an almost unexampled period of rest. Hardly a single ripple had disturbed the placid surface of the Underworld, and beyond a few trivial investigations, no case sufficiently interesting to occupy Blake's unique talents had cropped up.

Sexton Blake's shrewd, analytical mind was like a blade of tempered steel—incomparable in action, but inclined to lose its flashing keenness if left too long without being used.

"Anything interesting in the papers, guv'nor?" inquired Tinker.

Blake shook his head, and listlessly scanned the Personal column.

"Nothing new, my boy. I see our old friend, Silent Mike, is still using his favourite medium for communicating with his underworld friends. What fools the average criminals are. Like the Bourbons, they learn nothing and forget nothing. Five years ago Mike got put away through using the Agony Column to communicate with his fence, and here he is at it again."

He smiled as he read out the few lines of an advertisement which ran: "Lulu. Got to make amends. Swear again to love you. Meet me at Tony's usual time Monday.—Michael."

"Clumsy as ever, my poor Mike," added Blake. "Ah, well, I'm afraid I must ask Coutts to interfere in his courtship with the fascinating Lulu."

"What do you mean, guv'nor?" demanded the mystified Tinker. "It's probably only a poor chap that's quarrelled with his girl and wants to make it up——"

"Sorry to disappoint your romance," Blake cut in incisively. "It is not generally known that Mr. Isodore Roseblum is referred to by his intimates as Lulu."

"Izzy Roseblum the fence?" echoed Tinker.

Blake nodded. "If you will re-read the message, my boy, in the light of that knowledge, you will find it illuminating. That 'swear again to love you,' in conjunction with the first part of the message, reads: 'Got swag.'

"Notice the first two letters of the words 'swear' and 'again'—sw and ag?"

"Well I'm dashed!" Tinker said blankly. "I suppose Tony's is an Italian joint?"

"Precisely. Antonio Guiseppi's unsavoury cafe in Shadwell. I know the place well."

Blake stretched out his hand for the receiver, and called up a familiar number. "Might prove a nice little haul for friend Coutts," he drawled.

A moment later the voice of the C.I.D. man twanged over the wires.

"'Mornin', Blake! Seasonable weather, what? No, not a thing doing. Looks as if we're in for a crimeless Christmas."

Blake chuckled.

"Like to pull in an old friend of yours—Silent Mike—Coutts? I believe you want him for that Carstairs necklace affair?"

"I'd like to find the villain!" Coutts answered emphatically.

"Then send a couple of plain-clothes' men to Tony Guiseppi's to-night," replied Blake; "and, if you're not busy, drop in for a chat. You were saying something about being at a loose end this Christmas?"

"Thanks, awfully, old man!" came Coutts' gratified voice. "Fact is, the missus has gone off to some relatives in Wales, and a policeman's Christmas ain't a happy one without his wife. I was thinking maybe——" The worthy inspector's voice was rather wistful.

"Come right over and discuss it," said Sexton Blake cordially. "That is, when you've attended to Silent Mike." He replaced the receiver, and thoughtfully filled his briar.

"Even old Coutts is feeling the

draught," he remarked to Tinker. "I wonder——"

But what Blake wondered was never revealed, for at that moment a knock sounded on the door, followed by the entrance of Mrs. Bardell, the detective's worthy and incomparable housekeeper.

Her portly bosom heaved with the effort of mounting the stairs, and her rich voice gasped a little painfully.

"Which I sez good-morning to you, sirs, and wishing you all the condiments of the season!" she began in her usual breathless torrent of words. "Not 'aving seen you for some time, being hoccupied with my collandery dooties, now 'appily over, and as nice a turkey, though hexpensive, mind you, that ever you——"

She paused for breath and frowned at Tinker, who with difficulty repressed a grin.

Mrs. Bardell's cooking was unex-

ampled; she was a treasure that was the envy of every discriminating gourmet who had the good fortune to be invited to dinner at Baker Street, but her English was weird and wonderful at times, especially in moments of stress.

Blake, who knew her harmless idiosyncrasies, waited patiently for the flood to abate.

"But all this is what you might call irreverent," she said, with a wave of her podgy hand. "Which I wishes to remark that I 'ave a cablegraft."

She presented Blake with an orange envelope, and waited his decision majestically.

The detective ripped it open, and an amused smile hovered about his lips.

"We shall probably have an extra guest at our Christmas dinner, Mrs. B.," he said. "I hope it won't upset your arrangements?"

Mrs. Bardell beamed.

"Not in the least, sir." She smoothed her black satin dress, and departed.

Tinker looked curiously at his master.

"Who's the guest, guv'nor?" he asked.

Blake tossed over the telegram.

"Speaks for itself, doesn't it?"

The lad read the laconic message with a wide grin: "Hit Paris. Don't like it. Bum burg. May I spend Christmas with you?—Hanson."

"Gee whiz! Ruff Hanson, the hard-boiled egg!" said Tinker. "What on earth's he doing in France?"

Blake shook his head.

"I haven't the vaguest idea, my lad; but if his threatened visit eventuates, we ought to have a stimulating Christmas."

"I'll tell the world an earful!" quoted Tinker. "Jove, I'll be glad to see old Ruff again, guv'nor. He's a live wire all right."

Blake and Tinker had a genuine affection for the shrewd "go-getter" inquiry agent from New York. "Hard-boiled" Hanson, as he loved to call himself, was no Adonis to look at, but when it came to action Ruff Hanson was a human tornado. Blake and he had first met in the thick of a street battle in Damascus, and again in the mysterious affair of Shakespeare's Skull, when Hanson had succeeded in evading almost every policeman in England, until he proved his innocence of the crime attributed to him.

A visit from Ruff Hanson was like a tonic, and Blake looked forward pleasurably to it.

"Best get along to Covent Garden, youngster," he suggested. "Get some holly and evergreens to make these austere walls a little more festive."

Tinker rose to his feet and as he did so a loud nasal voice boomed from the stairs:

"Don't you worry, Maggie. I'll go right upstairs. I guess friend Blake's expecting me."

Tinker grinned.

"Swift, as usual, guv'nor," he said, opening the consulting-room door.

"Wal, here's a sight for sore eyes!" drawled the big, burly man in a voluminous overcoat and a broad-brimmed Stetson hat. "Howdy, kid? I've just hit l'il old London by the air-mail, and I came right along. Get my cable, or have I raced it?"

A huge, ham-like hand descended in an affectionate bear hug over Tinker's shoulders as Ruff Hanson entered.

"Howdy, Blake, old side-kick? Still wearing that darned old rag-bag, I see." He pointed derisively at Blake's stained dressing-gown, discoloured from

The Coast is: 'SEXTON BLAKE!'

See Page 12.

the acids of countless chemical researches. "I guess friend Joseph's coat had nothing on that, old hoss!" he drawled.

Blake smiled as he rose to greet his visitor.

"Come right in, Ruff. Welcome to our home town. What has sent you to Europe this time?"

The American parked his wide hat on the desk and sank into a saddlebag chair. He grinned as Tinker made pleasant noises with a decanter and glasses.

"Prohibition, I guess," drawled Ruff Hanson. "This durned Prohibition's getting me down, Blake. What with hijackers and bootleggers, crime in New York is getting as gosh-darned monotonous as a film star's smile in Hollywood. Me, I like action, plenty of it, but when the action's all about cases of alleged Scotch, I reckon it makes me tired.

"So when Bill B. Bevan, the big beezezus of the Bevan Automobile Works, Detroit, hired me to escort his wife and daughter over to Yurrup on the Gigantic, I grabbed the chance with both mitts.

"Big Bill Bevan's been sorta bitten with this culture bug. Funny that; but I guess it's Mrs. Bill's fault. I remember when Bill and I were out West together, years back, he was the toughest puncher that ever handled a steer, but he made his pile in the automobile boom, while I trekked East to be a 'dick.'

"And now Bill's got a swell house on Riverside Drive, and is as full of culture as Boston is of highbrows. He rolled into my office one night, all dolled up in a tuxedo, with one of them swell-looking Janes with glasses on a stick that's calc'lated to make a guy feel like ten cents.

"'Meet my wife, Mr. Hanson,' says Bill, in a funny, still, sorta voice. Mrs. Bevan stares at me like I was something outa an aquarium. Very toney she was.

"'Is this the—er—person you wish to escort us to Europe?' she asked, in a voice she'd kept on ice for years.

"Bill fidgeted, kind o' uncomfortable, and went all warm and worried under his soup and fish. 'Yes, my dear. I—er—place the utmost reliability in Mr. Hanson. I've known him for years. He is—er——' And he chokes like a carbonised carburetter, did old Bill Bevan."

Ruff Hanson paused, and sipped his drink.

Tinker grinned at the American's characteristically racy account of the incident. To the lad, both Mrs. Bardell's English and Ruff Hanson's Americanisms were things of beauty and joys for ever.

"Yep!" continued the hard-boiled egg. "Big Bill Bevan, the terror of Lone Pine centre, so tough he could dent a Nasmyth hammer in the old days, quailed before five foot nix of femininity. That's what marriage does for a man!

"Wal, to shingle the narrative, Blake, old timer. It seems Mrs. Bevan was keen on taking her l'il daughter, Chloe, to France, to what they call a finishing school, in Paris.

"Unfortunately, Big Bill couldn't accompany 'em. There was big trouble brewing in the Detroit plant, and some of the Reds had been threatening to kidnap Chloe.

"I guess Bill wouldn't have minded much if they'd threatened to kidnap Mrs. B., but I reckon not even the Red Army'd tackle that job. He pulls out a wad of bills. 'Mr. Hanson,' he says, 'I want you to guard my wife and daughter, and see that they reach Paris without mishap.'

"'Bill,' says I, 'I guess Mrs. B. can look after herself, but I ain't averse to picking up a coupla thousand berries for the job. I'm kinda pining for a real drink.' He smiles at that, and peels off five grand.

"Pine! Now, Annabel, my dear, I can return with a relieved mind to Detroit. You'll find Ruff Hanson a pillar of strength, a man who will treat you and little Chloe with the utmost courtesy and——'

"'Bill,' says I—my old side-kick's highbrow line of talk was getting me rattled—'you've sure slobbered a canful. This job's just in my line. The Reds that'll stop your little filly getting culture in Paris'll have to reckon with Willy and Wally.' With that, I introduced my assistants——"

With a gesture so quick that the eye could scarcely follow it, Ruff Hanson produced, seemingly in mid-air, two vicious automatics.

Blake laughed softly.

"My dear Hanson," he said, "I hate to revive painful memories, but your disconcerting habit of producing your ironmongery at inopportune moments once landed you in a murder charge."

Ruff Hanson grinned joyously.

"Oh, boy, what a trail! Poor old Coutts and the harness bulls of Scotland Yard. Willy and Wally and me sure led 'em a dance.

"Sure, I'll park the hardware," he added, and again, with incredible speed, the pistols disappeared, whereat Tinker heaved an involuntary sigh of relief.

Ruff Hanson was probably the quickest man on the draw in America, but his playful habit of "pulling his gats" amidst incongruous surroundings, was apt to lead to trouble.

"Well, we reached Paris O. K." Hanson continued imperturbably. "I guess the Reds got wise I was on the case. I was glad to park the Janes at the culture academy, and I bumped around that French burg for a coupla days, looking for trouble, but I guess that peace-on-earth stuff's bitten the Froggies mighty bad, because I ain't seen one solitary scrap.

"Then I thought I'd look on here, an' maybe we could beat up a pretty good sockdolager, and have a Merry Christmas together somewheres."

There was a gleam in the American detective's eyes as he spoke, and Sexton Blake laughed.

"What a regular fire-eating old tough you are, Ruff," he said. "You're never happy unless you're in the middle of what you call a shemozzle, or a sockdolager. But, come, I'll see that Mrs. Bardell fixes your room. I won't hear of your staying at the Savoy. We can put you up, and I guarantee Mrs. Bardell's Christmas dinner will compensate you for any excitement you may miss by spending Yuletide in Baker Street."

"Then you ain't on any case?" echoed Ruff Hanson, a trifle crestfallen.

Blake shook his head.

"I'm afraid not, old friend. The Christmas spirit seems to have permeated even the Underworld—but—one never knows!"

Ruff Hanson grinned.

"Gosh darn my pyjamas, Blake! I guess you're as peeved as I am that the crooks ain't planning a Christmas treat."

As the two detectives left the cosy consulting-room, Tinker became very thoughtful; then suddenly he chuckled:

"By gum! I wonder!" he murmured. "If they've ever reckoned with the Phantom Crook!"

The Colossus of Crime.

"INTEET, what-teffer, what are we, I ask you, a newspaper, or a drapers' catalogue?"

Mr. Julius Jones, that dour but efficient Welshman, who was the News Editor of the "Daily Radio," glowered furiously at Perks, the dapper little advertising manager. In moments of stress, Julius' accent was almost incomprehensible to the mere Sassenach.

"Dear me, that the 'Radio' should be reduced to piffling paras about crepe-de-Chine cammies, and Lady Bianca's blooming bazaar!" he groaned, as he viciously blue-pencilled a "flimsy" announcing a flood at Llanfairynymynyddion.

Mr. Jones was so upset that he hardly noticed that the flood had swept away, fortunately without casualties, the bridge of his own home town in Wales; the bridge where, years back, as a boy, he had dreamed of conquering Fleet Street with his pen.

"I want news, roast you!" he roared. "Not finnicky fal-de-lals about Christmas gifts for maiden aunts!"

"Pardon me, my dear fellow," expostulated the dapper little Perks. "That hardly comes into my province. I handle the ads, and the life-blood of a newspaper is the constant stream of publicity——"

Julius Jones' lean fingers closed meaningly on a heavy-laden paper-weight.

"Avaunt!" he roared. "A newspaper should give news. It's you bloodsucking parasites, with your ads, that have ruined——"

"Hallo, hallo, hallo! Julius, my old dear, that way apoplexy lies! Mornin', Perks! Heed not the gentle Julius!" called a cheery voice from the doorway of the glass-panelled room.

"Where have you been, you slacker?" growled Julius, as he spun round in his chair and glowered at Derek Page, the star crime reporter of the "Daily Radio," known throughout the Street of Ink as "Splash" Page, because of his amazing knack of securing sensational news stories.

Mr. Perks took advantage of the journalist's smiling entry to slip out furtively. He was a dapper little man, and Mr. Jones' violent tirade might have led to actual bloodshed if he had stayed, or, what was even worse, the rumpling of Mr. Perks' immaculate morning dress.

Splash Page grinned.

"What's bitten you, Julius, my old warrior?"

"Huh!" grunted the news editor. "That tailor's dummy submits an article, a full column, mark you, on 'Mannish Modes For Male Mannequins,' or some such tripe!"

There was ineffable scorn in the news editor's voice. Splash Page laughed heartily. The antagonism between Julius Jones and the advertisement side of the great paper was a long-standing one, but not very serious really.

Each knew that both departments were essential to the paper, but occasionally, when news was scarce, and the ads encroached too much on precious Editorial pages, Julius Jones was apt to get peeved.

"Have a cigar, and cheer up!" said Splash Page. "Anything doing?"

"Anything doing? By the tin horn of Tonypandy!" wailed the excitable Welshman. "Here I am, craving for news, and you, an alleged reporter, whose job it is to get it by hook or by crook—and you ask if there's anything doing!"

The telephone bell jingled, and with an anticipatory gleam in his eye, Julius lifted the receiver.

"What's that? An accident to the Western express at Lindforth? Ran off the line, you say? Crashed into the buffers at the station and—— Hold on!" He scribbled the particulars on a pad.

"What's that—nobody killed?" His pencil drooped. "What! No casualties! Jumping Jehosaphat! I thought you said you had a story!" He replaced the receiver, with a queer oath in Welsh.

"Timpkins, the fool, rings up to report a train smash, with no casualties. I'll fire him when he comes back!"

"You bloodthirsty old ghoul, Julius!" said Splash Page. "I believe you'd murder your own father for the sake of a headline."

Which was only relatively true. Julius Jones, in private life, was an esteemed churchwarden at the Welsh Wesleyan Church in Ealing, and was a humane and kindly father. But professionally he revelled in the most sensational crimes and disasters.

"Splash," he cajoled, "nigh on Christmas we are, and not a single scare head. Can't you find a ghost, or—or something?"

The newspaperman grinned.

"Ghosts are getting so durned respectable these days, old hoss; besides, nobody's scared of 'em now that Spiritualism's fashionable. A nice juicy murder, now——"

He broke suddenly, as a tap sounded on the glass-panelled door, and Tinker, looking very spick and span in a new Raglan overcoat, entered the news editor's sanctum.

"'Morning, Mr. Jones! 'Morning, Splash!" began Tinker cheerfully. "Merry Christmas, and all that!"

"Hallo, youngster! Same to you! What brings you here to the Street of Ink?"

"News. Ruff Hanson's hit town, and is staying for Christmas with us——"

"Egad! That bad American?" Julius Jones brightened visibly, for the chronicle of Ruff Hanson's exploits in quest of Shakespeare's Skull had been one of the most sensational stories the "Radio" had ever scooped.

"Has he killed anybody yet?" he demanded hopefully.

Tinker laughed.

"Not yet, but give him a chance, he's only been here a couple of hours. I've been doing some Christmas shopping, and thought I'd drop in on the way back. Splash, are you doing anything at the moment?"

The journalist glanced at the wrist-watch, and whistled.

"Cocktail time, Julius! Mayhap over a Manhattan I'll evolve a murder to gladden your heart. Mayhap not. C'mon, Tinker, I'll run you down to Romano's in the flivver. You can tell us all about Ruff. By-bye, Julius!"

Seven minutes later, Splash Page and Tinker were seated in a cosy alcove at Romano's bar, in the Strand.

"You've got something on your chest, my lad," said Splash quietly. "You don't visit Fleet Street unless you've got a job on."

Tinker grinned.

"Got it in one, my pippin! Did you ever hear of the Phantom Crook?"

The journalist shook his head.

"Can't say I have, old fruit. Most crooks are pretty tangible — when they've got the bracelets on. Come on, loosen up and spill the beans, as Ruff Hanson would say."

"The Phantom Crook," said Tinker impressively, "is the master crook of all time, the Colossus of Crime, the Dictator of Dastards, the Bonaparte of Blackmailers, and the Monarch of Mystery!"

"Good Lord!" gasped Splash. "What's up with you, youngster? Has your brief sojourn in Fleet Street made you talk in headlines?"

Tinker winked.

"Splash, are you game to put across the biggest joke ever?" he demanded.

The journalist's blue eyes twinkled mischievously. For all his brilliant exploits as a war correspondent and crime reporter, Splash Page was very boyish at heart. "I'm on—if it's workable, old son. What's the big idea?"

Tinker lowered his voice.

"I came in at the tail-end of your little chinwag with Comrade Julius, and it seems to me he's a bit peeved at the dearth of news."

Splash Page nodded.

"Well," proceeded the lad, "what d'you say if I gave you an exclusive scoop—a real front-page splash?"

The reporter grinned.

"Half my bally kingdom, youngster!"

"Then you're on. Fact is, Splash, the guv'nor's getting fed-up. You know how grouchy he gets when there's nothing doing in the crime line? Well, for days now we've been stagnant. Lord knows what's happened to the crooks; maybe they've lost their nerve, or perhaps they're lying low and saying nuffing. But the fact remains—the guv'nor and I look like retiring from criminology and taking up a new profession."

"Good Lord!" gasped the startled reporter. "As bad as that, is it? And what profession were you thinking of adopting—journalism?"

"Nothing so low," said Tinker. "I'm thinking of taking up crime."

Splash Page looked curiously at the lad.

"You're not feeling well, old hoss?"

"But, seriously," continued Tinker, "here's the guv'nor, and dear old Ruff Hanson, simply aching to get back into harness, and both as miserable as a wet week because there's nothing doing in the crime world."

"But there may be," Splash persisted. "Look at last Christmas—when we thought we were in for a quiet time, the exciting events that followed the theft of Mrs. Bardell's Christmas pudding."

"That's just it—Mrs. B. has got to provide us another thrill this year," said Tinker.

"Listen! Supposing you and I, and Mrs. Bardell, combine to give the guv'nor and old Ruff a Christmas after their own hearts? Let's pit our brains against theirs, and see who wins."

Splash Page grinned. His nimble wits had already discerned some glimmering of Tinker's scheme.

"That's why I've doped out the Phantom Crook," said Tinker. "Have you any pals who are dead game sports, and have pluck enough to carry it off?"

Splash Page grinned.

"There's young Viscount Rockcliff, the priceless chap who's always up at Vine Street for pinching policemen's helmets and such-like. He's game for any mischief, and a white man through and through."

"Splendid!" said Tinker. "If he's a pal of yours, he's the very man. Now, we'll have to think out the details mighty carefully, my lad.

"To-night I'm due to dine with the guv'nor and Ruff at home. I think old Coutts'll be there, too. Let's chase along to your flat now, and ring up Viscount Rockcliff; then we can map out our plan of campaign."

"Good enough, youngster! Lead on —I'm with you to the last ditch. Forward the Phantom Crooks!"

SPLASH PAGE'S flat in Chelsea was small but commodious. It had once been an artist's studio, and was furnished in a luxurious but haphazard fashion, eminently typical of its owner.

At three o'clock of a chill December afternoon, when the leaden skies darkened, and a few desultory snowflakes fell feather-like to earth, the journalist pulled back the curtains and switched on the light.

Round the fireplace three comfortable armchairs were drawn. Tinker lounged back in one, his clean-cut, boyish face reflecting the light of the cheerful fire, while in the other sat the Right Honourable Algernon George Actley St. Aubyn Montague, fourth viscount and seventh baronet Rockcliff — to give him his official Debrett title—known to his intimates as "Rocky" or "Monty."

A tall, thin youth, this Viscount Rockcliff, with fair hair slicked back from his long forehead, a thin, but shrewdly humorous face, and a pair of lazy, good-tempered blue eyes.

He affected a monocle, but even in this common attribute of conventional aristocracy, Rocky maintained his reputation for originality. It was an oblong monocle, with a heavy tortoiseshell rim, and lent an air of distinction to an otherwise ordinary visage.

"Jolly old pen-pusher, squat!" drawled Rocky. "And let us proceed to review the situation."

Splash Page sank into the vacant chair with a yawn, and stretched out his hand for a cigarette.

"I'll fix the newspaper end of it all right, Rocky," he said. "It's up to you ard Tinker to kick off; the onus lies on you, my gilded scion of nobility. Tinker has a far more ticklish game to play. His guv'nor can see through a brick wall, and the smoke screen we've got to put up is considerable."

Viscount Rockcliff pulled thoughtfully at his cigarette.

"Leave the first exploit of the Phantom Crook to me, laddie," he said gravely. "It's a good job you've called in the services of my massive brain, but I pity Tinker here if his guv'nor tumbles to our scheme. I had the pleasure of meeting jolly old Blake once, and he struck me then as a pretty shrewd bird to have his leg pulled."

Tinker laughed.

"Leave it to me. He'll be so bucked at having something to occupy his mind that he'll be grateful for the interlude; besides, it's an absolutely fool-proof scheme."

The journalist nodded.

"My lad, it's a good job that you and Rocky haven't criminal tendencies. The question that naturally arises, however, is, how will Mrs. B. take it all?"

"Don't you worry, Splash. You know she's got a soft spot in her heart for you, and I'll bet she'll be as pleased as Punch to fall in with the idea—especially as she'll be royally entertained."

Viscount Rockcliff rose to his feet with a yawn, and glanced approvingly through his oblong monocle at the immaculate set of his clothes.

"Well, old things, me for Clarkson's! You'll hear anon about the tragic affair at Jermyn Street. To-morrow we'll fix up the grand slam." He reached for his glass from the mantelpiece, and raised it in a toast.

"Here's to the Phantom Crook and a hectic Christmas—what!"

The toast was drunk enthusiastically, and thus was unfolded the great Christmas plot which was to have such far-reaching and unforeseen results.

The Phantom Crook Strikes.

"THAT woman is a treasure—a masterpiece."

Detective Inspector Coutts pronounced the dictum weightily as he pushed back his chair and snipped off the end of his cigar.

The C. I. D. man's face was redder than usual that evening. Probably the exertion of climbing into a boiled shirt had something to do with it, or it might have been the ample justice he had done to the incomparable dinner which Mrs. Bardell had cooked for the four detectives now grouped round the snowy tablecloth in Sexton Blake's cosy dining-room.

At the head of the table sat Blake, looking, as usual, a picture of sartorial perfection in his well-cut dinner-jacket.

At his right was the burly, broad-shouldered Ruff Hanson, in a plain, dark lounge-suit. Tinker sat opposite, while Coutts graced the foot of the table, his close-clipped moustache fairly bristling with satisfaction as he beamed at the pathetic remnants of what had been a poem of culinary art.

"Say, I guess Heinz, in his fifty-seven variety kitchens, would pay Mrs. Bardell a hundred thousand dollars per annum just for advice," drawled Ruff Hanson. "I guess we ain't got a cook to touch her in the States. D'ye think she can make waffles and corn-pone?" he asked, rather plaintively.

Blake laughed.

"Very probably, my dear fellow. Now, what do you say to a liqueur? I have a very choice brandy here—the gift of a grateful client from Cognac."

"Oh, my!" breathed Hanson ecstatically. "That's sure worth crossing the pond for."

Outside the cosy room the winter wind blew tempestuously, and roared with mocking glee down the chimney. Tinker raised the blind and pointed to a thick scurry of snow. It was as if the genial giant of Dickens' "Christmas Present" was pouring the sauce-cup over this great plum-pudding of a world.

Faintly, from the street below, came the shrill treble of childish voices, singing the old, old carol: "Good King Wenceslas looked out, On the feast of Stephen . . ."

"Say, Blake! The old country kinda gets ya——" said Ruff Hanson suddenly. "I guess there's a lot to this Dickens fella! I remember reading a book once by that guy. I was snowed up in a bunk-house out West. Rum kinda book it was; all about a plug-ugly named Sikes—a tough from Toughville, if ever there was one.

"Well, this ere Sikes guy was a pal of a Yidd fence with an Irish monniker—Fagan, or some such name. He had a moll named Nance that spilled the beans to the harness bulls on account of a crash she had for a kid named Twist, who wouldn't eat his grapenuts.

"I guess cereal breakfasts must have originated in England," he added. "Well, anyways, it was a darned fine book, and first taught me about England. I plumb forget whether Sikes went to the chair or not, but that guy Dickens sure knew a lot about crooks."

"It had always been a moot point whether Christmas made Dickens, or Dickens Christmas," said Blake gravely, suppressing a smile as he heard Hanson's summing up of the master of Christmas. "And talking of the festive season, have you any suggestions of how we can spend the holiday? You'll come to dinner, of course, Coutts?"

The C.I.D. man cleared his throat.

"Well, it's very kind of you, Blake—very kind. If professional duties permit, I—er—shall be delighted to accept."

"Splendid! I suggest we book seats for a pantomime on Boxing Day," said Blake, "and give our friend Hanson a chance of seeing a characteristically English show. By the way, Coutts, I suppose you have fixed Silent Mike's Christmas quarters for him?"

The Yard man nodded grimly.

"You bet! Harker and Edwards have been watching Tony's all the evening. We want him pretty badly——"

"Brr-ting!" went the telephone-bell, and Tinker crossed over to the instrument. He listened for a few moments, and then turned to Coutts.

"Harker got him, old man. The Yard speaking. They roped in Silent Mike and Roseblum half an hour back, caught red-handed with the swag. Swift work —what!"

He replaced the receiver and crossed over to the cabinet wireless-set, which was an inconspicuous feature of the well-furnished dining-room.

"How about a little music, guv'nor? It's too stormy to-night to go to a show.

I see they're broadcasting the second act of the 'Mikado.' Like to hear it?"

Blake nodded absently as Tinker tuned in, and soon the immortal music of Sullivan filled the room.

"That's a dandy radio-set you've got, Blake," said Hanson admiringly, as the familiar words and music issued from the loud-speaker. It was the despairing song of Ko-Ko that was conveyed from the crowded theatre through the snow-laden ether, and the words seemed a little incongruous:

"The flowers that bloom in the spring,
   tra-la,
   Have nothing to do with the case.
I've got to take under my wing,
   tra-la,
A most unattractive old thing, tra-la,
   With a caricature of a face."

Then suddenly the singer's voice trailed away abruptly, and there was a sharp crackling sound.

"Atmospherics——" began Tinker, and then a weird, unearthly voice sounded from the black, cavernous depths of the loud-speaker:

"Ladies and gentlemen. The Phantom Crook speaking. To-night I have declared war against Society. The time has come for the rich to disgorge their ill-gotten pelf—— Brr, brr, click——"

The voice ceased abruptly, and the startled listeners again heard the orchestra, a confused murmur of voices, then silence.

Sexton Blake's eyes gleamed with excitement.

"The Phantom Crook!" he echoed. "What on earth's that, Tinker?"

The lad shook his head.

"I can't say, guv'nor. Probably some silly ass larking about in the audience—an undergrad, or one of these Bolshies."

"Extraordinary!" gasped Coutts. "I say, Blake, this matter wants looking into."

"You bet it does," said Ruff Hanson briskly. "C'mon, Blake, old war hoss, let's have your view on the matter."

The criminologist thoughtfully lit his cigar.

"It is an extraordinary announcement, as you say, Coutts. I wonder if the B. B. C. are playing a practical joke, or what? They did it once before, you remember, when one of their lectures was interrupted by a——"

The telephone bell tinkled sharply, and the detective lifted the receiver. He smiled as he recognised the voice of Splash Page at the other end of the wire.

"Good evening, Splash! Hard at it, I suppose? What can I do for you?"

"Say, Blake, have you ever heard of the Phantom Crook?" queried the newspaper man.

Blake whistled softly.

"No. At least, not until half a minute ago."

A groan sounded over the wires.

"Good lor', then, he's started! I say, old man, I feel I ought to warn you! A most extraordinary letter's arrived at the office ten minutes back, and it concerns you vitally."

Blake listened intently, and there was a hushed, expectant silence in the room.

"It came by a messenger we cannot trace, and was addressed to the editor. It's signed 'The Phantom Crook.' It's a darned fine 'story,' and I was wondering if you'd care to let me use it for our country edition. The paper goes to bed in less than half an hour."

"Come on, old man, let's have the story!" said Blake sharply.

"Half a mo'! I'll read it to you as it stands!" replied the journalist.

Blake reached for the jotting-pad and scribbled the following extraordinary statement in rapid shorthand:

"To the editor of the 'Daily Radio.'

"Sir,—I trust you will grant me the hospitality of your columns to make known a matter of public interest, and one that cannot fail to appeal to the charitable this Christmastide. I have long felt that the rich are not making sufficient sacrifices, in view of the widespread sufferings among the poorer classes since the disastrous coal stoppage.

"I propose to remedy these matters forcibly. To-night I declare war on the capitalists, and solemnly declare that I shall steal some of their surplus wealth, all of which shall be converted into cash, and the whole of the proceeds presented to deserving charities.

"I am the head of a powerful organisation of what can be called revolutionary philanthropists. My plans are too well perfected for me to fear the police, and as an earnest of my intention, and of my complete invulnerability, I propose to rob the celebrated detective, Mr. Sexton Blake, of most of his treasured possession within the next twenty-four hours.

"He once criticised crooks as being deficient in a sense of humour, and so I take this opportunity of issuing a challenge.

"If Mr. Blake succeeds in recovering his property and piercing my identity I shall pay over the sum of £1,000 to any charity he cares to nominate. If, on the other hand, he fails to do so, I shall expect him to forfeit a cheque for £500 to St. Bartholomew's Hospital.

"For obvious reasons I must remain anonymous, but I think there is sufficient news value in this letter to admit of its widespread publication, and I hope it reaches you before the paper 'goes to bed,' so as to allow of its inclusion.

"With the compliments of the season. —Yours, etc.

"THE PHANTOM CROOK."

Sexton Blake's face was perfectly expressionless as he finished transcribing.

"Well, Blake, what do you think of it?" came the journalist's eager voice.

"An amazing document," replied the detective quietly. "Can you come along to Baker Street right away, and bring it with you?"

Splash Page hesitated.

"Well, in about twenty minutes. The chief wants to get a scoop on it—that's with your permission, of course! Do you mind if we publish it? It's a great story, and its publication won't do any harm. It'll catch the country editions,

and I can slam in an interview with you for the later ones."

Blake drummed thoughtfully on the desk with his fingers and smiled a little at the newspaperman's enthusiasm.

"Oh, you journalists!" he said at length. "To misquote the Duke of Wellington—publish, and be hanged to you! You can also announce that I accept the challenge."

"Good old Blake! I knew you'd be a sport!" said Splash triumphantly. "I'll bung it into the sub-editors and bring you a copy of the first edition within the half-hour."

Coutts' red face purpled as he found himself gazing down the barrels of Ruff Hanson's pair of six-guns. They had appeared as if from nowhere. "P-put the dashed things away, man!" stuttered the inspector.

Blake's face was very thoughtful as he replaced the receiver. The others, who had listened in silence during the telephonic communication, looked at him searchingly.

"Well, what's the big idea?" began Ruff Hanson. "Sounds as if there's something doing in the offing."

The detective nodded, and Tinker, who knew every phase of his guv'nor's usually impassive face, noticed the involuntary twitch of Blake's nostrils, which showed that his interest was keenly aroused.

"It rather looks as if we're in for a strenuous Christmas. The Phantom Crook has shown his hand."

"But who and what is the Phantom Crook?" demanded the aggrieved Coutts. For answer, Blake quietly read out his shorthand notes, and repeated the conversation with the reporter.

"Well, I'll be hornswoggled!" cried Ruff Hanson. "If that ain't the centipede's spats and the porcupine's cork tips! I like that guy's style, Blake. What are you going to do about it?"

Blake shrugged.

"Why, accept the challenge, of course!" he said quietly.

Ruff Hanson patted his hip pockets lovingly.

"Well, if Willy and Wally are of any use to you, old hoss, they're at your service. I'd kinda like to meet this hombre."

"But it's monstrous—ridiculous!" spluttered Coutts. "And I'll tell that chap, Splash Page, that he's abusing the Press by printing such a—a criminal document. It should have been submitted to Headquarters. The Yard's got a way of dealing with anonymous letters."

He puffed out his cheeks importantly.

Blake smiled.

"I'm afraid you can do nothing, old man. A letter remains the property of the recipient. There is nothing to prevent the 'Daily Radio' printing its own property. No, Coutts; I confess the problem intrigues me vastly. It is a very entertaining affair, and I'm looking forward with interest to the duel."

"Count me in on this!" said Ruff Hanson, with a joyous light in his hard blue eyes.

"But I say, guv'nor, when you come to think of it, what is the most valuable possession you've got. There's that ruby pin the Syndic of Andorra gave you for solving that dope smuggling business, the cigarette-case the King of Greece gave you during the War, that buhl cabinet, and the Ming vase, to say nothing of the jade tobacco-jar and your first folio Shakespeare."

Blake laughed.

"For I have great possessions," he quoted, "I assure you that each are equally valuable, in my opinion. But you haven't mentioned one unique possession, a remarkable oversight on your part. What about the Index?"

Tinker winced. Blake's reference to that monumental and unique criminological record got him on the raw. It was part of Tinker's less spectacular detective training to keep it up to date, but he loathed the job, while fully realising its immense importance.

"I wish he would pinch the bally thing," he said gloomily. "The millions of hours I've spent on it have put years on me."

Coutts laughed.

"He'd be a clever crook to pinch thirty-five volumes, each about the size of a tombstone, my lad. Honestly, though, Blake, do you really think there's anything in it, or is it merely some practical joker getting a little cheap publicity?"

"Hardly publicity," suggested Blake. "He hasn't honoured us with his name, you know. However, about that a little later. In the meantime we'll await the arrival of Splash Page, and see if he has any additional information.'

A curiously thoughtful silence fell on the group until they adjourned into the consulting-room, the walls of which were now gaily decorated with festoons of evergreen and holly. A fire of logs crackled merrily in the grate, and the snowflakes outside made the cosiness inside all the better by contrast.

"Proper Christmassy weather," grunted Coutts, subsiding into a chair, and stretching a pudgy hand towards the box of cigars near by.

An electric bell trilled sharply from the basement. It was exactly eleven o'clock.

"Splash Page. Let him in," said Blake. "He might have some more news.'

The lad crossed over to the door, to return a few minutes later with the journalist.

"Hallo, people! You lazy loafers, lounging indoors!" he called cheerfully, removing his snow-covered motor-coat, and hurling his gauntlets on to the sideboard. "Howdy, Ruff, my hearty! What brings you over to effete Europe?"

"Put it right there, if it weighs a ton, you darned old newshound!" cried Ruff Hanson, who had met Splash Page before on many an adventurous trail.

Splash sank into an easy chair.

"Beer, someone! Cause stoops of mulled ale to be produced. Zounds, but I'm thirsty!" he ejaculated.

Tinker poured out a whiskey-and-soda, and after a preliminary sip, Splash Page plunged his hand into his pocket and produced a copy of the first edition of the "Daily Radio," still limp from the press.

"Some story, kiddos," he chuckled, pointing at the screaming headlines: "Phantom crook and famous sleuth— mystery man's audacious challenge— Sexton Blake accepts!"

"Good old 'Radio,' first with the news again!" said Splash cheerfully. "It's dashed good of you to let me have the scoop, Blake, old man."

Sexton Blake read the few words of introduction, and smiled wryly as he pointed to a smudged photograph in the centre of the column.

"Is this blob of ink supposed to be me, or a photo of our friend, the Phantom?" he bantered.

"You, old man," replied the unabashed Splash. "Can't you recognise the massive and 'awk-like beak? But seriously, Blake, what do you make of it all? I've got the original letter here. Perhaps you'd better see it."

From an envelope he produced a neatly typewritten document, on a sheet of octave paper. The detective scrutinised it carefully, held it up to the light, and examined the envelope minutely.

"H'm! No watermark, few fingerprints; in any case, they'd be useless, as the letter must have been handled by at least four people."

"What do you mean?" asked Splash.

"The sender, the recipient (presumably the editor), yourself, and the linotypist who set it up," was the quiet reply.

"That's so," agreed the journalist.

"Who delivered it? Got any description?"

Splash Page shook his head.

"Only a very vague one. You know how busy one is just before the paper is put to bed. It was delivered to Sims,

the janitor, about ten-fifteen, by a man in a Burberry and a bowler hat, but whether he was dark or fair, or clean-shaven, he couldn't say."

"H'm!" said Blake thoughtfully, replacing the letter in its envelope. "That doesn't help us much. Frankly, what do you think of it?"

Splash Page grinned.

"It's a darned good story, and has gladdened Julius Jones no end. He's only hoping the Phantom Crook'll provide us with a nice, juicy murder, so's he can have a real, happy Christmas."

"You gosh darned newspapermen!" said Ruff Hanson. "Durn me if you ain't a gang of buzzards, the whole bunch of you!"

"Well, I think it's a disgraceful business," growled Coutts. "What the chief will say to this unauthorised handling of the case I don't know." He shook his head gloomily. "I think the Yard ought to see that letter, Blake. Maybe we can pull in this humorous crook for you. I'll send a couple of plain-clothes men to keep guard over the house, if you like?"

"Take a slant at these, pard," said Ruff Hanson, with his wide grin. "I guess you've met 'em before. We don't want no dicks snopin' around here."

Coutts' red face purpled as he found himself gazing down the barrels of the pair of six-guns held in the American's unwavering hand. They had appeared as if by magic—from nowhere.

"P-put the dashed things away, man!" stuttered the inspector. "Have

SATIRA NEXT WEEK!

(See page 24.)

you got a licence for them?" he added suspiciously.

"I sure have. Got it from the Yard last time your boneheads chased me up to Wales."

"H'm!" said Coutts doubtfully, "we don't care for gunplay on this side, Mr. Hanson."

"Guns is guns!" replied that worthy. He pointed to Blake. "And brains is brains, as I've always said. But neither of 'em seem to apply to Scotland Yard."

"Now, you two," Blake admonished. "I don't think I shall need either the Yard or your guns in this purely personal matter between myself and the Phantom Crook."

"Yes, but look here, guv'nor," broke in Tinker. "Supposing——" He broke off suddenly, as a loud peal of the bell, followed by a thunderous knock on the door, sounded through the quiet house.

"Great Scott! Who's making that frightful din?" he demanded, as he raced to the corridor. The others glanced significantly at the clock. It was nearly midnight. An electric tension had crept suddenly into the cosy atmosphere of the room. They heard the sound of a departing taxi, the slam of the front door, and Tinker's footsteps, followed by another's, ascending the stairs.

"Guv'nor," said the lad excitedly, as he burst into the room, "the Phantom Crook's started! Here's his first victim. This is Viscount Rockcliff—and he tells me the famous Rockcliff coronet's gone!"

First Blood to the Phantom.

BLAKE rose courteously to greet his distinguished visitor.

"We've met before, I fancy, my lord," he said. "May I introduce my friends. This is Detective Inspector Coutts, of Scotland Yard, Mr. Ruff Hanson, and Mr. Page."

"By Jove! A gathering of the clans — what!" drawled Rocky, with his infectious smile.

"Beastly sorry to barge in on you like this, Mr. Blake, but the most doocedly unpleasant thing's happened. Fact is, I've been bally well burgled!"

"Pray let me help you to a drink," said Blake suavely. "You may rely on the discretion of all these gentlemen. I take it you have received a visit from the Phantom Crook?"

Rocky paused, with the glass between his fingers.

"Gad! You're positively uncanny! How the dooce did you know that?"

"Elementary, as you had already informed my assistant of the purport of your visit, downstairs. It needed no great power of deduction to repeat it."

Rocky laughed.

"Of course. How stupid of me! Fact is, I'm a bit rattled. 'Pon my sam, it's enough to rattle any chappie! I'd been along to my club, chatting idly of this and that, trickled home, and found my man, Rice, in a frightful state.

"He'd retired early, I'd given him permission, but he awoke suddenly and heard a sort of creaking noise in my study. He crept cautiously to the door, opened it, and found a chappie in a black mask kneeling at my safe.

"Now, old Rice is a doocedly efficient sort of cove, or bloke, and he decided to creep silently out and give the alarm, when the burglar johnny jumped to his feet, and covered him with a revolver.

"Rice, as I say, is no fool. You can't argue with the chap behind a gun, and when the burglar forced him back into his bed-room, and turned the key on him, he couldn't say nay. Rice was in a fearful state; he waited for about twenty minutes, but not a sound came from the study.

"Then, thinking it was safe to give the alarm, he starts to pound on the panel. Still no sound from the next room, and Rice decided the burglar had gone. He burst open the door, and found my safe door wide open, and on top of the safe this bally impertinent note."

Rocky fumbled in his pocket, and withdrew a typed sheet of paper. Blake noted instinctively that it had been typed by the same machine as the Phantom Crook's audacious challenge to the "Daily Radio." Brief and laconic, it ran as follows:

"You have been signally honoured as my first victim. The Rockcliff coronet, a useless bauble, I have, like Cromwell, removed. The proceeds of this feudal survival will go to charity.

"(Signed) THE PHANTOM CROOK."

"Dog my catskills, but he's a cool card!" ejaculated Ruff Hanson. "Say, Mr. Viscount, can you put me wise to this coronet stuff? I thought it was only in story books that dooks and such wore crowns."

A spasm of pain seemed to twitch the classic features of Viscount Rockcliff.

"The Rockcliff coronet is unique, my dear Mr. Hanson. As you know, Blake, most coronets are mere silver-gilt affairs, but my ancestor, the first viscount, was a very rich man—made his pile in the East India Company.

"A viscount's coronet is the same as a duke's; that is, the cap is of crimson velvet turned up with ermine, having a gold tassel at the top, but instead of strawberry leaves, it has sixteen silver balls round the gold circlet.

"The Rockcliff coronet is a deuced heavy affair, being made of pure gold, and the circlet studded with priceless gems—rubies and emeralds."

"A pretty expensive bauble!" commented Blake. "I trust you informed the police at once?"

Rocky nodded.

"Yes. Poor old Rice was so bally unnerved that it was some minutes before I could get sense out of him. I phoned up the Yard, and Rice fetched a copper, who is now in charge. Then I decided to breeze right along, Mr. Blake, because the chappie on duty said I'd find Inspector Coutts and you here.

"'Pon my sam, it's the most extraordinary affair I've ever heard of, and if you can explain it, or tell me anything about the Phantom chappie, I'd be infernally obliged.

"It's dashed serious, you know. The coronet is a bally heirloom, and though I don't take much stock of the thing intrinsically, I've got the family to consider—what!"

Coutts cleared his throat impressively, and rose to his feet.

"You did quite right, my lord, in calling me in so promptly. Now, if you are ready we'll get on the scene of the crime at once. Care to join me, Blake?"

Sexton Blake nodded absently. There was an abstracted look in his shrewd grey eyes.

"Fetch the Grey Panther, Tinker, my boy," he commanded.

"I say, my lord," began Splash Page, a little breathlessly, "do you mind if I report this exclusively for the 'Daily Radio'? I can just about catch the late London edition, and——"

"Certainly, dear old boy, anything to oblige," replied Rocky magnanimously. "Lead on, Mr. Blake, the carriage waits without. 'Pon my sam, it's dooced exciting!"

"Mind if I keep Ruff Hanson company, Blake?" queried Splash, as the criminologist, accompanied by Coutts, took his departure. "I'll phone this to the rag."

"Not in the least," said Blake. "Throw another log on the fire. Come on, Tinker, sharp with that research case!"

The three detectives left the room, leaving Hanson and the journalist alone in the cosy consulting-room.

"Hot dog, but there's sure some action to-night!" said Ruff Hanson emphatically. "Wisht I was on the trail."

"Better stay here, old hoss, and guard Blake's treasures. The Phantom Crook might pay us a nocturnal visit."

Hanson brightened.

"Oh, boy, I'll inform the universe there'll be some scrap if he does!"

Splash Page smiled as he raised the receiver and called up the "Daily Radio," and there was a peculiar gleam in his dancing eyes.

"WHAT sort of man was this alleged burglar, Rice?" queried Coutts importantly, of the grave-faced, grey-haired manservant.

They had arrived in less than a quarter of an hour, at Viscount Rockcliff's magnificent maisonette in Jermyn Street, and Blake, Coutts, and Tinker surveyed the scene of the robbery.

The C.I.D. man had promptly started to interrogate Rice, recording the valet's answers in his black, official notebook. Meantime, Blake had crossed over to the safe in the corner of the room.

It was a massive affair, with a combination lock, the door of which stood slightly ajar. Coutts' interrogation of the valet did not reveal much that was illuminating. Substantially, his story was the same as that reported by his noble master.

"I couldn't see the man's face, sir," he said. "It was covered by a sort of black silk mask, reaching nearly down to his chin. He was about medium height, and wore chamois leather gloves. His voice was low, with a peculiar harshness about it."

"H'm!" said Coutts thoughtfully. "That will do, my man. You may retire, but"—and here the inspector's cold eye fixed the valet with a menacing stare—"you'll remain within call. I'm not at all satisfied yet."

"Certainly, sir," said the imperturbable Rice, and vanished like a well-oiled automaton.

"And now for the safe!" said Coutts briskly. "Er—your lordship, has anything else been abstracted beside the coronet?"

Rocky shook his head.

"Not a thing, as far as I can see; that's the rummy part of the business. Here are fifty quid in Treasury notes on the top shelf. You'd think, when the enterprising burglar started burgling, he wouldn't have overlooked such an obvious haul."

Sexton Blake smiled.

"Fond of Gilbert and Sullivan, I see," he said.

"Yes, rather!" agreed Rocky enthusiastically. "Topping stuff—what! But, I say, inspector, how on earth did the crook manage to open the safe? As far as I am aware, I'm the only person in the world who knows the combination."

"Are you sure that this man Rice is trustworthy?" asked Coutts suspiciously. "I don't mind telling you, my lord, I wasn't impressed by his manner." He knelt down suddenly and examined the safe. "H'm! If he wore gloves, there's not much likelihood of fingerprints."

"The results are purely negative," replied Blake, dusting his fingers lightly, and replacing a small box in his research-case. "I have already dusted the dial with grey powder."

"Good heavens! Then there aren't any clues?" gasped Rocky. "I say, Blake, that sounds bad. There'll be the dooce to pay when the family learn the coronet's pinched!"

Coutts grunted, and, like a lumbering bull-terrier, searched every corner of the room.

"This, I take it, is your sleeping apartment?" he demanded, moving to an elegantly appointed bed-chamber. "Have you a hall-porter downstairs who noticed anything particular?"

Rocky shook his head.

"No. He goes off duty at ten-thirty. Every inhabitant of this block has his own private pass-key."

"H'm!" You haven't lost your duplicate, by any chance?" demanded the Yard man.

The viscount thought for a moment.

"By Jove! Now you mention it, I mislaid the key about six weeks back. I meant to have another one cut, but you know how these things slip one's memory."

Coutts scribbled a few lines in his notebook, and turned to the stolid police-sergeant at the door.

"Sims, you'd better remain on duty to-night. I'll send you a relief in the morning. It seems a clear-cut case to me, but I haven't yet decided whether there's any inside complicity in it yet.

"Watch that man Rice, and on no account allow him to leave the premises without my permission."

"Very good, sir," said the stolid Sims.

"It looks like an inside job to me," Coutts muttered to Sexton Blake, who seemed to be taking a most detached view of the whole affair.

"Possibly. But I should be inclined to consider that the idea emanated from outside," said Blake quietly. "The Phantom Crook has a piquant sense of humour." He turned to the viscount.

"Was the coronet insured?" he demanded.

Rocky nodded.

"Yes—the Consolidated Risk people—for fifty thou."

"H'm!" said Blake thoughtfully. "That's bad."

"Bad?" echoed the other blankly. "I think it's a darned good job it was insured. If it's never recovered——"

The strident ring of a telephone-bell interrupted his remark, and Rocky lifted the receiver with a surprise expression on his face.

"What's that? Gad!" he ejaculated, with a startled expression on his face. He turned to Sexton Blake. "It's that American chappie, Henson, or Hanson. Wants to speak to you urgently. The Phantom Crook's in Baker Street!"

"What!" gasped Blake, startled out of his wonted impassivity. He grabbed at the receiver, and Ruff Hanson's nasal tones vibrated the diaphragm like a thunderstorm.

"Hi, Blake! By the Holy Highball, this Phantom Crook's pulled his stuff. He's a thug, a low-down, no-account yegg!" The American's voice was quivering with indignation.

"What's happened, man?" snapped Blake.

"Happened? The worst! While me and Splash were chinwagging here, that doggone Crook's pinched your greatest treasure. By the Great Horned Toad, if I lay my mitts on him——"

"Cut the cackle! What's the matter?" rapped Blake incisively.

"Why, dog my cats, he's pinched Mrs. Bardell!" roared Bluff Hanson.

"What!" gasped the dumbfounded detective. "My dear Hanson, you're drunk!"

"Drunk—Hades!" came the reply. "I went up to my room to get down some press clippings to show Splash, when I bumped into the door at the end of the first landing, where Mrs. Bardell sleeps, I guess. There was a sheet of paper fixed to the doorway, and I jumped like as if I'd been shot, because it was signed, 'The Phantom Crook.'"

"Good heavens!" said Sexton Blake. "The colossal audacity! What did it say?"

"Merely: 'Your move, I think, Mr. Blake. I have taken the greatest treasure a man can have—an incomparable cook. Come and find her within forty-eight hours—if you can.—THE PHANTOM CROOK.'

"I knocked at the door; there was no reply. I turned the knob; the room was empty; and then I chased down to the consulting-room, to find Splash Page. We've searched the whole darned house, but there ain't a sign of Mrs. B. since she served the coffee at dinner, at eight o'clock."

Blake's lips tightened grimly into a firm, straight line, as he said quietly:

"I shall be back in twenty minutes, Ruff."

He replaced the receiver with a deliberate gesture, and faced his curious listeners. "Gentlemen," he said quietly "the Phantom Crook has won the first round. He has kidnapped Mrs. Bardell. By Heaven, if he has dared to injure a hair of the good soul's head, I'll—I'll——"

He did not finish the sentence, but the silence was more eloquent than words.

"Kidnapped Mrs. B.," echoed Tinker, with staring eyes. "Oh, what rot, guv'nor! Perhaps she's just gone out to her sister's, or——"

"Come," said Blake briefly. "Rest

assured, my lord, that I shall do everything in my power to apprehend this Phantom Crook, not only on behalf of yourself, but for urgent reasons of my own."

IT was a very silent trio that arrived back in Baker Street a little after two o'clock that morning. Coutts scratched his bristly chin in a perplexed fashion, and plied Blake with questions that received only a monosyllabic reply.

The snow had thickened perceptibly as Blake urged the huge grey car through the boisterous December night. The wind whistled shrilly, and it was with difficulty that Blake forged his way ahead through the slushy streets.

Tinker took the Grey Panther back to the garage, while Coutts and the criminologist entered the consulting-room to hear the latest amazing developments in the Phantom Crook's career. Ruff Hanson was pacing restlessly up and down before the hearth, while Splash was frantically scribbling sheet after sheet for the to-morrow's issue of the "Daily Radio."

"Thank Heaven you're back, old hoss!" said the American heartily. "This waiting sure plays hades with my nerves. I'm a go-getter. Hanging about, warming my Oxfords at a Yule fire, ain't my idea of action."

Blake sank into a chair.

"Let's have the full story in detail, old man."

He rammed a wad of tobacco into his capacious briar, as Ruff Hanson described his dramatic discovery. Coutts fidgeted uneasily. The unwonted exertion of the past hour had reduced the boiled shirt to a limp rag. He had not Blake's ability to relax, and consequently his irritability rose.

He blew his nose like a trumpet once or twice, and finally rose.

"Well, Blake I think I'd better turn up at the Yard. Supposing I cover the coronet end of the affair, and you tackle the mystery of Mrs. Bardell. I'll give you a ring in the morning. Confound that Phantom Crook! I was looking forward to my Christmas dinner!" he added disgustedly.

Splash Page yawned.

"Think I'll accompany you, Coutsy. It's too late for the last edition. Me for bye-byes. Thanks for the story, Blake, old man, and don't worry unduly about Mrs. B. A crook with a sense of humour is seldom violent. I'll call in the morning to hear if there's any news."

Blake nodded.

"It's Thursday morning, the day before Christmas Eve. Look here, Splash, I authorise you to say that not only do I accept the Phantom Crook's Christmas challenge, but I'll double the stake money if I don't recover Mrs. Bardell by midnight on Christmas Eve."

Splash grinned.

"You're a dashed sportsman, Blake! Here's luck to you!" he added as Tinker entered eagerly.

"Any news of Mrs. B.?" he queried anxiously.

Blake shook his head.

"Better get to bed, youngster; you'll need all your faculties about you to-morrow."

There was a chorus of good-nights, and finally Ruff Hanson stretched his massive frame.

"Good-night, Blake old hoss! Guess I'll hit the hay, too. Let's know when

you want me in action," he said, with a cavernous yawn.

Silence fell on the house in Baker Street, save for the moaning of the wind in the chimney, and an occasional sputter of the logs.

But Sexton Blake still sat back, wrapped in thought and tobacco smoke.

His shrewd, analytical brain was probing, sifting, assembling masses of seemingly irrelevant evidence, weaving each separate fact until he had formed a coherent whole.

It was nearly 4 a.m. when he finally stretched his cramped limbs, and there was a suspicion of a twinkle in his eyes as he knocked out the final dottle from his pipe. "I was never a very convinced believer in ghosts—or phantoms," he said cryptically to his reflection in the overmantel mirror.

Mrs. Bardell Enters Society.

THAT excellent woman, Mrs. Martha Bardell, who had attended so long to the creature comforts of Sexton Blake and Tinker since the unfortunate demise of her husband, a highly-respected water-rate collector of Bermondsey, smoothed her black satin dress over her ample bosom, and took one last approving look at herself in the cheval glass.

Her chubby red face shone with the afterglow of a vigorous wash as she adjusted a voluminous feather boa to her satisfaction, and she bridled self-consciously at her becoming black hat with its top-hamper of nodding ostrich feathers.

"I 'olds with a bun. It's genteel—that's wot, genteel and lady-like," she murmured, patting her back hair.

"Shingles, indeed! In my young days shingles was a disease, and it still is," she added. "I don't know wot we're coming to, these days, with grandmothers bobbin' their 'air, and these 'ere Bolshevik boots!

"Russian boots, hindeed!" she said truculently to no one in particular. "Shows 'ow them Bolshies are getting a grip on the country. Give me the old elastic sides, every time!" she added, with a coy glance at her comfortable boots.

Mrs. Bardell, after serving a magnificent dinner to her master and his two guests, Ruff Hanson and Detective-Inspector Coutts, had retired to "tittervate," prior to sallying forth for an evening's chat and gossip with her widowed sister, Mrs. Amelia Cluppins, at Pimlico, and also to give final instructions regarding the poultry manager regarding the gigantic turkey she had ordered for Christmas Day.

Blake never interfered in the good soul's domestic affairs; they ran as smoothly as clockwork under her supervision, and so, with a final sigh of complete satisfaction at her personal appearance and the world in general, she sallied forth, majestic as a full-rigged ship, umbrella aloft, and her nodding plumes waving, into the snow-laden air of Baker Street.

She headed for Messrs. Peabody & Palmer, the famous poulterers, at the corner of Endil Street, and, having claimed the turkey, sallied forth triumphantly with the shop-boy carrying the colossal bird in a straw bag.

As she rounded the corner a luxurious Rolls-Royce car glided gently to the kerb.

Mrs. Bardell scanned the luxurious limousine with unconcealed interest. Inside the tonneau it looked very warm and inviting. A beautiful lady, clad in a rich ermine cloak, lounged back on the cushions, and with her was a young man in an ordinary lounge suit.

Suddenly the door of the limousine opened, and the young man emerged and, raising his hat, bowed politely.

"Goodness me!" gasped Mrs. Bardell. "Mr. Pige—'ow you startled me! Which I wishes to remark, and no offence intended, that your motorcar——"

"Hallo, Mrs. B. I thought I recognised you! Fact is, I just missed you at Baker Street, and I chased after you to catch you up. Lucky I found you."

Mrs. Bardell bridled. She had a soft spot in her heart for the engaging young newspaperman, "an imp like Master Tinker, only wuss," was her mental description of him.

"Here is a note from Tinker, Mrs. B," said Splash, with his cheerful grin. "But do come inside out of the snow. I want you to meet the Honourable Cynthia Montague; she particularly wants to know you."

"Lawks!" said Mrs. Bardell. "Fancy me 'obnobbing with the gentrey at my time o' life. Is this one of your larks, young man?" she asked suspiciously.

"Splash, bring Mrs. Bardell in out of the cold at once," called an imperious young feminine voice, and the newspaperman grinned triumphantly as he gallantly escorted that dazed soul into the cushioned tonneau.

"Cynthia, this is Mrs. Bardell, one of the best. If I were a little older, 'pon my sam, I'd marry her. The number of proposals she gets every year is alarming. She's broken the heart of every police-inspector of Scotland Yard. They have yearned all their lives to marry a woman who makes such incomparable pies. I believe Inspector Coutts would commit bigamy if he thought he'd get away with it——"

"Oh, go along, do, Mr. Pige," said Mrs. Bardell, blushing furiously. "Don't mind his nonsense, miss. He's one of these 'ere newspaper importers, 'e can't 'elp 'isself."

The Honourable Cynthia flung back her pretty head, and laughed musically. Sister of Viscount Rockliff, she was the leader of the younger set of society, and had entered whole-heartedly into the plot arranged by Tinker and Splash Page for the enlivenment of Blake's Christmas.

"Now Mrs. B.," said Splash Page earnestly, as the limousine purred through the snow-laden night. "I know you are a sport, and I want you to listen very carefully. Tinker and I have arranged with Viscount Rockcliff, Miss Cynthia's brother, to give Mr. Blake a surprise Christmas party. Please read Tinker's note, and you will see that it is quite O.K."

Mrs. Bardell tore open the envelope and scanned Tinker's boyish scrawl:

"Dear Mrs. B.,—We're planning a Christmas surprise for the guv'nor. Do be a sport, and agree to our scheme. We've arranged to have a real old-fashioned Christmas dinner at Goreham Grange, and, of course, the guv'nor'd be furious if you weren't there to supervise. So Splash and I have arranged

for you to go ahead, and it'll give the guv'nor a surprise to find that you're still in charge. Do please agree. Cheerio, Tinker."

"The young limb!" breathed Mrs. Bardell. "The owdacious young willain. It's nothing more or less than 'olesale kidnappin'."

The twinkle in the good woman's eyes belied the severity of her words, however, and when the Honourable Cynthia leaned forward and flashed her radiant smile, Mrs. Bardell chuckled.

"You see, Mrs. Bardell, it's so difficult to get Mr. Blake to accept a dinner engagement, but he'll come like a shot if he knows you're there. We've prepared a lovely room for you, with all you require, and of course you'll be one of the guests of honour at the feast."

"Well—er—it's mighty kind of you, miss," Mrs. Bardell temporised. "But wot Mr. Blake'll say, 'eaven only knows. There's 'is socks to darn, and that there dressing-gow-l of 'is, which is a disgrace, and 'as got another big 'ole——"

"Now don't you worry about household affairs. You're on a holiday now, Mrs. B.," broke in Splash Page cheerfully.

"But where are we goin'?" gasped Mrs. Bardell, as the great car hurtled out from the traffic-laden streets, and headed for the country.

"Goreham Grange, Mrs. Bardell. It's a lovely old place, some little way out of town. You'll fall in love with my brother's ancestral home," replied Cynthia.

Mrs. Bardell snuggled back against the cushions, and gave a sigh of resignation. "Oh well, what will be, will be, as my 'usband said when 'e broke 'is leg coming 'ome from the Buffaloes."

Splash Page winked at the girl. His stratagem had worked without the slightest hitch. Thanks to Tinker, he had learned of Mrs. Bardell's intended visit to the poulterer's, and no suspicion of the real plot had reached her.

On through the blinding snowstorm the great car rolled, and soon they passed through sleepy hamlets that looked for all the world like Christmas cards, with their snow-covered, thatched roofs, and their lighted windows reflecting the glow of cheerful hearth fires.

From an ancient church belfry the bells pealed merrily, and Mrs. Bardell smiled in blissful content. Her thoughts were very pleasant. What an adventure to tell her sister, Mrs. Cluppins—'obnobbing with dooks and earls! Rolls-Royceing to ancestral 'omes. That young limb, Tinker, always up to some mischief, and Splash Page no better. Ah, well!

Suddenly she sat up with a jerk, and a look of alarm came into her face.

"Good 'evings! The turkey!" she gasped. "I was that flustered I forgot to h'issue instructions to the boy——"

"Don't worry about the turkey," said Splash soothingly. "There's tons of 'em at the Grange. Besides, the boy'll take it back to the shop. There—er—won't be any need of it at Baker Street."

At which the worthy housekeeper lapsed into a puzzled mood.

The warmth of the car, and the novelty of her surroundings at last lulled the good soul into a gentle slumber, and she awoke with a start as the Rolls drew up before the magnificent entrance gates of Goreham Grange.

The grey old pile looked stately and dignified, wrapped in its white mantle of snow. The quaint, twisted Tudor chimneys, the leaden windows aglow with yellow light, the background of dark, mysterious trees, added a glamour to the scene that was irresistible.

The liveried chauffeur opened the door with a low bow. Splash leapt down first, and gallantly helped out Cynthia and then Mrs. Bardell.

"Welcome to Goreham Grange!" he said cheerfully, as he led the way to the spacious terrace.

Mrs. Bardell, impressed and awed, hung on grimly to her umbrella. Two flunkeys, clad in knee breeches and the gorgeous silk liveries of the Rockcliff family, stood like statues at the open door.

A pontifical butler bowed low as they crossed into the hall, one of the most famous halls in England, gaily decked now in honour of Christmas, with festoons of evergreens and gay paper chains.

Mrs. Bardell could hardly believe she was not dreaming, as Cynthia turned to the butler.

"Soames, show Mrs. Bardell to the guest-room. I presume dinner will be served soon?"

The stately butler bowed.

"Precisely, madam. Pray may I relieve you of your encumbrance." He turned to Mrs. Bardell. That worthy woman blushed: she was not quite sure what an encumbrance was, and had half a mind to tell the butler to leave her encumbrance alone, but she was awed into silence by his overpowering dignity.

Very solemnly the butler relieved her of her umbrella, and handed it to a waiting menial as if it had been a jewelled sceptre. "Pray step this way, madam," he said pontifically. "You are doubtless fatigued after your journey."

"I am that!" Mrs. Bardell agreed, as she followed him up the magnificent staircase.

"Hallo! Hallo! Hallo!" called a cheery voice, and from the library emerged the elegant figure of Viscount Rockliff. "Where's the incomparable Mrs. B.?"

"She's upstairs, Rocky, old sport. It worked like a charm. But look here, old boy, I've got to scoot back to London. Have you fixed up that wireless call?"

Rocky grinned. "Prompt at the time we agreed. Tinker tunes in to my wave length, and I've given Soames strict instructions. Come on, let's dash back, and fix our alibis. Now Cynthia, old thing, you know your job. Keep your end up, and see that Mrs. Bardell's kept thoroughly amused. She must have no suspicion of how things are."

Cynthia laughed. "The dear old soul is probably too excited to inquire too closely into the matter. Ring me up as soon as you've framed the Jermyn Street business. Lord, I'm as excited as a cat on hot bricks. This beats treasure hunting hollow."

Splash Page grinned.

"Wait till you see to-morrow's 'Radio' old fruit. C'mon, Rocky." He grabbed the peer by the arm, and, scarcely waiting for Rockliff to don his overcoat, hustled him into the waiting car.

"Back to Jermyn Street, Jenkyn, and drive like blazes," said Rocky. "Now for the Phantom Crook's next exploit."

Meantime, Mrs. Bardell, in the palatial guest-room of Goreham Grange, gazed in awe at the vast four-posted bed, the imposing wardrobe, and the magnificent silver toilet set on the Jacobean dressing-table.

"Lawks!" she ejaculated, removing her black hat, and preening herself at the mirror. "Is this 'ow the gentry live? Fancy sleeping in that there

(Continued on page 17.)

The Xmas Round Table

SCENE: Dinner of representative gathering of UNION JACK readers. The toast of "Sexton Blake," proposed by the Editor, has just been drunk with acclamation. In response to musical honours, and insistent demands for a speech, Blake rises to reply.

"MR EDITOR, Ladies, and Gentlemen" (said Sexton Blake), —"It is with great pleasure —and a somewhat acute sense of my unworthiness of the honour —that I reply to your toast.

"One of the finest innovations which have been made possible for us in late years is, in my humble opinion, the institution of the Round Table.

"This board at which we are now assembled for our Christmastide meeting is more than a mere convenient table at which we can debate our affairs during the year, or at which we can forgather at a dinner such as this at the season of reunion and festivity. It is the outward and visible sign of comradeship in our allegiance to the Old Paper—the paper that is ever new. (*Applause.*)

"My friend the Editor has made it a sort of slogan, I believe, that the paper is intended for readers of all ages and both sexes. He might have added: 'All nationalities that can read the King's English,' too.

"It is an established fact that everybody can enjoy a good detective story, and I think that if the contents of our paper were translated every week into, say, the language of the Cannibal Islands, the inhabitants of those places would refrain from their usual habit of greeting the stranger with spears, and would gibber with joy—or however it is that they express their delight—on the arrival of the boat with the weekly supplies of the UNION JACK.

"You will notice that I said one could enjoy 'a good detective story,' and not 'stories of a good detective.' The fact that I happen to be the individual whose doings are chronicled is merely incidental. I cannot claim that my activities are the best that could be chosen for the purpose. (*Cries of "No, no!"*)

"I see that you are inclined to disagree with me on that point, so I will not press it. I think it will not be disputed, however, that even my commonplace exploits are presented to you in such a way as to be not entirely uninteresting. That, of course, is through no merit of mine, and I must regretfully accuse my chronicler of a little occasional exaggeration, especially with regard to my alleged versatility, perspicacity, or prowess."

(*Here the speaker was interrupted by cries of dissent, in which the author of "Mrs. Bardell's Xmas Eve," was particularly observed to join, with a somewhat guilty air.*)

"Nor will I protest against his descriptions of my personal appearance. He means well, and may be excused on the grounds of literary zeal. But I would remark in passing that it is news to me that I have a 'hawk-like beak,' or that my eyes are 'orbs of steel-grey, set beneath a lofty, intellectual dome.'

"I will also forgive the same writer, in his account of my recent visit to Gorcham Grange, in emphasising the tobacco-burnt, chemical stained, and faded condition of my dressing-gown. I will assure you—and him—that it is quite a comfortable garment, and that although my worthy housekeeper, Mrs. Bardell, has kindly made me a present this Christmas of a new and very handsome one to replace it, I shall experience a pang to be off with the old love and on with the new.

"To do our writer friend justice, however, I must admit that he invariably refers to my evening rig-out as 'immaculate,' or 'faultless' and sometimes both. (*Laughter.*) I am not aware whether or not he is in league with my tailor for advertising purposes, but if not, I am sure that gentleman would be pleased to hear of his unsolicited testimonial.

"But enough of this banter.

"There is one thing I must mention, while I have the opportunity of addressing you, and that is my gratification at seeing at our Round Table such a representative gathering of those to whom the UNION JACK is a weekly boon.

"Boys and girls, aunts and uncles, mothers and fathers—grandfathers and grandmothers, even, are here. Readers from At Home; readers from each and every one of our Colonies; and readers from lands which owe no allegiance to the Union Jack as a flag, but which distinctly owe it to the UNION JACK as a paper.

"My friend the Editor tells me that the easiest way of becoming a stamp collector is to be the editor of such a paper as the UNION JACK, and to 'freeze on to'—the term is his own—the foreign stamps that decorate his morning mail from readers in all parts of the earth.

"He is to be envied as regards the stamps, but he is to be envied even more so as regards the splendid loyalty and enthusiasm in the letters themselves. And, speaking for myself, I must say that I am honoured, and at times embarrassed, at the laudatory things that those letters often say about me personally. I suspect the Editor of attempts to undermine my modesty by insisting on my seeing them.

"One thing I learn is that there is a persistent demand for stories recording a visit of mine to that particular part of the world from which the sender of the letter writes; it might be Kamchaka, Zanzibar, Backwash, Ga., Walla-Walla, or Bing-Bang-Bong, China. (*Laughter.*)

"I do not think I can claim acquaintance with literally all those places; but, as you know, I have had occasion to travel a bit, and I am sure the Editor is doing his best to oblige you with tales about as many of your home-towns as he can. It is, I understand, mainly a matter of selecting the material concerned from the records of my past cases, which I have already placed before him.

"But, as my time is drawing short, I will refrain from going further into the matter, except to say that you may rely on him doing his best for you; and that the material, whatever it may be, will be served up to you by our clever writing friends in the same palatable and enjoyable form for which the paper has so long held a reputation.

"To conclude, I must thank you very sincerely for your hearty reception of my name, and as I see that the next toast on the list is 'Mr. Tinker,' I will no longer intervene between you and the remarks of my young assistant, who, I can see, is already itching to make his speech."

(*Laughter, during which Tinker was observed to shake his head emphatically.*)

"My best thanks, then, for your toast. May your Christmases, now and to come, be everything that you can wish them; and if the periodical with which my name is unworthily associated can succeed in adding to your enjoyment of this festive season, I am honoured indeed." (*Cheers and prolonged applause.*)

Your Editor

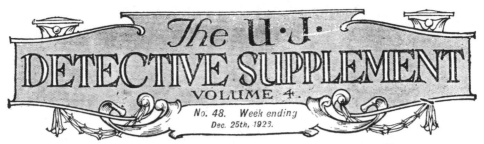

The U·J·
DETECTIVE SUPPLEMENT
VOLUME 4.

No. 48. Week ending
Dec. 25th, 1923.

A Crime of Christmastide

The horror of assassination where a public man is concerned is always acute; but when that man is a great and popular actor of the first rank, and when in addition the crime occurs at the season of peace and goodwill, the horror is intensified a hundredfold. Such was the tragic murder of William Terriss at Christmastide, 1897.

THE season of "peace on earth and good will to men" is one that, in an ideal state of things, would be observed by the criminal, as well as by the rest of us. Unfortunately, however, this is an imperfect world, and even at this time of year humanity's baser impulses cannot be suppressed, and the newspapers that reappear after the Christmas holiday, brief as it is, may confidently be expected to yield their tale of good will gone sadly astray.

Minor misdeeds, apparently, we shall always have with us; but, happily, this joyous season is seldom marred by crimes of such tragic importance as the Christmastide murder of William Terriss, nearly thirty years ago.

The mere fact that a popular actor named William Terriss was murdered at the height of his fame conveys to the present generation nothing of the horror that was felt when the crime was a vital affair of the moment.

At this distance of time the name and fame of the unfortunate victim have become dimmed by the ascendance of other stars. But those of us whose memories go back to the late 'nineties, and who saw William Terriss at the zenith of his powers, will recall something of what his name meant to the public of that day and generation. The genius of the stage is unfortunate in that he can bequeath no record of his art to posterity —or, at least, he could not until the coming of the films —and so the artistry of Terriss died with him, leaving only fading memories behind.

The wheel of Time has spun apace since the closing years of last century, and the stars of the theatrical firmament to-day have rival attractions to compete against for public attention. But in those days, before the coming of the microphone, and the film, an actor of any eminence was indeed a famous figure, and Terriss was in the very forefront of them.

The sensation caused by his untimely death in 1897 can, in short, be compared only to that which would be aroused nowadays by the news of a similar assassination of any great film actor of world-wide renown.

Such, then, was the horror of the deed committed in the dark, clustering shadows of the Adelphi stage-door that Christmas week thirty years ago.

NOW we come to a study of the murderer himself, the unbalanced instrument in the hand of an insensate Fate for the destruction of a worthy and gifted man.

The name he was most commonly known by was William Archer, but he also called himself on occasion William Archer Hunt. His real name, however, was probably Richard Arthur Prince.

Prince's antecedents, so far as can be traced, takes us back to Dundee, where he had been an engineer's labourer. From boyhood the stage, and the idea of becoming a great actor, had fascinated his weak and defective mind, and his labours in the engineering shops ceased as soon as he could obtain a "super's" job at a Dundee theatre.

Intoxicated by this success —or, rather, lack of failure— he came to London, and was lucky to the extent that he obtained another walking-on part at the Adelphi Theatre. Two or three tours in the provinces with various companies provided him with other jobs, but there is no record that he ever made much of a hit, or attained to anything more than the smallest parts.

His provincial experience was varied with occasional returns to London and small-part jobs at the Adelphi, where the great William Terriss—William Lewin was his real name—was nightly packing the theatre as the result of his masterly performances in such plays as "Harbour Lights," "The Corsican Brothers," and "The Vicar of Wakefield."

There seems no doubt, as revealed by the facts later, that Prince was of weak character, and mentally deficient. He had been known as "Mad Archer" amongst his theatrical associates, and the men of the engineering works had con-

William Terriss—a photo taken a short time before his tragic death at the hands of the assassin Richard Arthur Prince.
[Photo: L.E.A.

sidered him "soft," and had been in the habit, as we should say nowadays, of pulling his leg.

At all events, it is certain that for many years the ability and popularity of William Terriss had acted on his mind like a canker.

He had a way of standing in the wings when the great man was on the stage, glowering and muttering to himself. "Fools may succeed where genius fails," he was once heard to say—evidence of the small esteem in which he held the popular actor's ability, and of the great esteem he had for his own.

Growing side by side with this contempt of Terriss' work was a conviction in Prince's mind that the more influential man kept him down and prevented him from getting the parts he thought he deserved. And so, eventually, did insane jealousy merge into murderous hate.

In actual fact, Terriss' only intervention in the man's affairs was when he had given him money at a time when he was "down and out," and again when he wrote to the Actors' Benevolent Association recommending them to help him. In short, the unfortunate Terriss had done his murderer nothing but good.

In the month of December, 1897, came the final weeks of a period of unemployment for Prince, and the chaos of his unbalanced mind was fast whirling to its calamitous climax.

During those weeks he had been persistently hanging round the stage door of the Adelphi, worrying everyone who came in and out with his hard-luck story, and making himself a nuisance generally. Particularly were his importunities directed at the successful star, William Terriss.

And, as afterwards came out at the trial, all that time the desperate, mentally deficient "super" carried concealed in his pocket a sharp-pointed knife, of the type butchers use.

He had bought it about a month before the murder, a fact which pointed to his premeditated intention to commit the deed. The defence, however, contended that it pointed to no such thing, in view of the man's unsound mental condition. But of that later.

At all events, it was common knowledge that the out-of-work

A hansom cab, containing Terriss and a friend, came jingling along Maiden Lane, and stopped at the corner to set down the two men. There they parted, and Terriss walked the short distance that separated him from a small door set in the rear wall of the Adelphi, which was his own private entrance into the theatre.

As he unlocked it, with his back turned towards the street, a figure stole up behind him. It was Richard Arthur Prince. He had been lying in wait, for the great actor's habits were quite familiar to him.

He raised his butcher's knife and stabbed downwards, twice. The wounds were just under the left shoulder-blade.

With a cry Terriss staggered round and tried to grapple with his murderer. But the knife had done its work too well, and almost in the same movement he fell to the pavement.

Maiden Lane was not a busy thoroughfare, but it happened that there were a few passers-by, who were attracted by the commotion. Several of them flung themselves on the frenzied man, and, after a short, sharp struggle, overcame Prince and held him down, while police who had been hurriedly sent for came up and took the murderer into custody, rescuing him, incidentally, from the enraged crowd which soon gathered, and from which he stood in danger of being lynched.

Meantime, poor William Terriss was carried into the corridor of the theatre, and doctors from Charing Cross Hospital, near at hand, sped to the spot. They exerted all their efforts and skill to save his life, but he had received a mortal thrust. In twenty minutes after the fatal blow he had died.

By this time the orchestra inside the theatre were just concluding the finishing passages of the overture, and a crowded house was awaiting the rise of the curtain on a piece called "Secret Service," in which Terriss took the leading part.

Instead of the curtain rising, the stage-manager appeared before it, and in a few words announced that he regretted there could be no performance that evening.

No reason for this surprising news was given,

The fatal knife. Prince carried this about with him for weeks in contemplation of his insane deed.
[Photo: I. B.]

PRINCE by this time had been taken to a cell at Bow Street Police Court, hard by, and, after a preliminary appearance in the dock there, he came up for his trial at the Central Criminal Court before Mr. Justice Channell, in the beginning of January, 1898.

In view of his having been caught red-handed, there was no doubt as to his guilt; but the defence was insanity, and the trial resolved itself into one of his mental responsibility.

Many eminent doctors were called to give expert evidence in the case, and one and all they were unanimous that he was, in fact, insane.

Apart from more technical reasons, this was indicated by his demeanour immediately after the crime. He had made no attempt to escape, and had seemed delighted with the success of his stroke. He had made wild statements to the effect that the murder of William Terriss was an act of justice, and his conversation generally was shown to be incoherent and excitable. He was also found to be suffering from paranoia, or persecution-mania, and imagined that everybody had been scheming against him.

Testimony from members of his family brought out the facts that he had always been passionate, fiery-tempered, and inordinately proud of himself. Further proof of his mental shortcomings was given by a provincial theatrical manager, who had once employed him in a small speaking part. Prince had been incapable even of learning the few words required of him.

The prisoner's attitude of impenitence and his insane idea that he was the instrument of righteous justice on his victim, was, of course, not accepted by the law, however significant it might have been from a medical point of view as indication of his mental condition.

"Do you consider that the accused was less insane if it is shown that by buying the knife a month before the crime he must have premeditated murder?" the judge asked one of the medical witnesses.

"No," was the reply; "because it is well known that the insane do premeditate."

The doctor's version of Prince's motives and actions was that he—the doctor—believed Prince had, in fact, premeditated murder, and had bought the knife with the sole object of killing Terriss. Also, that Prince knew he was attacking Terriss. The doctor believed that he was mentally unsound, and had been affected by persecution-mania, until he had been urged by his delusions to kill his supposed persecutor. In the medical sense, added the expert, the prisoner did not understand the quality of his act.

The jury had a difficult task before them, as is always the case when insanity is the plea in a crime of this sort, for conservative lawyers and up-to-date medical men are very much at variance on the point. Even in these days—thirty years after the Terriss murder—when the mind and its maladies have been studied to an extent which would have amazed the older generation, the law and medicine have still been unable to find common ground where insanity is concerned.

The jury's verdict, however, was this: "We find the prisoner guilty of wilful murder. We say he knew what he was doing, and to whom he was doing it, but, on the medical evidence, that he was not responsible for his actions."

A very awkward verdict to act upon, this. It implied that the jury had found

actor had often threatened Terriss with violence; but he had often said the same thing of others, and no notice was taken of him—a disastrous policy, in view of the crime.

CAME the evening of December 17th, a Thursday, and just seven days before the Christmas Eve performance, the last show before the holiday.

and the audience wonderingly left their seats and filed out into the Strand. And there, for the first time, they learned the reason for their disappointment. The streets were a-buzz with the news of their favourite actor's tragic death, and the knowledge that William Terriss would never delight them with his art must have silenced many a little grumble at the loss of an evening's pleasure.

that Prince was guilty, and, since he knew what he was doing, that he should be punished for it. On the other hand, that they could not ignore the medical evidence of irresponsibility, and its corresponding exemption from the usual punishment.

It will be noticed that the jury did not say outright that the murderer was insane, but only that they recognised the medical evidence which said that he was.

The judge extricated himself from this dilemma by pronouncing sentence that Prince should be detained during her Majesty's pleasure, and Prince was consigned to Broadmoor.

Such was the tragedy of William Terriss that Christmas week of thirty years ago. A madman's hate, a mortal wound, and the stilling for ever of a voice and presence that had charmed thousands with the magic of art.

Well it is that the crimes of Christmastide, unhappily numerous as they are, include few so calamitous as this.

Pages from my Past

By Sonia Shirling.

Part Three of our enthralling series of articles recording incidents in the life story of a one-time adventuress. The following is the narrative of the very curious events which befell her in Naples after her Paris escapade, which was chronicled here last week.

THE Italians have a saying: "See Naples and die." The idea meant to be conveyed, of course, is that one can die quite content in the knowledge that life can hold no other sight more fair than the view of the city.

The view recommended, by the way, is that from the sea. The foreigner visiting Naples is, however, more often disposed to take the proverb to mean that, seeing Naples will result in his death from the Neapolitan street-smells.

Certainly they are offensive, but it must be admitted that the view is all that is claimed for it.

After my separation from my accomplice Pete at Rome, when he had attempted to shoot me, I decided to see Naples and determine for myself her much-lauded beauties—and, incidentally, look out for any business which might come my way.

The sale to a certain shady jeweller in Rome of the proceeds of the Paris jewel robbery had enriched me by many thousands of lira, and, although I knew that I was badly "wanted" by the Paris police, I did not worry unduly.

I had visited a coiffeur in Rome, and had my hair dyed, and altered my appearance to such an extent that I do not suppose my old, hard-headed father away back in Florida would have recognised me.

And so I went to Naples.

Arrived in the city of sights and smells, I took a bed-room and a sitting-room at the Hotel Santa Lucia, and commenced to enjoy myself.

I did all the sights, ascended Vesuvius, visited Pompeii, and took a trip in a motor-boat over to Capri. At night-time I decided, with perhaps pardonable curiosity, to see some of the underworld life of the city. I had been told way back in the States, by sons of Sunny Italy in that great republic, that Naples possessed the most vicious underworld of all the cities in the land. I soon discovered that I had not been misinformed.

I wandered one evening into one of those very dirty and disreputable cafes along the Quai Partinope. I had taken the precaution to bring a gun with me, and, later, I was to congratulate myself on my forethought. I had scarcely sat down at the dirty, wine-slopped table and called for a vermouth, when a big, scowling ruffian lurched drunkenly across the cafe, and sat down opposite to me. I ignored him.

The waiter brought my vermouth, and before I could raise it to my lips the brute opposite to me picked it up and swallowed it at a gulp. Now, I am

naturally quick-tempered, and able to take care of myself. I have learnt how to keep my end up in a rough-and-tumble in the hard school of New York's Bowery and Tenderloin.

Flushing angrily, I picked up the empty glass and smashed it into the leering face opposite to me. I do not know to this day if I blinded the man or not. With a yell he sprang to his feet, and, with blood streaming from his face, picked up the chair he was sitting on, swung it high above his head, and aimed it at me.

I jumped aside, and it crashed against the wall behind. Simultaneously almost a shot cracked, and the drunken rough swayed unsteadily against the wall, his arm hanging limply by his side.

I swung round in the direction from which the shot had come, to see a girl of about my own age standing in the doorway, a smoking pistol in her hand. Suddenly, as I was about to address her, she was pushed aside, and two Carabinieri swaggered into the cafe and demanded an explanation.

My girl saviour quickly soothed them in Italian, and slipped a hundred lira note into each of the Carabinieri's hands. Then she took my arm and led me out of the filthy hovel.

BY the moonlight I examined my companion. She was dark, with the sallow complexion of the South, had fine dark eyes, and was dressed quietly but well. To my astonishment she spoke English with a slight American accent.

"That was a near thing for you, wasn't it?" she said.

"Yes; but I am always getting into trouble," I replied. "I must thank you for saving my life."

"It is nothing, caro mio," she smiled back at me. "You are American, are you not?"

I confessed that I was.

"I have been to America," my companion continued. "I was born in Boston."

"I am staying at the Hotel Santa Lucia, quite near," I said. "Won't you come and have some supper with me?"

Eagerly she agreed, so eagerly that I was somewhat surprised; but, looking closely at her, I noticed that she looked white and faint.

Could the girl be hungry?

I did not question her, however; but, arriving at my hotel, ordered a tempting supper to be served in my sitting-room.

She ate ravenously, and her cheeks began to glow as she drank a glass of Chianti. Eventually she sighed deeply, accepted the cigarette and a cup of coffee I offered her. Suddenly she got to her feet and walked over to a divan near the window, where she sank and burst into tears.

"Poor child," I thought, "she shall have her cry, and tell me all about it afterwards."

When she grew more composed she told me a story which seemed startlingly impossible. Yet I saw no reason to doubt its authenticity.

Her name, she told me, was Luisa Continelli, and she was an orphan under the control of a virago of a stepmother. Her father, it appeared, had died in Boston some years previously, leaving her several thousand dollars. Her stepmother, an Italian woman, had come to Italy on her share of the deceased man's estate, and, arrived in Naples, had straightway committed her daughter to the care of nuns at a nunnery but a few miles from the city. Having thus got rid of her stepdaughter, the mother proceeded to appropriate the girl's fortune.

Three days previously the daughter had escaped from her religious prison, and made her way to her stepmother's house. There a violent scene had taken place, during which the girl's step-parent had thrashed the girl with a whip. Driven to frenzy, the girl had retaliated by picking up a revolver which happened to be lying in the room and shooting at her stepmother. Three shots she had fired, and at the third the woman had fallen.

Terrified, the girl had fled from the house and had hidden in the lowest haunts of the city ever since. Such was her amazing story.

"Did you kill your stepmother?" I asked

"I do not know," she replied.

Crossing the room, I picked up a copy of the "Il Giorno," a Neapolitan paper, and, handing it to the girl, told her to look through it to see if there was any report of the occurrence. I did not read Italian sufficiently well myself to look. For a few minutes there was silence in the room, save for the rustling of the paper. Suddenly the girl uttered an exclamation.

Falteringly she read to me a short account of how her stepmother had been found wounded in her house, but that she was not in a dangerous condition. The motive for the crime was stated to be one of robbery, as a valuable pearl necklace which had been on the neck of the wounded woman was missing.

The victim said that she did not see her assailant. Apparently, she did not wish to implicate her stepdaughter in the scandal.

Lighting a cigarette, I pondered on the best way I could help the girl. Eventually I decided on a course of action.

"I am going to see your stepmother," I told Luisa.

AT first she demurred, but agreed at last, on condition that I allowed her to wait in my rooms while I went. Making a note of the address, which was that of a very aristocratic street off the Via Roma, I called a taxi and drove to the house. I was admitted by a very correct man-servant, and after much trouble succeeded in getting taken to his mistress, who was lying in bed, suffering from the revolver shot.

I expected to see a somewhat hard-featured woman, but, instead, saw a grey-haired old lady who really didn't look as if she could be capable of thrashing her stepdaughter as Luisa had told me she had done.

I commenced by saying that I might be able to give her news of her step-daughter. At this she tried to sit up, and asked me anxiously whether Luisa was quite all right. I assured her that she was, and then told her, somewhat indignantly, what I had heard—of her ill-treating her daughter.

The invalid listened quietly till I had finished, and then, to my astonishment, turned her face to the wall and began to weep bitterly.

I waited. Was the woman acting, or was her grief real?

Presently she turned over and took my hand.

"My dear, I can see that you have been deceived terribly. I will tell you the truth."

I was certainly not prepared for the story she told me. It appeared that Luisa was not her stepdaughter, but her daughter, and that the girl had run away from home and taken to a vicious life in the Neapolitan underworld. For months the aged and broken-hearted mother had sought her in vain.

Then one night she had discovered Luisa robbing the house. She had besought her on her knees to return home, but brutally the girl had demanded money. The mother had refused. Luisa had then snatched at the pearl necklace her mother wore, which had been a gift from her dead husband.

Violently she fought with her daughter for its possession. Luisa, crazed with drugs, had eventually drawn a revolver and shot at her, afterwards disappearing in the night with the necklace.

I was horrified at the story. I had been completely taken in—I, a crook. True, she had saved my life, but a girl who could treat her mother as she had done, did not deserve the slightest pity. I told the wounded woman how I came to meet her, and that she was at that moment at my hotel.

With tears in her eyes, the mother besought me to go and try to use my influence with her to come home. I promised I would.

As fast as a taxi could take me I hastened back to the Santa Lucia, and up into my rooms.

They were empty—there was no sign of Luisa.

She had known I would learn of her duplicity and had fled, I suppose. Suddenly I rushed into my bed-room. A startling thought had flashed through my mind.

Yes, the little vixen had robbed me! All my trunks were turned out, my jewellery stolen, and the ten thousand lira which had been in my jewel-case. Well, I was a crook, and now I knew for the first time what it is like to be robbed oneself!

I saw the funny side of the matter, but my heart ached for the grey-haired mother pining out her heart for the daughter who was devoid of the smallest spark of affection. Savagely I lit a cigarette and strolled to the balcony.

The moon rode high over the Bay of Naples. Vesuvius reared her imperious head to the sky. All was at peace. I thanked Heaven I hadn't got a mother to break her heart over me!

AN ingenious New York crook, whose most profitable operations took place at this season of the year, was "Christmas" Kurwood. He gained that alias through specialising in looting his victims during the Yuletide shopping week.

His method was to go into a jeweller's shop and select various costly articles. In payment for these he would tender a traveller's cheque or a banker's draft drawn on a bank in some distant town. Any possible suspicions of the shopman would be lulled by the fact that the cheque was for very much more than the article's price, and that the customer always laid emphasis on the statement that he would return later to collect the change.

He made a habit of never turning up to claim the money, mainly for the reason that in the meantime the cheque would have been recognised as a forgery by the bank officials.

Detectives who were detailed to trace him found that "Christmas" had rented a safe-deposit box in the vaults of a Fifth Avenue jeweller, and they forthwith obtained an order from the Court and had it opened.

Their curiosity was justified. Inside was a sum in dollars amounting to £400 and a quantity of jewellery. The jewellery probably represented that portion of his "earnings" which he had not been able to translate into cash; and, strangely enough, each piece bore a little label with the name of the shop from which this Yuletide crook had illegally obtained it, and the date of its acquisition.

From certain clues found in this hoard, the detectives got on the swindler's track, and he subsequently became a non-paying guest at the

Christmas Crackers.

Government hotel at Joliet, Illinois, for a protracted period. And there, as each December came round, "Christmas" Kurwood doubtless realised that Christmas can be a far from festive season.

It all depends, of course, where one spends it.

ONE of the most welcome Christmas-boxes ever received was handed to eleven men in Albany, New York State, two years ago. The men were convicts, serving long sentences in the Albany Prison, and the Christmas-boxes were free pardons entitling them to immediate release. Two of the men were serving "life" for murder, and the crimes of the others included attempted murder, forgery, burglary, and robbery.

Christmas comes but once a year, but a free pardon less often.

HARD times during the winter of 1923 led to a Christmas scare in London, when it was persistently rumoured that the organised unemployed intended to launch an offensive against tradesmen and shoppers during the last week of the year.

Official action gave credence to the rumours, for Scotland Yard drew up and circulated to the Press a list of the plans said to have been agreed to by the ringleaders of the scheme. Among other things, it was alleged, the conspirators proposed to drop "stink-bombs" in public places of entertainment such as theatres and cinemas, in Tube-trains, and in the large stores; to raid restaurants and tea-shops and sing revolutionary songs; to disfigure the windows of West End shops with "Red" placards—which would have carried anything but the compliments of the season; and to march in a body on the Prime Minister's house at midnight on New Year's Eve.

The police made all necessary preparations to cope with possible disturbance, but the officials of the Unemployed Council denied that any such scheme was contemplated. Nor, in fact, did the rumoured happenings ever take place.

A MAN who bought a box of chocolates in Ottawa last Christmas Eve had a surprise when he opened it next morning and saw what looked like an unexpected present, but was not.

The chocolate-box contained 867 dollars —about £170. It turned out, however, when he returned to the shop to inquire about the matter, that the proprietor had used the box as a till, and had put the day's takings into it, intending later to put it in the safe. He had afterwards sold the box of money in the belief that it contained its original contents, whereas another box, full of nothing more valuable than chocolate, had been put in the safe.

(Continued from page 11.)

great bed! The dusting of them knobs and things must h'occupy hours."

A tap sounded at the door, and a trim maid, .dressed in a neat short-skirted black dress, with a snowy, frilled apron, and a dainty, be-ribboned cap, entered. Mrs. Bardell glanced disapprovingly at the girl's slim silk-stockinged legs.

"'Ussy!" she breathed.

"Does madam require the services for the coiffure?" she asked, with an accent.

Mrs. Bardell's worst forebodings were realised. Not only was this girl an 'ussy, but a French 'ussy at that. She sniffed superciliously.

"No thank you, miss. For over fifty years I've done me own 'air, and I ain't goin' to 'ave it mucked about now. Which I may add, that I was doing it before you were born or thought of."

"Very good, madam," said Tonette, with a saucy tilt to her chin, and soundlessly departed.

"Huh!" said Mrs. Bardell expressively, and murmured something about "the likes of 'er." It was half an hour later that the dinner gong pealed sonorously through the house, and Mrs. Bardell emerged at the head of the stairs, a very dignified figure in black satin and bombazine.

Cynthia, with that courtesy that characterised her class, had in deference to her guest's feelings not changed into evening dress, and she awaited Mrs. Bardell's stately descent with a charming smile.

"I hope you found everything you need, Mrs. Bardell? It must be a frightful inconvenience to you, this short notice, but you quite understand, don't you?"

"Perfectly, my dear," said Mrs. Bardell. She had felt instantly drawn to this pretty, attractive girl, who had neither side nor snobbery, and who treated her like a perfect lady.

Together they passed into the vast dining-room at Goreham Grange, and it was at that precise moment that the voice of the Phantom Crook startled the little group of listeners in the far-off Baker Street.

THE next moment, the world—or that proportion of it which had sufficient determination to buy that go-ahead paper, the "Daily Radio"—was startled, amused, and a little shocked, to read of the astounding exploits of the Phantom Crook.

Towards noon the evening edition of the Radio—the Evening Wireless—contained a full account of the disappearance of Mrs. Bardell. Splash Page had let himself go all out on his scoop, and Sexton Blake smiled grimly when Tinker returned, shortly before lunch, clutching the paper.

"Great Scott, guv'nor. everybody's talking about it!" he cried excitedly. "Look at the headlines: 'FIRST BLOOD TO PHANTOM CROOK—Scotland Yard Baffled—Sexton Blake's Housekeeper Vanishes'."

"Where do you think Mrs. Bardell is,

" Here's a note from Tinker, Mrs. B," said Splash Page. " But do come inside the car out of the snow. I want you to meet the Hon. Cynthia Montague." "Lawks!" replied Mrs. Bardell. "Fancy me 'obnobbing with the gentery at my time o' life! Is this one of your larks, young man?"

guv'nor?" asked Tinker. "The colossal cheek of the blighter!" he added, indignantly.

"Let me lay my mitts on that guy, and I'll knock seventeen different kinds of stuffin' out of him!" growled Ruff Hanson. "This hits me where I live. Here we've gotta go out to lunch, instead of having our eats right here. It's tough, durned if it ain't."

Blake filled his briar absently.

"Of course, there are several clues," he said quietly. His eyes were half closed, or he would have noted Tinker's imperceptible start.

"In the first place, I have established the fact that she was last seen at Messrs. Peabody & Palmer's. We have the messenger boy's evidence for that, and that she entered a limousine."

Tinker could have kicked himself.

Both he and Splash had overlooked the fact of the turkey, and that morning a hurried conference of the conspirators had been called to decide further manoeuvres to draw the criminologist's attention from that dangerous clue.

"Yep. We've got the bird all right—literally and metaphorically," said Ruff Hanson gloomily. "Can't that bonehead Coutts and his harness bulls trace that automobile? Hades! Gimme action!"

Blake laughed.

"We have several valuable hours yet. Ruff, to solve the problem. I vote we adjourn to the Carlton for lunch."

"You're taking this business blamed cool," snorted the American. "Gosh all Friday, if a crook had put this one over me, I'd be shootin' up the whole blame' burg."

"Perhaps our temperaments differ," replied the detective suavely. "Hallo, what's this?" he added, as a ring sounded at the door.

Tinker sprang to answer it, and returned a few minutes afterwards accompanied by a grubby-faced, carrotty-haired urchin, with tattered clothes and a perpetual sniff.

"News, guv'nor," he cried excitedly. "Now, sonny, tell us what happened."

"Coo!" said the urchin. "Are you the Mr. Sexton Blake?"

Blake nodded.

"I am. What can I do for you?"

The boy gazed up in speechless awe at the great detective.

"Crikey, guv'nor, d'ye mind if I shakes 'ands with yer? I'd like to tell the blokes daan our court abaat it." He rubbed his grubby hand on the back of his trousers, and Blake clasped it solemnly.

"And now, laddie," he said kindly. "What's it all about?"

"Well, it was like this 'ere," began the urchin, who, it seemed, answered to the name of Ginger.

"I was a-coming aat of our 'ouse in Sugar Court, just orf Seven Dials, wen somethink dropped and copped me a biff on the side of me 'ead. Yer can see the lump naa!" he added, showing a marked protuberance in the flame-coloured thatch.

"Lumme, says I, thinking it was Alf 'Uggins, the leader of the Daisy Court gang, and I starts to scrap, but there ain't no one there. Then I picks up the stone, and I found it was wrapped up in this bit o' paper."

So saying, the youngster pulled out of his pocket a crumpled piece of paper in a mud bath.

Blake scrutinised it carefully and gave

a soft whistle. "Dear me, most interesting!" he commented. "It's written on the back of Messrs. Peabody's bill for the turkey. The scoundrel! He is keeping Mrs. Bardell a prisoner, but that resourceful woman has outwitted him. Look at this, Hanson!"

He handed over the slip to the American, who read the scrawled, illspelt missive aloud

"Help! I'm being held pris'ner in this plase. Take this to Mr. Sexton Blake, Baker Street. Finder will be rewarded."

"Gosh all Friday!" roared Ruff. "Suffering cats! Let's be moving. Maybe we'll have her back in time for dinner," he added hopefully. "Here, son! Here's a two-dollar bill for you. Go and get yourself a merry Christmas!"

The urchin's grimy hand closed with avidity on the ten-shilling note. Blake produced another from his wallet.

"Where do you say the house was, sonny?" he demanded.

"Number seven, Sugar Court, guv'nor, just back of Slimy Joe's doss-'ouse in Seven Dials."

"H'm! an unsavoury neighbourhood. Come on, Ruff! Let's be moving. Tinker, you'd better hang on here in case you get any message from Coutts."

Ginger reached for his cap.

"I've gotta be moving, mister. I'm late on my job," he said. "Thank you, sir, and I wish yer all what yer wish yerself!"

___

The House in Seven Dials.

TWENTY minutes later Sexton Blake and Ruff Hanson trudged through the slush and mud of Covent Garden. The famous market was a riot of colour and clamorous sound. The Christmas market was thronged with shoppers, the stalls gay with holly and mistletoe; golden pyramids of oranges gave a splash of vivid colouring to the dingy background, but the two detectives were too intent on their quest to notice the picturesque scene.

Sugar Court, an oddly-named place, seemed to have done its best to hide itself in the dirtiest and darkest region of Seven Dials.

They had no difficulty in finding Slimy Joe's doss-house, for a faded sign hung over a filthy, gloomy-looking building with broken windows and an evil-smelling kitchen: "Good Beds, 4d.," and Slimy Joe himself, a villainous-looking fat man, with an oily face, sat on the steps of his select establishment.

He it was who surlily directed their steps to No. 7, Sugar Court. It proved to be a dilapidated building, with windows boarded up, and its grimy brickwork showed through the dingy snow like some leprous scab. The paint-blistered door had no knocker, and there was an atmosphere of decay and desolation about the building.

"By gosh, I'll pound the guy to a pulp who brought Mrs. B here!" said Hanson savagely. "C'mon, Blake, let's break the door down."

The detective shook his head.

"Better leave force as a final resort. Gently does it."

He rapped smartly with his knuckles on the door and waited. Not a sound emerged from behind the forbidding portal.

Again he rapped, and from a distance came the sound of a protesting squeak, as if an ancient door had creaked on rusty hinges. Then came the shuffle of feet down the corridor, and a high-pitched, quavering voice called out: "Who's there?"

"Open the door, and I'll tell you!" said Blake crisply.

Cautiously they could hear a rusty bolt being withdrawn, and the door was opened a few inches.

Framed in the aperture stood an extraordinary apparition—a tall, thin old man, with a bloodless face, that looked almost like that of a mummy. He wore a greasy astrachan cap, and long, greasy ringlets of dirty white hair hung low over his scalp.

A scanty goatee beard waggled on his thin chin as he demanded their business.

"Come, now, no nonsense!" snapped Blake, pushing back the old man's feeble resistance. "I'm a detective, and I've reason to believe that you are illegally detaining a lady in this house."

"Vy, no," replied the other, and his mouth gaped oddly. "Dere is no ladies in dis place. I live 'ere all by myself."

"We'll soon see about that, Ikey!" said Ruff Hanson, and with his burly shoulders he sent the door back with a bang that nearly broke it off its crazy hinges. The old man gurgled in protest, but they took no heed.

There was a musty, dank odour about the passage, ill-lit by a flickering gas jet, that seemed to find difficulty in keeping alight at all in that foetid atmosphere.

"FORTY WINKS"

"I'll examine the basement, you search the top part," said Blake grimly.

Ruff Hanson grinned. "Leave it to me, kiddo!" He raced up the ricketty stairs, gun in hand. On the landing he paused by a green-painted door. From behind it came the sound of a woman sobbing.

"Tarnation!" roared Ruff, and with one hefty kick he burst open the door, which splintered into fragments at the force of the impact.

Hanson tripped as he burst into the room. He had a swift vision of two men, each of whom wore a sinister black cowl that hid the face, and a harsh, vibrant voice called out sharply:

"Drop that gun! We've got you covered."

"The Hades you have!" roared Hanson.

With a tigerish spring he leapt forward, two sixguns in his hands.

"Drop your gats, you swabs, or I'll drop ya both where you stand! Mebbe you don't know me—Ruff Hanson, who shoots the pip at fifty paces. Drop them gats before I count three or I'll fill ya so fulla holes you'll think you're a colander."

Not a murmur came from the masked pair. Their eyes seemed to glint evilly through the slits of their masks. Two seconds passed in silence. The situation was a complete deadlock. Each person was menaced with a lethal automatic.

Then Ruff Hanson got into action. He pressed the triggers of both guns. Came a faint click.

"Durn it! Jammed!" he swore.

Bang! A spurt of flame leapt from the muzzle of the masked man's weapon. Hanson felt its scorching tongue on his cheek as he grappled with his assailant. He was mad with rage. For the first time in his career Willy and Wally, his two sixguns, had failed him in a crisis.

He lashed out savagely with the butt-end of his weapon, but stumbled over one of the masked men's foot. Ere he could recover the other man stuck the snout of his revolver in the back of his neck.

"One move, and you die!" he hissed.

With the feel of cold steel on the base of his skull Hanson was powerless.

"Durn ya!" he growled. "I'd stiffen you galoots——"

His utterances were cut short by the clinging embrace of a filthy sack which was dragged over his bullet head. He struggled fiercely to escape from the clammy folds of the stuff, choking, spluttering, and lashing out savagely with his feet.

He laughed grimly at the sudden ouch of pain from his assailant as a savage hack to the shin went home. He felt the bite of steel on his wrists, and a sudden vicious snap.

"Suffering catskills!" he muttered, with a final desperate effort. "The bracelets!"

"Sit on his chest, and blow his brains out if he makes a move!" came the harsh command, and the helpless American groaned as he felt himself flung forward like a sack of coals.

"If my gats hadn't jammed," he muttered, "I'd have——"

"Quiet, or I'll silence you for keeps!" hissed a sibilant voice.

Ruff Hanson strained his ears. If only Blake would come. He heard the slam of a door somewhere, and footsteps descending the stairs. He stirred feebly, but through the sacking he felt the hard muzzle of his assailant's pistol.

MEANWHILE Sexton Blake had descended to the basement of the house. An incredibly dirty kitchen, with a tiny apology for a fire in the grate, was empty, to all appearances, and he merely gave it a rapid cursory inspection.

Beyond the kitchen was a small scullery, almost choked with a pile of dirty dishes and garbage pails. He retraced his steps and entered a low-ceilinged room, evidently used as a bed-room. A bed, rickety and ramshackle, stood in the corner of the room, and on it lay, coiled like a snake, a feather boa.

Blake's keen eyes recognised it at once. It had once adorned Mrs. Bardell's handsome ensemble. He strode over towards the bed and pounced on the trophy, and as he did so something whistled through the air, and he felt his arms gripped in a clinging embrace.

"Keep perfectly still, Mr. Sexton Blake," came a mocking voice above his head. Blake looked up, and found an open trap-door above the bed. In the aperture he saw a man in a hideous black cowl, with a pistol pointed straight at the detective's heart.

He noticed, also, that in his left hand the stranger gripped a rawhide lariat, and the increasing pressure which lashed his arms to his sides convinced Blake that resistance was useless.

He had been neatly lassooed while momentarily off his guard.

"Sorry to inconvenience you, Mr. Blake, but your investigations are getting too warm for my peace of mind. I regret I must keep you a prisoner until the stipulated twenty-four hours have elapsed. Mrs. Bardell is quite safe, and will be restored to you uninjured, after I have received your cheque as an acknowledgment of your defeat."

Blake laughed softly.

"You talk very confidently, Mr. Phantom Crook. May I remind you I'm not defeated yet?"

The Phantom Crook wagged his revolver suggestively.

"If you will give me your word of honour not to attempt to escape I will see you are comfortably fixed until to-morrow."

"Thanks. I prefer the discomfort," said Blake quietly.

"So be it. I'm afraid you will not enjoy the company of Vladimir Dobrofski. He is rather eccentric in his habits."

"If you refer to the old gentleman with the beard and the aversion to washing, I can quite believe it," returned Blake smoothly.

He listened intently. From upstairs there came a crash and the splinter of woodwork, then the crack of a pistol.

"That, I believe, is your colleague, Mr. Hanson, being attended to by my assistants," said the Phantom Crook suavely. "I hope he will not be foolish enough to struggle."

Blake laughed.

"The disadvantage of these pinioned arms is that one cannot smoke," he said quietly.

The man in the cowl turned his head for a fraction of a second and issued a curt command. In that fraction of time Blake acted. He leapt on the bed, and, handicapped as he was with his arms lashed to his sides by the rawhide noose, endeavoured to scramble towards the trap-door.

He was too late, however, for into the room two figures entered— old Dobrofski and another masked man. They hurled themselves at Blake, who overbalanced from his precarious perch. Dobrofski

showed surprising strength for so old a man.

His lean, sinewy hands twined round Blake's leg in a vice-like clutch, and from the outset there could only be one conclusion, menaced on three sides as Blake was. Limp, panting, and dishevelled after his struggle, he found himself lashed firmly to the iron bedstead.

He glanced up defiantly at his captors, and the cool, mocking voice of the Phantom Crook said quietly:

"You asked for it, Mr. Blake. Had you promised not to resist, your treatment would have been more gentle. It may interest you to know that Mr. Hanson has also been foolish enough to fight, and he shares your captivity.

"I'm afraid you're not going to spend a very merry Christmas Eve, but it's the fortune of war."

The Phantom Crook laughed mockingly, and the trap-door closed with a bang. The Russian, Dobrofski, and his companion, after one final look to see if the bands that bound the detective were intact, shuffled out of the room. Blake heard the key grate in the lock, the faint murmur of voices, then silence.

The Phantom Crook had won the second round.

IN the humming news-room of the "Daily Radio" Mr. Julius Jones munched a sardine sandwich with an air of abstraction, as he automatically blue-pencilled twenty lines from some luckless reporter's story.

"Indeed whateffer, Splash!" he said between mouthfuls. "This Phantom Crook's a pretty story. Pity you couldn't fasten a murder or two on him."

Splash Page, who was leaning negligently on the news editor's desk, grinned.

"You carping old critic. Never bally well satisfied, are you? Here's me unearthing the biggest scoop in years, and you grouse."

"Wonder who this Phantom Crook really is," mused Julius Jones. "He seems to have a darned good sense of humour indeed."

Splash nodded.

"Blake seems to be up a gum-tree on the business. Wonder how old Coutts of the Yard's faring with his end of it?"

Julius Jones pressed a buzzer, and a freckled-faced printer's devil, with a flaming red thatch and a perpetual sniff, entered the room.

Splash winked knowingly at the urchin.

"Ginger, take these flimsies to the 'United Press' at once!" he commanded.

"Yes, sir!" said Ginger, and decamped.

"Smart lad that, Julius," commended Splash.

"Blowed if I can see it! A lazy, unwashed little devil!" growled Julius. "Where does his smartness come in?"

"Ah! You don't know Ginger as I know Ginger. He's got a genius for romance, that kid!"

"Pah!" snorted the news editor. "If instead of discussing the morals of printers' devils—which they haven't got, anyway—you'd try and find this Phantom Crook feller, you'd——"

"Is Splash Page about, Mr. Jones?" called a gruff voice from the doorway, and Detective-Inspector Coutts' burly figure entered the room—his billycock hat at an aggressive angle.

"Lo, here am I," grinned Splash. "Anything I can do for you, Coutts?"

The C.I.D. man frowned.

"Blowed if I know what's happened to everybody since last night. Every-

body seems to have gone mad, or drunk, or both."

"What's bitten you, old chap?" Splash asked gently. "Why this thusness?"

"It's this dashed Phantom Crook!" Coutts exploded. "Where's Blake? Where's Tinker? Where's Hanson? Blowed if they ain't all disappeared!"

The inspector scratched his bristly chin, and there was an expression of ludicrous dismay on his face.

Julius Jones swung round in his swivel chair, his eyes sparkling.

"What! You mean to tell me that the whole boiling bunch of 'em have vanished?"

"That's what I said," replied Coutts. "I've phoned, called a dozen times, but can't get a reply. It's the rummiest thing I've ever heard of!"

The news editor smiled happily as he tentatively scribbled a couple of sensational headings on his jotting pad— "Great Detective's Disappearance. Blake, of Baker Street!"

"Go to it, Splash. Get the low-down dope on this!" he commanded.

The newspaperman grinned, and linked his arm through that of the indignant Coutts.

"Come on, old sleuth! When the Yard fails—that's where the Press steps in!" he said boisterously.

"What? Why?" began Coutts, in a dazed fashion, as he found himself piloted towards the door.

"Never mind questions, let's get back to Baker Street," he said cheerfully.

"But who is this Phantom Crook, Splash?" he demanded. "I tell you frankly, this business is getting on my nerves. First the bally Rockcliff coronet's lifted, then Mrs. Bardell disappears, and now Blake and the rest of 'em vanish. It—it's uncanny!"

Splash Page pressed the self-starter of his little runabout, and smiled.

"That's nothing to what's going to happen, old scout. I tell you, Coutts, you're up against the biggest brains in the history of Scotland Yard!"

MEANWHILE things were happening at Goreham Grange. That treasure of a woman, Mrs. Maria Bardell, had, to use Tinker's expressive phrase, taken to Society as a duck takes to water.

Under the guidance of Cynthia she had inspected the palatial kitchens of the fine old manor house, and her housewifely instinct had been revolted at the wasteful extravagance of Alphonse, the French chef.

She had a minor passage of arms with that volatile man, and after a few pungent home truths, she emerged victorious from the fray—much to the amusement of the Hon. Cynthia.

"These Froggies ain't no good, miss! A lot of wasteful, extravagant fellers!" she began volubly. "Now, I ses the proper way to cook a turkey is to baste it slow on a low jet, an'——"

She wandered off into technicalities, but Cynthia was not a very interested listener. She seemed to be abstracted, and glanced out of the leaded casement over the white expanse of snow that mantled the spacious grounds of Goreham Grange, with anxious eyes.

It was nearly three o'clock, and if everything went "according to plan," the Viscount Rockcliff was due to arrive with a triumphant report.

The winter sun, like a great red ball of fire, sank slowly in the west, dyeing the sky a vivid crimson.

The gaunt, black branches of trees stretched their skeleton arms in a sinister fashion skyward, and a curious little chill of foreboding seized her.

Had anything happened?

The adventure, begun with such high spirits, in the cold light of day, looked mad and dangerous. Supposing Blake had outwitted the conspirators?

Cynthia shivered. Sexton Blake was not the kind of man on whom one could play jokes with impunity.

A loud and triumphant honk of a motor-horn sounded from the roadway as the Viscount Rockcliff's luxurious Rolls rounded the bend.

"At last!" breathed Cynthia thankfully. "Mrs. Bardell, be a dear and fix up the decorations in the morning-room," she asked.

Mrs. Bardell nodded.

"Suttingly, miss. I'll see as 'ow they're all in order."

Cynthia bustled the good soul out of the room just as the great car drove up to the driveway.

She ran to the terrace and stood, a slim, elegant figure of femininity, against the sombre background of the old house.

The cheerful voice of Viscount Rockcliff hailed her from the interior of the car.

"Hallo, Cynthia, old girl. We've got the goods!" he exclaimed cheerfully.

"Meet Mr. Ruff Hanson from New York City."

"Gosh darn my catskills!" growled a Transatlantic voice from the tonneau. "Am I in a fit state to meet a lady? See here, viscount—there'll be one heck of a rough house when friend Blake gets wise to this stunt——"

"Shucks!" called Rocky cheerfully. "You gave us your word not to start anything, Ruff. It's the fortune of war, old boy."

Ruff Hanson, with his coat rumpled and bedraggled, his Stetson hat awry, glowered at his captor.

Cynthia smiled bewitchingly.

"Oh, Mr. Hanson, I've heard such a lot about you. Rocky, bring Mr. Hanson in at once. The poor dear must be starving!"

The hard-boiled egg's tough face split into an amiable grin as he stepped out of the car, followed by a slim youth clad in a dingy suit several sizes too large for him.

"You've said a mouthful, miss. I could eat a coupla whales on toast!" said Ruff fervently. "Gosh all Friday, your brother's a dandy scrapper."

Cynthia led the way into the oak-panelled dining-room, and Ruff Hanson sank gratefully into a luxurious chair.

Rocky adjusted his oblong monocle in his eye and beamed as his sister poured out three whiskies-and-soda from a cut-glass decanter.

"What happened?" she asked breathlessly. "Did everything go off according to plan?"

Rocky grinned joyously.

"It did—and it didn't!" he said. "Unfortunately, in the scuffle, my bally mask slipped, and old Ruff here recognised me. It would have been too dangerous to leave both Blake and him in the house—so we brought him along here!"

"Oh, Mr. Hanson, I do hope they

didn't hurt you," Cynthia asked solicitously.

Ruff Hanson laughed.

"Hurt me! No, I guess not, but if Willy and Wally hadn't gone back on me, mebbe you wouldn't have had a brother by now. I suppose that gosh darned Tinker pulled their fangs."

Rocky nodded.

"Yes. Tinker attended to that end. We knew your fondness for gunplay, old boy, and couldn't afford to take any risks. Tinker loaded your gats up with the cartridges—after he had taken out the powder."

"Waal, I guess the joke's on you, old hoss," said Ruff Hanson ruefully. "Losh knows what'll happen when Blake finds out. You'd better spill the whole can of beans so's I can get the right slant on this business."

Viscount Rockcliff sipped his drink.

"In the first place," he began, "Tinker and Splash Page worked out the scheme—and roped in me and the Hon. Freddie here."

He waved gracefully to the languid youth who was stretching his long fingers towards the comfortable blaze in the wide, old-fashioned hearth.

The Hon. Freddie Deepwood laughed.

"Jove! I never enjoyed anything so much in my young life. It was perfectly priceless, old fruit."

Rocky grinned reminiscently.

"You should have seen Freddie, Cynthia—his make-up as Vladimir, the Russian, was gorgeous. He must have spent hours on it."

Freddie waved a deprecating hand.

"'Wigs, by Clarkson,' old boy. I give him the credit for the disguise."

"Yeah, but I don't quite get the hang of it, yet," protested Ruff Hanson. "I'll admit you got me and Blake fazed. You pulled a mighty good bit of team work between you, I'll admit. I suppose Splash worked the noose end of the business, and Tinker attended to the domestic side."

Rocky nodded.

"It was Tinker's idea in the first place. He knew you and Blake were pining for some action stuff—and well, we provided it all right. The only hitch as far as I can see, is that you recognised me in the rough house. Otherwise——"

"I suppose I'd have been left in that darned joint in Sugar Court," finished Hanson.

"Oh, well, it's a show-down all right, but I'm durned if I envy you when Blake gets free. He'll be hopping mad."

"Don't you worry about that, old hoss—he won't escape. We've got him fast," said Rocky.

"Splash Page is going to lead jolly old Coutts to him at seven o'clock—and he'll have to admit that the Phantom Crook's got him beat."

"Don't be too sure, guy. Blake's a wise bird," said Ruff Hanson. "He's got outa worse scrapes than this. Say, it was a cute idea that wireless stunt, I suppose youse got a radio set here? What I can't understand is how you pulled it off—and' came round with all that goff about the missing coronet."

Rocky laughed.

"Soames, my butler attended to that. Tinker had only to tune in my wave length—and there you are."

"'Hexcuse me, miss—but that there French maid of yours——" broke in the voice of Mrs. Bardell suddenly.

Ruff Hanson leapt to his feet as the housekeeper entered the room.

"Barking dogfish, Mrs. B. By Gee! You're looking dandy!" he exclaimed enthusiastically. "I'm feeling mighty relieved you're here—there's a chance

of getting a decent Christmas dinner anyways."

Mrs. Bardell bridled.

"Why, Mr. 'Anson, this is an unexpected pleasure! 'Ow is Mr. Blake?"

"Mr. Blake?"

Ruff Hanson chuckled.

"Very busy at the moment, I guess, but I reckon he'll be along later!" he added significantly.

"I was just saying as 'ow that mademoiselle 'as started argufying as to where to put the Christmas-tree. If I remembers rightly, miss, you said it was to be in the 'all."

Cynthia nodded.

"Certainly, Mrs. Bardell. I wonder if you'd mind helping me to unwrap the presents."

Deftly she guided the unsuspecting housekeeper out of the room, leaving the men to discuss their affairs.

"You don't bear any malice, do you, old thing?" queried Rocky.

Ruff Hanson grinned.

"I reckon I was a saphead. It ain't often a guy puts it across me—but between you and me, you managed it. Put it right there!"

He held out a massive hand.

"All that was worryin' me was the fact that my Christmas dinner was going west. But if you say Mrs. Bardell's attending to that—well, I guess we'll call it quits."

"Good for you, old dear!" laughed Rocky. "Tinker'll be along later with your suitcase. How about a nice hot bath—and after I'll show you round the house."

"Attaboy!" agreed the American, as he drained his drink. "I'll inform the universe I'm in for a Merry Christmas—but what friend Blake'll say, I'm durned if I know."

The Ghost of Goreham Grange.

"WAAL, I swow! Y'know, the more I see of Britishers, the more I like 'em," said Ruff Hanson heartily. "Rocky, ol' hoss, I useter think a galoot that wore a window in his eye and talked like as if he had a prune in his chops was just a plumb ornery mutt. But I'll tell the cockeyed world he ain't—no, sir!"

The American, after a bathe and a shave, was restored to his customary good-humour, and now stood admiring the spacious oak panelled dining-room of Goreham Grange.

It was nearly seven o'clock. The chill winter wind moaned eerily round the gables of the old manor house—but its mournful cadence merely served to heighten the cosiness within.

The huge dining table, with its spotless napery and its cut glassware, was a poem of harmonious colour. The light from the chandelier reflected the amber glow of champagne, and the rich crimson of old port, and gilded everything with its warm and kindly radiance.

A roaring fire of Yule logs crackled merrily in the grate. Round the walls, covered with holly and mistletoe, were grouped the family portraits of the Viscount Rockcliff's ancestors.

To the American, usually unimpressionable, the whole scene was redolent of romance.

"Christmas Eve at Goreham Grange!" he said. "Gosh my bed-socks—it sounds like a tale outa a Christmas number! Tell us some more about your ancestors, Rocky. I kinder like hearing this old-timer stuff."

Rocky laughed.

"They were a pretty dissolute crew, by all accounts," he said. "See that old boy there. That's Red Sir Rupert—the first baronet and founder of the family. He was a precious scoundrel—a pirate, a murderer, and a few other things as well."

He pointed to a faded portrait of a man clad in a doublet and hose of the Eliabethan period. It was a striking picture, painted by a master hand. Despite its age, the figure looked startlingly real. The face was that of a man about thirty-five, with red hair and a red torpedo beard. He had a thin, cruel mouth, a nose like an eagle's beak, and a pair of crafty black eyes that looked unutterably evil.

"He looks a tough guy all right!" said Ruff Hanson. "I guess I'd have needed Willy and Wally if I had had any dealings with him!"

Rocky nodded.

"Don't be too sure he's done with. As a matter of fact, there's an old tradition that his ghost still walks!"

"Shucks!" said Ruff Hanson, who had a healthy contempt for the supernatural. "What's this line of talk you're handing me?"

"No; honestly I'm not spoofing," said Rocky earnestly. "I don't believe in ghosts myself—but this is pretty well authenticated. My father swears he saw Red Rupert in the grounds about twenty Christmases ago—and he was a hard-headed, sceptical chap not given to romancing.

"The story goes that Red Rupert—who was beheaded finally for treason—had hidden part of the loot from a Spanish galleon in the grounds of Goreham Grange. He was arrested before he could divulge the hiding-place to his heirs—and they say that every so often his restless spirit haunts the grounds."

"Mighty interesting. Say, a ghost hunt on Christmas Eve sounds real dandy!"

Rocky chuckled.

"We'll have no time to think of ghosts by the time old Blake's finished his opinion of the Phantom Crook."

"You said a mouthful, bo!" agreed Hanson. "When d'ye expect them along?"

"About seven-thirty, if all goes well. Come on, let's see how the ladies are getting on with the Christmas-tree."

He led the way into the spacious hall. Flunkeys stood like graven images beneath the old minstrels' gallery, gay now with evergreens and paper lanterns aglow with colour.

In the corner stood a gigantic Christmas-tree, ablaze with colour, and a sparkle of gold and silver. There were mysterious-looking bundles, each labelled with the name of a guest—and on the topmost branch a beautifully modelled doll—a fairy with wide, sparkling wings, and a silver wand.

Mrs. Bardell, who had been tying the presents on to the lower branches, beamed good-humouredly as the two men expressed their admiration of her handiwork.

"It's the loveliest Christmas I've ever spent!" she said. "My cup of 'appiness is full! Kind 'earts is more than connorets, but I wishes to remark——"

Rocky patted her shoulder.

"My dear lady, we haven't started on Christmas yet. You wait until Mr.

Pausing only to fling back the window, Ruff Hanson leapt down on to the snow-covered lawn in front of the spectral figure of Red Rupert. *Bang—bang!* Hanson's gun spoke twice, but the phantom continued to glide soundlessly on.

Blake arrives—and that young imp Tinker."

He glanced at his watch.

"Jove! Nearly seven-thirty!" he said. "I hope the blighters won't be late."

Arm-in-arm with Ruff Hanson they strolled into the library, where they found the Hon. Freddie, immaculately clad in evening-dress and deep in conversation with Cynthia, who looked enchanting in a decollete frock of pearl pink.

"I've been telling Ruff all about our family skeletons," said Rocky. "He's taken a fancy to Sir Rupert—of infamous memory."

Cynthia laughed.

"That old reprobate! It only needs his ghost to walk to-night, and we'll have the best Christmas ever."

"Ghosts are all tommy rot!" said the Hon. Freddie sententiously.

"Abso-bally-lutely!" agreed the girl. She rose to her feet and switched on the gramophone. "Do you Charleston, Mr. Hanson?" she asked.

"I shake a mean foot!" replied the American. "I guess my hoofs are too darned clumsy for terpsichore!"

"Why, I thought all Americans danced!" pleaded Cynthia. "Come on; I'll show you how—it's perfectly simple!"

She clasped the unresisting American around his ample waist, and began to initiate him into the intricacies of the dance.

"Oh, boy! If the yeggs could see me now!" Ruff mused mentally. "Me, the tough from Toughville, prancing around with a skirt in the most exclusive aristocratic circles! Wow!"

But he was enjoying it—he admitted that you are under arrest on a charge frantically, when, at the second attempt, he managed some clumsy imitation of the Charleston.

The door opened, and, soundless as a well-oiled automaton, Soames the butler entered.

"Detective-Inspector Coutts and Mr. Page, and Mr. Tinker!" he announced pompously.

A moment later the trio entered the room. Coutts' red face was even redder than usual, and he bowed stiffly to Rocky.

"Durn my hide, Tinker! You double-crossing old galoot! Here's a fine business to put over a poor American citizen! As for you, Splash, I don't expect morals or manners from newspaper men——"

"Viscount Rockcliff," Coutts cut in abruptly, "it's my duty to inform you that you are under arrest on a charge of conspiracy, and, furthermore, of causing grievous bodily harm——"

"What!" gasped Rocky. "You're joking, Inspector. Haven't Splash and Tinker explained the jape to you? Come on, old boy! Have a drink?"

Coutts shook his head, and an electric tension crept into the atmosphere. Rocky stared at Splash and Tinker, and noticed that they were strangely silent.

"Good Lor', what's up? Has anything happened?" he asked helplessly.

"The worst's happened, Rocky old boy. We're all under arrest. Blake's vanished!"

"What!" roared Ruff Hanson. "Durn my hide! The big, two-fisted old he-man! Gosh all Friday! The old-timer's beaten you to it! Where's your Phantom Crook now?"

"Blake gone? But I don't understand!" said Rocky in bewilderment. "How can he have disappeared? We locked him in, and tied him down. Where is he, anyway?"

"And it's my duty to inform you that anything you say will be used in evidence against you," continued Coutts in an official tone.

"It's all U.P., Rocky old man!" said Splash. "As we arranged, I took old Couttsy—ahem!—Inspector Coutts to the house in Seven Dials; but when we got there there was absolutely no sign of Blake. We searched the whole house—it was empty as Mother Hubbard's cupboard.

"Then I explained the joke to Coutts. We went back to Baker Street; there was no sign of Blake there. And then—well, Coutts put Tinker and I under arrest."

Ruff Hanson roared with laughter.

"Good for you, old hoss! Take these desperate villains and lock 'em up. It'll do 'em good!"

He winked at the C.I.D. man, who winked back.

"I suppose you'll come gently?" he asked.

"But, I say, Couttsy, hang it, it was only a jape!" protested Tinker. "We didn't do anything criminal. Be a sport! You know we've planned to have you as a guest over Christmas."

"Bribing a police-officer in the execution of his duty is a serious offence!" persisted the inspector woodenly.

"Oh lor'!" gasped the dismayed Tinker.

"I would like a word with you, Mr. Hanson," said Coutts meaningly.

Ruff Hanson grinned, and the two conversed in low undertones.

The crestfallen conspirators eyed each other glumly. The great scheme had fallen as flat as the proverbial pancake.

Their great idea of kidnapping Blake had resulted in his neatly outwitting them; and, as Ruff Hanson remarked, they found they had bitten off more than they could chew.

"Very well, Mr. Hanson," they heard Coutts say. "If you don't press the charge, we won't proceed any farther on that count. But Mr. Blake has not yet been found, and the second charge therefore stands."

Tinker bit his lip with vexation. Where was the guv'nor? Why hadn't he turned up?

These were the questions that worried him incessantly.

Coutts cleared his throat.

"At Mr. Hanson's request, and in view of the prisoners' previous good conduct," he said magnanimously. "Also, in view of the season, I have decided to bind over the prisoners to be of good behaviour over the holiday!"

"Couttsy, you old kidder, you've been spoofing us all the time!" said Splash Page.

The C.I.D. man chuckled.

"You're not the only spoofer, my lad!" he said cheerfully. "But you're not out of the wood yet, by long chalks! Wait until Blake turns up—there'll be ructions!"

"Dinner is served, my lord!" called the sonorous voice of Soames from the doorway.

"By Jove! I wonder where the deuce Blake really is?" said Rocky to Splash, as they followed the ladies into the dining-room.

"Old Coutts gave me the fright of my life just now. He seemed so bally official!"

Splash nodded.

"The bally thing's been a frost. First Ruff recognises you, because your bally mask slipped—and now, here's Blake disappeared!"

Rocky thoughtfully polished his oblong monocle. "He's a downy bird, Blake. I bet he's got some scheme on."

In the vast dining-room the table groaned with viands, and Tinker eyed the assortment of good things hungrily.

There was a real old-fashioned Yuletide spirit over the whole place, and Mrs. Bardell's comfortable presence gave it a home-like appearance to the lad.

The curtains had been drawn back from the mullioned windows—and as a contrast to the warmth and jollity within, the gleaming white expanse of snow beneath the rays of a winter moon in a star studded sky, looked bleakly desolate.

The guests grouped themselves round the table—Mrs. Bardell, by general consent occupying the place of honour at the head.

Round the panelled walls the liveried flunkeys hovered like some priestly acolytes, while behind them glimmered the faded portraits of the Rockcliff ancestors.

"Say—that guy Sir Rupert's got my goat!" drawled Ruff Hanson to his neighbour the Hon. Freddie. "I've

never seen a tougher looking stiff. Those eyes of his are like chilled steel!"

The Hon Freddie nodded. "He was a pretty restless spirit while he lived, old man—and I shouldn't wonder——"

He never finished the sentence, for suddenly, in the silence of the night there rang out a shrill, high-pitched scream.

"Gosh! What's that!" gasped Ruff Hanson. "Dog my catskills!" he added, and flung out his hand dramatically at the window. "There's Red Rupert—as I'm a living sinner!"

A sudden dead silence fell on the crowded room. For an instant no one stirred; they simply stared at a weird phantom shape that stood for an instant framed in the leaded casements.

It was the figure of a man, clad in an old fashioned doublet and hose. A steel cuirass ornamented his breast, and beneath the brim of his quaint hat a ghastly luminous face peered forth.

It was the face of a fiend. Implacable eyes, cold as an iceberg, a beak of a nose jutting forth over a thin tight-lipped mouth—and what added to its horror, a red torpedo beard from which emanated a weird phosphorescent glow.

An instant it stood there—an instant which struck the watchers dumb with horror—and then Ruff Hanson roared.

"By the great Horned Toad. I'll get him!"

He leapt to his feet, his automatics appearing magically from somewhere.

He paused for an instant to unhasp the window, and followed by Splash Page and Tinker he leapt down on to the snow-covered lawn in front of the spectral figure.

Tinker felt his hair bristling on the nape of his neck, as he saw the ghostly shape flitting silently in the cold moonlight.

Bang! Bang!

Hanson's gun spoke twice, but the phantom seemed to glide soundlessly on his way, and finally passed between two high bushes and vanished.

Ruff Hanson cursed vehemently.

"Blister me. It's a real ghost, the bullets musta gone right through him!"

Tinker gasped out:

"Hang it! I'm sorry, Ruff, it was my fault. You forget I put blanks in your magazine!"

Explanations!

RUFF HANSON scratched his chin ruefully.

"Sure. Durn it, it rattled me for a moment. But who or what is the darned thing, that's what beats me."

Splash Page pointed to the ground.

"Do ghosts have footprints?" he demanded.

"Search me!" was the reply. "C'mon boys, let's beat up the grounds, we'll find the joker."

They raced through the shrubbery in separate directions, but not a vestige of a clue rewarded their efforts. The footprints vanished at the end of the driveway, and fuming with impatience they trooped back to the dining-room.

"It must be someone playing a practical joke!" said Rocky. "Great Scott! It gave me a turn. I've never seen a more ghastly apparition in my life."

"But if it's a joke," persisted Splash Page. "What's the idea of it. To scare us or—or what. Are you sure you had nothing to do with it, Rocky?" he demanded suspiciously.

"On my honour, I know nothing at all about it," said the viscount gravely.

"Hallo!" called Coutts suddenly. "Where's Mrs. Bardell gone to?"

He pointed to a vacant chair at the head of the table.

A sudden apprehension seized Splash Page, he pushed back his chair and stared at a white visiting card placed on Mrs. Bardell's plate.

He glanced stupidly at it for a moment, then his face broke into an admiring grin.

"Well, I'm dashed. He's diddled us."

"Who has?" chorused the others.

"Blake," said Splash. "Here's his card. He's scribbled on the back. 'What I have, I hold!'"

"Well, this licks creation!" boomed Ruff Hanson. "Durn me. Old Blake scores again. He's fooled you wise guys all along the line. Three cheers for the old timer! Call yourselves a bunch o' phantom crooks!" he added witheringly.

At that moment the door opened and Sexton Blake, in faultless evening dress entered, with Mrs. Bardell on his arm.

A veritable salvo of cheers greeted their entrance—and the detective's austere features relaxed into a smile as he bowed his acknowledgments.

"Welcome to the feast. We acknowledge defeat, Mr. Blake!" said Rocky. "We were fools to try and bluff you."

Blake smiled.

"You didn't bluff me at all, my friend. I just played up gently to you—and let you fall into your own trap."

"Let's have the whole caboodle, Blake. They fooled me all right, all right."

Sexton Blake's face was inscrutable.

"I'm hungry—the story will keep until after dinner."

WHAT a dinner that was! Almost bursting with the combined forces of food and curiosity Tinker could scarcely contain his impatience—but it was not until the toast of Sexton Blake and the incom-

---

parable Mrs. Bardell had been drunk enthusiastically, that Blake condescended to explain.

He lit a cigar and leaned back in his chair.

"In the first place it was Tinker's unusual request for opera that first aroused my curiosity."

Tinker started and blushed a little.

"My assistant, amongst many admirable qualities, has one peculiar foible—he didn't betray such sudden enthusiasm for the works of Gilbert and Sullivan prior to the Phantom Crook's dramatic announcement.

"I notice you have a broadcasting licence, Viscount Rockcliff. I presume you were responsible for that end of it."

Rocky nodded.

"Yes, but we didn't think you'd get on to that so quickly. What other brick did we drop?"

"Splash Page's picturesque effusion was full of the most valuable information," replied Blake, with twinkling eyes.

"It was so obviously written by a trained journalist. The term: 'putting the paper to bed'—nobody but a newspaper man could possibly write that phrase. It's a technical term. Then again, the machine, an Underwood, had a journalistic keyboard.

"Few people, other than journalists, use an exclamation mark; indeed, the symbol is missing from most keyboards.

"Then, again, my dear Splash, you forget that I have a most retentive memory. I noticed long ago that the alignment of the letters 'r' and 's' on your typewriter was not true. It was a simple matter to compare the 'Crook' missive with a letter you sent me recently on that Hatton Garden affair."

Blake paused, and Splash glanced ruefully at Ruff Hanson.

"Can you beat it?" he demanded. "He knew all along, and was just kidding us!"

"Furthermore," continued the detective, "if any further clues were needed to prove that my assistant contemplated kidnapping Mrs. Bardell—there was the unmistakable evidence of

the turkey. It was unfortunate that I should interview the shop-boy and that he was able to give me quite an accurate description of the motor-car, including the number.

"It was, therefore, a simple matter to ascertain that Mrs. Bardell was at Goreham Grange. I knew, of course, she was in perfectly safe hands, and I just emulated Brer Rabbit by lying low and saying nuffin'.

"You evidently realised your error regarding the turkey, Splash—hence your masterly handling of the affair thereafter."

The journalist winced at Blake's quiet sarcasm.

"I thought it was a jolly good stunt. Tinker pinched the bill from the turkey and forged Mrs. Bardell's writing. You've got to admit young Ginger was a darned good actor. He's a printer's devil, as a matter of fact."

Blake laughed softly.

"An admirable youth—he will go far some day. But really, really, Splash: Why didn't you get him to wash his hands? His thumb and forefinger was black with printers' ink, and his sleeve was thick with it, showing immediately that, like you, he was connected with the press."

There was a roar of laughter at Splash's expense.

Ruff Hanson beamed admiringly at Blake.

"Ain't he a world-beater! Gosh all Friday, but there's machinery in that brain of his. You might have put me wise, old timer," he said reproachfully.

Blake shook his head.

"I was afraid you'd accidentally reveal your knowledge, old man—and then, of course, the whole thing would have collapsed.

"I gave Coutts a hint that the coronet affair was in the nature of a hoax, and he therefore did not pursue his inquiries too far—which is perhaps as well for you, Rockcliff! Otherwise, there would have been serious consequences from Scotland Yard."

"But, I say, guv'nor, how did you escape? Of course, we didn't want to

hurt you or anything. We were as gentle as anything—you'll admit we took you off your guard."

Blake nodded.

"A very commendable bit of work—unfortunately I was expecting it—and acted accordingly. I had a razor-blade and a pick-lock hidden in my waistcoat lining; I flexed my muscles when you bound me and had plenty of 'slack' when you so obligingly left me alone.

"I departed ten minutes after you, and I believe Mr. Deepwood Dobrofski here left the building. Anything else?"

"Yes, guv'nor! I—I—suppose you were the ghost?"

Blake smiled.

"Well, it struck me as an apt return for a Phantom Crook's attention to haunt him with a real phantom. Luminous paint and an Elizabethan costume make a very convincing apparition.

"I changed in the car on the way down here; and, in the confusion, changed back into evening dress and merely requested Mrs. Bardell to come into the library. You were all too busy ghost hunting to notice us!"

Ruff Hanson leapt to his feet.

"By the 'Fifty-Seven Varieties of Henry Heinz' we'll drink the toast again! Here's to Sexton Blake and his treasure, Mrs. Bardell—between 'em they've beaten the Power of the Press, the Landed Aristocracy, and the detective force as well!"

Viscount Rockcliff rose to second the toast, and it was drunk with acclamation.

"Pile up the Yule logs, my beauties," cried Splash. "It's Christmas Eve and the night is yet young.

"The Phantom Crook is laid forever—peace to his ashes, and a Merry Christmas to us all!"

"Thank you all very much," said Sexton Blake, as he rose to respond. And then, with a smile: "If you don't mind, I'll collect in due course your thousand-pound cheque for the Hospital Fund."

THE END.

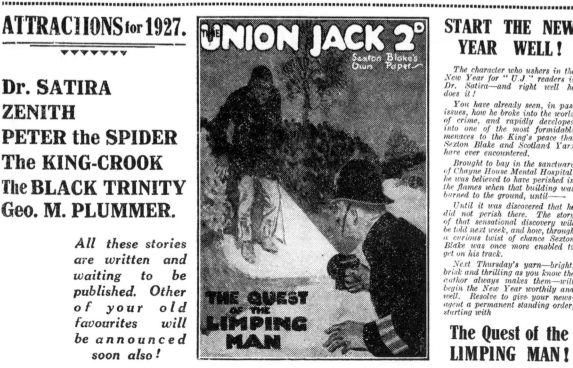

EDGAR WALLACE ALWAYS THRILLS!

The Three Just Men
by EDGAR WALLACE

(Author of "The Four Just Men," etc., etc.)

YOU CAN BEGIN HERE.

THE Triangle Detective Agency, of No. 233, Curzon Street, is run by George Manfred, his ostensible chauffeur-footman, Gonsalez, and his equally ostensible butler, Poiccart. This trio is known as the Three Just Men—a name they have earned for their chivalrous deeds in the past in risking life and liberty in the cause of the oppressed.

Sam Barberton seeks their aid in finding Mirabelle Leicester, a young girl, who seems to be the centre of some mysterious plotting, and who has vanished from her home at Heavytree Farm. Before the Three Just Men can communicate what they have learned, however, Barberton is mysteriously killed in broad daylight, while standing on the Embankment, apparently by snake bite.

Meantime, Mirabelle Leicester has fallen into the hands of two villains—an alleged Swede, named Dr. Oberzohn, and "Monty" Newton, a crook of the "flash" type. She is rescued from them by the Three Just Men, and sent back to her home by car.

Next morning she receives a visit from a wealthy blind man, a Mr. Johnson Lee. He questions her at some length about her father's activities in Africa as an astronomer. He also asks whether she had ever received a message written in Portuguese, and mentions Sam Barberton's death.

Later in the day a pedlar appears at the farm, trying to interview Mirabelle. He is refused access by one of the two men who have been set by Gonsalez to guard the property, upon which the pedlar enters a small barn in the orchard at the rear. Following him there, the second guard is overpowered by the pedlar, and a few minutes later the first guard, Digby, is attacked by the driver of a car which has just arrived at the gate.

Mirabelle sees the man struck down with a spanner wielded by the car-driver, and she straightway slams the door and thrusts home the bolts.

There is a mysterious offensive opening against Mirabelle and her Aunt Alma, the solitary occupants of Heavytree Farm!

On the Defensive!

MIRABELLE was calm; the hand that took the revolver from the hall-table did not tremble.

"Alma!" she called; and Alma came running downstairs.

"What on earth——" she began, and then saw the pistol in Mirabelle's hands.

"They are attacking the house," said the girl quickly. "I don't know who 'they' are, but they've just struck down one of the men who was protecting us. Take the gun, Alma."

Alma's face was contorted, and might have expressed fear or anger or both. Mirabelle afterwards learnt that the dominant emotion was one of satisfaction to find herself in so warlike an environment.

Running into the drawing-room, the girl pushed open the window, which commanded a view of the road. The gate was unfastened, and two men, who had evidently been concealed inside the trolley, were lifting the unconscious man, and she watched, with a calm she could not understand in herself, as they threw him into the interior and fastened the tailboard.

She counted four in all, including the driver, who was climbing back to his seat. One of the newcomers, evidently the leader, was pointing down the road towards the lane, and she guessed that he was giving directions as to where the car should wait, for it began to go backwards almost immediately and with surprising smoothness, remembering the exhibition it had given of decrepitude a few minutes before.

The man who had given instructions came striding down the path towards the door.

"Stop!"

He looked round with a start into the levelled muzzle of a Browning, and his surprise would, in any other circumstances, have been comical.

"It's all right, miss——" he began.

"Put yourself outside that gate," said Mirabelle coolly.

"I wanted to see you—very important——"

Bang!

Mirabelle fired a shot, aimed above his head, towards the old poplar. The man ducked and ran. Clear of the gate, he dropped to the cover of a hedge, where his men already were, and she heard the murmur of their voices distinctly, for the day was still, and the far-off chugging of the trolley's engine sounded close at hand. Presently she saw a head peep round the hedge.

"Can I have five minutes' talk with you?" said the leader loudly.

He was a thick-set, bronzed man, with a patch of lint plastered to his face, and she noted unconsciously that he wore gold ear-rings.

"There's no trouble coming to you," he said, opening the gate as he spoke. "You oughtn't to have fired, anyway. Nobody's going to hurt you——"

He had advanced a yard into the garden as he spoke.

Bang, bang!

In her haste she had pressed butt and trigger just a fraction too long, and, startled by the knowledge that another shot was coming, her hand jerked round, and the second shot missed his head by the fraction of an inch.

He disappeared in a flash, and a second later she saw their hats moving swiftly above the box. They were running towards the waiting car.

"Stay here, Alma!"

Alma Goddard nodded grimly, and the girl flew up the stairs to her room. From this elevation she commanded a better view. She saw them climb into the van, and in another second the limp body of the guard was thrown out into the hedge; then, after a brief space of time, the machine began moving, and, gathering speed, disappeared in a cloud of dust on the Highcombe Road.

Mirabelle came down the stairs at a run, pulled back the bolts, and flew out along the road towards the still figure of the detective.

He was lying by the side of the ditch, his head a mass of blood, and she saw that he was still breathing. She tried to lift him, but it was too great a task. She ran back to the house. The telephone was in the hall; an old-fashioned instrument with a handle that had to be turned, and she had not made two revolutions before she realised that the wire had been cut.

Alma was still in the parlour, the gun gripped tight in her hand, a look of fiendish resolution on her face.

"You must help me to get Digby into the house," she said.

"Where is he?"

Mirabelle pointed, and the two women, returning to the man, half lifted, half dragged him back to the hall.

Laying him down on the brick floor, the girl went in search of clean linen. The kitchen, which was also the drying place for Alma's more intimate laundry, supplied all that she needed. Whilst Alma watched unmoved the destruction of her wardrobe, the girl bathed the wound, and the frightened nurse—who had disappeared at the first shot—applied a rough dressing. The wound was an ugly one, and the man showed no signs of recovering consciousness.

"We shall have to send Mary into Gloucester for an ambulance," said Mirabelle. "We can't send nurse—she doesn't know the way."

"Mary," said Alma calmly, "is at this moment having hysterics in the larder. I'll harness the dog-cart and go myself. But where is the other man?"

Mirabelle shook her head.

"I don't like to think what has happened to him," she said. "Now, Alma, do you think we can get him into the drawing-room?"

Together they lifted the heavy figure and staggered with it into the pretty little room, laying him at last upon the settee under the window.

"He can rest there till we get the ambulance," began Mirabelle; and a chuckle behind her made her turn with a gasp.

It was the pedlar, and in his hand he held the pistol which she had discarded.

"I only want you," he nodded to the girl. "You other two women can come out here." He jerked his head to the passage. Under the stairs was a big cupboard, and he pulled the door open invitingly "Get in here! If you make a noise, you'll be sorry for yourselves."

Alma's eyes wandered longingly to the gun she had left in the corner, but before she could make a move he had placed himself between her and the weapon.

"Get inside!" said the pedlar.

And Mirabelle was not much surprised when Aunt Alma meekly obeyed.

He shut the door on the two women and fastened the catch.

"Now, young lady, put on your hat and be lively!"

He followed her up the stairs into her room, and watched her while she found a hat and a cloak. She knew only too well that it was a waste of time even to temporise with him. He, for his part, was so exultant at his success that he grew almost loquacious.

"I suppose you saw the boys driving away, and you didn't remember that I was somewhere around? Was that you doing the shooting?"

She did not answer.

"It couldn't have been Lew, or you'd have been dead," he said. He was examining the muzzle of the pistol. "It was you all right." He chuckled. "Ain't you the game one? Sister, you ought to be——"

He stopped dead, staring through the window. He was paralysed with amazement at the sight of a bare-headed Aunt Alma flying along the Gloucester Road. With an oath he turned to the girl.

"How did she get out? Have you got anybody here? Now speak up!"

"The cupboard under the stairs leads to the wine-cellar," said Mirabelle coolly, "and there are two ways out of the wine-cellar. I think Aunt Alma found one of them."

With an oath, he took a step towards her, gripped her by the arm, and jerked her towards the door.

"Lively!" he said, and dragged her down the stairs through the hall into the kitchen.

He shot back the bolts, but the lock of the kitchen door had been turned.

"This way!"

He swore cold-bloodedly, and, her arm still in his powerful grip, he hurried along the passage and pulled open the door.

It was an unpropitious moment. A man was walking down the path, a half-smile on his face, as though he was thinking over a remembered jest. At the sight of him the pedlar dropped the girl's arm and his hand went like lightning to his pocket.

"When will you die?" said Leon Gonsalez softly. "Make a choice, and make it quick!"

And the gun in his hand seemed to quiver with homicidal eagerness.

Two "Accidents."

THE pedlar, his face twitching, put up his shaking hands.

Leon walked to him, took the Browning from his moist grip, and dropped it into his pocket.

"Your friends are waiting, of course?" he said pleasantly.

The pedlar did not answer.

"Cuccini too? I thought I had incapacitated him for a long time."

"They've gone!" growled the pedlar.

Gonsalez looked round in perplexity.

"I don't want to take you into the house. At the same time, I don't want to leave you here," he said. "I almost wish you'd drawn that gun of yours," he added regretfully. "It would have solved so many immediate problems."

This particular problem was solved by the return of the dishevelled Alma and the restoration to her of her gun.

"I would so much rather you shot him than I," said Leon earnestly. "The police are very suspicious of my shootings, and they never wholly believe that they are done in self-defence."

With a rope he tied the man, and tied him uncomfortably, wrists to ankles. That done, he made a few inquiries and went swiftly out to the barn, returning in a few minutes with the unhappy guard.

"It can't be helped," said Leon, cutting short the man's apologies. "The question is, where are the rest of the brethren?"

Something zipped past him; it had the intensified hum of an angry wasp, and a second later he heard a muffled plop! In a second he was lying flat on the ground, his Browning covering the hedge that hid Heavytree Lane.

"Run to the house!" he called urgently. "They won't bother about you!"

And the guard, nothing loath, sprinted for the cover of walls.

Presently Leon located the enemy, and at a little distance off he saw the flat top of the covered trolley. A man walked slowly and invitingly across the gap in the hedge, but Gonsalez held his fire, and presently the manœuvre was repeated. Obviously they were trying to concentrate his mind upon the gap whilst they were moving elsewhere. His eyes swept the meadow boundary—running parallel, he guessed, was a brook or ditch which would make excellent cover.

Again the man passed leisurely across the gap. Leon steadied his elbow and glanced along the sight. As he did so the man reappeared.

Crack!

Gonsalez aimed a foot behind him. The man saw the flash and jumped back, as he had expected. In another second he was writhing on the ground with a bullet through his leg.

Leon showed his teeth in a smile and switched his body round to face the new point of attack. It came from the spot that he had expected—a little rise of ground that commanded his position. The first bullet struck the turf to his right with an angry buzz, sent a divot flying heavenward, and ricochetted with a smack against the tree. Before the raised head could drop to cover, Gonsalez fired; fired another shot to left and right; then, rising, raced for the shelter of the tree, and reached it in time to see three heads bobbing back

to the road. He waited, covering the gap, but the people who drew the wounded man out of sight did not show themselves, and a minute later he saw the trolley moving swiftly down the by-road, and knew that danger was past.

The firing had attracted attention. He had not been back in the house a few minutes before a mounted policeman, his horse in a lather, came galloping up to the gate and dismounted. A neighbouring farm had heard the shots and telephoned to the constabulary headquarters. For half an hour the mounted policeman took notes, and by this time half the farmers in the neighbourhood, their guns under their arms, had assembled in Mirabelle's parlour.

She had not seen as much of the redoubtable Leon as she could have wished, and when they had a few moments to themselves she seized the opportunity to tell him of the call which Lee had made that morning. Apparently he knew all about it, for he expressed no surprise, and was only embarrassed when she showed a personal interest in himself and his friends.

It was not a very usual experience for him, and he was rather annoyed with himself at this unexpected glimpse of enthusiasm and hero-worship, sane as it was, and based, as he realised, upon her keen sense of justice.

"I'm not so sure that we've been very admirable, really," he said. "But the difficulty is to produce at the moment a judgment which would be given from a distance of years. We have sacrificed everything which to most men would make life worth living, in our desire to see the scales held fairly."

"You are not married, Mr. Gonsalez?"

He stared into the frank eyes.

"Married? Why, no," he said, and she laughed.

"You talk as though that were a possibility that had never occurred to you."

"It hasn't," he admitted. "By the very nature of our work we are debarred from that experience. And is it an offensive thing to say that I have never felt my singleness to be a deprivation?"

"It is very rude," she said severely, and Leon was laughing to himself all the way back to town as at a great joke that improved upon repetition.

"I think we can safely leave her for a week," he reported, on his return to Curzon Street. "No, nothing happened. I was held up in a police trap near Newbury for exceeding the speed limit. They said I was doing fifty, but I should imagine it was nearer eighty. Meadows will get me out of that. Otherwise, I must send the inevitable letter to the magistrate and pay the inevitable fine. Have you done anything about Johnson Lee?"

Manfred nodded.

"Meadows and the enthusiastic Mr. Washington have gone round to see him. I have asked Washington to go because"—he hesitated—"the snake is a real danger, so far as he is concerned. Elijah Washington promises to be a very real help. He is afraid of nothing, and has undertaken to stay with Lee and to apply such remedies for snake-bites as he knows."

He was putting on his gloves as he spoke, and Leon Gonsalez looked at him with critical admiration.

"Are you being presented at Court, or are you taking tea with a duchess?"

Printed and published every Thursday by the Proprietors, The Amalgamated Press (1922), Ltd., The Fleetway House, Farringdon Street, London E.C.4. Advertisement offices: The Fleetway House, Farringdon Street, London, E.C.4. Registered for transmission by Canadian Magazine Post. Subscription rates: Inland and Abroad, 11s. per annum; 5s. 6d. for six months. Sole agents for South Africa: The Central News Agency, Ltd. Sole agents for Australia and New Zealand; Messrs. Gordon & Gotch, Ltd; and for Canada, The Imperial News Co., Ltd. (Canada).—Saturday, December 25th, 1926.

"Neither. I'm calling upon friend Oberzohn."

"The devil you are!" said Leon, his eyebrows rising.

"I have taken the precaution of sending him a note, asking him to keep his snakes locked up," said Manfred, "and as I have pointedly forwarded the carbon copy of the letter, to impress the fact that another exists and may be brought in evidence against him, I think I shall leave Oberzohn & Smitts' main office without hurt. If you are not too tired, Leon, I would rather prefer the Buick to the Spanz."

"Give me a quarter of an hour," said Leon, and went up to his room to make himself tidy.

It was fifteen minutes exactly when the Buick stopped at the door, and Manfred got into the saloon. There was no partition between driver and passenger, and conversation was possible.

"It would have been as well if you'd had Brother Newton there," he suggested.

"Brother Newton will be on the spot: I took the precaution of sending him a similar note," said Manfred. "I shouldn't imagine they'll bring out their gunmen."

"I know two, and possibly three, they won't bring out," Gonsalez grinned at the traffic policeman who waved him into Oxford Street. "That Browning of mine throws high, Manfred, I always had a suspicion it did. Pistols are queer things, but this may wear into my hand." He talked arms and ammunition until the square block of Oberzohn & Smitts came into sight. "Good hunting!" he said, as he got out, opened the saloon door and touched his hat to Manfred as he alighted.

He got back into his seat, swung the little car round in a circle, and sat on the opposite side of the road, his eyes alternately on the entrance and on the mirror which gave a view of the traffic approaching him from the rear.

Manfred was not kept in the waiting-room for more than two minutes. At the end of that time, a solemn youth in spectacles, with a little bow, led him across the incurious office into the presence of the illustrious doctor.

The old man was at his desk. Behind him, his debonair self, Monty Newton, a large yellow flower in his buttonhole, a smile on his face. Oberzohn got up like a man standing to attention.

"Mr. Manfred, this is a great honour," he said, and held out his hand stiffly.

An additional chair had been placed for the visitor: a rich-looking tapestried chair, to which the doctor waved the hand which Manfred did not take.

"Good-morning, Manfred." Newton removed his cigar and nodded genially. "Were you at the dance last night?"

"I was there, but I didn't come in," said Manfred, seating himself. "You did not turn up till late, they tell me?"

"It was of all occurrences the most unfortunate," said Dr. Oberzohn, and Newton laughed.

"I've lost his laboratory secretary and he hasn't forgiven me," he said almost jovially. "The girl he took on yesterday. Rather a stunner in the way of looks. She didn't wish to go back to the country where she came from, so my sister offered to put her up for the night in Chester Square. I'm blessed if she didn't lose herself at the dance, and we haven't seen her since!"

"It was a terrible thing," said Oberzohn sadly. "I regard her as in my charge. For her safety I am responsible. You, I trust, Mr. Newton——"

"I don't think I should have another uneasy moment if I were you, doctor," said Manfred easily. "The young lady is back at Heavytree Farm. I thought that would surprise you. And she is still there: that will surprise you more, if you have not already heard by telephone that your Old Guard failed dismally to—er—bring her back to work. I presume that was their object?"

"My old guard, Mr. Manfred?" Oberzohn shook his head in bewilderment. "This is beyond my comprehension."

"Is your sister well?" asked Manfred blandly.

Newton shrugged his shoulders.

"She is naturally upset. And who wouldn't be? Joan is a very tender-hearted girl."

"She has been that way for years," said Manfred offensively. "May I smoke?"

"Will you have one of my cigarettes?"

Manfred's grave eyes fixed the doctor in a stare that held the older man against his will.

"I have had just one too many of your cigarettes," he said. His words came like a cold wind. "I do not want any more, Herr Doktor, or there will be vacancies in your family circle. Who knows that, long before you compound your wonderful elixir, you may be called to normal immortality?"

The yellow face of Oberzohn had turned to a dull red.

"You seem to know so much about me, Mr. Manfred, as myself," he said in a husky whisper.

Manfred nodded.

"More. For whilst you are racing against time to avoid the end of a life which does not seem especially worthy of preservation, and whilst you know not what day or hour that end may come, I can tell you to the minute."

The finger of his gloved hand pointed the threat.

All trace of a smile had vanished from Monty Newton's face. His eyes did not leave the caller's.

"Perhaps you shall tell me."

Oberzohn found a difficulty in speaking. Rage possessed him, and only his iron will choked down the flames from view.

"The day that injury comes to Mirabelle Leicester, that day you go out—you and those who are with you!"

"Look here, Manfred, there's a law in this country——" began Monty Newton hotly.

"I am the law." The words rang like a knell of fate. "In this matter I am judge, jury, hangman. Old or young, I will not spare," he said evenly.

"Are you immortal, too?" sneered Monty.

Only for a second did Manfred's eyes leave the old man's face.

"The law is immortal," he said. "If you dream that, by some cleverly-concocted coup, you can sweep me from your path before I grow dangerous—be sure that your sweep is clean."

"You haven't asked me to come here to listen to this stuff, have you?" asked Newton, and though his words were bold, his manner aggressive, there were shadows on his face which were not there when Manfred had come into the room—shadows under his eyes and in his cheeks where plumpness had been.

"I've come here to tell you to let up on Miss Leicester. You're after something that you cannot get, and nobody is in a position to give you. I don't know what it is—I will make you a present o. that piece of information. But it's big—bigger than any prize you've ever gone after in your wicked lives. And to get that you're prepared to sacrifice innocent lives with the recklessness of spendthrifts who think there is no bottom to their purse. The end is near!"

He rose slowly and stood by the table, towering over the stiff-backed doctor.

"I cannot say what action the police will take over this providential snake bite, Oberzohn, but I'll make you this offer: I and my friends will stand out of the game and leave Meadows to get you in his own way. You think that means you'll go scot free? But it doesn't. These police are like bulldogs; once they've got a grip of you they'll never let go."

"What is the price you ask for this interesting service?"

Newton was puffing steadily at his cigar, his hands clasped behind him, his feet apart, a picture of comfort and well-being.

"Leave Miss Leicester alone. Find a new way of getting the money you need so badly."

Newton laughed.

"My dear fellow, that's a stupid thing to say. Neither Oberzohn nor I are exactly poor."

"You're bankrupt, both of you," said Manfred quietly. "You are in the position of gamblers when the cards have run against you for a long time. You have no reserve, and your expenses are enormous. Find another way, Newton, and tell your sister "—he paused by the door, looking down into the white lining of his silk hat—"I'd like to see her at Curzon Street to-morrow morning at ten o'clock."

"Is that an order?" asked Newton sarcastically.

Manfred nodded.

"Then let me tell you," roared the man, white with passion, "that I ta no orders for her or for me. Got swolle heads since you've had your pardon, haven't you? You look out for me, Manfred. I'm not exactly harmless."

He felt the pressure of the doctor's foot upon his and curbed his temper.

"All right!" he growled. "But don't expect to see Joan."

He added a coarse jest, and Manfred raised his eyes slowly and met his.

"You will be hanged by the State or murdered by Oberzohn, I am not sure which," he said simply, and he spoke with such perfect confidence that the heart of Monty Newton turned to water.

Manfred stood in the sidewalk and signalled, and the little car came swiftly and noiselessly across. Leon's eyes were on the entrance. A tall man standing in the shadow of the hall was watching. He was leaning against the wall in a negligent attitude, and for a second Leon was startled.

"Get in quickly!"

Leon almost shouted the words back, and Manfred jumped into the machine as the chauffeur sent the car forward with a jerk that strained every gear.

"What on——" began Manfred, but the rest of his words were lost in the terrific crash which followed.

The leather hood of the machine was ripped down at the back, a splinter of glass struck Leon's cap and sliced a half-moon neatly. He jammed on the brakes, threw open the door of the saloon, and leaped out. Behind the car was a mass of wreckage. A great iron casting lay split into three pieces amidst a tangle of broken packing-case. Leon looked up. Immediately, above the entrance to Oberzohn & Smitts' was a crane, which had swung out with a heavy load just before Manfred came out. The steel wire hung loosely from the derrick. He heard excited voices speaking from the open doorway, three floors above, and two men in large glasses were looking down and gabbling in a language he did not understand.

"A very pretty accident. We might have filled half a column in the evening newspapers if we had not moved."

"And the gentleman in the hall—what was he doing?"

Leon walked back through the entrance. The man had disappeared, but near where the had been standing was a small bell-push, which, it was obvious, had recently been fixed, for the wires ran loosely on the surface of the wall, and were new.

He came back in time to see a policeman crossing the road.

"I wish to find out how this accident occurred, constable," he said. "My master was nearly killed."

The policeman looked at the ton of debris lying half on the sidewalk, half on the road, then up at the slackened hawser.

"The cable has run off the drum, I should think."

"I should think so," said Leon gravely.

He did wait for the policeman to finish his investigations, but went home at a steady pace, and made no reference to the "accident" until he had put away his car and had returned to Curzon Street.

"The man in the hall was put there to signal when you were under the load—certain things must not happen," he said. "I am going out to make a few inquiries."

Gonsalez knew one of Oberzohn's staff—a clean young Swede, with that knowledge of English which is normal in Scandinavian countries, and at nine o'clock that night he drifted into a Swedish restaurant in Dean Street and found the young man at the end of his meal. It was an acquaintance—one of many—that Leon had assiduously cultivated. The young man, who knew him as Mr. Heinz—Leon spoke German remarkably well—was glad to have a companion with whom he could discuss the inexplicable accident of the afternoon.

"The cable was not fixed to the drum," he said. "It might have been terrible. There was a gentleman in a motor-car outside, and he had only moved away a few inches when the case fell. There is bad luck in that house. I am glad I am leaving at the end of the week."

Leon had some important questions to put, but he did not hurry, having the gift of patience to a marked degree. It was nearly ten when they parted, and Gonsalez went back to his garage, where he spent a quarter of an hour.

At midnight Manfred had just finished a long conversation with the Scotland Yard man, who was still at Brightlingsea, when Leon came in, looking very pleased with himself. Poiccart had gone to bed, and Manfred had switched out one circuit of lights when his friend arrived.

"Thank you, my dear George!" said Gonsalez briskly. "It was very good of you, and I did not like troubling you, but I——"

"It was a small thing," said Manfred, with a smile, "and involved merely the changing of my shoes. But why? I am not curious, but why did you wish me to telephone the night watchman at Oberzohn's to be waiting at the door at eleven o'clock for a message from the doctor?"

"Because," said Leon cheerfully, rubbing his hands, "the night watchman is an honest man; he has a wife and six children, and I was particularly wishful not to hurt anybody. The building doesn't matter; it stands—or stood—isolated from all others. The only worry in my mind was the night watchman. He was at the door—I saw him."

Manfred asked no further questions. Early the next morning he took up the paper and turned to the middle page, read the account of the "Big Fire in City Road" which had completely gutted the premises of Oberzohn & Smitts; and, what is more, he expected to read it before he had seen the paper.

"Accidents are accidents," said Leon the philosopher that morning at breakfast. "And that talk I had with the clerk last night told me a lot. Oberzohn has allowed his fire insurance to lapse!"

(Even Oberzohn's employees find his sinister plotting too much for them! Can the Three Just Men beat him after all? Breathless action resumes next week. Have you booked your copy?)

UNION JACK

Special Christmas Number.

The Affair of the
BLACK CAROL

A seasonable story of detective adventure, animated throughout by the gladsome spirit of Christmastide. Complete, and introducing: Sexton Blake, Tinker, Ruff Hanson, Splash Page and Mrs. Bardell.

No, 1,260,   EVERY THURSDAY,   December 10th, 1927,

The Affair of the BLACK CAROL

The story of how Sexton Blake foiled a sinister plot; and
how he spent a real old-fashioned Christmas in the
jolly company of Splash Page, Tinker, Ruff
Hanson, and—not least—the worthy
Mrs. Bardell.

Chapter 1.
"Christmas Comes But Once a Year!"

TINKER, Mr. Sexton Blake's assistant, sang heartily if unmelodiously, accompanying himself on the dinner gong with enthusiastic gusto.

"When on an elephant's back I pass,
Somebody beats on a sounding brass
Gong!
I'm the Rajah of Bong!"

It was lunch-time in Baker Street, and Tinker was hungry. A fire crackled cheerfully in the dining-room grate. The usually austere walls, crammed with curios and trophies, and relics of many a grim adventure, were now gaily festooned with holly and multi-coloured decorations.

The white tablecloth, with its sparkling cut glass and napery, looked inviting enough; but the steaming joint and vegetables which Mrs. Bardell had just deposited were what made Tinker's mouth water.

"Where on earth is the guv'nor?" the

lad inquired peevishly of Pedro, who also sniffed the appetising odour of roast beef with keen anticipation.

Tinker lifted his gong-stick again and continued his booming ditty:

"When I'm at home, I have poets who bring
Chorus of praise in a kind of sing-
Song!
I'm the Rajah of Bong!"

He hit the long-suffering instrument another terrific thwack, just as the dining-room door opened and Sexton Blake entered. There was a pained expression on his clear-cut face.

"My dear Tinker, is there any necessity to impersonate a mythical rajah by denting the gift of a real one?" he inquired, with mock gravity.

Tinker replaced the gong-stick, and stared in dismay at the dent in the beautifully engraved silver gong which had been presented to his master by the Maharajah of Kurdistan.

"Jove! I'm sorry, guv'nor. But I'm feeling so dashed chirpy—and so jolly hungry that——"

They sat down at the head of the

table, and Tinker proceeded to carve the joint, while the detective toyed abstractedly with the stem of his wine-glass.

"Only four more days, guv'nor," said the youngster brightly, "and then it's Christmas Day."

Blake nodded abstractedly. He had spent the whole morning in the "stink shop," as Tinker irreverently termed the laboratory. The dinner gong had interrupted his experiment, and it seemed as if he was inclined to be touchy.

Tinker passed the well-filled plate and waited in silence until Mrs. Bardell's cookery had soothed his guv'nor's irritability. The charm worked at length, and Blake helped himself to a glass of wine.

"Of course! How incredibly foolish of me. I had quite overlooked the fact!" he ejaculated.

"My hat! Fancy overlooking Christmas," broke in Tinker. "Of all things——"

"I was not referring to Christmas, my boy," replied Blake. "But to the new Van Luyten blood test. I overlooked the fact that the reagent amidobenzene chemolyzes——"

None were too busy or preoccupied to turn and smile and wave their hands as the coach rumbled by. Somewhere the kindly shade of Charles Dickens smiled down on the incarnation of his immortal dream children—Splash Page's Dickensian party, bound for the delights of Christmas at Lyveden Manor.

A tap sounded at the door and Mrs. Bardell entered, breathing a trifle stertorously. In her hand she gripped a telegram. Tinker heaved a sigh of relief at the interruption of Blake's chemical dissertation.

"That dratted varmint of a telegraft boy 'ad the cheek to demand 'is Christmas box," began the worthy woman. "Which it's a week afore Boxing Day—though, if I 'ad my way with the young limbs, the way they work the bell, I'd box 'em on the ear-'oles. Calls 'emselves civil servants. Why, a more uncivil lot o'——"

"Er—quite, Mrs. Bardell," said Blake, as he ripped open the orange envelope. "Please tell him there is no reply."

Mrs. Bardell sniffed, and made her exit. Tinker chuckled as Blake re-read the wire.

"Anything wrong, guv'nor?" he inquired. "I hope it's not a bally case. I want to spend Christmas in peace——"

Blake chuckled as he threw over the telegram. It was brief, pithy, and characteristic.

"Howdy. Just landed. Coming to wish you a Merry Christmas.—RUFF."

"Hurrah, guv'nor!" ejaculated Tinker. "Gosh! I'll be glad to see the Hard Boiled Egg again. We're bound to have a merry Christmas with him around, anyway!"

Blake smiled.

"If he doesn't start getting gay with Willy and Wally that is, young 'un. Friend Ruff has a diabolical knack of getting into trouble. I wonder what brings him over from New York at this time of the year?"

The detective rose to his feet, and slowly filled his briar pipe as he entered the consulting-room. Outside, in Baker Street, a faint flurry of snowflakes fell and a chill December wind rattled the window panes, enhancing the warmth and cosiness of the room within. Blake stirred the fire into a ruddy glow, and sank back into his favourite chair.

"We haven't seen our dynamic friend for some considerable time. I'm rather intrigued by his telegram, young 'un," he remarked.

"Ruff Hanson doesn't usually come to Europe on a joy-ride."

"That's so, guv'nor," agreed Tinker, staring into the glowing embers of the fire with the retrospection that a winter day evolves.

THE American gunman sleuth held a warm corner in the affection of the famous Baker Street trio. They had shared peril and adventure on many a dangerous trail in many lands, and none had a greater admiration for Ruff Hanson's breezy personality and essential straightness than Sexton Blake.

The admiration was mutual; for Ruff Hanson had often expressed in his own pungent fashion his equally high opinion of Sexton Blake.

"Talking of Christmas," continued Tinker, who was a youth with a single-track mind when an idea obsessed him, "what are we going to do about it, guv'nor—spend it quietly at home, or at one of the big hotels?"

Blake frowned.

"Christmas in a hotel, Tinker!" he echoed. "I trust I am fairly progressive, but this modern, new-fangled idea of Yuletide at a West End hotel, with jazz bands and cocktails, is to me disgusting. Christmas is essentially a private affair—where there is a reunion of old friends to yarn over old times.

I'm afraid there'll be little of peace on earth and good will at the Hotel Stupendous, with its cosmopolitan crew of multi-millionaires and dyspeptic dowagers."

A loud bang sounded above the ceaseless hum of the traffic in Baker Street.

"Talking of old friends," chuckled Tinker, "here's one of 'em, guv'nor. If I'm not mistaken, that sounds like Splash Page's Red Peril outside."

He crossed over to the window, just in time to see the newspaper man park his vermilion roadster at the kerb; and a few moments later the journalist breezed into the consulting-room, removing his leather gauntlets.

Derek Page—known in Fleet Street as Splash Page—grinned amiably.

"'Mornin', Blake! 'Mornin', Tinker! How's tricks?" he greeted cheerfully. "Jove, it's nippy outside!"

He warmed his numbed fingers at the cheerful fire.

"What-ho, my old ink-slinger!" retorted Tinker. "I suppose you're hard-up for a story, and come here scrounging for a scoop, as usual?"

"Well, as a matter of fact," replied Splash, "I don't want to break it too suddenly, but I came along here to ask you two if you'd give a poor, lorn journalist a bite of dinner on Christmas Day. I'd ask you to my place, but you know what a bachelor flat is——"

"By all means, my dear chap!" exclaimed Sexton Blake cordially. "Tinker and I were just discussing the subject. You know you are always welcome here."

He broke off suddenly as a nasal voice sounded on the stairway.

"Don't you worry about me, Mrs. B.! I kin find my way up blindfold. Say, ma'am, you sure are keepin' that schoolgirl complexion! You don't look a day older——"

"Oh, Mr. 'Anson, get along, do!" came Mrs. Bardell's coy reply.

"Ruff!" yelled Splash and Tinker simultaneously, and they leapt to their feet, as the door of the consulting-room swung open to admit the gigantic American.

Ruff Hanson, the New York detective, and an old friend of Sexton Blake, was clad in a tweed suit of transatlantic cut. In his hand he carried a huge, broad-brimmed Stetson, and on his battered, ugly face was a good-humoured grin, as he advanced with outstretched hand.

"Howdy, Blake, old timer?" he boomed. "Put it there if it weighs as much as the Woolworth Building! Well, well, folks! Howdy, Tinker? Dog my cats if you ain't got the tame news hound!"

"Ruff, you old villain!" yelled Tinker delightedly. "Park yourself in this chair and make yourself comfy!"

The American sank his huge bulk into an armchair and beamed genially on the trio. Some of the breeziness of his own Western prairie had been swept into the cosy consulting-room at Ruff Hanson's entrance.

Sexton Blake chuckled softly.

"Very glad to see you again, Ruff! Is it business or pleasure, this trip?"

"Pleasure, old timer—real pleasure! You're in for the merriest Christmas of your lives—and it's all on Hard-boiled Hanson!"

"Come into a fortune, Ruff?" queried Tinker.

"Something like that," explained the other carelessly. "Are you doing anything to-night?"

Blake shook his head.

"No. Christmas week is usually an off-time as far as I'm concerned. How about you, Splash?"

"Well, unless a murder happens, I'm my own boss," answered the journalist. "What's the great idea?"

"Meet me for dinner at the Hotel Splendide, and I'll wise you up," came the reply. "I want to introduce you to my sparring partner—greatest little kid you've ever struck. Say, my kid's a wonder——"

Sexton Blake stared speechlessly at the American.

It took a good deal to surprise the famous detective, but even his impassive face betrayed astonishment.

"Good heavens, Ruff!" he remarked. "Surely you've never committed matrimony?"

"For the love of Pete—NO!" roared the American. "You know my motto where fee-males are concerned—forget 'em all!"

"Then, to use your own transatlantic phrase," asked Blake, "how come? Whose is this 'kid'? And why? And so forth."

"He's young Cayterer—son of the Film King," explained Ruff. "And I'm his dry-nurse. Old man Cayterer——"

And Ruff Hanson went on to account for his unexpected presence in Europe at this Christmas season. Shorn of his picturesque and expressive—sometimes explosive—Americanisms, the facts were, broadly, these:

Ruff Hanson had been engaged some time previously by Mr. Benjamin Cayterer, president of the Lion Film Corporation, on a somewhat unusual mission.

Mr. Cayterer, an Englishman by birth, was one of the best-known and respected film magnates in Hollywood. For years he had been waging a relentless war against shady film pirates and producers, and had agitated for sweeping reforms in the motion-picture industry.

His policy was to weed out the undesirable elements which brought disgrace on Hollywood, and he was contemplating a drastic Censorship Bill to curtail the activities of, among others, his chief rival, Mr. Isidore Solmann, an unscrupulous financier with an unsavoury reputation.

Solmann was the head of a shady film corporation, and he hated Cayterer's reformative schemes, and did his best by bribery and graft to bring the Englishman's studios into disrepute. Cayterer, however, had managed to circumvent Solmann's machinations, and persisted with his self-imposed task to "clean up Hollywood."

Solmann realised that once Cayterer's proposed Bill became law he would be ruined. With the assistance of two unscrupulous crooks, Solmann determined to force Cayterer into a corner by striking him through the individual he loved most in the world—his eight-year-old son, Junior.

The boy, a dreamy, wistful child, had been lame from birth with some obscure disease.

The film magnate had been horrified to receive a blunt note informing him that unless the sum of fifty-thousand dollars was paid over and a written promise made to drop the Film Reform Bill, the unknown criminals would kidnap Junior and kill him.

Instantly Cayterer suspected Solmann as the prime mover in the plot, and hence his request for the services of Ruff Hanson. That hard-boiled sleuth was already aware of Isidore Solmann's shady reputation, and learned also that Cayterer held a trump card.

Cayterer had come into possession of evidence implicating his enemy in a disgraceful dope orgy in a Hollywood Road House in which a man had been killed.

It was a statement from a crook named Guiseppe Spagoni, who was at that time serving a term of four years in a penitentiary. It implicated Solmann in the shooting, and gave proof that if not actually the chief, Solmann was at least a ringleader in the dope-smuggling ring of California.

Unfortunately, the affidavit was given to Cayterer on the express condition that it was not to be used until Spagoni had served his sentence. The Italian swore that his imprisonment was a "frame-up" and he gave it to Cayterer as a precautionary measure in case he died in prison. Furthermore, unless backed up by additional proof, it had little value. Also, as Cayterer explained to Ruff Hanson, the film magnate was averse to hitting below the belt.

To use his own words as Hanson reported them to Sexton Blake:

"I may be quixotic, but I want to fight my battles cleanly and carry this Bill through on its merits."

Ruff Hanson admitted having been immediately attracted by Ben Cayterer's personal charm, and had agreed to guard Junior or, as he expressed it, "act as a dry nurse" to the little boy.

Cayterer refused to submit to the blackmailer's demand for the surrender of the letter—and frankly proposed that Ruff Hanson should act as a personal bodyguard for the next two months until the Film Reform Bill became law.

He had informed the gunman that he was leaving for England with Junior that week. It was only ten days from Christmas, and he was hankering to spend Yuletide in his native land, which Junior had never seen.

"You see, Mr. Hanson," he explained. "I promised Junior that I'd let him see what a real old-fashioned English Christmas is like—with snow, holly, Yule logs, and the thousand-and-one things that have made Christmas essentially a children's festival."

The prospect of a trip to England appealed tremendously to Ruff Hanson, especially as Ben Cayterer explained that he had rented from Lord Sylvester a fine old English manor house in the heart of the Dickens country in Kent, where he proposed to stay for three months before embarking on the film production of the great novelist's works.

"And that," concluded Ruff Hanson, "is why I'm here. Acting as personal bodyguard ain't much in my line. Blake," he added, "but that kid Junior's got a sorta appealing look to him that grips me somehow. Besides—the guest of a millionaire with all expenses paid, feels mighty good to a hard-boiled sleuth that generally gets more kicks then cents! And that's why the beanfeast to-night is all on your Uncle Ruff!"

Chapter 2.

Splash Page's Scheme.

THE gorgeously-uniformed be-ribboned linkman of the Hotel Splendide moved majestically towards the opulent Rolls Royce limousine that had drawn up soundlessly at the entrance of the equally opulent hotel.

In his hand he gripped a large umbrella to shelter the august arrivals at that up-to-date caravanserai from the feathery snowflakes which fell from the chill and leaden sky. He opened the door of the automobile with ponderous deference, and the tall distinguished figure of Mr. Ben Cayterer emerged, clad in an expensive fur-lined coat.

The millionaire's face glowed with good humour as he turned to the other occupant of the tonneau—a small boy with solemn eyes and a wan, rather wistful face, who was hugging in a tight embrace a large brown-paper parcel, from which protruded various shining wheels and a fascinating funnel.

"Hang on to your locomotive, Junior," he said cheerily. "We'll have the rest of the stuff sent up by the elevator man."

"Allow me, sir!"

With a courteous bow the commissionaire assisted the little boy to alight. He was a strange and almost pathetic contrast to the gorgeously-clad giant as he stood there, an eager excited look in his large brown eyes. He limped a little as he walked, and round one of his slender legs was clamped a hideous contraption of leather and steel.

His little hand crept forward trustingly towards his father's as they passed from the chill wind that sent the snow-flakes whirling down the crowded Strand, and together entered the warmth of the hotel lounge.

It was the cocktail hour at the Splendide. From the ball-room came the liquid strains of the orchestra, and in the lounge the usual crowd of social butterflies made a hum of light-hearted conversation.

Many people glanced curiously as father and son passed towards the lift. There was something so trustful and winsome about the little lame boy as he limped along eagerly by Ben Cayterer's side. A white-haired old lady smiled kindly at the boy as he passed, and Junior gave a shy little smile in return.

"Such a delightful child!" murmured the old lady to her companion. "Poor little chap—although he's lame, he was the life and soul of the ship, crossing over."

"That's the famous cinema magnate, is it not?" queried her companion. "I understand he is to open a new branch in England here."

Her companion nodded.

"Yes, Mr. Cayterer is English by birth—a most charming man," she remarked. "I understand he's taken Lord Sylvester's old place at Lyveden for Christmas."

They passed to other topics. But the man, sitting alone at the near-by table gazed speculatively after the lift that bore Ben Cayterer and his son to their suite.

He was a loose-limbed man of about thirty-five, handsome in a flashy, superficial fashion, with dark, oily hair slicked back from a smooth forehead, and a tiny moustache that rested like a black moth on his upper lip.

His eyes were peculiarly ill-assorted, one blue and the other hazel, and set a little too closely together on either side of his long, lean nose to be prepossessing. He was clad in conventional evening kit, and wore a double collar and black tie, American fashion, with his frilled white shirt-front.

"Lyveden, huh!" he muttered, lighting a cigar. "I guess that's as good as anywhere."

He beckoned to a waiter.

"Say, get me a time-table, will ya?" he commanded.

He drummed an impatient tattoo with his fingers on the table as he waited, and gazed at their slender, tapering length with an amused twinkle. Those fingers meant a good deal to Sam McCalla, crook, cardsharper, and con man. He was as vain of his carefully-

manicured hands as a debutante or a master pianist, and had once seriously thought of having them insured. But insurance companies have an awkward knack of instituting inquiries, and Mr. McCalla loathed inquiries.

Several awkward episodes in his past career would have undeniably cropped up, in which those slim, clever fingers had played an active part. The theft of 20,000 dollars from the safe of the Farmers' National Bank at Denver City, for instance, or the unfortunate poker game on the s.s. Poseidon, in which the spendthrift son of Gertler, the millionaire pork-packer, lost fifty thousand dollars. Mr. McCalla's fingers had also figured rather prominently in another interesting, if slightly humiliating, manner, when, from information received, he had been pulled in by police headquarters, and had suffered the indignity of having their slender tips besmirched by printer's ink for the

To my hosts of readers, near and far, here's wishing you this Christmastide the most that health and happiness can bring, and may our friendship never dwindle.

enhancement of the U.S. Government collection.

That was an unfortunate episode on which Mr. McCalla did not care to dwell, especially in the aristocratic surroundings of the Hotel Splendide.

The waiter reappeared with an A B C, and, having sipped his cocktail, Mr. McCalla studied the hieroglyphs under the name Lyveden with absorbed interest. He was engrossed in concocting a cablegram to a certain Mr. Isidore Solmann in New York when the swing doors of the lounge opened to admit a fellow-countryman of his, accompanied by three other individuals.

He looked up. Suddenly a flicker of fear crept into his ill-assorted eyes as he recognised the burly, broad-shouldered American with the humorously ugly face.

"Ruff Hanson, by all the gods!" he muttered. "But I guess he won't see me for dust."

He cupped his face in one hand, but his fingers trembled a little as he concluded the cablegram—the cablegram that was destined to have serious and far-reaching results on the lives of several people.

"NOW, Blake, old-timer," Ruff Hanson was saying heartily, as they entered the palm court, "wrap yourself round a Manhattan, while I climb into my glad rags, and then I'll present you to Ben." He held up a pudgy finger. "George, Manhattans all round for these gentlemen, and make it snappy. Has Luigi got the table all set?"

The waiter bowed.

"Certainly, m'sieu, for six, as you ordered," he announced.

"Good! I shan't be long, folk," explained Ruff. "I hate wearing a Tuxedo, but durn me, you feel like a bent nickel among all these guys if you don't."

Splash Page chuckled as the American took his departure.

"Poor old Ruff! He has never taken kindly to the amenities of civilisation, Blake. He longs for the chaps and sombrero of his Texas days."

Blake smiled his agreement as he sipped his cocktail.

"I can't imagine Ruff——" broke in Tinker. "Why, hallo, look who's here, guv'nor!"

Blake turned as a burly, familiar figure entered the lounge, and recognised his old friend, Detective-Inspector Coutts, of Scotland Yard. The C.I.D. man looked a trifle hot under his unaccustomed starched collar. And his boiled shirt was creased in several places. His red face was redder than ever, and his little bristly moustache more than usually aggressive. A look of relief passed over his face as he recognised Blake, however, and he hurried towards the little group with obvious satisfaction.

"What cheer, Couttsy?" called Splash. "Why the glad rags? Don't often see you hitting the high spots!"

Coutts sank into a chair and wiped his forehead with a violent-hued bandana.

"I'm a bit late," he grumbled. "The missus has gone away to her confounded relatives in Shropshire to spend Christmas. Couldn't find a blamed collar or a tie or——"

"Then you're a grass widower, my dear fellow," said Blake, with a smile. "And dressed to kill!"

The Yard man glowered.

"Dressed?" he snorted. "This confounded collar's got an edge like a saw. These blamed laundries ought to be abolished by Act of Parliament. Huh!" he grunted. "Have you seen that crazy Yank yet? He phoned me up this afternoon and asked me to dine with him here. Said it was most important."

"You mean Ruff Hanson?" queried Blake. "Then I presume we are all guests of his?"

"Who else but?" grumbled Coutts. "Rang me up in the middle of my after-noon——"

"Nap!" cut in Tinker, but the Yard man went on unheeding.

"My afternoon interview with the Chief, and told me to come and gnaw a bone with him at the Splendide, and bring a licence for those ridiculous guns of his in my pocket. Bribery and corruption, I call it."

Blake smiled with secret enjoyment. Inspector Coutts and Ruff Hanson were temperamentally diametrically opposed—the stolid, unimaginative Yard man instinctively recoiled from the American's spectacular hustle and his fondness for gun-play; yet, deep down, Blake knew that both were firm friends and had a great deal of respect for each other.

"Ruff has some dark and sinister motive in arranging this banquet," he said slowly. "It rather looks as if we're in for an exciting Christmas."

"Howdy, folk! I wanna interdooce yuh to two mighty good friends of mine," boomed the voice of Ruff Hanson. "Mr. Ben Cayterer and son."

They rose to their feet, and Blake turned and found himself face to face with the tall, handsome millionaire and a frail little figure with round, luminous eyes and a pale, pinched little face. He shook hands with Cayterer.

"I'm very glad to know you, Mr. Blake," said the millionaire. "I have often desired the privilege of meeting you personally, for my own sake, and also for Junior here, who is one of your most loyal hero worshippers."

Blake smiled down kindly at the little fellow, who gazed up with awe at the famous detective.

"Dad, is this *really* Mr. Blake?" he said in a piping voice, like the chirp of a cricket.

"Sure is, sonny!" laughed Ben Cayterer as Blake solemnly shook hands with the boy. "Junior," he added, "can't go in for games much yet, but he's one great little reader, and has followed many of your exploits and adventures in the Press."

Blake shrugged his shoulders deprecatingly.

"I'm afraid they are rather exaggerated, Mr. Cayterer," he said modestly. "I understand you're to be in this country for some time?"

"Six months at least, I reckon," replied the millionaire. "It's great to be back again. I'm hoping to get busy with some real honest-to-goodness English films early in the New Year; but just now Junior and I are on holiday."

"Yes, sir," piped Junior gravely. "We're going to have a real old-fashioned Christmuss—like Bob Cratchit, an' tiny Tim, an' Scrooge, an' everythin'."

"I see you're fond of Dickens, sonny," said Blake a smile softening his austere countenance.

"He gets it from me, I guess," said Ben Cayterer. "Say, Mr. Blake, it's my great ambition to film the master's works as they should be filmed in the country he knew and loved so well.

"We can make million dollar sets in Hollywood, but it isn't the same thing. Dickens is too English for cardboard sets in California, that's why I came home to make a pilgrimage round all the places he describes in his novels, and get the genuine authentic background for my pictures."

He turned as Ruff Hanson tugged his sleeve.

"This is Blake's side-kick, young Tinker, Mr. Cayterer. Likewise Splash Page, a newshound; and my old buddy Inspector Coutts, the grand bezeus at Scotland Yard."

Ben Caterer smiled a welcome at the group.

"I'm very glad to meet you, gentlemen. My friend, Ruff Hanson, has already told me about you, and our little dinner this evening is an excellent idea of his for us to get better acquainted."

He turned to his son and patted his shoulder affectionately.

"Now, son. You've had your wish. Run along to Mrs. Brown and get your supper. You'll have a chance to see Mr. Blake and Tinker later on."

"You're coming to my Christmuss party, sir, aren't you?" queried the boy anxiously. "Dad says he'd ask you to. An' I want to see Pedro."

Blake nodded.

"Why surely, sonny, you shall see Pedro," he promised.

Junior shook hands gravely with the group, his luminous eyes shining with happiness as he limped painfully towards the lift.

"It's his bed-time," explained Cayterer, "but he insisted on seeing you before he went, Mr. Blake, and hearing from your own lips that you would be present at his party."

"He seems to be a remarkably bright little boy," commented Blake, with a twinkle. "How old is he?"

"He'll be ten next month, Mr. Blake. Poor little chap, he's debarred from the usual boyish games, and he spends most of his time reading and imagining all sorts of thrilling adventures and situations in which he plays the role of hero. I intend taking him to Sir Julius Rome, the great Harley Street specialist, to-morrow and see if anything can be done for that lame leg of his. I've spent thousands on the best surgical advice, but——"

Ben Caterer shrugged his shoulders expressively.

"Now what about eats, folk?" chimed in Ruff Hanson. "Mr. Cayterer here has got a proposition to put in front of you, and it's some proposition, I'll tell the world!"

"You dashed old conspirator, Ruff!" chuckled Tinker. "You've got something up your sleeve! I believe you fixed up all this show to-night!"

"You betcha!" said Ruff Hanson, with a wink. "You'll like Ben—he's a white man."

The movie magnate led the way into the private dining-room, and Tinker's eyes sparkled as he saw the invitingly-laid table with its flowers, shaded lights, glittering cut glass, and napery.

"The stuff to give 'em—eh, Couttsy?" he whispered to the Yard man. "I wonder what's in the wind?"

It was not, however, till the wine and dessert stage had been reached, after a dinner that was a gastronomic poem, that Ruff Hanson enlightened the assembled guests.

He rose to his feet after the door had shut behind the discreet head waiter, and raised his glass

"Folk, I ask you to drink to Ben Cayterer and son—the founder of this feast," he proposed.

The toast was drunk with acclamation, and Coutts furtively unfastened a button of his white waistcoat as Ruff sat down.

"Mebbe you're wondering what's the great idea of this feed," he continued. "Wal, I'll put you wise. I'm a kinda personal bodyguard of Junior Cayterer, and believe me, that job suits my style of talent. There's a plug-ugly back in Noo York that's got it in bad for Ben here, but I guess we've slipped him. That being so, we can all take a deep breath and enjoy ourselves."

He sipped his champagne with keen enjoyment.

"'Christmas comes but once a year,' as the poet guy says. And, therefore, Ben has a great idea—blamed if that ain't po'try——" he added.

Splash Page chuckled at the look of astonishment in the face of the American at his unconscious rhyme.

"Now, Ben—you spill the beans. I've done my job and rounded up four of the best guys I know, as requested. It's up to you now."

"Well, gentlemen," said Cayterer. "Briefly told, the proposition is this. I have promised my son, Junior, to give him a real Dickens Christmas party. I have rented a place at Lyveden, near the Kentish Coast—Lyveden Manor, said to be the original of the famous Dingley Dell of the 'Pickwick Papers.' It

is the property of Lord Sylvester, and, judging from the photographs I've seen, is a beautiful old-world manor house. Unfortunately, however, I know very few people here in England, and I asked my friend, Hanson, if he could suggest names for a suitable house party on Christmas Eve.

"I have already communicated with the Reverend Ambrose Dale, the vicar of Lyveden, announcing my intention of giving a party to the poor children of the parish on Christmas Eve, and he is very enthusiastic about the idea.

"One or two friends of mine have agreed to join the house-warming, and I hope very much that you will accept my invitation for the Christmas holidays as my guests at Lyveden Manor.

"You are a busy man, I know, Mr. Blake," continued Cayterer, turning to the detective; "but even the busiest people relax at Christmas-time. Please forgive this somewhat unconventional invitation; but my son, Junior, ever since Ruff mentioned he was a friend of yours, is just crazy on having you at the party. I shall feel honoured to entertain you all at Lyveden Manor."

Sexton Blake lit a cigar and his eyes twinkled.

"I might have known from Ruff's elaborate secrecy that there was something in the wind," he remarked. "It is very kind indeed of you, Mr. Cayterer. Speaking personally for myself and Tinker, I shall be delighted to accept your invitation. A Christmas party at Dingley Dell sounds most attractive and original."

"Hear, hear!" said Splash Page and Tinker enthusiastically. "What do you say, Coutts?"

The Yard man cleared his throat.

"Well, Mr.—er—Cayterer, personally, speaking unofficially, I'm faced with rather a dull Christmas, what with the missus going to her folk at Shropshire. I'd very much like to accept—providing, of course, that I'm not on duty at the Yard."

Ben Cayterer's kindly face was wreathed in smiles.

"That's fine!" he said enthusiastically. "I'm leaving to-morrow for Lyveden, and I shall expect you gentlemen early on Christmas Eve. I—er—thought it would add greatly to the fun of the party if we all dressed in the costume of favourite Dickens characters."

"Jove! That's a topping idea," agreed Splash Page, "It looks like being a real, old-fashioned, merry Christmas—one that Dickens himself would love!"

Ruff Hanson bit off the end of a dubious-looking cheroot which Coutts had proffered him.

"I'm kinda hazy about this guy Dickens," he remarked. "But Junior's been putting me wise—and lemme tell the world that kid's got it all under his hat!"

I T was nearly midnight when the joyous little dinner party broke up.

Ruff Hanson and Blake exchanged several diverting reminiscences of the past; but it was not until his departure that the criminologist broached the subject of Ruff's real mission in England.

"I shouldn't relax my vigilance, my dear fellow!" he said gravely. "From what you tell me, danger still threatens the boy. I doubt if the fact of his being in England will prevent an attempt at kidnapping. This Solmann person may be desperate enough to cross the Atlantic to 'fix' Cayterer."

"Let him try!" laughed Ruff Hanson, patting his hip pockets significantly. "I guess Willy and Wally'll attend to him."

As they passed through the lounge together, a dark, saturnine face appeared from behind a sheltering palm. Two ill-assorted eyes glared malevolently after them.

"You wait, Hard-boiled Hanson, my bucko!" muttered Sam McCalla vindictively. "This is where it's 'finish' for you!"

He turned to his companion, a slim, Eton-cropped girl, clad in a close-fitting black-and-silver dress. Her eyes were slant, and her lids plentifully daubed with bistre, but she had a certain arresting, barbaric beauty that carried off her outre clothes and exotic colouring.

"Who's the lean guy talking to Hanson?" queried Sam McCalla.

Lil Brady, alias Liverpool Lil, narrowed her slanting eyes, thus revealing her half-Mongolian origin. Her face whitened beneath its rouge. Her fingers dug into McCalla's arm.

"That's that tec Sexton Blake!" she hissed. "Say, Sam, if—if you want to keep in good with me you've gotta——" She paused, and her full, sensual lips curled into an evil smile. "You've gotta croak that feller!" she whispered. "He's the snitch that sent Larry the Bat to the rope!"

Sam McCalla recoiled from the flaming hatred that shone in the woman's eyes.

He licked his dry lips nervously.

"Sexton Blake, eh?" he repeated. "And yuh want him croaked? You said it, kid. I'll see he gets his Christmas present!"

Chapter 3.

The Coach for Dingley Dell.

IT was the day before Christmas. The streets were crowded with parcel-laden people bending and battling manfully against the keen wind which swept a scurry of snow into their smarting faces. Though it was but early afternoon, the shop windows were gaily lit, and exposed their tempting wares to the hurrying passers-by.

The wind was keen, but there seemed to be a seasonable, boisterous gaiety about it that whipped colour into the cheek of many a tired City worker hurrying to complete his shopping in readiness for the morrow. Tired mothers and fathers forgot their cares and troubles in the joy of spending hard-earned and long-saved money, so that the children's Christmas should indeed be merry. Even the tattered kerbstone hawkers looked less wan and hopeless as they called their wares, for hearts are warmed at Christmastide, and uplifted with the reckless joy of giving.

Fleet Street—that thoroughfare which never sleeps—was thronged with the homeward-bound traffic of the City workers as Mr. Derek Page, the star reporter of the "Daily Radio," emerged from the imposing offices of that go-ahead journal, tucked himself in behind the steering-wheel of his little vermilion two-seater, and tootled off (as he expressed it) in the direction of the Strand.

The darkening twilight had turned suddenly to evening when Splash Page had concluded one or two mysterious errands, including a final visit, by ap-

pointment, to a brightly-lit public-house close to an ancient mews in Covent Garden. There, for some time, he was in conversation with a corpulent, red-faced man, with innumerable chins and a seemingly inexhaustible thirst. The conversation was largely on the subject of horses and how to handle them.

IN Baker Street, Sexton Blake, Tinker, and Detective-Inspector Coutts, of Scotland Yard, were grouped about the fire in the cosy consulting-room. Mrs. Bardell, who had brought up some wine from the cellar, had remained to zealously brush up some ashes in the grate.

"Splash said he'd fix all the costumes," remarked Tinker, with a glance at the clock. "It's nearly five o'clock, and Ruff Hanson ought to be here by now. Wonder what's gone wrong with——"

Even as he spoke a knock sounded at the consulting-room door, and Ruff himself breezed in.

"Howdy, folk! I just had to beat it down from Lyveden," he began in his blunt, unceremonious fashion. "Poor old Ben's nutty! The cook he engaged for Christmas has caught the flu, and was taken to Lyveden hospital this morning. He's beatin' the air and generally raisin' Cain at the employment agencies; but there ain't nothing doin.'"

"By gum! That's hard luck," began Tinker. "Just when we were looking forward to——"

"Forget it, kiddo!" broke in Ruff Hanson. "This is where my Ideas Department comes in! What's wrong with Mrs. B., the English queen of the kitchen, playin' deputy?"

Mrs. Bardell coloured and fidgeted nervously with the fireirons.

"Lawks, Mr. 'Anson, you do say sech things!" she murmured coyly.

"A perfectly splendid notion," said Blake, with a twinkle. "Mrs. Bardell, you see our difficulty. If it doesn't inconvenience you, or upset your previous arrangements, we would be delighted if you came down to superintend the culinary department at Lyveden Manor."

"Lawks!" said Mrs. Bardell. "You mean as 'ow you'd like me to cook your Christmas dinner for you?"

"Precisely," replied Blake. "I think Mr. Hanson's suggestion an admirable one. I'm perfectly certain that no one could cook the meal better than you."

Mrs. Bardell simpered a little and then curtseyed.

"I shall be delighted to oblige, Mr. Blake. I've allus wanted to see the kitchings of them stately 'omes of England, 'ow beautiful they stand, as poor dear Bardell allus used to say when we 'ad our own 'ome—and a nice 'ome it was, too, with adasperisterers——"

Blake's lips twitched slightly. He guessed she meant aspidistras. Paragon among housekeepers and admirable cook though she was, Mrs. Bardell's English was weird and wonderful at times. She used words with the haziest notion of their meaning, so long as they sounded right.

"Then that's settled," said Ruff Hanson, with a grin. "I came down specially to plead with you, Mrs. B. Them waffles you made for me last time I stayed here sure were the kind that momma useter make."

"Pardon me, Mr. 'Anson," she replied. "I presoom I'm to be primerrily in sole charge of the colandery apartment. I don't want no 'ussies of 'ousemaids to dictate to me in the kitching. I am monarch of all I purvey, as B. useter say on a Saturday night when 'e came 'ome from the Dog and Duck."

"You will be in sole charge," Blake

promised. "You needn't worry about the shopping. The provisions are already arranged for, I take it—eh, Ruff?"

"Sure. We've got all the eats," agreed Ruff Hanson.

Down below sounded the tinkle of a bell, and Mrs. Bardell waddled across the consulting-room to answer it.

"By Jove! That was a brain-wave of yours," commented Coutts. "My missus is a bit of a dab at cooking, but Mrs. Bardell beats her hollow."

"God rest you merry gentlemen; may nothing you dismay," called the cheery voice of Splash Page from the doorway a few moments later.

The newspaperman's motoring coat was powdered with snow, and he staggered under the weight of three bulky parcels.

"Costumes, fancy, tecs for the use of, as they used to say in the Army," he announced, with a grin. "Catch, Tinker!" He flung a bulky package at the lad, who caught it deftly. "I've fixed 'em all up. I got the best in the shop. Question is, who's going to wear which?"

Coutts grinned sheepishly.

"I'm not much of a hand at this carnival business, Splash," he muttered. "I don't quite see where I fit in, somehow."

Splash Page chuckled.

"I've got the very character for you to impersonate, Coutts. Fit you like a glove. The most popular in 'Pickwick,' after Sam Weller, which is Tinker's role."

"Suits me all right," grinned Tinker. "But what have you got for old Coutts?"

"He takes the part of the Fat Boy—always asleep, when he's not trying to make our flesh creep," replied Splash.

There was a roar of laughter, in which Coutts joined good-humouredly.

"Symbolic of Scotland Yard, I call it," added the newspaper man, with a chuckle.

"You ought to be Mr. Potts, the editor of the 'Eatanswill Gazette,' my lad!" retorted Coutts. "A bully journalist who always made a hash of things."

"Say. Where do I fit in this outfit?" cut in Ruff Hanson. "Dickens don't seem to have written a part for a hard-boiled egg."

"Hasn't he though!" protested Splash, unwrapping a parcel. "Here's your rig-out, my lad." He uncovered a shabby-looking surtout, a curly-brimmed felt hat, and nankeen trousers. "Here's the very garb for you, Ruff. Fit you like a glove!"

"D'ye expect me to wear them duds?" ejaculated Ruff, recoiling from the costume. "Who in tarnation ever wore clothes like this?"

"Bill Sikes, the celebrated burglar," replied Splash sweetly.

Blake's eyes twinkled.

"And what role has your fertile imagination assigned to me, Splash?" he inquired.

"Sydney Carton!" replied the journalist promptly. "Because it's the Only Way, and this Christmas is a far, far better thing than you have ever done."

"How about you?" demanded Tinker.

For answer Splash Page opened his leather motoring-coat, revealing a bottle-green surtout of old-fashioned cut, with a dirty shirt and a wispy collar. A monocle dangled from a threadbare piece of cord, and with a flourish he placed a battered high felt hat at a rakish angle on his head.

"Behold in me, Alfred Jingle, of No Hall, Nowhere!" he said, striking a theatrical air.

"Jove! That's good!" said Tinker enthusiastically. "Come on, Coutts, let's climb into our glad rags; we've got tons of make-up in the dressing-room!"

"I refuse to go as the Fat Boy," grumbled Coutts. "It'd bring disrespect on the Yard, and—and——"

"Don't be an ass, Couttsy!" chuckled Splash. "That was only my fun. Look at this handsome and elegant costume, my lad. You're going to be Mr. Tracy Tupman, that stout and gallant breaker of hearts."

"Say, can't you give me a line on this guy Sikes?" pleaded Ruff Hanson, as he dubiously tried on his faded felt hat. "Was he a second-story man, or a dip, or what?"

"He murdered Nancy and kidnapped Oliver Twist," explained Splash soothingly.

Ruff picked up the nankeen trousers and scratched his head dubiously.

"I'm all of a twist myself, I guess," he remarked. "But I'll try anything once. Let's go."

HALF an hour later Mrs. Bardell tapped at the consulting-room door and gave a little scream of alarm at the amazing transformation that met her gaze.

Lounging in a saddlebag chair, with his lean, ascetic face in startling contrast to the long, untidy wig he was wearing, was Sydney Carton, who looked vaguely like that famous criminologist, Sexton Blake.

A hulking ruffian with a muffler round his bull-like neck leered horribly at the good soul, while a corpulent-looking gentleman in tights and a navy blue surtout winked at her deliberately.

"Ouch!" gasped Mrs. Bardell.

Splash Page, in his role of Jingle, bowed sweepingly.

"Your pardon—should explain—Christmas Eve—spirit of carnival—revelry by night—sorry to alarm you—very," he said in the staccato, telegrammatic manner of Dickens' immortal Jingle.

"Mr. Pige!" squeaked Mrs. Bardell. "Lawks, 'ow you did give me a turn! I 'ardly reckernised you in that there get up. Which I was wondering when we was a-goin' to start for Lyveden Manor."

"At once," answered Blake. "I hope you're ready, Mrs. B.? Tinker, phone for the Grey Panther."

Tinker, who made an admirable Sam Weller in his dark livery and striped waistcoat, set his cockaded hat at a jaunty angle.

"Granted as soon as asked, as the Balham skivvy said when the ten stun gen'l'man trod on 'er toe," he remarked.

He was about to cross over to the instrument when, above the ceaseless hum of traffic in Baker Street, sounded the clear, high note of a coaching-horn.

T'an-ta-ra tantiry tantiry!

It was followed by the clip-clop-clippetty clop of horses' hoofs.

"What the deuce——" began Coutts, crossing over to the window.

Through the whirling, feathery snowflakes he saw the dim shape of an ancient stage-coach drawn up before the door, and already surrounded by a gathering crowd. The four horses snorted and pawed the ground impatiently. The driver, an enormously fat man clad in a multiplicity of overcoats, drew in the reins, while at the back a guard continued his fanfare.

SPLASH PAGE chuckled with delight.

"A little surprise for you, my lords; the stage-coach waits without!"

"Holy Heinz!" ejaculated Ruff Hanson. "You've gone crazy, Splash."

"You utterly preposterous person!" said Sexton Blake, with twitching lips.

"Do you seriously expect us to travel down to Lyveden in that, Splash?"

"Sure I do!" said the newspaperman blandly. "Hang it all, it's Christmas Eve! Let's give these poor perishing moderns a thrill. Their lives are grey and unromantic enough. Think how it'll cheer 'em up in the little Surrey villages to see Dickens' characters bowling through on a stage-coach at Christmas Eve!"

"Who's the lean guy talking to Hanson?" queried the man at the table. "That's that 'tec, Sexton Blake," hissed the girl. "Say, Sam, if you want to keep in good with me, you've gotta croak that feller!"

Tinker's eyes sparkled with excitement.

"Fine! What a lark, Splash! Come on, guv'nor! I've never ridden in a stage-coach. We can stop at all the old-fashioned inns on the way—if any—and I bet we'll be welcomed with open arms!"

"We'll be had up for causing an obstruction, Blake—see if we won't," Coutts grunted. "Of all the fool things this crazy journalist's put over, this is the daftest!"

"Now that the carriage waits without, I see no help for it," exclaimed Blake. "If we keep it waiting much longer there certainly will be an obstruction in Baker Street, and we shall spend Christmas at Bow Street!"

TAN-TA-RA! Tan-ta-ra!

A shrill blast rose above the busy hum of traffic in Baker Street. The corpulent driver, his red face purple in the keen north wind, clucked his tongue and gathered in the reins.

"Merry Christmas, everybody!" yelled Splash Page joyously, from the top of the coach.

"Merry Christmas!" roared the crowd as the stage-coach, with the accompaniment of jingling harness and rumbling wheels, started its historic journey through the snow-laden twilight of Baker Street for the open road beyond.

Tinker felt his blood thrill in the keen wind as he and Splash Page waved their hats gaily to the staring throng below.

"This is great, Splash!" he chuckled enthusiastically. "A Christmas in a lifetime!"

There was a smile of beatific happiness on the red face of Detective-Inspector Coutts as he lit up one of Blake's excellent cigars in defiance of anachronisms.

"Does one good to relax a bit, eh, Blake, old friend?" he exclaimed. "Too much hustle and rush about modern life. This is the way to travel!"

Sexton Blake nodded. His eyes were a trifle abstracted as he stared at the twinkling lights in the shop windows, with their tempting array of presents. The greengrocers and poulterers were doing a roaring trade, and the provision stores were packed with eager shoppers, as they passed on their triumphant way; yet none were too busy or preoccupied to turn and smile and wave their hands as the coach rumbled by.

It was a spontaneous tribute from the people of England to the noble genius of Dickens, who, more than anyone, has kept alive the spirit of Christmas. Somewhere, his kindly shade smiled down on the incarnation of his immortal dream-children, well content that Yuletide was still a "kind, good, forgiving charitable time," and that even in the twentieth century, with its radio and aeroplanes, Englishmen still kept his memory green.

The streets of Town gave way to the pleasant, winding roads of Surrey,

white and ghostly beneath their mantle of snow. The wind whistled eerily through the gaunt branches of the trees, overcoming the fainter noise of the horses' hoofs on the snow-muffled road.

"Kinda hits me where I live, Blake," said Ruff Hanson—"this England of yours. I ain't a sentimental guy, but it kinda holds you."

He pointed through the snow to where the orange glow of a cottage window shone a welcome through the trees; and across the heath was borne the chime of the Christmas bells ringing out their message of peace and goodwill to men.

Tinker and Splash Page slewed round

in their seats and grinned cheerfully at the older men, to whom the spirit of Christmas Eve and the peaceful countryside had brought back memories, grave and gay, from the years that had passed.

"How about a little community carol singing, Coutts?" suggested Splash. "We change horses at the next village, and I'm going to stand Mrs. B. a bottle of pineapple rum, blamed if I don't!"

With that Splash and Tinker began lustily, if unmelodiously, to burst out with

"Good King Wenceslas looked out
On the feast of Stephen,
When the snow lay round about,
Deep and crisp and even."

There was something so infectious about the age-old carol and the exhilaration of that romantic ride that soon everybody joined in, including a voice from the interior of the coach itself, as that excellent woman, Mrs. Martha Bardell, quaveringly took up the melody.

Chapter 4.

The Spirit of Christmas.

LYVEDEN MANOR was en fete. The old house, with its mullioned windows agleam with light, its age-old eaves glistening beneath a mantle of snow in the wan moonlight, against a background of whispering elms, echoed and re-echoed to the happy laughter of delighted children.

"Yoicks and tally-ho!" roared Tinker, as the coach clattered through the lichened stone gateway, with its carved griffins on either side, and swept up the snow-covered drive.

"Tom, give her a toot!" urged Splash to the red-faced guard, a Covent Garden ostler, delighting in the new role he was enacting.

Tan-ta-ra! blew Tom on his silver trumpet.

"Whoa, there!"

Old Jim Ridge, ex-cabby, and now, for one night only, driver of the Christmas stage, drew in his horses with a flourish as the ancient oak doorway of Lyveden Manor opened and a white-haired butler stood blinking in astonishment at the sight before him.

Ruff Hanson nudged Sexton Blake.

"That's old Parsons, the butler I was telling you about. Been in Lord Sylvester's service for donkeys' years. More like an archbishop than a blamed butler!"

Tom, the guard, hurriedly fixed the ladder to the rail of the coach, just as the rotund, well-knit frame of Ben Cayterer emerged from the hallway.

He stared in astonishment as Splash Page, not waiting for the ladder, clambered down the side of the coach and bowed, with a flourish of his battered hat.

The snow had almost ceased falling, and he made a ghostly, impressive figure with his early-nineteenth-century garments on the lawn of the ancient manor-house.

"Alfred Jingle—your hand, sir! Glad to see you—very!" said the journalist.

Ben Cayterer flung back his head and gave a gargantuan roar of laughter, in which Splash joined.

He noticed that the movie magnate was clad in the swallow-tailed coat, the white tights, and immortal gaiters of the founder of the Pickwick Club.

"Lands sakes, Mr. Page!" said Cayterer. "Did you travel all the way by stage-coach? By Jove, how topping! I wish I'd thought of it!" he added enthusiastically.

"Ooh, dad," chirped a boy's voice, "is it real?"

From the hallway emerged a tiny, pathetic little figure, clad in the quaint peg-top trousers and tasselled hat of the schoolboys of a century ago.

He had a crutch under one arm, but his little face was radiant with happiness as he beheld the champing, steaming horses and the brilliant paintwork of the stage-coach.

"Tiny Tim, as I live!" yelled Ruff Hanson delightedly. "Say, Sydney Carton, clap your eyes on Bob Cratchit's youngest son!"

Little Junior Cayterer's eyes sparkled with joy as he saw Tinker and Splash and Blake descend from the roof of the coach. Suddenly a bonneted head emerged from the interior of the coach and Splash rushed to open the door.

"Mr. Cay—er—I mean Pickwick,

meet an old friend of yours—Mrs. Bardell—direct descendant of the famous Mrs. Bardell, of Goswell Road, whom you doubtless remember."

Ben Cayterer smiled as he helped the somewhat breathless housekeeper from the coach.

"Say, Mrs. Bardell," he said cordially, "this is more than good of you to fill the breach, in the circumstances."

Mrs. Bardell gazed about her rather helplessly for a moment. Her black bombazine dress rustled as she followed the others into the spacious hall.

"Which I'll have you know, Mr. Pige," she announced, in a loud whisper, "that, fancy dress or no fancy dress, I ain't agoin' to wear trousers—not at my time of life, young man."

"Wear trousers?" gasped the astonished newspaper man. "Who on earth suggested it, Mrs. B.?"

"'Im in the gaiters," replied Mrs. Bardell, with dignity. "He said something about me filling somebody's breeches—but not if I know it!" she added, clutching her umbrella pugnaciously.

"Oh, my hat!" exploded Tinker. "He means he's glad you are going to do the cooking, Mrs. B., and that it's jolly decent of you to come."

"Ah!" said Mrs. Bardell, somewhat mollified; then she turned as a tiny hand clutched her sleeve and the piping voice of Junior demanded earnestly:

"Please are you reely Mrs. Bardell?"

The housekeeper smiled kindly.

"Why, in course, my lamb—Martha Bardell, a widow woman this past twenty years."

"And, please, do you still let lodgings to single gen'l'men, like it says in the Pickwick Papers?" persisted Junior, his large, grave eyes looking up seriously.

Mrs. Bardell gave a rich chuckle.

"Mr. Blake and Mr. Tinker are still single gen'l'men, my dear," she said, "and I does my best to look arter them."

Junior smiled his sweet grave smile, as he hobbled painfully along at her side.

"When Parsons has shown you your room, I'd like you to see my Chrissmuss tree. I like you, Mrs. Bardell—I wish you were my nurse instead of Miss Brown. She—she thinks 'magination is silly."

"Bless the child!" said the good soul, her heart warming to the motherless bairn. "You and me's going to be great friends."

Blake and Cayterer winked significantly at each other, and Parsons, the butler, hovered like some grave archdeacon at the foot of the stairs.

"Show Mrs. Bardell to her quarters, Parsons—she must be fatigued after her journey. What about something warming, gentlemen, before we join the party? You must have had a cold ride."

"Sound idea!" agreed Splash Page. "I presume, by the way, you've got room for Jim Rudge, the coachman, and Tom? I had a deuce of a job to hire that stage-coach, Mr. Cayterer."

"By all means, my dear fellow—there's plenty of room in the servants' hall." He signalled to a footman. "Williams, see that the driver and his mate have a good meal, and—er—plenty of beer. This way, Mr. Blake!" he added, passing through the spacious hallway, gaily decked with paper streamers, holly, and mistletoe, and branches of yew. From behind a closed doorway came the merry strains of fiddles, playing away for dear life, and the laughter of children.

Ben Cayterer opened the door, and Tinker stared at the cheerful scene that met his gaze.

IT was a long room—brilliantly lit by a glittering chandelier.

A huge log fire blazed in the wide, old-fashioned brick fireplace.

The raftered roof was hung with festoons of evergreen, and coloured lanterns gave a rosy glow to the happy faces of some thirty children who were playing musical chairs to the tune of the fiddle, played by a thin-faced, lank-haired man, who looked like Uriah Heap.

In the corner was a gigantic Christmas-tree, glittering with dozens and dozens of tiny candles, sparkling with silver, and glinting with gold. It was laden with crackers, bon-bons, chocolate boxes, toys, and all sorts of enchantments to gladden the hearts of the little ones.

Ben Cayterer's kindly face glowed as he led his party up the old time-worn stairs that led to the minstrel gallery. A group of people sat there, watching the children romping below with the care-free innocence of childhood. They were all clad in Dickens costume, save for a tall, silver-haired old gentleman, who wore clerical clothes.

"Mr. Blake, I want you to meet Rev. Ambrose Lane, the Vicar of Lyveden, to whose good offices I owe the success of my kiddies' party," said Cayterer.

The vicar smiled as he shook hands with the distinguished criminologist.

"Delighted to know you, Mr. Blake," he said warmly. "Mr. Cayterer told me you were coming down. I am not in costume at the moment," he added, with a laugh—for a reason that may later on be apparent."

"The reverend's gonna play Santa Claus," explained Ruff Hanson, in a Bill Sikes-ish whisper.

"My daughter Enid, Mr. Blake," said the vicar, as he presented a slim, piquantly pretty young lady, bewitchingly attired in the charming costume of Dolly Varden.

One by one the members of the little house party were introduced. Sir Anthony Trent, the bluff squire of Lyveden Hall, the neighbouring estate; his wife and daughters; Colonel Rushton, who made an imposing Mr. Bumble; and several other people prominent in Lyveden, completed the grown-up element of the party.

"I guess Junior's lost his heart to your housekeeper, Mr. Blake," said Ben Cayterer, as they strolled into the adjoining lounge. "It's mighty good of her to come down and help us out over Christmas."

Blake laughed.

"She is only too delighted, poor soul. She would have been very lonely in Baker Street," he remarked. "By the way, what was Sir Julius Rome's verdict about the little fellow, Mr. Cayterer?"

Ben Cayterer's eyes shone.

"There's hope, Mr. Blake!" he said earnestly. "Sir Julius thinks an operation, though risky, may prove successful. He is willing to perform it on the understanding that I take a fifty-fifty chance. But it's worth it! I intend to put Junior in a nursing home after the holidays, and then—well, we can only hope."

Blake nodded, and sipped his drink.

"Sir Julius is a very cautious man," he remarked. "If he thinks there is a chance, then it's most certainly worth taking. I hope sincerely the operation will be a success."

"Thanks, Mr. Blake," said Ben Cayterer huskily. "It—it means a good deal to me."

"By the way," resumed the criminologist, lowering his voice, "have you heard anything further re the fascinating Mr. Isidore Solmann? It would be as well not to relax your

vigilance—he seems to be a dangerous enemy."

Ben Cayterer laughed.

"Hang Izzy! I've heard nothing since I sailed. I guess he's too cautious to try any tricks in England; he might have done in New York, but with Ruff Hanson around—he's got a fat chance!"

A knock sounded at the door of the lounge, and the handle turned slowly. A moment later Pedro, the majestic bloodhound, entered, accompanied by little Cayterer Junior, his boyish face flushed with excitement.

"Look, daddy!" he piped. "Mrs. Bardell interdooced me to Pedro. Isn't he a scrumptuous dog—and so polite! Why, he knocked at the door with his tail before coming in."

Pedro's noble head and mournful eyes rose a little as he saw his master, and Blake's eyes twinkled.

"I think Master Pedro ought to go to bed, don't you, Mr. Cayterer?" he suggested. "He's getting rather too old for Christmas parties!"

"P'raps you're right, Mr. Blake," said Junior gravely. "May I give him a bone, and make him comfy?"

"Surely, son, but mind you take Parsons with you. Pedro can sleep in the stables and dream about rabbits. Hurry up, or you'll be late for Santa Claus."

The little boy clutched Pedro's collar, and obediently trotted out of the room.

"Fine dog that, Mr. Blake," commented Cayterer. "Gentle as a lamb, with children, eh?"

"With children, yes," repeated Blake, with emphasis. "But I'm afraid Mr. Isidore Solmann wouldn't notice much gentleness."

"Hey, you guys!" boomed Ruff Hanson from the doorway. "What's the big idea? The stage is all set for Santa Claus, and here you are mopping up hooch like a coupla bootleggers."

Blake rose to his feet with a cluck of annoyance.

"Of course—how careless of me! I've forgotten the parcel. See you in a moment, Mr. Cayterer."

He strode rapidly down the hallway and climbed the stairs to his bed-room.

MEANWHILE the fun in the raftered dining-room was growing fast and furious.

Musical chairs had given place to blind man's buff, and the shrieks of laughter when Splash Page chased the corpulent Colonel Rushton, until they both fell sprawling over the coal scuttle, rang throughout the ancient manor. Blake found the Rev. Ambrose Dale busily affixing the long white beard of St. Nicholas when he returned to the minstrel gallery with his parcel.

"A few toys for the little ones, vicar," he said.

The Rev. Dale smiled his thanks.

"Very kind of you, Mr. Blake," he said. "Do you know, I think Christmas is the best time, because it is the kindest time. Lyveden is a very poor parish, and for weeks I have been worried about the kiddies and how to give them a Christmas treat—yet, here, as though it was an answer to prayer, Mr. Cayterer throws open this house for their benefit. Bless you both, Mr. Blake!"

Sexton Blake's austere face flushed a little.

"Christmas belongs to the children, vicar," he said quietly. "It is the least we can do in return for the joy that Dickens gave us—to see that the youngsters have theirs."

Splash Page and Tinker, hot, perspiring, but thoroughly happy, were the life and soul of the party. Ruff

Hanson in one corner was regaling a crowd of small boys with tales of breathless adventure in Texas, when the magic name of Santa Claus was announced.

Instantly there was a hush as the scarlet-robed figure descended the stairs and took his place at the Christmas tree.

Ben Cayterer, beaming down benevolently from his seat in the minstrel gallery, was joined by Ruff Hanson. The American grinned cheerfully.

"Say, Ben, I'm all-fired glad I took this job!" he said. "I'm tickled to death with a Dickens Christmas."

It was a merry ceremony that followed. Thirty pairs of eyes gazed eagerly and expectantly at the Christmas tree as Santa Claus began to distribute its glittering gifts.

Amid frantic happiness and noisy jollity, the evening passed, and about ten o'clock thirty tired, but thoroughly happy children left for home in charge of parents or guardians, their arms full of toys and heaven knows how many delectable enticements.

"Well, that's that!" breathed Ben Cayterer at length. Enjoy your real Dickens party, son?"

Little Junior's eyes glowed like stars.

"It was splendiferous, dad," he said eagerly. "I enjoyed it more'n anything I've ever had. I—I think Mr. Dickens would have enjoyed it, too. Don't you think so, Mr. Blake?"

Blake's look softened as he met the gaze of those serious brown eyes.

"I'm sure of it, sonny," he said gravely.

"Run along to bed, son," counselled his father. "Santa Claus will drop in on you soon. He's busy getting some more toys."

Junior turned obediently and raised his little tasselled cap.

"Good-night, everybody!" he piped, in his cricket's chirp of a voice. "I'm Tiny Tim, you know, so I can say, God bless us every one!"

And there was an unwonted tenderness in the eyes of even the youthful Tinker as he gazed after the frail little figure limping slowly out of the room.

Chapter 5.

Christmas Ghosts.

SUPPER had been served. Round the crackling oak Yule logs in the spacious fireplace of the library were grouped the remaining members of Ben Cayterer's Christmas house-party.

Colonel Rushton, still clad in his robes of Bumbledom; Sir Anthony Trent, who made a rollicking Micawber; Ruff Hanson, looking ferociously villainous as Bill Sikes; and the famous Baker Street trio—Blake, Tinker, and Mrs. Bardell—and, finally, Detective-Inspector Coutts.

The vicar of Lyveden and Enid had been prevailed upon to stay the night, for the wind howled menacingly down the chimney. The vicarage was a good four miles from the manor, and the good clergyman was loath to exchange the comforts of the cosy hearth for the blustering north-easter that rattled the mullioned windows with boisterous glee.

Ben Cayterer had invited Mrs. Bardell to join the guests, and that good soul, embarrassed at first by the attention shown to her, lost a good deal of

her shyness after sipping the excellent '51 port from Lord Sylvester's well-stocked cellar. Enid Dale, looking bewitchingly pretty in her flowered Dolly Varden dress, was deep in conversation with Ben Cayterer.

Splash Page was arguing about the War with Colonel Rushton, while Blake was discussing the conclusion of Dickens' unfinished novel—"Edwin Drood"—with Sir Anthony Trent.

Ruff Hanson winked slyly at Tinker on the couch and whispered below his breath:

"Look at old Ben, kiddo! Seems mighty interested in Miss Dale, don't he?"

Tinker nodded, and slyly jerked his thumb over his shoulder.

On the sofa that fascinating Lothario, Mr. Tracy Tupman—alias Detective-Inspector Coutts—was gazing up admiringly at Mrs. Bardell, who was evidently holding him enthralled with pearls of culinary wisdom.

Scraps of their conversation reached Tinker, and he grinned with amusement.

"It's the hoysters that do it, Susspector," she said. "I'll write out the reci-pie for stuffing roast turkey so's your missus kin 'ave it 'andy. You beards the hoysters, mix 'em with the breadcrumbs, 'erbs, and seasonin', add a little more egg to bind the forcemeat, an'——"

The worthy C.I.D. man hung on every word of that admirable cook's recipe. Coutts was a good trencherman, and had a terrific admiration for Mrs. Bardell's cooking. There were times when he privately compared that estimable woman to his wife, and felt faintly resentful that Blake should have secured such a paragon.

A mocking hoo hoo! sounded down the chimney, followed by the hiss of the blazing logs as a shower of sleet, blackened by soot, fell into the grate. Mrs. Bardell clutched Coutts' sleeve, and her left hand flew to her black bombazine bosom.

"Oh, Mr. Coutts, I'm that skeered! That old himage, Parsons, told me as 'ow this 'ouse is 'aunted."

There was a lull in the general conversation, and Ruff Hanson's nasal voice drawled.

"Say, Ben, Mrs. B. says there's a spook in this place. Did you rent that along with the rest of the house?"

The millionaire shook his head.

"No, there was no mention of any ghost, as far as I know," he remarked.

Splash Page chuckled and pointed to the ancient grandfather clock which tick-tocked solemnly in the corner.

"'Tis now the witching hour of night, when churchyards yawn and graves give up their dead!" he chanted solemnly.

Mrs. Bardell gave a stifled scream.

"I declare, Mr. Pige, you give me the fair creeps!" she protested. "As poor B. useter say, 'There's more things in 'eaven than are dreamt of in your phrenology.'"

Tinker's lips twitched. He felt a malicious desire to draw Mrs. B. out. Her malapropisms were things not exactly of beauty but joys for ever.

"Did you ever see a ghost, Mrs. B.?" he queried innocently.

"That I did, Master Tinker, and a gashly sight it were," she said. "It was while me and poor B. were courting. 'E took me to a circus one day, and we went to see 'Marier Marten, or the Murder in the Red Barn.' It froze the marrer in my bones, as the saying is. I was all worked up. The ghost of the pore murdered Marier came to the wretch in the condemned cell, howling somethink awful. Her nightdress was

all covered in blood, and the willain screeches out somethink about 'Remorse—remorse! My kingdom for remorse!' and she varnishes before my very hyes into thin hair, as the saying goes."

The company's exclamations or smiles, or even laughs, were suddenly stilled as the old clock in the corner began to chime the midnight hour. Sir Anthony Trent glanced up at the large, sombre oil-painting of a dark, saturnine man dressed in Elizabethan costume.

"I say, padre, it's Christmas Eve, and all that, what? How about telling us that ghost story of yours about jolly old Hugo the Headless? You know all the facts, and his portrait up there will give us all the right atmosphere."

The Rev. Ambrose Dale smiled benignly and lit his cigar.

"Well, ladies and gentlemen, it is a Dickens' Christmas Eve, and, in short, I am quite agreeable. It's certainly a weird story, and——"

"Lawks, sir, you give me the fair creeps already!" broke in Mrs. Bardell, glancing at the painting hurriedly. "If it's worse than Marier Marten——"

She broke off suddenly. Above the sough of the wind and the pelting hail that lashed the mullioned windows came a long, mournful wail that seemed to hold a world of agony in its depths.

"What's that?" gasped Splash Page, starting to his feet.

Crash!

EVEN as the newspaper-man spoke that unnervingly sudden sound startled the occupants of the cosy library. Enid Dale, white and trembling, pointed a shaking finger at the panelled wall.

"Daddy, daddy, look—the portrait of Sir Hugo!" she cried.

A dazed silence fell on the group—for the portrait in its heavy gilded frame had crashed to the floor, face downwards.

Sexton Blake quietly crossed over to the fallen picture. His action was so deftly methodical that it soothed their overwrought nerves. The criminologist examined the worn wire that had held the portrait to the picture rail—then he shrugged his shoulders.

"H'm! Queer coincidence, gentlemen. The wire has snapped. It is evidently very old and brittle."

Mrs. Bardell rose to her feet, her usually placid face was flushed.

"Which I says that I'm going to bed, gen'l'men," she announced firmly. "I don't 'old with 'orrors—not by no means. I'm also locking my bed-room door. Gen'l'men didn't oughter wander about arter midnight, with or without 'eads, as this 'Eadless Gentleman must have done. The vicar 'ere is a spirituous adviser, and I 'opes 'e advises this 'ere spirit to for ever 'old 'is peace."

She turned to the Reverend Ambrose, who coughed a little uneasily.

"Er—I'm sorry if I have scared you, ladies," he stammered. "Perhaps it was a little injudicious of me to offer to tell that particular story—but you demanded a ghost story, you know!"

Sexton Blake smiled.

"I presume the apparition of Sir Hugo is supposed to haunt the manor in the approved headless ghost fashion?"

"That is the legend—but whether it is true or not, I cannot say," replied the clergyman.

"I'd like to see that spook," broke in Ruff Hanson grimly. "Willy and Waliv are mighty good psychic investigators!" He patted his hip-pocket significantly.

Ben Cayterer yawned and glanced at the clock.

"Guess I'll slip up and see how Junior is," he remarked uneasily. "I've got a pillow-slip full of toys to deposit by his bed. He's still a firm believer in Santa Claus."

Sexton Blake was very thoughtful as Mrs. Bardell and Enid took their departure. The vicar followed their example later, and Coutts, Tinker, Ruff Hanson, and Blake were left to themselves, and began to discuss the curious incident of the fallen picture.

They broke off suddenly as a strangled exclamation from the doorway caused them to turn their heads.

Ben Cayterer stood there—his face livid. In his hand he held a dagger and a slip of paper. From his open mouth came strange, unintelligible noises that were scarcely human.

But it was his eyes that gripped Blake's attention—they were terror-filled and almost protuberant.

"My—my Heaven, Mr. Blake!" he gasped. "They—they've got Junior!"

He swayed and would have fallen had Blake not supported him.

"Brace up, Mr. Cayterer!" commanded the detective sharply. "Brandy, Tinker——"

The youngster leapt to the sideboard and poured out a stiff peg of the cordial. Gradually Ben Cayterer's face cleared, but his fingers were trembling as he held out the crumpled slip of paper.

"I found this, transfixed by the dagger to Junior's pillow!" he said huskily. "My kiddie's gone! For Heaven's sake, Mr. Blake, advise me! I—I don't—What shall I do?"

Blake took the document, which was typed on an ordinary sheet of slate-grey notepaper. The dagger-slit in the top right-hand corner was about half an inch wide. The message, though brief, was sinister with import:

"Got your kid. Twenty thousand bucks and Spagoni's spiel, and you'll get him back. Wire acceptance to Juniper, 4a, Sago Street, Pimlico—and keep out the bulls or—it's curtains."

— —

Chapter 6.

Business as Usual.

"**B**LUEBELLS!" roared Ruff Hanson. "They've got the kid! C'mon, Blake, let's go! Ben, I'm a gink that oughta be kicked from here to Hoboken! But by the Great Horned Toad, I'll get these guys, and get 'em good!"

The dynamic American had leapt to his feet, a grim, fighting look on his weather-beaten face.

"It's not your fault, Ruff," said Ben Cayterer wearily. "I might have known that——"

"Not my fault!" roared Ruff. "Say, you hired me to protect that kid, and while I was down here the plug-ugly Yid——"

"Never mind that now!" snapped Sexton Blake. "Where is Junior's bedroom?"

Ben Cayterer unsteadily led the way up the wide, old-fashioned staircase. He halted on the first landing, and pushed open a bed-room door, revealing a bright, cosy room in which a gas-fire glowed, and an oaken bedstead took up most of the room. There was a communicating door, and Ben jerked his finger towards it.

"That leads to my bed-room."

"H'm!" said the detective slowly. "Was this door locked?"

The millionaire shook his head.

"No, sir, I never dreamt it was necessary, with so many of us in the house," he said brokenly. "My kid!"

His voice trailed off miserably, and his eyes held a stricken look.

"Help! There it goes again!" roared Ruff Hanson, holding a stubby finger

aloft. "What the blue blazes is it, Blake?"

The wind had now fallen somewhat, and, high and shrill, came a repetition of the ghastly, inhuman wail that had startled Mrs. Bardell in the library.

Sexton Blake rapidly took command of the situation.

"Ruff, you and Splash make a tour of the grounds," he ordered. "Coutts, you'd better investigate the hallway and first floor, and see if any doors have been left open. Tinker, you join Ruff—take Pedro."

He stopped and picked up a tiny shoe and handed it to his assistant. His calm, matter-of-fact manner did a good deal towards steadying the millionaire's almost frenzied anxiety.

Ruff and Splash, with Tinker at their heels, hurried downstairs. Parsons, in the hallway, approached the American deferentially.

"Er—is anything wrong, sir? I was about to retire when——"

"Report to Mr. Blake!" snapped Ruff as he unbolted the hall door. "Mr. Cayterer's son has been kidnapped!"

The manservant's jaw dropped.

"Good 'Eavens, sir! Master Junior kidnapped?" he echoed. "You don't mean to——"

"Snap into it!" snarled Ruff, and the butler recoiled at the ferocious fashion with which the American produced his wicked-looking six guns as he stepped out into the blustery night.

It was pitch-dark in the gardens of Lyveden Manor. The wind soughed through the branches of the elms, and the sleet cut and stung their faces like a thousand thongs.

"You take the rear of the house, Splash!" ordered Ruff. "Tinker, go

get the dawg! I'll scoot up the driveway."

The American parked one of his guns at his hip, and flashed on his electric pocket-lamp. He made a queerly sinister figure in the storm, clad in the rough garments of Bill Sikes and a scowl twisting his battered features.

He flashed his light on the gravelled drive, which was now ankle-deep in sleet and slush. Many motors had arrived at Lyveden Manor that night; the ruts and tracks of various makes of tyres crossed and re-crossed each other in hopeless confusion. He could make out faintly the wheel-marks of the stage-coach, but, in view of the sodden state of the ground and the incessant sleet, it was almost hopeless to pick out anything less unusual in that mass of motor-car tracks.

Suddenly there came a deep-throated bay, and Tinker appeared from the dark outline of the stables, holding Pedro on a leash.

"Found anything, Ruff?" he yelled.

"Nary a thing!" roared the American. "What about the dog—gotta line on the trail yet?"

Tinker shook his head.

"Seems a bit fogged—and I don't blame the old boy! If, as I suspect, the kidnappers came by car, Pedro won't be able to pick up the scent."

Ruff Hanson and Tinker plodded on silently towards the huge ornamental gates of the Manor house. Then, sud-

13

denly through the storm, they heard the chug-chug of a high-powered motor-car, and two yellow beams cut through the darkness.

Together they raced to the gates, just as a gleaming yellow car hurtled along the roadway. They caught a glimpse of a dark figure crouched over the wheel, and Ruff Hanson flashed his torch at the vehicle. In one split second he caught a glimpse of the driver. His face was hidden behind a black mask.

Crack!

With the speed of light Ruff Hanson's

They met Splash Page at the entrance, but the journalist had little to report. All the windows were securely fastened, and the back door was locked and bolted.

"Whoever pulled the coup must have got in by the front, or one of the bed-room windows!" he announced.

MEANWHILE, Sexton Blake was conducting a minute examination of the missing boy's bed-room. Most of the little fellow's Tiny Tim clothes were neatly

The detective strode towards the communicating door and pulled it open. Instantly a keen current of air blew in from an open window.

"Ah!" said Blake significantly, as he crossed over to the sill and flashed his torch to the depths below. "See! A most convenient stack-pipe, Mr. Cayterer! The mystery of ingress and egress is solved."

"But I can't understand why Junior didn't cry out or scream, Mr. Blake. I always warned him not to speak to strange men or to accept anything from them. He was an obedient little kid, and I bet he'd have hollered like blazes if there was a stranger in his bed-room."

Blake stooped, and his keen gaze fell on the heavy portiere curtains that bellied out in the night wind from the open window.

Suddenly he shot out a finger and thumb, and seized a minute fluffy object from the heavy plush, and placed it carefully in his wallet.

"Found a clue, Mr. Blake?" Ben Cayterer was watching him curiously.

"Maybe," was the cryptic reply. "I'm inclined to think that it was not a stranger that entered Junior's room to-night, but a very old and very familiar friend."

The millionaire stared at Blake with astonishment.

"An old friend?" he echoed. "Good heavens, Blake, you don't mean to insinuate that——"

"I insinuate nothing at the moment," was the quiet reply. "Come, I see Tinker and Ruff racing across the lawn. There is evidently something doing."

Together they descended to the hall-way, and while Ruff recounted their adventure with the yellow car, Tinker called up the local police at Lyveden.

"The man was masked, you say?" demanded Sexton Blake.

Ruff Hanson nodded.

"I only caught a glimpse of him, old-timer, but I swear his dial was covered from eyes to chin. Then again, he returned Wally's compliment pronto—or perhaps it was his pal in the tonneau. They're the crooks all right, Blake, and I bet they'll be nabbed within an hour."

Sexton Blake shook his head slightly.

"In the first place, that may be a fake number," he remarked. "Furthermore, they can easily abandon the car, and I confess I'm curious to know why they loitered about so long, once they had kidnapped the boy.

"Junior was abducted at least an hour ago; why, then, should these miscreants in the yellow car hang about the neighbourhood when it was all to their advantage to get away?"

Ruff Hanson scratched his bullet head.

"Beats me," he said. "But say, how d'you figure it out that it was an hour back since Junior left?"

Blake waved the question aside as almost annoying.

"There was a gas fire in the lad's room," he said briskly. "He retired to sleep before 10 p.m., and yet the bed was cold when we entered. In a warm room a bed retains the warmth of a person's body for a considerable time."

"You're a whale on the grey matter, old-timer," said Ruff Hanson admiringly.

Sexton Blake turned to Ben Cayterer.

"My dear fellow," he said quietly, "if you will be guided by me, you will try and rest. There is nothing we can do until the morning. I'm convinced that no harm can come to Junior; it's not him they want, but Spagoni's confession, primarily, and twenty thousand dollars incidentally. The latter demand, I imagine, is a sort of private

Mrs. Bardell gave a little scream of alarm at the transformation that had taken place. "Your pardon—should explain—Christmas Eve—spirit of carnival—sorry to alarm you—very!" said Splash Page, in the manner of Dickens' immortal Alfred Jingle.

Dickens characters, left to right : Alfred Jingle (Splash Page); Sydney Carton (Sexton Blake); Sam Weller (Tinker); Tracy Tupman (Insp. Coutts); Bill Sikes (Ruff Hanson).

gun spoke. He had aimed for the back tyre. The car swerved slightly, but did not falter on its way. A tongue of flame leapt from the rear of the tonneau.

There was a soft phut, and a bullet embedded itself in a trunk of a tree, four inches away from the American's bare head.

"By the great horned toad!" roared Ruff. "Them's the guys, Tinker! C'mon! I guess I punctured their back wheel an'——"

He pulled back the bolt of the wrought iron gate and raced down the roadway. There was no sign of the yellow car, and the American scratched his chin ruefully.

"Don't tell me I can't shoot straight, kid! I never miss!" he remarked, pointing to a fresh wheel-track in the road. "It's just my blamed luck them guys have solid tyres—or luck!"

Tinker turned back with Pedro.

"I'm going to phone!" he announced. "I've got the number and description of that car. The police will stop it!"

"Say, kiddo, you sure use your eyes!" said Ruff Hanson approvingly, as they retraced their steps towards the Manor House.

folded on the back of a chair, and the metal frame that supported his lame leg was a pathetic relic propped against the side of the bed.

"Can you tell me if any of his every-day clothes are missing?" Blake queried.

Ben Cayterer fumbled in the wardrobe, his usually rubicund face grey with apprehension.

"I guess I can't find his little Norfolk suit, Mr. Blake—the one he was wearing before the party!" he announced. "But how the blazes did they get into the bed-room? That's what beats me! D'ye think Junior was drugged, or——!"

Blake shook his head and pointed to the bed, the counterpane of which was neatly drawn back, disclosing a pillow, in which was the soft depression caused by the little boy's head—and a minute slit to the right through which the dagger had been plunged.

"No; I do not think they used violence. There is no mark of a struggle," he announced. "As to his method of entry—this window is locked on the inside. He either walked in through the passage door or through your bed-room."

(Continued on page 16.)

CHRISTMAS!

* * *

CHRISTMAS! It's been a long time getting round, but we shan't have much longer to wait (to quote the remark of the old lady when she saw the balloon being inflated).

Well, the first and most pressing duty for me is to give you the jolly old glad hand, and wish you all the best!

Here's to all of you—dark or fair, fat and forty, frail, freckled, or frabjous! Old, young; mothers, fathers; uncles, aunts—I salute you all, whether you're here at home in Britain or in some un-Christmassy climate beyond the seas! Here's the glad hand of Yuletide greeting my patient readers who have survived my weekly burblings for so many weeks—and I wish I could greet you in person!

This is the first Christmas I have had the opportunity of getting over my own individual greetings.

Duty, did I say? Why, it's a pleasure!

* * *

In the Dickens' Manner.

I AM especially bucked to know that you are going to have the story of that memorable Christmas of ours at Lyveden Manor.

That was a real corker of a Yuletide, if ever there was one! A bit disturbing at times, with an element of tragedy cropping up, but all atoned for by a No. 1 sized happy ending, as you'll see.

It was a very sound scheme, too, of my pal, Splash Page's, to make us all rig ourselves up in Dickens costumes and journey down in the good, old-fashioned way by stage-coach, with the guard tootling on his horn all the time, and the dogs howling in harmony, and people cheering and waving as if they were enjoying it as much as ourselves—as perhaps they were.

I'm sure Mrs. Bardell never had such a treat in the span of her natural life; and as for Ruff Hanson, of course he'd never seen anything like it. Christmas in the States, apparently, still awaits the Dickens touch.

* * *

Willy and Wally Intrude.

YOU'D have been tickled to death to see Ruff as Bill Sikes, I know. This hard-headed, say-it-with-lead Yank wasn't at all anxious to get himself into the rig, and (between ourselves) only did it so as to be sociable.

But you ought to have seen him when he got himself into that Bill Sikes outfit! He was the living image of the character—certainly the best of all of us. The favourite implement of the original Bill was, I believe, a bludgeon, but Ruff Hanson wasn't at all at home with the one Splash supplied him with, but brandished his two-guns, Willy and Wally, most of the time.

It was as strange to see the legendary Bill Sikes with a couple of six-shooters as it would be to see Robinson Crusoe dusting out his little wooden hut with a vacuum cleaner.

* * *

Symbolic.

BY the way, the gifted artist who is entrusted with the illustrations to this Yuletide yarn of ours—and I specially like his version of us dressed in our Dickens costumes—looked in at Baker Street yesterday to talk over a few details.

He caught me in the midst of hanging the decorations in the consulting-room, and forthwith made a sketch. This appears above, and I want you to notice the beautiful symbolism in the foreground.

My paste-pot and other paraphernalia of the horrible Index are rather obscured on this occasion by the more festive clutter of paper-chains.

Which is distinctly as it should be!

A Kind, Forgiving Time.

ONE of the people who have the real, right Christmas spirit is Mr. Mead, magistrate of the Marylebone Court.

"I don't like to send anyone to prison at Christmas-time," he said to an erring member last year, and let him off with a caution.

Good luck, Mr. Mead! I second that remark of yours!

Here's wishing you a happy time *this* Christmas, with no thoughts of newly-prisoned gaol-birds to disturb you!

* * *

Yule Agree!

THIS is a sadly imperfect world, I'm afraid, and even at this season of jollity and good will, when we are all doing our best to be friendly disposed towards the whole world, crime rears its ugly head.

Like Mr. Mead, we none of us want to see a crook sent to prison at Yuletide, but you've got to draw the line somewhere, and there are times when I shouldn't shed even a glycerine tear to see it happen—cases of mean theft, for example.

I remember an instance where a workman, who had been paying into a Winchester slate club for nearly twelve months, drew out his share to buy Christmas fare and Christmas luxuries for the children, and took it home and left the money in his bed-room while he left the house for a few minutes.

The money—£61—had vanished when he returned.

The thief who did that—well, I hope he swallowed the sixpence in the Christmas pudding!

Hard Luck!

AND here, while I think of it, I offer my sincere commiserations to all imprisoned juries, if there be any such.

It doesn't often happen, I know, that the twelve good men and true are shut off from their wives and families all through the Christmas holidays, and I don't recall a case in this country.

But one jury was unlucky in New York last year. They were trying the notorious oil scandal case, involving a multi-millionaire oil king and a very high U.S. Government official in charges of bribery.

It was expected that it would sort of weaken the jury's resolution if they were allowed out within sound of the chinking of gold—and the defence had an illimitable supply—so the judge ordered them to be closely guarded during the whole course of the trial.

This imprisonment lasted for a period of months, including Christmas.

It could hardly be called the festive season in their case; but let's hope they made up for it by having a prosperous New Year!

* * *

Take This Tip.

I HOPE that none of my long-suffering readers get run in this Yuletide, by the way.

Sexton Blake's jocular assistant decorates the con[sulting-room] pages with [...]

Not that I'm hinting you're an a[ban]doned set of ruffians. On the contrar[y,] I feel certain that all of you regu[larly] scooped the pool of the Sunday-sc[hool] prizes in your youth. No; but wh[at I] mean to say is that lawbreaking at Y[ule]tide is perfectly easy, if you go the r[ight] way about it.

Do you happen to know that if you [give] the road-sweeper or the dustman [a] Christmas-box, on the understanding [that] your street or dustbin will receive [the] honour of his special attention du[ring the] coming months (and he having ca[rried it out] without the knowledge or consent [of the] mayor and corporation), you are liab[le to] a term of imprisonment not exceeding [...] years, or a fine of not more than £[...] (And quite enough, too, I should say!)

Anyway, if you don't believe me, [it's] 99 Vic., cap. 72, para. (d), sub-section [...] clause XI.—or some such number.

On the other hand, you may have no [end] of bread and water and a plank bed if [you] bestow your largesse on the postman. [He] has the sanction and authority of [the] Postmaster-General for his Christmas-[box.] Besides which, he can't deliver more [letters] than the tradesmen send you.

* * *

Cooked *His* Goose!

THE mention of postmen brings up [the] subject of the unfortunate man f[rom] Vienna.

**Robert may have his duty to [do, but he has his]
pleasures, too! Here's a m[ember of the]
City of London police statio[n ... with a]
Christmas pudding on his w[ay ...]**

NOTE BOOK

...oom at Baker Street with paper chains—and these
...ble brevities.

...Some altogether absurd period after his
...letide dinner the postman brought to his
...r a goose which had been sent him by
...riend in Hungary, and which it was in-
...ded should have been the star turn on
...Christmas bill of fare.

...ts condition by that time was—well, it
...sn't as fresh as a rosebud. All we need
...about it was that the postman was doing
...duty nobly in delivering it at all, and
...s not at all sorry to be rid of it.

...The postman (between gasps) explained
...t the bird had been detained over the
...idays by the Customs officials for some
...-tape reason or other.

...After giving the remains decent burial,
...recipient grabbed his pen and wrote
...her a stinger of a letter to the Customs.
...mentioned sarcastically that the
...ennese were not in the world solely
...pay taxes and be the playthings of
...cialdom, and other items to that effect.

...Result : He was hauled off to the police
...rt, and made to pay a fine for the crime
..."insulting official honour."

...ally Ghostly !

...HIS being the merry season of Yule,
...and the Yule log being in position
...burning bright, draw up your chairs
...let's have a ghost story.

...hristmas Day, but he has his
...oto of the cook at one of the
...ing an advance sample of the
...n. They're passing it as O.K.
...ly.

How's this for a start?

You may remember there was a sensation some time ago about a ghost having been seen by a night-watchman at Barnet. Soon after this a local J.P. wrote to the Press, giving his own experiences.

At the extreme northern boundary of the Grange (he wrote) is an old house which has been partly rebuilt, and underneath are some large cellars from which, for many years, at intervals low rumbling noises as of heavy weights being moved, short, sharp tappings, and sounds like muffled voices are distinctly heard.

At the invitation of the occupier of the house I have on several occasions been inside. I have heard a kind of suppressed report, like the discharge of an air-gun, and more frequently a jingling noise, which seemed to move about the room.

Once I saw quite plainly a spirit. Looking at it closely, I saw right through it. Gradually it passed away. I have seen strong men walk away from the house with wide, staring eyes and trembling limbs.

Other and bolder people have sought excitement—women have been seen to hurry away with their shawls wrapped closely round them, seemingly anxious to get away from the scenes they had witnessed.

Pretty eerie, that ! But listen !

*　*　*

Accurate, but Misleading.

PERHAPS you've guessed it ?
Yes, it was merely a bit of very clever spoof.

The mysterious house referred to was actually a public-house. The noises in the cellar were made by the trundling and tapping of casks, and the suppressed reports were nothing more alarming than the popping of corks.

The uncanny jingling which was heard all over the place was caused by glasses on the bars, and the spirit which the facetious J.P. saw, and which gradually passed away, departed down the usual channels; while the trembly people who hurried away from the place were generally making their exit from the bottle and jug department.

The publication of this explanation caused a good deal of amusement in the district, for even Barnet people failed to recognise a description of a house well known to them.

On the other hand, there were many believers in the other kind of spirits who were somewhat peeved, for they had written offering explanations of the phenomena which accounted for everything but spirits of the bottled variety.

*　*　*

Notice to Quit.

TO be serious, however.
Here is a ghost story for which I have no humorous explanation to offer.

A newly-married couple were spending their honeymoon in a certain house in Rome. One night the bride awakened to see the shadowy form of an old woman sitting on the table at her bedside.

Frightened, she hid her head under the bedclothes. Immediately a shower of heavy blows fell on her shoulders. She said afterwards that they felt as if they were from a stick, wielded by a strong arm.

She shouted in alarm. Her husband woke up, heard her story, and bravely searched the whole premises. Nothing could be seen. Also, the windows and doors were all fastened on the inside.

Stranger still, the same thing happened the following night, except that the husband saw the apparition this time—and got the beating, too.

They didn't pause to investigate again, though, but ran out into the street.

This spectre with a grudge against married couples seems to be rather amusing at first sight, but the curious fact is that, about a year previously, another couple had been driven from the same place in exactly the same way.

Talking of Spectres—

"WHAT is your husband's occupation ?" asked the magistrate's clerk of a lady in trouble at one of the London police courts.

"He's an inspector," she replied.

"Inspector !" interrupted the other lady in the case indignantly. "The only things he inspects are the bottoms of beer-glasses !"

*　*　*

For One Day Only !

REFERRING back to my sad suggestion about some worthy reader of mine being led away in clanking chains this Christmastide—in other words, falling foul of the law—let me reassure you.

According to that ponderous tome, "Halsbury's Laws of England" (which I have just got down from the guv'nor's bookcase, so as to use it as a bit of uplift in hanging the Christmas decorations), "no summons, warrant, or other process may be served on Christmas Day."

There appears to be an exception, however.

There is nothing to stop a writ from the King's Bench or Chancery Division on the (otherwise) glad day.

But stay ! Even those formidable writs cannot be served on a Sunday, and Christmas Day this year is also a Sunday.

Harassed readers who have spent most of their time looking round corners for bailiffs can therefore slink under the shelter of their family roof-tree this Yule and defy the whole bunch of them.

*　*　*

The Policeman's Lot.

THERE is at least one London policeman who stands a chance of having a happy Christmas, and—what is more to the point—a prosperous New Year.

A few weeks ago he heard that a more or less legendary uncle of his had died in America worth £2,000,000, and that he was entitled to a part of the share-out.

When I last heard of him he was writing to the lawyers in the United States putting in his claim, and I expect he is watching the morning postal delivery eagerly just about now, sorting out the letters from America from moneylenders' circulars offering to lend him ten thousand pounds on note of hand alone.

*　*　*

Query ?

SEVEN women, one after another, applied at the Willesden Police Court for separation orders from their husbands a week or two back.

"Are all the women in Willesden trying to get rid of their husbands?" asked the magistrate. "Is it in preparation for the Christmas festivities?"

Surely not ! How can families be festive without father dressed up as Santa Claus?

(Continued from page 13.)
commission for Mr. Isidore Solmann's agent for the kidnapping."

"I guess you're right, Blake," said Ruff. "To-morrow, when this cursed storm lets up a bit, we kin get busy. How about covering this Juniper chap in Sago Street?"

Inspector Coutts, who had strolled into the study, grinned.

"4a, Sago Street is very well known to me," he remarked. "It is run by a barber named Wilton, and is an accommodation address much used by the criminal class. There's very little chance that the real kidnapper will call for the letter in person; he'll probably send an entirely blameless individual to collect Mr. Juniper's wire."

"Then you think——" began Cayterer.

"I think I'll get rid of this rig-out, sir," said Inspector Coutts, indicating the blue surtout of Mr. Tracy Tupman. It looked foolishly frivolous now that tragedy had appeared on the scene. "The police are bound to be on the look-out for a yellow car, and if we turn in now we can tackle the case freshly in the morning," he added.

Sexton Blake nodded.

"No harm will come to your son for a day or two, at least, Mr. Cayterer," he said kindly. "I have a theory that he will be restored to you very shortly indeed."

The millionaire looked at the detective, but Blake's face was impassive as the Sphinx.

"I hope to Heaven you're right!" he said fervently. "Er—good-night, gentlemen! I shan't sleep, but—— You'll excuse me, I—I have had rather a shock."

He turned slowly and mounted the stairs in the direction of his room.

"Poor old Ben!" said Ruff. "Blake, I feel real mean about this. I should have slept outside that kid's door instead of listening to fool ghost stories. Dog my cats, if I get hold of that plastering plug-ugly I'll—I'll——"

"Police have sent out an A.S. message, guv'nor," broke in Tinker, coming in from the telephone.

"They've traced the number of the motor-car already to——"

"Ah!" said Blake, with a significant lift of his eyebrows. "And to whom does it belong?"

"The Rev. Ambrose Dale," said Tinker.

"Holy smoke!" growled Ruff Hanson. "Wouldja believe it? That hoary-headed old sinner that was splitting the spook stuff!"

Sexton Blake said nothing, but there was a queer expression in his grey eyes that Tinker alone understood.

T HERE was a subdued atmosphere of gloom at Lyveden Manor on Christmas Day, which dawned clear and frosty, with the added seasonableness of snow in place of the pelting hail of the night.

Ben Cayterer, hollow-eyed and distrait, took his seat at the head of the breakfast table and turned to Blake.

"No news, I suppose?" he said dully.

Blake shook his head.

"Coutts took an early tramp to the station at Lyveden early this morning, and up till now the police have been unable to trace the yellow car."

"Ah, good-morning, Mr. Cayterer, good-morning!" boomed the mellifluous voice of the clergyman from the doorway. "Parsons has just informed me of the terrible tragedy that has befallen you. My dear fellow, why didn't you call me? I was too far away in the east wing to have heard anything, and I'm afraid I selfishly luxuriated in my really comfortable bed. Good-morning, my dear!"

He turned to Enid, who had just entered the room, looking very fresh and winsome in her simple, tailor-made frock.

"Oh, daddy!" she said. "Isn't it dreadful! I've just heard the news from Mrs. Bardell." Her grey eyes clouded with sympathy as she turned to the millionaire. "Mr. Cayterer, I can't tell you how shocked I am at this awful news. I do so hope that you'll hear something soon."

"Thank you for your sympathy, my dear!" said Cayterer huskily. "We didn't disturb you last night—what was the use? I—I'm hoping that Mr. Blake here will soon discover what's happened to my boy. He's been a veritable tower of strength to me."

"I'm afraid the situation at the moment is rather obscure," said Blake. "In this sort of case time is an important factor. We must not be too precipitate. Junior, I am convinced, will be safe for a time, for the kidnappers have no reason to treat him harshly if they are under the impression that you will pay the ransom."

"I suggest you wire to this address in Sago Street. Coutts has already advised Scotland Yard to keep the shop under observation."

"Yes, but—what shall I wire?" queried Cayterer helplessly. "I hate submitting to these curs. It's not the money I object to, Mr. Blake, but the principle of the thing. Yet these scoundrels have me utterly at their mercy now, and they know it."

"Well, bear up," smiled Blake. "There are always three rounds in this blackmailing game. They may be described as the demand, the acceptance, and payment, either by cash—or, if the luck holds, penal servitude."

He helped himself to some toast and marmalade, then turned to the Rev. Ambrose.

"By the way, vicar," he inquired, "can you recall the number of your automobile?"

The reverend gentleman paused in the act of conveying a devilled kidney to his mouth.

"I haven't got a motor-car, Mr. Blake," he said, with the trace of a smile. "I'm afraid my stipend is too slender to maintain what is, after all, only a luxury."

Tinker stared blankly at the vicar and gave a smothered "ouch!" of pain as Ruff Hanson's heavy boot kicked him significantly under the table.

Chapter 7.

The Black Carol.

S AGO STREET, Pimlico, on Christmas morning, looked even more depressing than it did on the three hundred and sixty-four other mornings of the year.

The snow which had fallen during the night had been ploughed by passing traffic into a brown, porridge-like mess. A blood-red sun hung low in the sky, and completed the slush-making process by rapidly melting the snow on the dingy slate roofs, so that it dripped mournfully on to the pavements, to the discomfort of the pedestrians.

Two places only were open on Christmas morning in Sago Street. At the corner the Spotted Dog, a gimcrack gin palace, was crowded with most of the male inhabitants of that unsalubrious thoroughfare. Across the road, the hairdressing establishment of Mr. William Wilton was likewise crowded with several blue-chinned gentlemen in various stages of deshabille, awaiting their turn for the barber's ministrations. The dingy, faded windows of the shop were crammed with dummy packets of cigarettes which, gaping and bulging from sheer age, exposed their spuriousness the more; various pomades and unguents for beautifying hair and moustachios; corn cures; mysterious envelopes of many colours purporting to contain certain winners for forthcoming races, and similar tawdry stuff.

A rat-faced little man, clad in a plum-coloured suit, a check cap and lemon-topped boots, sidled furtively from the Spotted Dog into Mr. Wilton's saloon and glanced inquiringly at the knight of the lather brush.

"Anythink for Juniper—Jas. Juniper?" he queried, in a wheezy voice.

Mr. Wilton jerked his pomaded head in the direction of a letter-rack.

"Telegram. Just come. Thrippence!" he said laconically.

The rat-faced man handed over three coppers, and snatched an orange envelope from the rack. He did not trouble to open it, but sidled out of the shop without troubling to express his hope that Mr. Wilton should have a Merry Christmas. In Sago Street he paused, glanced furtively to the right and left, and then crossed over to the Spotted Dog.

A husky-looking loafer in corduroys who was leaning against the wall of that decrepit hostelry, expectorated slowly and sidled up alongside the apprehensive Mr. Juniper.

"Merry Christmas, Wally," he said affably. "Nice new style in suitings you've got on. Christmas present?"

"You go to blazes!" snarled Mr. Juniper. "And mind your own business!"

"Tut, tut! Harsh words on a Christmas morn, Wally! I'm surprised at you!" reproved the other, affectionately tucking his arm through that of the incensed Mr. Juniper.

"You leggo my arm, or I'll——" began Wally, baring his yellow teeth in an ugly grimace.

"You're taking a little walk with me," said his imperturbable companion. "You haven't opened your telegram yet, I see. Might be an invitation to dinner with the Lord Mayor. 'Tisn't the first time you've been a guest of his, is it, Wally?"

"I don't know what you're talking about," growled the other, changing colour. "My name's not Wally. I don't know you, and if you don't leggo my arm, I'll call a cop."

"Dear, dear!" replied the other, in the same cool, maddening tone. "Here's Constable Jervis at the corner. Remember him, Wally. Now, are you going to come across—or shall I put you in stir for Christmas?"

A terrified look came into the little crook's face as he saw the implacable look in the other's eyes.

"'Swelp me, sergeant! I ain't done nothink!" he whimpered. "I'll swear I ain't!"

"Tut, tut!" clucked Sergeant Steele, of the C.I.D. "A double negative makes a positive. If you ain't done nothing you must have done something. Let's take a look at that wire."

Mr. Juniper saw that resistance was useless. With a sigh, he pulled out the unopened telegram.

"Here you are, rot yuh! Blowed if I reckernised you as a busy in that rig-out! I don't know nothink about wot's in the wire, and I don't care!"

The plain-clothes man scarcely glanced at the orange envelope. Still keeping his grip on the little man's arm, he hailed a passing taxi.

"You're coming a little ride with me, Wally," he said softly. "How long you stay in stir depends on yourself. D'ye get me?"

The rat-faced man said nothing; but his face was murderous as the cab rolled on towards the Westminster police station.

"Let's see, you came out two months back, didn't you, Wally?" said Detective Steele. "I can hold you for failing to report, you know."

"Listen here, Steele! A bloke offered me a fiver to collect that telegram for him. Who he was I dunno—s'welp me bob, I ain't ever seen 'im before!"

"Ah!" said Steele softly. "And where were you to meet this philan-thropist with the telegram?"

Wally hesitated. He licked his dry lips nervously.

"I wasn't to meet him anywhere. I 'ad to post it on to him to a certain place—miles away from 'ere," replied Wally.

"I see," drawled the detective. "What's this fellow's name? And what's he like?"

The little crook glanced nervously out of the window as the cab drew up before the dingy portals of the police station.

"I don't know 'is name. 'E called 'imself Robinson," he said; then added, with sudden animation: "Rum sort of cove 'e was, too—'e was dressed as a clergyman, and talked like a sky pilot, too!"

Detective-Sergeant Steele glanced shrewdly at the unfortunate crook.

"A clergyman, eh?" he echoed softly. "And you weren't to meet him. Then how was he to get the telegram?"

"S'welp me—I 'ad to post it on to 'im," mumbled the wretched man. "I 'ad to send it to Mr. Richard Robinson, care of the G.P.O., Saxenham."

"Ah!" said Sergeant Steele softly. "Mebbe you'll get a Christmas dinner, after all. Come in the cooler a bit, my lad, while I check up on your statement."

SEXTON BLAKE and Tinker were alone in the library of the Manor-house when a laconic message arrived from Scotland Yard, reporting the detection of the man the Yard detective had familiarly addressed as "Wally."

Blake scanned the telegram, and his grey eyes narrowed.

"H'm! Saxenham is a few miles from here, young 'un. The unknown kidnapper has evidently covered his traces pretty completely. He seems to be a person of considerable resource. I think you and Coutts should take a little run over to Saxenham immediately and keep tabs on the post office. In accordance with my instructions, Steele has forwarded on the wire of acceptance, and I fancy the elusive Mr. Richard Robinson will fall into the trap."

"But, I say, guv'nor," began Tinker earnestly, "I hate to suspect a person without definite proof; but it looks to me as if the Rev. Ambrose is acting kind of queerly. Why should he deny that he has a car? Or, for that matter, there's the hint you let fall that young Junior was kidnapped by an old and intimate friend. It seems inconceivable to me—unless it all points to the vicar."

Blake smiled cryptically.

"As usual, young 'un, you are deduc-ing from false premises. Your job is

to hang around the post office at Saxen-ham. I'll put a phone call through to the local postmaster to advise him of your coming. Get Coutts and the local inspector to detain anybody asking for letters addressed to Robinson, and we shall see—what we shall see."

Tinker rose to his feet, a puzzled ex-pression on his boyish face, just as Ruff Hanson entered the room.

The gunman sleuth's battered counten-ance was unusually grave.

"Say, Blake," he drawled, "this case is kinda getting me down. Poor old Ben Cayterer's hit durned badly. He's just walking around and around the house like a guy who's been hoodooed. The suspense is killing him; and we can't do a darned thing. Our hands are tied until this skunk shows out in the open——"

"Which will be very soon, I trust," interrupted Blake. "The police have already got the kidnappers' go-between in London."

Briefly the detective described the turn events had taken.

"Well, that's something!" ejaculated Ruff Hanson. "Guess I'll travel with Coutts and Tinker to this Saxenham place."

He squared his massive shoulders, and there was a purposeful look on his weather-beaten face.

"Hot dog! You lemme get at him!" he muttered vindictively. "I'll show the skunk where he gets off!"

Blake did not reply; he was wrapped in thought and pungent clouds of tobacco-smoke. None knew better than he that it was a waiting game, and he had a shrewd notion that the unknown kidnapper was not likely to walk blindly into a trap.

The afternoon shadows of Christmas Day were lengthening into twilight.

Big Ben Cayterer sat hunched in his armchair, his leonine head in his hands—a picture of despair.

Even the ebullient high spirits of Splash Page could not dispel the gloom that seemed to enshroud the Manor-house. The Rev. Ambrose and his daughter had returned to the vicarage; and the other local guests, after express-ing their sympathy with the stricken millionaire, had unobtrusively with-drawn from the house of sorrow.

Splash Page, after wandering gloomily round the grounds of Lyveden Manor, re-entered the library just as Parsons wheeled in the tea-wagon.

The butler's face was grave as he an-nounced that tea was ready.

Ben Cayterer looked up vaguely from his reverie.

"Er—yes! All right, Parsons," he said listlessly.

"I beg your pardon, sir," coughed the manservant. "I suppose there ain't —ahem!—isn't any news of young Master Junior yet, sir?" he inquired. "We are naturally very concerned in the servants' hall, and——"

"Yes, quite! I appreciate your sym-pathy, Parsons. No; I'm sorry to say there is no news. Mr. Blake is just telephoning through again to Saxen-ham."

"Now, don't you worry, Mr. Cayterer," said Splash. "You've got Blake's word that he'll see this through, and believe me when he says so—it goes.

"This blighter Robinson—or whatever his beastly name is—will call for the telegram, and friend Coutts'll be wait-ing for him with a pair of handcuffs."

"I doubt it," said the voice of Sexton Blake himself. He had quietly ap-peared in the doorway.

"This man Robinson seems to be an exceptionally cautious and clever criminal," he went on. "I have just rung through to Saxenham, and I'm

afraid I have nothing encouraging to report."

"What's that?" demanded Cayterer, his face grey.

"A small urchin named Joe Fowler called at the post office, inquiring for a letter for a Mr. Robinson. Coutts cross-examined him, and the boy's story was a simple one. A tall gentleman in a fur-lined coat in a motor-car stopped him on the outskirts of Saxenham village and offered him five shillings to collect the letter and bring it to him.

"His description of the man was vague. He was more explicit about the car—a yellow coupe. Coutts and Ruff Hanson promptly bundled the boy into their automobile and drove hurriedly to the rendezvous at Saxe Bridge."

"Yes, yes; go on!" urged Cayterer eagerly.

"And there was no sign of the elusive Mr. Robinson," concluded Blake.

"By heavens!" groaned Ben Cayterer hollowly. "We're done, Mr. Blake! We're licked!"

"Nonsense!" said the detective sharply. "The situation is complicated, perhaps, but not hopeless."

"Tell me, Blake," began Splash Page curiously, "what you meant precisely when you said Junior didn't cry out because he met an old friend?"

For answer the criminologist un-earthed the little fluffy object he had discovered in the missing boy's bed-room, together with a tiny scrap of red material.

"White crepe hair, my dear fellow; and on the stackpipe I found a shred of this red flannel. What does that suggest to you?"

"Good heavens! I see it now!" ejaculated Splash Page. "Junior didn't cry out because he, like most other kids last night, was expecting Santa Claus."

"Precisely," said Blake. "Our crook is an enterprising and versatile individual; it was a touch of genius to disguise himself in the one costume which would allay a child's suspicion."

"The cunning rat!" growled Ben Cay-terer. "I suppose he pinched the Rev. Ambrose's costume after the vicar had dispensed with it?"

Blake shook his head.

"On the contrary, I have taken the opportunity of examining that costume, and this material is an entirely different texture to that of the vicar's. There were two Santa Claus' here last night!" he added significantly. "By the way, Mr. Cayterer, do you happen to know of anyone named Lemuel Clay?"

The millionaire shook his head.

"Why, no——" he began.

Parsons, the butler, who was deftly removing the empty tea-things, dropped one of the fragile cups with a crash. His fingers fumbled as he bent over the debris, and Blake's eyes narrowed.

"I'm sorry, sir!" mumbled the man-servant. "I'm afraid I've been very clumsy!"

His back was towards the detective as he picked up the broken pieces of porcelain, but when he straightened his face was as white as death.

A loud knock sounded at the front door of the house, and a look of relief came into the butler's face as he hurried to answer it.

Splash Page and Tinker exchanged significant glances. The newspaper-man had noticed the butler's agitation at the mention of Lemuel Clay's name. What did it mean, and who was the mysterious Mr. Clay?

Parsons returned a few moments later with a round, flat package in his hand.

"One of the villagers left this for you, sir," he said deferentially.

Cayterer took the parcel and examined it curiously. It was wrapped in brown paper and was about eight inches in diameter.

He undid the string and revealed a black waxen gramophone record.

"Now I wonder who sent me that?" he said blankly. "Blamed if I know any musical villagers!"

He scanned the disc with some bewilderment. The hand-written label of the record was, "A Christmas Carol. Specially Recorded," and it was obvious that most of it had not been recorded on, only a narrow ring of sound-impressions being visible.

"That looks like a new and up-to-date form of Christmas waits," laughed Splash Page.

Blake leaned over and examined the record curiously. Suddenly a queer expression crept into his grey eyes, and his mouth tightened into a grim, firm line. From his pocket he whipped out a silk handkerchief, and with it he took the disc gingerly from the millionaire's hand.

"Say, what's the idea?" began Ben Cayterer blankly.

Blake did not reply verbally, but crossed over to the gramophone in the corner of the library.

He fixed a needle in the sound-box of the instrument and gently placed the record on the turntable.

A faint whirring sound followed, and then through the library a scream of agony rang out, piercing and shrill.

"Don't! Don't! Oh, daddy, daddy, he's hurting me!"

It was the voice of Junior Cayterer!

The millionaire leapt to his feet, his face bloodless, his lips twitching spasmodically.

"Blake," he croaked hoarsely, "what devilry is this? What——"

His voice trailed away as a metallic, incisive voice came from the gramophone.

"Say, Ben, how d'ye like your Christmas carol? The kid gets more of the hot iron unless you come through with the dough and call off your 'tecs."

Chapter 8.

Ruff Runs Into Trouble.

WHITE and trembling in every limb, Ben Cayterer stared at the diabolical disc which had so faithfully recorded the voice of his little son screaming under the torture of his captors.

"The fiends! The cunning fiends!" he croaked "By Heaven, Blake, this is more than flesh and blood can stand! I —I——"

With a moan, he crumpled into his chair. His iron constitution had snapped under the intolerable strain of hearing the anguished cries of the son he idolised. Sexton Blake snapped off the ghastly record with its mocking title. An unwonted spot of colour blazed in his cheeks.

"By Heaven, Splash," he hissed, and his fists clenched savagely, "I'll get this man, if it costs me all I possess! Quick! Get Mr. Cayterer to bed and let him rest; the strain's proved too much for him. Ring up the doctor."

With the aid of Parsons, the journalist managed to half drag, half carry the comatose figure of the movie magnate to his room.

Meanwhile, Blake took off the record and carried it to his bed-room, wrapped in his silk handkerchief. He switched

on the light and opened his research-case, from which he took a phial of white powder. He lightly dusted both sides of the record and examined it minutely through a powerful lens.

An hour later Tinker found him, on his return, busy with a pad of telegraph-forms and a pencil. The criminologist hardly looked up from the columns of abstruse figures he had jotted down on a pad when the lad entered the room.

"I say, guv'nor," began Tinker, "we've had a deuce of a wild-goose chase!" he began.

"This cunning blighter Robinson sent a kid——"

"I know, I know!" snapped Blake irritably. "Go down to Lyveden post office, tell them it's police business, and get these wires off immediately."

He handed his assistant a sheaf of forms and relocked his research-case.

Tinker gave one glance at the grim, strained expression on his guv'nor's usually impassive face and hurried out of the room.

Blake sat for a while drumming his fingers in a ceaseless tattoo on the arm of his chair, then he doffed his lounge suit and changed into his dinner jacket.

DOWNSTAIRS, Ruff Hanson, Coutts, and Splash Page were talking in whispers when Blake entered the library. The American looked up with a haggard expression.

"Say, old timer, the doc's been. Ben's had a slight stroke, and mustn't be disturbed on any account. What's happened exactly?"

"Happened?" echoed Blake. "It means that this man Robinson—or whatever his name is—is the most heartless and brutal blackmailer I have ever experienced in a fairly lengthy professional career!"

The detective's voice was vibrant with passion.

"He is torturing that child; and with callous devilry has actually recorded the poor little fellow's screams of agony on a gramophone record. I tell you, Ruff, that if I lay my hands on him I'll——"

His fists clenched and his voice was a trifle unsteady.

"By the Holy Heintz, I'll—I'll croak him for sure, Blake!" declared Ruff passionately. "I ain't ever killed, except in self-defence, but this time——"

An ugly look crept into his blue eyes, and his hand dropped significantly to his hip.

"Dinner is served, sir."

Parsons' imperturbable voice broke in suavely as he entered the room with his peculiar, cat-like tread.

Coutts gave a slight grimace.

"I'm afraid it's not going to be a very cheerful meal, Blake," he remarked. "Poor Mrs. Bardell, she's spent hours preparing it! We mustn't disappoint the old girl."

Together they filed into the dining-room, just as Tinker returned, cheeks aglow, from his errand to the village.

"Sent 'em off, guv'nor. The local inspector O.K.'d them; but the telegraphist didn't half curse at having to work overtime on Christmas Day!" he announced.

Blake nodded abstractedly as he sat down to the table.

It was a far from hilarious meal. The screams of the crippled boy still rang in Sexton Blake's ears, and the illness of their host added to the gloom that reigned like an evil miasma about the house.

The turkey—beautifully cooked, and stuffed with Mrs. Bardell's famous oyster forcemeat—did not receive the appreciation it deserved; and even the advent of the plum-pudding, in its glory

of holly and rum, was greeted in a subdued fashion.

Mrs. Bardell herself sensed the tension as she entered with the pudding.

The good soul had luxuriated in what she called "a reel good cry," and she had uttered several blood-curdling threats in the servants' hall relative to the fate that lay in store for the kidnappers of her "little lame lamb," as she dubbed Junior Cayterer.

It was the most dismal Christmas dinner that Tinker ever remembered, and there was a sigh of relief when the meal was over and they adjourned to the library.

"Blamed if I know what we kin do!" said Ruff Hanson plaintively. "The dragnet's all out; but we ain't got a description of the skunk. The auto with the masked men belongs to the vicar, according to the cops; yet, according to the reverend, he hasn't got one."

"That is easily explained," retorted Sexton Blake. "The vicar did at one time possess a car, but he sold it to a local garage. He couldn't afford to keep it up. I've checked that end of the case, and also ascertained that the car was recently bought by a Mr. Lemuel Clay."

"Who's Lemuel Clay, guv'nor?" asked Tinker eagerly.

"That's what I should like to know myself," was the quiet reply. "The police have no record of the man—nor, by an oversight, had they noted the fact that the vicar had sold his car."

"Fact is, we're up a darned gum tree!" said Ruff Hanson bitterly. "And it's my durned fault! I've acted like a cheap skate! I reckon it's about time I quit this game and——"

"You are not to blame, my dear fellow," broke in Sexton Blake. "We are all equally culpable, for that matter. This man Robinson is an unusually resourceful and daring criminal. To-morrow, very probably, there'll be a further demand from him—with instructions how to pay over the money. It is then that I shall act."

"Well," announced Splash Page gloomily, as he dug his hands into his trousers pockets, "it isn't often I regret a scoop, Blake—and, talking journalistically, this is a big beat for me—but I wish to Heaven it hadn't occurred! That little kid tortured, and——"

He smiled cynically. From the village church came the peal of Christmas bells in a glad carillon—clanging joyously their Yuletide message of peace on earth—goodwill to men. It seemed a ghastly mockery—one that failed to drown the agonised shrieks of the winsome little boy with the serious brown eyes.

"Don't! Don't! Daddy, they're hurting me!"

None of the four friends were sentimentalists, but the thought of a cripple child being tortured in cold blood at Christmas-time—the happy feast of childhood — filled them with berserker rage.

The Dickens Yule that they had planned was darkened by the thought of Tiny Tim alone—helpless—scared—and they were all powerless to help.

A silence fell. In the grate the logs crackled, and the flames roared gleefully up the chimney.

Outside the snow began to fall—thickly, heavily. The high wind of the previous night had fallen, and for a while each one present was occupied by his thoughts.

Tinker was the first to break the silence.

"I think I'll turn in, guv'nor!" he

announced. "It's not particularly bright, and I'm feeling a bit tired."

He yawned lustily, and with a fugitive smile left the room.

"Poor kid, I'm afraid I've landed him —and all of you—into a tough kinda Christmas!" said Ruff Hanson lugubriously.

Blake smiled.

"It's not your fault, Ruff—let us hope to-morrow will bring some definite news. I have distinct hopes that the identity of Mr. Robinson will be revealed—and likewise that of Mr. Lemuel Clay."

opened the door. His room was situated in the east wing of the manor house, and overlooked the servants' quarters. For a moment or two he stood tensely in the passage, listening. Silence—a brooding hush, sinister with menace.

The gunman sleuth exchanged one of his weapons for an electric-torch, and in his bare feet tiptoed soundlessly down the corridor. At the head of the stairway he paused and flashed the light into the cavernous gloom of the hallway below.

The hall was empty.　　An ancient

The cupboard-like elevator was fairly roomy, but the big American had to crouch in an uncomfortable attitude before it would accommodate his bulk. He tugged at the cord. Soundlessly, the lift descended into the basement.

It stopped with a jerk—and Ruff found himself in the well-stocked wine-cellar of Lyveden Manor. An electric light bulb gleamed in the arched roof. The bases of innumerable wine bottles glinted in the light. That much Ruff saw as he cautiously emerged from his cramped position—and then it happened.

A couple of masked men sprang from the shadow of a wine bin, and unluckily for Ruff his foot caught in the lift rope as he turned to grapple with his assailants.

"Crack!"

His six-gun spoke. One of the masked men gave a squeal of rage as his upraised arm spurted blood. Ruff's bullet had found a billet—but he was hampered by his position. Before he could disentangle his foot from the clinging rope the second man brought down the barrel of a heavy Smith-Wesson revolver on the American's skull.

It was a brutal and savage blow. Ruff Hanson collapsed limply, his body half in and half out of the lift.

"It's that nosy Yank!" muttered the man with the shattered wrist. "Quick, get him away before the others start investigating."

Together the two crooks dragged Ruff Hanson's unconscious body out of the lift and dumped it unceremoniously on the floor of the cellar.

The wounded man cursed lividly as he surveyed his limp forearm.

"Quick, get Jean and Jules!" he snarled. "I'll have to bandage this before I bleed to death."

He scowled at the helpless American, and kicked him brutally in the ribs.

"Is the tide on the turn?" he demanded hoarsely. "We'll have to clear out before that hound Blake gets wise."

"Clear out nothing!" rasped the other. "You stay on till that next consignment comes. That fool Blake's too darned busy looking for Cayterer's brat to mosey around here."

He crossed over to one of the wine bins and pressed a small button let into its side. Immediately the bottle-laden shelves swung back, revealing a cavernous passage from which came a breath of the fresh, clean air of outdoors.

"You get back to your room, Parsons!" snapped the man in the mask. "Pitch what yarn you like to account for that broken wrist. The sound of the shot won't penetrate upstairs. They knew what they were doing when they built these cellars. No jerry-building Council-house stuff down here."

Parsons, the silent and irreproachable butler of Lyveden Manor, removed his mask and his face worked strangely.

"I'm getting windy, Clay," confessed the man addressed. "That hound Blake's got X-ray eyes. Once he finds out about——"

"Don't be a fool!" snarled the other. "I tell you that after to-morrow we're on velvet. Jules'll look after this beauty. It's a dark night, and 'no names no pack drill,'" he added, with a significant scowl at the unconscious American.

From the cavernous aperture in the wall of the wine cellar there came the sound of approaching footsteps.

"Upstairs with you, quick! We'll attend to this brute!" snapped Clay.

With trembling fingers Parsons tied a handkerchief round his injured wrist,

Sam McCalla crumpled up with a gasp of agony as Mrs. Bardell's umbrella caught him a vicious dig; and then the indomitable woman turned to belabour Liverpool Lil.

"**W**HOOO! Hooooo!"

A long, inhuman wail rang eerily out through the night silence that enshrouded Lyveden Manor.

Ruff Hanson awoke with a start. Even before his eyes were really open, his great fists had reached under his pillow for his beloved six-guns. It was nearly three a.m., he noted, glancing at the illuminated dial of his watch that hung on the bed-rail.

"What in tarnation?" he growled. "Sounds like a blamed owl, and yet——"

Again that eerie wail cut into the night silence. The gunman sleuth leapt noiselessly from his bed—pistols in hand. It was the same sound that he had heard during the vicar's ghost story the previous night—mocking, menacing.

"If that's Headless Hugo," rasped the American, "this is where he gets his!"

Ruff Hanson drew on his flamboyantly-coloured dressing-gown and softly

grandfather clock ticked solemnly in the corner. In the small grate a few red embers smouldered.

"Queer!" muttered Ruff Hanson. "I could have sworn I heard——"

He broke off suddenly. His trigger finger tightened. A queer metallic clank, as if someone was dragging heavy chains along a stone floor.

He crept down the stairs. The clanking was fainter now. He turned abruptly to the doorway that led to the butler's pantry.

It was ajar. He saw a panelled room with plain but serviceable furniture and a service lift that communicated with the wine-cellars. Ruff Hanson's eyes narrowed as he glimpsed a yellow line of light behind the doors of the lift.

"Now, what in tarnation——" he breathed, tiptoeing towards the panelled wall. "It looks as if——"

Again came the eerie inhuman wail.

"Hot ziggety dog!" snapped Ruff, tugging at the doors of the service lift.

and without a backward glance slowly ascended the cellar stairs that led to his sanctuary.

SEXTON BLAKE and Tinker entered the breakfast-room punctually at 8 a.m.

They occupied the west wing of the manor-house, and the queer sound that Ruff Hanson had heard during the night had not penetrated so far to disturb their slumbers.

"How is Mr. Cayterer this morning?" inquired Blake as Parsons entered with the coffee.

The butler shook his head gravely.

"Not very bright, sir. He says he'd be grateful if you'd drop in on him after breakfast. He had a very troubled night."

"You don't look any too bright yourself, my man," said Blake, after a keen scrutiny of the butler's pale face and restless eyes. "What's happened to your wrist? Had an accident?"

"I—I—er—strained it, I think, sir. I slipped going down the wine-cellar stairs," was the halting reply.

Blake shot a keen glance at the man and noted his embarrassment. He said nothing, however, but smiled a greeting as Detective-Inspector Coutts and Splash Page entered the room.

"Good-morning!" said the Yard man cheerfully. "Topping morning for a walk, eh, Blake?"

He jerked his head towards the window. The lawn of Lyveden Manor was white with frozen snow, and there was a keen, healthy tang of frost in the air.

"Ruff's late this morning, guv'nor," announced Tinker. "He's generally an early bird."

The youngster helped himself to toast and marmalade as the butler re-entered the room with a bundle of letters.

"The morning post," he announced. "A letter and a telegram for Mr. Blake, one for Mr. Hanson, and the rest for Mr. Cayterer."

"Good! Better see if Mr. Hanson's coming down, Parsons," said the detective, ripping open the telegram.

"Ah!" he gave a sigh of satisfaction as he read the brief message it contained.

"We progress, my dear Coutts—we certainly progress. The Record Department, with their unfailing efficiency and dispatch, have already fathomed the identity of the elusive Mr. Robinson."

Coutts paused with an impaled kidney midway between his plate and his mouth.

"What's that?" he inquired. "C.R.O. have him taped? By Jove, that's good news, Blake! Who is he?"

Blake tapped the telegram with his lean fingers.

"Mr. Robinson is an American crook named Sam McCalla, who has already served a term or two in the States. Here's a full description of him, with the additionally interesting information that he is believed to be in England and working with a notorious woman crook named Liverpool Lil."

"I know the vixen," said Coutts. "She works the blackmailing stunt. Unscrupulous as she is pretty. Jove, that simplifies matters, Blake! With those descriptions, it won't be a few hours before——"

"If you please, sir, Mr. Hanson does not appear to be in his room," announced Parsons, in an agitated voice. "His morning cup of tea is untouched on the floor of the corridor——"

"What's that?" Blake snapped sharply; and his eye narrowed as it

fell on Parsons' wrist. Hastily the butler tried to conceal it behind his back, for creeping through the plentiful supply of bandage was a crimson stain.

With a bound the detective rose to his feet and twisted the butler's left arm behind his back. Parsons gave a squeal of agony.

"Queer sort of sprain that bleeds, Parsons!" snapped the criminologist. "Let's have a look at that wrist!"

The butler was powerless in Blake's vice-like grip. He writhed and squirmed, but his struggles were useless.

"Take off that bandage, Splash," ordered Sexton Blake. And, despite the man's struggles, the newspaper man unbound the injured limb. The fresh, clean bullet-wound, hidden by its protective wrapping of gauze and oiled silk, was revealed.

"Ah!" said Blake softly. "Now, Parsons, come across—and come across quick. Who shot you?"

Parsons licked his dry lips nervously.

"I—I don't know!" he quavered. "As Heaven's my witness, Mr. Blake, I——"

"Coutts"—Blake's eyes were very stern as he turned to the Yard man—"take charge of him! Perhaps a few hours in a cell might loosen his sullen tongue. I charge him with being concerned in a conspiracy to demand money with menaces."

"Before Heaven, I'm innocent, Mr. Blake!" cried Parsons. "I don't know anything about Master Cayterer! I—I had nothing to do with it, and that's Gospel truth!"

There was a ring of sincerity in the man's voice, and Blake looked at him searchingly.

"If you are innocent, how, and why, were you shot?" he demanded.

"I—I can't tell you!" said the man sullenly. "It was nothing to do with Junior Cayterer—that I'll swear on the Book!"

Coutts grabbed hold of Parsons' sound arm.

"You're going to take a little walk with me, my man!" he announced grimly.

Parsons looked wildly round the room, but escape was impossible. Cursing, protesting his innocence at the top of his voice, he was led out of the library between Coutts and the elated newspaper man.

"By Jove, guv'nor!" ejaculated Tinker. "The plot certainly thickens. What made you suspect Parsons, guv'nor?"

Blake shrugged.

"Whether he is implicated with this man McCalla remains to be seen. One thing is certain—he knows Mr. Lemuel Clay, who, it seems, is the owner of the yellow car that Ruff Hanson saw on Christmas Eve. His agitation in the library when I mentioned the name to Mr. Cayterer was palpable proof of the fact. I have a hunch that an hour or two in the cooler, as the Yanks say, will induce him to confess."

"But where's Ruff, guv'nor? After all, we've no definite proof that Parsons is implicated."

"If I'm not much mistaken, that bullet-wound came from either Willy or Wally," said Blake quietly. "That means that friend Ruff has already tumbled to Parsons' duplicity."

He opened the envelope, which had been forgotten in the excitement, and read its typewritten contents with a frown. It ran as follows:

"Clear out of this case, you poor 'tec. Tell Cayterer that unless he comes

across by to-morrow midnight the kid'll die—slowly. Hand the money and Spagoni's spiel to the man you'll find waiting at the cemetery gates at 11 p.m. Boxing Day.

"He is unaware of the contents of the package you give him, so keep the cops out of it, or——"

"This man McCalla means business." said Blake grimly. "Come along, young 'un! I'll phone his description to the police-station, and then we'll make a search of the estimable Parsons' room."

Chapter 9.

Mrs. Bardell to the Rescue.

WHEN Ruff Hanson recovered consciousness it was nearly daybreak. His mouth was parched and dry, and his tongue felt like a piece of scorched flannel.

He was conscious of a numb, aching pain in his limbs, and it did not take him long to realise that he was as trussed and helpless as Mrs. Bardell's Christmas turkey.

He tried to rise painfully, but his throbbing head pained abominably, and he let loose a pungent string of Texan profanity as his eyes became accustomed to the dim light of dawn.

He found that he was bound hand and foot, and confined in a dark, noisome cubby-hole that smelt of tar and seawater. By the gentle rocking motion he deduced that he was aboard ship, though whereabouts on the ocean he could not gather.

"Blue bells, what a blamed fool!" he muttered bitterly. "Hog tied like a poor simp—me, Ruff Hanson—the tough from Toughville!"

He racked his brains to account for his presence aboard this malodorous craft. There was no throb of engines, and the rocking motion of the boat was rhythmic and gentle.

"I guess we're at anchor somewhere, but where and how I'm blamed if I know!" he murmured. "Hot dog! If I c'd lay my mitts on that guy Parsons I'd——"

He broke off as the door of his prison opened cautiously and a swarthy, bearded individual clad in a blue jersey and an oily peaked cap surveyed him with arms akimbo.

"Ha! Zo you haf gonsciousness recovered!" said the newcomer, expectorating neatly into a pool of rancid bilge-water.

"Say, listen, squarehead!" demanded Ruff. "What's the big beezezus?"

The other grinned sardonically.

"You Yankee fool, your nose into odder beoble's business 'ave boked, never again vill you do dat!"

"I'd like to poke a gat into your blamed ribs!" growled Ruff. "You herring-faced Hun!"

"You vait till der boss come, you another song vill sing," was the stolid reply.

"Say, listen, squarehead!" pleaded Ruff, though it went much against the grain with him to plead with any man. "If a thousand dollars are any good to ye—hand me a knife!"

The other laughed harshly.

"You tink I a fool am? My orders are to see you don't escape."

He stooped over the prostrate American and scanned his bonds with approval.

"Ha! Jules have a goot job of dose knots made," he announced gutturally. "Later you take a voyage, and you ain't coming back!"

He slammed the door behind him, leaving Ruff Hanson to his thoughts.

Who was the mysterious boss, and how did he come aboard the ship?

Vainly he tried to answer the questions.

"If I only had my gats now!" he groaned. "There might be a fighting chance to——"

He broke off suddenly, for, as the ship gave a slight lurch, he slipped from the coil of rope on which he had been flung and felt a knubbly protuberance beneath his armpit.

"Blue bells!" he chuckled. "They've left me Wilbur!"

Wilbur was the whimsical name with which he had christened his little Bolt automatic, which he carried sleeping or waking, Texan fashion, in a shoulder holster. Evidently his captors had been content with removing his two six-guns, Willy and Wally, and had overlooked the tiny, but equally deadly, weapon smuggled beneath his armpit in its oilskin holster.

"Oh boy!" breathed Ruff Hanson happily. "This is where I pull some Houdini stuff, and then 'say it with lead.'"

The gunman sleuth knew all there was to know about ropes. In his earlier life in Texas as a cowboy he was an expert lariat-thrower, and had amused his comrades in the bunkhouse and at Rodeos by imitating some of the late Houdini's spectacular escapes.

It was a knack once learned as a source of amusement that had proved him in good stead in his later career as a detective. Heartened by the knowledge that he was armed, Ruff squirmed and wriggled to manœuvre the necessary "slack" which was a preliminary to freedom.

It was a tough job. The knots had evidently been tied by a seaman, and were cunningly placed in the salt-stiffened rope that was wound like a hammock lashing round his body.

For over an hour he squirmed and wriggled to ease his cramped wrists, the rope fraying his flesh, and his strong white teeth aching with the effort to unfasten the knots.

He was forced to desist from his efforts at length to take a breather.

Panting and exhausted, he lay back just as the door opened and the bearded man peered in. He seemed to be satisfied that his captive was safe, for he gave a sardonic chuckle and made a grimly suggestive gesture with his finger across his throat as he took his leave.

Gradually Ruff's perseverance was rewarded, and he succeeded, at the cost of bleeding wrists, in wrenching his hands free from their bonds. Though his head still throbbed like a steam-hammer, he feverishly set to work to untie his pinioned legs.

The pain was excruciating as the blood circulated into his cramped limbs again.

His rugged face twisted into an ugly grin as he slid his hand into his armpit, and his fingers closed round the cold, comforting butt of his automatic.

He was a strange spectacle, with his bloodstained head, bare feet, and flowered silk dressing-gown; but there was grim purposefulness in his face as he crept towards the door, that boded little good for his captors.

MEANWHILE, Mrs. Bardell, having superintended the luncheon arrangements, had arrayed herself in her best black bombazine dress and her black straw bonnet, with its nodding osprey plume and glistening jet ornaments.

"Jane Ellen," she announced, "I'm going to take a little institutional afore lunch. Now that that 'umbug and hippogriff Parsons 'as been pinched p'r'aps you'll believe what I said about 'im. Let this be a warning to you, my gel. Dill-water runs steep, as the proverb says; tho' what the price of baby's dill-water as got to do with it I can't condescend."

. She sniffed audibly, and, grasping her umbrella, sallied out of the kitchen into the spacious grounds of Lyveden Manor.

She passed through the lodge gates to the winding roadway that led to Lyveden on the one hand and the little fishing village of Saxenham on the other. By the signpost she halted and peered at the indicator.

Wind and rain had almost obliterated the faded lettering, and Mrs. Bardell turned to the right.

Even as she did so a powerful automobile turned the corner at a great pace and churned a gout of slushy mud from a puddle, depositing the greater part of it on Mrs. Bardell's precious bombazine dress.

"Hi, you willain!" she screamed, shaking her umbrella at the rapidly-disappearing juggernaut. "I'll have the lore on you, I will! You great 'ulking road-'og, a-splashing and smashing your way as if you owned the blooming earth!"

With her pocket-handkerchief she strove to repair the damage, but with little effect. Grasping her skirts and displaying an alarming expanse of elastic-sided boots and striped stocking, the good soul hurled objurgations at the heedless motorist.

"That means I'll have to tramp to Lyveden for some petrol to clean this mess, if there's a chemist open," she said bitterly.

Resolutely gripping her umbrella, she trudged down the road, fulminating against motorists in general. She paused for breath on the outskirts of Lyveden village, then suddenly her eyes glittered. In the driveway of a house set a little back from the highway she caught a glimpse of a high-powered car.

It was the green Hispano that had ruined her dress.

There was a "To Let" sign flanking the gateway, and the place had a dilapidated appearance, although the house showed signs of occupation.

Mrs. Bardell grasped her umbrella in her left hand, and with the light of battle in her eyes marched through the gateway.

The automobile was empty, but she approached the house wrathfully, her black bonnet nodding and its jet ornaments clattering with her indignation.

"I'll let 'em know who's 'oo!" she muttered. "The owdacious——"

She broke off suddenly. A curtain had been raised for an instant in an upper room and a small white face appeared for a second at the window.

It was the frightened face of little Junior Cayterer!

"Well I'm blest!" gasped Mrs. Bardell indignantly. "The pore lamb! I'll——"

Even as she spoke the boy's face vanished and the white curtain was replaced. Mrs. Bardell's face grew crimson with wrath. She approached the paint-blistered doorway and tugged at the bell. It pealed reverberatingly through the house.

A hurried movement sounded from behind the portal and the door was opened a bare inch or two.

"What d'ye want?" queried a female voice ungraciously.

"Open this door, you 'ussy, or I'll scream the place down!" retorted Mrs. Bardell promptly. With a lightning lunge like a fencer she thrust her umbrella into the aperture and levered open the door.

"How dare you!" shrilled the tall, well-dressed woman on the other side. "What is the meaning of this unwarrantable outrage?"

Mrs. Bardell stood there, bosom heaving, umbrella raised defensively.

"Outrage, you woman you! I'll show you outrage! Not only 'ave you kidnapped a pore innercent, but ruined my best bombazine, which pore dear B——"

"For Heaven's sake, Lil," called a masculine voice from the head of the stairs, "what's all the row about?"

"This woman's crazy!" said Liverpool

Lil, nonplussed for the first time in her life. "She came barging in here like a mad woman, and——"

"Crazy, am I, you scarlet 'ussy!" screamed Mrs. Bardell.

Thwack!

Her umbrella caught the woman a resounding blow across her shoulders.

Liverpool Lil gave a scream of rage, and she leapt at Mrs. Bardell, who sidestepped nimbly. The woman crook's eyes flashed with fury, her fingers curved like the talons of a hawk about to strike.

"Sam, you fool! Get this she-cat out of it, or——" she cried hysterically.

Sam McCalla bounded down the stairs, his saturnine face working convulsively.

"Get out of here, woman!" he thundered, "or by heaven I'll——"

"Ouch!"

He crumpled up with a howl of agony as Mrs. Bardell's umbrella caught him a vicious dig.

Liverpool Lil gave a snarl of fury and scrambled at Mrs. Bardell's bonnet, but that indomitable woman belaboured her with her trusty gamp, emitting piercing screams at the top of her lusty lungs at the same time.

"For — Heaven's — sake——" gasped McCalla, painfully trying to recover his breath. "What is the matter? What does all this mean?"

"It means," snapped a quiet voice from behind the half-open door, "that the game's up, Sam McCalla. Stick 'em up!"

The door swung open, and on the steps stood Sexton Blake, an automatic in his hand.

———

LIKE a cat, Ruff Hanson tiptoed along towards the door of his prison.

To his delight he found that it was merely latched, and not barred. Evidently his captors had trusted to the skill of the man who had tied the ropes to keep him effectually a prisoner.

Cautiously he opened the door, and found himself in a narrow companionway. The sound of low voices reached him from the end of the passage, and he advanced cautiously, gun in hand, towards it.

He paused at the door of a cabin, and heard the voice of the man who had felled him the previous night in the wine cellar of Lyveden Manor.

"It's all U P, boys! That white-livered cur Parsons'll bound to squeal!" he snapped.

"Better go while the going's good, and let the other consignment go. How the blazes were we to know Blake and the Yard were spending Christmas at the manor?"

"That's true enough, boss; but are you sure it was only on account of the Cayterer kid they're down here? These local police are fools, anyway—they think smuggling passed away a hundred years back. But you never know."

"I tell you this Cayterer business ain't anything to do with us. Why couldn't the blamed fool stay in the States?" growled the other. "After all, we're only bootlegging in silks and whisky—it's one of the learned professions over there. If that fool Lord Sylvester hadn't sub-let the manor we'd have been safe, with Parsons in charge of the old smugglers' cellar that leads to Saxenham Cove."

Ruff Hanson grinned. He was beginning to see daylight. Parsons and the masked men he had seen in the yellow car had nothing to do with the kidnapping of Junior—they were smugglers.

Evidently the extensive cellars of Lyveden Manor were used as a secret

storing-place for smuggled goods, and were connected by a subterranean passage to the sea.

"What about the Yank?" queried another voice.

"Oh, him?" The boss' voice was contemptuous. "Let him rot! Best thing we can do now that Parsons' pinched is to clear. The Sea Sprite'll take us to Rochester, and then we'll put——"

"Your blamed mitts as high as they'll go!" snapped Ruff Hanson, as he flung open the cabin door with a crash and levelled his gun at the three occupants of the cabin.

One was the bearded German, another was a tall, powerful-looking man with a bald, egg-shaped head and a fierce black moustache, while the third was a squat, grizzled Frenchman.

Ruff was enjoying himself.

"Sorta hits you where you live—eh, boys?" he remarked pleasantly. "Now, don't try no funny business, Mr. Lemuel Clay. I kin hit the pip blindfold at forty paces!"

"Curse you!" snarled Clay, the smugglers' leader. "I'll get you yet, you hound! Pierre's on deck, and——"

———

NEXT WEEK!

Another long complete story of

FURG, the FUR-MAN.!

Sexton Blake and Tinker in the wilds of the Canadian backwoods, and a plot that overshadows anything that Furg has ever attempted before. You must be certain to get—

CAPTIVE CARGO!

———

Order it now for next Thursday.

———

A sudden commotion sounded overhead, and a police-whistle shrilled.

Down the companion-ladder came the sound of heavy footsteps, and the voice of Inspector Coutts snapped out:

"This way, Splash and Willis! Grab 'em before they——"

"Howdy, Coutts, old timer?" said Ruff Hanson pleasantly, as the Yard man appeared at the cabin door. "Pleasant l'il bunch, ain't they? Take 'em as a Christmas-box—it's Boxing Day!"

A volley of imprecations broke out from Lemuel Clay.

"I suppose that white-livered hound Parsons squealed?" he cried shrilly. "By Heaven, I'll get him, if I wait ten years!"

"Yes, Parsons squealed," answered Coutts. "You're under arrest, so come quietly! And a very nice little Christmas-box, too!" he added, with a grim chuckle as he snapped the handcuffs on the wrists of Mr. Lemuel Clay.

Epilogue.

MRS. BARDELL was indeed "monarch of all she purveyed," to quote her own words, a few hours after Mr. Sam McCalla and Liverpool Lil were placed behind prison bars, there to meditate on the meagreness of their Yuletide fare.

It was nearly 7 p.m., and Blake's redoubtable housekeeper queened it regally in the spacious kitchens of Lyveden Manor.

She was clad, as befitted her majesty, in a spotless white apron over her black bombazine, and she wielded a wooden spoon as a sceptre, while her minions hastened to do her bidding.

A delicious odour of roast turkey permeated the atmosphere.

Splash Page sniffed appreciatively and cocked the battered beaver of Alfred Jingle over his forehead.

"Oh, boy, lead me to it!" he grinned at Tinker, who had likewise donned his Dickensian costume. "What a day!"

Everyone was in high spirits now that the dark shadow of tragedy had been lifted from Lyvedon Manor. At Ruff Hanson's suggestion everybody present had resumed their Dickens' costume, and were now assembled before the crackling log fire.

"We ain't gonna be cheated outa our Christmas feed for the sake of a bunch of plug-uglies!" Ruff remarked.

It had been an easy matter to persuade Mrs. Bardell that her triumph in tracing the kidnapper of young Cayterer should be celebrated by another Christmas dinner in place of the one that had been spoiled.

Everyone had lent a hand with the preliminary arrangements, with the result that the unregretted absence of Parsons had made little difference to the household routine.

Little Junior Cayterer, despite his alarming experience, seemed very little the worse for his adventure, and had slept solidly through most of the afternoon. Sexton Blake himself had departed on a rather mysterious errand to London shortly after McCalla's arrest, and Tinker glanced uneasily at the clock, which had just struck seven.

"Wonder what the guv'nor's up to?" he murmured to Splash. "Queer he should dash off like that! He said he'd be back for dinner, but if this storm gets much worse, I doubt it."

The mullioned windows rattled in the keen east wind as if skeleton fingers rapped on the panes, and down the chimney, soot-blackened sleet sizzled in the glowing coals. Suddenly the long siren hoot of the Grey Panther was heard, and Ben Cayterer's rather tired eyes brightened.

"Sounds like Mr. Blake," he said eagerly. "I'll go and see."

He crossed over to the hall, and Tinker and Splash heard Blake's quiet voice outside, together with other deep, resonant tones, that were unfamiliar. The door shut softly, and they heard feet mounting the stairs.

"Something dashed mysterious is going on," muttered Tinker. "I wonder what the deuce it is?"

"Possess your soul in patience, my lad," reproved Splash.

Ruff Hanson and Coutts were playing a weird and wonderful game at the card table in the corner.

"What the deuce are you playing at?" chuckled Splash Page.

"Game of Noo York—which is 'Rollen de bones' in the vernacular. He's skinning me alive. Where'd you learn to play dice, Coutts?" he demanded of the Yard man. "You'd win a fortune in the States."

The inspector grinned widely as he pocketed a pile of silver. "I ran a Crown and Anchor board when I was in the Army!" he said complacently.

Over half an hour went by, and the dinner gong reverberated throughout the house, but still there was no sign either of Blake or Ben Cayterer.

The minutes passed, and Splash glanced uneasily at Tinker.

"What on earth's happening?" he queried. "Dinner was fixed for seven-thirty, and here it is after eight o'clock."

Suddenly a tap sounded at the door, and a moment later the footman and housemaid entered, bearing aloft great silver dishes.

They were followed by Mrs. Bardell, red of face, triumphant of mien.

"Dinner is served, gents!" she said, and with a flourish, took off a gleaming dish cover and revealed a vast turkey.

"Hurrah!" yelled Tinker. "Jones, tell Mr. Blake that dinner is ready. I believe he's with Mr. Cayterer somewhere."

The footman nodded, and withdrew, while Mrs. Bardell, knife and fork poised above that gigantic bird, beamed round the table.

"Which I sez it as shouldn't," she remarked, "a more lushus or tender bird I've never cooked, genel'men."

"You're right, Mrs. B.," agreed Splash. "The last was great, but this is a champion! They say that Christmas comes but once a year, but this time we're having it twice."

"And rightly so," said the voice of Ben Cayterer from the doorway. "Gentlemen, thanks to Sexton Blake and Sir Julius Rome, this is the happiest day of my life——"

A tense, amazed silence fell on the assembled guests; for, on the threshold, his hand in his father's own, stood Junior, again clad in the costume of Tiny Tim. But—miracle of miracles—he had no crutch, and the ugly iron strut which had disfigured his frail little leg was gone.

The boy's brown eyes were shining with excitement as Sexton Blake, accompanied by a tall, grey-bearded man in evening dress, followed them into the room.

"Mrs. Bardell and gentlemen, may I present to you Sir Julius Rome, the distinguished specialist," he said quietly.

The great physician bowed, and Tinker understood at last. This, then, was the reason for Blake's mysterious errand to London.

"Heaven bless you, sir!" said Ben Cayterer huskily. "Gentlemen—you will, I am sure, rejoice with me that Sir Julius, at the urgent request of Mr. Blake here, came down to see Junior, instead of waiting until after the holiday, as we had planned.

"I was afraid that the ordeal through which he had passed might have affected him seriously, but I am pleased to tell you that not only is he little the worse for his adventure, and—best of all—he will be able to walk normally in a few days.

"An operation which Sir Julius performed to-night, together with a course of treatment, and I hope Junior will be able to romp with the best of us."

Splash Page whistled softly.

He had heard, of course, of Sir Julius Rome and his miraculous cures and uncanny skill as a bone-setter. Looked on askance by the medical profession at first, his great work during the War, when he had cured literally thousands of so-called hopeless cases, had earned for him his knighthood and a warm public esteem.

To-night, in a few minutes almost, he had diagnosed the trouble that had baffled the best doctors of America, and here before them, in the person of the shining-eyed boy, was the proof.

"Look, dad, I can walk to the table by myself," piped the child, in his boyish treble.

Rather slowly he walked towards his chair, and, as he reached it, a great roar of applause burst out from the table.

Mrs. Bardell's honest face beamed with happiness. Tears of joy rolled down her red cheeks. Ruff Hanson gave a mighty bellow that he had not used since the far-off days when he had punched cattle on the Texas prairie. He pumped Ben Cayterer's hand till it ached.

"Say, ain't that a grand and glorious feeling? The best Christmas present of the lot," he boomed.

A flush crept into the great doctor's cheek's, and Blake, noticing his embarrassment, steered him to a chair.

"Come, Sir Julius. Mrs. Bardell is anxious to show you another instance of manipulative surgery," he said, glancing with twinkling eyes at the turkey.

That dinner beneath the raftered roof of Lyveden Manor, was a momentous and memorable one. The cheery companionship of old and tried friends: the mellow influence of good wine and incomparable cooking; and the fact that the dark shadows had been lifted, all served to make that second Yuletide feast easily the happiest Blake and Tinker had ever known.

The spirit of Dickens with his kindliness and humour pervaded the whole meal, and when the speeches came, Mrs. Bardell was toasted till the rafters rang, to the chorus of "She's a jolly good fellow."

The good soul's heart was too full for words, and it was, appropriately enough, little Junior Cayterer that echoed her sentiments when he piped the immortal Christmas benediction of Tiny Tim: "God bless us—every one!"

THE END.

DEAD MAN'S ROCK

By Sir A.T.Quiller-Couch ('Q')

A Tale of Treasure—and Vengeance!

Begin this absorbing serial now!

YOU MAY READ ON FROM HERE.

MY father was hounded to death by a scoundrel named Simon Colliver. He had been searching for clues which, according to the will of my grandfather, Amos Trenoweth, would reveal the hiding-place of the Great Ruby of Ceylon and other treasure, and I, Jasper Trenoweth, with naught in the world save the apparently useless clues to the treasure which my father had discovered before his death, and a burning desire for vengeance on Simon Colliver, had come to London to seek my fortunes.

With me came my only friend, Thomas Loveday. We were both young, and through the follies of youth and my unquenchable desire to avenge my poor father, we fell on hard times indeed. So hard, in fact, that we were faced with nothing but starvation, and as a last wild chance, we decided to try our luck at gambling.

Accordingly, we went to a strange place known to Tom, over which presided one of the most extraordinary women I have ever seen. After a painfully short time, we found that we had lost all our few shillings.

We were stunned. This, then, was to be the end! Miserably we were about to leave, when I suddenly remembered that I had in my pocket the half of a golden belt-clasp—one of the clues to the treasure on which certain signs, meaningless to me, were inscribed. What use was it to me now?

Returning to the roulette table, I placed the clasp, which was accepted by the strange woman as the equivalent of £5, on the square marked 13. This stake would decide between life and death for me, but I did not feel it. My passion had fallen upon an anti-climax, and I was even yawning when the murmur of many voices, and a small pile of gold and silver at my side, announced that I had won.

"So the luck has changed at last," said the woman. "Be brave whilst it is with you."

In answer, I again placed the clasp upon the number 13.

Once more I won, and this time heavily. Tom laid his hand upon my shoulder and said, "Let us go," but I shook my head and went on.

Time after time I won now, until the pile beside me became immense. Again and again Tom whispered in my ear that we had won enough and that luck would change shortly, but I held on. And now the others surrounded me in a small crowd, and began to stake on the numbers I chose. Put the clasp where I would, the needle stopped in front of it.

They brought a magnet to see if this curious piece of metal had any power of attraction; but our hostess only laughed, and assured them, at any rate, there was no steel in the pointer, as (she added) some of them ought to know by this time. When eight times I had put the buckle down and eight times had found a fresh heap of coin at my side, she turned to me and said:

"You play bravely, young man. What is your name?"

"Jasper Trenoweth."

Again I fancied I caught the gleam in her eyes; and this time it even seemed as though her teeth shut tight as she heard the words. But she simply laughed a tranquil laugh and said:

"A queer-sounding name that—Trenoweth. Is it a lucky one?"

"Never, until now," said I.

"Well, play on. It does my heart good, this fight between us. But you are careful, I see. Why don't you stake your pile as well while this wonderful run lasts?"

Again Tom's hand was laid upon my shoulder, and this time his voice was urgent. But I was completely deaf.

"As you please," said I coldly, and laid the whole pile down upon the black.

It was madness. It was worse than madness. But I won again; and now the heap of my winnings was enormous. I glanced at the strange woman; she sat as impassive as ever.

"Play," said she.

Thrice more I won, and now the pile beside her had to be replenished. Yet she moved not a muscle of her face, not a flash of her mysterious eyes.

At last, sick of success, I turned and said:

"I have had enough of this. Will it satisfy you if I stake it all once more?"

Again she laughed.

"You are brave, Mr. Trenoweth, and indeed worth the fighting. You may win to-night, but I shall win in the end. I told you that I would readily lose to you, and so I will; but you take me at my word with a vengeance. Still, I should like to possess that clasp of yours, so let it be once more."

I laid the whole of my winnings on the red. By this time all the guests had gathered round to see the issue of this conflict. Not a soul put any money on this turn of the wheel, so engrossed were they in the duel. Every face was white with excitement, every lip quivered. Only we, the combatants, sat unmoved—I and the strange woman with the unfathomable eyes.

"Red stands for many things," said she, as she lightly twirled the needle round. "Blood and rubies and lovers' lips. But black is the livery of Death, and Death shall win them all in the end."

As the pointer of fortune circled on its last errand, I could catch the stifled breath of the crowd about me, so deep was the hush that fell upon us all. I felt Tom's hand tighten its clutch upon my shoulder. I heard—or fancied I heard—the heart of the man upon my right thump against his ribs.

I could feel my own pulse beating all the while with steady and regular stroke. Somehow I knew that I should win, and somehow it flashed upon me that she knew it, too. Even as the idea came darting across my brain, a multitude of pent-up cries broke forth from thirty pairs of white lips. I scarcely looked to see the cause, but as I turned to our hostess her eyes looked straight into mine and her sweet voice rose above the din:

"Gentlemen, we have played enough to-night. The game is over."

I had broken the bank!

I STOOD with Tom gathering up my winnings as the crowd slowly melted from the room, and as I did so, cast a glance at the woman whom I had thus defeated. She was leaning back in her chair, apparently indifferent to her losses as to her gains. Only her eyes were steadily fixed upon me as I shovelled the coin into my pockets. As she caught my eye she pulled out a scrap of paper and pencil, scribbled a few words, tossed the note to the man with the shovel, who instantly left the room and said:

"Is it far from this place to your home?"

"Not very."

"That's well; but be careful. To win such a sum is only less dangerous than to lose it. I shall see you again—you and your talisman. By the way, may I look at it for a moment?"

We were alone in the room, we three. She took the clasp, looked at it intently for a full minute, and then returned it. Already the dawn of another day was peering in through the chinks in the blinds, giving a ghastly faintness to the expiring candles, throwing a grey and sickening reality over the scene—the disordered chairs, the floor strewn with scraps of paper, the signs and relics of the debauchery of play.

Ghastlier than all was the yellow face of the woman in the pitiless light. But there she sat, seemingly untired, in all the splendour of her flashing gems as we left her—a very goddess of the gaming table.

We had reached the door and were stepping into the darkness of the outer passage, when Tom whispered:

"Be on your guard; that note meant mischief!"

I nodded, swung open the door, and stepped out into the darkness. Even as I did so, I heard one quick step at my left side, saw a faint gleam, and felt myself violently struck upon the chest. For a moment I staggered back, and then heard Tom rush past me and deal one crashing blow.

"Run, run! Down the passage—quick!"

In an instant we were tearing through the open door behind, in the glare of all the candles, the figure of the yellow woman still sitting motionless and calm.

We gained the door, and plunged into the bright daylight. Up the alley we tore out into the street, across it and down another, then through a perfect maze of by-lanes. Tom led and I followed behind.

Still we tore on, although not a footstep followed us, nor had we seen a soul since Tom struck my assailant down. Spent and breathless at last we emerged upon the Strand, and here Tom pulled up.

"The streets are wonderfully quiet," said he.

I thought for a moment, and then said:

"It is Monday morning."

Scarcely were the words out of my mouth when I heard something ring upon the pavement beside me. I stooped and picked up the Golden Clasp.

(Continued overleaf.)

BABS —the famous high-powered racer that was wrecked on Pendine Sands. A coloured metal model of this car, made to stand square and solid on its own four wheels, is given with every issue of this week's NELSON LEE Library. This is a great opportunity to get one of these splendid models. Nothing like them has been given with any other paper.
Ask for the

NELSON LEE LIBRARY
On Sale Everywhere.   Price 2d.

"Well," said I, "this is strange."

"Not at all," said Tom. "Look at your breast-pocket."

I looked and saw a short slit across my breast just above the heart. As I put my hand up, a sovereign, and then another, rolled clinking on to the pavement.

Tom picked them up, and handing them to me, remarked:

"Jasper, you may thank Heaven to-day, if you are in a mood for it. You have had a narrow escape."

"What do you mean?"

"Why, that you would be a dead man now had you not carried that piece of metal in your breast-pocket. Let me see it for a moment."

We looked at it together, and there surely enough, almost in the centre of the clasp, was a deep dent. We were silent for a minute or so, and then Tom said:

"Let us get home. It would not do for us to be seen with this money about us."

We crossed the Strand, and turned off it to the door of our lodging. There I stopped.

"Tom, I am not coming in. I shall take a long walk and a bathe to get this fearful night out of my head. You can take the money upstairs, and put it away somewhere in hiding. Stay, I will keep a coin or two. Take the rest with you."

Tom looked up at the gleam of sunshine that touched the chimney-pots above, and decided.

"Well, for my part, I am going to bed; and so will you if you are wise."

"No. I will be back this evening, so let the fatted calf be prepared. I must get out of this for a while."

"Where are you going?"

"Oh, anywhere! I don't care. Up the river, perhaps."

"You don't wish me to go with you?"

"No. I had rather be alone. Tom, I have been a fool. I led you into a hole whence nothing but a marvellous chance has delivered us, and I owe you an apology. And—Tom, I also owe you my life."

"Not to me, Jasper; to the Clasp."

"To you," I insisted. "Tom, I have been a thoughtless fool, and—Tom, that was a splendid blow of yours."

He laughed, and ran upstairs, while

I turned and gloomily sauntered down the deserted street.

An Age-Old Story

WHEN Tom asked me where I was going, I had suggested an excursion up the river; though, to tell the truth, this answer had come with the question. Be that as it may, the afternoon of that same Sunday found me on the left bank of the Thames between Streatley and Pangbourne; found me, with my boat moored idly by, stretched on my back amid the undergrowth, and easefully staring upward through a trellis-work of branches into the heavens.

I had been lying there a full hour, wondering vaguely of my last night's adventure, listening to the spring-time chorus of the birds, lazily and listlessly watching a bough that bent and waved its fan of foliage across my face, or the twinkle of the tireless kingfisher flashing down-stream in loops of light, when a blackbird lit on a branch hard by my left hand, and, all unconscious of an audience, began to pour forth his rapture to the day.

Lying there I could spy his black body and yellow bill, and drink in his song with dreamy content. So sweetly and delicately was he fluting, that by degrees slumber crept gently and unperceived upon my tired brain; and as the health-giving distillation of the melody stole upon my parched senses, I fell into a deep sleep.

•   •   •   •   •

WHAT was that? Music? Yes, but not the song of my friend the blackbird, not the mellow note that had wooed me to slumber and haunted my dreams. Music? Yes, but the voice was human, and the song articulate. I started, and rose upon my elbow to listen. The voice was human beyond a doubt—sweetly human. It was that of a girl singing. But where? I looked around and saw nobody. Yet the singer could not be far off, for the words, though softly and gently sung, dwelt clearly and distinctly upon my ear. Still half asleep, I sank back again and listened.

"Flower of the May,
    Saw ye one pass?

'Love passed to-day
    While the dawn was,
    O, but the eyes of him shone as a glass.'"

"Flower of the May,
    Bird of the——"

The voice quivered, trailed off, and stopped. I heard a rustling of leaves to the right, and then the same voice broke out in prose, in very agitated and piteous prose:

"Oh, my boat—my boat! What shall I do?"

I jumped to my feet, caught a glimpse of something white, and of two startled but appealing eyes, then tore down to the bank. There, already twenty yards down-stream, placidly floated the boat, its painter trailing from the bows, and its whole behaviour pointing to a leisurely but firm resolve to visit Pangbourne.

My own boat was close at hand. But when did hot youth behave with thought in a like case? I did as ninety-nine in a hundred would do. I took off my coat, kicked off my shoes, and, as the voice cried. "Oh, please, do not trouble!" plunged into the water.

The refractory boat, once on its way, was in no great hurry, and allowed itself to be overtaken with great good humour. I clambered in over the stern, caught up the sculls which lay across the thwarts, and, dripping but triumphant, brought my captive back to shore.

"How can I thank you?"

If my face was red as I looked up, it must be remembered that I had to stoop to make the boat fast. If my eyes had a tendency to look down again, it must be borne in mind that the water from my hair was dripping into them. They gazed for a moment, however, and this was what they saw:

At first, only another pair of eyes, of dark grey eyes twinkling with a touch of merriment, though full at the same time of honest gratitude. It was some time before I clearly understood that these belonged to a face, and that face the fairest that ever looked on a summer day.

So we stood, she smiling, and I dripping, while the blackbird, robbed of the song's ending, took up his own tale anew, and, being now on his mettle, tried a few variations. So, for all power I had of speech, might we have stood until to-day had not the voice repeated:

"How can I thank you?"

I looked up. Yes, she was beautiful, past all criticism—not tall, but in pose and figure queenly beyond words. Under the brim of her straw hat the waving hair fell loosely, but not so loosely as to hide the broad brow arching over lashes of deepest brown. I had scarcely spoken to woman before, never to beauty. Tongue-tied and dripping I stood there, yet was half inclined to run away.

"And yet, why did you make yourself so wet? Have you no boat? Is not that your boat lying there under the bank?" There was an amused tremor in the speech.

Somehow I felt absurdly guilty. She must have mistaken my glance, for she went on:

"Is it that you wish——" and began to search in the pocket of her gown.

"No, no," I cried, "not that!"

I had forgotten the raggedness of my clothes, now hideously emphasised by my bath. Of course, she took me for a

Printed and published every Thursday by the Proprietors, The Amalgamated Press, Ltd., The Fleetway House, Farringdon Street, London, E.C.4. Advertisement offices: The Fleetway House, Farringdon Street, London, E.C.4. Registered for transmission by Canadian Magazine Post. Subscription rates: Inland and Abroad, 11s. per annum; 5s. 6d. for six months. Sole agents for South Africa: The Central News Agency, Ltd. Sole agents for Australia and New Zealand: Messrs. Gordon & Gotch, Ltd.; and for Canada, The Imperial News Co., Ltd. (Canada).—Saturday, December 10th, 1927.

beggar. Why not? I looked like one. But as the thought flashed upon me it brought unutterable humiliation. She must have divined something of the agony in my eyes, for a tiny hand was suddenly laid on my arm and the voice said:

"Please forgive me. I was stupid, and am so sorry. But it was odd to swim when your boat was close at hand, was it not?"

I looked, faltered, met her honest glance, and we both broke into shy laughter. A mad desire to seize the little hand that for a moment had rested on my arm caught hold of me.

"Yes, it was odd," I answered slowly, and with difficulty; "but it seemed—the only thing to do at the time."

She laughed a low laugh again.

"Do you generally behave like that?"

"I don't know."

There was a pause, and then I added: "You see, you took me by surprise."

"Where were you when I first called?" she asked.

"Lying in the grass close by."

"Then"—with a vivid blush—"you must have——"

"Heard you singing? Yes."

"Oh!"

Again there was a pause, and this time the blackbird executed an elaborate exercise with much delicacy and finish. The brown lashes drooped, the lovely eyes were bent on the grass, and the little hand swung the creeper nervously backward and forward.

"Why did you not warn me that I had an audience?"

"Because, in the first place, I was too late. When you began I was——"

"What?" she asked, as I hesitated.

"Asleep."

"And I disturbed you. I am so sorry."

"I am not."

I was growing bolder as she became more embarrassed. I looked down upon her now from my superior height, and my heart went out to worship the grace of her. With a touch of resentment she drew herself up, held out her hand, and said somewhat proudly:

"I thank you, sir, for this service."

I took the hand, but not the hint. It was an infinitesimal hand as it lay in my big brown one, and yet it stung my frame as with some delicious and electric shock. My heart beat wildly and my eyes remained fixed upon hers. The colour on the fair face deepened a shade; the little chin was raised a full inch, and the voice became perceptibly icy.

"I must go, sir. I hope I have thanked you as far as I can, and——"

"And what?"

"Forgive me that I was about to offer you money."

The hat's brim bent now, but under it I could see honest eyes full of pain.

"Forgive you!" I cried. "Who am I to forgive you? You were right. I am no better than a beggar."

The red lips quivered and broke into a smile. A tiny dimple appeared,

vanished, and reappeared. The hat's brim nodded again, and then the eyes sparkled into laughter.

"A sturdy beggar, at any rate."

It was the poorest little joke, but love is not exacting of wit. Again we both laughed, but this time with more relief, and yet the embarrassment that followed was greater.

"Must you go?" I asked, as I bent down to pull the boat in.

"I really must," she answered shyly. And then, as she pulled out a tiny watch: "Oh, I am late—so late! I shall keep mother waiting and make her lose the train. What shall I do? Oh, pray, sir, be quick!"

A mad hope coursed through me. I pointed to the boat and said:

"I have made it so wet. If you are late, better let me row you. Where are you going?"

"To Streatley; but I cannot——"

"I also am going to Streatley. Please let me row you."

Before my persistency she wavered and was conquered. "But my boat?" she said.

"I will tow it behind." And in the glad success of my hopes I allowed her no time for further parley, but ran off to my own boat, tied the two together, and gently helped her to her seat.

(A great love has entered the life of Jasper Trenoweth—a love which is bound up, as events will show, with the rest of the events in this fateful story. Long instalment next week!)

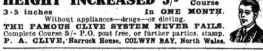

BOYS!

When you are asked 'What do you want for Christmas?' Say "ERECTOR"

It may be dad, or mother, or an uncle or aunt—it matters not who asks the question—make sure of an "Erector" set this Christmas. In the meantime there's a very interesting little book that you can have free. It tells all about these wonderful sets of "Erector" parts with which you can make innumerable models—cranes, bridges, motor cars and steam engines for instance. And they work too! For there's a powerful electric motor with some of the sets to drive the models. Send for the free book now, look through it, mark the set you fancy in pencil. We suggest No. 4, it makes 500 models and has a motor. Keep the book handy, wait for the question—'What do you want for Christmas?'—Say "ERECTOR" and hand the book over for inspection. The chances are you'll get the very set you've marked. So don't forget, but send for the free book now.

Nothing delights you more than to possess a real good mechanical model, but no matter how wonderful that one model may be you get tired of it eventually. But with a set of "Erector" parts you can never tire, for models can be built and taken to pieces again, and there's always something different. And as you build each model you will be proud of it. For "Erector" now has innumerable new parts which make it possible to build more realistic models and bigger and better ones than ever before. Besides, many complete units are now included according to the size of the set, and such items as a boiler, 3-drum hoist, car hood, steering-wheel, disc-wheel, truck body, digger scoop, clam shell bucket, tip bucket, and reverse switch attachments must surely convey to you how truly wonderful "Erector" is. The new solid brass perfect gear standardisation adds another useful feature, and the new Udylite finish on the bright parts and electrically baked enamelled colour parts ensure that your "Erector" set will remain new in appearance always. There is certainly no other constructional toy to beat "Erector" and you must certainly have a set even if you have to wait until Christmas. But get a set before if you can.

ERECTOR

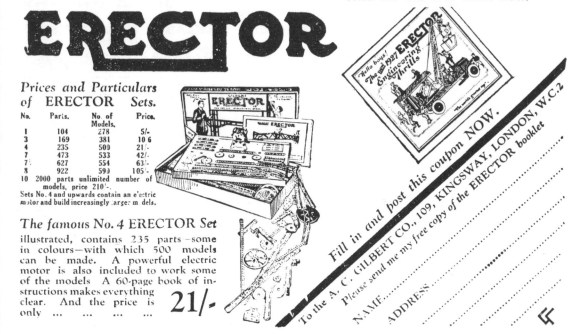

Prices and Particulars of ERECTOR Sets.

No.	Parts.	No. of Models.	Price.
1	104	278	5/-
3	169	381	10/6
4	235	500	21/-
7	473	533	42/-
7½	627	554	63/-
8	922	590	105/-
10	2000	unlimited number of models, price 210/-	

Sets No. 4 and upwards contain an electric motor and build increasingly larger models.

The famous No. 4 ERECTOR Set

illustrated, contains 235 parts—some in colours—with which 500 models can be made. A powerful electric motor is also included to work some of the models. A 60-page book of instructions makes everything clear. And the price is only ... ...

21/-

Fill in and post this coupon NOW.

To the A. C. GILBERT CO., 109, KINGSWAY, LONDON, W.C.2

Please send me my free copy of the ERECTOR booklet

NAME

ADDRESS

Manufactured by the A. C. GILBERT Co., 109, Kingsway, London, W.C.2

The Crime of the Christmas Tree

Specially written Christmas Sexton Blake story, introducing Splash Page, Inspector Coutts and Tinker. By the author of previous successes such as "The Black Carol," etc.

A Christmas Tree – symbol of Yuletide fun and frolic, and yet . . . . Who but Sexton Blake could have solved the mystery of the tragic tree o. Huntingley Manor, standing sentinel over the silent form of Jabez Bruff?

Prologue.

The League of Robin Hood.

"BENTLY, old egg, the scheme sounds fruity to me — distinctly fruity — ripe, in fact, for the plucking."

"An ominous metaphor, sir, if I might vouchsafe the remark," said Bently, factotum in chief and mental and sartorial adviser of that cheerful young man, the Hon. Toby Cripps.

The Hon. Toby surveyed his slim, elegant figure in a cheval glass, and beamed approvingly through his oblong, shell-rimmed monocle at his reflection. Solomon in all his glory was dowdy compared to that exquisitely-garbed young man.

From the tips of his white-spatted, glossy shoes to the crown of his resplendent silk hat he was sartorially perfect. Not even the editor of "The Tailor and Cutter" could have found fault with his braided morning coat and harmoniously-striped trousers.

His one eccentricity was his oblong monocle—an invention of his own that caused a sensation when he first appeared with it in the Burlington Arcade.

"Ominous, did you say, Bently?" he asked, a slight furrow creasing his smooth forehead. "What d'you

mean, ominous? Be brief, be pithy—explain yourself."

"I was referring to your metaphor, sir," said Bently, with a resigned expression.

"Metaphor? That's the sort of thing that's generally mixed, isn't it, like vermouth, and grill?"

Bently's solemn face flickered for a moment.

"You said, sir, that the scheme was ripe for the plucking. I merely suggested, sir, that in view of the circumstances, the — er — advertiser might also consider it ripe, but in a somewhat more sinister light."

"Ominous! Sinister! Come, come, Bently, you've been reading too much crime stuff! Why carp? Blithe is to-day's password—blithe and gay—what!"

"Very good, sir," said Bently. "I merely ventured to warn you—er—in case of eventualities."

"Now look here, Bently, you old croaker. Out with it! What are you insinuating?"

The Hon. Toby pushed back his silk hat and leaned negligently against the wardrobe.

"Do you, or do you not, want to spend Christmas at Barchester Towers? You know my Aunt Anastasia of old," he added.

Bently nodded.

"I do, sir; but——"

"But me no buts, you old goat!"

said Toby. "Can you imagine anything more soul-corroding than spending Christmas with my aunt? She is certain to invite a party of earnest young women, whose wildest idea of dissipation will be charades or hunt the slipper. I know 'em! Blights, likewise blots, on the Yuletide escutcheon, whereas this cove seems to be one of the lads, judging by his letter and advertisement."

"There may be a catch in it, sir," persisted the sceptical Bently.

The Hon. Toby pulled out his notebook and extracted a newspaper cutting from the personal advertisement columns of the "Daily Radio."

"Catch or no catch," he remarked, "it sounds like the elephant's elbows to me. Now listen, Bently—it's plain and straightforward."

And he read out the following advertisement:

"Christmas guest wanted to join novel Yuletide party. Must be young, ex-Service, Public school, with taste for adventure. Excitement and thrills guaranteed to right applicant.—Write Box 0968."

"There's nothing wrong with that, as far as I can see, Bently," said Toby. "As I say, I wrote to the merchant, and his reply this morning seems all in order. He simply asks me to meet him in Room No. 11

" I think, gentlemen, we are all agreed on one point at least— the League of Robin Hood is going to make itself felt this Christmas ! "

at the Hotel Splendide, to discuss the matter. Now the old Splendide's a pretty sound sort of show. The appointment's fixed at a decent hour —cocktail time, just before luncheon —and, as I said before, the whole thing sounds very fruity.

"Have I a taste for adventure? I ask you, Bently—did I or did I not attempt to play 'Loch Lomond' on that fat police-sergeant's whistle on Boat Race night?"

"You did, sir. That little effort of improvisation cost you twenty shillings and costs."

"Don't be sordid, Bently," said the Hon. Toby, with a pained expression. "I've made up my mind. I'm going to see this merchant and find out all about his novel Christmas binge. If it's the goods I'll send a wire to Aunt Anastasia. Her bally Christmas parties always remind me of that carol chappie, you know—Wincarnis, or some such name."

"Wenceslas, sir—good King Wenceslas !"

"That's the bloke ! The line I always remember applies to Aunt Anastasia's party: 'For the frost was cru-el !' Cheerio, Bently ! I may see you anon !"

"Will you be back for lunch, sir?" asked the valet.

"I doubt it, Bently—I very much doubt it," said the Hon. Toby.

Bently helped him into his fur-lined coat, and, humming the latest snatch of a musical comedy success, the Hon. Toby descended the stairs of the Jermyn Street flat and strolled briskly towards the Haymarket.

IT was a crisp, frosty December morning. Christmas was ten days off. The shop windows were gay with seasonable fare, and the pavements thronged with people taking the advice of the much-advertised slogan : "Shop Early !" He hailed a taxi and directed the driver to the Hotel Spendide. Lolling back in the tonneau he considered the project again.

The Hon. Toby was the youngest son of the Earl of Haredale, that eccentric peer who spent most of his time abroad in his quest for lepidoptera, or bally butterflies, as his son called them.

Toby had served in the R.A.F. during the War, and, being in receipt of a handsome allowance from his father, he emulated, as far as possible, the excellent example of the lilies of the field. He toiled not, neither did he spin anything except the whimsical yarns which made him such a popular figure in various cocktail lounges in the West End.

The taxi drew up at the Splendide, and Toby grinned cheerfully at the bemedalled commissionaire who saluted him.

"Deal with the jehu, William," he said airily, and strode into the

lounge of the famous hotel. The reception clerk bowed. The Hon. Toby was a familiar figure at the Splendide.

"Tell me, Carlos, there is some sort of doings on in Room No. 11. Know anything about it?"

The reception clerk smiled.

"Why, yes, sir; that is Lord Huntingley's suite. Are you expected, sir?"

"What ! Old Robin Huntingley !" gasped the Hon. Toby. "But I thought he was in Africa, potting big game. Lend me one of these buttoned myrmidons of yours, Carlos. I always get lost in your bally corridors."

"Show Mr. Cripps up to eleven !" Carlos commanded to a diminutive page-boy.

The Hon. Toby adjusted his famous oblong monocle as he followed his guide into the lift. This was a surprising development. Young Lord Huntingley, V.C., D.S.O., had been Toby's O.C. in France. Could it be possible that he and the anonymous advertiser were one and the same?

He followed the boy along the carpeted corridor of the hotel, and waited until he was announced. A low hum of voices came from behind the open portal, and suddenly someone called: "Come in !"

The Hon. Toby entered, and found five young men and a pretty girl grouped about the centre table.

"Hallo, hallo !" he said cheerfully, as he recognised a plump, pink-faced young man in the corner, helping himself to a cocktail. "If it isn't old Pongo !"

"Wot cheer, Toby, old fruit !" grinned Pongo. "Are you in on this mystery beano?"

"Looks like it," replied Toby, a trifle bewildered. "What's the merry idea?"

"Search me !" said Pongo Paget, who held down a more or less arduous post in the Foreign Office. The girl, slim, shingled, and sophisticated, looked over at Toby and smiled. That susceptible person coloured. She was extraordinarily attractive.

Her cornflower blue eyes seemed to dance with mischief, and a fascinating dimple lurked at the corner of soft, red lips. She was dressed in a simple little frock of apple green georgette.

"What ho! What ho!" drawled Pongo. "You've clicked, my boy," he added, as the girl crossed over towards Toby and held out her hand.

"You are Mr. Cripps, I presume, she said, in a voice that matched the charm of her appearance.

"Toby of that ilk," he replied.

"I'm so sorry to keep you all waiting," said the girl, "but my brother will be along quite shortly to explain. Won't you help yourself to a cocktail, Mr. Cripps?"

"Rather!" agreed Toby, with alacrity. "Er—does your brother happen to be Lord Huntingley, by any chance?"

She nodded.

"Old Robin Huntingley! Bless my soul, then you must be his kid sister, Marion—er—I beg your pardon," added Toby. "But old Robin used to speak a lot about you in the mess. I served under him in France, y'know. You were about eight or nine then, I think. I remember you knitted him a chest protector, or something——"

Lady Marion coloured faintly.

"Fancy you remembering that," she said. "Why, it seems centuries ago, and you don't look very old."

"I'm frightfully senile, really," retorted Toby. "I've had my face lifted and my glands removed, so you don't notice it at first glance!"

She gurgled with laughter.

"Robin told me about you. He was frightfully braced when he got your letter in reply to his advertisement. You see, he's been abroad so long that he's quite out of touch with his old friends. He only came back from Africa two months ago. It's his first Christmas at home since the Armistice."

"I see. And that ad. of his was to get in touch with some convivial blokes, so's to make sure of a merry Christmas, eh?"

"Partly," said Lady Marion, and her face became grave for a moment. "There was another reason, too. We had very many replies to the advertisement, but Robin winnowed them out, leaving——"

She made a graceful gesture towards the five men who were chatting quietly in various parts of the room. They were all young, well dressed, and bore the indefinable, but unmistakable stamp of money and good breeding.

"I see Many were called, but few are chosen!" laughed Toby. "I'm glad you've included old Pongo, there. Great chap, Pongo! His imitation of a pneumatic road drill must be heard to be believed. Positively amazing, it is."

"You mean Mr. Paget?"

"That's the chappie," said Toby, beaming through his monocle. "The Glaxo babe of the Foreign Office. Sleeps peacefully from ten till four every day."

"Is that lounge lizard libelling me as usual?" drawled the plump Pongo, lumbering to his feet. "My dear lady, let me warn you against this man Cripps. Beneath that guileless, not to say fatuous, exterior, he hides a soul steeped in villainy. He

is a secret gum chewer, a frequenter of low taverns, a——"

Pongo broke off suddenly, and the conversation subsided as a tall, handsome man entered the room, accompanied by a burly, red-faced clergyman.

"Why Robin, what a time you've been!" said Lady Marion reproachfully. "These gentlemen have all been here since eleven-thirty."

"My fault, Lady Marion—my fault entirely!" boomed the clergyman, in a rich, jovial voice. "Robin and I had an—altercation with a certain gentleman in Shinwell that delayed us considerably. Bless my soul," he added, and his broad, red face creased into a delightful grin—"Toby Cripps, by all that's wonderful!"

Toby's monocle dropped in astonishment.

"Why, padre!" he exclaimed delightedly. "Do mine optics deceive me, or is it the one and only Jovial John?"

"Jovial John it is, Toby, my boy!" laughed Lord Huntingley. "As large as life, if not larger. But park yourselves around, gentlemen," he added, taking his stand against the fireplace. "Cigarettes and drinks are at your elbows."

The little groups drew up their chairs in a semi-circle before the warm glow of the electric fire. There was a sudden little silence, full of expectancy, as their host cleared his throat, and smiled down at them.

LORD HUNTINGLEY, V.C., D.S.O., big, broad-shouldered, and extraordinarily handsome, was known by reputation at least to everyone present. During the War he had been one of the most famous and audacious Aces in the R.A.F., and since the Armistice, his career as an explorer and pioneer in darkest Africa had added fresh laurels to his name.

He was not yet thirty-five, and his keen grey eyes still glowed with the enthusiasm of youth, as he turned to his assembled guests.

"Well, gentlemen, I presume you are all waiting to hear further details regarding the advertisement to which you replied," he began. "I may say that it was inserted with a particular object in view, and what that object is I will come to later.

"The point is, I want half a dozen young men who are not afraid of public opinion, who are willing to act under my leadership this Christmas-time to help give a square deal to the poor devils of ex-Servicemen who are not so fortunately placed as we are.

"I have chosen you six out of many applications—chiefly fraudulent begging letters—because I know something of your War records, and a good deal about your personal characters. You are all tolerably well off, all sportsmen, and—I'm not sure about Toby here—endowed with a certain amount of sense."

"For those kind words many thanks," said Toby Cripps. There was a ripple of laughter, and Lord Huntingley continued.

"Now, this isn't going to be a pijaw, you chaps, nor is there going to

be any snivelling sentiment about it. You all know how the present wave of industrial depression is affecting the country. We have over a million unemployed, and many of them served with us in France. They're going to have a pretty thin time of it this Christmas, gentlemen, and the question is, what are we going to do about it?"

He paused. There was an uncomfortable little silence. Pongo and Toby Cripps looked embarrassed.

"What about a whip round?" suggested a lean young man on Toby's left.

Lord Huntingley smiled.

"Less than a drop in the ocean, my dear Dale. No, we've got to think out a better scheme than that, and that's why I called this conference. You want a Merry Christmas—we all do. We want to recapture the Dickens spirit and mix charity with jollity.

"We also have to tackle the Scrooges and the selfish blighters who won't stir a finger to help rally round the poor devils who are out of work. I admit, quite frankly, we nine persons cannot hope to solve the unemployment problem, but we can make Christmas jolly for a few families.

"That's where Padre Brown comes in. You all know what magnificent work he did out in France? Let me tell you, he's tackling a harder job and fighting a worse enemy than the Bosche, in his slum parish in Shinwell. I've been there, and seen it."

"Yes, but dash it all, Robin," broke in Toby, "that's all very well! We all know that slums are bally rotten places, but short of burning 'em down, I don't see what we're going to do about it."

"I'll tell you what I intend to do, with your co-operation, gentlemen," said Lord Huntingley. "There are several people known to us who have made pots of money during the War, and afterwards, who don't care two hoots in Hades what happens to ex-Servicemen, or anybody else.

"And there are not only profiteers. We all know scaly blighters who seem to take a delight in kicking a man when he's down, mealy-mouthed magistrates on the bench, who, because they've got a touch of liver, sentence some poor devil of a coster to a month's hard; raddled old harridans who spend half their time in mud baths, and the other dancing or gambling, and bullying their servants; crooked company promoters; defaulting slate club secretaries—the list is endless."

"Agreed," broke in Pongo Paget. "But what are we going to do about it? And where does the novel Christmas party of the advertisement come in?"

HUNTINGLEY smiled. "It occurred to me that it would be an excellent scheme if we formed ourselves into a society. A provisional name for it would be the S.S.S., meaning the Society for the Suppression of Scugs. If we could kidnap a few profiteers, and hold 'em up for ransom, and with the money buy a new parish hall, a gymnasium, and a slap-up Christmas dinner for everybody in the padre's parish, it strikes me we would give practical assistance to the down-and-outs, teach the scugs a lesson, and, incidentally, give ourselves a thrill or two."

"A sound scheme—very sound," said Toby, brightening. "If you could kidnap my Aunt Anastasia, for instance, I'd galumph for joy."

Padre Browne chuckled.

"I suggest, gentlemen, that we start on a very small scale. In my parish at Shinwell we have, Heaven help us, three of the worst type of—er—scugs in existence. I am not exaggerating. For callous indifference to suffering, selfishness, and mean, vengeful natures, these three men are unsurpassed. They deserve to be boiled in oil."

The padre's usually jovial face was set and stern. Known in Shinwell as the fighting parson, the Rev. John Browne, M.C., had deliberately turned his back on the large emoluments and easy living which were offered to him on his demobilisation.

He deliberately chose the harder path, and toiled amidst the squalor of the slums to lighten and alleviate the lot of his poor and needy parishioners. There was nothing namby-pamby about the Rev. John. He knew how to use his fists, as many a drunken, wife-beating bully learned to his cost down at Shinwell.

"Who are these blighters, padre?" demanded Toby. "How about making a list of 'em, like thingummy in the 'Mikado.' You know, 'we've got him on the list, he never will be missed,'" he hummed. "Suppose we all cudgel the grey cells and work out a scheme to give all the scugs we know a dashed good hiding?"

"I can name my particular candidates quite easily," said the clergyman. "There is Sir Marcus Grossman, who, incidentally, owns most of the property round Shinwell, and has battened on the rents of the wretched slum-dwellers for years. I asked him for a donation for a Christmas treat for the kids; he gave me a cheque for a pound!

"Then there's the magistrate of Shinwell Road Police Court, Mr. Jabez Bruff, one of the most unpleasant men it has been my misfortune to meet. He is a bully, a braggart, and takes a perverse pleasure in sentencing the poor wretch who has the ill-luck to appear before him to the maximum penalty allowed by the law.

"He sentenced a poor little half-starved servant girl, who stole an apron and a pair of shoes from her mistress, to three months' hard labour. And it was a first offence."

"Good glory!" ejaculated Lord Huntingley. "Why didn't she appeal?"

"Appeal?" The padre laughed bitterly. "She hadn't got the price! Her legal representative—it was a dock brief—is a toady of Bruff's. The poor girl was too dazed to understand exactly what had happened to her.

"Then there's Mr. William Snape. I should like to lay my hands on that cunning, treacherous devil. He was a secretary to the local Christmas club. The poor people of my parish invested their sixpences and their shillings—money they could ill afford—in order to provide their kiddies with some extra Christmas cheer.

"Yesterday they discovered that Snape had decamped with the whole lot. It came to about three hundred and fifty pounds!"

"Put him on the list, Pongo," said Toby. "Snape, the Swindler, to be scragged!"

Lord Huntingley smiled.

"Now supposing, for example, that the S.S.S. were to tackle the three men the padre has just mentioned? We would obtain plenty of excitement, I fancy if, for instance, we kidnapped Sir Marcus Grossman, or Mr. Jabez Bruff, and gave them a taste of their own medicine."

"Robbing the rich to help the poor, eh, like Robin Hood?" said Toby.

Lady Marion, who had hitherto been silent, leapt to her feet and clapped her hands.

"Oh, I've got it! Why on earth didn't we think of it before? Let's call ourselves the League of Robin Hood. Robin here is descended, according to legend at least, from the original outlaw of Sherwood Forest. It all fits in so beautifully. Padre Browne, you are hereby christened Friar Tuck!"

The clergyman chuckled.

"I' faith, wench, had I a quarterstaff, I'd show thee how a son of the church could crack a pate wi' the best of them."

"By Jove, that's a splendid idea, Lady Marion," broke in Pongo. "I was almost afraid you were going to suggest we could wear costumes."

"Why not?" broke in Lord Huntingley. "They're easy enough to procure. In Lincoln green, with masks, no one would know us."

"Robin, dear old egg, I said from the first this was a fruity scheme," broke in Toby Cripps. "Suppose we all sort ourselves out, and make a plan of campaign. Who are these chappies, for instance? None of us has been introduced."

"So sorry," said Huntingley. "On your left is Dougles Dale, commonly known as Dodger. This chap here, with the pugnacious jaw, is Billy Bruce, home on leave from India, and with him is his bosom pal, Babe Rivers.

"The saturnine-looking merchant over there is Hank Moran, one of Ould Oireland's misfortunes."

The big, dark Irishman grinned self-consciously, as Huntingley made the introduction.

"Splendid!" ejaculated Toby. "Now we know where we are. There are eight sturdy wights ready to deal with all comers."

"Don't you dare leave me out!" broke in Lady Marion.

"Shouldn't dream of it," said Toby hastily. "Eight sturdy wights, and one charming wench, hereby pledged to scrag scugs, put pep in the padre's parish, and revive the glories of an old English Christmas."

"That's the ticket!" said Huntingley.

"I propose," broke in Pongo Paget, "that Robin becomes leader. Toby, possessing the perfect valet, will fix up the costumes, and the rest of us suggest various scaly scalliwags who should be put through the hoop."

"I second that entirely!" broke in Hank Moran.

"Any dissentients?" asked Pongo, looking round the room. "No? Carried nem. con."

Robin Huntingley turned to the padre. "Suppose we deal with your little lot, first, padre? This man, Grossman, you say, is a rotten landlord, and a pretty scurvy knave in general. How about making him spend his Christmas in the slums he owns?"

"I'd like to," said the padre grimly. "He's giving a big party in his house in Park Lane on Wednesday, spending thousands of pounds in sheer vulgar display. It's a fancy dress affair——"

"Wait! I have an idea!" announced Dodger Dale. "Let's make a list, and we'll discuss the best methods of making their punishments fit their crimes."

"Pity we haven't got a bally greenwood," grumbled Toby. "Jolly old caves, haunches of venison, and all that."

"Don't worry about that. My place down in Essex has plenty of room."

"By Jove, yes!" broke in Pongo. Huntingley Manor—the ideal spot. It's off the beaten track, and Robin, being lord of the manor, can do pretty well what he likes there."

"D'you know, Robin, old bean, the more I think of this scheme of yours, the fruitier it gets," said Toby Cripps. "I'll see Bently this afternoon about the costumes. Suppose we meet to-night, either here or in my place, and map out the plan of campaign. That blighter, Bruff, sticks in my gullet, padre. I bag Mr. Bruff. He's my meat!"

"And I," announced Marion, with a determined little lift of her chin, "will deal with that awful Lady Rumplestein. She is a hag of hags, mean as they make 'em, a scandal-mongering snake in the grass, who makes everyone she comes in contact with miserable."

"Go to it, Lady Marion!" chuckled Toby. "You can deal with my aunt as well, but Bruff's the boy for me."

"I think, gentlemen," broke in Huntingley, "we'll adjourn for lunch. We are all agreed on one point, at least—the League of Robin Hood is going to make itself felt this Christmas. We may have to break the law, but that is immaterial. The people we are going to punish are those whom the law cannot touch, and before we're through with them they'll have to part with a good deal of their ill-gotten gains."

"Hear, hear!" said the padre. "Boys, I'm with you! This is a time for deeds, not words."

"Good old Friar Tuck!" chuckled Toby. "Ods bodikins, and likewise gadzooks. Fair Robin, I am hungry. Bring forth the viands, the capons, and the pasties. Let mulled sack be brought in jugfuls that we may drink the health of fair Maid Marion and the lads in Lincoln green!"

END OF PROLOGUE.

Chapter 1.

Some Unpleasant People.

MR. JABEZ BRUFF nodded curtly to the policeman on duty at the door of Shinwell Road Police Court and wrinkled his thin nose with disfavour as he emerged from the dingy court precincts into the murky gloom of a December afternoon.

It was bitterly cold, and a chill east wind blew boisterously down that dingy and malodorous thoroughfare.

As the magistrate emerged and stood for a moment or two on the steps to button up his coat collar, a hulking, ruffianly-looking dock labourer, leaning negligently against a pillar at the corner, spat in disgust.

"Bruff, curse 'is eyesight!" he muttered below his breath. "I'll get yer one of these days, you old rat!"

Mr. Bruff, by some telepathic sense, seemed to be aware of the waves of hatred that emanated from that scowling figure in the corner.

"Constable, what the devil do you mean by allowing that lazy loafer to lounge about near the station for?" he snapped irritably. "Move him on at once!"

"Yes, sir! Sorry, sir!" said the policeman, moving majestically towards the labourer.

Mr. Bruff's thin lips pursed tightly, his cold, beady little eyes smarted in the biting east wind.

"Confound it! I suppose there isn't a taxi handy, as usual!" he grumbled.

The magistrate, if anything, was feeling more splenetic than usual that afternoon. It was three days before Christmas. Whether it was the approach of the festivities or the cold weather was not quite apparent, but the number of drunks charged at Shinwell Police Court had increased to alarming proportions.

Jabez Bruff was, fortunately for the honour of British justice, a rare exception to the usual metropolitan magistrate. There was a streak of cruelty in his nature that gloried in inflicting the maximum penalty on the unfortunate persons who appeared before him.

Where another man would have dismissed a common or garden "drunk" with a five or ten shilling fine, Bruff always clapped on a pound, or even five pounds, knowing full well that the poor wretch could not pay the sum, and would have to go to prison in default.

It now pleased his mean, vindictive nature to think that a good many persons who had anticipated the Christmas revels too early would eat their Christmas dinners in gaol. He took a perverse pleasure in the thought.

He was, probably, the best hated man in Shinwell. "Cruiser" Cray,

the hulking bully whom the policeman had just moved on, voiced the opinion of the whole district. The Cruiser himself was a brutalised specimen of humanity, a drunken, dissolute ruffian who terrorised the neighbourhood with his fists and ill-treated his ailing wife; but, brute as he was, he was more human than the little, dried-up, vindictive magistrate who seemed to glory in inflicting pain from his position of power.

His mean, ratlike face was nipped with the cold as he descended the steps. It was his custom to hail a taxi, to take him as far as the nearest Tube station. He bitterly resented the necessity of the cab, but Shinwell Road was a dangerous district for him to walk through in the gloom of a December afternoon. He knew well enough how unpopular he was with its inhabitants.

As he reached the pavement a taxi swung round the corner. Mr. Bruff hailed it with his upraised umbrella.

"Aldgate Tube, quickly!" he snapped to the driver—a red-faced individual, swathed round with innumerable capes and wraps. He was about to slip into the vehicle when a deep voice hailed him.

"Merry Christmas, Mr. Bruff! Seasonable weather, isn't it?"

The magistrate turned and found the burly, broad-shouldered figure of the Rev. John Browne gazing down at him with a jovial smile creasing his round, red face.

"For those that like it!" he snapped. "Er, I reciprocate your wishes," he added stiffly. Mr. Bruff disapproved of the Vicar of Shinwell; he disliked big, boisterous men who beamed and clapped one on the back. "You'll excuse me, vicar," he said, opening the door of the taxi, "I'm in rather a hurry."

"Quite—quite!" said the Rev. John amicably.

of light, then suddenly consciousness left him in complete darkness, as if one had snapped out an electric-light switch.

"You dare to imprison me, a magistrate, you murderous cutthroat!" *"Don't be a fool, Bruff!" snapped Robin Hood. "You have been sentenced to an indefinite term of imprisonment."*

When the door had closed a wink passed between the big clergyman and the driver of the taxi, who gave what seemed to be a wholly unnecessary toot on his horn. The next moment the cab was on its way.

Mr. Bruff muttered an imprecation below his breath.

"Confound the driver! Why had he left one of the windows open on a bitterly cold day like this?"

He sprang to his feet and jerked viciously at the strap. The sash sprang upward violently. There was a slight tinkle as of breaking glass and a sweet, sickly smell pervaded the interior of the cab.

Bruff swayed dizzily, his head seemed to be whirling round and round. His knees sagged under him, and he collapsed to the floor. He seemed to be enveloped in a greyish fog, shot through with little specks

"BY my halidom! A right merry sight, friend Robin," grinned the Hon. Toby Cripps, as Lord Huntingley steered his powerful Mercedes car through the winding driveway that led to Huntingley Manor.

The fine old Elizabethan building on the borders of Herts and Essex was discreetly screened from the main road by about two hundred acres of woodland, and one came upon it with almost a shock of surprise. It was as if one had stepped back through the centuries. In the twilight of a late December afternoon, the ancient manor looked its picturesque best. Its mellow, ivy-clad walls, mullioned, latticed windows, behind which shone the warm, yellow glow of light, seemed to beckon a welcome to the calm of a bygone age, away from the rush and roar of modern life

And at the moment snow was falling. Whirling, generous flakes, soundless and beautiful, fell in a thick cascade.

"Egad!" said Bill Bruce. "This is something like it, Robin, my boy. To think that a month back I was sweating and swearing in Aden! It's a treat for poor devils of exiles

like Babe and me to see that there are bits of the Old Country still unspoiled by blighters like Grossman & Co."

Huntingley smiled grimly.

"Comrade Grossman's going to taste a little Anglo-Saxon justice to-night, Bill," he said, deftly steering the car to a standstill before the great oaken door of the manor. He gave three blasts on his Klaxon, and the door swung open, revealing the warm glow of a vast hallway, in which a roaring log fire blazed.

A grizzled-haired manservant, with a mahogany-hued face and a slight limp, bowed stiffly as Robin, followed by Bill Bruce and Babe Rivers, entered the manor.

"Hallo, Rigg! Have the rest of the party arrived?"

"They 'ave, me lord," replied Rigg, Huntingley's ex-sergeant, and now his devoted servant. "Mr. Cripps and Padre Browne are in the smoking-room. Her ladyship phoned up that she'd be along later. The rest of the gentlemen are in the billiard-room."

"Splendid!" laughed Huntingley. "Now we shan't be long. Er—how are the prisoners?"

A grin split Rigg's mahogany face.

"Carrying on somethink awful, sir," he announced. "That there Bruff's the worst. You expecting any more, sir?"

"A few," said Robin, with a chuckle. "Don't forget to see that Bruff does his half-hour P.T.I. in the morning."

"I won't, sir," said Rigg grimly. "'E's bad-tempered and downright vicious. 'E must 'ave broke 'is mother's 'eart, but 'e won't break mine."

Rigg's face twisted suddenly into the ferocious frown which had struck terror into the breasts of a whole battalion a few years before.

Huntingley chuckled.

"Heaven help Bruff!" he murmured. "Boys, this is certainly going to be the merriest Christmas of our lives."

He strode down the hallway, the walls of which were crammed with trophies of his prowess as a big game hunter.

"Rigg'll show you to your rooms," he remarked. "You'll find us in the dining-room when you've changed."

"Right-ho!" said Bill, and his inseparable companion, Babe Rivers. "On with the motley, the drinks, and the doings."

Huntingley turned the knob of the door to the right of the hallway, and removed his heavy fur-lined overcoat, which he hung on a convenient peg. He glanced at himself in the cheval mirror, and grinned joyously.

He was clad in a doublet of Lincoln green, his straight, muscular legs in hose of the same colour. Beneath the doublet he sported a buff leather jerkin, from the girdle of which dangled an ivory hilted hunting-knife.

His feet were cased in buskins of soft suede leather, and he reached up for a jaunty cap, from which a pheasant's plume streamed gallantly. Over his shoulder was a narrow belt, which carried a tanned hide quiver, and at his side was a wallet and silver-tipped hunting-horn.

He made a gay and gallant figure as he emerged from the dressing-room into the spacious dining-hall across the hallway. He lifted the hunting horn to his lips, and blew three long blasts, then strode over to the wide hearth, in which a log fire of pinewood blazed with cheerful warmth.

Few men in this drab age can wear costume successfully; they are inclined to be self-conscious or ludicrous in the flamboyant garments of a more colourful age, but the Earl of Huntingley, with his dark handsome face, upright carriage, and air of gay nonchalance, seemed to be even more at home in Lincoln green than conventional evening kit.

THE echoes of his hunting horn were just dying away in the rafters of the magnificent timber roof of the dining-hall of the ancient manor, when there came a joyous shout from the minstrel gallery, and three figures, also in doublets and hose of Lincoln green, appeared on the balustrade.

"What ho! What ho!" cried the Hon. Toby Cripps, and, quite unabashed by the incongruity of the act, he jammed his oblong monocle in his eye, and slid down the banister.

"Slit my weasand, and likewise stap my jolly old vitals, Robin, you're back early," he greeted his leader.

Huntingley smiled, as Hank Moran and Pongo Paget followed decorously in the wake of the exuberant Toby. "Where's the Padre?" he demanded.

"Here, i' faith, good Robin," boomed the jovial voice of the Rev. John Browne, emerging from the hallway. The Fighting Parson of the Shinwell Road was now clad in a grey friar's robe, which seemed infinitely more in keeping with his ample girth and jovial red face than he drab habiliments and dog collar f his usual clerical suit.

"We're all here except Marion," announced Huntingley. "She's dealing with the Bernstein hag. Now, my lucky lads, let's have your reports."

Seven sturdy specimens of English manhood in Lincoln green, and one in the robes of a friar, grouped themselves round the leader, who stood with his back to the fireplace in the magnificent dining-room of Huntingley Manor. Round the oak-panelled walls the pictures of long-dead Huntingleys gazed down on the picturesque scene, and seemed to smile approval.

The spacious room, wth its ancient minstrel gallery at one end, its wide hearth, on which an ox could have been roasted with ease, the solid oaken furniture and suits of armour, was a perfect background, lit by the mellow glow of a vast candelabra and the flickering flames of the pinewood fire.

Huntingley smiled approvingly.

The scheme he had mooted, seven days before, had met with the joyous and enthusiastic acclamation of his seven colleagues. Each had his allotted task, and now, three days before Christmas, they had assembled to report progress.

"Robin, my boy," chuckled the Hon. Toby Cripps, "the scheme worked like a charm! That blighter, Bruff, now reposes in durance vile, 'a meditating of 'is sins,' as old Rigg would say. I went round to the padre's taxidriver pal, borrowed his clothes and his cab, fixed the little phial of anæsthetic in the jamb of the window, and let Bruff do the rest.

"He was still unconscious when we brought him here. Rigg and the others dumped him into the cellar. Later on I hope to have the joy of hearing what he's got to say when he wakes up."

Huntingley grinned.

"He's already done so. I'm told that his language even brought the blush of shame to the weather-beaten cheek of Sergeant Rigg. You've done splendidly, Toby! How did you and Hank get on, Pongo?"

Pongo Paget chuckled.

"Gosh, Robin, you should have seen old Hank with a walrus moustache and a policeman's helmet! He looked the part to the life. It

---

**This Week's Issue
is
SPECIALLY ENLARGED
to
32 pages.**

---

was as easy as falling off a log, really! You know that blighter, Manly, who calls himself a militant champion of the working-class?"

"I've heard of him," said Huntingley. "I haven't the doubtful pleasure of his acquaintance. Wasn't he the chap who incited all the Shinwell button-makers to come out on strike, and then, when they were on the verge of starvation, told 'em to close with the bosses' offer? They accused him of being in the bosses' pay, didn't they?"

"They did, and rightly," broke in Padre Browne. "And the name of the boss is Sir Simon Grossman. Manly, while posing as the workers' champion, is a creature of Grossman, subsidised by him to foment trouble, and then to counsel acceptance of decreased wages."

"The scug!" said Huntingley, and his handsome face darkened. "What a pleasant parish yours must be, padre. Go on, Pongo; let's hear how you slipped it across Manly."

"WELL, old Hank and I thought out a fruity wheeze," said Pongo Paget. "Manly, because of his inflammable speeches, generally falls foul of the police.

'Why,' says I to Pongo—'why not rig ourselves up as slops, cops, rozzers, or flatties, and call round at the unspeakable Manly's house?'

"Hank says: 'Phwy not?' So we toddled round to jolly old Willie Clarkson's and hired out uniforms, two, police, wheeze for the use of. I made an inspector that Scotland Yard would have been proud to acknowledge, while Hank's policeman would have inspired confidence in the commissioner himself. I took the old bus with me, and called at Mr. Manly's salubrious abode in the Shinwell Road."

"Splendid!" chuckled Robin. "A distinct brain-wave, Pongo! What happened?"

"Well, I knocked very sternly and officially, and a frightened-looking woman opened the door. Putting on my best official manner, I rapped out: 'I'm Inspector Hawk, of Scotland Yard, and I want to see your husband.' She screamed. But I pushed my way in. And there was Mr. Ratface Manly in the back parlour, busily trying to bundle an unwholesome specimen of humanity into the boot cupboard. On the table there was about a hundred quid in silver and notes."

"Which I promptly took charge of, in the name of the law!" chuckled Hank Moran.

"The johnny who was trying unsuccessfully to disguise himself as a boot was none other than our friend, Mr. William Snape, the slate club secretary. He was in hiding in Manly's house, and the precious pair were going fifty-fifty with the stolen money."

"The cursed villains!" ground out Padre Browne savagely. "I knew Manly was a firebrand, but I never thought he was a crook as well!"

"What happened then?" queried Huntingley, with a grin.

"Ah!" said Pongo. "You should have seen your little Pongo doing the stern, official stuff! 'Sergeant, slip the bracelets on 'em!' I snapped. Manly swore like a trooper, raved he was the victim of class warefare, threatened me with the Third, Fourth, and Fifth International; but I cut him short and bundled him into the bus.

"Hank dragged the wretched Snape in after him, and the capture was complete. To bingle a long story, both Manly and Snape have joined Bruff in our private menagerie of unspeakable scugs. They couldn't make out why we didn't stop at the police station, but I stepped on the gas and didn't stop until we reached here.

"Rigg took charge of 'em in his usual efficient fashion—and there you are!"

"Excellent!" laughed Huntingley. "We now have Sir Simon Grossman to deal with. And what was the name of that playful chappie who knocks his wife about, padre?"

"Cray—Cruiser Cray," said Padre Browne. "He's my particular meat, Robin," he added, pulling up the sleeve of his cassock and baring a brawny arm. "That man has made life hell for the poor devils in Shinwell. He's a great bullying braggart, who can only be tamed by physical force!"

"Good old Friar Tuck!" chuckled the Hon. Toby Cripps. "May I be there to see!"

"I think," drawled Huntingley, "it wouldn't be a bad idea if we had a little chat with our prisoners."

"Sound scheme!" agreed Pongo Paget. "I bet Rigg's put the fear of death into 'em by now!"

"Better put on your masks, boys," counselled Robin. "We don't want to be recognised."

TOGETHER they filed out of the spacious dining-hall into the grounds of the ancient manor. It had stopped snowing; a fitful moon illumined the scene, which was one of ethereal beauty. Across the virgin whiteness of the lawn the wind rustled eerily in the fir-trees. Their dark branches were powdered with snow, and each branch seemed as if it were loaded with glistening jewels.

Huntingley waved an arm towards the nearest fir-tree, a tall, graceful sapling, that cast a dark purple shadow on the snow.

"Just the right size for a Christmas tree, you chaps! Marion's got all the decorations and stuff handy for the party. One of you will have to lend a hand with an axe to-morrow!"

"Topping!" said the Hon. Toby. "And if Sir Simon bloomin' Grossman's going to have any Christmas pudden, it's going to cost him five quid a teaspoonful!"

Huntingley paused as they neared the right wing of the ancient Manor House. It had never been occupied since the death of the Dowager Lady Huntingley, many years before. It was connected to the main building by a straggling passageway, and was, to all intents and purposes, a separate building.

Huntingley raised the horn to his lips, and blew three long blasts. Instantly a man's figure emerged from the darkness and touched his cap. He was clad in a khaki overcoat, and under his arm he carried a shot-gun.

"Ah, Roberts! Everything O.K.?" demanded Huntingley.

"Yessir, Sergeant Rigg 'as done the rounds. Pris'ners all present and correct, sir!" replied Roberts.

All Huntingley's male staff were ex-Servicemen, who had served under him in France. They worshipped the gay sportsman, who, when the War was over, had not forgotten the lads who had served under him "over there." Though he had spent most of his time abroad, Huntingley still maintained his staff at the manor, and there was not one man who was not prepared to carry out even his most fantastic order.

The sentry marched towards an oaken door, and unlocked it. A dank, musty smell came from the interior of the bare whitewashed hallway. Huntingley led the way down a winding stairway that gave access to the vast wine-cellars of the Manor House. He pressed a switch, revealing a long vaulted room, scrupulously clean, with bare, whitewashed walls.

At the end of the room were six compartments, which had originally been wine-bins, but had now been converted into replicas of prison cells.

As Huntingley strode into the vaulted chamber, in his suit of Lincoln green, his face masked by a black silk domino, a startled gasp came from the occupant of one of the cells. He leapt from the bare plank bed on which he had been seated, and peered, with a bewildered expression, through the bars.

"My Heaven! I'm going mad!" he groaned. "What—what does it all mean?"

Huntingley laughed softly.

"It means, Mr. Jabez Bruff, that you're having a taste of your own medicine!" he drawled. "You are now experiencing a foretaste of the punishment you have so wantonly inflicted on others."

"By Heaven!" gasped the magistrate, and his mean, vindictive little eyes glittered with rage. "You dare to imprison me, you murderous cutthroat! Release me at once, and explain your outrageous conduct!"

"Don't be a fool, Bruff!" snapped Robin Hood. "You have been sentenced to an indefinite term of imprisonment, and it depends entirely on how you behave yourself how long that term will last."

"Manly"—Huntingley turned to the occupant of the next cell, a redhaired, undersized individual, in a nondescript suit, who was beating hysterically against the bars of his cell—"if you don't stop that foul language," he snapped, "you'll get solitary confinement on bread-and-water. I'm in command here. Understand that!"

"Curse you!" snarled Amos Manly. "You have absolutely no right to detain me here against my will. I'll see——"

"I have the right," broke in Huntingley, with a slow smile beneath the rim of his mask—"the fine old Anglo-Saxon right of conquest and capture. In a little while you will be joined by others, and then, perhaps, I will enlighten you further.

"Meanwhile, I will simply remark that if you are hungry food will be provided, on conditions. The conditions will probably repel you, my friends, especially Manly, who prates so much about labour, and hasn't done an honest stroke of work in his life."

Huntingley pointed to a huge pile of logs in the corner of the vaulted room.

"The renowned Mr. Tom Tucker sang for his supper," he continued: "Having already had a sample of your vocal ability, gentlemen, I'm not anxious to have my ear-drums lacerated further. You will accordingly work for your supper. The

three of you should, in three hours' time, have succeeded in chopping up those logs, and thus earned your evening meal."

He signalled to the sentry.

"Unlock the cells, Roberts!" he commanded. "Remember, no work, no food!"

"Very good, sir!" said the sentry, clicking his heels.

Mr. Jabez Bruff was speechless with fury. Flecks of foam dabbled his thin, cruel lips, as Roberts unlocked the door.

"I—I—I——" he stuttered.

"Don't be so egotistical!" chuckled Huntingley. "Come, you chaps, there's work to be done! Sir Simon Grossman is now just about climbing into evening-dress, an inconvenient costume, I fear, for scrubbing and wood-chopping; but he'll get used to it in time."

— — —

Chapter 2.

The Fighting Parson.

"I SAY, guv'nor!" Tinker, balanced precariously on a step ladder, turned with a spray of holly in his hand, towards Sexton Blake, the celebrated detective, who was seated in a saddlebag chair before a roaring fire in the consulting-room grate.

Blake, deeply immersed in a bulky volume, his favourite briar between his teeth, a whisky-and-soda at his elbow, and his dilapidated carpet slippers within an inch of incineration, made no reply.

"I say, guv'nor!" Tinker repeated, a little more loudly. "What are we going to give Mrs. B. for a Christmas present?"

Blake gave a deep chuckle of amusement, and turned over the pages of his book, but did not seem to have heard Tinker's question, for he snuggled back farther into his chair, and continued his reading.

Tinker sighed, carefully adjusted the holly above the picture-rail, and gingerly stepped down the ladder to survey his handiwork. The usually austere consulting-room had an unwonted gaiety this blustery December night. Festoons of evergreen ornamented the bookcases and picture-rails, a bunch of mistletoe hung over the door, while Chinese lanterns and paper-chains flaunted their colourful length diagonally from corner to corner.

It was ten-thirty p.m., three days before Christmas, and Tinker, for once, had ignored his job on the Index, and concentrated on decorating Blake's quarters in honour of the Yuletide festivities.

Blake, himself, however, seemed to have taken little interest in the youngster's efforts towards brightening the place. He had been out all day, in the dingy precincts of the Record Office, and after dinner had donned his woeful scarlet dressing-gown, piled up the fire, and immersed himself in his book.

"I say, guv'nor," repeated the long-suffering Tinker again.

"Huh?"

Blake looked up from his book, and seemed suddenly to realise that he was back in a workaday world again.

"What is it, my lad?" he demanded. Then, suddenly, his eye fell on the decorations. His eyes twinkled.

"Splendid, young 'un. Very festive," he remarked.

"I've asked you three times, guv'nor," said Tinker reproachfully, "what are we going to give Mrs. B. for Christmas?"

"Sorry, young 'un," said Blake, "but I was immersed in my book," he remarked.

"I suppose it's some bally treatise on the habits of the lesser streptococcus, or the larger protozoa, or something?"

Sexton Blake smiled, and held up his book.

"Nothing half so abstruse, my lad," he said, with a chuckle. "I'm indulging in one of my few relaxations—one of the greatest books ever written—'The Pickwick Papers.'"

Used as he was to his guv'nor's moods, Tinker was surprised. It was very seldom, indeed, that Blake indulged in novel reading. Not that he disliked novels, but time was usually so fully occupied that he seldom had an opportunity. It was, moreover, an infallible sign that when Blake took down "Pickwick" from its shelf, he intended to give criminology a rest.

"Then you've finished the Denman case, guv'nor?" said Tinker.

"This afternoon," said Blake. "I verified the title deed, after wading through about three hundred dusty parchments, and, as I expected, my theory was correct. However, I don't want to discuss crooks or crime until after Christmas, young 'un.

"I've decided to have an orgy of Dickens. It's almost a year since I read Pickwick for the eighteenth time, I think, and it's like a breath of fresh air, after the dingy atmosphere of the Old Bailey. I have my pipe, my glass, a blazing fire, and 'Pickwick'; what more can a man wish for? No power on earth will prise me from my chair to-night, young 'un."

"Good!" chuckled Tinker. "Now, what about these Christmas presents? I hope to Heaven Mrs. B. won't present us with some more of those ghastly knitted ties, guv'nor," he added. "She means well, poor old dear, but——"

THE telephone-bell rang.
"I'm engaged on an important case at—er—Dingley Dell, Tinker," said Blake warningly. "I'm not leaving Sam Weller and Pickwick for anybody."

"Right-ho, guv'nor!" said Tinker, lifting the receiver. He grinned as he recognised the voice of Inspector Coutts, of Scotland Yard.

"That you, Blake?" snapped Coutts gruffly.

"No, it's me—Tinker. Merry Christmas, Couttsy! How's your poor old feet?"

"I don't want any of your impudence, young Tinker," snarled the Yard man. "Where's Blake? I want to speak to him urgently."

"Hang on a sec!" said Tinker, and, covering the mouthpiece, turned to the detective. "Guv'nor, Couttsy seems to have something on his mind," he explained.

Blake sighed wearily, and held out his hand for the instrument.

"Well, Coutts, what is it?" he asked, without enthusiasm.

"Sir Simon Grossman's been kidnapped," said Coutts.

"And a good thing, too," drawled Blake. "Is that all you've got to say?"

"B-but you don't seem to understand," spluttered the inspector. "That's the fourth time to-day it's happened."

"He's been kidnapped four times," said Blake incredulously. "Is he making a hobby of it?"

The imprecation Coutts vented twanged in the diaphragm.

"No, no! Four people have been forcibly abducted. The latest is Sir Simon Grossman," he explained. "He had a big party at his Park Lane place to-night, and six masked men in fancy-dress held up the whole ballroom, and two more literally forced Sir Simon into a closed car."

"Very interesting," said Blake. "Thanks for the news! I daresay Splash Page will have the picturesque details in to-morrow's 'Radio.'"

"But look here, Blake," pleaded the Yard man. "I—er—wanted your help. I'm in an extraordinary tangle down here. Hysterical women, angry men, fool servants, and—and——"

"I'm sorry," cut in Blake decisively. "I'm not stirring out to-night, Coutts, old man. I'm far too comfortable. Besides, I dislike Sir Simon Grossman intensely, and it would cause me no pang of regret if he never came back."

Blake replaced the receiver, and glanced across whimsically at Tinker.

"Poor old Coutts is worried," he remarked. "He looks like having a strenuous Christmas." He yawned,

and snuggled more comfortably into his chair.

Tinker stared curiously at Blake. It was very unlike the detective not to offer his advice and assistance to his friend, Coutts, and the youngster ventured to say so.

"My dear Tinker," drawled Blake, "it's not that I object to helping Coutts, but I do strongly object to stirring from my comfortable fireside to find an unconscionable scoundrel like Sir Simon Grossman. Coutts has some extraordinary story about a hold-up by masked men in fancy-dress. I wouldn't be surprised if he turned up in person shortly."

Blake's prophecy proved correct, for less than half an hour later there was a thunderous rat-tat on the front door, and Mrs. Bardell ushered the Yard man into the consulting-room. His broad, red face glowed like a flame, the rim of his aggressively cocked bowler-hat was powdered with

A man in a khaki overcoat and carrying a shotgun unlocked the gates, and the limousine swept up the driveway. "By James, there is something fishy about this!" said Splash Page.

snow, and his manner was distinctly irritable.

"Park yourself, Couttsy," said Tinker, with a chuckle. "You look hot and bothered."

"Pah! So would you be, my lad, if you had my job! Got a cigar, Blake?" he queried.

"At your elbow, my dear fellow. Have some hot toddy, to keep out the cold. Tinker, slice another lemon for the inspector."

Somewhat mollified by his reception, Coutts bit off the end of a Cabana, and settled back in his chair.

"It's a queer business, Blake—dashed queer!" he said. "Hanged if I can make head or tail of it! What with old Bruff, Amos Manly, and now this chap Grossman——"

"WHY not begin at the beginning, Coutts?" said Blake. "Let's have the depositions in order of precedence. Which Bruff is that—the magistrate?"

"Yes. That's what makes it so dashed queer," said Coutts. "The start of the whole thing was this evening, about six o'clock. Walters, the Divisional Inspector of the Shinwell Road district, rang me up about

this firebrand Labour chap, Manly. It seems his wife was very upset about his arrest, and called at the station to try and bail him out.

"But here's the point—Walters knew nothing about an arrest, neither does anybody else at the Yard. We sent out an A.S. message to the whole metropolitan area, and nobody knows anything at all about Manly. Yet his wife swears that an inspector and a police-sergeant came round about four p.m. this afternoon and took her husband away in a fast car."

"H'm!" said Blake. "It sounds as if some ultra patriotic Fascist has been at work. Incidentally, six months' hard wouldn't do Manly any harm. He's a mischievous devil, and runs with a queer crowd."

"Granted," said Coutts. "But that doesn't alter the fact that he's missing, and his wife's raising Cain about it. She calls it a police conspiracy. Says her husband's probably been deported for his political views. All rot, of course."

"Well," said Blake tentatively.

"But that's not the half of it, Blake," continued Coutts, with a rush. "No sooner had I got back to the Yard—it was about eight o'clock —than a frantic message came through from Mr. Bruff's housekeeper, asking if there was any news about her employer. She feared there'd been an accident, or something. He invariably arrived home about six o'clock. His habits were as regular as clockwork.

"If, by any chance, he couldn't be back for dinner, he always telephoned to her. I told the woman not to worry, and thought no more about it. You know the queer fancies these hysterical women get. Then, somewhere about ten o'clock, when I was packing up to go home, she rang up again. She had received a letter, by district messenger, wishing her a Merry Christmas and——

"But see it for yourself," said Coutts, pulling out a folded piece of notepaper. "I sent a constable round to interview her."

Blake took the letter. It was brief, but pointed; typed, he noted subconsciously, apparently, on a Remington portable.

"Dear Madam," it ran,—"You are now assured of a Merry Christmas, for we cannot imagine you spending a joyous Yuletide in the sole company of the unpleasant Mr. Bruff. We have, therefore, removed him, and trust you will enjoy Christmas untrammelled by his blighting presence. He is well, and will come to no harm if he behaves himself. Faithfully yours,

"'THE LEAGUE OF ROBIN HOOD.'"

Blake's lips twitched as he read the document.

"What d'ye make of that?" demanded Coutts.

"Very amusing," said Blake, with a chuckle. "Have you got any more like that?"

"Amusing!" echoed Coutts. "Good glory, Blake! A Metropolitan Magistrate disappears. According to that letter, he's in the hands of some fantastic league, and you call it amusing!"

"But where does Grossman come in?" asked Blake, ignoring Coutts' indignation.

"Ah!" said Coutts. "I'm coming to that. To-night he held a Carnival dance at his Park Lane house. According to the guests I've interviewed, the ballroom was crowded.

"Shortly after half-past ten, the music stopped suddenly, and six men, dressed in some fancy costume—Robin Hood stuff—appeared from somewhere, and posted themselves at the four doorways of the ball-room. They were all masked. Most of the guests thought it was some gag or joke, and waited to see what would happen.

"Then, suddenly, one of the men— he was obviously the leader—crossed over to Grossman, and said: 'I want you,' quite quietly, like that, with-

out any fuss. Then he turned to the dancers on the floor, and said: 'Ladies and gentlemen, don't move! Don't be alarmed.' He signalled to his five accomplices, who immediately whipped out five automatics, and covered the whole room.

"People were so stunned with astonishment that they just stood there and stared for a minute or two. Grossman went ghastly pale and started to yell for help, but this masked chap jammed a gun in the small of his back, and marched him out of the room. The others could do nothing. They were covered from every part of the ballroom by his accomplices."

"Great pip, Couttsy, are you serious?" broke in Tinker. "Hadn't anybody got the sense to rush 'em, or make a fight for it?"

Coutts emitted a jet of cigar smoke and snorted contemptuously.

"Never saw a more spineless lot in my life," he grunted. "When I was called in they were babbling like an aviary of parrots; hysterical women screaming—a lot of Grossman's pals jabbering away in Yiddish—I couldn't get any sense out of 'em at all.

"According to the servants, the man in green escorted Grossman to a car; there were dozens of 'em parked outside the house. The butler said he didn't suspect anything wrong, and thought his boss was just seeing a guest off."

"WHAT happened upstairs meanwhile?" asked Blake.

Coutts shrugged.

"As far as I can see, the five others simply waited till their leader got clear, and then locked the doors on the dancers. It all happened so smoothly that scarcely any of the household staff realised what was amiss. It was only the banging and shouting of the imprisoned guests that aroused 'em. The butler phoned up the Yard, and I was along there in ten minutes."

"Very interesting!" said Blake "This League of Robin Hood seems to have highly organised methods."

"Yes, but hang it all, Blake," protested Coutts, "you don't seem to realise. The blighters have kidnapped Grossman, and disappeared without a trace. None of the servants can give any coherent account of what happened.

"Nobody noticed what particular type of car they used, and, beyond the fact that the men were dressed in Lincoln green, and wore masks, I have no description to go on. It's extraordinary. They don't seem to be crooks, in the ordinary sense of the word. They may, of course, be holding Grossman for ransom, but why should they kidnap Bruff; he's not a wealthy man?"

"And Manly! You've forgotten Manly!" broke in Sexton Blake "I'm willing to bet that the so-called policemen who arrested him also belong to this romantically named league. Let's have a look at that letter again, Coutts."

He studied the document carefully

through a lens, and then tossed it aside.

"Nothing much to go on. Hand-woven, linen-grained paper of good quality. 'Remington' typewriter. Almost certainly typed by a man not very familiar with the machine. Where did that District Messenger come from?"

"Southampton Row."

"H'm!" said Blake thoughtfully. "Whoever runs this Robin Hood League seems to have a sense of humour. Have you noticed, incidentally, that the three people you've mentioned, Manly, Bruff, and Grossman, are all connected, in some way, with Shinwell Road? Furthermore, none of them has a very savoury reputation. Old Bruff, I noticed in to-day's paper, has been particularly severe with his sentences. I don't like that man, Coutts. He's a disgrace to the bench."

"He's a nasty-tempered fellow, I admit," assented the Yard man. "But hang it all, if that letter's genuine, this bally league's got to be stopped. This is a law-abiding country, and kidnapping is against all the rules."

BLAKE yawned. "I confess, Coutts, to a sneaking sympathy for this league," he said quietly. "Hitherto, they seem to have confined themselves to the—er—elimination of people whom we could well do without. As far as I'm concerned, I don't intend to lift a finger to help either Manly, Bruff, or Grossman."

"So that's that!" murmured Tinker.

"But hang it all, Blake, that's compounding a felony," spluttered Coutts incoherently. "Here's a multimillionaire held up at the point of a gun and taken away, Heaven knows where. He may be murdered by now, for all I know."

"I fail to see in what way I'm compounding a felony, Coutts," said Blake, smiling. "I'm quite at liberty in accepting or rejecting a case at my discretion. I know nothing at all about this League of Robin Hood, have never heard of it until to-night; but if their policy consists in removing people who are likely to interfere with the Christmas festivities of poor people, then more power to their elbow."

"Blake!" gasped the scandalised inspector. "Do you mean to tell me that you, of all men, countenance this wholly illegal action? What's come over you, man?"

Blake sipped his drink slowly, then tapped the volume of Pickwick that lay face downward on the table.

"It's Christmas-time, Coutts," he answered. "I want a rest from this eternal battle against crime and criminals, and to forget the seamy side for a little. Just now I was reading of that immortal Christmas party at Dingley Dell, and it seemed to me that we're fast losing the kindliness and jollity and good fellowship for which Christmas stands.

"Men like Manly, with their ranting anarchism, would abolish Christmas altogether. Bruff, the old curmudgeon, is another Scrooge, but worse, inasmuch as he has the power

to sentence less fortunate devils. As for Grossman, he never has, nor never will, understand what Christmas means.

"And so I say their fate does not worry me in the least. This league, whatever it is, and whatever its object, has taken its name from an English outlaw who did much for the common people, and, providing they do not overstep the law to any serious extent, I shan't interfere with them."

Coutts jammed on his bowler hat and prepared to leave.

"I never heard such rot in my life, Blake!" he growled. "I thought you'd be only too pleased to help round up this gang of thugs. Instead of that, you seem to side with them."

Blake laughed.

"Let me know if any new developments crop up, old chap. Splash Page would be very interested in the story. Perhaps he'll help you."

"Pah! That newshound!" retorted Coutts contemptuously. "That's final, then, Blake—you're not going to trouble about the case?"

Blake shook his head.

"Just a word of advice, Coutts. Perhaps this league consists of persons who have a personal grudge against Bruff or Grossman. I'd make discreet inquiries around the Shinwell district if I were you. Grossman owns most of the property there."

"I will," said Coutts grimly. "I'll give 'em Robin Hood when I round 'em up!"

Tinker grinned as the door closed behind the incensed inspector.

"Good old guv'nor!" he said. "I agree with you entirely about Robin Hood. I'd like to join the bally league myself!"

Chapter 3.
The Nose for News.

SPLASH PAGE, star crime reporter of the "Daily Radio," emerged from the Shinwell Road Police Station and glanced at his wrist-watch beneath the sickly blue rays of the police lamp.

It was nearly ten p.m., and Splash, who had been on the track of a newspaper story in that unsalubrious quarter, shivered as he descended the steps and entered his swift, vermilion roadster, which Tinker had nicknamed the Red Peril.

He turned up his collar and pressed the self-starter. It had stopped snowing, but the road was sloppy with mud and slush. Belated Christmas shoppers, carrying bundles of holly and mistletoe, hurried homeward, heads well down to protect them from the biting east wind.

"Gosh! What a night!" muttered Splash. He would be glad to get back to the warm news-room of the "Daily Radio," to write up the few facts he had gleaned about the Manly Mystery, as he subconsciously thought of it.

"It certainly is a rum business," muttered Splash, guiding his car dexterously between a loaded van and a taxi. "The woman's holding something back, I'll swear, and yet——"

He broke off suddenly, as he noticed crowds of people assembled at the corner of a dark side street just off the Shinwell Road.

"Hallo! What's up?" ejaculated the newspaperman. Crowds, to Splash Page, meant news. He jammed on his brakes just before a glittering gin palace and leapt out of his seat.

"Go ahead, padre! Sock 'im in the jore!" yelled a hoarse, red-faced man, hovering excitedly at the edge of a circle of nondescript loafers, who had formed themselves into a ring round two strangely assorted combatants.

Splash, with the ease born of long practice, pushed his way into the front, and grinned delightedly as he saw a big, red-faced parson hammering lusty blows into the body of a huge man in corduroys.

The latter made a poor show of it. He blundered about dazedly, whirling his arms like flails in every direction, and staggered groggily on his pins as the parson slammed home two vicious punches to the point.

"Curse yer!" he panted. "I'll kill yer fer that!" His breath came in sobbing gasps. He made no effort to parry the padre's blows, but strove to bear down on him and crush him by sheer bulk and brute force.

Crack! One of his ham-like hands caught the parson a buffet on the side of the head with a quite audible sound.

The Rev. John Browne gave vent to a very unclerical oath, and rocked unsteadily on his feet. Cruiser Cray gave a short laugh and tried to follow up his advantage. The padre was too quick for him, however.

Amid hoarse cries of encouragement from the delighted audience he feinted with his right, neatly side-stepping the Cruiser's blundering attack.

"Look out, padre! 'Ere's the cops!" yelled the red-faced man.

"Curse the cops!" roared another. "Spoilin' a good fight. Stand up to 'im, Cruiser!"

"I'll eat the Bible-punchin' rat!" snarled Cruiser Cray. "Dog-collar an' all!"

"Come and try, my friend!" laughed the padre, and his left fist shot out, swift as the dart of a snake, straight for the other's jaw. It was a perfectly timed blow. The Cruiser's head jerked back with an audible snick, and he collapsed to the pavement like a sack of coal.

Even as he did so a police whistle shrilled in the distance. Padre Browne, breathing a trifle heavily, looked down at the unconscious Cray, while several vociferous sympathisers patted him on the back.

"Good for you, padre! 'E deserved it, the sodden pig!"

The fighting parson grinned a trifle self-consciously, and donned his clerical hat, which some sympathisers had held for him during the fight.

"Look out! The cops!" yelled the red-faced man again. The door of a big blue limousine, drawn up near the kerb, opened suddenly, and out of it stepped two young men. They lifted the body of the unconscious Cray from the pavement and bundled him unceremoniously on the floor of the tonneau.

"Hop in, padre!" jerked one of them.

The crowd melted away as the sound of running footsteps rounded the corner. Padre Browne took a running jump at the footboard of the limousine, and was dragged in by willing hands. Splash Page noticed that the overcoat of one of the young men had flapped open, revealing a jerkin and tunic of Lincoln green. He saw it for less than a second, for the big blue car shot off down the road just as a burly police sergeant appeared at a run.

"Gosh! That's queer!" muttered the newspaperman. "There's a story there somewhere."

For Splash Page to think was also to act. He took a flying leap into his Red Peril, and, heedless of the shouts of the exasperated policeman, followed the blue limousine.

Shinwell Road, with its clanking trams and slush-laden gutters, was soon left behind, and Splash wondered what the outcome of the scene he had just witnessed would be. It would make a picturesque story, he reflected, as he gradually overtook the big blue car, which seemed to be heading for the country

Through crowded Islington he almost lost it, and narrowly averted a collision with a slow-moving dray. He picked up the trail, however, on the road to Epping Forest, and the keen night wind whipped his cheeks into a glow of colour, as he drove on grimly in the wake of his quarry.

It was not apparent whether the occupants of the car knew they were followed, or not. Splash did not much care. He was out for a story, and when the star crime reporter of the "Radio" was out for a story, no power on earth would stop him getting it.

T HE Manly affair, while interesting enough in its way, did not satisfy Splash Page. He had interviewed Mrs. Manly and the divisional inspector at Shinwell Road, but could get no satisfaction out of either of them.

He had meant, on his return to the office, to ring up Sexton Blake and ask his opinion of the matter, but that could wait, he reflected.

The news agencies would carry the broad details of the story. Splash Page's speciality was scoops.

The fight he had just witnessed promised to develop into a first-class front-page yarn. The Fighting Parson was always a picturesque figure with the public, and it was Splash Page's intention to interview him, and, if possible, secure a photograph That, at least, had been his first intention, but the queer behaviour of the young men in the blue limousine. in dragging both combatants into the car and driving at full speed to an unknown destination, suggested a startling development.

"What's the game, I wonder?" mused Splash, as they roared through the dark shadowed roadway of Epping Forest. "That chap in fancy dress seemed to know that padre all right. Were they afraid of the police, or what? In any case, why drag the bruiser chappie in with them?"

He shook his head in bewilderment. The situation was distinctly intriguing Ahead of him the blue limousine swerved to the right off the Cambridge Road. The going was heavier now. The hedgerows and banks were laden with snow, and the winding country road was choked with slush.

Splash kept about three hundred yards to the rear of the limousine, and wondered when the long journey would end The wind moaned eerily in the leafless boughs of the lofty elm-trees that girded the roadway, and the newspaper man's fingers were numbed with cold.

Suddenly the blue limousine slowed down before a pair of wrought-iron gates leading into a fine old Elizabethan mansion beyond a noble avenue of fir-trees. Splash Page stopped his car, and watched from the shadow of the hedgerow.

A man, clad in a khaki overcoat, and carrying a shotgun, unlocked the gates, and the car swept up the driveway. The gates were locked again, and Splash saw the figure of the armed sentry pacing slowly up and down the snow-laden avenue.

"By James! There's something fishy about this!" said Splash Page. "Fighting parsons, armed sentries, blokes in fancy dress—they don't seem to fit in somehow."

He squared his chin, and, leaving the Red Peril in the shadow of the elm, approached the gates. His boots crunched on the heavy snow. It was freezing hard here in the country, and watery clouds obscured the fitful moon.

A high wall divided the manor from the roadway, and Splash glanced up at it speculatively. Should he risk a climb, and trust to luck when he got over on the other side, or have a chat with the johnny in the khaki overcoat?

He stiffened suddenly as he heard the sound of an approaching motor-car. He had just time to hide himself behind a moss-covered buttress of the wall, as a Rolls-Royce purred to a standstill before the gates.

He gave a gasp of astonishment as the blinds of the tonneau were suddenly released, and in the sudden light he saw five masked men in Lincoln green; and between them, his face the colour of death, that eminent financier, Sir Simon Grossman!

"Jumping Jehosophat!" said Splash Page. "Waat a peach of a story!"

His eyes glowed with excitement as he watched the gates being swung open, and the Rolls sweep up the avenue towards the manor.

"I'm not going back till I've found out what it all means," decided Splash Page. "It looks like being an all-night job—but it's worth it!"

" P ARTY, 'shun!" Ex-sergeant-major Rigg's voice rang out in a bull-like bellow in the vaulted cellar of Huntingley Manor.

Three haggard-faced men rose wearily to their feet, as Rigg unlocked the gates of their cells. They had been prisoners for less than six hours, but even that short period had felt like an eternity of torment beneath the despotic sway of ex-sergeant-major Rigg.

Jabez Bruff blinked stupidly in the sudden blaze of light in the vaulted roof. His hands were raw after the unaccustomed toil to which he had been submitted The pile of logs in the corner had been neatly chopped, and Bruff writhed inwardly at the indignity of it. He, Jabez Bruff, stipendiary metropolitan magistrate, to be forced to chop wood, and perform degrading and menial tasks in the company of a low Bolshevik like Manly, and a thieving scoundrel like Snape. Somebody would suffer for this, dearly, he vowed venomously. The police would be sure to trace him, and then——

He exulted at the thought of the penalty that would be meted out to his captors, and his thin lips writhed unpleasantly as he emerged from his cell into the vault.

"Take that grin off your face, Bruff, or I'll knock it orf!" snapped Rigg. "Manly, stop that slouching. Stannatenshun when I speak chuh!"

"I protest——" began Manly, but a good deal of the truculence had gone out of his voice.

"You protest, do you, me lad!" said Rigg grimly. "You bread-pudden-faced Bolshie, I'll learn yer to protest! Corporal, see as 'ow this man does an hextra hour's pack drill in the morning."

Corporal Roberts nodded.

"Very good, sir."

Manly swore sullenly beneath his breath and suddenly the heavy wooden door of the vault opened, and five masked men in Lincoln green entered, accompanied by two dazed and badly frightened men.

"Two more for your fatigue-squad, sergeant!" laughed Huntingley. "This chap's name is Grossman— Gross by name, and gross by nature."

"Sir Simon!" gasped Bruff, scarcely believing his eyes, as he recognised in the fat, grey-faced man in evening dress the prospective Conservative candidate for Shinwell.

"Bruff!" gasped the millionaire hoarsely. "You here! What, in Heaven's name, does it mean?"

"Lumme!" said Cruiser Cray, and passed a shaky hand over his battered face. "If it ain't old ratface!" A twisted smile played about his puffy lips, and his great ham-like hands closed convulsively "So you're getting a taste of stir, eh, you perishing old blighter? Cripes! And 'ere's Manly, an' Soapy Snape!"

He flung back his head, and laughed hoarsely.

"'Scuse me, gents! This is the

funniest dream I ever 'ad. I'll wake up shortly, I know. This is too good to be true!"

"Yus, you'll wake up all right, me lad!" snapped Rigg, fixing him with a cold eye. "Line up with Bruff and Manly 'ere! An' you, Grossman, snap into it!"

"Ach!" groaned Grossman. "I shall die! I know it! My heart!"

He clutched convulsively at the front of his rumpled dress shirt.

"Rubbish!" snapped Huntingley. "A little exercise'll do you the world of good. Get that fat paunch of yours down. Remember, Grossman, if you want food, you work for it. If you want sleep, you also work for it.

"How have these other three been behaving, Rigg?"

"Fairly well, sir. Bruff was inclined to be obstropulous, but 'e calmed down."

"Good!" said Huntingley. "See that Grossman and Cray pick half a pound of oakum before they go to sleep. The others can turn in now."

"'Ere!" began Cruiser Cray truculently. "Wot's orl this? You ain't catching me pickin' no oakum!"

"Cray!" With a bellow like a bull of Bashan, Rigg turned to the mutineer. "Do you know what the cat is?"

Cruiser Cray's bruised face blanched. Rigg crossed over to a door in the wall, and opened it. It gave into another and smaller room. He snapped on the light, disclosing an upright triangle of wood, from which dangled leathern thongs.

From a ledge near by Rigg pulled down a short, stubby whip of rhinoceros hide, with nine knotted lashes of thin leather, lashes that could flay the flesh from a man's bones.

"Reckernise that, you gaol-rat?" he demanded. "The cat-o'-nine tails?"

Cray stared dumbly at the weapon, and his face was ashen.

"I guess I'll—I'll get on with the job, sarge!" he muttered thickly.

Rigg grinned, and drew his gnarled fingers lovingly over the leathern thongs.

"Then put a jerk in it, my lad," he commanded, "or you'll taste another dose of the cat!"

Huntingley glanced at the wretched Grossman, who was quivering with fear.

"That applies equally to you, Sir Simon!" he said pointedly.

Chapter 4
Tragedy.

WHILE these things had been going on inside the manor, Splash Page, outside, had already decided that the fantastic chase of the men in Lincoln green promised to develop into a red-hot feature story, provided that it was handled properly. Seldom in his chequered career as a newspaper-man had he encountered such a queer set of circumstances as the fight in the Shinwell Road and its sequel at Huntingley Manor.

"It certainly looks like a hold-up to me!" he reflected. "But why the mummery?"

He glanced speculatively at the high stone wall that surrounded the grounds, and drew a deep breath of decision.

"Over the top for it!" he muttered. "Sentry or no sentry!"

With cat-like agility he muscled himself up between the buttress and the crumbling face of the wall, and reached out for a convenient cluster of ivy. Luckily it held, and a few moments later, breathless but exultant, he reached the top and stared over snow-covered lawns gleaming white and ghostly in the rays of the fitful moon.

Suddenly, from the direction of the Manor House, came the high, shrill note of a horn. The khaki-clad sentry near the lodge gate became alert, and raced at the double towards the west wing of the building.

Seizing his chance, Splash Page poised himself for a jump, and landed, breathless and slightly shaken, into a snowdrift. He was in the manor grounds. He picked himself up hurriedly, and brushed the snow from his leather motoring coat. Now, in the darkness, and beneath the whispering leaves of the fir-trees, he watched a procession of men in doublets and hose emerging from the right of the manor and entering the main hallway.

He drew in his breath sharply in a sibilant whistle; then, very cautiously, still hugging the shadows, he moved towards the Manor House itself.

Suddenly, he squared his shoulders, and a cool, confident grin played about his lips.

"By heck!" he muttered. "I'll bluff it through!"

He strode towards the oaken door, and lifted the ponderous knocker. A moment later a thunderous rat-tat-tat echoed through the silent night. Splash Page, braced and tense, waited on the steps. He had no idea of the sort of reception that awaited him, but he was too old a newspaperman not to be prepared for all eventualities.

The door swung open suddenly, and facing him stood a tall man clad in Lincoln green, his face masked by a black silk domino.

"Good-evening!" said Splash Page calmly. "Sorry to call at such an unconventional hour, but I represent the 'Daily Radio,' and——"

"You won't represent it much longer, my friend, if you don't put up your hands!" snapped the Earl of Huntingley grimly. And, as if by magic, a nickel automatic appeared between his slim fingers and pointed straight at the journalist's heart.

Splash did not turn a hair.

"A highly melodramatic gesture, my dear sir," he drawled; "but, unfortunately, it cuts no ice with me." So saying, his hand snaked with lightning rapidity to his hip.

Huntingley saw the gesture, and barked a harsh command. Instantly half a dozen masked figures appeared in the hallway and swooped down on the newspaperman.

Splash backed away hastily, but he was surrounded on all sides.

"Have it your own way, gentlemen," he said, with a shrug of resignation. "I don't know what game

you're playing, but it looks a good one to me."

A low laugh broke from Huntingley.

"Boys, it looks as if we've found a new recruit," he murmured. "The League of Robin Hood has need of a scrivener, by my halidom. And what better scribe can we obtain than the doughty Page of the 'Radio'?"

"Thou hast spoken a mouthful, bold Robin," agreed the irrepressible Splash. "If you give me the exclusive rights of reproduction, my pen is at your service!"

"Manfully spoken i' faith!" chuckled the Hon. Toby Cripps. "Come on in and join the gang!"

Splash Page stared at the speaker. He recognised the voice, and gradually some inkling of the evening's strange events dawned on him. It was with alacrity that he doffed his motoring-coat and followed Huntingley into the panelled dining-room.

INSPECTOR COUTTS, of Scotland Yard, was a much-worried man on the day following the amazing kidnapping of Sir Simon Grossman. He had acted on Blake's hint, and made several inquiries round the Shinwell Road district, but had been unable to glean any definite information, either about Manly or Bruff.

He returned to Scotland Yard in a distinctly disgruntled state of mind, and was confronted with an imposing number of depositions dealing with the case.

He chewed savagely at an unlit cheroot, and hoisted his feet on the desk to cogitate on the problem. Blake's inexplicable attitude in the affair annoyed Coutts. He was a clever, painstaking official, but he lacked imaginative qualities. To him crime ran in well-defined grooves, and anything bizarre or out of the ordinary irritated him. Also, it was Christmas-time, and Inspector Coutts was hoping, if not altogether expecting, that crime would ease up a bit.

The phone bell rang suddenly, and with a grunt of annoyance he raised the receiver.

"That you, Coutts?" queried Tinker. "Heard the latest? Splash Page's disappeared!"

"What?" gasped the inspector, in astonishment.

"That jolts you a bit, doesn't it?" laughed Tinker. "The guv'nor rang through to his flat, and to the office, but nobody's seen or heard of him since last night."

"There's nothing unusual about that!" growled Coutts. "These newshounds are erratic birds!"

"I know," said Tinker. "But Splash always communicates with the 'Radio' office wherever he is at ten a.m., and no message has come through. It's now nearly one o'clock, and no message has arrived."

"That's his trouble!" said Coutts callously. "I've got worries enough of my own, without investigating Splash Page's disappearance. He'll turn up all right. How's Blake to-day?"

"Quite fit," said Tinker. "He's

intrigued that Splash hasn't followed up the Grossman disappearance, though. The story in the ' Radio ' this morning's by that chap Dexter. In the usual way, Splash would have handled the whole business, but he's conspicuous by his absence."

"H'm! That's certainly queer!" said Coutts. "Coupled with the fact that the office doesn't know where he is. I think I'll drop in and see Blake after lunch."

"Do!" said Tinker. "But don't expect him to trot around with you. He's dug himself in over Christmas, and he says that Grossman, Bruff, and Mauly can stew in their own juice, for all he cares!"

Coutts snorted explosively and rang off.

MEANWHILE, at Huntingley Manor, Splash Page, the newly-elected scrivener to the League of Robin Hood, stood on the snow-clad terrace and watched with amusement the salutary methods of Sergeant Rigg and his henchmen as they drilled their unhappy prisoners.

Sir Simon Grossman, Jabez Bruff, Manly, Snape, and the hulking Cray were already and completely cowed by Rigg's basilisk glare and bull-like bellow. Panting and perspiring, they doubled round the snow-mushy lawn, clad only in trousers and singlets. Bruff's wizened little figure looked ludicrous beside that of the burly Cray, and Splash Page chuckled.

He had entered wholeheartedly into Huntingley's scheme, a n d h a d promised that no inside story of the League of Robin Hood should appear until after Christmas.

He turned to the monkish figure of Padre Browne on the terrace of the manor.

"Is it true that Grossman offered a thousand quid to be excused early-morning wood-chopping, padre?"

The clergyman nodded.

"He did, and the offer was duly accepted," he replied. "It'll cost him another thousand to be excused his oakum-picking. Meanwhile, the poor of Shinwell benefit. They'll get their Merry Christmas all right! Sir Simon will pay through his thoroughly unpleasant nose before we've done with him! Huntingley's cashing the cheque through his own bank."

"Emphatically the stuff to give 'em!" chuckled Splash Page.

"Squad!" boomed the voice of Sergeant Rigg. "Right wheel! Back into your cells! There'll be an hour's break for lunch!"

Five wretched and weary men broke into a jog-trot beneath the gaze of the armed and watchful guards and returned into the vaults of the west wing. Sir Simon Grossman's pendulous chins quivered, and tears of rage were in his eyes as he collapsed on the hard plank bed in his cell.

"Ach! How long will this torture last?" he wailed. "Bruff, that such a thing could happen in England now is incredible!"

"They shall suffer bitterly never fear!" rasped Jabez Bruff from the

adjoining cell. The partitions between each were not thick, and each man could, and did, converse when the outer door of the vault had been closed and they were left to their own devices.

"Do they mean to bleed us white and then kill us?" demanded Grossman wearily. "One thousand haf I paid to be excused that dreadful wood-chopping!"

"Yus, you rat! And I've got a double dose of it to do," rumbled the deep voice of Cruiser Cray from the end cell. "It's lucky for you, hog's face, that I can't get at yer," he added vindictively.

"Don't talk to me like that!" snapped Bruff. "You are an unconscionable villain and deserve your fate, but I, a magistrate, should——"

"Aw, shut your trap!" broke in Cray wearily. "We're all in the same boat. I'm making a dash for it to-night, guard or no guard. You 'eard that tall bloke say as we 'ad to chop dahn some of them Christmas-trees. Lemme get my 'ands on an axe in the open and watch out There'll be murder done!"

Jabez Bruff shivered.

UPSTAIRS, meanwhile, the League of Robin Hood were in full session. Lord Huntingley and Toby Cripps had returned from a hurried dash to town after cashing Grossman's cheque, the proceeds of which were now entrusted to Padre Browne.

Splash Page had accepted Huntingley's invitation to stay over Christmas at the manor, but at the back of his mind there was a vague uneasiness as to how the mad escapade would end.

"You're looking a bit worried, Splash," said Huntingley. "What's the trouble?"

"I was thinking how I can handle this business in the Radio, you chaps," he confessed. "I'm entirely with you in sentiment, but, after all, there'll be a devil of a lot of trouble when this comes out. Have you decided what you're going to do with the prisoners?"

Huntingley nodded.

"Sure! We'll dump 'em all in the wilds of the Essex marshes—I've got a shanty there—and let 'em all find their way back. None of them has recognised us. Besides, their story'll sound so fantastic that no one'll believe them. If they blab too much they'll be the laughing-stock of England. It's a good job that old Splash Page here promised to hold in his hand; otherwise, the police would be here now."

"It's not the police I'm worried about so much," said Splash. "Suppose Sexton Blake gets on the job? It's just the sort of case that would appeal to him."

"Sexton Blake," echoed the padre. "If I know anything of the man, he's with us."

"Maybe. But Blake isn't the sort of man to compound a felony, even for the best of motives. I think Lady Marion's scheme of adding Lady Rumplestein to our specimens a bit too dangerous. Don't forget that all Fleet Street are hot on the scent of the story as it is. I'll have to ring up the rag and tell 'em I'm covering one end of it—give 'em a bowdlerised version. Heaven forgive me for letting the paper down."

"Don't worry," soothed Huntingley. "It'll all come right. I'll stand all the racket if it comes to a showdown."

"We're all in this together," insisted Padre Browne, whereat there was a chorus of approval.

The short December afternoon gave place to dusk. It was nearly five o'clock when Sergeant Rigg reported that the prisoners had completed their task of cutting down the fir saplings which were to be distributed later in the poorer quarters of London.

"The man Cray was hobstropulous sir," he reported to Huntingley. "We 'ad to put 'im in irons. 'E made an unprovoked attack on Corporal Green with a haxe!"

"Did he, by Jove, the murderous brute!" said Huntingley.

"'E didn't succeed in wounding 'im, 'owever," said Rigg, who was still a trifle breathless after the encounter. "I marched all the prisoners back to the cells, and am waitin' for further orders."

"Good!" said Huntingley. "Let's go and see what sort of a job they've made of it."

He and the others were still clad in Lincoln green. Splash Page alone wore ordinary kit, but in the presence of the prisoners he donned a black domino. He and Huntingley strolled on to the terrace of the manor and gazed over the white expanse of lawn. It was a cloudless night, and the moon was already a bright silver disc above the dark fir-trees.

Together they strolled over the crisp, powdery snow towards the wood. The wind rustled eerily in the branches, and the lights of the ancient manor splashed golden on the white carpet of snow.

Suddenly Splash gave a startled gasp and pointed with an outstretched finger to where, beneath a tall and graceful fir, sprawled the motionless body of a man.

"Good heavens!" gasped Huntingley. "It's Bruff. What's the matter with the chap?"

They raced over the snow beneath the frosted branches of the tree, which glittered diamond like in the rays of the moon. A thrill of horror shot through Splash Page as he gazed at the motionless body sprawled face downward.

A trickle of crimson had oozed from a wound in the man's neck; his

(Continued on page 18.)

16

"U.J." Calling The World.

GREETINGS, everybody! The marching months have been doing their usual stuff and bringing us nearer and ever nearer—some of us fast, and some slow—to the good old feast of Yule, and here we are now, right upon it!

CAN'T BEAT!

And before we can turn round we shall be right in the midst of it.

So, right now, let me shake you by the hand and wish you the Compliments of the Season.

No use in trying to ring the changes on that time-honoured theme in new, high-flown language; one can't beat the old, old wish: A Happy Christmas.

And that I wish you, with all my heart.

* * *

The Glad Hand.

AS that creator of Modern Christmas, Charles Dickens, said, it is a kind, forgiving time.

So may it be for all "U.J." readers the world over—may you have plenty to be kind to, and few to forgive.

Here's to your health and gaiety. and your enjoyment of the season's mirth, wherever you may be. Whether Christmastide finds you amongst the blizzards of Canada or the blossoms of "Down Under," may you have a real fine time!

* * *

Counting My Chickens.

AND, as I am in the sleuth game, let me do a bit of deducing in the best manner of my respected guv'nor.

I shall soon receive a flattering number of Christmas cards and greetings from my "U.J." friends in all parts of the globe. How do I know this? The deduction is easy; it has happened at previous Christmases, and, with luck, it should happen again.

So let me take time by the forelock and thank in advance all those staunch pals of mine who have rallied round with the glad hand and the seasonable smile, as it were, and caught the post with their Yuletide greetings by the time these words are read. Also, of course, those who do not need to do so till later.

Naturally I always try and acknowledge these compliments individually, and I'm hoping I shan't be altogether buried by the heap before I can answer all these letters.

* * *

Hand-picked.

I THINK you will agree that I have picked out a really good, seasonable case from the "Index" for this week's yarn.

Weighing it up from all points of view, I really think that this affair of the Robin Hood League is as good a combination of a detective story and a Christmas setting as one could hope to find.

I imagine it will be to your taste, so I'll leave you to get on with it, as the

kind-hearted warder said to the convict when he slipped a plateful of roast turkey into his cell one Christmas Day.

* * *

Br-r-r !

OUR yarn referred to seems to be equipped with everything Christmassy except the usual ghost.

Never mind; let's have a real ghost story on this page instead !

Ghosts and garages don't seem to go together any more than crape and crackers, but this is a genuine case, and it happened in the heart of London, near Hyde Park.

The garage in question is situated next to a Tube station just north of the park. There is a basement to the building—which has been converted to its present use—and in this basement one evening before Christmas one of the assistants was busy opening some packing-cases.

Suddenly he was consternated to see an awesome figure at the foot of the stairway leading to the garage above.

* * *

All Agreed.

"IT was dressed in black and wearing a bowler hat," he reported afterwards. "It made no sound whatever, and seemed to glide towards me. There was a horrible leer on the face, and if expression counts for anything, it meant no good.

"The thing approached to within a few feet of me, and then simply vanished before my eyes.

So far, so ghastly.

But inquiries began to be made, and there was unexpected confirmation of this weird story.

Another assistant then admitted he had seen the same uncanny visitant about a month before, and described it. He had not told the story before, for fear of being laughed at. Also, another employee probably had the same experience, for he would never enter the cellar at night without taking a weapon of some sort with him, and eventually left without any apparent reason.

* * *

A Grave Matter.

BUT the most convincing thing was the discovery that the garage was built on the site of an old graveyard, and that one of the stones of the basement floor was, in fact, an old gravestone.

WORKING

The name on it had long since been worn away, but the words: " . . . lies Middlewyck, who passed . . ." could be distinguished.

It is worth mentioning that, at the time when the employee was working in the cellar, every door in the building was properly locked, and there was no way in but the stone stairs at which the apparition appeared. The employee declared he would never venture down there again, day or night, unless he had to.

I don't blame him, either.

Tinker's Xr

Cheery Yuletide Chat fro

Whisky Wassail.

CHRISTMAS comes but once a ye A well-known fact, of course, what I meant to say was that there people who are duly thankful for it.

Among them may be included th who are tempted to indulge in Ameri bootleg whisky, and similar corros chemicals, as an addition to the seaso luxuries.

In short, if they indulge only Christmas-time, they must be glad t there is only one December 25th in calendar. Unless, of course, they not survive "the morning after," which case the frequency of the fest season interests them no more.

Last year there were nearly a hund deaths in the United States due so to drinking bootleg liquor at Christm time.

This is a cause for great satisfact in Government circles in the States.

* * *

The Undertakers' Friend.

LEST you should suspect me of be funny at Uncle Sam's expense would explain that I do not mean suggest that the Government wants kill off the population.

Nunno; there were less than a hund deaths at Christmas, 1927, but at same period in 1926 there were m than twice as many. In short, th has been a gratifying decrease in t bootleg death-rate.

Less alcohol was consumed last Chri mas than at any other since Prohibit became law.

In New York and Chicago, example, there were fourteen deaths l year; and in the same towns, w Detroit added, fifty at Christmas, 1920

At one time the U.S. Government a poisonous substance in industr alcohol, and published the fact. people persisted in drinking it, so officials had to put in a harmless distasteful ingredient instead.

"Undertaker cocktails," the Yar called them. And rightly so.

* * *

Ice See !

IT doesn't seem to have much to with our Robin Hood story at t moment, but an ingenious way of wat

s Notebook.

Baker Street Dinner=table.

crops in the rainless parts of
...rica has been tried out with some
...ess.

...stead of making irrigation canals
...dams and reservoirs at great ex-
...se, the latest idea is to steer a sort
...ractor between the rows of growing
...s, and shoot ice bullets into the
...und, where they rapidly melt and
...er the roots.

...uite a brainy gadget, one gathers.
...re is a freezing machine aboard the
...tor which fills a mould with water
...produces an ice bullet; and as the
...le contraption moves along, the
...lets are conveyed to a compressed
...gun which fires them into the soil.

...ust shows you what can be done with
...you see. For further uses, refer to
...week's story.

* * *

...sn't Cobble Now.

...HILE it is America's turn, let me
...mention the case of Patrick Can-
...g, the poor cobbler of Haverhill,
...ssachusetts.

...eeping a wife and three daughters on
...proceeds of half-sole-and-heeling was
...ill work, Patrick found. He was,
...efore, rather interested to hear, a
...le of days after Christmas Day, that
...elative living in Monte Carlo had
...d, and that he inherited £2,500,000.

...hope he got some of the money away
...n the lawyers, and if so, that he in-
...ds to celebrate the anniversary of his
...d luck by something really lavish in
...way of Yuletide entertainment to
...se who have been less lucky in life's
...ery.

* * *

...der the Influence.

...was last year, too, that a curious
...murder case was reported from
...many.

...man named Schafer travelled over
...n Zurich to Buer, in Prussia, to
...nd the holiday with his old friend
...hlwurt.

...verything went off in merry fashion
...il just after Christmas. And then,
...en the two men were sitting together
...the fire, Schafer suddenly produced
...evolver, fired several shots at Wohl-
...t, and fatally wounded him.

He was arrested, and then gave his
reason for the crime.

He said that he had been undergoing
a course of hypnotic treatment at Zurich,
and while he was under their control
the doctor and Wohlwurt had caused him
to commit a number of criminal acts.

On discovering this afterwards, he
decided to be revenged on the man he
had thought to be his friend, and had
accepted his invitation for Christmas
with the deliberate idea of killing him.

Police investigations proved that this
somewhat unusual explanation was quite
true, but I don't know whether the man
was acquitted on the strength of it or
not.

* * *

False Alarm.

"WILL you adjourn Christmas for
fourteen days?"

This was the question which was
asked of the Lewes magistrates, so a
friend of mine who happened to be present tells me, by their clerk some little
time ago.

But the magistrates' surprise at being
asked to juggle with the calendar was
explained away when they were told that
Christmas was the name of a man whose
case was down for hearing.

IN THE NEWS

tion, is receiving
close consideration
by Law Officers of
the Crown."

That little item
appeared in the
news last Febru-
ary, and intimated
that such pleasant
little flutters as the
Stock Exchange
"Help Yourself" Society were going to
be called upon the carpet.

Apparently it hasn't happened yet, for
this particular scheme is again much in
evidence this year, and besides benefit-
ing a much-needed and needing cause, is
giving people the thrill of their lives
in the meantime, wondering what they
would do if they won the prize of a bag
of winkles and a paper of pins.

If you're in it—as I am—I hope you
will win this prize.

I myself have tried to reserve one of
the motor-cars.

* * *

By the Way.

DURING the present shopping season
shoplifters will be specially busy.
They will, in fact, have their hands full.

'What's all
this about
Christmas?'
demanded
the turkeys,
bobbing up
on their way
to market.
Alas for
them, they
have ceased
to wonder
now!

Love-ly!

A LITTLE bit of comedy from Wild
Wales:

Last Christmas Eve a man of Aberdare
was on the point of being escorted into
the police station by one of the local
cops, when he turned round and smote
him one and disappeared.

He was at large for some months, and
very elusive at that.

Finally he was arrested again.

In the quietness of a certain Lovers'
Lane he was passing along in the dusk
one evening, when suddenly two of the
lovers sprang out of the shadows at
him, and after an exciting scrap escorted
him once more to the station.

The lovers were two policemen, disguised, one as a railwayman, and the
other as a woman.

A case of courting—caught—court.

The Draw of the Draw.

"THE whole question of the legality
of Christmas draws . . . which
depend on the result of public subscrip-

A Snappy Christmas.

WHILE we are pulling the joyous
cracker in the cosy neighbourhood
of the blazing Yule-log—or heaped-up
Household Nuts—spare a thought for the
man of the North-West Mounted Police
on his lonesome job in the frozen wastes
of our Dominion.

Just after Christmas last year, Constable Truelove, of the Mounties, struggled into Cochrane, Ontario, with an
Indian.

This Indian was his prisoner, and the
constable had penetrated into the fast-
nesses of the far North-West to get him.
A thousand miles was that little excursion, and on winter trails. But Truelove
went after his man, and got him, which
is the tradition of the service.

What a thousand miles on winter
trails really means, only those of us
who have experienced the same conditions
can know. So we'll leave it at that.

But here's to the health of Constable
Truelove.

(Continued from page 15.)

hands were outstretched and rigid. One glance was sufficient to tell them that Jabez Bruff was dead.

Huntingley's face blenched.

"My heaven!" he gasped huskily. "Murder!"

Splash Page dropped on his knee beside the body, and his face was tense and set.

"Stabbed from behind — that's obvious," he remarked. "Gosh, Huntingley, there's trouble looming up for us all in this!"

Chapter 5.
A Tragic Turn.

SENTON BLAKE was nothing if not consistent. Despite all the blandishments of Inspector Coutts, he resolutely refused to move in what Fleet Street described as the most sensational kidnapping case of recent years.

The Yard-man himself was hopelessly at sea, and confessed as much to Blake, but beyond indicating certain lines of inquiry, the private detective dissociated himself from the matter.

Coutts had departed in high dudgeon, and Blake and Tinker had just changed into evening dress before spending the evening at the theatre, when the telephone rang.

Blake took up the receiver, and his eyebrows lifted slightly as he heard the agitated voice of Splash Page at the other end of the wire.

"For Heaven's sake come at once to Huntingley Manor, Essex, Blake!" he said urgently. "Something frightful's happened. I can't explain on the phone, but I'm in the worst mess I've ever been in."

It was not often that Blake betrayed surprise, but the compelling urgency in the journalist's voice made him whistle softly. It was certainly unlike Splash Page to be agitated.

"Can't you give me a hint, my dear fellow?" he said. "We were just going out; you were lucky to catch me."

"For goodness' sake cancel all your engagements, Blake, old man!" said Splash. "It's murder, and I'm afraid I'm in it!"

Blake's face became grave. He and Splash Page had been colleagues on many an adventurous trail together, and this appeal for help could not be disregarded.

"Right: I'll come," he said briefly. "Keep cool, Splash. I'll be there as quickly as the Panther can bring me."

"Thank Heaven!" said Splash fervently. "Make for Widdingdean, on the Cambridge Road; the manor's a little beyond the village."

"I know the place, I believe," said Sexton Blake; and turning to Tinker told him to fetch the Grey Panther from the garage.

The youngster glanced inquiringly at his guv'nor as he donned his coat.

"Splash Page's in trouble," announced Blake. "Hurry, young 'un!"

They were both very silent on that moonlit drive to Huntingley Manor. Blake's mind was preoccupied. He knew that something out of the ordinary had happened to make Splash's appeal so urgent, but he did not guess at the astonishing revelations that were to be made to him on his arrival.

They reached the huge, wrought iron gates of the manor a little after seven o'clock. Blake blew the Klaxon loudly, and from the adjacent lodge emerged a khaki-clad figure with a gun held in

the crook of his arm. His face, Blake noted, had a furtive expression as he peered through the iron scroll work of the gates.

He seemed a little more reassured, however, as he recognised the detective's features in the moonlight.

"Thank Heaven you've come, Mr. Blake!" he said. "'Is lordship's bin on tenter'ooks!"

He took a massive key from his pocket and unlocked the gates. Tinker steered the Grey Panther up the driveway towards the manor, then gave a startled exclamation as three figures emerged from the shrubbery.

"Great Scott, guv'nor!" he ejaculated. "Look at this lot!"

TWO men, garbed in Lincoln green, accompanied by a grey-garbed friar, were illumined in the headlamps on the car, and a second later Splash Page appeared from the shadows. Tinker brought the Grey Panther to a standstill, and Blake and he joined Splash and the curiously dressed trio on the snow-covered lawn.

"Blake, old man, I'm so glad you're here!" said the journalist huskily. "We need your advice badly. Jabez Bruff's been murdered, and we, in a way, are responsible."

"Bruff?" echoed Blake; and his keen grey eyes swept the little group. "What was he doing here?"

"I'll explain all that in a minute," said Splash. "Meanwhile, I thought it best to leave the body undisturbed until your arrival. It's over here. Ghastly business."

He led the way towards the slightly swaying fir-tree, and pointed to that stark, grim thing that sprawled face downward on the snow.

"We didn't touch a thing," said Splash. "I know your methods pretty well by now, Blake, so we left everything just as we found it. The man was stone dead. We couldn't do anything for him, anyway."

"Good!" said Blake, with a nod of approval. He dropped on his knees beside the body, and in his calm, methodical fashion proceeded to examine it.

"Dead about two hours, I should say," he announced. "Stabbed by some sharp instrument that pierced the jugular."

The motley figures in Lincoln green stood by silently, as the detective scanned the snow, his alert eyes questing for clues. There were many footprints, but mostly indistinguishable, and Blake frowned thoughtfully.

He glanced up at the growing Christmas-tree speculatively, as if its whispering branches could tell the secret of the dead man's violent end.

"Have you informed the police yet?" he inquired suddenly.

Lord Huntingley, who had hitherto been silent, shook his head.

"I—er—that is, we—er—didn't dare, Mr. Blake," he said uneasily. "You see, we kidnapped Bruff, and, morally, I suppose, we can be held responsible for his death. Heaven knows we didn't expect—"

"Quite! Quite!" said Blake, and turned to the newspaperman.

"Better give me a short precis of the situation, Splash," he announced. "I take it you are all also responsible for the kidnapping of Grossman, Manly, & Co.?"

Splash nodded.

"We are, Blake. Come into the house, and we'll put all our cards on the table. It's got to come out now, and we need your advice desperately."

IT was a strangely silent party that assembled in the oak-panelled dining-room of Huntingley Manor. Sexton Blake drew out his briar and listened gravely, as, in terse sentences, Splash Page outlined the motives and actions of the League of Robin Hood.

Occasionally the detective would interject a question or two, but for the most part he remained seated, with half-closed eyes, puffing slowly at his pipe.

"And so," concluded Splash, "according to Sergeant Rigg, in the melee, when they were disarming the man Cray, Bruff must have slipped away unobserved. Who stabbed him, and why, are the problems. One doesn't want to speak ill of the dead, and all that, but Bruff was a pretty scaly specimen of humanity. Nearly everybody hated him, and it's just as likely that Manly, Snape, or Grossman did the murder."

"You are assuming too much, and too quickly," said Sexton Blake quietly. "I pass no opinion at the moment, Lord Huntingley," he added, "about the less you fully realise the gravity of the situation; the question remains that the police must be informed at once."

"Gosh, Blake!" said Splash Page. "Can't we hush up the matter? I mean to say, think of the scandal that——"

"I'm afraid there can be no question of hushing it up," broke in the criminologist. "However, I will compromise to this extent. I myself will make a preliminary inquiry. Maybe I shall discover a few facts which will put a different complexion on the case. One thing is certain, however, you cannot evade the unpleasant consequences of being accessories in the sudden end of Jabez Bruff."

"Accessories!" gasped Lord Huntingley. "But dash it, Mr. Blake, I swear we never intended to kill Bruff."

"Perhaps not," said Sexton Blake non-committally. "But you admit that you committed the serious crime of detaining him as a prisoner against his will. However good your motives may have been, the law cannot possibly overlook that fact."

"My Heaven!" groaned Huntingley hoarsely. "This is terrible! Look here, Mr. Blake, can't I take all the blame for this business? Let Splash, Toby, Padre, and all the rest of 'em clear off, and I'll face the music."

"Not on your life!" broke in Padre Browne. "We stand or fall together."

"Sure we do!" chimed in Toby Cripps.

Splash Page tugged at Blake's sleeve.

"Hadn't you better cross-examine the prisoners, Blake? After all, there's a chance that Manly or Cray did it. They both hated Bruff like poison. If you could extract a confession out of them now, perhaps——"

"I think, in the circumstances, it would be advisable," said Sexton Blake.

Huntingley pressed a bell-push, and a moment or two later Sergeant Rigg entered.

Blake scanned the man's face keenly.

"You, I take it, were the last to see Jabez Bruff alive, Rigg?" he said.

"I was, sir."

"About what time was that?"

"Just about five-fifteen, sir. The working party was scattered about the plantation, sir. Grossman was workin' with Snape, Cray on his own, while Bruff's job was to tie the upper branches of the smaller trees together in bundles o' three."

"I see," said Blake quietly. "How many did the guard consist of?"

"Three, sir. Meself, Green, and Jones."

"What happened when Cray attacked Green?"

"The three of us closed in on 'im, 'sir, and brought 'im down."

"And the prisoners?"

"I didn't notice pertickler, sir. I was too occupied with Cray. I believe Bruff must 'ave run away. 'Is body was found some distance from where 'e was workin'."

"H'm!" said Blake thoughtfully. "I think I'll take a look at your prisoners. By the way——" He wheeled suddenly on Huntingley, and pointed at the leather belt that hung loosely from his doublet.

"I notice your knife is missing, Lord Huntingley," he said quietly.

For a moment or two deathly silence followed the detective's words. Huntingley's handsome face paled suddenly, and he clutched nervously at the empty sheath that dangled from his girdle. The implication of Sexton Blake's words was unmistakable, and each man looked uneasily at the other.

The detective's features, however, were perfectly impassive as he stood with his back to the fireplace and surveyed the oddly assorted group. Huntingley wetted his dry lips.

"Good heavens, Mr. Blake!" he gasped. "You're not suggesting that I am responsible for——"

"I'm suggesting nothing yet," interposed the criminologist. "I merely draw your attention to the fact that your knife is missing; so also is the weapon which slew Jabez Bruff."

"But great Scott," ejaculated Splash Page, "surely you can't think that Huntingley's had a hand in this ghastly business? I admit we've all laid ourselves open to a charge of conspiracy. But murder——" Splash Page's face expressed righteous indignation.

"I'm not insinuating anything, Splash," said Blake. "I'm anxious to help you all, but the gravity of the situation cannot be minimised."

"I swear none of us 'ad owt to do with it, sir!" broke in Sergeant Rigg. "It must 'ave bin Snape or Manly. I've 'eard 'em threaten Bruff with my own ears, only last night."

Sexton Blake stroked his chin thoughtfully.

"You had better all stay here, gentlemen," he said quietly. "I trust to your honour to attempt no escape until I have interrogated your prisoners. Sergeant, please conduct me to the vault."

SPLASH PAGE swallowed hard, and glanced across at Tinker. The youngster's face was troubled. He and the newspaperman were old friends, and had much in common, including youth and high spirits, but this was the first time he had found the journalist perturbed and definitely involved on the wrong side of the law.

Huntingley stared sombrely after Blake's retreating figure as he accompanied the burly sergeant out of the panelled room.

"My Heaven, you chaps!" he gasped huskily. "Our idea of a Merry Christmas seems to have gone all wrong. As for this——"

He handled the empty sheath, and his face was grey.

"Surely you don't think that I could have been capable of—of——"

"Nonsense, Robin!" boomed the padre. "You trust Sexton Blake! If any man can get us out of this mess, he can!"

"Yes, leave it to the guv'nor," said Tinker reassuringly. "He'll see you through. As a matter of fact," he added, "he sympathises with the League of Robin Hood. I'm not betraying any confidences when I say that

he definitely refused to help Coutts—of Scotland Yard, you know—to trail you all for the kidnapping of Grossman. I've an idea that the guv'nor suspected all along that you were mixed up in the business, Splash."

"H'm!" said the newspaperman glumly. "If it was only kidnapping it wouldn't be so bad, but murder——"

He shivered involuntarily, and the silence that followed his words was chill with the menace of the Law's outraged majesty.

What had begun in a spirit of revelry, and with the best of motives, had now turned to tragedy. Splash Page's vivid imagination visualised the aftermath that would follow the inevitable arrival of the police on the scene.

Not even his friendship with the famous criminologist could avert the resultant scandal. More than all, he feared the censure of his newspaper, the "Daily Radio," for committing the unforgivable sin of falling down on a story. He had been swept off his feet by the romantic glamour of the situation at Huntingley Manor, and had meant to hold up the inside story of the kidnapping until after Christmas, when he would have scooped the pool with the startling account of the missing men's discovery in Huntingley's shack on the Essex marshes.

Now, however, he was swayed by opposing forces. Loyalty to his paper demanded that he should instantly apprise them of the true facts of the situation; loyalty to his new-found friends, sportsmen to a man, impelled him to hold his hand.

He wondered what Mr. Blake was doing in the vaults of the west wing. Was the murderer among the four

prisoners? Or was there some deeper mystery to be solved, and one that would react in a still more sinister fashion on the League of Robin Hood?

Chapter 6.

Putting the Wind Up.

SEXTON BLAKE'S face was very thoughtful as he followed Sergeant Rigg through the rambling passageway in the west wing, and descended into the cellars.

"It's a queer business, sir," muttered the sergeant. "But one thing I'll

The padre's fist shot out straight for the Cruiser's jaw. It was a perfectly timed blow. He collapsed to the pavement even as a police whistle shrilled in the distance.

take my oath on, sir. 'Is lordship ain't 'ad nothink to do with the murder. 'E's one of the whitest men breathin', sir, an' we're with 'im to a man in this business.

"Lord Huntingley certainly knows how to inspire loyalty," said Sexton Blake drily. "Tell me, Rigg, did you notice whether Bruff and the other four prisoners had any opportunity of converse alone?"

"Not to my knowledge, sir," replied Rigg. "As you'll see when you get into the vaults, they're pretty well caged. If that big feller, Cruiser, 'adn't run amuck this wouldn't 'ave 'appened," he added bitterly.

He took out a huge key from the pocket of his khaki overcoat as he spoke, and inserted it in the lock of the door. It swung back easily without a creak, and, pressing a switch to the right of the lintel, Rigg revealed the four sullen prisoners in their cells.

Cruiser Cray sat with his massive wrists encircled by a pair of shining steel bracelets, and leapt to his feet with a snarl as Sexton Blake entered. Grossman, crouched in the corner of his cell, was moaning miserably to himself. His grey, unwholesome face was covered with a stubble of beard. Manly and Snape blinked uncertainly in the sudden glare of light.

For a moment or two Sexton Blake surveyed them dispassionately; then he spoke, and his voice was quite impersonal.

"Cruiser Cray, Jabez Bruff has met with a violent death. Have you any information to volunteer on the subject?"

"Rat-Face dead?" said Cruiser. "Gosh! That's the best bit o' news I've 'eard for years!"

"Ach! Who are you?" wailed Sir Simon Grossman, clutching convulsively at the bars of the cell. "You have murdered Bruff, and now you have come to murder me!"

He fell on his knees, and streams of perspiration poured down his flabby face.

"Have mercy! Have mercy!" he wailed. "I will pay anything——"

"Be quiet!" snapped Sexton Blake; and his voice was icy with contempt. "You four men are in a dangerous position, how dangerous you do not yet realise. Jabez Bruff was found stabbed in the neck, and I happen to know that you, Cray, and Manly had a long-standing grudge against the man.

"Cripes! I know yer now!" said Cruiser Cray, his jaw dropping. "You're Sexton Blake!"

"Sexton Blake!" echoed Sir Simon Grossman. "The great detective! Mr. Blake, I implore you to tell me what all this means. I—I feel I'm going mad!" He raised a shaking hand to his head.

"It means, Grossman," said Blake quietly, "that you and your three amicable associates stand a very good chance of appearing in the dock on the charge of murder!"

"Murder!" gasped the wretched financier. "I swear I don't know what you're talking about! I was kidnapped, brought here against my will by a gang of armed ruffians. So was Jabez Bruff. These others will bear out what I say."

"That's true enough, Mr. Blake," said Manly. "And I want to know, as a free born Englishman, by what right we are detained here, when——"

"It is news to me that you are suddenly proud of your British citizenship," broke in Blake quietly. "In your public capacity you seem to be singularly eloquent on the subject of your spiritual home in Russia."

H E glanced across at Snape. That foxy-featured crook wilted beneath the stern gaze of the criminologist.

"You, Snape, are already wanted by the police on a charge of embezzlement. I have also reason to know that you, Manly, are an accomplice of his. Cruiser Cray, you are already an old lag, and you appreciate how very precarious your situation will be when the police learn that Jabez Bruff was last seen alive in your company, and were repeatedly heard to threaten him."

The coarse, brutal face of the Cruiser whitened.

"S'welp me, guv'nor!" he protested. "I didn't lay a finger on the white-livered rat! We were all in the same

boat—that tall bloke in the fancy costoom and the bow and arrers must 'ave done it. Shot 'im in the neck, like as not, when 'e tried to run for it."

"How do you know Bruff attempted to escape?" demanded Blake suddenly.

"I—I didn't! I only guessed from what you was a-tellin' of me, guv'nor!" said Cray uneasily.

Rigg stood by uneasily, as Blake confronted the four prisoners.

"Don't believe what that big brute says, Mr. Blake," he said earnestly. "I swear one of these four did for Bruff."

Blake pulled at the silken lapels of his dress suit, and abruptly turned on his heel. "I shall be back very shortly," he announced. "In company with the police. Meanwhile, you have an opportunity to consider the situation. I warn you, however, that you are all four in the shadow of the gallows."

He signalled to Rigg, and together they left the vaulted chamber. When the door had closed behind them a burst of profanity broke from Cruiser Cray's lips.

"Curse 'em! It's a frame-up, that's what. I never touched Bruff! Manly, you sneaking rat, you was nearest to 'im. I saw you edging close to 'im when 'e was tyin' up them trees——"

"You liar!" roared Manly, his voice rising to a shriek. "It was you who threatened to do 'im in. I saw you slip that knife into your pocket, the one you found by the terrace after exercise this morning."

"Knife?" echoed Cray. "I tell you I ain't 'ad no knife, curse you!"

He seized the bars of his cell in his manacled hands, and shook them until they rattled. Stark berserker fury held him in its grip, and he looked more like a gorilla than a human being as he glared ferociously through the grille.

"Stop yer row!" whined Snape. "We're for it now all right, Cray. Point is, if we 'ang together, and tell the same tale to the cops——"

"We'll 'ang together all right," cut in Cray grimly. "I'm getting out of 'ere afore they come."

S EXTON BLAKE dismissed Sergeant Rigg, and strolled slowly over the moonlit lawn towards the fatal fir-tree. His shrewd, analytical brain was busy with the problem of how to spare his colleague, Splash Page, and his companions of the League from the unpleasant consequences of their original action. He lit a cigarette and reviewed the situation in his kind.

Jabez Bruff was a person of some consequence. His disappearance had already been broadcast by the Press, and Scotland Yard were already in possession of the letter written to his housekeeper, announcing that the League of Robin Hood were responsible for the deed.

Had Bruff been an unknown man it would have been comparatively simple to hush up the affair, but Blake was essentially straightforward, and not likely to resort to subterfuge and evasive tactics.

Indubitably the police would have to be called in. He glanced at his watch. It was nearly eight p.m. Time was fleeting, and the longer he refrained from calling in the police the more serious would the situation become.

He glanced down dispassionately at the figure of the dead man, and shrugged his shoulders. His duty was clear. However much he sympathised with Huntingley, it was obvious that the police would arrest the whole lot, and it looked as if they would spend their Christmas in a prison cell.

Suddenly his face lightened, and a faint, fugitive smile played about his finely-chiselled lips.

"It would teach them all a lesson," he murmured. "It is the only possible solution of the problem."

He strolled slowly towards the terrace of the manor, and was admitted into the hall by Padre Browne. The cleric's usually jovial face looked pale and perturbed.

"Lady Marion has returned, Mr. Blake," he announced gravely. "We haven't yet informed her of the—the murder, but she senses there is something wrong. None of us wants to drag her into the matter; she has been away the whole day, and obviously can have no connection with the affair."

Sexton Blake flung away the stub of his cigarette into the glowing fire of pine logs in the hallway. The flickering flames gilded the suits of armour until they shone like gold, the raftered ceiling festooned with evergreens, the holly and mistletoe above the carved oak mantelpiece made the scene festive and gay—an incongruous background to the tragedy that had befallen the ancient manor.

"It is better that she should learn the truth at once," announced Blake.

He followed the padre into the dining-room, where a strangely silent group sat before the wide hearth. Lady Marion was seated on the arm of her brother's chair, a puzzled expression on her piquant little face. Blake bowed courteously over her slim fingers, as Huntingley introduced them.

"Is there anything wrong, Mr. Blake?" she asked anxiously. "Everybody seems so glum and silent, and, excuse me, your presence here is rather surprising. I have just motored from town, expecting to find revelry, and instead——"

"I am afraid something rather unpleasant has happened, Lady Marion," interposed Blake quietly. "You, I take it, have been quite cognisant of—er—the activities of the Robin Hood League?"

"Certainly," she answered. "Topping idea, isn't it?" Her eyes twinkled mischievously. "Don't say we are all under arrest. After all, it's Christmas time, you know, and Sir Simon Grossman and his friends are really rather horrid people who can be dispensed with until Christmas is over."

"Marion, my dear!" broke in her brother. "Mr. Blake has come down to advise us what to do. It would be much better if you went back to town, something rather awful has happened. Jabez Bruff has been murdered!"

"Murdered!" She rose to her feet, her eyes dilated with surprise. "How awful! I—I—is this really so, Mr. Blake?"

Sexton Blake nodded.

"From superficial appearances, everything points in that direction, Lady Marion," he announced. "Of course, the inquest will decide the matter. The point is, Lord Huntingley"—he turned to her brother—"we cannot safely delay the advent of the police any longer. If you will allow me to take charge of the arrangements, I will do my best for you, but you must be guided by me in your conduct before the police."

"We are in your hands entirely, Mr. Blake," said Huntingley.

"In that case," said Sexton Blake,

crossing over to the telephone in the hall. "The sooner the matter is sifted, the better. Your nearest station is Widdingdean, is it not?"

Huntingley nodded.

"About five miles away from here," he announced.

"Good! That will give us time to formulate our plan of campaign," replied Blake.

For a moment or two there was a pause. The Hon. Toby Cripps felt a queer sinking sensation in the pit of his stomach. Splash Page fidgeted uneasily with his tie, while Blake was away telephoning.

"Now we're for it, Tinker," he murmured. "There's no escape."

"Trust the guv'nor," said the lad confidently. "I've a hunch that we'll still have a Merry Christmas."

"I doubt it," said Splash Page gloomily.

———

Chapter 7.

Enter the Police.

INSPECTOR EPHRAIM, of the Essex police, was dozing at his desk in the tiny police station at Widdingdean, when Sexton Blake's telephone call came through. He muttered an imprecation below his breath, as the harsh ring of the bell jarred on a comforting dream of roast turkey and plum-pudding, but the name of the famous private detective from Baker Street was sufficient to jerk him out of his chair like a hooked minnow.

"Mr. Blake? Bless my soul!" he ejaculated. "Fancy you being in this district! Why, it must be years since I had the honour of serving with you on that Goncourt case. You probably remember me. My name's Ephraim."

"Ephraim? Oh, yes! Why, certainly," said the voice of Sexton Blake over the wire. There was distinct cordiality in his tone. He remembered the Goncourt affair well. Inspector Ephraim had then been a village constable, and had shown undoubted intelligence, so much, in fact, that when the murderer was run to earth, Blake had dropped an influential hint to the authorities, which resulted in Ephraim's rapid promotion.

"There's trouble, bad trouble, at Huntingley Manor, inspector," he announced. "Will you come over at once with a couple of men? It looks like murder."

"Murder?" echoed the inspector, and his eyes glistened. "I'll be along as quick as I can, Mr. Blake. Lord Huntingley is in residence, is he not?"

"Yes," said Blake laconically. "He's naturally tremendously upset at the tragedy. The case has several unique features, inspector. I will explain in detail on your arrival."

Inspector Ephraim, a red-faced, bucolic-looking man, possessed that estimable quality, in a policeman, of looking more stupid than he actually was. He rang the bell for the two constables, who, with himself, represented the law in Widdingdean district, and issued curt instructions.

Meanwhile, Sexton Blake had hung up the receiver, and re-entered the dining-room.

"And now, gentlemen," he announced quietly, "we must arrange our plan of campaign. By a stroke of good fortune I have just learned that the inspector at Widdingdean is an old acquaintance of mine, and that may possibly save a good deal of unpleasantness when he conducts the investigations."

"Jove! That's a bit of luck, Blake," said Splash Page enthusiastically. "Perhaps we can square him to——"

"Attempted corruption of the police in the execution of their duty is a very serious offence," Blake reminded him.

"Hang it all, Mr. Blake!" said Huntingley. "I am mainly responsible for the whole business. Couldn't all these others go back to town, as I suggested before, and I'll bear the brunt?"

"I'm afraid that's impossible," said Blake. "By the way, your prisoners are also experiencing a good deal of uneasiness as to the outcome. Sir Simon Grossman will undoubtedly be glad to drop any proceedings against you for the kidnapping to avoid scandal; as for the others, they're in trouble with the police already. Whatever happens, it will be a very big feather in Inspector Ephraim's cap."

"What about old Coutts, guv'nor? He'll be hopping mad when he discovers what's happened."

Blake smiled briefly.

"Get on to him at the Yard, young 'un," he said. "Tell him to come down at once; you needn't specify why, but hint that I have solved the secret of Sir Simon's disappearance."

TINKER rose to his feet, and the detective turned to Huntingley.

"Don't be too downcast, my friend," he murmured. "I see a glimmer of light in this dark affair. Remember, surface appearances are often deceptive. That knife of yours, for instance, might quite conceivably have been extracted from your belt by design, or have fallen out by accident. I think a further parley with your prisoners would be advisable."

He turned to Rigg, who was hovering near by.

"Give me the key," he ordered curtly. "By this time they've had a chance to talk things over; maybe they have come to a decision."

He crossed into the hallway and opened the heavy oaken door. A blast of icy wind swept into the place, and Lady Marion shivered.

"Oh, it's dreadful, Mr. Blake!" she murmured. "Poor Mr. Bruff, he—he wasn't a good man, but to meet his death so suddenly on the eve of Christmas seems horrible. We'd planned to have such a jolly time, too." She pointed to the decorations, and her face was wistful.

"One thing is certain," said Sexton Blake. "The poor of Shinwell will have a happy Christmas, Lady Marion, and perhaps you, too, will not be disappointed."

With which cryptic remark, he went out on to the terrace to the west wing. Nearing tne vaults, his keen eyes became aware of a dull thudding sound, and, quickening his pace, he descended the steep stone steps into the basement.

He unlocked the arched door, and his jaw set grimly as he saw the gigantic figure of Cruiser Cray hurling himself with maddened frenzy against the bars of his ceil.

"By heck!" roared the Cruiser. "Lemme get at the snivelling Snape! I'll do for 'im, the lying skunk! 'E says I knifed Bruff in the back. The bloomin' liar! I'll—"

He spluttered incoherently, flecks of foam appeared on his gibbering lips.

Blake's eyes narrowed.

"What's all this about a knife, Snape?" he rasped out sharply.

"Cray did it, I swear, Mr. Blake," said the ferret-faced Snape. "'E picked up a knife by the terrace this morning. Manly and I saw him do it."

"It's a lie, a foul lie!" screamed the Cruiser. "I ain't got no knife. It was Manly wot picked it up!"

"H'm!" said Sexton Blake thoughtfully. "This is getting a little more clear, my friends. Obviously, one of you has a knife. The question is—who?"

He turned to Sir Simon Grossman, who cowered wretchedly in the dark corner of his cell.

"I think I shall interrogate you all separately," announced Blake. "You first, Sir Simon."

He unlocked the door of the cell, and Grossman licked his flabby lips.

"I—I swear I know nothing— nothing, Mr. Blake," he quavered.

Blake's fingers closed slowly round Grossman's arm.

"Come with me!" he commanded. Keen psychologist that he was, Sexton Blake had deliberately left the four prisoners in the dark and uncertainty in the hope that they would reveal some new factor in the case.

T HAT his surmise was sound, was evidenced by the abject terror of Sir Simon Grossman. Blake's carefully w o r d e d warning about the shadow of the gallows had had its effect on all four. They were like cornered rats, ready to bite anyone or anything within reach, to accuse each other, and lie indiscriminately, in the hope of saving their necks.

"This way," said Sexton Blake, leading the trembling financier towards the stone stairs. "The police will be here at any moment now." he added significantly.

"As Heaven's my witness, I'm innocent!" bleated the wretched man. "Won't you help me, Mr. Blake? I will pay anything, anything, to escape from the dreadful scandal. My son is to be married next month to Lady Hamblin. Royalty has promised to be present, and if any whisper of this murder, and my connection with it,

should leak o u t, I—"

"Your connection with it?" snapped Sexton Blake, and his steely e y e s narrowed.

"No, no! You misunderstand me," quavered Grossman. "I—I mean Bruff and I were b o t h friends, in a way, Mr. Blake, but if it should leak out that he and I were kidnapped and imprisoned in company with such men as t h a t brute Cray—"

"Ah, I see!" said Sexton Blake. "You are afraid that some of yours and Bruff's little stunts together in Shinwell would leak out, eh?"

It was a shrewd thrust, and it went home. Both Bruff and Grossman had b e e n concerned together on many a shady deal in that unsalubrious quarter.

"My fee will be a thousand guineas to extricate y o u from this trouble," said Blake gravely. "And you will have to follow my instructions to the letter."

"I will do anything you ask," said Sir Simon Grossman.

Blake could see that he was nearly at the end of his tether, and piloted him gently up the stairs towards the Manor House. On the way, he outlined in quick, rapid sentences, the plan he had devised and, like a drowning man, Grossman clutched eagerly at the straw contemptuously tossed to him by the criminologist.

"You understand?" said Blake, as they reached the hallway. "My assistant, Tinker, will coach you in your part; until then——"

He placed a significant finger on his lips.

"I will do all you say," said Sir Simon Grossman humbly.

Blake signalled to Tinker, who had just completed his telephone call to Inspector Coutts, and whispered a few words to his assistant. Tinker grinned as he listened. He already had an inkling as to what was passing in his master's mind.

"Right-ho, guv'nor!" he said briskly. "Coutts will be along in an hour's time. He seemed very excited about the news."

"Take Sir Simon upstairs," Blake commanded briefly. "And, remember, no word to the others."

Just as the two disappeared together up the wide oaken staircase, there came a thunderous rat-tat-tat at the door.

"The police!" said Sexton Blake, as the butler appeared from the dining-room. He motioned to Huntingley and the others who trooped into the hallway. Padre Browne's plump fingers played nervously with the cord of his monkish robe, and the League of Robin Hood looked apprehensively at each other.

"Tell them to come in," said Sexton Blake quietly.

Splash Page glanced at the detective's face, but it was as impassive as that of the Sphinx itself. A moment later the door was opened, and into the mediæval atmosphere of the hall entered the prosaic, blue-uniformed figure of Inspector Ephraim, accompanied by a stolid-looking constable.

For a moment or two no one spoke. There was a tense and dramatic silence. The inspector glanced curiously at the men in Lincoln green, and then turned inquisitively towards Sexton Blake, who smiled a welcome.

"Ah, come right in, inspector!" he said cordially. "We are very glad to see you!"

It was a remark which Splash Page considered to be inaccurate in the extreme.

Chapter 8.

The Vanishing Dagger.

INSPECTOR EPHRAIM coughed a trifle uncertainly.

"What's the trouble, Mr. Blake?" he queried. "I understand Lord Huntingley——"

He broke off, and glanced rather dubiously at the tall figure of Robin, who stood uneasily with his back to the fireplace.

"Perhaps I had better explain," said Sexton Blake "Come into the dining-room, inspector. I have a story to tell you which is rather a curious one, and one with a distinctly Christmasy flavour."

"But you said something about murder, Mr. Blake," said the puzzled inspector.

The door opened, and into the mediæval atmosphere of the hall entered the police. For a moment or two no one spoke. There was a tense and dramatic silence.

"I did," replied the detective, as they trooped into the panelled dining-room. "It is now the eve of Christmas," he added, and his grave eyes twinkled. "A time that Charles Dickens has called a kind, forgiving, charitable time, when even the rigors of the law can be relaxed a little. As you know, even in our convict prisons, a charitable spirit pervades."

Splash Page glanced curiously at Sexton Blake. What on earth was he driving at? Blake took out his favourite briar, and filled it leisurely.

"I want to tell you, before we view the body, a small parable," he continued.

"It concerns the fate of a man whose cold heart never quickened to the kindly spirit of Yule, who abused his position to punish, without mercy, the poor, the unfortunate, and the afflicted, and who met his end by a dagger that was never manufactured, and that doesn't exist."

Lord Huntingley stared in bewilderment at Padre Browne. Blake's parable was incomprehensible to them all. Inspector Ephraim scratched his bullet head.

"I'm afraid I don't understand you, Mr. Blake," he said, in a puzzled voice. "Seems to me there's been murder done, and with all due respect to you, Mr. Blake, this is hardly the time for parables."

"As you will," said Blake, with a shrug. "You are a man of action, inspector. I, too, appreciate action, but this is a case where imagination may lead more directly to results than cold, implacable facts. If you prefer the latter," added Sexton Blake, "there is no colder or more implacable fact than the body of Jabez Bruff, who

lies, stark and stiff, beneath that symbol of Yule, the Christmas Tree. Pending your arrival, nothing has been disturbed."

"Jabez Bruff!" ejaculated the inspector. "The missing London magistrate!"

"Exactly!" said the detective quietly. "And if I am not mistaken, here is another of the missing men," he added, as the door opened, and Tinker appeared on the threshold, accompanied by Sir Simon Grossman, looking slightly less dishevelled now, after a wash and brush up.

Lord Huntingley leapt to his feet, and a deep flush suffused his handsome face. Blake held out a restraining hand, and glanced meaningly at the financier.

"Sir Simon will tell you, inspector, how much he has been enjoying his unconventional visit to Huntingdon Manor. He is so pleased that he has already promised a further donation of a thousand guineas to Padre Brown's mission at Shinwell, of which constituency—as you doubtless know—Sir Simon is prospective candidate."

Padre Browne's jaw sagged open. The Hon. Toby Cripps adjusted his oblong monocle in his eye, and gazed blankly at Babe Rivers. The whole group were dumbfounded at the unexpected denouement. Splash Page himself had seldom found Sexton Blake so inexplicable in his actions. He was, in fact, seeing what it looked like from the suspect's point of view. Hitherto he had always been in the know, working with Blake.

Sir Simon Grossman rubbed his pudgy hands nervously together, and smiled a sickly smile.

"Mister Blake is right, inspector," he

said nervously. "I have enjoyed myself thoroughly; it has been a good joke, and there is no one who regrets more than myself that it should have ended in tragedy."

Splash Page whistled below his breath. By what magic had Blake metamorphosed the blustering financier?

Blake turned, with a smile, to Ephraim.

"You are in for a night of surprises, inspector," he prophesied. "But come, you want facts. You shall have them."

WITH that, Sexton Blake led the way towards the terrace, and on to the lawn. Beneath the Christmas Tree lay the body of Jabez Bruff. The dark stain that dyed the virgin whiteness of the snow glistened in the moonlight.

"My Heaven!" gasped Ephraim. "Murder! How did this happen, Mr. Blake?"

Blake gazed down reflectively at the corpse.

"I understand," he said quietly, turning to Huntingley, who had averted his gaze from the grim sight, "that this was the Christmas tree you intended for your own party at the manor?"

"It is," said Robin dully. "I meant to give a real, old-fashioned treat to the villagers. But now, of course——" He broke off with a shrug.

"Strangely symbolic," said Blake, gazing upward at the dark foliage of the fir-tree. "Queer that the criminal should be marked down for so early an execution."

"The criminal?" echoed Inspector Ephraim. "Then you know who killed Jabez Bruff."

"I know what killed Jabez Bruff," amended Blake. "As I hinted he was killed by a weapon not made by mortal hands, a blade that completed its work, then vanished as silently as it came."

"For Heaven's sake, Blake," said Splash Page irritably, "tell us what on earth you are driving at!"

"Look——" said Blake quietly, pointing upward. "There is the murderer! This is the Crime of the Christmas Tree. Strange that a man who hated Christmas like Bruff should meet his end by the very symbol of Christmas."

"That's all very well, Mr. Blake," broke in Ephraim. "It looks to me as though Mr. Bruff was stabbed through the neck. I'm not at all satisfied with all this fantastic symbol stuff of yours."

"Very well, then," rejoined Blake swiftly. "Have facts, hard facts. Obviously, if Bruff was stabbed in the back of the neck by human agency, there would be signs of a struggle, or at least the footprints of his assailant. See, within a radius of twelve yards of the body there is no other sign of a print save the dead man's own, mine, as you can easily verify, and that of Splash Page, as you can see from the print of his overshoe. It has frozen hard to-night, and they are held firmly in the snow."

"That's so!" agreed Inspector Ephraim, scratching his chin, and glancing at the plainly-outlined footprints. "Mr. Page, I take it that you were the first to discover the body?"

Splash nodded.

"I was near with Lord Huntingley," he announced. "I was the only one who knelt near it, however, except for Mr. Blake. See, there's a depression where my knee pressed into the snow."

"About what time was this?" demanded the inspector.

Splash Page looked a trifle embar-

AWESOME—WEIRD—UNCANNY!

A MAN lying dead in the snow, and, bending over him, was the figure of the local doctor. That is what a terrified local labourer gasps out to Sexton Blake. But—and this is the uncanny thing—the doctor has been dead for months!

Whose, then, was the crouching figure, and why does the victim, and other victims later, show signs of bloodlessness? Is a vampire at work?

The villagers say there is. There is trouble in that village—and a reign of superstitious terror.

But, after terrifying peril, Sexton Blake solves the mystery of the vampire. Here is a Christmassy story of the right sort—thrills of the unseen, unnerving incidents, and a tangled problem with a first-class surprise at the end which you will not expect.

Just the right yarn to get that Yuletide feeling. Out on Thursday next—

The Mystery of the SIPING VAMPIRE.

UNION JACK 2ᵈ

The Mystery of the SIPING VAMPIRE
A tale of the weird

"Hercules, Esq.," one of the most brilliant yarns to appear in this or any other paper, reaches its final instalment in this issue. It has a very worthy successor. For full details, see page 30.

For full details, see page 30.

---

rassed. "Er—two hours ago!" he announced.

"Two hours!" echoed the inspector. "But surely you could have rung up the police immediately if——"

"We had Mr. Blake to rely on," interposed Splash diplomatically.

"Exactly!" said the detective smoothly. "You will see, inspector, that this first theory of the man being stabbed by a human being is ruled out by the lack of footprints indicating a struggle."

"I don't see that at all," the inspector persisted. "I've heard of men who could throw knives a distance of thirty yards with deadly accuracy."

"I can do it myself," said Blake calmly. "But that theory is also unsound. Where is the knife?"

"The murderer may have removed it," said Ephraim.

"Highly improbable," said Blake. "To remove it he would have to have approached the body. You can see for yourself that there are only Mr. Page's footprints within twelve yards of it. I can vouch for Mr. Page's complete innocence. Lord Huntingley and the rest will be able to furnish a complete alibi if necessary."

"Yes; but——" temporised the inspector. "I don't see how else he could have been murdered. You said yourself——"

"I said that it looked like murder!" said Sexton Blake, with emphasis. "I have called it the Crime of the Christmas Tree because, in a sense, the Christmas-tree is the criminal. Look!"

He pointed towards the lower branches of the fir. The foliage was powdered with frozen snow; from the underside of several branches hung dozens of icicles, some as much as six inches in length. Each sharp sliver of ice glittered to a sharp point in the moonlight.

"Jack Frost's daggers!" said Sexton Blake dramatically "Each one sharper than steel. Now do you understand my parable, inspector? You will see by Bruff's footmarks, heavier at the toe than at the heel, that he was running towards the coppice of fir. There are indications that there was a particularly strong wind when that occurred; it has dropped a little now. And this is what happened——"

So saying, Sexton Blake seized hold of the sapling in his firm, muscular hand and flexed his shoulder muscles. The wondering group stared at him, half comprehending as he shook the tree.

Instantly a dozen icicles detached themselves from the branches of the tree and fell tinkling to the frozen surface of the snow.

Blake stepped back hurriedly and brushed his hands on his silk handkerchief.

"That is the way Jabez Bruff, hater of Christmas, met his death," he said quietly. "I brought you to witness, inspector, for, believe me, at the inquest, there can be no other possible verdict than accidental death. That is what I meant when I told you that the weapon was non-existent a day ago. The icicle which fell on this unfortunate man, piercing the soft, fleshy part

of his neck and piercing the jugular, was actually melted by contact with his warm blood; thus no weapon will ever be found!"

IT was two hours later.

Detective-Inspector Coutts, of Scotland Yard, stared wonderingly at his Baker Street colleague as Blake welcomed him at the entrance to Huntingley Manor.

He had come post haste from London, in response to Tinker's trunk call. He was cross, travel-stained, and weary when he knocked at the door; but his eyes glinted appreciatively as they fell on the cheerful glow and warmth within.

"What's all the trouble, Blake?" he demanded, removing his overcoat, and moving towards the pinewood fire.

"No trouble at all," he announced calmly. "You seemed to be at a loose end for Christmas, so I persuaded Lord Huntingley, my host, to invite you here over the holiday."

"What!" gasped Coutts. "I understood from that young rip, Tinker, that you had traced Grossman, and that you wanted my help."

"That also is true," said Sexton Blake. "But come into the dining-room, my dear fellow. A hot toddy and cigar would be very grateful and comforting after your drive."

"They certainly would," said Coutts.

Blake led the way to the dining-room and opened the door. Coutts blinked his eyes as they fell on the occupants grouped about the hearth. Eight young men, each clad in Lincoln green, were talking animatedly to a pretty girl in evening dress. Sprawled negligently in a chair, his long legs stretched out to the glowing logs, was Splash Page, while Tinker grinned a welcome from a low stool in the corner.

"Detective-Inspector Coutts, of Scotland Yard," announced Blake; and the hum of conversation was hushed

The C.I.D. man's moustache bristled importantly at the effect his entrance had created. A tall, handsome figure in green advanced towards him with outstretched hand.

"Glad to know you, inspector," he said. "My name is Huntingley, chief of the League of Robin Hood."

Coutts gasped in astonishment as he sat down.

"What does all this mean, Blake?" he inquired.

"Sit down, my dear chap," replied the other. "Help yourself to whiskey and a cigar. You shall now learn the true history of the league, and the decision rests entirely with you as to what attitude the authorities will take in the matter. Personally"—here he smiled whimsically at the group—"I think our modern outlaws have decided to use less dangerous and spectacular methods in future."

"You bet on that, Mr. Blake," said the Hon. Toby Cripps fervently. "You gave us all the fright of our lives when you led us to think that Jabez Bruff had been murdered."

"I meant to, young man!" retorted the criminologist. "While sympathising with your ideals, it was necessary to give you a sharp reminder that the law of England cannot be flouted with impunity."

"Jabez Bruff?" echoed Coutts blankly. "Is he dead?"

"He died suddenly three or four hours ago, in the grounds of this house. The matter is already in the hands of the local police."

"Is there something fishy about his

death, then?" queried the surprised inspector.

"Not in the least," replied Blake calmly "It was quite accidental." With that, he briefly outlined his theory of Bruff's dramatic end.

Coutts listened with close attention, allowing his cigar to go out.

"Well, I'm dashed!" he ejaculated. "Killed by an icicle! I've never heard of such a thing!"

"It is not without precedent!" retorted Blake smoothly. "A similar occurrence took place in Nome, Alaska about fifteen years ago, a n d if my memory serves me, there was the case of a woman in North Wales killed by an icicle during t h e blizzard of '08 or '09."

"But what on earth was Bruff doing here?" demanded Coutts.

"Ah!" said Blake, with a twinkle. "That is where we need your official advice. The decision rests entirely with you, Coutts."

The Yard Man swelled importantly.

"I understand from the depositions of witnesses that Sir Simon Grossman was forcibly kidnapped by a band of men clad like Robin Hood," he began sternly.

Huntingley looked a trifle uncomfortable beneath his gaze.

"You'd better ask Sir Simon himself," Blake interjected. "Tinker, see if he's in the library, please."

TINKER rose to his feet, and a few moments later reappeared with the financier, who wilted a little under Blake's keen scrutiny.

"Ah, Sir Simon," said the detective pleasantly. "I understand, from Inspector Coutts here, who is down investigating Mr. Bruff's—er—unfortunate demise, that Scotland Yard believe you to have been forcibly kidnapped. Is that so?"

Grossman spread his hands in a Semitic gesture.

"Ach! It was a joke," he said. "High spirits, that was all, inspector. Lord Huntingley always was one for jokes, you know."

"H'm!" said Coutts. "It certainly didn't sound like a joke to me, Sir Simon. I understood you were held up at pistol point, and forcibly detained against your will."

The financier shuffled uneasily.

"Well, perhaps they were a leetle rough," he conceded; "but it is Christmas-time, and we must all be friends together, is it not?"

"Sir Simon has paid his ransom," said Huntingley. "He is free to go at any time, inspector, or free to stay over Christmas, as you are."

"I'm hanged if I can understand all this," grumbled Coutts. "Seems to have been just a crazy, practical joke. But what was Bruff doing here?"

"You'd better come with me, Coutts, and perhaps I can enlighten you a little further," said Blake. "Incidentally, I have two interesting Christmas presents to give you—Messrs. Snape and Manly. I believe you want 'em."

"Badly," said Coutts, in bewilderment. "But still I don't understand what you're driving at."

"You'll see," said Sexton Blake briefly.

In the dining-room, Huntingley and Splash Page looked across at Tinker.

"Your guv'nor's a living marvel!" said t h e newspaperman. "How the dickens he d e d u c e d accidental death, when everything pointed to murder, beats me. He put the wind up us all, until he chose to explain."

"I told you he'd see you through,' said Tinker. "As a matter of fact, there were two reasons why he did not let on at first that you were mistaken when you thought Bruff had been murdered.

"Firstly, he wanted to frighten Grossman, Manly, and the rest, so that when the showdown came they wouldn't insist too much on the fact that they'd been kidnapped. You see the effect it had on Grossman. He's terrified of any scandal spoiling his son's marriage to Lady Hamblin; that's why he's pretending the whole thing was a joke.

"As for Cray, Snape, and Manly, they're wanted by the police, anyway."

"What was the other reason?" inquired Huntingley.

"Well, he also wanted to scare you chaps from going too far with this outlaw business," explained Tinker. "Fortunately, Inspector Ephraim didn't inquire too closely as to why Bruff was here. Coutts will, of course, but he'll be so darned pleased at having roped in Snape and Manly, and solving the mystery of Grossman's disappearance, that I doubt if he'll make any fuss."

TINKER'S prophecy was confirmed later on that night. Mellowed by whisky and an excellent supper, Detective-Inspector Coutts lolled back in his comfortable armchair, and smiled over at Lord Huntingley.

"My lord," he said, and his voice was less gruff than usual, "my friend, Mr. Blake, has given his word that any further escapades indulged in by the League of Robin Hood will be strictly within the law. I shall have to word my reports to headquarters in a very tactful fashion, but seeing that it is Christmas-

time, and the objects of your league have been to give a Merry Christmas to those less fortunate than ourselves—well——"

He broke off, slightly embarrassed at this, for him, unprecedently lengthy speech.

"I doubt if the Commissioner will take any further action."

"Bravo, Coutts!" ejaculated Splash Page. "You're a sportsman! I'll see that my report to the 'Radio' is also very tactful, and pride of place will be given to the sagacity, acumen, and tenacity of Inspector Coutts in solving the sensational disappearance of Sir Simon Grossman, rounding up Snape, the embezzler, Manly, the mealy-mouthed mobsman, Cray, the——"

"Shut up!" interrupted Coutts, reddening. "You know very well that it was Sexton Blake who did it all. If he hadn't have fathomed the real cause of Bruff's death, you'd all have been in prison over Christmas."

Huntingley rose. Very picturesque he looked in his doublet and jerkin as he stood amid the mediæval splendour of the old manor. In his hand he held a brimming goblet, and as he raised it up, jovial Padre Browne followed his action.

"My merrie men!" cried Robin. "We might i' faith have been mumchance and sad this Yule. As it is, thanks to Sexton Blake, the revelry will continue unabated. Fat capons, boar's head, turkeys, groaning boards, and bowls of wassail shall grace our festive fare this Christmas-tide."

"Hear, hear!" broke in Toby Cripps. "Gosh! Think of skilly for Christmas!" He shivered slightly.

Coutts leant forward.

"Snape and Manly will!" he said meaningly.

"Serve 'em dashed well right!" retorted Toby. "They pinched hundreds of poor devils' Christmas feeds. I hope they get seven years!"

"Men," said Robin Hood, in a ringing voice, "I give you the name of our benevolent patron, one whose sympathies are with us, one whose aid has never been withheld from the poor, the needy, and the unfortunate. I refer to Sexton Blake—prince of good friends!"

There was a roar of acclamation that rang to the raftered roof of the Manor House. Sexton Blake's lean face flushed with pleasure at the spontaneous tribute.

"Gentlemen," he said modestly, "I thank you all for the tribute, which is all too undeserved——"

The rest of his speech was drowned in loud cries of dissent, and the League of Robin Hood, led by the brawny figure of Friar Tuck, burst out heartily into the strains of "He's a jolly good fellow" until the rafters rang again.

"Oh, boy!" chuckled Splash Page to Tinker. "It certainly looks as if we're in for the Merriest Christmas yet!"

The End.

HERCULES Esq

By GWYN EVANS.

Conclusion of Our brilliant serial of millions and mystery.

" My Million, I think ! "

INSTANTLY pandemonium raged. Porters dropped their trucks with a clang, men swore, a woman screamed hysterically. The cry was taken up by a hundred throats.

"Where's the extinguisher? Stamp on it, fool!"

Thick clouds of black, poisonous-looking smoke rose, sluggishly, followed by the staccato crackle of burning wood. Flames licked the paintwork greedily. A dozen station police leapt on to the ledge over which the luggage was handed, each one armed with a fire bucket.

"Keep back, there!" roared a voice. "Keep back!"

The crowd surged and swayed forward and backward, while smoke-grimed figures within the office battled with the leaping flames. Bill Kellaway stood rooted to the spot for a moment, too stunned with surprise even to think coherently. Then suddenly he realised.

"My stars!" he babbled. "The million quid! It'll be burnt to ashes!"

Like a madman he leapt forward into the crowd, pushing and fighting to get near that blazing inferno.

"Keep back there!" bellowed a blue-uniformed figure.

"Back, nothing!" roared Bill. "I've got my whole fortune in there, and I'm grabbing it, fire or no fire!"

He wrenched his arm away from the policeman's restraining grip, and his sleeve was ripped to tatters. Heedless of the smoke that tore at his throat and almost blinded him, he took a flying leap on to the smouldering ledge, and as the raging flames fanned his cheeks with their burning breath, he glared wildly round for the little attache-case for which he had endured so much.

Three burly station police, their faces running with sweat, their eyes blood-shot and red-rimmed, stamped and trampled on the blazing embers, while two clerks, overcome by the heat,

choked and spluttered their way out on to the platform.

Bill had no eyes for anything but the attache case. By the red glare of the flames he saw piles of trunks and parcels on shelves, along which the fire tongues flickered and advanced inexorably.

"Come down, you crazy fool!" roared one of the policemen, as Bill made a sudden grab for the topmost shelf, on which reposed a neat leather valise.

"Go to hades!" roared Kellaway. "I want my luggage! I——"

His fingers closed greedily on the handle, and, with a sobbing breath of relief, he jerked down the million-pound attache-case from the shelf. The leather was warped and blistered by the heat; but Bill, capering like a madman, emerged from the blazing office flourishing the case like a triumphant banner above his head.

He was greeted by a half ironical cheer from the crowd.

Suddenly there was a loud swoosh of water, and as Bill collapsed, spent and exhausted on to a porter's truck, the station fire staff brought the hydrant into play, and the jet hissed and steamed as it met the now roaring flames.

Bill hugged his attache-case on his knee, and his eyes shone with triumph. His silk hat was lost, somewhere in the fire, his morning coat was in tatters, his resplendent cravat was a sooty rag, but he had the million pounds!

He groped in his pocket for a cigarette, and his fingers encountered an unfamiliar object. Wonderingly, he brought it out. It was Colonel Eustace Reed's wallet. Opening it he saw a pink ticket—No. 0767.

"Pardon me, sir," said a voice civilly enough. "'Ave you any proof that this is your luggage?"

Bill Kellaway laughed a trifle hysterically.

"Proof!" he said. "D'you think I'd risk my life if it wasn't? Here's my bally ticket."

"Very good, sir!" said the stationmaster. "Sorry, sir, but rules are rules." He took the pink slip and compared it with the number of the label pasted on the attache-case. "That's

all right, sir. I think we've got the fire under control. Very little damage done, considering."

Bill chuckled. He was thinking of Inspector Barker, and the wiliness of Wally the Dip. The little crook, with colossal nerve, must have slipped Reed's wallet into Bill's pocket right under the Yard man's nose!

"Good old Wally!" said Bill, rising shakily to his feet. "No wonder he went quietly!"

At that very moment Inspector Barker was engaged in the salutary but bitter task of mentally kicking himself, while Wally the Dip hilariously boarded a west-bound bus, to exercise his talent on the matinee queues.

MR. JAMES THURWOOD, that discreet but unpopular man, was not a keen psychologist, nor did he suffer from nerves to any extent. He still slept peacefully and dreamlessly in his bed, undisturbed by the thought of the forty-seven fellow creatures he had so expertly turned off in the course of his ancient but necessary profession.

Mr. Thurwood, to paraphrase the poet, was the mildest-mannered man who had ever hanged a murderer. His mildness was equalled only by the bland and impassive Chang, one-time public executioner of Pekin.

Both of them were sincerely and honestly grateful to that perverse individual, Dr. Lenoir, for providing them with light and congenial tasks in the evening of their days—tasks which were not arduous and were liberally remunerated.

Mr. Thurwood was a simple soul, and, as he often remarked, took life as it came. Yet even he was aware of a new and electric tension in the atmosphere of the bizarre upper room, when Dr. Armand Lenoir rose to address what was destined to be the last meeting of the Secret Six.

Mr. Thurwood stood, as usual, on the right side of the fireplace, with his colleague, Chang, on his left. Between them, on the wall, was the shining sword, the pride of Chang's heart, neatly flanked with the coiled ropes which Mr. Thurwood had once so lovingly handled.

In the centre of the black-walled room the five masked members of the Secret Six sat round the horseshoe table, with Lenoir at the top centre. Lenoir's dark eyes were unusually brilliant to-night, as he rose to his feet, the ivory pallor of his face enhanced by his black imperial beard.

The five round the table leant forward eagerly as he began to speak in his soft, caressing drawl.

"Well, gentlemen," he began, "I have to announce—provisionally, of course—that Hercules, Esq., has successfully accomplished his fifth task. I received a telephone call shortly after six o'clock this evening, stating that he secured the million pounds from Charing Cross Left-Luggage Office, and would bring it to our headquarters to-night.

"I note from this evening's papers there was an outbreak of fire in the office this forenoon. Whether that has anything to do with our friend Hercules we shall probably learn later."

"We should have taken action at once, as I suggested, Lenoir!" snapped Colonel Reed. "It was waste of time ringing up Lee and Jarvie and the rest when I found that cloak-room ticket was missing."

"Hades!" broke in Phineas Lee irritably. "Quit that Shylocking, No. 4! I reckon the kid's done blamed well. What do you say, Jarvie?"

Sir John Jarvie coughed as he studied his ancient enemy. "He has certainly been phenomenally lucky," he said stiffly. "He has, also, I grieve to say, been helped considerably by that minx Dorothy. I have spoken to her very seriously on the matter, and I believe she has now seen reason."

"Aw shuck!" said Phineas Lee. "Young Herc beat me fair and square, and he's the first guy that's ever done it."

"Pardon me," broke in Jarvie, with icy politeness. "I seem to remember hammering you over that Los Angeles deal when——"

"Gentlemen, please!" broke in Lenoir suavely. "The time grows short. I have many things to say. Assuming for the moment that Hercules has fulfilled his fifth task, there remains one more to perform. The setting of that task devolves upon myself."

"Sure," chimed in the American. "And I'll bet you five grand he does it."

"I'll take you," said Jarvie. "If I know anything of Lenoir's inventive brain, and his perverse humour, he'll set a task that will make the first five look as easy as falling off a log."

"That remains to be seen," chimed in No. 5. "Hercules isn't here yet. Don't forget, in addition to getting the million, he's got to bring it here in person."

Lenoir glanced at the clock. It was eleven-thirty p.m.

"If I know anything of Kellaway's love for the dramatic, it will be midnight when he arrives. There is a lot of say for melodrama, as you have already seen, gentlemen," he added. "You must admit, I think, that up to now I have carried out my promise, and you have experienced in turn the thrill of the gaming table, the joy of battle, and even the rare and refreshing tonic of defeat. Too many victories are apt to cloy, I think you'll agree."

"Waal, I'll say I've enjoyed the game, Lenoir," said Phineas Lee.

"I also must admit that I shall be sorry to see the end of the contest," admitted Sir John Jarvie. "At first I was highly dubious about the whole business, Lenoir, but I've found it very exhilarating to watch."

"There is still the final task to perform," broke in Lord Radstoke's thin, acidulated voice.

"Well," commented Colonel Eustace Reed, "though I've lost a fifth of a million, Lenoir, I'm not complaining. I've had a good flutter, and, incidentally, I'm grateful to Hercules, Esq., for the information about Drew. I called at his place this afternoon, and found he was in bed, suffering from neuralgia. I insisted on seeing him, and discovered that he was most shockingly battered about the face. I tackled him at once about Kellaway, and he was in such a state of nerves that he broke down completely, and "—he paused, with a smile—"the story would be laughable were it not so serious—he actually believed that Kellaway was a Soviet agent."

"And I bet he played up to it. Hercules is nothing if not resourceful."

"Anyway," said Colonel Reed, "Drew is no longer in my employ. He should consider himself lucky that he is not arrested for conspiracy."

"If you did that," drawled Lenoir, "I'm afraid the whole of the Secret Six would be in gaol. Our friend, Inspector Barker, is getting decidedly suspicious of——"

Rat, tat, tat! A thunderous knock sounded at the door. Instantly dead silence fell on the little group.

Lenoir smiled.

"Hercules, Esq., I think," he murmured softly. "Thurwood, will you go——"

Rat, tat, tat! The knock was repeated louder and more vehemently; then a gruff voice shouted:

(Continued overleaf.)

The Meccano Boy of to-day will design the Air Liners of to-morrow

The conquest of the air has progressed so rapidly in recent years that in five or ten years' time our skies may be thick with busy air-craft—single-seater business 'planes and huge sky-liners. The men who will design and pilot these machines are the Meccano boys of to-day.

When a boy builds with Meccano parts he has all the thrills of a real engineer, for he builds his models, piece by piece, and when they are completed he works them in exactly the same manner as an engineer would work the corresponding machines in real life.

This year Meccano Outfits are bigger and better than ever. They all contain a greater number and wider selection of parts than previously, enabling hundreds of new models to be built. Ask your dealer to tell you all about the latest developments.

Prices of Outfits from 3/6 to 380/-

Send for this fine New Book

Every boy should read this splendid book. You can obtain a copy from your dealer, price 3d. If you prefer it, send us three penny stamps and we will send you a copy post free, providing you send us the names and addresses of three of your chums. Write clearly and be sure to put No. 28 after your own name for reference.

Meccano £100 Model Building Contest

Here is a splendid opportunity for Meccano inventors! Cash prizes totalling over £50 are being awarded for the best Meccano models entered in the new Meccano model building contest, and, in addition, there is a large number of other splendid prizes, making a total value of £100. Ask your dealer for full particulars and an entry form.

MECCANO
The Toy that made Engineering famous

MECCANO LTD.: Old Swan: LIVERPOOL.

"Open, in the name of the law!"

"My stars!" gasped Sir John Jarvie. "Barker, of Scotland Yard!"

Lenoir rose to his feet. His face was unnaturally pale.

"Keep cool, gentlemen," he said. "Keep your masks on. Maybe I'll be able to bluff the fool!"

He crossed over to the back door, and stealthily unlocked it. In the darkness of the corridor outside he glimpsed a burly blue-clad figure, and behind him loomed a helmeted figure in gleaming oilskins.

"Ah, good-evening, inspector!" said Lenoir. "What can I do for you?"

"I want you, Dr. Lenoir!" snapped the other, his red face and waxed moustache bristling. "Sergeant, stand by the door while I see what's going on in here."

Lenoir, for once in his life, was unable to cope with the situation. He fell back as the other entered and swept the room with a comprehensive glance.

Sir John Jarvie's face turned pale beneath his mask, and Phineas licked his dry lips uneasily. Lenoir recovered a little. Fingering his pince-nez nervously, he approached the dumbfounded group round the table.

"Er—by the way, inspector, this seems a little irregular. Have you a warrant to search these premises? We're doing nothing illegal, you know. It's merely——"

"Warrant!" laughed the other hoarsely. "I've been watching you folk for some time. You can't pull any wool over my eyes, Dr. Lenoir. This is a criminal organisation——"

"I—I say," bleated Jarvie nervously. "You—you know me, Barker. Surely this matter can be arranged amicably between friends?"

His hand slid to his pocket, and he pulled out a bulging wallet.

"Sergeant," snapped the other, "you're a witness of this! Attempted bribery and corruption!"

"My stars!" said Sir John again, and sank down heavily into his chair.

Lenoir was the only one who retained some semblance of composure.

"I insist on seeing your warrant, inspector," he said.

"You do, eh?" said the other grimly. "Sergeant, will you bring in——"

The black onyx clock on the mantelpiece began to chime the hour of twelve. There was a deathly silence, save for the staccato chime.

The man in uniform pushed something into his chief's hand, and as the last stroke of midnight died, the clear voice of Bill Kellaway cried triumphantly:

"My win, gentlemen!"

With that the alleged inspector flung down a leather attache-case on the table, and ripped off the waxed moustache, revealing the rather parboiled but unmistakable features of Hercules, Esq.

"Well, I'll be hornswoggled!" ejaculated Phineas T. Lee.

Lenoir opened his mouth to speak, but for a moment or two he could not utter a word.

"Kellaway!" he gasped at length. "Kellaway, you—you young devil!"

Bill grinned joyously.

"You all deserved that scare, gentlemen," he chuckled. "I owe the Secret Six many a fright."

Sir John Jarvie spluttered incoherently.

"I—I never heard such insolence. I—I——"

Suddenly Phineas T. Lee laughed, peal after peal of deep, rumbling laughter that was infectious. The tension was broken. Even the acidulated Radstoke joined in the merriment. The relief of the five millionaires was so overwhelming that they behaved like schoolboys for a few minutes. They clapped each other on the back, looked at Kellaway, whose face was a queer blend of Barker's and his own, and from Kellaway to the man in policeman's clothes.

"Take your face fungus off, Henry," chuckled Bill. "Gentlemen, meet Henry Squared, the world's most perfect valet. I wouldn't part with him for the contents of this case. By the way, Lenoir, you might open it and see that the million's O.K.," he added.

Lenoir produced a key from his chain and unlocked a bag. Tied neatly in bundles within lay the thousand £1,000 Bank of England notes, crisp, new, and undisturbed.

"Gentlemen," said Lenoir, holding his hand for silence. "I think we may safely admit that Hercules, Esq., has satisfactorily performed his fifth task. In the circumstances, I think he was entitled to play his little joke upon us. It at least introduced a new and unexpected thrill into our gathering."

"It sure did," chuckled Phineas T. Lee. "Say, Thurwood, I guess we'll celebrate this with a magnum of bubbly!"

"One moment, please," said Lenoir suavely. "You forget that, according to the compact, Hercules has six tasks to perform. He has triumphantly achieved the first five——"

"Oh, help!" said Bill helplessly.

His day had been so crammed with excitement that he had forgotten all about his sixth and final task. Dr. Lenoir's dark eyes were agleam with mischief as he turned to face the expectant millionaires.

"The sixth task still remains to be performed, gentlemen," he continued, "and, according to our rules, I am empowered to set it."

"That's true enough," cut in Sir John Jarvie; "but don't be too hard on him, Lenoir. I reckon he's earned his million."

Sir John's relief was so great at Bill's dramatic denouement that his tone was unusually magnanimous. He had visualised disgrace and arrest, perhaps penal servitude, and the sudden reaction had softened his truculence considerably.

Lenoir shook his head solemnly.

"I'm afraid we must adhere to the rules, No. 1. Much as I should like to be lenient—er—M'sieu Hercules." He turned to Bill, who scowled savagely at him.

"All right, curse you, have your pound of flesh, Lenoir," he said wearily. "Shoot!"

Lenoir smiled, that queer, lopsided smile of his that gave a touch of diablerie to his pale face.

"I beg to submit task No. 6, gentlemen," he announced. "One which I think is eminently worthy of its predecessors."

Bill thrust his hand into his trousers-pocket, and his fingers closed over the grotesque mascot with which the whole of his fantastic adventures had started. He drew it out and studied the grinning crocodile head with a wry smile.

Would Sebak still bring him luck, or——

"Task No. 6, my dear Hercules," drawled Lenoir, "can be very simply expressed. To be brief, you must marry Miss Dorothy Jarvie within one week from to-day, or you forfeit the million pounds!"

"What's that?" spluttered Sir John, starting to his feet. "What the devil d'ye mean, Lenoir? I never heard such confounded——"

He broke off suddenly as Bill Kellaway, with a wild whoop, bounded to his feet, and raced across the room so quickly that he had reached the landing before anyone could stop him.

"Gee!" said Phineas Lee, with a chuckle. "I guess you've scared him at last. Even Hercules jibs at matrimony!"

Lenoir's dark eyes twinkled, and he glanced at Henry whose face was wooden. Suddenly Bill Kellaway reappeared. With him, looking radiantly beautiful, with eyes like twin stars and her face aglow with happiness, was Dorothy.

She gurgled with laughter as her eyes fell on the dumbfounded millionaires. Bill raised her slim hand aloft. On her third finger glittered a plain gold wedding ring.

"Gentlemen," he announced, "as all the best murderers say: 'I done it!' We were married by special licence this afternoon."

Sir John Jarvie's mouth sagged open. He stared at Bill, stared at Dorothy, and uttered never a word.

Dorothy looked up at her husband with shining eyes, and suddenly he kissed her tenderly. He grinned, utterly unabashed, at the Secret Six, and reached out for the attache-case.

"Our million, I think," said Hercules, Esq.

"Indubitably, sir," said Henry, imperturbable to the last.

For a moment there was complete silence, then an extraordinary sound escaped from Mr. Thurwood's scrawny throat. It was a cross between a sneeze and a death-rattle.

Mr. James Thurwood had laughed for the first time in his life.

The End.

BEGINS NEXT WEEK—

Our Brilliant New Serial to follow "Hercules, Esq."

The ISLE of STRIFE

By that popular and
talented author,

STACEY BLAKE.

Author of "From Prisoner to President."

OUT of the ether came the call. Jim Southcroft lay back in a cane chair on the veranda of the Hotel de la Plage, looking at the purple strip of Channel, fast disappearing into the approaching night, and listening by turns to the chatter of his companions and the braying of the orchestra that played jazz murderously in the salon.

The band ceased suddenly. It was the moment when the nightly news bulletin from 2LO was picked up for the benefit of the British clientele and handed out from the loud-speaker.

Jim usually was quite uninterested. But all at once the magic of his own name, articulated from the loud-speaker, called him to alert attention:

"*Will James Southcroft, of Hounslow, Middlesex, believed to be touring on the Normandy coast, come at once to his home, where his father is lying dangerously ill.*"

He sat up, rigid. He went to the hotel office and asked for a time-table. No words of explanation were needed. Every soul in the hotel knew that it was he who was called. A man at his side butted in.

"You'll not get the boat at Dieppe," he said. "You've got half an hour to do sixty miles, and the road is not too good. And the express from Bouvaincourt is gone. You'd better drive farther, to Ault Aerodrome, and hop the Channel by air. A special plane——"

Jim nodded. The man obviously talked sense.

"And if you want a chum for the journey, I'll go with you. I want to be in London in a hurry myself. I'll pay half the cost of the plane, if you like. I've got a deal in London—a shift in market prices."

"I shall be ready to start in five minutes," said Jim.

And in five minutes the stranger's hundred-an-hour sports car backed out of the hotel garage, and slid out on the road to Ault—the road to adventure.

From that very moment things started. Action—desperate, dangerous action—even before he can reach his dying father's bedside and learn the story of the Isle of Strife—San Fernando.

It is Jim's troublous legacy. His grandfather, owner of San Fernando, was killed by the islanders; and now, a week later, Jim's father has been knifed in broad daylight in England.

"Leave it all alone! A quiet business life. What could be better?" urges his father.

"But I'm going to fight! I've got to pay somebody back!" says Jim.

And fight he does. Jim is not one to avoid this sort of trouble. Nor is his pal Tommy Wilford. In fact, he loves it for its own sake—thrives on it. And there is plenty for both of them in the Isle of Strife, which is no pleasure resort at the best of times.

Treacherous Spanish half-breeds; plot and revolution; cunning commercial entanglements; danger by land and sea; danger by bullet and knife. Those were the things these two found at San Fernando before Jim Southcroft laid hands on his legacy.

This is a tale of high adventure under the brazen sun and the glamorous moon of tropic skies, written by a man who can spin a yarn of this sort with spell-binding intensity. Never does the interest slacken from one dramatic, breath-catching situation to another. UNION JACK serials are famous; they are selected on sterling merit alone.

The fairest thing one can say about this yarn is that it is fully entitled to its place in these pages, and a worthy successor to the extremely popular "Hercules, Esq."

(*It begins in next week's issue. Despite the preoccupations of Christmas-time, realise that you simply must follow this yarn from the beginning. An order NOW to your newsagent will ensure a regular weekly copy—even if you have to postpone the actual reading of the serial until after the holiday. If you find you've missed first instalments, you'll be sorry.*)

Printed and published every Thursday by the Proprietors, The Amalgamated Press, Ltd., The Fleetway House, Farringdon Street, London, E.C.4. Advertisement offices: The Fleetway House, Farringdon Street, London, E.C.4. Registered for transmission by Canadian Magazine Post. Subscription rates: Inland and Abroad, 11s. per annum; 5s. 6d. for six months. Sole agents for South Africa: The Central News Agency, Ltd. Sole agents for Australia and New Zealand: Messrs. Gordon & Gotch, Ltd.—Saturday, December 15th, 1928.

THE GREY LADY OF THE BELL.
A Ghost Story with Seasonable Thrills.

To begin with, let it be stated that this account is literally true in every particular.

The events here narrated not only actually happened, but were the subject of a most thorough investigation by no less a body than the staff of the "International Psychic Gazette," and were reported in part by that journal. The additional details here given were the outcome of later inquiry from other sources.

The thing happened on a dark country road in Warwickshire. A Mr. Brown (that is not his name, but it will do) was driving a party of friends—another man and two ladies—to London by car. They left Stratford-on-Avon at about eleven-thirty at night, but had not gone more than a few miles when their petrol tank ran dry, and the car came to a stop alongside a solitary old barn.

The two men got out, Mr. Brown walking back to obtain fresh supplies from a petrol pump they had just passed, and the friend standing in front of the car near a hedge.

The driver found there was nobody in charge of the petrol pump at that time of night, and started for the car again. "It was then," said Mr Brown, in his account, "that he heard the ringing of a bell, though he took little notice of this, being intent on getting back to the car and refilling the tank from an emergency can of petrol."

Then he heard the bell again, nearer. He looked up and saw a woman dressed in grey coming towards him.

"She was holding a handbell which she kept ringing," said Mr. Brown.

"The sight of her in that solitude struck me as unearthly. I called to my friend to get into the car, hoping he would not see the strange figure, and avoid frightening the two women.

"Just as I called to him he rushed back into the car and jumped in. He slammed the door behind him, exclaiming 'My Heavens! What do you think I have seen?'

"I turned round to him and said: 'Don't be silly; let's get away.' I was anxious to avoid scaring the ladies."

"With some difficulty, for I felt very nervous, I managed to pour about a cupful of petrol into the tank and threw the can into the back of the car. Then I heard the bell ringing again and saw the strange apparition walk straight through the hedge. I knew then, for certain, that it was no ordinary mortal we had to do with."

The report goes on to say that, in a very nervous agitation, he drove the car up a long, steep hill. One of the women had fainted, but he did not stop till he reached the top. By that time she had recovered, and shrieked in a terrified tone: "Did you see the ghost?" She declared that a woman in grey had come up to the car before it started, leaned over the side, and touched her forehead. That was what had caused her to faint.

An interesting development occurred when the party reached London and Mr. Brown began delving into the history of the district where the spectre had appeared. He found an old engraving of a farmhouse at the approximate position of the barn at which the car had stopped, known as Haunted Hillborough.

In a book published in 1857, entitled "The Legend of Shakespeare's Crab Tree," there is also another picture of Haunted Hillborough, and a woman wearing a cloak and a poke bonnet.

This tale, which was widely circulated, naturally interested the people of Warwickshire, and especially those in the haunted district. Investigations were made, and—alas! for this perfectly good ghost story—this is what came to light:

The aged, solitary barn was in reality a large shed. "Haunted Hillborough" was actually the village of Pillerton Priors. The Lady in Grey was really a pet lamb; and the ghostly bell was worn round the lamb's neck.

This lamb is a local celebrity in its way. It is very large and tame, and has a habit of standing in an erect position, begging for food from passers-by.

When the motorist knocked at the door of the petrol station, the proprietor, who had gone to bed, got up and looked out of his bedroom window. He plainly saw the lamb in the field and heard its bell.

He also saw it advance towards the motorists—according to his description, in a friendly way.

The touch of its clammy nose on the lady's forehead was also a gesture of friendship, and not meant to be any more unnerving than its spectral walking through the hedge.

But, of course, the motorists didn't know that.

Be a Railway Manager

BING 'VULCAN' ENGINE

Powerful clockwork loco., with tender. Coupled wheels. Heavy hand-rails. Brass buffers. L.M.S., G.W.R., or L.N.E.R. Gauge 0.

260 coupons

BING TANK ENGINE

Beautifully finished, weighty tank engine. L.M.S. or L.N.E.R. Gauge 0.

120 coupons

PASSENGER COACH

Four compartments with doors to open. Strongly made, well finished. Gauge 0

90 coupons

SIGNAL BOX

Realistic signal box. With steps, one-arm signal and candle-holder. Height 5 in.

120 coupons

Operating your own railway system . . . controlling . . . directing . . . fast traffic running to the 'tick' . . . 'locals' interweaving with main-line trains . . . planning schedules . . . organising . . . dictating. What fun to be a Railway Manager! Everything you need to build your own model railway you can get—FREE—in exchange for B.D.V. Coupons. Begin saving to-day and ask your friends to help.

GET THE 84-PAGE GIFT BOOK

worth 5 coupons. It contains full particulars of the Bassett-Lowke and Bing model railway systems. Godfrey Phillips, Ltd. (Gift Dept. U.J.), 112, Commercial Street, London, E.1.

B.D.V
CIGARETTES

"—just like hand made"

10 for 6d 20 for 11½d. Plain or **Cork** Tips

Coupons also in every packet of B.D.V. Tobacco, 11d per oz.

COMPARE THE VALUES WITH OTHER GIFT SCHEMES

BASSETT-LOWKE ENGINE

Scale model 'Duke of York' clockwork loco. Forward, reverse, and stop levers. L.M.S., L.N.E.R., G.W.R., or S.R. Gauge 0. Complete with tender.

375 coupons

ELECTRIC RAILWAY

Complete miniature electric railway. The real thing on a small scale. Full particulars in the B.D.V. Gift Book.

TIME-TABLE BOARD

Made in wood, finished dead black. With realistic time-table.

117 coupons

CORRIDOR BOGIE COACH

Correct colours, all first-class. 13 in. long.

380 coupons

(Also bogie brake third, to match, same coupon value.)

N.B.3.

S.O.S.! Sabatini's Own Story—CAPTAIN BLOOD!

THE UNION JACK 2ᴰ

Sexton Blake's Own Paper

The PAUPER of PENGARTH CASTLE

SEXTON BLAKE and **WALDO** the Wonder-Man!
in the first episode of a magnificent two-part story.

No. 1,131.   EVERY THURSDAY.   June 13th, 1925.

Captain Blood

By Rafael Sabatini

CONDEMNED to the slavery of the West Indian sugar plantations for a crime he did not commit, Peter Blood, a physician of the little Somersetshire town of Bridgewater, is sent to Barbadoes, and there bought for £10 by the brutal Colonel Bishop.

Blood is more fortunate than his companions, and his work as a doctor exempts him from the slave-labour in the plantations. His comparative freedom gives him a chance of escape for himself and a few of his friends, among whom is Jeremy Pitt, formerly a shipmaster.

Ere the plan can be put into effect, Barbadoes is raided by a Spanish ship, the Cinco Llagas. The Spanish commander, Don Diego, exacts a heavy ransom and returns to his ship. Meantime, however, a party of the slaves under Peter Blood has captured the vessel, and overpower him and retain the ransom.

Don Diego, as the only available navigator aboard, traitorously steers them for the island of Hispaniola, where they encounter a Spanish galleon, and are in grave danger of capture. By a ruse, however, Captain Blood disguises the true state of affairs, and later frees his captives, putting them in a boat and allowing them to land on Hispaniola. Two days later the Cinco Llagas sails into the rock-bound bay of Canyona.

These adventures of Captain Blood, as chronicled by his shipmaster, Jeremy Pitt, show that his original intention was to return to France or Holland; but, finding this impossible, he decided to throw in his lot with the slaves he had rescued and become one of the "Brethren of the Coast."

AND so, to condense all that Jeremy has recorded in the matter, Blood ended by yielding to external pressure, abandoned himself to the stream of Destiny. "Fata viam invenient," is his own expression of it.

If he resisted so long, it was, I think, the thought of Arabella Bishop that restrained him. That they should be destined never to meet again did not weigh at first, or, indeed, ever. He conceived the scorn with which she would come to hear of his having turned pirate, and the scorn, though as yet no more than imagined, hurt him as if it were already a reality.

And even when he conquered this, still the thought of her was ever present. He compromised with the conscience that her memory kept so disconcertingly active. He vowed that the thought of her should continue ever before him to help him keep his hands as clean as a man might in this desperate trade upon which he was embarking.

And so, although he might entertain no delusive hope of ever winning her for his own, of ever even seeing her again, yet the memory of her was to abide in his soul, as a bitter-sweet purifying influence. The love that is never to be realised will often remain a man's guiding ideal.

The resolve being taken, he went actively to work. Ogeron, most accommodating of governors, advanced him money for the proper equipment of his ship the Cinco Llagas, which he renamed the Arabella. This after some little hesitation, fearful of thus setting his heart upon his sleeve. But his Barbadoes friends accounted it merely an expression of the ever-ready irony in which their leader dealt.

To the score of followers he already possessed, he added three score more, picking his men with caution and discrimination—and he was an exceptional judge of men—from amongst the adventurers of Tortuga.

With them all he entered into the articles usual among the Brethren of the Coast under which each man was to be paid by a share in the prizes captured. In other respects, however, the articles were different. Aboard the Arabella there was to be none of the ruffianly indiscipline that normally prevailed in buccaneering vessels.

Those who shipped with him, undertook obedience and submission in all things to himself and to the officers appointed by election. Any to whom this clause in the articles was distasteful might follow some other leader.

Towards the end of December, when the hurricane season had blown itself out, he put to sea in his well-found, well-manned ship, and before he returned in the following May from a protracted and adventurous cruise, the fame of Captain Peter Blood had run like ripples before the breeze across the face of the Caribbean Sea.

There was a fight in the Windward passage at the outset with a Spanish galleon, which had resulted in the gutting and finally the sinking of the Spaniard.

There was a daring raid effected by means of several appropriated piraguas upon a Spanish pearl fleet in the Rio de la Hacha, from which they had taken a particularly rich haul of pearls. There was an overland expedition to the goldfields of Sancta Maria, on the Main, the full tale of which is hardly credible, and there were lesser adventures through all of which the crew of the Arabella came with credit and profit if not entirely unscathed.

And so it happened that before the Arabella came homing to Tortuga in the following May to refit and repair—for she was not without scars, as you conceive, the fame of her and of Peter Blood, her captain, had swept from the Bahamas to the Windward Isles, from New Providence to Trinidad.

An echo of it had reached Europe, and at the Court of St. James' angry representations were made by the ambassador of Spain, to whom it was answered that it must not be supposed that this Captain Blood held any commission from the King of England; that he was, in fact, a proscribed rebel, an escaped slave, and that any measures against him by his Catholic Majesty would receive the cordial approbation of King James II.

Don Miguel de Espinosa, the Admiral of Spain in the West Indies, and his nephew Don Esteban who sailed with him, did not lack the will to bring the adventurer to the yard-arm. With them this business of capturing Blood, which was now an international affair, was also a family matter.

Spain, through the mouth of Don Miguel, did not spare her threats. The report of them reached Tortuga, and with it the assurance that Don Miguel had behind him not only the authority of his own nation, but that of the English king as well.

It was a brutum fulmen that inspired no terrors in Captain Blood. Nor was he likely, on account of it, to allow himself to run to rust in the security of Tortuga. For what he had suffered at the hands of Man he had chosen to make Spain the scapegoat.

Thus he accounted that he served a twofold purpose; he took compensation and at the same time served, not indeed the Stuart king, whom he despised, but England and, for that matter, all the rest of civilised mankind which cruel, treacherous, greedy, bigoted Castile sought to exclude from intercourse with the New World.

One day, as he sat with Hagthorpe and Wolverstone over a pipe and a bottle of rum in the stifling reek of tar and stale tobacco of a waterside tavern, he was accosted by a splendid ruffian in a gold-laced coat of dark-blue satin with a crimson sash, a foot wide, about the waist.

"C'est vous qu'on appelle Le Sang?" the fellow hailed him.

Captain Blood looked up to consider the questioner before replying. The man was tall and built on lines of agile strength, with a swarthy, aquiline face that was brutally handsome. A diamond of great price flamed on the indifferently clean hand resting on the pummel of his long rapier, and there were gold rings in his ears, half-concealed by long ringlets of oily chestnut hair.

Captain Blood took the pipe-stem from between his lips.

"My name," he said, "is Peter Blood. The Spaniards know me for Don Pedro Sangre, and a Frenchman may call me Le Sang if he pleases."

"Good," said the gaudy adventurer in English, and without further invitation he drew up a stool and sat down at that greasy table. "My name," he informed the three men, two of whom at least were eyeing him askance, "it is Levasseur. You may have heard of me."

They had, indeed. He commanded a privateer of twenty guns that had

(Continued on page 27.)

The PAUPER of PENGARTH CASTLE

This story of Rupert Waldo, commonly known as the Wonder-Man, is better than usual, fine as Waldo yarns always are. You will realise the truth of that assertion when you have read to the end of it. Moreover, this is a double-length, two-part story. The first episode is complete in this number, and ends with a smashing climax that leads to even more surprising events in the second, which will be recorded next week. Our normal policy, as you know, is to have one long complete story each week. But we make an exception in this case, for we think the yarn itself justifies the experiment. Tell us what YOU think about this.

"... and yet here stands the castle, desolate and poverty-stricken!" said his lordship bitterly. "I, who should be reaping the benefit of this great estate, reap nothing."
(See page 7.)

THE FIRST CHAPTER.
"My Name is Sexton Blake."

RUPERT WALDO, behind the wheel of his rakish-looking two-seater, had some difficulty in keeping the car on the road. His pipe had blown out between his teeth, and it was useless to refill it. The wind was blowing at almost hurricane force.

Somehow, the fury of the elements rather appealed to this strange mixture of crook and gentleman. For Waldo, although as crooked as a corkscrew, possessed many surprisingly fine qualities.

He was nearing Launceston, in Cornwall, and was hardly over the border from Devonshire. It was afternoon, and the grey sky, with its ragged, scurrying clouds, looked more suitable to mid-winter than late spring. On every hand there were signs of approaching summer.

But on this particular afternoon, at least, the howling gale, sweeping in from the Atlantic, was buffeting Cornwall from end to end. Within the last half-hour the hurricane had increased enormously.

Waldo was on his way to Falmouth, having in mind a little stroke of business connected with a consignment of Brazilian gold specie. It was in the strong-room of a steamer, due in at Falmouth on the morrow.

Waldo was in no hurry, particularly as this gale had sprung up. The boat was bound to be a day late. In any case, he wasn't at all sure that the coup would come off. He was going down partly on chance.

The Wonder-Man had been enjoying himself for some weeks, touring the country and staying in different towns as the fancy pleased him. More often than not he carried loot away with him, and was not in the least troubled about any possible chase.

He was taking life easily, filling in a few odd weeks before he got down to his next big undertaking. He had several ambitious schemes brewing, but the time was hardly ripe for their exploitation.

Waldo was in no way disguised, and in his comfortable tweeds he looked less like a criminal than one would imagine. With his fine figure, his pleasant face, it was hardly to be wondered at that hotel proprietors welcomed him. He was open-handed to a degree, and popular with everybody.

The car was running well, and the road was practically devoid of any other traffic. Waldo enjoyed this battle with the hurricane. Even the car could scarcely be described as his own property, for he had obtained it quite cheaply some weeks earlier in one of the residential thoroughfares of Edgbaston.

Turning a bend, he entered upon a straight stretch of road, with the gale sweeping across broadside, and unchecked by any hedge. The car was nearly forced out of Waldo's control.

But with a laugh he accepted the challenge and pressed on the accelerator. In the distance he could see a solitary cyclist, and he instinctively slowed down again. Waldo was a keen motorist, and in normal circumstances he never indulged in road-hogging.

The cyclist, he could see, was a lady. He pitied her. She was struggling valiantly against the gale, and he rather wondered how she could maintain any control at all.

And it was at this moment that something occurred which led to a most surprising string of circumstances—something which neither Waldo nor anybody else could have possibly foreseen. It was just one of those tricks of fate for which there is no accounting.

A solitary tree grew by the roadside—a sturdy old warrior which had successfully battled against many a storm. But it seemed that it had met its conqueror now, for the gale was causing it to sway ominously.

The girl, fighting against the wind, probably knew nothing about the tree whatever. And Waldo was startled when a heavy branch tore itself away from the tree in the midst of a violent flurry and swept down on to the roadway, completely enveloping the fair cyclist in the lashing foliage.

Waldo's heart leapt. The tree itself, giving up the struggle, was about to crash over.

The girl, as it happened, had been hardly hurt. Knocked from her machine by the force of the impact, she was bruised and dazed, but otherwise unharmed. But to disentangle herself was impossible, for the twigs and branches of the great limb held her down.

And as the foliage lashed about it in the hurricane she caught a brief glimpse of the great tree. Groaning and straining, it was being literally torn up by the roots, and was on the point of falling.

It would be death—swift and sudden—if that trunk fell across the road where she lay. Panting with alarm the girl tried to struggle up. And again she glimpsed the tree falling.

She saw something else, too.

A man—goodness knows where he had sprung from—stood full in the path of the falling giant. With a final groan of anguish, accompanied by a shriek of triumph from the gale, the great tree leaned over.

And Waldo, his muscles tensed to their utmost, met that fearful weight. He was not mad enough to imagine that he could stop the tree falling. Even he, with his amazing strength, was not capable of miracles.

But as the tree fell he managed to divert it a trifle. Instead of falling upon the helpless girl it slewed partly sideways. The impact sent Waldo crashing over backwards, and he was aware of a thunderous, devastating commotion as the trunk fell.

The very ground shook; but Waldo was up in a moment, unhurt except for a slight graze or two. With a single heave he pulled the fallen branch aside, and found the girl lying amid the tangle.

"Hurt much?" he asked briskly.

"Splendid! that's the way! I'm afraid your machine's in a bit of a mess, but we must be thankful for small mercies, eh?"

The girl was on her feet now, pale and trembling, but rapidly regaining her self-possession. Waldo's cool, reassuring tones were good to listen to, and his smile was comforting.

She was rather tall, with a fine figure and deep grey eyes. Her dark hair was dishevelled, but in spite of these misfortunes there was a grace and dignity in her bearing which Waldo did not fail to observe.

He would not have called her shabby, but there was an indefinable something which indicated poverty. And yet, at the same time, the girl was obviously of high breeding. Every inch of her proclaimed the fact.

"Thank you! Thank you ever so much!" she said in a soft, husky voice. "How did you do it? I thought the tree was falling straight on me. You've saved my life!" she added simply.

"Don't mention it!" smiled Waldo. "A mere trifle, I assure you. That's the worst of these trees—they have a habit of falling upon one at awkward moments. Perhaps I may have the honour of giving you a lift? Your machine, I'm afraid, has met its Waterloo."

The bicycle was completely out of commission with a buckled front wheel and twisted forks.

"Thank you! I shall be grateful for——"

The girl swayed as she spoke, and was on the point of fainting. The reaction had left her weak. Waldo caught her just in time, and a minute later she was comfortably ensconced in the two-seater. But she was struggling to strengthen herself. Perhaps she felt that it was unwise to take advantage of this stranger's hospitality.

"Really, I ought not to bother you in this way!" she faltered. "I—I think I can walk——"

"You mustn't think that at all!" interrupted Waldo. "If you'll tell me where to go, Miss—Miss——"

"Pengarth Castle is where I live," she said. "I am Lady Betty Hamilton-Page. My father is the Earl of Pengarth. It is really too good of you to take all this trouble!"

"On the contrary," put in Waldo, with his reassuring smile. "I am highly honoured to be of service. My name is Blake—Sexton Blake."

The girl revealed sudden interest.

"Oh!" she exclaimed. "Mr. Blake! The—the great criminologist?"

Waldo smiled.

"My talents, I'm afraid, have been grossly exaggerated by certain young enthusiastic newspaper reporters," he answered calmly. "I can assure you, Lady Betty, that I am a mere ordinary mortal."

He jumped into the driving seat, and had soon turned the car round. He was feeling happier than ever, and took keen delight in the fresh battle with the elements.

His audacious assumption of Sexton Blake's identity was characteristic of the man. Quite on the spur of the moment, and without any previous premeditation, he had named himself as Sexton Blake. After all, why not? He would be away on his travels again within half an hour, and it was quite a piece of fun.

Waldo had a very real respect for Sexton Blake. Although the famous detective had frustrated him so many times, Waldo bore Blake not the slightest animosity. Quite the opposite. He held Blake in high esteem, for a man who could check Waldo was worthy of respect.

Both the occupants of the car were surprised. Lady Betty was pleased and thrilled that such a celebrated man had saved her from death. She had often wondered what Sexton Blake was like in the flesh, and she was not disappointed. After all, Waldo had a charming personality.

And Waldo himself was astonished that his fair companion was the daughter of an earl. True, her blue blood was obvious, but it struck him as rather incongruous that an earl's daughter should be alone on the high road riding a mere bicycle. Her dress, moreover, was hardly what he would have expected.

"If you will go down the next turning on the right we shall be at the castle within five minutes," said Lady Betty presently. "I can't understand one thing, Mr. Blake. How in the world did you save me from that tree?"

The point had been concerning her ever since she had been rescued. She had fully expected to see her rescuer crushed to death, and yet he had diverted the tree from her sufficiently to save her by the tiniest margin without any apparent injury to himself.

"Oh, that?" smiled Waldo. "It looked very much like a feat of miraculous strength, didn't it? Just one of those little deceptions, Lady Betty. I fancy the tree would have fallen as it did without my aid. My one object was to be at your service."

The girl was silent. He had made it no clearer. She was convinced that he had saved her life—and this, in fact, was the literal truth.

Proceeding down the side turning they had the gale behind them, and after a short run, mounting a rise, Lady Betty pointed.

"There is Pengarth Castle," she said.

The old place stood on the opposite hilltop—a fine granite pile, looking gaunt and almost forbidding in the greyness of the wild afternoon. Waldo eyed the scene with interest. It was a real old Cornish castle, the scene of many an historic battle.

Approaching nearer, they turned into a drive. There were no gates, and the lodge was empty, with boarded-up windows. The drive itself, with parklands on either side, was more or less a wilderness. Grass grew in profusion, and there was a ragged air of neglect—neglect of many years' standing.

Emerging from the drive, they came out in front of the grey old mansion. There was something indescribably impressive about the place. As far as Waldo could see, most of the ancient windows were bare and grimy. Only those adjacent to the great door were clean and curtained.

Poverty was written over the entire castle.

THE SECOND CHAPTER.
The Poverty of Pengarth.

LADY BETTY HAMILTON-PAGE was so far recovered that she was able to get out of the car unassisted. She looked very charming as she stood there, with the gale blowing her hair and bringing back the colour to her cheeks.

"You'll come in and meet my father, won't you?" she asked. "Please do, Mr. Blake. And I hope you'll excuse his manner. He is rather blunt and brusque, particularly with strangers. You must forgive him, for he is really the kindest and dearest old gentleman."

"I am afraid I shall be imposing——"

"No, no!" she interrupted. "Certainly not, Mr. Blake! You must come in! Please do!"

Waldo bowed.

"If you insist," he said resignedly.

He had intended slipping away at once, but his curiosity was now piqued. He was rather keen upon meeting the owner of this wild, dilapidated place. He couldn't help feeling a tinge of regret that such a stately castle should be so pitifully poverty-stricken.

Lady Betty went up the great steps and pulled at an enormous handle. Waldo, having stopped his engine, joined her. The castle doors were of an enormous size, of solid oak, and metal-studded. But instead of the doors opening, a kind of wicket was pulled back, revealing a barred square.

A face appeared behind the bars—an old, lined face which lit up with surprise at the sight of the pair outside.

"It's all right, Jelks," said Lady Betty quickly. "Open the door. I had a little accident, and this gentleman was kind enough to bring me home."

"An accident, m'lady!" ejaculated the face behind the bars. "The saints preserve us!"

His voice was agitated, and Waldo heard the pulling of bars and bolts. He was more interested than ever. The whole procedure seemed so quaint and extraordinary.

In these enlightened days, he had expected to find the castle replete with every modern improvement—with gardeners busy in the grounds, with footmen ready at the door, and similar up-to-date conventions.

He felt that there was something wrong. Lady Betty ought to be attired in old-time dress, and Jelks, the butler, was quite incongruous in his modern setting. Waldo felt that time had slipped back a couple of hundred years.

Why on earth was the castle barred in this fashion? Why was it made impregnable against even the return of its owner's daughter? Waldo was more than ever keen upon entering.

He had always hankered after the unusual. He was attracted by anything out of the ordinary. Commonplace crime had no interest for him whatever. He would much prefer a small reward and an interesting tussle to an easily-won fortune.

The big doors swung heavily open, and Lady Betty entered. Waldo, removing his cap, followed her. And he had already decided that he would indulge this whim of fate to the full. If necessary, he would even abandon his project in Falmouth. The latter had never appealed to him greatly, and this gaunt, old, poverty-stricken castle was already exerting its influence over the impressionable Waldo.

He found himself in a great hall, with massive oaken beams far overhead, a stone floor, and oak-panelled walls, with dingy, but probably priceless, tapestries.

There was an air of astonishing peace here. Scarcely any echo of the raging storm came within these massive walls. The silence, compared to the rush of wind without, was almost uncanny.

"If you will take a seat, Mr. Blake, I will go to my father, and bring him here," said Lady Betty. "I want him to thank you personally for your bravery and——"

"Please!" interrupted Waldo. "There's no need to tell him of that insignificant incident, surely?"

"Indeed, there is!" declared the girl firmly.

She tripped away up a great wide staircase which looked more suitable to

Waldo, even with his great strength, was not mad enough to think he could stop the tree falling. But with his muscles tensed, he met that fearful weight and managed to divert its direction a trifle. (*See page 4.*)

a feudal king's palace than to a twentieth century residence. Waldo seated himself upon a carved settee, and waited.

His fondness for the unusual was being gratified. And his audacity, his amazing strength, his extraordinary daring, made him quite easy in mind regarding the outcome. No matter what cropped up, he would be ready for it. And his assumption of Sexton Blake's identity—a mere caprice of the moment—now seemed likely to involve him in a far deeper deception than he had at first intended.

He heard voices on the staircase, and rose to his feet. Lady Betty was coming down with her father. There was no shadow of doubt that the old gentleman who appeared was the Earl of Pengarth.

His personality was a powerful one. He was talking angrily, petulantly, and with unrestrained force. He came into view round the bend in the staircase—a tall, bent-shouldered figure, with white hair and a grizzled moustache. He was dressed in rusty black, but in spite of his bent shoulders he had an unmistakably military bearing.

Rupert Waldo caught the old man's eye, and bowed.

The Earl of Pengarth advanced towards the visitor, paused a few feet away, and glared.

"Well, sir!" he growled, in a voice which could scarcely be called hospitable. "I understand that I must make you welcome to Pengarth. You saved my daughter's life, eh? I owe you a big debt—but I'm afraid it is a debt which can never be paid. I am grateful, sir—deeply grateful."

"Please refrain from mentioning the subject, sir," exclaimed Waldo, with real distress. "I am afraid Lady Betty has somewhat exaggerated the circumstances of the incident——"

"Nothing of the sort, sir!" interrupted his lordship. "I won't be contradicted! How dare you tell me that my daughter exaggerates! Blake, eh? Sexton Blake? H'm! I'm not sure that I altogether approve of you, sir. D'ye hear? One of those infernal spies, eh?"

"Really, sir——"

"I shouldn't be at all surprised if this is a piece of your clever trickery!" went on the Earl of Pengarth, adjusting his spectacles, and giving Waldo an even closer scrutiny. "Come, sir! Let me have the truth! Have you been sent here by that jackal, Slingsby, or have you not? A ruse to get into the castle—that's what it is! If such is the case, I'll kick you out with the toe of my own boot!"

Waldo was rather taken aback, particularly as the old earl had worked himself up into a towering passion. Lady Betty was standing by, flushed and distressed.

"Please, father!" she exclaimed, gripping his arm. "Oh, how can you? Just as if Mr. Blake would descend to such despicable methods! I am sure he doesn't even know who Mr. Slingsby is."

The Earl of Pengarth cooled down and grunted.

"Eh? Then he's fortunate!" he exclaimed gruffly. "Anybody who doesn't know Simon Slingsby is fortunate!" He glared at Waldo. "A rat, sir—a miserable, despicable rat! That's what Slingsby is! A robber, too—nothing more nor less than a blackguardly thief!"

Waldo had the grace to feel rather self-conscious. Somehow, this soldierly old fellow made him feel very mean and small. He was indulging in the basest form of deception, and was in such a position that he couldn't very well admit the fact. He resolved to make his excuses and leave as soon as possible.

"I regret to learn that Mr. Simon Slingsby is such an undesirable character, sir," he said smoothly. "Need I give you my word that I have never met the man, and have no association with him? My presence here is purely accidental. And as I have business in Launceston, I beg to crave your indulgence——"

"Rubbish, sir!" interrupted the earl sourly. "Nonsense! My daughter insists upon your staying to dinner—and I won't hear any refusal. What is more, the hospitality of Pengarth Castle—such as it is—is open to you for as long as you care to stay. You have acted like a brave man, sir, and my gratitude is very great."

Waldo hardly knew what to say. The old man's words contradicted his attitude. And Waldo remembered what Lady Betty had told him—that her father, in spite of his brusque tongue, was really one of the dearest old gentlemen.

"Nevertheless, Lord Pengarth, I must insist——"

"Insist!" roared the Earl of Pengarth. "And so do I insist, sir—in my own house, too! As for your business in Launceston, it can go to the devil! H'm! Launceston, eh? A disgraceful town—a place of iniquity!"

"Oh, father!" exclaimed Lady Betty.

"Simon Slingsby lives in Launceston! And that is enough!" rapped out Lord Pengarth. "Any town that harbours such a reptile is not deserving of recognition."

"Please, Mr. Blake, you really mustn't take too much notice of father," said Lady Betty, with a smile. "He doesn't mean what he says. Launceston is as dear to him as the castle itself. Mr. Slingsby, I may mention, is our family lawyer."

"Oh!" said Waldo, with a sudden smile. "That explains his lordship's vitriolic tirade. As I have every reason to know, lawyers are divided into two classes—honest and shady. When they are honest they are as true as steel, but when they are shady, they are worse than serpents in the grass."

Lord Pengarth rapped his stick on the floor.

"What are we standing here for?" he demanded. "Sit down, Mr. Blake! Your legs may be young, but mine are not! Sit down, sir!"

They seated themselves on the carved settee.

And to Waldo's embarrassment Lady Betty went into a full account of the mishap in the gale. The master-crook could easily see that Lord Pengarth was well disposed towards him, and accepted him without question as Sexton Blake.

His lordship's gruff manner of speech was only characteristic of him, and he meant nothing by it. Waldo was already beginning to reverse his decision.

He had been asked to stay. Well, he would stay—until the morrow, in any case, and perhaps two or three days. Being a shrewd man Waldo easily connected Lord Pengarth's poverty with Simon Slingsby's villainy. In all probability the old earl had a bee in his bonnet on the subject. But Waldo was now keen upon learning more.

He had sometimes read of impecunious noblemen who stuck to their ancestral castles in spite of straitened circumstances. But he had never met one before, and he had never imagined it possible that any peer of the realm could be so akin to a pauper as Lord Pengarth obviously was.

The Wonder-Man, in fact, was becoming exceedingly interested.

Half an hour later Waldo was an established guest.

Having accepted the invitation to stay, he obtained his traps from the car, and Jelks carried them into the castle. In the absence of any groom or chauffeur Waldo himself drove the car through a granite arch, into a vast weed-grown courtyard at the rear.

Here he found a colossal amount of storage room—stables, coach-houses galore, all of them decaying with disuse. By the time he had walked back to the front of the castle he found Lord Pengarth waiting for him.

"A wild day, Mr. Blake," grunted his lordship, who was wrapped in a shabby ulster. "We will go for a walk in the grounds. I have a mind to talk to you."

"Nothing will suit me better, Lord Pengarth," said Waldo promptly.

In the meantime Jelks, the butler, was having a word with Lady Betty in the great hall. At his feet were Waldo's bags. Following the practice of years, Waldo had seen to it that his baggage carried no labels or identification marks of any kind.

"Whatever is the matter, Jelks?" asked Lady Betty. "You are looking unusually thoughtful this afternoon."

"With good reason!" said the butler, shaking his head. "With good reason, m'lady! His lordship was saying that you nearly got killed this afternoon. Haven't I told you again and again, child, that I don't like that bicycle. Unnatural things—that's what they are!"

Lady Betty laughed.

"Well, Jelks, you needn't worry about it any more," she said, patting him on the shoulder. "The bike's finished—smashed beyond all hope of repair. Now, if you say you're glad, I shall hate you!"

"I'm glad, m'lady, and I'm sorry," said the butler. "Without that bicycle we sha'n't be so anxious when you're out. But I'm afraid it'll mean an awful lot of walking."

"Oh, well, Jelks, it can't be helped," said the girl. "One of these days, perhaps, we shall have a fine motor-car.

Oh, there's Mr. Blake's car, you know. I shall be all right for a day or two, Jelks, sha'n't I?"

Jelks stroked his hair slowly.

"Mr. Blake, m'lady?" he said. "Did ye say that gentleman is Mr. Sexton Blake?"

"Yes, the famous detective, of London."

"It's queer, m'lady—mortal queer!" muttered the old butler, as though to himself. "Maybe I'm wrong, but—— Oh, well, I don't suppose I ought to interfere. 'Tisn't my business."

"What isn't your business, Jelks?"

"Nothing, m'lady—nothing!" said Jelks, picking up the bags.

He moved off upstairs, and the girl looked after him wonderingly. Old Jelks had been born in Pengarth Castle, and had served the family throughout his life. He was a real example of the "old retainer," and even in these poverty-stricken times he was as staunch as ever. Nothing could have induced Jelks to desert his master.

Lady Betty wondered why he had seemed so strange while referring to Sexton Blake. She concluded, after a moment's thought, that his old-fashioned notions clung to him, and that he disapproved of a detective being a guest under the roof of Pengarth Castle. Jelks did not make any distinction between the common detective and the specialist.

And so, although Lady Betty dismissed the subject from her mind, Jelks deposited Waldo's bags in the guest chamber, and then made his way down by a rear stairway into the domestic quarters.

The castle was more or less a ruin. Although the roof was intact over the hall, the entire east and west wings were unused. Vast corridors, enormous halls and reception chambers, and other rooms by the score, were closed and empty. Furniture—ancient and decaying—reposed in some of them, but neither of these great wings was habitable.

Only the comparatively small frontage was used—with the great hall, a drawing-room, and Lord Pengarth's library. At the rear of this front block was an inner courtyard, and the windows which looked out upon it belonged to the domestic quarters.

The entire staff at the castle consisted of Jelks and his wife. Over a period of twenty years the household had grown smaller and smaller. First an under-butler, then a housemaid, then a footman or two, and so on until the once great domestic staff had been whittled down to two.

Only the residents in the immediate neighbourhood of Pengarth Castle knew the unhappy truth. But even these had no real knowledge of the cause of his lordship's fallen fortunes.

Affairs had started going wrong long before Lady Pengarth's death, sixteen years earlier. And since that sad event the magnificent castle parklands had grown ragged and more ragged, and the castle itself had taken on a forlorn, dilapidated appearance.

And now, according to local gossip, the end was not far off. There were even whispers about the famous old Pengarth curse. Nobody knew exactly what the curse was and how it had originated, but among the villagers in the neighbourhood it was said that once the curse placed its hand upon the castle nothing could prevent it passing from the Pengarth family. It certainly seemed that this disaster was approaching.

THE THIRD CHAPTER.
The Pengarth Spirit.

JELKS was an elderly man, and though he never grumbled his duties were long and arduous. When he got into the servants' hall he lowered himself slowly into a big chair and rubbed one of his knees.

"It's the rheumatism again, old lady," he said ruefully. "Can't seem to get rid of it no how. Getting ready to go to the village? I thought you weren't going until to-morrow?"

Mrs. Jelks, busy with the strings of her bonnet, glanced round across the long, quaint old apartment with its uneven stone floor. She was some years younger than her husband, an active, able woman.

"To-morrow, indeed! Law, Jelks, whatever are ye thinking of? Isn't there a fine gentleman come here to stay? M'lady told me, not ten minutes ago, that we've got a guest! The first guest this many a month!" she added thoughtfully. "It's more than I can make out."

"Ay, and it beats me, too!" said Jelks, looking at the housekeeper with a curiously intent expression. "Do ye remember, Martha, when we went to London five years ago?"

Mrs. Jelks could hardly repress a smile.

"Seeing that we haven't been to London since, it's hardly likely that I'd forget," she replied. "What about it? What's wrong with ye, father? You're looking rare worried!"

"When we were in London," said Jelks, "the master lent us to one of those relatives of his, and while you helped below stairs at that big wedding-party I announced the guests. Maybe ye'll know nothing about it, old lady, being five years ago, but Mr. Sexton Blake was at that party."

"Then ye know him?" asked his wife in surprise.

"I reckon so," replied Jelks, with a frown. "Leastways, I thought I did. I ain't got such a bad memory for faces, Martha, and it was Mr. Blake himself who picked me up when I fell down them stairs. Ye remember? There was a loose rod, and I gave my leg a rare twisting. Ay, and Mr. Blake was a real gentleman, too—gave me a pound, he did, and it isn't likely that I'd forget his voice and his smile."

"It's a wonder he didn't recognise ye to-day, father," said Mrs. Jelks. "They do say that Mr. Blake never forgets a face once he's seen it. But there, I dare say it's all so much talk. And I can't stay here, wasting my time. I've got to order eggs and butter and——"

"Wait ye a minute!" interrupted her husband. "It's queer, you think, that Mr. Blake didn't recognise me? Maybe, old lady. But it's downright puzzling why I can't recognise Mr. Blake!"

The housekeeper stared.

"What are you trying to tell me, Jelks?" she asked firmly. "I know your little ways. There's something you haven't said yet."

"Then I'll tell ye!" said Jelks, with sudden vehemence. "That gentleman who saved m'lady and who is now with the master is no more Mr. Sexton Blake than I am! Ay, ye can stare!" he added, rising to his feet. "It's a fact, Martha! I'd swear to it!"

Mrs. Jelks was aghast.

"Ye're daft, father!" she exclaimed breathlessly.

"But I'm not doddering!" said Jelks grimly. "And my eyesight's as good as ever it was, old lady, and so's my memory. That gent isn't Mr. Blake, that I know! But it's a real awkward thing to deal with. Maybe I'd better tell the master."

"Maybe ye'll do nothing of the kind!" interrupted his better half sharply. "Lor', father, whatever are ye thinking about? Mr. Blake has changed, I suppose, and, what with different clothes and——"

"It's no good, Martha—I know what I'm saying!" interrupted the old butler. "He ain't Mr. Blake. But if I tell the master he'll only call me a fool, and that'll make things worse."

Mrs. Jelks was thoroughly unconvinced.

"You'd best send the real Mr. Blake a telegram!" she said tartly. "That'll fetch him down here to prove that ye're right. Sakes alive, father, I can't make ye out! Just as if a gentleman would come here pretending to be Mr. Sexton Blake when he isn't Mr. Sexton Blake!"

She pulled her jacket on with an indignant tug, and prepared to leave.

"Wait!" said Jelks tensely. "A telegram, eh? You've hit it, Martha—you've hit it! That's what I'll do! I'll send Mr. Blake a telegram. If I'm wrong it won't do no harm, and if I'm right, as like as not Mr. Blake will send a reply. Then we'll know what to do. While you're in the village you'll send that telegram."

At first Mrs. Jelks flatly refused, saying that she wouldn't be a party to any such nonsense. But her husband was so insistent, and he was apparently so set upon the plan, that at last she gave in.

And so, all unknown to Rupert Waldo, a telegram to Sexton Blake was dispatched that very afternoon. The Wonder-Man seldom made a miscalculation, and in this instance he could hardly be accounted careless.

He had been accepted without question by Lord Pengarth and his daughter. What earthly reason should he have for assuming that Jelks, the old butler, knew the real Sexton Blake by sight? If such a thought had entered his mind, Waldo had naturally dismissed it without the slightest consideration. The chance seemed too remote for serious reflection.

The butler's position was rather a delicate one. To openly denounce the visitor was out of the question, and he knew his master too well to approach him on the subject even in private. His only course was to communicate with Sexton Blake, and await the result.

In the meantime, Waldo was beginning to obtain a grip on the situation.

Lord Pengarth stood upon a rising knoll, his back to the wind, gazing across at the gaunt old castle. He had said very little to Waldo during the walk, and Waldo himself had remained silent—keenly studying his host. He had an idea that the earl would soon lose his reticence.

"A fine old pile, sir!" he ventured at length.

"Eh? What's that?" said Lord Pengarth, with a start. "Yes, yes! Pengarth Castle is one of the most ancient—one of the most honourable—inhabited castles in the whole of Cornwall. None can compare with it, Mr. Blake. For eight hundred years a Pengarth has lived under that roof. Think of it! Eight hundred years!"

"A wonderful record!" commented Waldo.

"Gadso! And does that snake Slingsby think that he'll turn me out?" demanded Lord Pengarth fiercely. "Does he imagine that a Pengarth will relinquish the castle to a stranger—a moneyed upstart, a common usurper with nothing behind his name but a cheap party-bought knighthood?"

"I am afraid Mr. Slingsby is optimistic," said Waldo. "You must remember, however, that I am in a state of almost complete ignorance regarding your affairs, Lord Pengarth. Not that I desire to share your confidence in any way——"

"Nonsense, sir! Nonsense!" interrupted Lord Pengarth. "I want to talk to you. I don't often have the opportunity of talking to anybody, and perhaps you can give me some advice. Heaven knows that I need it! Not that I can pay you!" he added, frowning. "I can't! Paupers are hardly in a position to pay your fees, Mr. Blake!"

Waldo waved a deprecating hand.

"Really, Lord Pengarth——" he began.

"I'm not ashamed of it!" broke in his lordship. "I've been robbed, sir—swindled, victimised, betrayed by that viper Slingsby. I'll tell you about him, and then you'll be able to judge. Come, we'll walk."

They paced slowly back towards the castle, and it was some moments before Lord Pengarth broke the silence. Waldo was genuinely curious to hear about this mysterious Mr. Slingsby. He had an instinctive feeling that Lord Pengarth was a man with a real grievance.

"For over fifteen years the tragedy has been developing," said the earl. "Heaven granted me no son, Mr. Blake, and when the Countess of Pengarth passed away I was left lonely and desolate, with only my daughter for comfort. At that time Pengarth Castle was rich. There were scores of servants—grooms, carriages, everything!

"And to-day the great Pengarth estates are as rich as ever, Mr. Blake," he added, raising his stick and pointing. "As far as the eye can see these rich lands have been controlled by the Pengarth family for generations and for centuries."

"A wonderful vista!" commented Waldo.

"And yet here stands the castle, desolate and poverty-stricken," said his lordship bitterly. "I, who should be reaping the benefit of this great estate, reap nothing. It is Simon Slingsby who holds the reins. Not that I blame him any more than I blame myself. I am a fool, Mr. Blake—a weak, blundering imbecile! Had I possessed an ounce of common-sense in the past, had I possessed an inkling of business instinct, this disaster would never have come. The tragedy you see is the tragedy of one man's trust in another."

"Slingsby betrayed you!"

"Basely—hideously!" replied Lord Pengarth, his voice quivering with intense emotion. "Forgive me, Mr. Blake, for talking to you in this way, but I need it. For months I have been pent up—unable to speak to any save my own child. And she knows all. Moreover, why should I bring worry to her pretty head? Heaven knows, she has enough trouble managing my house. As for appearances, we gave them up years ago. Throughout Cornwall we are known as the titled paupers."

He bowed his head, and Waldo had nothing to say. The old man's agony was intense.

"From boyhood I had known Simon Slingsby as the family lawyer—the man who managed our affairs, and who had the implicit trust of the countess and myself," continued his lordship at length. "I never questioned his statements, I never even read his documents presented to me for signature. I signed them trustingly, believing this man to be my friend and adviser. At that time the Pengarth fortunes were considerable."

"And what caused the crash?" asked Waldo quietly.

"There was no crash, sir—no crash!" said the earl. "It has been a gradual process—extending over many years. Sometimes I am ready to convince myself that there is more than legend in the old family curse. For it was after the burglary, seventeen years ago, that the first signs of trouble commenced. The Countess of Pengarth's jewels were stolen at that time, Mr. Blake—and with them the historic Pengarth Cross."

"Possibly you have some recollection of the crime? The jewels were never recovered—the thief was clever enough to make his escape without leaving a trace."

Waldo remembered nothing of the affair, but he nodded.

"Yes, now you mention it, I recall the case," he replied. "And was there any special significance attached to this Pengarth Cross?"

"Only the significance of legend," replied his lordship. "Since that date, Mr. Blake, matters have grown gradually more serious. They have gone from bad to worse, until now—well, sir, I have been given to understand that I am virtually a trespasser on this property."

"A trespasser?" repeated Waldo.

"That reptile Slingsby holds the title-deeds!" exclaimed Lord Pengarth, his whole manner grim and fierce. "His scheming plans have at last matured, and I am on the point of being turned out. Indeed, Slingsby has sold the castle—he has sold the entire estate—and I am soon to be evicted, like any drunken cottager who fails to pay his rent!"

Waldo shook his head in silent sympathy.

"What is your advice, Mr. Blake?" demanded Lord Pengarth, turning upon his companion and grasping him. "What is your suggestion? Shall I resist this accursed villain? Shall I refuse to leave? Or shall I defy these usurpers?"

"Defy them!" replied Waldo promptly. "Stand your ground, Lord Pengarth, and send this Slingsby viper about his business!"

His lordship actually smiled, but it was a fierce smile.

"Splendid!" he said gruffly. "That's the advice I wanted. Not that it would have made any difference, whatever advice you had given me," he added frankly. "For no power on earth will force me out of the castle! A Pengarth has lived here for eight hundred years! The invader will conquer over my dead body! Here I am, and here I remain—and let those who would arouse me beware!"

He spoke with concentrated intensity, and Waldo could do nothing but admire the old man's spirit—that same spirit which had characterised the Pengarth family throughout the centuries.

THE FOURTH CHAPTER.
Sexton Blake is Amused.

MR. SEXTON BLAKE, the celebrated criminologist, looked round rather impatiently as Tinker appeared at the door of the laboratory.

"I distinctly told you, Tinker, that I didn't want you to disturb me!" he said irritably. "This experiment is delicate, and——"

"Sorry, guv'nor," interrupted Tinker, "but it's a telegram!"

"Take it away! I don't want to see it!"

"But it seems urgent——"

"Confound you, Tinker, nine telegrams out of ten seem urgent—and they are no more urgent than four meals a day are necessary for the human frame!" said Blake curtly. "People bother me with their trivialities, and are aggrieved when I refuse to pander to their whims! Go away, Tinker! Open the telegram yourself and deal with it!"

"I've opened it, guv'nor," said Tinker. "You told me to attend to all business this evening——"

"Then for Heaven's sake carry out your instructions, and leave me alone!" broke in the detective tartly. "My mind must be concentrated on this stuff. Peculiarly enough, Tinker, at the present moment you inspire me with fury. And unless you get out of that doorway I shall have no alternative but to throw a bottle at you!"

Tinker hesitated.

It was evening, and Sexton Blake's Baker Street chambers were quiet. He was intent upon completing this laboratory task, and he had given strict orders that he was not to be disturbed. Under ordinary circumstances Tinker would have refrained from interrupting his master. But this telegram seemed to require special attention.

"I think you ought to read it, sir," said Tinker firmly.

He dodged in alarm and closed the door, for Sexton Blake had picked up a big glass retort in a most suggestive manner. Tinker retired to the consulting-room and grunted.

"He's always the same when he's messing about with those chemicals!" he grumbled. "Like a bear with a sore head! The chances are he won't appear until about three o'clock in the morning. So what am I going to do about this business?"

He looked at the telegram again, and frowned.

"Sexton Blake,
Baker Street,
London.
"Gentleman arrived this afternoon calling himself Sexton Blake. Now staying here as Lord Pengarth's guest. Please wire if in order or not. Suspect deception.

"JELKS (Butler),
"Pengarth Castle."

"I don't know who Jelks is, but he's a pretty smart chap for a butler," mused Tinker thoughtfully. "And if this isn't urgent, what is? Somebody staying at Pengarth Castle as Sexton Blake! And the guv'nor's here, wasting his time on that silly laboratory work!"

Tinker was rather disgusted. He sat down in a chair and glared round the room helplessly. He had been having a trying time for the past two days, and was longing for a change.

His famous master had got into one of his "touchy" moods. There had been no case to interest him for some time, and he had been irritated for weeks by spending his energies on affairs which turned out to be trivial and uninteresting.

As a balm to this period of inactivity Blake had now turned to his laboratory. It wouldn't have mattered so much if the experiment had been essential to a criminal investigation. It wasn't. And Tinker wondered what he should do about this telegram.

He decided that it would be better to send an answer, telling Jelks that Sexton Blake was in London, and that he had better get the police on the job. Then he concluded that it would be better to give his master a couple of hours. The telegram wouldn't be delivered until the morning, anyhow, so there was no hurry about its dispatch.

Within forty minutes Blake made an unexpected appearance.

"A success, Tinker!" he observed, yawning. "I reached my desired end long before I anticipated. Well, has anything startling happened? There's no need to look at me so morosely, young 'un."

"What about this telegram, sir?" asked Tinker. "Perhaps you'll be good enough to look at it now? It may not be important, but there's no telling. Personally I think something ought to be done."

He spoke indifferently, being rather huffed, but he watched Blake with intentness as the latter glanced over the message. Sexton Blake's only emotion was amusement.

"This appears to be interesting, Tinker," he murmured. "So a gentleman is now staying at Pengarth Castle under my name? I can only conclude that he is there for nefarious purposes. What is the time? Barely eight o'clock. We will look in at one of the musical comedies. I am in the mood for a little relaxation."

"But what about this wire?"

"To the best of my belief, there is a midnight train to Cornwall," said Sexton Blake smoothly. "We will travel down personally, and have a look into this affair first hand. It will probably be a wicked waste of time, but as I shall be neglecting no important work it won't matter."

Tinker was quite pleased. He hadn't expected his master to go all the way down to Cornwall to investigate the little mystery. But it was just as well, for perhaps the journey would bring Sexton Blake out of his present contrary mood.

Fate was working overtime against Rupert Waldo!

THE FIFTH CHAPTER.
The Invader.

"GOOD - MORNING, Mr. Blake!" said Lady Betty briskly as Waldo came downstairs. "You're just in time! My father ought to be here in less than a minute, and breakfast is waiting."

The hall at Pengarth Castle was used as a dining-room—not the entire apartment, but a small corner of it, where an old-fashioned window allowed one to look out upon the weed-grown terrace and the ragged lawns.

It was a brilliant morning—as summer-like as the previous day had been wintry. The storm had gone, leaving the air peaceful and balmy, with a hot sun shining down from a cloudless sky.

Waldo had slept well, and he was very interested in his novel surroundings. The more he thought of Lord Pengarth's position, the more he was convinced that the old earl was a victim of misplaced trust. There had been no riotous expenditure of money in his lordship's past—no reckless gambling which had resulted in his own downfall. The unknown Simon Slingsby was the villain in the case.

From Waldo's point of view, there was nothing to be gained by remaining. There was not much chance for him here—in an impoverished castle, where there was nothing worth stealing except one or two rare "old masters." Even these were not Lord Pengarth's property, since they had been sold over his head.

But Waldo lingered. He decided to wait and see how things developed. He was personally interested, and from his point of view that was all that mattered. The Wonder-Man was no common grabber, but a real artist. And a dim plan had already begun to take shape in his fertile mind.

Lord Pengarth came downstairs, grumbling about the draughts in his bed-room, and he took his seat at the table and gave Waldo a curt nod. As a host, he was scarcely the ideal.

"Any letters?" he demanded. "Yes, yes! What's this? Upon my soul! One from that infernal Sir William! I won't open it! Do you hear me, Betty? I won't open it!"

"I wouldn't if I were you, dad," said Lady Betty, as she prepared to pour out the coffee. "It'll only upset your appetite, and you'll be cross all day. Leave it until you get into the library."

The earl glared at her over the top of his spectacles.

"I shall do nothing of the sort!" he snorted. "Have I to ask my daughter's permission before I can open my own letters? Upon my soul, Betty, you're getting impudent!"

She smiled, and took no further notice. And Lord Pengarth, seizing a knife, slit the envelope open with a vicious thrust. He pulled out the letter, adjusted the glasses, and commenced reading. Then, to the surprise of Waldo, and the consternation of his daughter, he leapt to his feet, sending the heavy chair over with a crash.

"I won't admit him!" roared Lord Pengarth, pacing up and down. "No, by gad! I won't let him set foot into the place! The rascal—the upstart! This is more than flesh and blood can stand!"

"What ever is the matter, father?" asked Lady Betty, running over to him.

"Matter!" thundered his lordship. "That rascal, Sir William Brag, is coming here this morning to take possession! We are to be turned out, Betty—pitched out of Pengarth Castle this morning! Do you understand—this morning?"

Lady Betty was distressed and alarmed.

"There must be a mistake, father," she ventured.

"There is no mistake!" snapped the earl. "The man states his intentions in plain language. Good gad! He's blunt to the point of insolence. He has bought the property, and intends to enter into possession to-day. And he will be pleased, mark you, if I can make arrange-

"You'll hear more about this!" gasped Sir William as he bolted for the car. "Drive away, Parker—Mr. Slingsby's house. And hurry! That old man's mad—raving mad!" (See page 19.)

ments to hand him the keys upon arrival, and make my own arrangements for leaving!"

Lady Betty lost some of her colour.

"Oh, dad," she exclaimed, "what shall we do?"

Lord Pengarth paced up and down, hitting his heavy stick fiercely upon the floor. And Waldo watched silently. The crisis, apparently, had arrived.

Sir William Brag had something to be said in his favour. In all probability, he had bought the property in good faith, and naturally he expected to take possession of it. But it was characteristic of Lord Pengarth to vent his wrath upon any head that happened to be nearest.

"What shall we do?" repeated his lordship after a while. "I'll tell you what we shall do! Jelks—Jelks! Confound the man! Where the deuce are you, Jelks? Never about when you're wanted——"

"Are you calling, sir?" asked Jelks, as he appeared breathlessly from one of the angles of the old hall.

"Yes, confound you, I am!" shouted Lord Pengarth. "Bolt every door! Put every bar in position! And if anybody comes here, refuse them admittance. If necessary, shoot them!" he added grimly.

"Yes, your lordship!" said Jelks, with a kind of feverish joy. "I'll get the gun ready at once!"

Lord Pengarth sat down at the table again and breathed hard.

"I'll show them whether I'm in earnest or not!" he said fiercely. "I'll show them whether a Pengarth will tamely submit to being ejected from his own castle! I'll shoot them, by gad! That's what we did hundreds of years ago. And that's what we'll do now! Death to the invader!"

"But, father, we're not living in the Middle Ages now!", protested his daughter gently. "It'll be dreadful if you resist Sir William. He has bought the property, and we ought to explain to him——"

"I'll explain nothing!" roared her father. "I don't care what he's bought—I don't care whether we're in the Middle Ages or not! This is my castle, and no usurper will set foot inside it! What's this? Coffee? It's cold, Betty—stone cold! Haven't I told you fifty times that I won't drink cold coffee? Take the infernal stuff away!"

He stirred it vigorously and drank.

"You intend to defy Sir William when he arrives?" asked Waldo, with interest. "I don't want to interfere, Lord Pengarth, and perhaps I had better take my leave——"

"You will do nothing of the kind!" interrupted his lordship. "I want you here, Mr. Blake—I want you to help me in resisting these rascally invaders!"

Lady Betty looked alarmed.

"Oh, father, you can't ask Mr. Blake to do that!" she said quickly. "It isn't right—he's our guest. And if you resist Sir William, it's almost the same as resisting the law——"

"Who cares about the law?" rapped out her father, as he attacked the eggs and bacon. "Here, in my own castle, I make my own laws! The Pengarths have always done so—and always will, by gad! What do you say, Mr. Blake? Do you suggest that I should tamely submit—that I should leave my ancestral home at the command of this interloping jackanapes?"

Waldo shook his head.

"I strongly advise you to remain firm, Lord Pengarth," he replied. "Resist to the last ditch. The Pengarths have never surrendered in the past, and it is your duty to live up to the traditions of the family."

"Splendid, sir—well said!" roared Lord Pengarth approvingly. "And I will resist—as you say, to the last ditch! I am glad you are here, sir—infernally glad! Just the kind of man I want by my side! I've had enough of feminine weakness!" he added, glaring at his unhappy daughter.

Lady Betty glanced rather appealingly at Waldo, but said nothing. She didn't quite understand it. She had expected a man like Sexton Blake to talk Lord Pengarth round, and to show him the futility of resisting the law. It upset all her calculations to find that the guest was urging his lordship to fight.

But Waldo was not only amused, but thoroughly interested. And he was anxious to see how the affair developed. Resistance was the one thing necessary in order to precipitate some excitement. And Waldo lived for excitement. He grasped at the nearest possibility of it.

"Possibly my advice to your father struck you as being somewhat strange," said Waldo, after breakfast, when Lord Pengarth had gone off to make an inspection of the doors and windows. "But I can assure you, Lady Betty, I have excellent reasons."

"But, Mr. Blake it seems so futile!" said the girl earnestly. "We know that Mr. Slingsby has swindled us, but he cannot be touched by the law. My father has signed all the documents unwittingly, and Mr. Slingsby is lawfully in the right."

"Exactly!" agreed Waldo.

"And Sir William Brag is only exercising his legal claim when he demands possession of Pengarth Castle," went on Lady Betty. "It would be foolish to resist—it would only lead to terrible trouble. And I fear it would finally result in sheer humiliation. For Sir William will probably appeal to the sheriff of the county, and have us ejected. We couldn't stand that, Mr. Waldo. It would be too dreadful!"

Waldo smiled reassuringly.

"Take my word for it, Lady Betty, there will be no such disaster as that," he said smoothly. "I have decided to help your father, and although I do not wish to make any rash promises, I rather fancy your days of anguish will now be few. I admire Lord Pengarth's fine independence — his undying spirit of dogged resistance."

"Yes, he is a real Pengarth," said Lady Betty thoughtfully. "I wonder what you mean, Mr. Blake? How can you help us? As far as I can see, it only remains for us to go as quietly and as unobtrusively as possible. Perhaps I shall be able to obtain some employment——"

"Don't think of it!" interrupted Waldo lightly. "Leave everything to me. Hallo! A motor-car, unless I'm mistaken. Sir William has arrived to turn the despot out of his castle. The next episode promises to be rather entertaining."

He walked to the nearest window and looked out upon the terrace. A fine limousine had just driven up, and it held a solitary occupant, in addition to the chauffeur.

Sir William Brag had come to take over his new domain.

THE SIXTH CHAPTER.
Two Different Things.

SIR WILLIAM BRAG looked what he was—a merchant prince who had risen from the lowest rung. He was, in fact, a woollens manufacturer. Brag's Invincible Serge was famous throughout the cloth-trade.

He was a short, stoutish man, but in no way resembled the typical parvenu. His face was not red, and his voice was not blaring. In repose, as now, he had a refined, almost aristocratic, appearance. There was a certain dignity about him as he stood surveying the gaunt old castle.

Finally, he approached the great door and pulled at the bell. Waldo heard it jangling somewhere in the rear. By looking through one of the side mullioned windows, the Wonder-Man could just see Sir William as he stood there waiting.

Jelks answered the ring, but he did not open the door. Instead, he slid back the small wicket, and gazed out through the strong iron bars.

"Open the door, please!" said the visitor. "What's the idea of this extraordinary business? I have come here to see Lord Pengarth. I am Sir William Brag."

"I am sorry, sir, but Lord Pengarth is not at home to any visitors," replied Jelks firmly. "If you will be good enough to communicate by letter——"

"I will do nothing of the sort!" interrupted Sir William angrily. "My correspondence with Lord Pengarth has been absolutely one-sided. I have never received a line from him, and his attitude is beyond all understanding. I am here to settle this matter once and for all."

Jelks sighed.

"I am sorry, sir, but the master gave very strict orders," he replied.

"Open this door at once, and don't stand there arguing!" shouted Sir William. "Do you hear me, you infernal lackey? Do you think I'm going to be defied by a common servant? Open the door!"

Sir William's manner betrayed his origin. He had schooled himself for years to look dignified and refined. But when he was angry his repose vanished. He became almost vulgar in expression, and his carefully trained voice lost all its polish.

"I regret, sir, that I cannot open the door," said Jelks.

"You—you fool!" roared Sir William. "Do you realise that I'm the owner of this property? It's mine—every inch of it! Bought and paid for! Why, confound you, I hold the title deeds in my pocket! Open this door at once!"

But Jelks merely shook his head again.

"Lord Pengarth's orders were final, sir," he replied. "I will take him a message if you desire it."

"I've never heard of such idiocy in my life!" raved Sir William. "Yes, take him a message. Tell him that I want to speak to him. That's all. Here, give him this card!"

Fairly quivering with indignation, Sir William Brag scrawled something on one of his cards and passed it through the bars. Jelks took it with becoming dignity and retired. And Waldo, watch-

ing from the little window, chuckled with enjoyment.

There was something really original about this affair. And Sir William Brag, for all his arrogance, was more to be pitied than blamed. He had bought the property from the Launceston lawyer, and, quite naturally, he desired to take possession.

Neither he nor Mr. Simon Slingsby had dreamed that Lord Pengarth would resist. It had never occurred to them that the stubborn old earl might bolt himself in his castle and refuse to shift. Here, in this twentieth century, his lordship was acting in exactly the same way as his ancestors might have acted in medieval times.

There was a quaintness about the situation which attracted Waldo's whimsical mood. And he was determined to do everything possible to spur his lordship on. Something of the spirit of Pengarth Castle was entering his own veins, and he, too, looked upon Sir William Brag as an impudent intruder.

Mere money and title deeds counted for nothing. This was a case of man against man, and Lord Pengarth, with the knowledge that his ancestors had always owned this property, had the moral right on his side.

His lordship was waiting in the big hall, pacing up and down, and muttering to himself. He glared at Jelks as the butler stood before him. Jelks was holding out the card.

"What's this?" rapped out Lord Pengarth.

"Sir William asked me to present it to you, my lord," said Jelks.

"Then take it away!" roared the Earl of Pengarth. "Do you hear me, Jelks? Take it away! I won't look at it."

He grabbed the card and adjusted his spectacles so fiercely that he nearly knocked them off.

"H'm! What's this? 'A few words in private will be much appreciated.' Oh, will they?" he exclaimed grimly. "We'll see about that, Jelks. We'll see about that. Like his confounded impudence!"

"Sir William is waiting, my lord!" exclaimed Jelks tentatively.

"Let him wait!" stormed Lord Pengarth. "And I won't see him, either! I won't demean myself by arguing with the rascal! Go and tell him that he can get off my premises, Jelks!"

"Yes, my lord," said Jelks.

"Come here, sir! Don't walk off like that!" thundered the earl. "What on earth's the matter with you, Jelks? I'll go to the door myself, and, what's more, I'll let this impudent tradesman have a piece of my mind! Gad, I'll send him off!"

"Please, dad," urged Lady Betty, taking his arm, "you'll only excite yourself, and you know the doctor has told you to be careful! Besides, Sir William is probably acting in all innocence."

"Fiddlesticks!" shouted her father. "As for the doctor, he is a fool! All doctors are fools! For twenty years they've been telling me that I'm on the point of dying, and I'm stronger than ever I was. Go away, child, and leave this to me!"

He pushed her arm away, set his shoulders back, and marched towards the great door with a light in his eye which boded ill for the waiting Sir William Brag.

* * * * *

Fuming and fretting, Sir William waited.

He was in a fine state of fury and indignation. For weeks he had been negotiating about this castle. He had seen an advertisement in one of the

(Continued on page 19.)

The U·J
DETECTIVE SUPPLEMENT
VOLUME 3.

No. 24. Presented with
the UNION JACK for
the week ending
June 13th, 1925.

TRUTH   JUSTICE

Troublesome Tests

The tests used on unwilling visitors to police stations by police surgeons are troublesome in more ways than one. Not only do the tested usually find them difficult, but the experts who set them are never agreed as to their efficacy.

TO be intoxicated is, in itself, no offence in the eyes of the law, however much it may be in the eyes of decent people.

This being so, any charge involving drunkenness must be supported by the evidence of another, and punishable, offence—as, for instance, "drunk and incapable," or "drunk and disorderly." Moreover, before the charge of drunkenness can be proved in court, the police, who are prepared to back up their allegation of incapability or disorderliness, have to establish without doubt that the accused was in a state of intoxication at the same time.

And, be it observed, this proving of drunkenness is one of the things that form life's little problems for our perplexed police.

Medical science has progressed a long way, and our physicians will now undertake to cure diseases that their grandfathers had never even heard of. But, so far, the doctors have been unable to tell us what it is that causes the simple cold in the head, and, for that matter, are unanimously backward about guaranteeing a cure for one.

So it is with the law. Our medico-legal experts will cheerfully undertake to prove that a murder victim was killed in such-and-such a manner, or that he was not killed at all, but just died. But when it comes to proving definitely that a man is intoxicated or not—well, they haven't found out yet exactly how it's done.

A man may be so far removed from his normal self for the ordinary person to say without hesitation that he is in that condition, but the trouble about it from the police-surgeon's point of view is that he has got to find an answer to the question: "Is he legally drunk?"

To do this, numerous tests have been devised, but the accused who has been gathered in and who is going through his paces at the police-station has the laugh after all, for nobody seems agreed as to what the tests prove, or where the line is to be drawn between drunk and sober.

"I don't think very much importance can be attached to the tests applied," said a physician of St. Paul's Hospital in a recent case that was heard at the Marylebone Court. "I think that mistakes can very easily be made. I have examined many patients who might have been mistakenly passed as being, to a certain degree, drunk."

To which the magistrate, Mr. Wilberforce, asked:

"According to you, the diagnosis of drunkenness is in its infancy?"

"It is a very difficult thing," responded the doctor. "I'm glad I don't have to settle it."

Well may he have been glad. The "British Medical Journal" a short time ago published an article entitled: "The Definition of Drunkenness," in connection with the increasing number of motor-car accidents as a result of intemperance, but even this eminent medical

"It requires the suspect to shut his eyes . . . even Blondin might have boggled at it."

authority had to admit that it couldn't be done.

"Unfortunately, there can never be a clear, scientific definition of drunkenness," it admitted. "Scientific tests can give very little help."

However, for want of a better, the harassed police-surgeon has to go on using them—and very curious some of these attempts to give a plain "Yes" or "No" to the legal question are, too.

One of them is the Rhomburg test, invented presumably by a gentleman of that name. This consists in making the

suspect stand in an upright position, with the eyes closed.

This seems simple enough, and if you try it you will probably find it presents no difficulty; but to the reveller who has looked on the wine when it is red the thing may be less easy of achievement. In one reported case—that in which the hospital physician already quoted gave his opinion—the suspect undergoing the test had to open his eyes and fling out his hands to maintain his balance after fifteen seconds.

Whether that is a fair test is still doubtful, however, for the doctor stated in defence that many people came out of it hopelessly. Sir William H. Willcox, the eminent adviser to the Home Office, asserts that this variety of shut-eye balancing is not a test for alcoholism at all, but for locomotor ataxia.

Another semi-gymnastic feat which it is claimed will decide whether a man is sober or not, goes a step farther than the Rhomburg test. It requires the suspect to shut his eyes and balance himself on one foot. If the first is difficult for some who are admittedly quite sober, what about the one-foot ordeal? Even Blondin might have boggled at it.

Yet another way in which the police-surgeon seeks to establish the proof of control of mind over muscle is that known as "toeing the line."

This merely consists in asking the unsteady one to walk along a chalk line for a distance of six yards or so. Here again the experts are at variance. Sir William Willcox says that a man who can accomplish it should be considered sober, because it is rather difficult to do it in normal circumstances; and a judge at the Old Bailey, whose name was not reported at the time, asserted that it "is the unfairest test in the world—enough to make a man drunk."

Again, Dr. Halstead, who has recently retired from the post of divisional surgeon to the Sutton police after more than twenty years' experience of this kind of work, suggests an improvement on it.

"I have known men walk along a straight line without difficulty," he says, "but they usually fail at a curved one." This added entanglement for the feet of the captured hilarious has proved the undoing of many of them, in the doctor's experience. In an interview reported in the "Evening News," he related an incident concerning one of these occasions, when, as he was drawing his curved line, the reveller remarked: "Now, if

"Picking up a pin from the floor would be somewhat more trying . . ."

you'll only keep your end still, mine will stop wiggling."

Touching the nose with the forefinger of one hand, and then the other, is yet a further trial to convivial gentlemen going through the mill. This also is sometimes complicated by the surgeon demanding it to be done with the eyes closed.

A defending counsel once ridiculed this test as "old-fashioned muddling, popular in the Victorian era, but utterly unsuitable." He declared that he himself had tried it the day before, but was unable to do it even with his eyes open.

After that, telling one's correct name and address and putting one's finger on a spot on the wall—two further tests sometimes employed—would probably come easy. Picking up a pin from the floor would be somewhat more trying, especially if the suspected party were inclined to equatorial plumpness and had thick fingers; and so would rising on the toes and bending the knees. This is demanded of the unwilling visitor to the police-station, but even many people who have no acquaintance with the bottle will agree that it wants doing at the best of times.

Apart from the bodily contortions necessary to prove oneself guiltless of over-indulgence, there are those good old tongue-twister tests: "British Constitution," "Truly rural," "Ragged rascals ran," and "Methodist Episcopal."

When a man replies "Bri'sh Con'shooshon," the inference is obvious.

The divisional surgeon of the Metropolitan "S" Division once gave evidence to the effect that a non-abstainer whom he examined failed dismally at getting his tongue around some of these tricky syllables.

"I asked him to say 'Truly rural' and 'Methodist episcopal,'" he testified, "but he only succeeded in saying 'Toor-a-loor-al' and 'Episticle.'"

The time sense is another obstacle over which the unwary suspect may trip up—and the man who is not suspect, too. The test is in giving a correct answer to a question which involves an estimate of the length of time which has elapsed from, say, the moment the victim entered the station.

Some people are born without the sense of time, and for this reason, apart from the excited condition of even a sober person in the novel situation of being questioned in a police-station,

the test must be regarded as unfair.

In one case a police surgeon gave evidence to the effect that an accused man stated that he had been under detention for twenty minutes, whereas the right time was thirty-five.

"Well," countered Sir Henry Curtis-Bennett, who defended, "how long have you been under cross-examination?"

"A quarter of an hour," replied the doctor.

"You have been timed!" retorted Sir Henry blandly, "and the time is less than ten minutes, but I am quite prepared to give you a certificate that you are sober."

At which there was the usual "laughter in court."

Yet a further variety of the mental-alertness test is the rather uncommon one of asking a man to turn up particulars in a railway time-table. In a case which was tried at the Mansion House police-court the detained one came out of it very well indeed. The police surgeon stated that the accused had stood on one leg and walked the chalk-line very well.

"You then asked him to look up the A.B.C. and tell you the last train to Harwich?" asked the defence.

"Yes; and he did it correctly," admitted the doctor. "He said it was a restaurant train—*and it was.*"

There must have been some mistake on the part of the policeman who gathered this person in.

One more test about exhausts the list —the light test. This is merely the sudden flashings of a light in the eyes

" . . . once had his hand badly bitten by an irresponsible gentleman."

of a man supposed to be intoxicated, and noting the speed with which the pupils contract. This is believed to be a reliable guide by many doctors, but here again authority is at sixes and sevens. The Home Office medical adviser gave it as his opinion that in ordinary cases it is valueless, and that he only attached importance to it in extreme cases of alcoholism.

So, you will perceive, this question as to when is a man drunk or sober is far from being solved. Police surgeons have a far from easy job in the perpetual search for an answer to it, and sometimes they have to put up with more than mere perplexity.

Doctor Halstead of the Sutton Force, previously mentioned, once had his hand badly bitten by an irresponsible gentleman whose peevishness came uppermost at the medico's questions.

It seems then, that the efforts of our scientific medical men of to-day have

failed to find a real definition of drunkenness, to say where the dividing-line exactly lies, just as they have failed to find the cause of a cold in the head.

"The crucial question whether a man's brain is so clouded that he is unfit to be in charge of a car," says the "British Medical Journal" on the subject of drunken motor-drivers, "is one which must be decided by common sense, and scientific tests can give very little help.

"A man who will in convivial surroundings become hilariously drunk may, with the same dose of alcohol in quiet surroundings, merely go to sleep. A skilled musician—who is also a chronic drunkard—may be able to play with considerable skill when he is too drunk to stand.

"Consequently it is very difficult to devise a fair test for drunkenness based on the performance of skilled movements, because the test depends so largely on the degree of practice the individual had had in the subject."

So that's that!

And, by way of conclusion, here is a story of a man who was undoubtedly in an unsteady condition, who failed in a simple colour test, and spent the night in a cell—but got off free the next morning when he interviewed the magistrates, on a technical point.

It happened at Enfield; the time, New Year's Eve. The gentleman had well begun his alcoholic preparations for seeing the Old Year out and, as a result, began to "come over" queer. Seeing a red lamp in the distance, he made for it, intending to consult the doctor whose house it denoted.

The red lamp was, however, in reality a blue one—the lamp outside the police-station. But all lamps were alike to the reveller, and he entered and demanded the services of the doctor. He got them. The police-surgeon attended to him, and certified that he was intoxicated. The patient was escorted to a cell, from the gloom of which he saw the New Year in.

Next morning he appeared before the justices. His intoxication was not denied. But drunkenness in itself, as has been explained, is not a crime, although it is a crime to be in that condition in a public place.

A police-station is not a public place. Nobody will assert that it is. The magistrates wouldn't, anyway. They discharged him, and our reveller started the New Year well by emerging after his night's lodging a free man.

" . . . the lamp outside the police station."

Detective "Luck"

By William Ardouin.

Crime investigators no less than criminals are aided by luck—and the great god Luck doesn't much care on which he bestows the good or on which the bad. There is an element of humour about some of the instances related in this article which surely must have tickled the official mind.

IN the detection of crime luck oftentimes plays no unimportant part, and even where a combination of fortunate circumstances gives the investigator an opportunity of using his powers of observation and deduction, there are in many instances associated with them some element of humour.

Tobacco ash has led to the undoing of a wrongdoer, so also has dust found in the nails and ears of suspected persons. Recently, for instance, in the South of France, an alibi was disproved by the contents of a keyhole.

One of the most amusing instances known to the writer occurred some years ago in the Transvaal. The liquor law as regards providing Kaffirs with liquor is very rigorously applied there, and in cases where an offender has been brought before the Court, on more than one occasion, an indeterminate sentence can be imposed.

The "bootleggers" in that part of the world are particularly wily in dodging the many and ingenious traps which are laid for them by the police. The law specifically lays it down, however, that indisputable, legal proof must be forthcoming on the part of the detectives engaged in a case to prove that liquor has actually been supplied, and for this purpose it has to be tasted, and the evidence of the taster given before the Court.

A suspected but elusive offender had been apprehended. He had been in the habit of supplying "tots" and not bottles, which latter is the more usual method of disposal. He would charge one shilling for a tot of the vilest brandy that the Colony produced, and no evidence was left, after the brandy had been swallowed, to convict him.

The liquor dealer had been traced to an underground cellar in an unsavoury suburb of Johannesburg known as Vrededorp—the well-known Mecca for these dealers in "forked lightning." Here he plied his business with profit to himself and bad heads for his numerous clients which consisted of the dusky population.

The services of a "trap boy" had been enlisted by the police. They are generally in possession of marked money, which in the event of a deal is found on the seller, after arrest. The trap boy had been specially instructed what to do. He was to enter the cellar, purchase a tot and retain the brandy in his mouth for transference to a receptacle held by a detective, who was waiting outside. This was duly done, and the corpus delicti brought into Court as evidence of the supply of liquor.

The case came before the magistrate, and the evidence seemed to be quite in order. Detailed information was given as to the "trapping" of the offender. At the conclusion of the hearing, the magistrate interposed with the remark that no one had actually tasted the liquor, in compliance with the Act, to prove that it actually was spirit.

The detective was certainly disinclined to undertake this unpalatable job, knowing the circumstances under which it had been obtained. The Court was in a dilemma, when one of the spectators, emerging from the rear, volunteered to taste the liquor and give evidence in the interests of justice. His services were welcomed. He entered the box, swallowed the liquor, every particle of it, leaving not a vestige behind—and then, with brazen effrontery, swore that it was water. The case, as can well be supposed, collapsed with surprising suddenness.

The following narrative has about it a touch of ironic humour:

Before the outbreak of the European War, a gold robbery on a large scale had been committed in South Africa. The manner in which it had been carried out indicated ingenuity of a rare order and several bars of gold had been removed practically under the eyes of the officials.

The police had a shrewd idea that an Australian mineralogist of some repute, a prospector who had travelled in different parts of the world, and was known to the police in both hemispheres, had a hand in the robbery. Several days elapsed, and they were no nearer a solution of this baffling mystery. Eventually they obtained a warrant to search the residential quarters of the mineralogist, and upon doing so they found he had flown. But he left behind him some discarded clothing, two or three pairs of old boots and other articles of little value.

ONE of the detectives engaged in the case was a botanical enthusiast. He discovered on the clothing after a careful examination of it, some thorns of "Prickly Pear," which is a wild South African plant. By a process of deduction he endeavoured to account for the appearance of the plant upon the clothing.

In a flash an idea occurred to him, which led to his patrolling adjacent areas of the mine for some days afterwards. Eventually he entered a plantation—in the centre of which was a prickly pear bush. He noticed that the ground in the vicinity of the plant had been recently interfered with. The soil was loose.

With a prospector's knife he dug it up, and found the stolen treasure.

Visions of rapid promotion began to dawn upon this ingenious officer. Not only would the reward for the recovery of the stolen gold be his, but fame was now within his reach. He conveyed the good news to his chief, and received his cheery words of encouragement.

The next day the stolen gold was examined. It was found to be a mixture of copper and brass known to the criminal fraternity of those parts as "schlenter."

The circumstances in which a broken matchbox led to the conviction of an offender and the recovery of stolen property are certainly not without a sprinkling of humour. The thief was masquerading as a gentleman of leisure on a punt on a river at Woking.

With a diplomacy worthy of a better cause, he entertained river parties on a somewhat lavish scale, which led to his being invited to wealthy houses as a privileged guest. On these occasions he would lose no opportunity of taking a careful lay of the premises, and sooner or later, with his boat unsuspectingly moored in the river at night time, he would, single-handed, perform daring and exceptionally clever robberies which defied the authorities for a long time.

He was eventually arrested. A piece of broken matchbox was found in his possession. There was nothing exceptional in this, and certainly nothing of an incriminating nature. But it was borne in mind by the astute officer of the law, who humorously remarked to his colleague that it might bring about a conviction, little dreaming at the time that it would do so. When, subsequently, a room was searched, in which the suspected man was known to reside when not engaged in his punting expeditions, property which was believed to have been stolen was discovered.

BUT instinct led the officer in charge of the case to look for the corresponding portion of the broken matchbox, which strangely enough was discovered in a pocket of one of the jackets hanging in the room. Careful investigation revealed that it was part and parcel of the same box.

Both portions were in the same stained and worn condition; they had evidently at some time or other been immersed in water. Such boxes, too, were retailed by Woking general dealers; they were the kind used in Surrey villages which the river punter used to frequent.

This link of evidence, circumstantial though it was, gradually became incontestable, and incidentally enabled the police to secure a well-merited conviction against this Raffles of the river.

There was a case at the Old Bailey in December last where dust was the silent testimony which gave the deliberate lie to a concocted story of a wholesale burglary of merchandise. It was a case of long-firm swindling, one of the partners entering upon the role of the insurance "bilker." £15,000 worth of goods had been obtained by fictitious means and insured. During one of the Bank Holidays, a policeman noticed the premises open, and apparently in disorder. The principal partner alleged that £5,000 worth of goods had been stolen, but——

The dust on the stock-room shelves, where the goods were reported to have been deposited, disclosed that no merchandise of any description had rested upon those shelves for a period of quite three months. Heavy sentences afterwards passed on all the partners doubtless gave them an opportunity to reflect on the humorous potentialities of dust.

Many years ago the forgery case of "D. S. Windle" created a sensation in the London courts. The ease with which letters of credit for large amounts were repeatedly negotiated made one marvel at the cool and daring nerve of the negotiator, who had the temerity to tell the judge at his trial that the business was only conceived with the object of exposing the laxity of the banks, as any bank manager with the slightest tendency to shrewdness could have seen that, as the name indicated, the whole thing was a "D——Swindle!"

GUARDIANS of the COAST

The old Coastguard Force is no more. But though it has officially ceased to exist as such, the majority of the disbanded coastguards are now serving in the new Coast Watching Force, about whose manifold and often adventurous duties you are told something here.

THE running of contraband—that is, smuggling into the country articles on which the Customs require an import duty to be paid—is a form of crime around which has gathered a glamour of romance which is never likely to be lost.

Heroic conflicts between Coastguards and smugglers have been embodied in countless stories, the readers of which cannot but have a sort of sneaking liking for the glorified villains of the piece, if only out of admiration for the manner in which the smuggling is conducted and the skill and bravery of the Coastguards encountered is parried—sometimes.

Spirits from Holland, lace from France, anything and everything from the four corners of the earth on which a duty is imposed big enough to make the adventure worth while, were at one time brought illicitly into England.

Then it was that the Coastguard Force had livelier days and nights than they know now, and the gusto with which they entered into hand-to-hand conflicts with the contraband runners spotted beaching their boat on some lonely stretch of the coast—as storied in history—leads one to suppose that the brawny men of the Coastguard welcomed the frequent diversions for taking part in which they were paid.

Excitement of the chase was easily roused in their veins. The cut-and-thrust of keen blades, the crack of pistol-shots, and the brisk clubbing of heads when it came to a melee, was a welcome interlude to relieve the tedium of eventless hours of staring out to sea.

But there was a darker side to the picture. The smugglers were men who gambled openly with the Coastguard. To most of them human life was

sacred. They drew the line at the capital crime, and if they were compelled to choose between their own life and liberty and the lives of the coast-watchers, when a chance encounter threw them together, their conduct was based on the principle of self first.

It was none the less murder, of course, when the life of a Coastguard was taken. But the smugglers did not set out with the deliberate intention of that sort of thing. The darker side of the picture is presented by the scoundrels who lured ships to their doom with false lights—the wreckers.

A rock-bound, storm-swept coast, and a moonless and starless night; the captain of a sea-washed vessel straining his eyes for some indication as to where the storm was driving him; the nearest Coastguard patrol some miles away; what a chance for the wreckers to send flashing out lantern rays which should be a perfect imitation of some neighbouring harbour lights!

Hard-over would go the vessel's helm, and the craft would be steered for the false light and the phantom harbour. In a minute or two she would be piled on the rocks, her hull battered and torn, and her crew washed to their doom.

And the object of the wreckers? The pilfering of the vessel's cargo; a profit

made at the expense of no matter how many lives. That, of course, is one of the basest of crimes; it is, indeed, a felony, as also is the removal or masking of any signal or light placed for the guidance of seafarers.

To-day, the wreckers' trade is an impossibility. Wireless has made an end of it. But at the beginning of last century it was a form of crime that was rife. The circumventing of wreckers was one of the chief tasks of the Coastguard.

Other jobs of theirs in connection with salvage and wrecks was, and still is, the rendering of help to distressed vessels, and the saving of life and property from the hungry maw of the sea. When wreckage was washed ashore, its safeguarding from plunder was their responsibility. That, too, is a very infrequent occurrence in these days, but the job is still theirs.

When goods from a wrecked vessel are washed ashore, the Coastguard has to take particular care of it, should the goods be such that an import duty is due to be paid on them. Until the money is forthcoming, the importer is not allowed to claim his wreckage.

Many other duties, besides the protection of the revenue and life-saving, devolved on the Coastguard when the administration of the force was taken over from the Board of Customs by the Admiralty in 1856.

It was the intention of the Admiralty to strengthen the Coastguard so as to use it more efficiently for the defence of our coasts, and also to use it, in the event of war or other national emergency, as a force from which could be drawn a number of men for immediate drafting to the ships of the Navy.

So the members of the Coastguard became not only

The tattered aeroplane wing shown here was found by coastguards on the beach near the ruins of Dunstanburgh Castle, on the Northumbrian coast. Deep mystery surrounds it, for investigation failed to discover whence it came or to whom it belonged.

coast detectives, but reservists for the Navy. In that capacity it became part of their daily routine to maintain communication between vessels of the Fleet and the Admiralty by means of visual signalling—semaphore and helio. Later, telegraphy and telephony largely superseded this manner of communication, and now wireless plays the greater part.

Others of their new duties comprised the recruiting of boys and men for the Navy, and the reporting of the movements of foreign warships off the English coast to the Admiralty.

Now, a Naval Signalling Section does the work for the Admiralty, and the old Coastguard no longer exists as such. In 1923, the old Coastguard passed out of Admiralty hands into the care of the Board of Trade. It lost its time-honoured title, and became the Coast Watching Force.

Many of the miscellaneous jobs performed by the Coastguard are still the concern of the new force, but their main duties consist of the salvage of wrecks, life-saving, the reporting to the nearest Customs officer of any craft approaching the coast about which they may entertain suspicions, and guarding the foreshore.

Every part of the foreshore of Great Britain is, in the first place, the property of the Crown. Though it would take a long time for the stealers of sand and gravel (and they are very numerous to-day along unwatched parts of the coast) to make away with the foreshore completely, serious damage is done in that way. It is all part of the day's work of the Coast Watching Force to round-up these foreshore robbers.

BUT a more serious aspect of the foreshore question is the risk the Crown runs of losing whole chunks of that property—right to claim it as personal property may pass to any ordinary, humble citizen, who can use it, unchallenged, for any personal purpose for a period of sixty years (twenty years in Scotland).

The coast Watching Force, therefore, have to see that no citizen starts to "build up" a title to any of the Crown's foreshore property in this way. Anyone who can produce evidence of having used a part of the shore for some particular personal purpose for the requisite sixty years has as much right at the end of that time to claim it as his own, as though possession had been expressly granted to him by the Crown.

It is not customary to shift the members of the Coastguard (or Coast Watchers) about from beat to beat. Thus the knowledge the patrols gain of some bit of the coast is invaluable. Not only do they become better acquainted in this way with the vessels that commonly pass by, and so are able at once to recognise strange vessels and keep a keen eye on them, but the vagaries of the winds and tides in that quarter become to them an open book.

Many of the Coastguard-stations have been given up to other uses now that the new force is less in numbers, an annual saving to the Exchequer of over £270,000 being effected in this way. The more lonely stations, in most cases, have been kept on, to the great convenience of the local folk, for the Coast Watchers, as part of their manifold duties, do public telegraph business where ordinary post-office facilities do not cover this work.

For that the men, or the members of their families, get a commission of one penny per message, plus the usual delivery fees. Other instances of the handyman nature of the work of coast watching are provided by the services rendered to the Society for the Protection of Wild Fowl.

Trappers and egg-gatherers breaking the law are warned, and if necessary the police are informed. On behalf of Trinity House, the Coast Watchers look out for, and immediately report, the irregularity or failure of lights at sea, shifting buoys, light-vessels broken adrift, and beacons that have gone wrong in any way.

Important observations are also carried out for Lloyd's, to whom reports of casualties at sea are telegraphed. The Air Ministry has a call, too, on the Coast Watchers' services. For them the Watchers operate storm warning signals, look after and take the readings of metereological instruments which the Ministry maintains at certain stations, and regularly chart air and sea temperatures.

The job gets back more closely to the old preventive work in the duties connected with the Government fishery departments. The important Sea Fishery Acts are enforced by the Coast Watchers, fishing vessels that dare to trawl within the three miles limit are "run in," and foreign fishing boats that encroach too near the coast are reported to headquarters.

The carriage of passengers by uncertificated ships is reported, and the regulations concerning the registration of fishing vessels enforced. The landing of dogs and other animals is another matter closely watched by the Coastguard of to-day.

Life-saving being one of the main concerns of the Coast Watchers, the men are invaluable allies of the Royal National Lifeboat Institution. Station officers serve on the local committees of the Institution, and the ratings—or rank-and-file—may be members of the local lifeboat crews.

From the vantage-point of some high eminence the men are usually the first to detect a vessel in distress. At once a message is flashed over the wires to the nearest lifeboat. If that, for any reason, is prevented from putting out to the rescue, neighbouring lifeboat crews are warned.

Ships of the Navy not infrequently do considerable damage to fishing-nets, for which the fishermen put in claims for

damages. The Coast Watchers concerned investigate these claims, and, knowing as they do from their long stay in one district, every local fisherman and his character, are sometimes able to reduce the seriousness of the claims to something more in accordance with the actual damage done.

In view of the reduction in numbers of the new force, some of the work formerly done by the old Coastguard in connection with preventive duties has been shifted to a body run by the Board of Customs and Excise, and known as the Coast Preventive Force, though some of the watching for this department is still done by the Coast Watching Force.

A big difference in the terms of service in the two forces has a bearing on the possibilities of another war. Both are recruited from Naval Pensioners, but the men of the Coast Preventive Force would not be called up for service under naval discipline as would the Coast Watching Force on the outbreak of war.

The Coast Preventive Force would continue its civilian work under the supervision of the Customs Waterguard

Coastguards in full war kit. Signalling with flags was formerly part of their ordinary daily routine, communication thus being maintained between ships of the Fleet and Admiralty headquarters, a method now largely superseded by wireless.

[Photos: Illustrations Bureau.

staff. The Coast Watchers, however, would at once pass from a peace-time organisation to form, along with the Naval Signalling Section, the nucleus of a shore naval force. They would become, that is, a real Coast Guard.

Their duties would be switched back again to what they were during the Great War. It would be a very simple change-over—just the adoption of a special cap-badge, and the Coast Watching Force would be no longer a civilian body, but a combatant force.

How valuable an addition to the Navy in time of emergency such a splendid force of naval pensioners would be is easily realised—all men in the prime of life, skilled in the ways of the sea, and trained to arms.

Recruits to the force are required to be between the ages of forty and forty-five. Length of service in the Coast Watching Force, to secure the gratuity that goes with completion of service, is

(Continued at foot of next page.)

TRUE STORIES OF DEVIL'S ISLAND.

By Marguerite E. Smith and Culpeper Chunn.

No. 6.—The Passing of "The Jackal."

This perfectly true story of the passing of "The Jackal," late official executioner of Devil's Island, is perhaps the most astounding of the many that came to the ears of the writers of this series. This story is told from a personal account of the "Jackal's" closing days, given to the authors by "El Tigre," a former Devil's Islander whose adventures were related recently on pages 162-65. It brings to a fitting conclusion our present series of true stories of the dreadful penal settlement of French Guiana.

A GOOD many of the sensational stories about Devil's Island that find their way into the newspapers from time to time are hard for the average mortal to believe; yet it is no exaggeration to say that few of them are without sufficient basis in fact.

Without first-hand knowledge of this veritable hell on earth, it is difficult to conceive of the frightful conditions that exist there, or of the desperate quality of the criminals for whom it is maintained. One has to visit the colony, or talk with ex-convicts who have been imprisoned there, to appreciate some of the things heard of it.

Of the many astounding stories that have come to the ears of the present writers during the course of their investigation of the colony, perhaps the most astounding of them all is that of the "Jackal" (or the "Chacal"). A personal account of the closing chapters of the life of this remarkable man was given to us by "El Tigre," himself a former Devil's Islander, whose adventures have been set before the readers of the Supplement in a previous article, and a man whose veracity we have no cause to doubt.

The Jackal was an apache. Born in the slums of Paris, as a youth he lived in the sewers of the famed "Gay City" by day, and, with companions as evil as himself, roamed the streets at night, picking pockets, robbing church-boxes, snatching purses, and—who knows?—slitting throats for a livelihood.

Most of his early history, however, is obscure. Up to the time he was deported to Devil's Island, little is known of him beyond the facts stated. Even the nature of the crime for which he was sentenced to French Guiana is a matter of conjecture, for the facts concerning it are buried in the official archives of France.

But it is not with his early history that we are concerned, interesting as it might be, but with his life on Devil's Island, which, in our opinion, affords one of the most dramatic episodes in the history of crime.

Immediately subsequent to his condemnation, alleged to have been for some major offence, the Jackal was deported to Devil's Island on the convict-ship which makes a semi-annual trip to French Guiana. Landed at Cayenne, the port of debarkation, he was transferred with a number of other incorrigibles to Ile St. Joseph, on which island France's most dangerous criminals are confined, and, as is customary in the case of all new prisoners, put immediately to work.

For a period of several years thereafter, he seems to have been lost sight of. Like the other prisoners, he became a cog in a ponderous wheel—a nonentity. Each day, each week, each month, was a continuous round of gruelling work, abominable food, blows and curses from the guards, and the tropical sunlight.

Prisoners condemned to servitude are driven without mercy. The newcomers are given the most arduous work—quarrying stone, chopping trees, and cleaning brush, digging endless ditches, crushing rock—anything that will break their spirits and their backs.

If their conduct warrants it, the survivors are "promoted," and become carpenters, bricklayers, and the like. But few of them live to be so honoured, for the pestilential climate and broiling sun kill most of them off before they can adjust themselves to the new conditions.

The Jackal was one of the fortunate ones. At least, he did not fall victim to the tropical miseries that were his daily portion. On the contrary, he applied himself to his work with such assiduity as to gain the favourable attention of the guards, as a result of which, when the opportunity presented itself, he was relieved of his pick and shovel, and elevated to a position of singular prominence. In fact, like Byron, he woke up in the morning and found himself famous.

As in the case of the other workers, the executioner of the colony is recruited from the ranks. In French Guiana the post is important in more ways than one, for the convict appointed to fill it is given full charge of all executions, which are numerous, and receives a small fee each time one takes place. He is also given a wider range of liberty and more privileges than the other convicts, in consequence of which, the job is much sought after.

As it is compulsory for the convicts to witness the executions, doubtless as a warning of what they might expect if they overstepped themselves too far, the Jackal had more than one occasion, when an ordinary convict, to see the victims pass over the Great Divide.

Like most of the other convicts, he manifested great interest in the gruesome proceedings, in fact, fairly gloated over them, and was often heard to say that the height of his ambition was to step into the shoes of the envied executioner. Thus it came about that, his ambition having been made known to the commandant, upon the death of the incumbent, he was appointed to succeed him as a reward for his good behaviour.

In appearance, the Jackal was well qualified for the office. A slender, slightly emaciated man he was, of medium height, with iridescent brown eyes, a pallid, almost chalky-white complexion, and a low, retreating forehead. Although he had a tigerish streak in him, he seldom exhibited it; ordinarily, he was urbane, spoke in soft, well-modulated tones, and seemed friendly disposed toward everybody. He seemed, in fact, exactly what an executioner should be. Inwardly as well as outwardly, he was born to the purpose. Had he not been, this story would never have been written.

As in France, convicts condemned to death on Devil's Island pay the penalty for their crimes on the guillotine. Still following the customs of the parent country, all executions take place in public, the guillotine being so placed that none of the proceedings will be missed by the onlookers. An exhibition of the kind at Devil's Island is attended by practically everyone in the colony, from the officials and guards to the prisoners.

Once installed in his new office, the Jackal took to his new duties like a duck takes to water. Indeed, since Dame Guillotine was first made the official instrument of death, it is doubtful if, either in France or French Guiana, she ever had such a lover as was he.

During his regime, which, because of his proficiency, lasted for several years, or up to the time of his own amazing death, as far as it was possible for him

---

(Continued from previous page.)

fifteen years, though it is possible for a fit man who wishes to "carry on" at the expiration of that time to serve for an additional five years.

The pay of the coast detectives is not on a sumptuous scale; though, of course, all the men are already in receipt of a naval pension. The rates of pay, leaving out of account the bonus calculated according to the Civil Service scale, is for Coast Watchers twenty-seven shillings a week, rising by annual increases of one shilling to thirty-four shillings per week.

Assistant superintendents start at thirty-five shillings a week, rising to thirty-eight. Superintendents start at £160 a year and rise to £225. Inspectors commence with £350 a year, with annual rises of £15 a year until £420 a year is reached.

Unfurnished housing accommodation is also provided for all ranks, plus free uniform. Where the conditions of service are unusually hard, such as where the look-out point is a long way from where the men are housed, or where the nearest town is miles away, extra pay is granted as compensation for the extra discomfort and inconvenience.

When the axe of economy began to fall heavily on public departments at the conclusion of the Great War, the possibility was considered of still further

reducing the numbers of the then existing Coastguard, and making shift as far as possible with civilians who would maintain a watch on a part-time basis.

Fortunately, this idea came to nothing. On a previous occasion it had been tried by the Board of Trade and found to be an impracticable system.

The ability to resort to physical force, where necessary, might not always be possessed by the part-time local watcher, and through fear for his skin, or from dishonest motives, he might cast a blind eye on the pillagers of wrecks and other law-breakers whom the handy naval man in uniform—the coast detective par excellence—now forcibly, or merely by his presence, scares away.

to do so, he dignified his work, and injected into it an element of humaneness it had never before achieved.

The guillotine in use at that time was a bunglesome affair, consisting, like all such machines, of two upright posts surmounted by a cross-beam, and grooved so as to guide an oblique-edged knife. Pulled up to the cross-beam by a cord, the heavily-weighted knife descended with great force when the cord was released.

Despite the crudity of his machine, the Jackal laboured over it as faithfully and contentedly as the average mother labours over her first-born. Never a day went by, whether the guillotine was in use or not, that he did not oil the machinery and polish the blade that decapitated his victims.

He not only took an extraordinary pride in his work, he really loved it, had an almost insane passion for it, in fact. He was never so happy as when called upon to put his machine to the test. An execution that went smoothly —as most of those at which he officiated did—gave him the most intense satisfaction, for he considered his work an art and himself an artist, with few, if any, equals.

"I am proficient in my work because I am wedded to it," he was once heard to say. "Any work, no matter what it is, can be made an art if one really loves it. This is particularly true of the work of the guillotineer. To decapitate a human being in the proper manner calls for the exquisite touch. No victim of mine has ever been made to suffer because of bunglesome work. It is my business to see that every prisoner condemned to the guillotine dies instantaneously and painlessly, and, understanding my business, I do it well.

"Even that M. Deibler, the official executioner for the whole of France, is not so good as am I. How can he be, when he does not even know his victims? With me it is different. I am personally acquainted with all of the miserables I am called upon to behead, and I do by them as I would have them do by me."

NOR was he speaking idly. On terms of social equality with his victims, and, in fact, numbering many of them among his friends, he had a personal interest in his work, and did his best to please the wretches condemned to kiss Dame Guillotine.

On the day preceding an execution he would visit the cell of the man whose life he had been ordered to take, amicably explain the fine points of his art to him, and tell him exactly what was expected of him if he wished to die gracefully, quickly, bravely, and without pain.

He would then kiss the doomed man on both cheeks, wish him Godspeed on his journey into the unknown, and, with tears in his eyes, pledge himself to expedite matters and try to give the other no cause to find fault with the manner in which he started him on his way. Nor did he ever fail to do his best to make his pledge good.

An execution on Devil's Island, to a man of normal feeling, at any rate, is probably more interesting to write about than to witness. Several hours before an execution was to take place, the Jackal, with much ceremony, started to work on his machine to get it in readiness for the great event.

After cleaning and oiling the machinery with the same degree of care a jeweller might take with a delicately adjusted watch, he whetted the knife to a razor-edge and put the wicker basket in the proper place to catch the victim's head.

The time for the affair having arrived, the Jackal took his place behind the guillotine, and the convicts, most of them shackled, were led from their cells and grouped in advantageous positions to witness the death of their brother in misfortune.

Surrounded by a ring of flashing bayonets, the heavily ironed victim was then brought from the death-house to the guillotine, where the eager, but dignified, executioner and numerous officials awaited him. Events thereafter, for a space of several moments, moved rapidly.

With swift, but sure fingers the Jackal opened the condemned man's shirt at the throat and rolled it away from the neck. Following a few other brief preliminaries, he was then courteously requested by the Jackal to assume the necessary position and submit to being strapped on the plank.

If he complied, he was assisted by the Jackal, and shown every consideration consistent with the latter's duties. If he resisted, he was forced, with the butts of the guards' guns, if necessary, to do the executioner's bidding. When all was ready, the Jackal would glance swiftly at the multitude of witnesses, as

---

THE DOOM OF DEVIL'S ISLAND!

THE ghastly horrors of the convict settlements of French Guiana about which we have been reading in this and preceding articles are now, happily, to be swept away for ever.

With the help of M. Renault, Minister of Justice, and M. Daladier, Minister of the Colonies, this great reform is being tackled, and arrangements are being made for the return of the prisoners to France, and their lodging in the prisons of Paris.

And here, back once more in the land they never hoped to see again, the unfortunates of Devil's Isle may hope for treatment more humane, and for release at last to their own folk, with the unforgettable memories of the sun-baked settlements but a nightmare of the past.

---

if seeking their approval or gauging their temper, and give the cord a quick pull.

Brutality, or even force, he positively refused to employ. His course of procedure was as different to that of most other French executioners—that of the infamous M. Samson, for instance, as night is from day. Skill, not brutality, he often declared, was the guillotineer's chief requisite.

If a victim balked at the critical moment, and tried to bolt or fight, the Jackal would step quietly to one side, fold his arms, and leave the handling of the unruly one to the guards. It was his business to behead his unfortunate friends and acquaintances, he said, not to fight them. If the officials ordained that one of them must die, he considered that he was doing him a real service by making his death as swift and painless as possible; but beyond that he refused to go.

In his personal relations with the prisoners, however, he seemed to hold opposite views, for at the very height of his professional career, he forsook his duties and the cloak of urbane restraint he wrapped himself in while performing them, long enough to settle in an arbitrary manner a little private affair of his own. That is to say, he deliberately and, according to the judges,

with malice aforethought, murdered another prisoner.

According to El Tigre, who knew the Jackal intimately, the trouble between the executioner and the victim of his wrath, one Dubray, dated back for several years.

DUBRAY, it seems, had aspired to the office of executioner as well as the Jackal, and upon the death of the latter's predecessor put in a bid for it. His application, however, was rejected, and the Jackal selected to fill the vacancy, as has been seen.

Incensed, Dubray then did everything in his power to discredit his successful rival in the hope of replacing him. But the new guillotineer had the confidence of the authorities, and could not be dislodged. Realising this, finally Dubray decided that the only way to remove him was to murder him. He therefore secured poison, in some manner not stated, and put it in the other's food; but the bitter taste warned the Jackal in time, and he did not partake of it.

Suspecting Dubray, he waited until dinner was over, and then, without saying anything to anybody, secreted a club in his blouse. That night, when the prisoners went in to supper, he called Dubray to account, wrung a confession from him, and, without warning, crashed in his head.

In the circumstances, the Jackal would seem to have been not without some justification for his act; but in French Guiana the laws, especially in their application to the convicts, are harsh and inflexible. Placed on trial for his life, the Jackal pleaded guilty to murder, and was promptly condemned to death—and to death on the very machine that was the pride of his heart and the apple of his eye!

The bitter irony of it! He, the peerless executioner, condemned to die on his own guillotine! Yet if the Jackal was conscious of the scurviness of the trick Fate had played on him, he gave no evidence of it. On the contrary, he arose to the occasion in the most astounding manner, and proved himself to be the master-artist he had always professed himself to be.

Accepting his condemnation with characteristic philosophy, he begged the pardon of the judges for putting them to so much trouble, and, with proper humility, capped the climax by asking permission to officiate at his execution!

Was such a request ever made before? What was the Jackal's motive? Was he prompted by sheer bravado? Was he trying to show his supreme contempt of Fate? Or did the grim humour of the thing appeal to him? Whatever it was, the permission he asked for was, still stranger to relate, granted him. Taking into account his good conduct, the officials decided that if it would give him any satisfaction to chop off his own head, the least that they could do for him was to see that that satisfaction was not denied him. Why not, forsooth? The Jackal was an executioner; why not let him execute himself?

Just what the Jackal really thought about the matter no one, of course, will ever know. Outwardly he was supremely indifferent. True, in his talks with the chaplain and guards he manifested some interest in the technicalities of his approaching execution; but it was impersonal and professional, and no more than he would have manifested in the approaching execution of anyone else.

Immured in a dark, four-by-six cell, with heavy iron balls riveted to his legs, and the upper part of his body secured by a series of straps and iron braces that

U.J. No. 1,131.
Page 18.

made it impossible for him to move, his chief regret seemed to be, not that he was to die, but that someone less skilful and with less exalted ideals than himself would fall heir to his beloved guillotine.

"Is it not the height of folly to suppress such an artist as I am when there are only fools and bunglers to take my place?" he was heard to lament. "Ah, monsieur, what have I done to merit such treatment as this? True, they say I murdered a cochon with a billet of wood. But what if I did? Is not the world better off with such as he in the ground? Diable! Had I not beat out his brains, would he not have been dead anyway? Oui! He would have been condemned to death for trying to murder me, and I would have been given a handful of francs for cutting off his head!

"Ah, it is strange! Is it not, monsieur? Because I knocked off his head, instead of cutting it off, I must die like a common assassin. Helas! I fear I am too ignorant to perceive the justice of this, but if it pleases messieurs les juges, who am I to find fault? My only fear is that my successor will be an ass, and that the office of executioner will sink to the level of common butchery from which I raised it. I am glad I shall not live to see that day, monsieur!

"But, after all, perhaps the grandeur of my death will so impress him as to make him realise the greatness of his office. Certainly, monsieur, I shall do my utmost to set him an impressive example, and show him how properly to behead a man!"

And do his utmost he certainly did. On the morning that he was to die, several hours prior to the time for his execution, the iron balls and strait-jacket that secured him were stricken off, and, after a hearty breakfast, he was led to the guillotine and permitted to oil and adjust the machinery and polish the knife.

Chatting amicably with the guards, he went about his task cheerfully, even whistling a snatch of ribald song occasionally, and remarking that the next man condemned to die on the guillotine would not be so fortunate as he, since his successor would probably be a clumsy fellow and make a mess of his first job.

Hard to satisfy as he was, on this particular morning, the guillotine was finally got in readiness. The Jackal himself admitted that it had never before worked so smoothly. Bowing to the official in charge, he signified his readiness to proceed, and a two-deep cordon of guards was thrown around the death machine in honour of the occasion.

The prisoners, who had been eagerly looking forward to the event for several days, were then led from their cells, and lined up behind the guard of honour. With one hand on one of the uprights and the other on his hip, the Jackal stood in his usual place behind the guillotine and smilingly watched them, occasionally nodding to an acquaintance, and once calling out a cheerful greeting to a pal.

At a word from the master of ceremonies he snapped to attention, and slowly and deliberately hoisted the knife to the top of the guides. Securing the cord, he unfastened his shirt, tucked his collar out of the way, and moved the basket that was to catch his head the fraction of an inch nearer to the machine.

One last, lingering glance he cast around him, then took up his position on the plank, which was swung level into position, and deliberately reached for the cord that was to bring the blade of death rushing down upon him. Above the excited whispering of the witnesses could be heard the drone of the priest:
"I am the resurrection and the life, saith the Lord."

A gentle sigh escaped the Jackal, perhaps at the thought that he was touching for the last time the machine he loved so well; then, his farewell given, he gave the cord the same quick pull that had launched so many others into the mystery of eternity.

Thus died the Jackal, late official executioner of Devil's Island. Like all of his executions, his last one was a complete success. Whatever may be said of the manner of it, it cannot be said that it lacked originality. If nothing more, the Jackal at least has the distinction of dying as perhaps no other man ever died before. Sentenced to death, he, in his capacity of official executioner, carried the sentence into effect with the sanction and approval of the authorities, and to their, as well as to his own, entire satisfaction.

Criminal and convict as he was, spawn of the Parisian gutters, he made an art of his duty, and faced death as unflinchingly as any hero to whose memory a monument may stand.

To-day his body lies in some obscure, unnamed grave under the brazen sun of that exile land, unhonoured and unsung. The victim of misguided youth and tortured age—a death-dealing fanatic, a merciful executioner, or what?

A man, at least, who faced death firmly in a strange cause.

THE END.

POLICE OF OTHER CLIMES.
No. 7.

A German Policeman.
[*Photo: Topical.*]

Law Talks.—No. 24.

The Law of "Infants."

UNTIL a youth reaches the age of twenty-one, he is, in the eyes of the law, an infant or minor.

Big things hang on the attainment of a boy's majority. Not only do his privileges and responsibilities alter when he celebrates his twenty-first birthday and becomes "of age," but he stands in a very different position from then onward in regard to punishment if he breaks the law.

But a boy does not have to live exactly twenty-one years before becoming of age and assuming the legal status of a man. His birthday is perhaps due for celebration on the last day of the year, the actual time of his birth being a few minutes previous to midnight. As, however, portions of days are not counted, at least for the purposes of the law, he becomes of age the moment after midnight strikes the previous night.

Until that time arrives, the infant remains hedged about by all kinds of restrictions, all of them for his own good. Up to the age of seven years, a youngster is deemed in English law to be incapable of committing a crime—or, rather, he cannot be punished as an adult criminal would be.

Between that age and fourteen years, the youthful wrongdoer stands his trial in court, and is perhaps convicted. His punishment, however, depends entirely on the opinion of the jury, on whom the decision rests, as to whether the young prisoner realised what his action meant when he broke the law. If the jury finds there is no knowledge of wrongdoing, then punishment is less severe than would be the case in ordinary circumstances.

A minor cannot be tricked into borrowing money on his written promise to repay when he comes of age; such a contract does not stand good at law. But an adult who enters into any agreement or contract with a minor is bound to honour it.

An employee who is still an infant may agree to an arrangement whereby he binds himself to the service of his employer for a certain wage and period. But if, in the agreement, there is a clause which is obviously unfair to the employee—such as the employer reserving to himself the right to discharge him when he has a mind to—the agreement is void. The law refuses to recognise it.

An infant who wishes to bring an action against someone may do so through a friend, but not in his own name, though he can be sued direct. He would have to make his defence in the same way—through his father or guardian or anyone specially appointed as his representative.

The law recognises the minor's responsibility no less than the adult's when a wrong is done. For example, there can be quoted the case of the youth who hired a horse for a day's riding on the condition that it was used for riding only. He loaned the animal to a friend, who ignored the stipulation and tried the horse over a fence. The animal came a cropper and hurt itself so badly that it had to be shot.

By his action in lending the hired horse, the minor broke the agreement and rendered himself liable to the owner as though he had borrowed the animal without asking. So the law is not all on the side of the minor.

The PAUPER of PENGARTH CASTLE

(Continued from page 10.)

papers, and had made inquiries. And although he had never seen the interior, this wasn't really necessary. For Pengarth Castle was one of the most historic piles in the West of England.

And, what was more to Sir William's liking, it was in the market cheap. The price of the castle and the magnificent park land struck the woollens merchant as being ridiculously low. He had interviewed Mr. Simon Slingsby, and he had heard all about Lord Pengarth's die-hard attitude.

And as it was not necessary to deal direct with his lordship, the entire transaction had been completed between himself and Mr. Slingsby. On the previous day the final deeds had been signed and witnessed, and the final cheque paid.

Pengarth Castle and Pengarth Park now belonged to Sir William Brag in their entirety. He was gazing upon his own domain, and the door of the castle was barred against him, and he could gain no admittance. The situation was not only irritating, but positively ridiculous.

This was no villa, a small house among hundreds of others. Pengarth was a veritable fortress, with oaken doors and iron bars that had withstood many a siege. If the earl was obstinate enough, he could withstand any invasion or attack short of artillery.

But Sir William refused to admit this possibility. A few private words with his lordship, and the latter would realise his position, and relinquish the castle.

Possibly there was a misunderstanding, and that could be cleared up in a very short time. Sir William paled as he thought of the other alternative. Why, the earl might resist for weeks—he might refuse to get out, even if the police were brought! It would require a regiment to take the castle by storm.

At this alarming point in his thoughts, Sir William observed the figure of Lord Pengarth behind the bars of the wicket gate. Sir William was rather startled. Seldom had he seen such a fierce, grim visage.

"Well, sir?" demanded the earl tensely.

"Er—really!" protested Sir William, confused. "If you will give instructions for the door to be opened, so that I may talk in private——"

"I have no private business with interlopers, sir!" thundered Lord Pengarth. "Leave this property at once, and never return! Do you hear me? The Pengarths have never surrendered, and never will!"

Sir William felt more helpless than ever.

"But—but this is preposterous!" he broke out. "Do you realise, Lord Pengarth, that I have bought this castle?"

His lordship laughed.

"I don't care if you have bought the whole of England!" he replied. "This is my home—the home of my ancestors—and no power on earth will make me shift from it! So you can go back to that rat, Simon Slingsby, and obtain what consolation you may!"

Sir William lost all control of himself.

"You're mad!" he shouted furiously. "I demand admittance! Good heavens! Do you think I have paid tens of thousands of pounds for nothing? This is my property, and I demand instant admittance! What is more, Lord Pengarth, I shall take full means to obtain redress for this extraordinary conduct!"

The Earl of Pengarth quivered.

"Go!" he thundered. "Good gad! Do you imagine that I will allow a man of your type to walk these ancient halls? Never, sir! I don't care what you have paid, and I don't care what you do! While I live, you will never cross this threshold!"

"I will have you ejected by force!" yelled Sir William.

"Get out, before I shoot you!" retorted the earl. "Jelks—Jelks! Bring that gun! By gad, sir, I mean it! I'll give you two minutes to get out of sight! Jelks, you old rogue! Where's that gun?"

"Coming, sir!" came the voice of the scared butler.

Sir William went a greyish colour. There was something about Lord Pengarth's attitude which meant grim business. And the prospect of being peppered at close quarters with a shot-gun was not exactly enticing.

"You'll hear more about this!" gasped Sir William frantically.

He bolted to his car like a rabbit, and leapt in.

"Drive away, Parker!" he gasped. "Drive to Launceston—Mr. Slingsby's house! And hurry! This old man's mad—raving mad!"

"Yes, sir," said the chauffeur breathlessly.

He went round the drive, and he had hardly taken the car a hundred yards before a shattering report came from the main door of the castle. A cloud of smoke hovered there. And Sir William went positively white.

The Earl of Pengarth had fired a shot into the air as an evidence of his determination. And Sir William drove off to Launceston with a sensation of unreality.

He had bought Pengarth Castle, but that was all it amounted to. Buying the place, and taking possession, were two entirely different things!

THE SEVENTH CHAPTER.
The Situation is Entertaining.

"LOOKS more like a ruin than an inhabited castle, guv'nor," remarked Tinker interestedly. "I say, it strikes me we've been hoaxed! Somebody has been having a lark, sir."

Sexton Blake shook his head.

"I think not, Tinker," he replied. "I will admit that Pengarth Castle has a deserted, dilapidated air, but I know for a fact that the earl lives here with his daughter. They are greatly impoverished, and Lord Pengarth is more or less of a hermit."

They had turned the bend in the drive, and were just driving up to the main frontage of the castle. Arriving in Launceston early, they had breakfasted, and Blake had easily hired a motor-car.

Pengarth Castle was looking picturesque in the sunshine. But no blue sky and no sunlight could disguise the pitiful air of neglect. Both Blake and Tinker regarded the old pile with interest as they drove up.

On the road from Launceston they had passed a big limousine, and had caught sight of a furious-looking man in the interior. Both had wondered if this stranger had just come from the castle. And they had received confirmation almost at once, for the neglected drive showed distinct traces of motor-car tracks.

Blake shut off his engine as they arrived opposite the moss-grown steps. Then they walked up, and Blake pulled the heavy bell. Dimly, they heard the jangling far away.

"I believe the place is ruined, guv'nor," murmured Tinker. "It seems impossible that anybody can live here. There's not a soul about——"

The little wicket opened, and the face of Jelks appeared.

"Mr. Blake!" he ejaculated hoarsely.

Jelks was trembling with excitement. At the very first glimpse, he recognised the famous detective. That five-year-old incident came back to him with perfect clarity. It was this gentleman who had assisted him to his feet, after he had fallen over a loosened stair-rod.

"You are Jelks, I take it?" said Sexton Blake. "I seem to remember your face, Jelks. It was you who sent me a telegram——"

"Yes, sir—yes!" whispered the butler. "There is a gentleman staying here who calls himself by your name! He's imposing on the master, and I'm glad you've come, sir! I'm mortal glad!"

"Well, Jelks, don't you think it would be a good idea to open the door?" asked Blake smoothly. "Surely it is not necessary to talk through this wicket?"

"No, sir—beg pardon, sir!" muttered Jelks. "But I'm afraid of his lordship, sir! I've got strict orders to admit nobody. So I'd be obliged, sir, if you'd keep as quiet as mice! The young gentleman is a friend of yours, sir?"

"I'm Mr. Blake's assistant," said Tinker. "What's the idea of this mystery? Anybody might think we were planning to burgle the place, or something!"

Stealthily, Jelks withdrew the bolts, and Blake gave Tinker a warning glance. When the great door opened, they stole silently in. And Jelks set the bolts once more, and then led the way to a narrow archway in the quaint old lobby.

Instead of taking the new arrivals straight into the hall, he led them down a narrow, solemn passage, and by a roundabout route into a cold, musty-smelling apartment, which had not been used for years.

"We can talk here, sir," said Jelks, resuming his normal voice. "Nobody can hear, and I'm relieved that the master doesn't know yet. There's been rare happenin's this morning, sir—only just before you came, too!"

And, in a somewhat scared voice, Jelks gave a brief account of Sir William Brag 's visit, and the outcome of it.

"By jingo, our worthy host appears to be a bit of a firebrand!" remarked Tinker, as he digested the story. "Sent him off, and fired a shot after him—eh? That's the real old-fashioned way, guv'nor! We shall have to be careful about meeting old Pengarth!"

"That ye will, sir, an' no mistake!" agreed Jelks earnestly. "Like as not, his lordship will turn ye out befor' ye can have time to explain! This other gent has wormed his way into the master's confidences, an' they're like brothers! The queerest thing I ever saw, sir! But, then, this other gent saved my Lady Betty's life, an' that makes a real difference!"

Sexton Blake was thoughtful for a few moments. This stranger had gained admittance to the castle by a mere chance, it seemed. Rendering a service to Lady Betty, he had brought her home, and had naturally been asked to stay. But it was a poser why he had given his name as "Sexton Blake." The man was obviously up to some mischief, or he would never have adopted such a subterfuge.

Blake did not quite understand the affair of Sir William Brag. He thought the butler had got hold of it wrong. If Sir William was really in possession of the title-deeds, Lord Pengarth would never refuse him admittance. It was unthinkable. But Sexton Blake didn't know Lord Pengarth yet.

"As far as you know, we have been admitted without anybody knowing?" he asked.

"Yes, sir! The master and the other gentleman are in the library, an' the windows overlook the north wing," explained Jelks. "My lady is upstairs, so I don't think your arrival is known yet."

"I would like to get a glimpse of this masquerader without his knowing it, if I could," said Blake thoughtfully. "It would be a big help——"

"Ay, sir, I've got it!" interrupted Jelks quickly. "I never thought of it before! There is a way, sure enough!"

Without explaining he led the way out of the apartment, and they went along a hollow-sounding paved passage with an arched roof. After one or two turns Jelks led the way through a tiny slit of a stone doorway. They were now in almost total darkness. And the passage which Jelks walked along was extremely narrow.

"This way, sir!" he whispered. "Just ye look here, an' you'll see right into the library. At one time o' day this was a secret passage, but his lordship had it opened years ago."

He fumbled in the darkness and slid something back along the wall at about the height of his shoulders. Then, drawing Sexton Blake further along, he whispered for him to look.

Blake found himself opposite a round kind of spy-hole as big as a tea-saucer. He was looking straight into Lord Pengarth's library. And at the very first glance Blake caught his breath in sharply.

For he was looking straight at Waldo, the Wonder-Man!

Waldo was taking his ease on a soft lounge, and indulging in a cigar. Lord Pengarth was standing with his back to the fireplace, and he was grimly declaring that he would never give way. He liked this visitor of his—this Blake. He was a man after his own heart!

For Waldo had been urging Lord Pengarth on from the very start, and was still doing so. After his daughter's continuous advice that they should quietly vacate the castle, Waldo's attitude of defiance was agreeable.

Neither of the men was aware of a change in the appearance of the wall. The spy-hole was high in the library wall, and cunningly concealed at the base of some ornamental moulding. And so, although the hole was so big, only the sharpest of sharp eyes could have detected it from the library.

Blake closed the little shutter, and he and Jelks and Tinker made their way out of the gloomy passage.

"Well, sir—well?" asked Jelks tensely.

"You acted with great discretion in telegraphing me last night, Jelks," said Sexton Blake quietly. "The man in Lord Pengarth's company is a famous criminal named Rupert Waldo."

Tinker clutched at the air.

"Waldo!" he gasped excitedly.

"There is no necessity to go into those melodramatic gestures, Tinker," said Blake. "I am very glad we came. I cannot possibly imagine what Waldo's game can be, but there is no question of its crookedness."

"The—the man is a criminal, sir?"

asked Jelks in alarm. "May the saints save us! What can he be doing here? An' he savin' m'lady's life, too! I don't believe it, sir! There's trickery——"

"No, Jelks, I can quite believe that Waldo saved Lady Betty's life in the way you have described," said Sexton Blake. "Although a dangerous criminal, he has a gallant side to his character. Waldo, indeed, is a most surprising man. And the situation is rather awkward. We cannot deal with him as we would with any ordinary malefactor."

"That's a fact, sir!" agreed Tinker. "With his terrific strength and his monkey tricks he can evade us without any trouble. And even if we brought a dozen policemen here, he'd still escape us!"

Blake frowned.

"For once, Tinker, you have not exaggerated," he said thoughtfully. "Your statement sounds absurd, but it happens to be the truth. I think I shall face Waldo at once and ask him what his game is. There is no sense in letting this deception go on."

"You'll take the bull by the horns, sir?" asked Tinker eagerly.

"Yes, it is the better way."

Blake had decided on brisk action. He believed that Waldo was merely pandering to his craving for the unusual. He could hope to gain nothing by staying in this poverty-stricken castle. And, obviously, he had given the false name in order to obtain Lord Pengarth's confidence. It was high time that his lordship was undeceived.

"Jelks, you will please go into the library and announce us in the formal manner—Mr. Blake and Mr. Tinker," said the detective. "You can then leave the rest to me."

"But the master gave orders, sir——"

"I will take all responsibility," interrupted Blake.

There was something about his manner which Jelks could not stand up against. Although agitated and worried, he led the way to the library, knocked at the door, and entered.

"If you please, my lord— " he began.

"Well?" barked Lord Pengarth, looking across the quaint, old-fashioned apartment. "What is it you want, Jelks? I distinctly told you not to bother me! Bless my soul, I can't have five minutes alone without an interruption from you! What do you want, sir?"

"Mr. Blake, my lord, and Mr. Tinker!" announced Jelks, with a kind of gasp.

Sexton Blake and Tinker entered quickly, and Lord Pengarth stared in anger and amazement. To Tinker's astonishment Rupert Waldo remained at his ease on the lounge. A genial smile played round his mouth.

"Splendid!" he murmured. "If there was one thing required to make the situation entertaining that one thing has happened. Blake, old man, how are you? Haven't seen you for weeks!"

The Wonder-Man's cool assurance was at his service on the flash. He rose leisurely, and for a moment he and Blake eyed one another.

"What are you doing here, Waldo?" demanded Blake quietly.

"Confound it, what's all this business?" roared Lord Pengarth, breaking in. "And who, sir, are you? And what do you mean by addressing Mr. Blake as Waldo? Jelks, didn't I tell you to admit nobody——"

"One moment, Lord Pengarth—please!" interrupted Waldo smoothly. "I must confess to a little deception. I had hoped that it would continue longer, but no matter. In one way the

situation has increased the interest, for it is always gratifying to meet old friends."

"I don't understand you, sir!" growled the earl.

"But you will, sir—you will!" said Waldo patiently. "I offer you my humble apologies. I am not Mr. Sexton Blake, as I intimated—for Mr. Sexton Blake now stands before you, accompanied by his brilliant young assistant, Tinker. Are they not a handsome pair?"

Lord Pengarth spluttered.

"Have you gone mad, sir?" he demanded, glaring.

"I am merely pointing out that I am not everything I have appeared to be," replied Waldo gracefully. "The time has arrived for me to make my bow and depart in peace. So, Lord Pengarth, with your permission—and yours, Blake—I will leave the stage. Good-morning, gentlemen! It is quite possible that we shall soon meet again!"

He bowed, smiled, and strolled leisurely out of the library.

———

THE EIGHTH CHAPTER.
Advice on Both Sides.

SEXTON BLAKE had made no attempt to hinder Waldo's departure, for the simple reason that any such attempt would have been foredoomed to failure. He, Tinker, Lord Pengarth, and Jelks, with their united efforts, could not have stopped Waldo from going, and he knew it.

For the Wonder-Man had earned his name by reason of his amazing strength and cat-like agility. He had been known to outwit a dozen detectives, even at close quarters. It was far better to let him walk out unhindered, and thus avert a scene—for he would have walked out, in any case.

Everybody was startled—at least, Lord Pengarth and Jelks were. They watched Waldo go rather blankly. He passed through the doorway and completely vanished. Even Lady Betty, who came in a moment later, had seen no sign of the Wonder-Man.

"Oh!" she exclaimed as she entered. "I am sorry! I did not know there were visitors——"

"Jelks!" thundered Lord Pengarth, recovering himself. "Jelks, go out and bring Mr. Blake back at once! I don't know what he means by that extraordinary story of his!"

"The man was speaking the truth, Lord Pengarth," interrupted Blake. "He is Waldo, a criminal, and I am Sexton Blake. If any doubt lingers in your mind with regard to that point I can prove my identity at once."

"Prove nothing, sir!" roared the earl. "Jelks, what the devil do you mean by admitting these people? More of Slingsby's spies? The sheriff, probably, with a warrant to have me ejected. You infernal fool, didn't I tell you——"

"It's Mr. Blake, sir!" exclaimed Jelks, scared. "I—I knew the other gentleman wasn't Mr. Blake, and I sent off a telegram."

"Wh-at!" ejaculated Lord Pengarth. "Do you mean to stand there, man, and tell me that you sent for this gentleman?"

"Yes, my lord. I—I——"

"There is really no necessity for this

confusion," interrupted Blake smoothly. "It can be explained in a few words. The situation is quite simple."

And, in his own level manner, Blake put the facts in a nutshell. Even Lord Pengarth was compelled to quieten down under the famous detective's calm, dignified manner. But even though Lord Pengarth was convinced, he didn't seem to like the change.

"We have no intention of intruding, Lord Pengarth, but it was necessary for us to come down in order to ascertain the facts," concluded Blake. "I must warn you, also, that Waldo is a dangerous man, although I do not fancy he was engaged in any criminal work under your roof."

"I should think not, sir, I should think not!" growled his lordship. "A fine fellow! I cannot doubt your word, although I am still astonished. But this Waldo, whatever you say about him, is a gentleman! You hear me, sir—a thorough gentleman!"

"Oh, father, you must be wrong!" exclaimed Lady Betty. "Mr. Blake tells us that the man is a criminal."

"I can't help what Mr. Blake tells us!" grunted Lord Pengarth. "The man's gone, and I'm infernally sorry. I liked him. A man after my own heart. Plenty of strength and determination."

He turned to Blake coldly.

"Don't think me inhospitable, sir, but you will oblige me by leaving these premises at the earliest possible moment," he said, with a defiant glare. "You gained admittance without my knowledge, and now you will please me if you take your departure."

Sexton Blake bowed.

"As you wish, Lord Pengarth," he replied quietly.

"Jelks," snapped the earl, "show the gentlemen out! And remember, open the door to nobody! I won't have my instructions defied!"

He turned his back and fumed. Lady Betty was greatly distressed, and hardly knew what to do.

Sexton Blake and Tinker left the library, and walked out into the big hall.

"Well, this is a rummy business, sir," murmured Tinker. "First we meet Waldo, and then we're politely kicked out! I can't say I think much of Lord Pengarth as a host. I've known more hospitable men."

"His lordship is a bit of a character," replied Blake. "I have never met him before, but I have heard quite a lot about him. His action in no way surprises me. We can do nothing but go."

"And what about Waldo?"

"I hardly know what to do," admitted Sexton Blake thoughtfully. "To attempt any search for him would be a mere waste of time. As we have good reason to know, he is as elusive as a will-o'-the-wisp. But I would give a great deal to know what his exact game is."

Tinker smiled.

"That's all right, sir; you'll know," he said confidently. "I can't imagine you leaving this district without getting to the root of things."

Lady Betty Hamilton-Page approached Sexton Blake and Tinker before they could take their departure. She was looking flushed and rather distressed. Her father's brusque behaviour was always a worry to her.

"Please don't go, Mr. Blake!" she said quickly. "You mustn't take any notice of my father. He doesn't mean to be rude. It's only his way."

"So I gather," said Blake, smiling. "But I am afraid we are mere intruders; and now that my mission is accomplished it only remains for us to go."

"But I don't understand, and I want

Somewhere in the castle a scream had sounded—a long, horrible sort of sound—which had been abruptly cut off before reaching its climax. Blake stood up, rigid. Instinctively he knew that a tragedy had happened.
(See page 24.)

you to explain!" insisted the girl. "Please come over by the window, and sit down. And you mustn't think of leaving the castle in this way. It would be dreadful!"

"It is very nice of you, Lady Betty, but I am afraid we must respect your father's wishes," said Blake gently.

"But you needn't—really!" she insisted. "I can soon talk him round. I always can. Of course, there's no doubt about—about——" She paused rather awkwardly.

"About my identity?" smiled Blake. "Well, hardly, Lady Betty. Jelks, for one, can vouch for me. It was he who sent me a telegram, telling me that somebody was masquerading here under my name."

"Forgive me, Mr. Blake, for appearing to doubt you," said Lady Betty. "But I am really quite confused. This man you called Waldo was so charming, so gentlemanly in every way. It seems incredible that he can be a criminal."

"Charm of manner is one of Waldo's greatest assets," said Blake gravely. "He is constantly using it to gain admittance to the best circles. I can assure you, Lady Betty, that Waldo is a dangerous man. At the same time, he has many gentlemanly instincts, and I do not believe that he was staying under your roof with the idea of personal gain."

"I agree with you when you say that he has gentlemanly instincts," replied the girl quietly. "He has been most charming ever since he arrived. At the same time, I am afraid he has done much to encourage my father in his obstinate attitude. I do wish you would stay, Mr. Blake, and convince my father that the position is hopeless."

"I am afraid I do not quite follow."

"But you know of our dreadful predicament?"

"Jelks gave me a hint or two, but they sounded so extraordinary that I gave them scant attention," replied Blake. "I understand that you are in danger of being evicted? Surely that is an incorrect statement?"

"Unfortunately, it is only too true," replied Lady Betty sadly. "The castle has been sold over our heads, Mr. Blake, and the new owner desires possession. It is only natural, of course. But my father refuses to leave. He swears that he will die rather than surrender."

Blake shook his head.

"I admire your father's spirit; but that sort of thing cannot be done nowadays," he replied. "And I hope you will not press me in this matter, Lady Betty. I should not like to interfere in this delicate situation."

"Oh, but you won't be interfering!" she said quickly. "The situation is now so extreme that you must stay, Mr. Blake—you really must! I don't know what we shall do if you go. It will all end up in some terrible tragedy."

"But Lord Pengarth wouldn't really shoot this Sir William Bragg, would he?" asked Tinker curiously.

"He would!" she declared. "I am sure of it!"

Sexton Blake looked grave.

"Your father is several hundred years behind his time!" he exclaimed. "He should have lived in the fifteenth century, and then this sort of thing would have been quite permissible. But he really cannot take the law into his own hands in such a drastic way. It will only end up in disaster and humiliation."

The girl took hold of Blake's arm in her anxiety.

"I am glad to hear you say that, Mr. Blake!" she exclaimed. "I want you to stay here, and please talk to my father and bring him round. This man—this Waldo—only had the opposite effect upon him, and I was getting quite frightened. Sir William Brag is not to blame. He has bought the property, and it is our duty to go. If you can only convince my father of that you will have done us an incalculable service."

Blake hesitated.

"It really seems like interfering in a purely family affair," he demurred. "Honestly, Lady Betty, it is not my style of thing at all. And, while agreeing that there is no other course, it certainly goes against the grain. My sympathies are all with your father. I have nothing but admiration for his rocklike attitude. At the same time, it won't do."

"No, we must go—there is no other course," said the girl. "It pains me as much as it pains him, for I love the old castle. It will be a dreadful wrench to leave it, and to know that it is in the hands of strangers. But having fallen victims to Mr. Slingsby's treachery, it is my father's duty to abide by the result. Please make him realise that, Mr. Blake."

Blake could not refuse her. But he only promised to stay on consideration that she told her father at once. The detective was certainly not going to remain an uninvited guest.

And thus it was that Sexton Blake and Tinker became involved.

Sir William Brag paced up and down like a cat on hot bricks. He was so furious that it was impossible for him to sit down.

"I tell you I'll have the police into this affair!" he threatened. "That's not a threat, Slingsby, it's a statement! Man alive, do you think I'm going to be fooled about like this? I won't have it! That castle is mine, and I mean to gain possession!"

Sir William was in the privacy of Mr. Simon Slingsby's study. The house was an old-fashioned one on the outskirts of Launceston, and its meanness of appearance matched that of its owner.

Mr. Slingsby was seated at his desk—a thin man, with drooping shoulders and a lean, cadaverous face. He was sixty, at least, and his clean-shaven cheeks were lined, wrinkled, and sallow. Two deep-set eyes watched Sir William as he paced up and down.

"It's all right, Sir William—there's no need to get excited," said Mr. Slingsby, in a soft, caressing voice. "It's only a matter of arrangement."

"Arrangement be hanged!" shouted the knight. "That's what you told me last time—and look what's happened. I'm not going to be fooled about like this!"

"Yes, but if you will only be calm——"

"Have I bought that property or have I not?" demanded Sir William, pausing in front of the desk, and bringing his fist down with a crash. "That's what I want to know, Slingsby! Have I bought that property, or have I not?"

"Of course you have bought it, Sir William," said the lawyer gently. "There has never been any dispute on that point. Pengarth Castle is yours——"

"My freehold property!"

"Exactly—your freehold property," agreed Mr. Slingsby. "But it won't help matters if you persist in this excited attitude, Sir William. We shall be able to deal with Lord Pengarth to our mutual satisfaction if you will only regain control of yourself."

Sir William Brag sat down heavily.

"Very well!" he panted. "If you are so clever, perhaps you will tell me what is to be done. Personally I am at a loss. I have bought this property—I have paid you for it—every brass farthing, and now I come to you for an explanation."

Mr. Slingsby shrugged his shoulders. "An explanation?" he repeated.

"Yes, confound you—an explanation!" rapped out Sir William. "Don't I deserve one? You are Lord Pengarth's lawyer—you have dealt with this transaction from first to last. And now, after everything is signed and settled, and with the title-deeds in my pocket, I can't even get in the place."

"Of course, it is perfectly preposterous——"

"It's insane!" snapped Sir William. "I've bought plenty of property in my time, Slingsby, and I've never had this experience before. And Pengarth Castle, too—my future home!"

Mr. Simon Slingsby leaned back in his chair and removed his glasses. He was upset and alarmed, but he took care not to show it. He had never suspected that Lord Pengarth would be such a hard nut to crack in the end. He had thought, indeed, that his lordship would knuckle under without a trace of fighting, after all hope had gone.

Slingsby had at last reached the point he had been striving at for years. He had drained the Earl of Pengarth to the last penny, and had sold his castle over his head. It was an awkward contretemps when Lord Pengarth refused to acknowledge the sale. Unless dealt with delicately, it might mean all sorts of inquiries.

And Mr. Slingsby was particularly anxious to avoid inquiries. There was no trickery about the documents—everything was in perfect order. But, at the same time, Mr. Slingsby's reputation would not be enhanced if all the facts were dragged into the light of day in a civil court.

"You tell me that Lord Pengarth flatly refused to admit you?" he asked.

"He not only refused to admit me, but he had the infernal impudence to fire a gun at me!" snorted Sir William, with righteous indignation. "I've a good mind to go and tell the police about it!"

"Do nothing rash, Sir William—it will only make things more difficult," said the lawyer. "Naturally, Lord Pengarth takes this thing to heart. He is an obstinate old man—a crank. You must bear with him, and where direct methods fail you must apply indirect methods."

"I don't know what you mean."

"I mean that you must gain admittance to the castle by stealth," said Mr. Slingsby smoothly. "I can supply you with several men——"

"No, I'll be hanged if I will!" interrupted Sir William, jumping to his feet again. "I'm not going to break into my own property! Keep your preposterous idea to yourself, Slingsby. I'll apply for an eviction order——"

"Well, of course, you can do that," said Mr. Slingsby coldly. "That is your own look-out. You will certainly gain your end, but it will be very costly."

"I don't care what the charges are!" stormed Sir William.

"I was not talking in terms of money, Sir William."

"What the thunder do you mean?"

"It is your intention, I think, to take up your residence in the castle?" asked Mr. Slingsby. "You will not be popular in Cornwall if you submit Lord Pengarth to such a grave humiliation. Socially, you will be an outcast, and life at Pengarth Castle will not be very pleasant. His lordship, although poor, is greatly respected."

Sir William paused, thinking of Lady Brag and her social ambitions.

"I hadn't looked at it in that way!" he growled. "Well, what alternative is there? What do you suggest?"

And Mr. Slingsby talked quietly for ten minutes, and Sir William Brag's eyes began to sparkle.

THE NINTH CHAPTER.
Tragedy.

DINNER was in progress at Pengarth Castle.

It was a picturesque little scene. Outside the dusk was deepening, and the corner of the big hall was illuminated by bunches of candles. The table was simple, but nevertheless dignified. At the head sat the Earl of Pengarth, and at the foot his daughter acted as an admirable hostess. On either side sat Sexton Blake and Tinker.

"I am glad you stayed, Mr. Blake,"

said his lordship gruffly. "Trust my daughter to know the right thing! But I'm an excitable old man, and it's just as well to take no notice of me."

"I shall know in future, Lord Pengarth," smiled Sexton Blake. "At the same time, I don't quite agree with you. In my opinion, you have every reason to be angered and incensed. The prospect of losing Pengarth Castle must be galling."

"Galling, eh?" said Lord Pengarth. "Not at all, Mr. Blake—not at all! For I have no intention of losing the castle. Not the slightest intention! I shall not shift. Not one foot will I set outside this house at the command of the intruder!"

His die-hard spirit was as strong as ever, and, even as he spoke, some of his old fire returned.

During the afternoon Lady Betty had "talked him round," as she had promised, and the old gentleman was now mightily pleased that Sexton Blake and Tinker were remaining as his guests. His one regret was that Blake failed to see eye to eye with him in this momentous crisis.

He had already told the famous detective the story of Simon Slingsby's treachery. And Blake inwardly sympathised with the unfortunate old peer. To express open sympathy was to invite an outburst, however.

"People declare that my fallen fortunes are all due to the Pengarth Curse," continued his lordship, as the meal was drawing to a close. "Sometimes I think they are right. It is certainly very extraordinary."

"The Curse?" asked Tinker interestedly.

"Yes, my boy," said Lord Pengarth. "Perhaps—who knows?—Slingsby is merely the ordained instrument. For generations—for centuries—there has been a Sacred Cross in the possession of our family. Legend has it that if this Cross leaves our possession, misfortune will fall upon the Pengarth family. Be that as it may, since the night the Cross was stolen misfortune has slowly and surely overwhelmed me."

"Perhaps it is merely coincidence," said Blake.

"That is my own opinion; but at the same time I sometimes find myself thinking differently," admitted the earl. "The Pengarth Cross was taken at the same time as Lady Pengarth's jewellery. We were rich then. The Pengarth fortunes were in a healthy condition. The first tragedy was the death of my dear wife. Did I suspect Slingsby of treachery? Never! In my folly, I allowed the reptile to have complete and absolute control over my affairs. It was not until recently that I received the shock."

Lord Pengarth's voice had dropped now, and he was talking quietly.

Sexton Blake could well understand the terrible blow that had fallen when his lordship had discovered the truth.

The man he had trusted all his life had basely betrayed him. And, what was more to the point, he had betrayed him in such a way that there was no possible redress.

In his own blindness, he had even signed away his rights to the castle itself. Things had grown from bad to worse. He had obtained mortgages, little realising what Slingsby had in mind.

And now, too late, he was a pauper—and Slingsby was wallowing in the spoils of his victory. He had drained his client of his last penny, and the end was in sight.

"But I won't go!" declared Lord Pengarth. "Never! They can bring police here—they can bring the British Army itself! But when I leave Pengarth Castle for good, I shall be carried out in my coffin! Never will I relinquish my rights!"

There was something rather fine about his bearing as he spoke, and Sexton Blake was at a loss. It was very difficult to deal with the old gentleman.

"I have nothing but admiration for your wonderful spirit, Lord Pengarth, but is this attitude wise?" asked Blake quietly. "Would it not be better to avert all further trouble and humiliation?"

His lordship shook his head.

"This affair is bigger than mere wisdom, Mr. Blake," he replied. "When I am calm and cool—as now—I realise that it would be wise to accept defeat. But I will never do that. I am a Pengarth—an old-fashioned man, perhaps, but that cannot be helped. I regard this castle as mine, and any man who tries to turn me out of it is my enemy. Let him arouse me at his peril!"

"But, dad, Mr. Slingsby and Sir William Brag have the law on their side," put in Lady Betty softly. "And we must bow before the law. That is inevitable."

"Your daughter is right, sir," said Sexton Blake. "I wish I could advise you otherwise, but I cannot. Let me urge you——"

"No! I won't hear a word!" interrupted Lord Pengarth, glaring fiercely. "Not a word, sir! This castle is the stronghold of the Pengarths—they have held it for centuries against the invader. My duty is plain. They will only enter over my dead body!"

And there was something in Lord Pengarth's tone which proved that he was in deadly earnest.

*   *   *   *   *

Like shadows of the night, a number of forms crept up towards Pengarth Castle.

It was later in the evening, and the dusk had deepened into night. It was, of course, still comparatively early, and Sexton Blake and Lord Pengarth were in the library. Tinker was with Lady Betty in the drawing-room, listening to a further account of Simon Slingsby's villainy from the worried girl.

But outside, unknown to all, lurked these forms.

There were five of them altogether. Sir William Brag had arrived with four helpers, and this time his mission was clear. He had decided to take Simon Slingsby's advice, and enter the castle by stealth.

He was doing nothing against the law. It was his own property, and so he had a perfect right to enter or leave it as he pleased, and in any way he pleased. And once inside with his men, it would be all plain sailing.

He would then be lord of his own castle. And he gloatingly pictured to himself what would happen then. Let Lord Pengarth rave and threaten as he pleased! If there was any nonsense, the old fool would be thrown out, and his own bolts and bars would be used against him!

Sir William was filled with glee at the very prospect. Not usually a ferocious man, his fight to gain possession of his own property had rendered him almost bloodthirsty. And he looked forward with acute pleasure to the coming meeting—once he was inside.

"I'll get my own back with interest!" vowed Sir William to himself. "I'll teach the old idiot to bar me out! Any nonsense, and out he'll go with his daughter and his two servants! Then they'll know what it's like to be bolted out! I'll have my own way in this affair, by Heaven!"

It was with real pleasure that he watched the proceedings.

The four men were quite honest fellows, and they had been told just sufficient to satisfy them that everything was above board. As Mr. Slingsby had explained, Lord Pengarth was an obstinate man, and this drastic course was being taken to save him from the humiliation of an eviction order.

One of the men was a blacksmith, and, having mounted some steps, he lost no time in getting to work upon one of the smaller windows. It was heavily barred, and impregnable against the bare hands.

But the blacksmith was armed with a hacksaw, files, and other tools. The hacksaw was sufficient. He commenced cutting the first bar, and soon conquered it.

The next one followed, and then a third. All were torn out from the upper sockets. The window itself proved no great barrier. Five minutes' work, and it succumbed.

"All ready now, sir," murmured the blacksmith, as he descended the steps. "I think you said you wanted to get in first?"

"Yes, yes!" exclaimed Sir William. "Splendid! You men had better remain out here."

"Won't ye want us to come in, sir?"

"Not yet—not yet!" replied the knight. "If possible, I wish to avoid all unpleasantness, much as I have been angered. You will only be required in case of need. It is possible that Lord Pengarth will resist. If so, I must reluctantly call you in. Otherwise, you will remain here until you get further orders from me."

Sir William mounted the steps, and a glow of triumph surged through him as he set foot inside the castle. In spite of the old earl's obstinacy, he had been conquered! It was the only way to deal with such pig-headedness! Ordinary methods were useless.

Outside, the men stood near the wall, talking in low tones. They didn't quite like the affair, but they were being well paid, and were assured that everything was in perfect order.

In the library, Sexton Blake and Lord Pengarth talked. They were discussing antiques now—one of his lordship's favourite topics. The earl excused himself, in order to fetch a particularly prized object of art. And, by a curious coincidence, Lord Pengarth left the library alone at almost exactly the same moment as Sir William Brag entered the castle by means of the window.

Thus the situation stood.

Sir William Brag entered by the window, and at the same time Lord Pengarth left the library and went out along the dim passages.

Not one soul in that gaunt old household suspected that tragedy—stark and horrible—was in the air. Sexton Blake, sitting in the library, was idly wondering what his course of action should be. He had half a mind to take Tinker with him on an exploration of the deserted buildings.

He finally decided upon this course. Then he started and rose sharply to his feet.

Somewhere in the castle a scream had sounded—a long, horrible sort of sound—which had been abruptly cut off before reaching its climax. Blake stood rigid. Instinctively he knew that a tragedy had happened.

*   *   *   *   *

Tinker, in the drawing-room, looked quickly at Lady Betty. She had paused in her playing, and was looking for another piece of music.

"Did you hear that?" he asked.

"What ever can have happened?" said the girl, catching her breath in. "Do—do you think——"

She didn't exactly know what she meant, and she ran from the room, with her cheeks paling. Tinker followed.

They found Sexton Blake in the big hall.

"Did you hear it, too, sir?" asked Tinker swiftly.

"Yes," replied Blake. "Lady Betty, please remain here."

Without another word he hurried down a corridor. His sense of direction told him that the sound had come from somewhere on this side of the building. He and Tinker made all haste.

Outside, the four men were running helter-skelter across the parklands. The sound had reached them more clearly than any of the others, and they were badly frightened. They fled.

Blake's electric torch was switched on, and he went down passage after passage, keen and grim. And then, turning a corner, he suddenly checked. The light from his torch revealed a dreadful scene.

The Earl of Pengarth was standing there, apparently dazed. In one hand he held a guttering candle. A window stood open near by, and the night wind was blowing in with a chilly touch.

In the earl's other hand he held his heavy stick—without which he never moved. And on the floor, huddled at his feet, lay something as still as death. It was the figure of a man.

"Keep back, Tinker!" muttered Blake tensely.

He moved forward, and, taking no notice of Lord Pengarth, he knelt down, flashing his light upon the huddled form. It was that of Sir William Brag. Blake had never seen the man before, but he recognised him on the instant from Lord Pengarth's description.

And Sir William Brag was dead.

Sexton Blake, who had seen death in many forms, knew this at the first glance. The unfortunate knight had met his end in a dreadful manner. The front part of his skull was crushed. He must have received one awful blow which had brought instantaneous death. His scream had evidently been uttered as the death-thrust was about to be dealt.

Grimly Blake rose to his feet and faced the Earl of Pengarth. It seemed to him that the facts were obvious. The earl had accidentally come upon Sir William Brag breaking in, there had been a second's altercation, and this tragedy was the result.

Instinctively Blake glanced at the earl's heavy stick.

"Lord Pengarth, what has happened?" asked the detective sternly.

The Earl of Pengarth looked at Blake in a strange way, his eyes burning with a kind of dazed-looking light.

"I—I don't know!" he muttered. "I came along this passage—I heard a scream—— Uuugggh!"

Suddenly he grew absolutely rigid, and a curious gurgle sounded in his throat. Then, before Blake could touch him, he just as suddenly became limp and collapsed into an inert heap. His eyes were open and staring, and his lined old face was almost waxen.

"Good heavens!" muttered Blake.

"He's dead, sir!" panted Tinker, coming up. "Apoplexy!"

"A stroke of some kind, certainly," agreed Blake swiftly. "Hold the light, Tinker—hold it! No, he's not dead. His heart beats and he breathes. But I am afraid it will be touch and go."

Gently they carried the stricken peer into the hall, where Lady Betty and Jelks and Martha were waiting in a little frightened group. The girl ran forward as she saw the still form of her father.

"Dad!" she breathed, with a little scream.

"Please, Lady Betty—please!" exclaimed Sexton Blake. "Your father has had a stroke, but he still lives. Tinker, you must go at once for the doctor and for the police. Every second is of value."

"The poor master—the poor master!" moaned Jelks, looking ten years older.

"What's happened, sir?"

But he soon knew what had happened, and so did the others. And the same thought was mutual. The Earl of Pengarth had settled this crisis by committing the act of murder!

In his grim determination to obtain possession of the castle he had struck the intruder down with all the strength of his fierce obstinacy. But as he was near to death's door himself the whole problem was solved.

* * * * * *

But Sexton Blake was not satisfied.

He could not forget the earl's last words:

"I came along this passage—I heard a scream."

If his lordship had spoken the truth, the crime had taken place before he arrived. On the face of it there seemed no possibility of Lord Pengarth's innocence being proved. His guilt was beyond all question.

Everything pointed to it from first to last.

If such was actually the case and he died, then the whole affair was over and there was no further problem.

But Sexton Blake could not forget that Rupert Waldo was probably within the castle. Did Waldo know anything about this tragedy? Even this seemed incredible, for the Wonder-Man was famed for his clean fighting. He never killed; he seldom even injured. It was not like him to commit such a pointless, needless murder.

On the other hand, the Earl of Pengarth had every motive.

"I rather fancy, Tinker, that our work here is done," said Sexton Blake a little later, while they were waiting for the doctor to conclude his examination. "The police will soon be here, but their presence is needless. With Lord Pengarth dead, the case ends."

But even as he spoke these words Blake inwardly felt that he was wrong. This episode was closed.

But there was another episode to follow!

End of Part One.

THE SEQUEL—

to the events narrated above will be recorded in next week's issue ∴ ∴ of the U.J. ∴ ∴

Therein you will read of the even stranger events that befell at Pengarth Castle—how the stricken earl fell under the shadow of suspicion for the death of Sir William Brag.

And rightly so. Had he not motive enough, according to his warped ideas? It is a clear enough case that stands against him, but there are complications.

What of Waldo? Has he any part in this mysterious affair? Yes, he has; but it's a different one from what you might think. You will read how he approached Simon Slingsby; how Sexton Blake took a hand in their affairs; and finally of the lifting of the castle's curse.

Moreover, there is a second climax to the yarn—a strange event which fully explains the death of Sir William Brag. You haven't guessed this, either.

All these things will be told next week under the title of "The Curse of Pengarth Castle."

One final remark: Make sure of getting your copy!

THE UNION JACK 2

Sexton Blake's Own Paper

The Curse of PENGARTH CASTLE

"WHY DON'T YOU PUBLISH TWO U.J.'s EVERY WEEK?"

That's what many readers have asked at various times. We can't do that; but, anyway, here's a suggestion!

When the summer evenings tempt you outdoors, and you don't feel so keen on reading, and you're inclined to forgo your weekly "U. J."—remember the winter. It's then that you want two every week.

Why not take this paper as regularly in the summer as you do in the winter, and, if you can resist them now, save the summer numbers, to brighten the dark, dismal evenings. They'll still be seasonable, and Sexton Blake never palls.

It's a good tip! Act on it from now on. Only a matter of the usual twopence, and you'll have your two copies a week just when you want them. Incidentally, you'll be able to read the serials as a whole, too, if you prefer them that way.

That's right! Place a standing order with your newsagent!

Our £10 Detective Competition

"WHO IS THE MAN?"

RESULT AND SOLUTION.

We are now glad to be able to announce the result of the competition in connection with the story entitled "Who is the Man?" which appeared in this paper of April 18th last, No. 1,123.

The problem of trying to answer the question embodied in the title of the yarn, and in finding the author's original solution to the mystery, proved a very popular one.

The name of the £10 winner, together with those of the twenty runners-up who have been awarded original U.J. cover designs as consolation prizes, are given overleaf. Meantime, in order to refresh your memory of "Who is the Man?" a short summary of the story appears here, followed by the concluding portion which contains the solution.

This was, of course, withheld pending the receipt of competitors' entries, but now, in conjunction with the summary, you will see how the various clues dovetailed into each other, and how the discoveries of Sexton Blake form a fitting and feasible conclusion to a very ingenious yarn.

THE STORY.

WILBUR KING, an eminent financier, is found dead in his City office by Miss Phyllis Dean, his typist, at 11.15 one morning. A look of intense fear is stamped on the dead man's face.

Harry Hall and Jonas Starke, members of the office staff, send for a doctor—Dr. Sylvanus Batterbee—who states that the financier is the victim of an unknown assassin.

Inspector Coutts, Sexton Blake, and Tinker arrive later from Scotland Yard, where the Baker Street man and his assistant happened to be when the news came through. The members of Wilbur King's staff are interviewed, with results that indicate suspicious circumstances.

Harry Hall, the private secretary, last saw his employer alive at 10-35, when he was in his usual health and spirits. Jonas Starke, a clerk, had not seen him that morning at all. Phyllis Dean gives an account of how she found her master.

The interview is interrupted by the sudden appearance of a snake in the room. The resulting scare is nullified by the discovery that it is not venomous, but quite harmless. It belonged to the financier, who kept it in a ventilated safe in the office with the object of scaring away burglars from the valuables the safe contained.

The private secretary knows the combination number, and opens the safe so that the snake may be replaced. It is then found that £20,000 worth of Chilian bonds are missing from it. The natural inference is that Hall has taken them, for he knows the combination; also, it comes out that Hall had quarrelled that morning with his employer, who had been pestering Phyllis Dean, the typist, with his attentions—and Hall was engaged to Phyllis.

Blake also interviews the commissionaire and the lift-man of the building, Joseph Turner and Michael O'Brien. They stated that the dead man had arrived at ten, had had no visitors during the morning, and that there was nothing unusual about him. Sexton Blake, however, finds that there was at least one visitor, who, being a regular caller, the two men had forgotten to mention—the waitress from a near-by café with a cup of coffee for the financier.

A visitor is announced at this point—a man named Horace Wills. He confesses that he poisoned King by means of a dose of atropine dropped into the coffee-cup unseen by the waitress. This confession is negatived later by the fact that the original cup of coffee was dropped in the street and spilt. Wills therefore did not poison the financier, for a second cup was taken to him. Meantime, however, a supply of atropine is found in Phyllis Dean's desk, which may or may not have been used in making-up her eyes.

A telephone call comes through for King, and Blake, answering it, receives a message intended for the dead man. He is warned to beware of "Bill," who has sworn to "get him." It is a girl speaking, and apparently Bill's anger against King is caused by jealousy. The man's full name is William Hoxon, of Rubenstein's Turf Agency, Blake discovers, and is further told that Bill has conveyed a warning about a rose. It seems that the speaker is employed in a florist's

shop, for she mentions having sold a rose to King that morning.

On Blake interviewing Jonas Starke, the "sporting" clerk, the man tries to attack Blake. The missing bonds are found in his room at the office, and he confesses to having stolen them, but denies having murdered his master. It is later definitely stated by Blake that King did not die of atropine poisoning, and this is confirmed by the doctor who made the post-mortem examination. He states that the poison used is unclassified.

Meantime, Sexton Blake has found, on the fire-escape overlooking the room in which Wilbur King died, the imprint of a pair of small shoes—those either of a man or woman—whose soles were of crepe rubber, and also a cigarette-end.

Blake sends Tinker to investigate the movements of William Hoxon, the racing tout who is friendly with the girl at the florist's from whom the dead man bought a buttonhole every morning. Tinker trails his man to the Oriental cookery establishment of one Idris Ben Hassan, in the East End, posing as a drug addict the better to spy on him.

His imposture is discovered, however, and he is overpowered, but eventually gets back to Baker Street with the information that the rose of which Wilbur King was warned was not the flower he wore in his buttonhole, but Abe Rosenblum's gang, the leader of which was usually referred to as "The Rose."

At a fancy-dress ball at the Hotel Olympic Blake is present, and, by means of a dictaphone, overhears a conversation between two masked dancers, a man and a woman. The man confides to his companion that he is morally guilty of the murder, but it was not his hand that did the deed. He says also that he has an unassailable alibi.

Next morning Sexton Blake and Coutts go to the building in which is Wilbur King's office. There a man is arrested, but his identity is not disclosed to the public, for he had hidden his face from the photographers.

Later during the morning Press reporters visit Baker Street, and ask for the identity of the prisoner, together with the names of two other persons Coutts has also arrested on Blake's instructions. Two visitors have also come at Blake's request, but it is arranged that the detective asks them to wait while he gives his disclosures to the Pressmen.

THE SOLUTION.

SEXTON BLAKE crossed over to the half-opened door, while Tinker, Coutts and Robson, the reporter, waited impatiently, consumed with curiosity. From behind the portal they heard the low hum of voices, and the closing of a door.

A moment later the detective re-entered—alone.

"I have asked our visitors to wait a few minutes in the waiting-room," he explained. "Their presence is not yet necessary."

He crossed over to his chair and sat down. The inevitable briar dangled from his finely-chiselled lips, his eyes were half-closed, and the tips of his

long, tapering fingers were pressed lightly together.

"The problem of the murder of Wilbur Wright," began Sexton Blake quietly, "is one of those fascinating tangles which occasionally occur in the history of criminology. A crime that at first seems extraordinarily simple, and yet develops into an exceedingly complex and intricate problem.

"You are all conversant with the bare facts of the case. Wilbur King was murdered at about eleven-fifteen yesterday morning. The post-mortem examination revealed traces of an obscure and unclassified poison. The features of the dead man were contorted with a look of horror and an unnatural fear.

"It is known that he had many enemies. From what I can gather he was a ruthless, unscrupulous man, with many shady and nefarious transactions in his past life. The problem of motive, therefore, was not hard to seek. Where the mystery deepened was the fact of so many people having a more or less strong motive for his death. That I think is sufficiently clear."

"Now the problem becomes more abstruse," continued the detective.

"When, accompanied by Inspector Coutts, I arrived at Threadneedle Street, my mind was ready to receive any and every impression from the facts. I suspected nobody in particular—and everybody in general.

"The first person I met was the commissionaire. He was obviously an ex-Service man, and was to be reckoned with as capable as the next man of murder—all things being equal.

"The next person was O'Brien, the lift-man. From a tattoo-mark on his wrist it was easy to deduce a sailor with plenty of foreign experience, for the tattooing was expertly done, and suggested Japanese work. I also noticed his large and extraordinary red hands, rather like sausages; and this drew my attention to a curious ring he was wearing."

Tinker coughed and broke in excitedly: "Now I see, guv'nor, a glimmer of light in those weird notes of yours."

Blake smiled.

"Perhaps you would read them out again, so that we can check up."

Tinker unearthed the scrap of paper torn from Blake's memo-book:

King—alive, healthy, normal. Time 11 a.m. (waitress corroboration.) No sign of virulent poison. Matossian cigarette. Sausages. Cæsar. Ring missing. Cigar butt. Was telephone disinfected?

Acid stain on Hill's finger—obviously chemical. Memo hobby? Starke's automatic. Typist's curious eyes. Corpse—Italian.

"You must remember," continued Sexton Blake, "that those notes were jotted down after I received the impressions, and are not, therefore, in strict sequence. It struck me as worthy of note, however, that ring of O'Brien's, the lift-man. I am rather a connoisseur of jewellery, and it struck me as strange that a man like that should wear an exquisitely-wrought gold ring, obviously dating from the Renaissance period of Italy.

"Association of ideas, as you will see from my rough memo. Sausages—his fingers reminded me of. The ring reminded me of Italy, and the Borgias.

"The Borgias, as you are all aware, were the most fascinating, powerful family of the mediæval period. They were utterly unscrupulous, and master-murderers, through their vast knowledge of poisons. Poison-rings were one of the many methods by which they got rid of their victims."

"Yes, but guv'nor, what's Cæsar got to do with it?" demanded Tinker.

Blake shrugged his shoulders, and Tinker blushed slightly.

"Sorry, guv'nor, I ought to have known."

"Well," pursued Sexton Blake, puffing slowly at his pipe. "That was interesting, but I did not attach undue importance to it. After all, O'Brien may have picked up the ring as a curio during his travels, and I concentrated on the expression of fear in the dead man's face.

"He was obviously frightened—almost to death. It was therefore safe to assume that Hall was not responsible for that look. According to Hall's own version King held him in his power, and a blackmailer is seldom frightened of his victim. The same applied to Starke and Miss Dean.

"I then noticed that the fire escape overlooked the window of King's office, so that if a man were to sit on the second step he would be able to watch Wilbur King.

"Investigation verified this—I found a Matossian cigarette and the footprints of crepe-soled shoes.

"The result of those clues clinched the matter. I had arranged with Dr. Batterbee for the photograph of the retina of the dead man's eye. I have already explained that phenomenon, and now you can see the photo of the man who sat watching the death agony of Wilbur King."

Blake handed the newspaper man an enlarged photograph of the image thrown on the screen in the laboratory the previous afternoon.

"Why!" gasped Robson. "I know this man, Mr. Blake. It's Marini. Mr. C. B. Marini—the famous inventor, at present at the Hotel Olympic."

Coutts chuckled.

"At present in the 'Hotel' Brixton, on remand, you mean."

"But—but I don't understand!" exclaimed the bewildered reporter. "Such a well-known man as Marini——"

"Notice his initials?" said Sexton Blake quietly. "C. B.—Cæsare Borgia. Another link.

"Now I will rapidly go over the rest. My suspicions were increased tenfold when O'Brien came to be interviewed by Coutts. The ring was missing from his finger! I noted that at the time; and then, in his excitement, the lift-man used the Italian word for body. He said 'The corpo'.

"Freud, and other psychologists have taught how important a lapsus linguæ, a slip of the tongue, can be, and from that moment O'Brien was suspect."

"Yes, but why should a lift-man poison his employer? And what's this inventor chap, Marini, got to do with it?" demanded Tinker.

"That," replied Sexton Blake, "as Coutts will recall, was one argument in O'Brien's defence. An ignorant liftman would hardly know the properties of a Borgia ring. It needed someone with a cunning brain and plenty of power, money, and determination.

"Well, a few discreet inquiries and a little eavesdropping on the detectaphone furnished me with the main part of the story. The rest I verified from O'Brien himself.

"Many years ago, Wilbur King, while on tour in Italy, fell in love with a beautiful Italian girl, Lucrezia Marini. She and her brother were the last representatives of the great Borgia family, as proud as they were poor.

King, who as I have hinted, was an unscrupulous blackguard, soon tired of his wife. He ill-treated her abominably, until finally she died of a broken heart. Her brother Cæsare now C. B. Marini, swore to be avenged on the scoundrel, but he was poor, and King a rich English 'milor.'

"For ten years Cæsare nursed his burning hatred of King, when suddenly fortune's wheel turned and the young Italian became famous and rich.

"He came to England with his fiancee and watched, planning with devilish ingenuity the death of the scoundrel who had ruined his sister's life. You must remember that all the force of the hot blood of one of the proudest and greatest Italian families burned in his veins, together with an inherited knowledge of poisons unequalled in the world.

"He laid his plans carefully, and fortune favoured him, by sending the Irish-Italian, O'Brien, across his path."

"Irish-Italian, did you say?" interposed Coutts.

"Precisely," said Blake. "The liftman's mother was a Sicilian. He was born in Italy, and later migrated to Ireland. While in the land of his birth, on one of his numerous voyages, he joined a Sicilian secret society. Don't forget he was half Italian. As it happened, the president of that society was young Marini.

"When O'Brien left Italy he probably thought that the wild escapades of his youth were over. A chance meeting with Marini, however, convinced him of his error.

"Marini paid him well to further his private vengeance, using the society as a bludgeon in the cause of remonstrance. Add to that the fact that O'Brien had little cause to love King, who was a domineering bully, and you have the motive—while Marini supplies the brains."

"By Jove, guv'nor, you're a giddy marvel!" said Tinker, with boyish enthusiasm. "But how was it worked? I mean the poisoning."

Blake smiled.

"I have written a small monograph on obscure poisons, and from what Batterbee tells me, coupled with a knowledge of Borgian toxicology, I should think this was the method used.

"An Italian chemist—this is a historical fact, not fiction or fantasy—has discovered a poison so nicely gauged that it can cause death in a given period—a day, or a week, or a month—or even an hour.*

"The poison is distilled from a special gland secreted in a particular variety of mussels, and I should deduce that Marini placed sufficient into the Borgia ring for his needs.

"He gave it to O'Brien, with instructions to prick King's arm with the ring as he was carried up in the elevator. The prick would have been hardly noticeable to a man suffering twinges of gout—or perhaps he may have noticed it and O'Brien explained it away by saying he had a pin sticking from his clothes, and apologising. There, I think, you have the explanation of the mystery in all its diabolical ingenuity.

"O'Brien has in part confessed, and Marini will, I am confident, corroborate. It was a foolish move on his part to watch King's death agony from the fire-escape, but Italians are fond of melodrama. No wonder Wilbur King's face was fear-stricken as he discovered his villainy avenged at last. It was the double clue of the small-size footprint and the cigarette end on the fire-escape which helped me identify Marini, and, once I had suspected him, I had no difficulty in discovering he was to dance at the Hotel Olympic with his fiancee, at which I overheard his admission of his part in the crime."

Sexton Blake yawned slightly, then suddenly rose to his feet.

"By Jove! I was forgetting! Tinker, ask Mr. Harry Hall and Miss Dean to come in. I want to tell them the good news. They have suffered enough to deserve a lasting happiness."

As Tinker crossed over to the waiting-room Coutts and Robson rose to their feet, with up-raised glasses.

"Here's to you, Sexton Blake! More power to your elbow!"

Sexton Blake's lean, clear-cut face flushed a little, but his keen grey eyes held an unwonted gleam of pleasure at the sincerity of the spontaneous tribute.

THE END.

* See UNION JACK Supplement, Vol. 2, Page 252, "Poisons You Cannot Buy."

THE RESULT
of our "Detective" Competition.

None of the entries received gave the correct solution of the mystery of Wilbur King's death as originally conceived by the author of this story and as revealed on this page.

Of those who succeeded in naming the actual murderer as Michael O'Brien, the lift-man, two were in the final selection, and they were of such equal merit as regards accuracy of observation and deduction that it has been decided to divide the Prize of £10 between them.

The sum of £5 has therefore been sent to the following two competitors:

MR. EDWARD S. HARDY, 82, Folkestone Road, Dover.

MR. GEORGE L. GREET, Filmore, Pinhoe, Devon.

To the twenty entrants, names and addresses as below, whose efforts came next in order of merit original UNION JACK cover designs have been sent, in accordance with the terms of the contest:

Mr. George Church, 6, Kitchener Road, East Finchley, N. 2; Mr. James Lynch, 59, Lr. Dominick Street, Dublin; Mr. S. J. Moffatt, 14, King's Road, Belmont, Surrey; Mr. H. Brownsing, 1, Back Marton Street, Lancaster; Mr. James E. Condon, 22, Greenmount Road, Terenure, Dublin; Mr. F. Spotsworth, 47, Clyde Street, Cheetham Hill, Manchester; Mr. T. Horrocks, 684, Warrington Road, Park Lane, Wigan; Mr. E. H. F. Bish, 15, Haldane Road, Fulham, S.W. 6; Mr. K. H. Flintoff, Belvedere Cottage, Burnham-on-Crouch, Essex; Mr. T. J. Phillips, 38, Bishopric, Horsham, Sussex; Mr. H. Hampton, 18, Vale Road, Camberley, Surrey; Mrs. M. Muntz, 37, Festing Road, Southsea; Mr. E. A. Royls, 232, Greame Street, Moss Side, Manchester; Mr. G. Trueman, 19, Ravensdon Street, Kennington, S.E. 11; Mr. Alfred Tranter, 33, Catharine's Cross, Darlaston, Staffs; Mr. A. Cook, 22, Middle Street, Hull; Miss Ethel Keays, Devon Villa, Richmond Hill Avenue, Clifton; Mr. R. J. Thomas, 7, Church Place, Neath, Glam, South Wales; Mr. Charles Wright, Groveley Road, Wilton, Salisbury, Wilts; Miss G. Keays, Devon Villa, Richmond Hill Avenue, Clifton.

Printed and published every Thursday by the Proprietors, The Amalgamated Press (1922), Ltd., The Fleetway House, Farringdon Street, London, E.C.4. Advertisement offices: The Fleetway House, Farringdon Street, London, E.C.4. Registered for transmission by Canadian Magazine Post. Subscription rates: Inland and Abroad, 11s. per annum: 5s. 6d. for six months. Sole agents for South Africa: The Central News Agency, Ltd. Sole agents for Australia and New Zealand: Messrs. Gordon & Gotch, Ltd.; and for Canada, The Imperial News Co., Ltd. (Canada).—Saturday, June 13th, 1925.

Captain Blood
by Rafael Sabatini

(Continued from page 2.)

dropped anchor in the bay a week ago, manned by a crew mainly composed of French boucan hunters from Northern Hispaniola, men who had good cause to hate the Spaniard with an intensity exceeding that of the English.

Levasseur had brought them back to Tortuga from an indifferently successful cruise. It would need more, however, than lack of success to abate the fellow's monstrous vanity. A roaring, quarrelsome, hard-drinking, hard-gaming scoundrel, his reputation as a buccaneer stood high among the wild Brethren of the Coast.

He enjoyed also a reputation of another sort. There was about his gaudy, swaggering raffishness something that the women found singularly alluring. That he should boast openly of his bonnes fortunes did not seem strange to Captain Blood; what he might have found strange was that there appeared to be some measure of justification for these boasts.

It was current gossip that even Mademoiselle d'Ogeron, the governor's daughter, had been caught in the snare of his wild attractiveness, and that Levasseur had gone the length of audacity of asking her hand in marriage of her father. M. d'Ogeron had made him the only possible answer. He had shown him the door. Levasseur had departed in a rage, swearing that he would make Mademoiselle his wife in the teeth of all the fathers in Christendom, and that M. d'Ogeron should bitterly rue the affront he had put upon him.

This was the man who now thrust himself upon Captain Blood with a proposal of association, offering him not only his sword, but his ship and the men who sailed in her.

A dozen years ago, as a lad of barely twenty, Levasseur had sailed with that monster of cruelty L'Ollonais, and his own subsequent exploits bore witness and did credit to the school in which he had been reared. I doubt if in his day there was a greater scoundrel among the Brethren of the Coast than this Levasseur.

And yet, repulsive though he found him, Captain Blood could not deny that the fellow's proposals displayed boldness, imagination, and resource, and he was forced to admit that jointly they could undertake operations of a greater magnitude than was possible singly to either of them.

The climax of Levasseur's project was to be a raid upon the wealthy mainland city of Maracaybo; but for this, he admitted, six hundred men at the very least would be required, and six hundred men were not to be conveyed in the two bottoms they now commanded. Preliminary cruises must take place, having for one of their objects the capture of further ships.

Because he disliked the man, Captain Blood would not commit himself at once. But because he liked the proposal he consented to consider it. Being afterwards pressed by both Hagthorpe and Wolverstone, who did not share his own personal dislike of the Frenchman, the end of the matter was that within a week, articles were drawn up between Levasseur and Blood, and signed by them and—as was usual—by the chosen representatives of their followers.

These articles contained, inter alia, the common provisions that should the two vessels separate, a strict account must afterwards be rendered of all prizes severally taken, whilst the vessel taking a prize should retain three-fifths of its value, surrendering two-fifths to its associate.

These shares were subsequently to be subdivided among the crew of each vessel, in accordance with the articles already obtaining between each captain and his own men.

For the rest, the articles contained all the clauses that were usual, among which was the clause that any man found guilty of abstracting or concealing any part of a prize, be it of the value of no more than a peso, should be summarily hanged from the yard-arm.

All being now settled they made ready for sea, and on the very eve of sailing Levasseur narrowly escaped being shot in a romantic attempt to scale the wall of the governor's garden, with the object of taking passionate leave of the infatuated Mademoiselle d'Ogeron. He desisted after having been twice fired upon from a fragrant ambush of pimento trees where the governor's guards were posted, and he departed vowing to take different and very definite measures on his return.

That night he slept on board his ship, which with characteristic flamboyance he had named La Foudre, and there on the following day he received a visit from Captain Blood, whom he greeted half-mockingly as his admiral. The Irishman came to settle certain final details of which all that need concern us is an understanding that in the event of the two vessels becoming separated by accident or design, they should rejoin each other as soon as might be at Tortuga.

Thereafter Levasseur entertained his admiral to dinner, and jointly they drank success to the expedition, so copiously on the part of Levasseur that when the time came to separate he was as nearly drunk as it seemed possible for him to be and yet retain his understanding.

Finally, towards evening, Captain Blood went over the side and was rowed back to his great ship with her red bulwarks and gilded ports, touched into a lovely thing of flame by the setting sun.

He was a little heavy-hearted. I have said that he was a judge of men, and his judgment of Levasseur filled him with misgivings which were growing heavier in a measure as the hour of departure approached.

He expressed it to Wolverstone, who met him as he stepped aboard the Arabella.

"You over-persuaded me into those articles, you blackguard; and it'll surprise me if any good comes of this association."

The giant rolled his single bloodthirsty eye, and sneered, thrusting out his heavy jaw.

"We'll wring the dog's neck if there's any treachery."

"So we will—if we are there to wring it by then." And on that, dismissing the matter: "We sail in the morning, on the first of the ebb," he announced, and went off to his cabin.

IT would be somewhere about ten o'clock on the following morning, a full hour before the time appointed for sailing, when a canoe brought up alongside La Foudre, and a half-caste Indian stepped out of her and went up the ladder. He was clad in drawers of hairy, untanned hide, and a red blanket served him for a cloak. He was the bearer of a folded scrap of paper for Captain Levasseur. The captain unfolded the letter sadly soiled and crumpled by contact with the half-caste's person. Its contents may be roughly translated thus:

Levasseur's Heroics.

"My well-beloved,—I am in the Dutch brig Jongvrouw, which is about to sail. Resolved to separate us for ever, my cruel father is sending me to Europe in my brother's charge. I implore you, come to my rescue. Deliver me, my well-beloved hero! — Your desolate Madeleine, who loves you."

The well-beloved hero was moved to the soul of him by that passionate appeal. His scowling glance swept the bay for the Dutch brig, which he knew had been due to sail for Amsterdam with a cargo of hides and tobacco.

She was nowhere to be seen among the shipping in that narrow, rock-bound harbour. He roared out the question in his mind.

In answer the half-caste pointed out

beyond the frothing surf that marked the position of the reef constituting one of the stronghold's main defences. Away beyond it, a mile or so distant, a sail was standing out to sea.

"There she go," he said.

"There!" The Frenchman gazed and stared, his face growing white. The man's wicked temper awoke, and turned to vent itself upon the messenger. "And where have you been that you come here only now with this? Answer me!"

The half-caste shrank terrified before his fury. His explanation, if he had one, was paralysed by fear. Levasseur took him by the throat, shook him twice, snarling the while, then hurled him into the scuppers. The man's head struck the gunwale as he fell, and he lay there, quite still, a trickle of blood issuing from his mouth.

Levasseur dashed one hand against the other, as if dusting them.

"Heave that muck overboard," he ordered some of those who stood idling in the waist. "Then up anchor, and let us after the Dutchman."

"Steady, captain. What's that?" There was a restraining hand upon his shoulder, and the broad face of his lieutenant, Cahusac, a burly, callous Breton scoundrel, was stolidly confronting him.

Levasseur made clear his purpose with a deal of unnecessary obscenity.

Cahusac shook his head.

"A Dutch brig!" said he. "Impossible! We should never be allowed."

"And who the devil will deny us?" Levasseur was between amazement and fury.

"For one thing, there's your own crew will be none too willing. For another, there's Captain Blood."

"I care nothing for Captain Blood!"

"But it is necessary that you should."

He has the power, the weight of metal and of men, and if I know him at all he'll sink us before he'll suffer interference with the Dutch. He has his own views of privateering, this Captain Blood, as I warned you."

"Ah!" said Levasseur, showing his teeth. But his eyes, riveted upon that distant sail, were gloomily thoughtful. Not for long. The imagination and resource which Captain Blood had detected in the fellow soon suggested a course.

Cursing in his soul, and even before the anchor was weighed, the association into which he had entered, he was already studying ways of evasion. What Cahusac implied was true: Blood would never suffer violence to be done in his presence to a Dutchman; but it might be done in his absence; and, being done, Blood must perforce condone it, since it would then be too late to protest.

(*Next week: "Kidnapped!"*)

THE UNION JACK · 2ᴰ

Sexton Blake's Own Paper

The Curse of PENGARTH CASTLE

SEXTON BLAKE and WALDO the Wonder-Man!
IN A MAGNIFICENT DETECTIVE MYSTERY STORY.

No. 1,132.　　　EVERY THURSDAY.　　　June 20th, 1925.

Captain Blood

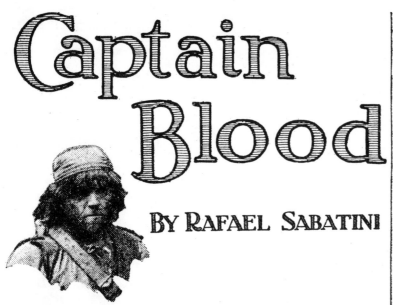

By Rafael Sabatini

CONDEMNED to the slavery of the West Indian sugar plantations for a crime he did not commit, Peter Blood, a physician of the little Somersetshire town of Bridgewater, is sent to Barbadoes, and there bought for £10 by the brutal Colonel Bishop.

A Spanish galleon, the Cinco Llagas, which comes to raid the island, is captured by Peter Blood and his comrades, and the crew and commander captured. They sail away from Barbadoes and release the Spaniards near the island of Hispaniola.

The original intention of Peter Blood—now Captain Blood—was to make his way back to Europe, but circumstances compelled him to remain with the crew and become, with them, "Brethren of the Coast"—in short, pirates.

He re-names the ship "Arabella,"—after Arabella Bishop, the daughter of the slavedriver who bought him for £10 and for whom he has a now hopeless affection, and puts in at Tortuga, the pirates' haven.

Here he is approached by a man named Levasseur, the captain of a French privateer, who proposes that they form a partnership with the object of raiding the city of Maracaybo, and as a preliminary make a cruise so that they can "acquire" additional ships for the enterprise. Blood agrees to this partnership.

Before sailing, Levasseur receives a note from Mlle. d'Ogeron, the daughter of the Governor of Tortuga, appealing for his help. She is being sent to Europe in a Dutch brig, the Jongvrouw, in her brother's charge, for she is in love with Levasseur, and her father intends to separate them.

The brig has already started, and, before the arranged time of his and Blood's sailing, Levasseur sets off in pursuit, against the wishes of his crew, and in spite of the fact that the French and English are at peace with the Dutch.

WITHIN the hour the Arabella and La Foudre were beating out to sea together. Without understanding the change of plan involved, Captain Blood, nevertheless, accepted it, and weighed anchor before the appointed time upon perceiving his associate to do so.

Levasseur's Heroics. (cont.)

All day the Dutch brig was in sight, though by evening she had dwindled to the merest speck on the northern horizon. The course prescribed for Blood and Levasseur lay eastward along the northern shores of Hispaniola. To that course the Arabella continued to hold steadily throughout the night, with the result that when day broke again she was alone. La Foudre, under cover of the darkness, had struck away to the north-east with every rag of canvas on her yards.

Cahusac had attempted yet again to protest against this.

"The devil take you!" Levasseur had answered him. "A ship's a ship, be she Dutch or Spanish, and ships are our present need. That will suffice for the men."

His lieutenant said no more. But from his glimpse of the letter, knowing that a girl and not a ship was his captain's real objective, he gloomily shook his head as he rolled away on his bowed legs to give the necessary orders.

Dawn found La Foudre close on the Dutchman's heels, not a mile astern, and the sight of her very evidently flustered the Jongvrouw. No doubt Mademoiselle's brother, recognising Levasseur's ship, would be responsible for the Dutch uneasiness. They saw the Jongvrouw crowding canvas in a futile endeavour to outsail them, whereupon they stood off to starboard and raced on until they were in a position whence they could send a warning shot across her bow. The Jongvrouw veered, showed them her rudder, and opened fire with her sternchasers. The small shot went whistling through La Foudre's shrouds with some slight damage to her canvas. Followed a brief running fight in the course of which the Dutchman let fly a broadside.

Five minutes after that they were board and board, the Jongvrouw held tight in the clutches of La Foudre's grapnels, and the buccaneers pouring noisily into her waist.

The Dutchman's master, purple in the face, stood forward to beard the pirate, followed closely by an elegant, pale-faced young gentleman in whom Levasseur recognised his brother-in-law elect.

"Captain Levasseur, this is an outrage for which you shall be made to answer. What do you seek aboard my ship?"

"At first I sought only that which belongs to me, something of which I am being robbed. But since you chose war and opened fire on me with some damage to my ship and loss of life to five of my men, why war it is, and your ship a prize of war."

From the quarter-rail Mademoiselle d'Ogeron looked down with glowing eyes in breathless wonder upon her well-beloved hero. Gloriously heroic he seemed as he stood towering there, masterful, audacious, beautiful. He saw her, and with a glad shout sprang towards her. The Dutch master got in his way with hands upheld to arrest his progress.

Levasseur did not stay to argue with him; he was too impatient to reach his mistress. He swung the poleaxe that he carried, and the Dutchman went down in blood with a cloven skull. The eager lover stepped across the body and came on, his countenance joyously alight.

But Mademoiselle was shrinking now, in horror. She was a girl upon the threshold of glorious womanhood, of a fine height and nobly moulded, with heavy coils of glossy black hair above and about a face that was of the colour of old ivory. Her countenance was cast in lines of arrogance, stressed by the low lids of her full dark eyes.

In a bound her well-beloved was beside her. Flinging away his bloody poleaxe, he opened wide his arms to enfold her. But she still shrank even within his embrace, which would not be denied; a look of dread had come to temper the normal arrogance of her almost perfect face.

"Mine, mine at last, and in spite of all!" he cried exultantly, theatrically, truly heroic.

But she, endeavouring to thrust him back, her hands against his breast, could only falter:

"Why, why did you kill him?"

He laughed, as a hero should; and answered her heroically, with the tolerance of a god for the mortal to whom he condescends:

"He stood between us. Let his death be a symbol, a warning. Let all who would stand between us mark it and beware."

It was so splendidly terrific, the gesture of it was so broad and fine, and his magnetism so compelling, that she cast her silly tremors and yielded herself freely, intoxicated, to his fond embrace. Thereafter he swung her to his shoulder, and, stepping with ease beneath that burden, bore her in a sort of triumph, lustily cheered by his men, to the deck of his own ship. Her inconsiderate brother might have ruined that romantic scene but for the watchful Cahusac, who quietly tripped him up, and then trussed him like a fowl.

Thereafter, what time the captain languished in his lady's smile within the cabin, Cahusac was dealing with the spoils of war. The Dutch crew was ordered into the longboat, and bidden go to the devil. Fortunately, as they numbered fewer than thirty, the longboat, though perilously overcrowded, could yet contain them. Next, Cahusac having inspected the cargo, put a quartermaster and a score of men aboard the Jongvrouw, and left her to follow La Foudre, which he now headed south for the Leeward Islands.

Cahusac was disposed to be ill-humoured. The risk they had run in taking the Dutch brig and doing violence to members of the family of the Governor of Tortuga, was out of all proportion to the value of their prize. He said so sullenly to Levasseur.

"You'll keep that opinion to yourself." the captain answered him. "Don't think I am the man to thrust my neck into a noose without knowing how I am going to take it out again. I shall send an offer of terms to the Governor of Tortuga that he will be forced to accept. Set a course for the Virgen Magra. We'll go ashore and settle things from there. And tell them to fetch that milksop Ogeron to the cabin."

(Continued on page 25.)

The Curse of PENGARTH CASTLE

This exploit of Sexton Blake and Waldo the Wonder-Man is a sequel to the events narrated last week under the title of " The Pauper of Pengarth Castle." This double-length story forms one of the most thrilling and intriguing of a long series concerning the Wonder-Man, and readers who have had the misfortune to miss the first episode will do well to secure it if possible. For those who wish to refresh their memory of the earlier events, a summary of the first story appears overleaf.

THE FIRST CHAPTER.
Strangers in Possession.

PENGARTH CASTLE, Cornwall, was a house of tragedy.

Darkness enshrouded the weed-grown park, and concealed the dilapidations which were all too obvious in the full light of the day. It was fairly late in the evening, and all was quiet.

Upstairs, in one of the bed-rooms, lay the Earl of Pengarth, hovering between life and death. And, locked behind the door of a lower room, lay the remains of Sir William Brag—struck down mysteriously, and killed on the instant.

In the drawing-room sat Lady Betty Hamilton-Page, Lord Pengarth's only daughter. Usually she was a smiling, cheerful girl. But now her eyes were wet and swollen with crying, and she was still sobbing as she sat on the lounge, waiting feverishly for the doctor's verdict.

It seemed to her that hours must have passed.

She knew that everything was wrong. Pengarth Castle was no longer the peaceful habitation she had known during the past few years. There were strangers in possession.

In the hall were two county constables. And in the library there were other strangers. In addition to Sexton Blake and Tinker, Colonel Flowerdew, the Chief Constable, was there—to say nothing of Police-Inspector Burgess, of Launceston.

Old Jelks, the butler, was going about in a semi-dazed condition. His legs, always a trifle unsteady, seemed no longer able to support his withered frame. Born in the castle, and serving the Pengarths throughout his life, the old fellow felt that this tragedy was to mean the end of all things.

It had come so suddenly—so unexpectedly.

Jelks and his wife were the only servants in this entire mansion. Poverty-stricken for years, Lord Pengarth had been unable to retain any other servants beyond these two. They had fulfilled the simple needs of his lordship and Lady Betty. For the girl was motherless and true to her father. It had meant loneliness and solitude remaining at Pengarth Castle. But she had never once complained.

And now it seemed that her father was to be carried off. She was momentarily expecting the doctor to come and announce that the old man had breathed his last.

He had been carried upstairs unconscious—the victim of a sudden stroke. And the girl's horror was further increased by the almost certain knowledge that her father was guilty of the murder of Sir William Brag. Her position was a dreadful one.

All her instincts urged her to hope for her father's recovery. In spite of his gruff manner, his bursts of temper, he was a dear old chap, and the thought of losing him filled Lady Betty with dumb misery.

But yet—wouldn't it be better?

She shrank from the thought. But it came back again and again. What if her father recovered? The problem, instead of being solved, would be intensified a thousandfold. For he would be obliged to stand

THE PAUPER OF PENGARTH CASTLE

—a summary of the events which preceded those of the present story.

RUPERT WALDO, the freakishly-strong, sportsmanlike crook, is motoring in Cornwall, when he is the means of saving from death or injury a girl cyclist. She is Lady Betty Hamilton-Page, the daughter of Lord Pengarth, and she invites her rescuer to return to Pengarth Castle with her and receive the thanks of her father.

Waldo, on the impulse of the moment, introduces himself as Sexton Blake, and under that name is received at the castle and entertained by the earl.

Lady Betty's father proves to be a curious personage. He has been the victim of a crafty lawyer named Simon Slingsby, who has defrauded him out of the title to Pengarth Castle, and sold the property to a new-rich knight named Sir William Brag. Lord Pengarth, however, refuses to give up possession, and intends to repel the invader by force of arms if necessary.

The butler at the castle, Jelks, knows Sexton Blake by sight, and realises that Waldo is an impostor. He telegraphs to the detective to that effect, and Blake later arrives at the castle.

Meantime, Waldo has encouraged the earl in his attitude, and the new proprietor has been turned away. Waldo, when exposed by Blake, cheerfully admits his imposture, and supposedly takes his departure. It is not unlikely, however, that he conceals himself somewhere in the disused part of the castle.

Sir William Brag, having been refused admission, returns at night, intending to force his way in. Lord Pengarth hears the noise of his entry, and goes out. There is a scream. When Blake arrives on the spot, it is to find Sir William Brag dead. The earl has an apoplectic stroke, and is himself at death's door.

It looks exceedingly like murder, and the finger of suspicion is pointed at the Earl of Pengarth

in the dock, to answer the most dreadful charge of all.

Murder!

The girl shuddered and prayed that her agony would soon be lessened. If she only knew, one way or the other! The suspense was beginning to tell on her, and her nerves were becoming ragged.

The door opened softly, and old Jelks appeared.

"Yes?" asked Lady Betty quickly.

"Yes, Jelks?"

"Dr. Stacey would like——" began Jelks quaveringly.

"Bring him in, Jelks—please bring him in!" exclaimed the girl. "I must know something—I must!"

Jelks retired, and a moment later a stout, grey-haired old gentleman entered. He had known Lady Betty since childhood. He had attended to her in all her childish illnesses.

"Oh, Dr. Stacey—please tell me!" exclaimed Lady Betty, as she approached him. "What news have you brought?"

"Calm yourself, child—I have the best news," replied the doctor gently. "Your father is unconscious, but his iron frame will, I believe, withstand this shock. He may recover his senses at any time now."

"You—you mean he will be well?"

"No, I don't mean that," replied the old doctor. "It will be many weeks before your father can walk again. It is possible, indeed, that he may never be able to use his legs any more. But that he will gradually recover I am convinced."

Lady Betty looked at him with dumb horror in her eyes.

"You are thinking of something else?" he asked softly. "Yes, child, I know, without you telling me. But I cannot believe it—I cannot possibly believe it! Your father never struck that blow!"

"But—if he did?"

"In that case the situation becomes terrible beyond expression!" said the doctor gravely. "But you must not allow such ideas to have any place in your mind, child! Good gracious! Can you think a dreadful thing like that of your own father?"

"Please, doctor—please don't scold me!" sobbed the girl. "I don't know what to think! But you—you know what happened! You know my father threatened Sir William Brag this morning, and——"

"I know one thing which inspires me with confidence," interrupted Dr. Stacey quietly. "Mr. Sexton Blake is here, and he has confided to me that he believes your father to be innocent. We can only wait, Lady Betty—wait and see what the night brings forth."

Colonel Flowerdew, the chief constable, was not only looking grave, but intensely troubled.

"You were here, Mr. Blake, and nothing could have been more fortunate than that," he was saying. "I think it will be better for all concerned if you tell us precisely what happened. All the details. And then possibly we may be able to gather some inkling as to the origin of this dreadful tragedy."

Sexton Blake, the famous criminologist, nodded.

"Yes, that is a good suggestion," he admitted. "We have talked at random—merely discussing the aspects of the tragedy. No doubt it will help Inspector Burgess if I give him a full account of what has happened from this morning onwards."

"That's the idea, Mr. Blake," said Inspector Burgess, nodding. "Nothing like having it all clear. If you don't

mind, I'll make a few notes while we're talking."

The little party in the library were looking grave. Even Tinker wore an expression of solemnity which was foreign to his cheerful disposition. But this tragic evening had left its mark.

"My first knowledge of the case begins with last night," said Sexton Blake, as he lighted a fresh cigarette. "I was in London—at home in my Baker Street chambers. A telegram came from Jelks, Lord Pengarth's butler. He informed me that somebody was staying under this roof and using my name."

"Good gracious!" ejaculated the colonel.

Neither he nor the inspector had heard anything about this aspect of the affair, and they were both surprised.

"Tinker and I came down by the night train," continued Sexton Blake. "We arrived this morning, and drove over from Launceston."

"And who was this man—this masquerader?"

"You will be astonished when I tell you," said Blake. "He was quite undisguised, and he made no attempt to impersonate me. He was Rupert Waldo—also known as the Wonder-Man."

"Waldo!" echoed Inspector Burgess, aghast.

"Yet I do not think he is really connected with this tragedy," said Sexton Blake. "I have an idea that it was merely a whim of his to masquerade under my name. It had happened by chance. In yesterday's gale, Waldo saved Lady Betty from a falling tree, and thus gained access to the castle. By using my name, his welcome, it appears, was even more cordial. He took his departure the instant I unmasked him."

"But, good heavens!" ejaculated the colonel. "Couldn't you detain the rascal?"

"If you had ever attempted to detain Waldo, Colonel Flowerdew, you would not ask me that question," said Blake. "I could not have detained him against his will, even if I had had half a dozen helpers. His strength is colossal—his agility startling in the extreme. Sometimes Waldo hardly seems to be human."

"I have heard that he is a hard nut," commented the inspector.

"However, we need not discuss him now," went on Blake. "I am convinced, at least, that he is not connected with the murder. You may, or may not, know that Lord Pengarth has been living in the direst poverty for some years—the culminating point arriving to-day. For Pengarth Castle has been

sold over his head, and was purchased by Sir William Brag—the man who now lies dead."

"It looks very significant," growled the chief constable.

"This morning Sir William arrived to take possession of his new property," continued Blake. "There was no question about the legality of his ownership. He had purchased the property through Mr. Simon Slingsby, Lord Pengarth's lawyer. And he brought the title-deeds with him, and all the necessary documents to prove his claim. Curiously enough, those documents were not upon him when he was found dead."

"You think he came to the castle this evening without them?"

"It certainly appears so, colonel," said Blake. "Well, during the earlier visit, Sir William was refused admittance, and Lord Pengarth plainly told him that if he returned he stood in peril of being shot."

"It grows worse and worse!" growled the colonel.

"Lord Pengarth had an unreasoning hatred against Sir William Brag," said Sexton Blake. "For, after all, Sir William had bought the property in good faith. The real viper, in the earl's mind, is undoubtedly Simon Slingsby. I am personally convinced that Slingsby has robbed Lord Pengarth right and left over a period of many years—until, indeed, he has almost converted him into a pauper,"

"Slingsby is a rogue," growled the chief constable. "I have known it for years. But he is clever—he always acts within the law."

"It was so in this case," said Sexton Blake. "He betrayed Lord Pengarth basely, and the earl did not realise his true position until it was too late. But he swore that he would never leave Pengarth Castle. A Pengarth has lived here for eight hundred years, and it was the earl's boast that no outsider would ever set foot in the castle as its owner."

"Significant!" muttered Colonel Flowerdew.

"Admittedly," agreed Blake. "Lord Pengarth was telling me the story of the old family curse. There is a Sacred Cross, it seems, and the legend runs that if that cross was ever lost misfortune would dog the Pengarths until they were forced to abandon the castle to the invader. That cross was stolen in a burglary sixteen or seventeen years ago, and the ill-fortunes of the family started at about that date."

"But that's all rubbish, surely?" asked Inspector Burgess.

"It may possibly be a coincidence,"

said Sexton Blake. "But the fact remains—and it is certainly rather curious. Well, this trouble came to a head to-day, for Lord Pengarth refused to acknowledge Sir William's claims, and sent him away."

"And Sir William returned this evening, and broke in?"

"That is obvious," said Blake. "He gained admittance by one of the numerous small windows—after having cut through three iron bars. So Sir William was obviously determined—and, after all, there was nothing to prevent him breaking into his own house. He was acting within the law. His plan, no doubt, was to confront Lord Pengarth, and to order him to leave."

The chief constable nodded slowly.

"We are left in no doubt as to what happened after that!" he exclaimed. "Lord Pengarth met the intruder, was infuriated, and struck him down. A most distressing affair, gentlemen. I am almost hoping that Lord Pengarth will die, and thus escape the dreadful ordeal which must otherwise inevitably follow."

THE SECOND CHAPTER.
Waldo Listens.

"THE facts fit in perfectly — there is no other possible way of looking at them," said Inspector Burgess. "I think you told me, Mr. Blake, that you were with Lord Pengarth in the library a few minutes before the tragedy?"

"Yes."

"And he left the library, alone, to fetch an antique he was to show you?"

"Exactly."

"Then, of course, the case becomes clearer and clearer," said the inspector. "Possibly Lord Pengarth heard a noise, went to look into it, and found Sir William getting through the window. One blow must have sufficed to cause that dreadful wound."

"We found Sir William lying dead on the floor," put in Tinker. "Lord Pengarth was standing over him. He said something about having heard a scream—and that looked as though somebody else had committed the murder. But the poor old chap went into a fit, and collapsed before we could ask him any questions."

"You don't think that this Waldo——" began the colonel.

"It is, of course, possible," admitted Blake, "but very unlikely. Waldo had no motive for the crime. He is not the type of man to commit an unnecessary murder—indeed, he has always hesitated at any kind of violence. It is not incorrect to say that his crimes have invariably been characterised by gentlemanly conduct. No, I do not think Waldo had a hand in this."

"But the title-deeds?" put in Inspector Burgess. "I can hardly imagine Sir William getting into the castle without them. He would naturally carry the documents, in order to prove his claim."

"That is one of the knotty points which we must attempt to solve," said Sexton Blake quietly. "So far, I have only made a very cursory examination of the body, and I have not even examined the corridor. As soon as you have finished with me, gentlemen, I shall be glad if you will let me pursue a few investigations."

Colonel Flowerdew nodded.

"By all means, Mr. Blake. We shall be only too delighted!" he exclaimed. "Eh, Burgess? We should be foolish to deny ourselves the services of such an expert. And if there is any possible hope that Lord Pengarth is innocent, nobody will be more delighted than myself. I have known him for years—a fine old fellow! To-night's tragic events fill me with dismay."

Inspector Burgess, bluff and stolid, felt that Sexton Blake's investigations would be rather unnecessary. There was no question whatever about the earl's guilt. From first to last the case was obvious.

Lord Pengarth had threatened Sir William, had even told him that if he came back he would be shot. In his grim determination to retain possession of the castle, the old die-hard had allowed his fury to get the better of him.

Sexton Blake's evidence alone would be enough to convince any jury.

Lord Pengarth had left the library, and two minutes later there had been a scream. And both Blake and Tinker had found his lordship standing over the stricken body of his enemy. It was as clear as daylight.

Moreover, there was no other possible culprit.

Jelks could be ruled out, since he did not possess sufficient strength—and hadn't been anywhere near the spot, in any case. Waldo was an elusive character, and there was no motive in him killing Sir William Brag. So he could be easily ruled out, too.

With Lord Pengarth it was quite different.

The motive was there without looking for it. The very fact that he had suffered a stroke was significant. Overcome by the horror of his action, he had collapsed—as Dr. Stacey had warned him he would collapse if he excited himself too greatly.

Upon the whole, Colonel Flowerdew was hoping that his lordship would pass peacefully away without recovering consciousness. The problem would thus be solved. There would be a brief scandal, but nothing more. If, on the other hand, the Earl of Pengarth recovered, the results would be distressing for all concerned.

So far, the tragedy was unknown to the outside world. Tinker had informed Inspector Burgess, and he, in turn, had communicated with the chief constable. They had told nobody else—except Dr. Stacey. So there were no inquisitive reporters hurrying to the scene. Pengarth Castle contained its own tragedy, and those outside were in ignorance.

Sexton Blake was allowed to go at last. The inspector had gained all the information he needed—he had gleaned every fact. And now, in his opinion, there was nothing further to be done.

On the morrow, of course, there would be an inquest, and the facts would be made public. But until then no action could be taken. As for investigating, the inspector considered that there was nothing to investigate.

Blake and Tinker were about to retire to the drawing-room, when Lady Betty came into the library with Dr. Stacey. They heard that Lord Pengarth would recover.

"Is there any hope, Mr. Blake?" pleaded the girl. "I am sure my father didn't do it. And yet—and yet——"

"My advice, Lady Betty, is for you to set your mind at rest as much as possible," put in Sexton Blake gently. "Lord Pengarth will recover, and the conviction is upon me that this crime was committed by some other hand."

"Please prove it, Mr. Blake," said the girl breathlessly.

But both Colonel Flowerdew and Inspector Burgess gravely shook their heads.

Pengarth Castle was a great, rambling pile, with only a tiny section of it inhabited. The north wing and the west wing were empty and deserted—damp, chilly places, where long corridors ranged, and where endless rooms were slowly falling into decay. For many years they had been neglected, and a considerable portion of the castle was falling into ruin.

The villagers round about declared that ghosts walked the old empty wings—that gruesome spectres were to be seen at the hour of midnight. But such tales, of course, were only to be expected.

It must be admitted, however, that a dim figure lurked spectrally in one of the corridors of the north wing. In one respect, however, this ghost was a novelty—for it paced up and down, enjoying a cigarette.

Furthermore, it was distinctly solid, being no less a person than Rupert Waldo himself.

As Blake had suspected all along, the Wonder-Man had not left the castle after his denouncement. Instead, he had simply made his way to the disused wings, and there had become lost in the wilderness of empty rooms and corridors. It would have been like searching for a needle in a haystack to look for him. And Waldo was elusive enough in any ordinary setting.

And Waldo, it seemed, knew more about this affair than anybody else.

He certainly had a full knowledge as to what had happened to Sir William Brag's documents. They were now in Waldo's own hands, and he was putting them back into his own pocket after a lengthy inspection by the light of his electric torch.

"Decidedly interesting," he murmured complacently. "I can't possibly go away from this place with things in their present stage of development. It goes against the grain."

He was his usual cool self. But how was it that he possessed these documents—which had certainly been upon Sir William Brag at the moment of his death—and which had been missing when Sexton Blake found Lord Pengarth standing over the body?

Was Waldo the murderer?

If the possession of these deeds indicated anything, he certainly was. It proved, at all events, that he not only knew about the murder, but had been present even before Lord Pengarth himself had arrived.

He paced up and down the dark corridor, thinking deeply. The gloominess of his surroundings—the eerie nature of this place—had no effect upon him whatever. Waldo's nerves were of iron.

He had taken an interest in Lord Pengarth ever since their first meeting the previous afternoon.

The old earl's steadfast stand had filled Waldo with admiration—for it was an affair after his own heart. Events had developed in a very different manner from what he had expected, but this only increased his interest.

In the first place, Blake had butted in. It was deucedly queer how Blake always butted into his affairs! Waldo simply couldn't start anything without Sexton Blake haunting him. There was something uncanny about it. But he realised that in this particular instance it was his own doing. For had he masqueraded under any other name than that of Blake, the famous Baker Street criminologist might never have come to Cornwall at all.

"Oh, well, these things are probably sent to try us," decided Waldo calmly. "I don't mind Blake's presence a bit—it gives the affair an added piquancy. But I think I ought to come in somewhere. If I can't make something for myself out of all these ingredients, it's high time I gave up the profession and started poultry-farming."

And Waldo could already see a way in which he could line his pockets. But he was not entirely selfish. His heart was large—as he had proved on many occasions—and if he could help somebody else at the same time, why not?

Besides, there was a certain spice about the decision he had taken which amused his whimsical nature. However, before anything could be done, it was necessary to learn a few definite facts.

He made his way calmly towards the inhabited part of the castle. He did this openly, and when he arrived in the vicinity of the library he was as collected as ever.

The corridor was empty, and behind the heavy library door he could hear voices. He listened. The prospect of being caught never worried him. In the matter of escape his natural gifts had never failed him.

To any normal ear only a blur of voices would have been distinguishable. But Rupert Waldo's hearing was amazing acute. Like all his other faculties, it was highly, abnormally, developed. He could hear Sexton Blake's words without any difficulty.

"My advice, Lady Betty, is for you to set your mind at rest as soon as possible," Blake was saying. "Lord Pengarth will recover, and the conviction is upon me that this crime was committed by some other hand."

"Please prove it, Mr. Blake," came Lady Betty's voice.

"You can be sure that I shall use every effort," said Sexton Blake. "If there is any way of unmasking the truth, I will do so. I wish I could make a definite statement, but at the moment it is not possible."

Waldo nodded to himself.

"There's no mistake about it, Blake's a cute beggar!" he murmured. "He knows all the time that old Pengarth didn't do it. I hope he doesn't suspect me! Surely Blake wouldn't think such unkind things about an old pal?"

He crept away, satisfied. He had learned the main thing he wanted to know—that the Earl of Pengarth would recover. His course was now decided, and he left the castle silently and mysteriously.

Waldo had made up his mind, and that meant he was going to act.

THE THIRD CHAPTER.
Waldo's Way.

MR. SIMON SLINGSBY sat in his study hunched up in an easy chair. It was rather chilly this evening, but the crafty old lawyer did not allow himself the luxury of a fire. His miserly spirit rebelled at the idea.

His house stood on the outskirts of Launceston — an old-fashioned, gaunt-looking house, characteristic of its master.

For Slingsby, the lawyer, was a tall, narrow-shouldered man, with lean cheeks, deeply-sunken eyes, and a sallow complexion. When in solitude, there was something almost repulsive about him.

His clients never saw this phase of his character, though.

With them he was always smooth-tongued, his smile was benevolent, and his plausibility irreproachable. Yet, in spite of his care to maintain an appearance of kindliness, he was well known in Launceston as being "an old devil."

At the present moment he was thinking about Sir William Brag.

Apparently, everything had gone well. Acting upon his—Slingsby's—advice, Sir William Brag had gone to Pengarth Castle to force an entry. True, the four men who had accompanied Sir William had returned, and one of them had reported that he had heard a scream.

But Slingsby took little notice of this. The earl, no doubt, had shouted out in rage at the sight of the intruder. And Sir William was now in possession. It was just as well the unfortunate affair was over.

It had been a worrying time.

Slingsby had drained the old peer to the last penny, and as a final blow he had sold the castle over his head, and had received a huge sum from Sir William Brag in payment. The cunning old lawyer had "wangled" the mortgages in such a way that Pengarth Castle had virtually become his own property before he had passed it on to the now deceased Sir William.

The transaction had only been finally completed that very day, and Sir William's cheque for the main payment reposed in Simon Slingsby's safe. The thought was a comforting one.

There had been a great deal of trouble—Lord Pengarth's obstinacy, Sir William's anger. It was just as well the affair was over.

Without warning, the window shot up, and a lithe form slipped over the sill, and sat there. The heavy curtains had been parted by the newcomer, and Mr. Slingsby stared at him with blank fright.

"Mr. Slingsby?" said Waldo pleasantly. "Yes, without any question! If I may say so, Mr. Slingsby, you have 'lawyer' written over every inch of your unpleasant features."

Rupert Waldo closed the window and stepped into the room with as much assurance as though he had just been announced in the usual manner. Mr. Simon Slingsby looked at him with growing alarm.

"Who—who are you?" he panted huskily.

"Names are of no account, surely?" smiled Waldo. "I am here on urgent business, and let that be sufficient. You may not be aware of it, Mr. Slingsby, but you and I are now about to have a cheery little heart-to-heart talk."

The lawyer was startled beyond measure. True, this intruder had no appearance of a footpad, and his smooth manner was reassuring. He was obviously a gentleman. But his unique method of entry left Mr. Slingsby in no doubt as to his motive.

"You—you rascal!" gasped the lawyer. "You have come here to rob me!"

"Exactly!" said Waldo. "How you do guess things!"

"But you sha'n't—you sha'n't!" shouted Slingsby.

"That, of course, remains to be seen," commented Waldo. "And why this little exhibition of your vocal powers,

Mr. Slingsby? Surely we can do without these animal effects?"

Very coolly he grasped Mr. Slingsby as the latter was about to make a dash for the door. The lawyer felt that he was in the grip of a gorilla. Without any apparent effort, Waldo forced him down into a chair, and while he held him there with one leg and arm he placed another hand over his victim's mouth.

"Now, Mr. Slingsby, surely we can talk quietly," he suggested. "I don't like doing this sort of thing, but unless you keep quiet I shall be compelled to bind you and improvise a temporary gag. How about it? Do we talk quietly, as one gentleman to another, or must you force my hand?"

Slingsby was quivering from head to foot with fear.

He nodded; and Waldo released his hand. Then he moved over to a chair and sat down.

"We might as well be comfortable," he said evenly. "Now, Mr. Slingsby, understand, I have your word that you will not make any outcry. As a gentleman, you would naturally keep the bargain. But as I know you to be several kinds of a tyke, I shall be well on my guard. And the next time I am compelled to silence you I may not be quite so gentle."

The lawyer breathed hard, his fear increasing.

"What—what do you want?" he asked huskily.

"All sorts of things," replied Waldo. "But, first of all, let me give you a little piece of news. Sir William Brag is unfortunately no more. He has been murdered."

"Murdered!" gasped Slingsby, slinking with horror.

"Unfortunately, he met with disaster within Pengarth Castle," said Waldo. "I have now come here to make you sign a few signatures, and pleasant little things of that sort."

He took the documents from his pocket, and Slingsby eyed him fearfully.

Waldo turned the parchments over leisurely.

"In glancing over these title-deeds, it strikes me that something is radically wrong," he commented, with a business-like air. "In the first place, Sir William Brag is not the owner of Pengarth Castle, and never has been. That somewhat moth-eaten pile is the sole property of the Earl of Pengarth."

"You are mad!" panted Slingsby, aghast.

"I have had it brought to my knowledge that for years you have been indulging in consistent robbery," continued the Wonder-Man. "You have betrayed your best client, and have reduced him to poverty. All this is now going to be changed."

"I—I don't understand you!"

"Possibly not; but you soon will," smiled Waldo. "I don't usually go about performing these little acts of restitution, but this time I couldn't resist the temptation. In passing, I might as well observe that I have a strong inclination to wring your neck, but I will be firm and resist it."

"What do you mean? I have been robbing Lord Pengarth?" asked Slingsby, recovering some of his composure. "You are talking insanely! You come here, without knowing any of the facts——"

"Whether I know any facts or not, one look at your face is sufficient," interrupted Waldo complacently. "Seldom have I seen such a crooked visage. It positively fills me with repulsion. Forgive me for being so frank, Mr. Slingsby, but I told you that this was going to be a heart-to-heart talk."

"I'll have the police on you——"

"Now, this is a mere waste of time," put in Waldo. "Come, Mr. Slingsby, you know as well as I do that you have been robbing that unfortunate old man. There are two things that you must do. Firstly, you must alter these deeds so that Pengarth Castle becomes the Earl's property once more; and secondly, you must hand me Sir William Brag's cheque which he gave you in payment of the estate. That has got to be torn up."

"Fool! Madman!" gasped Slingsby. "I will do nothing—nothing!"

"That's a pity," replied Waldo. "There's nothing I hate worse than violence, but unless I get what I want I use it. Come, Mr. Slingsby, it will be quite simple. A few documents, renouncing your ownership or title to Pengarth Castle and the surrounding estates. I am well aware that you are reaping a rich income from property which really belongs to Lord Pengarth. All that is now going to be changed, as I have said."

Slingsby laughed harshly and shrilly.

"I will sign nothing!" he declared. "In any case, my signature would be useless without witnesses——"

"That is a minor detail," interrupted Waldo. "When it comes to the actual signatures, we will see about the witnesses. In the meantime, you will prepare the documents according to my directions. And attempt no trickery. I have a passing knowledge of the law, and I shall see that you leave no loop-hole for yourself."

"And I refuse—point-blank!" snarled the lawyer. "Lord Pengarth has no claim on me! He can fight it out in the Courts if he chooses——"

"That, as you know, is impossible, as Lord Pengarth has no money for fighting purposes," interrupted Waldo. "Furthermore, you have gained everything so completely under your control that he would have no hope. My methods are more drastic, but they save a lot of trouble."

Slingsby sat there, quivering. Guilt was written over every inch of him. But, although he was cornered, he would never admit the fact.

"I will not be brow-beaten and forced into such a mad compact!" he exclaimed fiercely. "You can do your worst! I am at your mercy, but you will never get me to put my signature to anything!"

Waldo reached over to a heavy bronze statuette. Carelessly he took it in both his hands and bent it as though it were made of putty. Slingsby watched, scared out of his wits. Such an exhibition of sheer abnormal strength was an eye-opener. That statuette could never have been as much as distorted by any ordinary man, but Waldo calmly bent it until it snapped in two.

"I don't want to treat you like that, Mr. Slingsby, but you can see how things are fixed," he said smoothly. "Now then, about those documents."

Simon Slingsby panted for breath. He started screaming, but in a second Waldo was upon him. And when the lawyer felt that vice-like grip, and saw the grim, deadly light in Waldo's eyes, he knuckled under.

For the next hour Waldo rather enjoyed himself. At the end of that time he instructed Slingsby to sound the bell. Slingsby did so, and his eyes glittered.

But Waldo took out a long, dangerous-looking knife. He carefully pressed this against Slingsby's side as they sat close together.

Without warning the window shot up, and a lithe form slipped over the sill. Mr. Slingsby stared at the newcomer in blank fright. "Mr. Slingsby?" queried Waldo, pleasantly. (*Page* 6.)

"Remember," he murmured, "I shall not hesitate if you force me!"

The lawyer was on the point of fainting with fear. A moment later his housekeeper entered.

"Ah!" said Waldo smoothly. "Mr. Slingsby desires your signature to one or two documents as a witness. You will please be good enough to sign as I direct."

"Yes, Mrs. Raikes, it is quite right!" panted Slingsby, who had felt a sudden pressure of the knife. "This gentleman will direct you where to sign."

The housekeeper, rather astonished—for she had certainly not admitted this visitor—appended her signature to various documents, immediately following Slingsby's own signature.

"That will do, thank you, Mrs. Raikes!" said Waldo pleasantly. "You have been most obliging."

He handed the astonished woman a ten-shilling note, and she departed, flustered.

"And now, old friend, what about the key of the safe?" suggested Waldo. "What, you object? I am afraid it means more trouble."

He grasped Slingsby as he would grasp a child, swiftly bound his hands behind him, and gagged him with his own duster. Then, going through his pockets, he selected a bunch of keys.

A few minutes later the safe was open, and Waldo not only found Sir William Brag's cheque, which he tore up, but he was gratified to discover a totally unexpected hoard. He had anticipated riches within that safe, but they far exceeded his expectations.

Then he departed, leaving Mr. Slingsby to get free as best he could. Waldo was light-hearted and cheery,

although his pockets were heavy. He was more than pleased with himself.

"I must admit that I have been singularly smart this time," he told himself. "Congratulations, old boy! And if it comes to that, nobody but a gentleman of my profession could tackle this sort of work!"

———

THE FOURTH CHAPTER.
The Clue!

MEANWHILE, Sexton Blake was getting down to some real work.

While Inspector Burgess and the chief constable were talking in the library, gravely discussing what was to be done with regard to Lord Pengarth's arrest, Blake was busy.

He and Tinker were in the passage where the murder had taken place.

"I don't see that there's much to be done, sir," remarked Tinker. "Of course, if Lord Pengarth didn't commit the murder——"

"Hold that light, Tinker, and not quite so much talk!" interrupted Blake. "We are here for facts, not theorising. This is the spot where the murder was committed, and there ought to be some clues if we only know how to look for them. There is quite a lot of dust on this floor."

Tinker played the light steadily.

"I'm afraid it's stirred up too much, sir," he said. "Don't forget we've all been here, including Inspector Burgess and the colonel. There's only a confusion of marks."

Tinker was right.

Examining the floor, there was nothing to be seen, except faint traces of dust, disturbed in every possible manner. This particular passage was not used in the ordinary way. The floor was of stone, and the walls were bare and grim-looking.

Blake and Tinker were close against the window which the unfortunate Sir William had forced open. At this spot he had met his end. Someone had sprung upon him, and had killed him with one tremendous blow—presumably with a stick or a club.

Lord Pengarth's own stick could easily have dealt the blow; but Blake had examined it without finding any trace. It was possible that none remained, but not probable.

And if the earl had not committed the deed, who had? Certainly not Rupert Waldo.

Blake took the light from Tinker, and moved farther on. And here he met with more success.

"It has apparently been taken for granted that the murderer came from the direction of the inhabited section of the house," remarked Blake. "But there is no certainty of that. This passage leads directly into the deserted west wing, and, therefore, it has scarcely ever been used. Beyond this point, indeed, we may expect to find untouched ground. It may possibly reward us with something of an enlightening nature."

They had hardly walked four yards before Blake halted. Here, farther down the passage, and well beyond the fatal window, the dust of the floor was practically undisturbed. No ordinary eye could detect anything. But Blake's trained vision was not deceived.

"Hallo, Tinker! Look at this!" he murmured. "By Jove, this is interesting!"

Blake was bending down low over the floor. He played the light closely, so that it was directed upon one certain spot. Tinker could certainly see a kind of smudge, but it didn't mean much to him. He could not recognise anything distinctive.

"What is it, sir?" he asked keenly.

"A footprint, young 'un."

"Yes; but whose?"

"That is a question I should like the answer to," said Blake. "If you will look closely you will notice one or two very interesting details. In the first place, it is an impression of a naked foot."

"Well, I'm jiggered!" said Tinker.

He wondered why he hadn't seen it before. For now that it was pointed out to him, he could see that Sexton Blake was right. What had been a mere blur, now became something of distinct shape. That imprint had certainly been caused by a naked human foot. It was astonishing how simple it became once it was explained.

"Yes, it's exactly as you say, sir," went on Tinker. "But what did you mean—'in the first place'? You speak as though there's something else."

"And there is, Tinker. What do you think of that toe-mark?"

"You mean that smudge made by the big toe?"

"Yes."

"Well, it looks a little more distinct than the rest," said Tinker.

"I'm very much afraid, young 'un, that you are going backwards instead of forwards," sighed Sexton Blake. "You have missed the point altogether. The mark of that big toe is a surprising distance from the rest of the imprint. In other words, it means that the owner of this foot possesses a splayed toe."

Tinker stared, and gave added attention to the mark on the floor.

"A splayed toe, guv'nor?" he repeated. "But that's like niggers have out in the tropics, where they don't wear any boots."

"Precisely!" agreed Blake. "Perhaps you are not quite hopeless, after all. But I am not implying that this footprint was made by a nigger, as you may possibly imagine. I am merely remarking that it is rather strange that we should find such a thing here in Pengarth Castle."

"It's jolly rummy!" said Tinker, nodding.

And it was undoubtedly strange. The person who had made that footprint was in the habit of going about barefooted, and had indulged that habit for years, in all probability. Nothing else could explain the wide nature of the big toe.

Passing farther down the passage, Blake and Tinker found one or two other traces. But afterwards, in the deserted corridors of the west wing, they lost all trace of the marks.

"Well, we have discovered one thing, at least," said Sexton Blake. "Somebody has been along this passage with bare feet, and I don't think we are making a wild guess when we set that somebody down as the murderer. Before we proceed with this investigation any further, Tinker, I have an unpleasant task to perform."

Tinker looked grave.

"You're going to have a look at the body?" he suggested.

"Yes," said Blake. "The police have given me permission, and I might as well get it over as quickly as possible. So far I have had practically no opportunity, and such an examination is all-important."

Blake lost no time.

He and Tinker went back to the inhabited section of the castle, and found one of the rural constables guarding the room of death. He looked a bit scared when Sexton Blake announced that he wished to go in alone. Blake entered, and the door closed.

"It's more than my nerves could stand, anyway!" remarked the policeman, turning his ruddy face towards

Tinker. "A queer business this, young gent."

"Yes," said Tinker. "And it looks like being queerer, too."

"I hear as his lordship is gettin' better," went on the constable. "Likely he'll be recovered consciousness by now. I think the inspector has been anxious, too. Wants to get a confession."

"Don't you believe it," said Tinker. "He'll get no confession from Lord Pengarth—because he didn't do it. But I'm glad to hear he's getting better. It makes things a bit more cheery."

The constable shook his head gloomily.

"There ain't no doubt about it, sir," he said. "Inspector Burgess ain't fooled, an' he knows. He says that his lordship killed the poor gent, and that's good enough for me."

"I don't like to cast any doubts upon the inspector's brain power, but between you and me, he's a little bit slow," remarked Tinker. "Just you wait until Mr. Blake has finished, then you'll get a surprise."

Sexton Blake, in the meantime, was making his examination.

At first he discovered nothing that could possibly be called a clue. The unfortunate Sir William had been felled by a single blow—a devastating thrust which had caught him in the middle of the forehead, causing instantaneous death.

He had been found lying in the passage with the Earl of Pengarth standing over him. And if the earl's heavy stick had not caused that wound, then something equally heavy must have been used.

Blake could find no trace of the instrument on the wound itself. It had been a clean, direct hit. And that blow had been so swift that the weapon probably bore no traces. Yet, concluded Blake, it seemed strange that such could be the case, for the skin was deeply gashed, and blood must have sprung out in the split fraction of a second.

He turned his attention to other things.

When Blake made an examination it was thorough. He left nothing undone. And at last his persistence was rewarded. He not only found a clue, but a powerful, telling clue of the first importance.

In that moment he knew, absolutely for certain, that Lord Pengarth was guiltless; and this fresh item of evidence was also conclusive that Rupert Waldo had no hand in the killing.

Yet the clue itself was simple.

Examining the dead man's hands, Blake discovered that the right fingers were rigidly gripped. And as Blake was pursuing his inquiry he extracted four hairs from those rigid fingers.

Very carefully he placed the hairs in a little box and slipped the latter into his waistcoat-pocket. He was looking more keen than ever. But the rest of his examination proved futile.

However, he was not disappointed. He had met with far greater success than he had hoped for. Passing out of the death chamber, he relocked it, and handed the key to the constable on duty. Jelks was hovering near, and the old butler was looking awful. There was a haggard, hunted expression in his eyes, and he seemed on the point of a collapse. Blake glanced at him sharply.

"You had better go to bed, Jelks," he said. "This strain is proving too much for you."

The old butler trembled.

"I'm thinking about the master, sir," he muttered. "They're all sayin' that he killed Sir William. It's not true, sir. They oughtn't to believe it. His lordship never did it."

"Do you know who did?" asked Blake curiously.

"I, sir?" asked Jelks, aghast. "What should I know, sir?"

He walked off unsteadily, and Tinker came up to his master.

"Anything fresh, guv'nor?" he murmured.

"Well, yes," replied Blake softly. "One thing is certain, at all events. The murder was committed by a man with naked feet and a rough, unkempt, reddish-brown beard."

Tinker stared at his master blankly.

"Then—then it wasn't Lord Pengarth at all?" he asked. "But how do you know, sir?"

"Never mind how I know," replied Blake. "Come, Tinker; we are just going into the west wing again, and our search may be fruitful."

It was fruitful, but not in the way Sexton Blake anticipated.

THE FIFTH CHAPTER.
All Done by Kindness!

SOMETHING moved near the castle wall. The night was growing old now, and the blackness was intense. Pengarth Castle stood out against the skyline, grim and rugged. For the most part it was in total darkness, and only one or two dim lights shone from the mullioned windows of the inhabited section. The greater part of the castle was in a state of pitch darkness.

The something which moved passed beneath a high tree—a great giant which had stood there for well over a century. What was this object which lurked in the dense blackness? Not a man, surely? For it swung itself up into the tree with the panther-like agility of a forest beast.

Hand-over-hand, with extraordinary ease, the figure climbed to the topmost branch. It was almost uncanny to watch. But then, Rupert Waldo was always fascinating when he was performing one of his daring stunts.

There were none to watch on this occasion.

The man was more agile than a gorilla. Astonishingly enough, by the time he reached his high perch he was as calm and cool as though he had never exerted himself. His breathing was regular and even, and in no way strained. Such exertion had practically no effect upon Waldo's startling stamina.

"Everything seems to be nice and quiet," he murmured. "Now, I wonder what I'd better do? Go off somewhere for a little snooze, or act at once? It might not be a bad idea to ascertain how things are going inside."

He glanced down at the lighted windows, for in this high tree he was above the level of the roof.

"It's rather a nuisance, having to gain entry and exit by this manner," he told himself. "But for Blake I should have had a smooth time of it. However, I'm rather glad I took the job on. It's panning out splendidly. One of the nicest little affairs I've ever handled."

Selecting a strong, supple branch, he climbed out upon it, swung, and at the right moment he released his grip, thrusting himself outwards at the same moment.

The Wonder-Man swung from the branch to the parapet of the building in one clean jump. He landed perfectly, and stood there, recovering his balance.

He did this as a mere matter of course, never seeming to realise that his leap had been of a death-defying character. Possessing no nerves, this aspect of the case had never occurred to him.

But Waldo had really taken his life into his hands. One tiny slip, and he would have missed his mark, and would have gone hurtling down to the stone pathway below.

"So far so good!" he murmured. "Sounds like the villain in the play, but it comes rather apt at the moment. Now we shall have to see about making a re-entry."

He lowered himself over the parapet, clinging to the face of the building like a fly. If Waldo had chosen, he could have made a fortune for himself in the United States by climbing skyscrapers. There wasn't a man in the world who could have touched him at this particular line of business.

And his present task was all the more difficult because it was essayed in the darkness.

Feeling for niches with his toes and fingers, he gradually crept lower. And at length he stood upon a window-ledge, and felt carefully with his fingers. The window, old and decayed, opened with very little pressure. Waldo slipped in, and found himself in a deserted corridor.

He went along this, reached some stairs, and passed down. He was soon on the ground floor, and there he paused, irresolute. Down this corridor he could see an electric-torch gleaming, and he could hear low voices.

"So I am honoured with company," he murmured. "My old friends, Blake and Tinker, too! Shall I allow this opportunity to slip by? Assuredly not."

And, instead of making efforts to conceal himself, or to flee, he strolled calmly forward and met Blake and Tinker face to face.

"So we meet again—eh?" smiled Waldo, looking into the torchlight. "I saw you down this corridor, Blake, so I thought I'd have a few words. Better than coming into the other part of the castle. We can talk quietly here without any fear of interruption."

Blake regarded the Wonder-Man warily.

"You seem particularly pleased with yourself, Waldo," he said, in a replica of Waldo's own cool manner. "What's your exact scheme? What do you hope to gain by prowling about these deserted quarters of the castle?"

"Nothing whatever," replied Waldo. "It may seem strange to you, Blake, but the idea of personal gain did not occur to me. However, luck has come my way, but we needn't go into details about that."

"What have you been up to, you beggar?" demanded Tinker.

"Harsh words from such young lips," said Waldo, shocked. "Come, Tinker, have I ever treated you badly that you should be so cruel? And, whatever my shortcomings, I have never yet descended to begging."

"My hat! You're a caution!" grinned Tinker.

"Ah, that's better!" said Waldo pleasantly. "Let us smile, for I can assure you that everything in the garden is lovely, or it will be when Lord Pengarth has had a few gardeners on the job for a week or two."

The Wonder-Man's bantering tone was characteristic of him.

It was generally impossible to tell whether he was serious or not. He made a fine art of this assumed carelessness. And Blake had good reason to know that Waldo was generally in his grimmest mood when he appeared to be in his lightest.

"Look here, Waldo! We'll be straight," said Blake. "I know very well that I can't capture you single-handed, and you know that I wouldn't shoot you down in cold blood. But if you have no motive in this night prowling of yours, what in Heaven's name are you doing it for?"

"Spoken like a man," said Waldo. "Well, we'll get down to business. The police don't suspect me, do they? They have got it into their thick heads that Lord Pengarth is the murderer."

"Well, what about it?"

"Lord Pengarth is not the murderer. I can tell you that straight away," continued Waldo. "You see, Blake, I am even ready to help you in your little investigation. There's no end to my generosity. All the same, I'll be obliged if you'll refrain from asking me to give a personal account to the police. They may not understand my motives as you do. Besides, it's such a nuisance having the bother of breaking handcuffs, and all that sort of thing."

Blake could hardly help smiling.

"Perhaps you'll tell me what you know?" he suggested.

"Not only with pleasure but with eagerness," said Waldo smoothly. "I know this much, at all events. Sir William Brag was lying dead in the passage a full minute before Lord Pengarth arrived on the scene."

"How do you know this?"

"Because I was with the dead man before the earl appeared."

"You don't mean to tell me you——"

"Come, Blake," protested Waldo; "don't be unkind! Don't think such unwarrantable things of me. I may be several kinds of a rogue—you see, I admit it freely—but I am no murderer."

"You are too previous, Waldo," said Blake grimly. "I was not going to accuse you of the murder, because I know that you did not commit the crime. I was going to ask you if you saw the murderer."

"Unfortunately, no," said Waldo. "I was just too late for that interesting item. I heard the scream and I heard a scurry of feet. But when I arrived on the spot Sir William was quite alone. I seized the opportunity to act with my usual quick-witted agility. In short, I went through Sir William's pockets."

"You—you ghoul!" growled Tinker, startled.

"You misjudge me," said the Wonder-Man, shaking his head. "I only wished to obtain certain documents which the dead man had been carrying in his breast-pocket. I may say I obtained them, and I have since put them to good account."

"What in the world are you doing, Waldo?" asked Blake. "What is the meaning of all this activity on your part? If you are not out for personal gain, wouldn't it be better not to interfere?"

"I regret that you should use such a term in reference to my good offices," said Waldo sadly. "But the fact is, I'm acting on the square. I know that it will hit you sideways, but it remains a fact. And, what is more, I am particularly anxious to see Lord Pengarth at once."

"Your impudence is unbounded!"

"It is not impudence, Blake," said Waldo quietly. "I have a very good reason. Honour bright, old man, I wish to see Lord Pengarth urgently—vitally. You can take my word for it that I have no wrong intentions."

Blake shook his head.

"It amazes me, Waldo, why you don't change your tactics, and utilise your wonderful ability to good purpose!" he exclaimed. "Now and again you come out with something decent, and then you drop back into your bad habits. What is your game this time?"

"It is the excitement of it that appeals to me, Blake. You can't expect anything else after so many years," replied the Wonder-Man. "But about Lord Pengarth. Will it be possible for me to see him?"

"Your request is an extraordinary one," said Blake, frowning. "But for your assurance that I could take your word, I would never consider the matter. Even now, I do not know whether it is possible."

"Has the old chap recovered consciousness?"

"Yes; but he must not be disturbed."

"I shall not disturb him—I shall bring him happiness," said Waldo quietly. "It may seem strange to you, Blake, but I have taken a liking to old Pengarth—and his story rather knocked me. So I've been working on his behalf."

"You have been to Simon Slingsby?" asked Blake keenly.

"No good trying to keep anything from you!" growled Waldo. "I might as well admit it—and I must see Lord Pengarth at once!"

Sexton Blake only hesitated for another moment.

"Come with me," he said shortly.

Waldo made no comment, but there was an expression in his eyes which clearly told that he was grateful. There was nothing unusual in this "fraternising" between detective and crook. Sexton Blake and Rupert Waldo usually conversed as though they were old friends.

Somehow, it was almost impossible to regard Waldo as a dangerous criminal. He had such an air of open straightforwardness about him that even Tinker was sometimes deceived. It was small wonder that Waldo was about the cleverest confidence man in existence!

Sexton Blake led the way to a deserted staircase, and they mounted. By this means they got to the upper floor of the inhabited section. And within a few moments they were outside Lord Pengarth's door.

"Wait!" said Blake softly.

He entered and found the room empty, except for the patient. Many candles burned, and the Earl of Pengarth was propped up in bed, pale, drawn, and ill. But he was fully conscious, and his eyes kindled slightly when Blake appeared.

"I am glad you have come, Mr. Blake," he murmured. "Betty has gone out for a moment—to fetch me a drop of port, that is, if the doctor will permit. I don't like being alone. I cannot help seeing that huddled form. They think I killed poor Brag, don't they?"

"Do not upset yourself, Lord Pengarth."

"But I didn't, Mr. Blake—he was killed before I arrived on the spot!" exclaimed the old earl tensely. "I want you to prove that—I want you to establish my innocence."

"One moment, Lord Pengarth," said Blake softly.

He went to the door, and beckoned Waldo and Tinker to enter. Lady Betty appeared at the same moment, carrying a glass of port on a tray. She gazed open-eyed at the Wonder-Man.

"If you will please leave us, Lady Betty——" began Blake.

"Not at all!" interrupted Waldo. "Lady Betty, I shall be honoured if you remain. What I have to say to your father concerns you quite as much as it concerns him."

She was too surprised to answer, but Blake said no more. They all entered the sick-room.

"What's all this—what's all this?" demanded the earl, with a slight return of his old manner. "Gad! Am I to be disturbed by a whole regiment? Can't I be decently ill without this invasion?"

"First of all, Lord Pengarth, I wish to tell you that I shall be able to establish your innocence almost at once," said Blake quietly.

"Oh, Mr. Blake!" ejaculated Lady Betty, clasping her hands.

"Good!" growled his lordship. "That's a fine piece of news, Mr. Blake! I'm glad you stayed here—upon my soul I am! But what's this man doing here? Bless my life! It's the fellow who came here at first—masquerading as you, Mr. Blake."

"Pray let me apologise for disturbing you, Lord Pengarth," said Waldo quietly. "But I happen to have some of your property in my possession, and I wish to return it to you."

Lord Pengarth, in spite of his weakness, tried to sit up.

"Good gad!" he ejaculated. "Then you did try some of your thieving tricks? You infernal rascal——"

"You misjudge me," interrupted Waldo. "While I was under your roof, Lord Pengarth, I respected your hospitality—even though I was a rank impostor. This property of yours has been missing for years—and that is why I am more than ever delighted to restore it."

He placed a number of documents on the bed.

"What are these?" demanded the old earl. "Papers—legal documents! Take the accursed things away! Haven't I seen enough of them? Haven't they brought me ruin?"

"But this time they have brought you fortune," put in Waldo smilingly. "You will find them quite in order. Mr. Simon Slingsby has had a revulsion of feeling, and, after due consideration, he has decided to restore everything of yours that he has filched. You will find that these documents legally give you back full titles and ownership of Pengarth Castle, Pengarth Park, and the rich farmlands surrounding this district. In other words, Lord Pengarth, you are practically restored to your former position of affluence."

Lord Pengarth was stunned—he was in no condition to receive such a surprise as this. Even Sexton Blake was startled. And Lady Betty stood there, pale with excitement. It seemed that she was listening to some wild fairy tale.

"Is this true, Waldo?" asked Blake quietly. "Heaven forgive you if you have deceived Lord Pengarth!"

"While admitting that I am a pastmaster in the art of deception, I have practised nothing of that nature this time," replied Waldo calmly. "I am grateful to you, Lord Pengarth," he added, "for having given me the opportunity of interviewing Mr. Simon Slingsby. I can assure you it was a most enjoyable hour."

"Has Slingsby agreed to this?" panted his lordship.

Waldo smiled.

"Well, I can hardly say that he agreed to the affair, but he certainly signed these deeds, and they are duly witnessed," replied the Wonder-Man. "Let him bring what legal action he chooses, he will lose the case. This property is now yours, Lord Pengarth. It is just a case of poetic justice. Slingsby robbed you—and I have robbed Slingsby. It has all been done by sheer kindness."

Blake pursed his lips. He was in a delicate position. He turned aside, feeling that it would be far better for him to be officially ignorant of this transaction. That it was morally right there could be no question. And as Sexton Blake was not concerned, he thought it better to remain in ignorance.

THE SIXTH CHAPTER.
A Self-Confessed Burglar.

THE Earl of Pengarth clasped Waldo's hand.

"I cannot thank you for what you have done," he said quietly. "They call you a criminal, but I cannot regard you as such. Yet you have proved that you are accustomed to such work—by your visit to Simon Slingsby."

"There is something else, Lord Pengarth," said Waldo. "And I fancy it is something which places Slingsby entirely in your hands, and brands him for all time as a criminal far worse than myself. I would rather starve in the gutter than be a man like Simon Slingsby."

"What are you referring to?" asked his lordship.

"If it is as I think, the rascally reptile will have no chance of claiming restitution," replied Waldo. "And you, for your part, will be able to take legal proceedings, if you think it advisable —if you consider that this method of mine is not quite—well, the thing."

He pulled out a velvet bag from his pocket. This he emptied on to the coverlet, and a number of jewels fell out—a diamond necklace, rings, brooches, a wonderful pearl bracelet. And there was something else, too—something which Lord Pengarth seized upon with a hoarse cry.

"The cross!" he panted. "The Pengarth cross!"

He clutched it to him, and Lady Betty bent over the bed.

"Dad," she breathed, "please, dad! You mustn't excite yourself——"

"Child, child!" broke in her father. "Don't you see? It's the Pengarth cross! It means the end of the Curse—the end of the Pengarth ill fortunes!"

The girl was white with excitement and joy.

"And it means also that I can now freely acknowledge Waldo's work," put in Sexton Blake, turning. "That cross was stolen sixteen or seventeen years ago, Lord Pengarth, and it has remained in Slingsby's possession ever since. If you wish, it is within your power to send him to penal servitude."

"He shall go!" vowed Lord Pengarth grimly.

"Do you recognise these trinkets?" asked Waldo.

"Recognise them?" repeated the earl. "Why, yes! They are my poor wife's jewels. They were stolen at the same time as the cross. So Slingsby was the thief! The cur—the villainous viper!"

"He must have taken them on purpose, so that he could work on your feelings regarding the curse," said Sexton Blake. "That, undoubtedly, was his scheme. If all these facts come out, Lord Pengarth, there is not the slightest doubt that you will win—both in a civil court and in a criminal court. I am not sure that it would not be better to let things rest as they are, and thus avoid all scandal and publicity."

(Continued on page 19.)

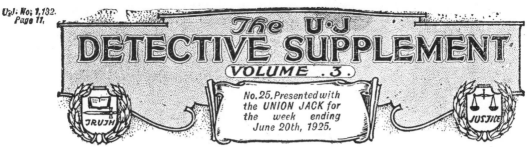

The U·J
DETECTIVE SUPPLEMENT
VOLUME .3.

No. 25, Presented with
the UNION JACK for
the week ending
June 20th, 1925.

"Looney" Laws

Legal lapses that lead to little but laughter.
By Kerslake Carr.

OPINIONS are divided as to which is the most "comic" law on our Statute Books. Those who have witnessed a tobacconist, say, calmly defying the law after the regulation serving hours might be inclined to award the palm to that law which forbids anyone to buy or sell tobacco in any form after the clock strikes eight at night—nine on Saturdays.

All tobacconists are not as bold as the one the writer saw the other day. It was Saturday evening, and the clock was striking nine. Promptly on the last stroke the tobacconist wrapped his arms around a slot machine which stood in his shop and shuffled with it to the doorstep.

There he planted it, and there by its side he remained, whilst customers, whom the law forbade to purchase cigarettes from the owner of the machine, dropped their sixpences into the slot and got packets of cigarettes in exchange.

The reason the tobacconist stood there

was to supply customers with change. And the reason his shop lights remained on after he had officially closed for the night was to guide to his slot machine these customers who were not customers —inasmuch as no one served them.

To complete the comic performance, a policeman stood a few feet away, anxiously waiting for the supply to run out and for the defiant tobacconist to retreat into his shop for more cigarettes. Then, of course, the shopman would have been "for it," with no technical niceties to save his bacon.

Only a few months ago English Members of Parliament were backing a Bill which was designed to wipe out idiotic laws purposely made to annoy Roman Catholics in the reigns of Edward VI., Queen Elizabeth, and Georges I. to IV.

Scores of years back those particular laws began to be ignored, until at last no one took any notice of them. But they were still on the Statute Book. Among them were a law forbidding Roman Catholic books of religion "ever to be kept in this realm"; preventing any priest wearing his vestments outside a Roman Catholic church, or performing Roman Catholic rites other than in his church, the penalty for each offence being fifty pounds; and another ordering the banishment for life of any member of a religious order daring to enter England.

In spite of those and numerous other "comic opera" laws, this country does not take the palm. We have not by any means a monopoly of freak laws.

Even now they are being passed briskly by some of the State legislatures in America, where the "blue sky law" season seems to have something in common with England's "silly season" —when legitimate news runs short and the newspapers are driven to find giant gooseberries and to locate the ever-popular sea-serpent.

The comical ease with which the prohibition regulations are evaded in the States has grown stale; people no longer smile at it. But their grins are lengthening at the result of America's latest law-making campaign.

The legislators of Texas, in particular, are looking after prohibition interests, the latest move being directed at doctors who prescribe alcohol for imaginary complaints, and at patients who thus endeavour to quench their thirst.

Now the doctors of Texas have to publish the names of such patients, that all and sundry may know. Doctors and patients who thus strain the prohibition laws become linked together by name, and it is the sort of notoriety they do not like.

That the prohibition laws are thought deserving of the epithet "looney" is owing to the manner in which they are not carried out. Those whose duty it is to enforce the laws are sometimes the leading spirits in bootlegging enterprises, but even their worst efforts to make the law laughable are feeble compared with the law-breaking of the doctors and chemists.

The Prohibition Director of New York last month made his report on the

"Rushed into the hotel . . . and turned the lot into the street."

general lawlessness which results from the open contempt shown for the liquor laws.

He is reported as declaring that the New York chemists hand out drinks freely and impartially, and no less than 5,000,000 forged medical prescriptions calling for liquor by way of medicine are held by them.

It is the countless thousands who defy it who have made that law a "funny" one. Not so the anti-dancing legislation that surprised San Francisco a while back. Where innocent dancing is enjoyed it can surely be the concern of no one but the dancers as to how long the dancing continues.

So thought the dancers of 'Frisco, until two clergymen suddenly unearthed an ancient law which forbade dancing after midnight. At the head of a posse of police, the clergymen rushed into the hotel where the dancing was in progress and turned the lot into the streets.

The kill-joy Puritan spirit showed plainly there. Somewhat similar is the old law, still on the Statute Books of this country but now seldom if ever

"A policeman stood a few feet away, anxiously waiting for the supply to run out."

enforced, which empowers church-wardens to turn the drinkers out of any public-house on a Sunday directly the church-bells stop ringing.

But to revert to 'Frisco. A number of well-to-do citizens were collecting money for the purpose of giving poor kiddies of the city a Christmas treat. To augment the funds they were running a raffle.

The local clergy dug up an old law which said that sort of thing was criminal. So the would-be benefactors of the poor were run in and put on trial.

There are many other laws which the folk of 'Frisco object to as silly, but which they still have to put up with as relics of the old Puritan misery-spirit previously alluded to.

Among the funniest of them are a few which harm no one in these days, but which no doubt were irksome to some in times gone by—as, for example, those who took their sport by way of rabbit shooting from the city tramcars.

That may have been possible when San Francisco was a little more rural than it is at present, but it certainly isn't possible to shoot rabbits—from tramcars or in any other way—in the city limits now.

Other acts which 'Frisco knows to be unlawful—because the Statute Book still says so—are the giving of snuff to children below the age of sixteen, the selling of snakes in public streets, and the washing of two babies simultaneously in one tub.

Remarkable habits those, and surely do not need much suppressing in these days. But youngsters who defy the old laws by playing in the streets with a ball or popgun are terrible criminals. The worst part about it is the unwillingness of the kiddies, when caught in the act, to wait for the policeman to lay hands on them and complete the arrest.

They persist in "beating it." So the puritanical-minded of 'Frisco are agitating for another humorous law, whereby

"Illegal to drive a donkey at more than six miles an hour —past a cemetery."

the juvenile popgun players and ball bouncers will be compelled to stand their ground when called on by the police to do so—and not to resist arrest !

In Ohio there is a law which discourages "speed" to such an extent that it is illegal for anyone to drive a donkey at a swifter pace than six miles an hour —past a cemetery. The last clause seems to have been thrown in to make it funnier still.

The legislators of Ohio are seriously considering erasing that law from their Statute Book and substituting for it one that prohibits the attendance of more than five couples at any one dance on a Sunday.

A freak law which is worrying the sportsmen of Pennsylvania puts a ban on Sunday fishing; it is to be presumed that the kill-joys who defeated the late movement to have that law rescinded

consider the fishes should have one day's rest in seven, too.

The teaching of the theory of evolution is illegal "way down in Tennessee." But Alabama rightly threw out a Bill cast on similar lines. The length of hatpins which the ladies of Massachusetts employ to skewer on their headgear has been furiously debated on in that State. A movement was made to amend the law which kept the said length down to a respectable number of inches, but the anti-hatpin legislators would have none of it.

In Massachusetts, too, the law makes baseball on Sunday illegal; and the ladies are definitely classed among the irresponsible lower animals by being sternly refused the privilege of serving on juries.

The wildest of these legal restrictions become almost sane in comparison with the action of one of the legislators of Rhode Island, who moved the adoption of a resolution to severely censure President Coolidge because of his refusal to buy a new hat.

It is a widespread custom among Americans to celebrate Easter by purchasing new headgear. The President did not want a new one, and, Easter or no Easter, refused to fall in line with the custom. Naturally, Rhode Island legislature turned the astonishing resolution down.

Jury law in France is a mass of technicalities. The jury who were umpiring a case in Paris tripped up over one of them, and in consequence the alleged murderer who was on trial was acquitted in face of the verdict.

The correct legal term which the jury should have used in giving their answers to the various questions put to them is, "By a majority." The term the jury used was, "Yes, unanimously." But a fresh trial followed the accused man's acquittal, and this time the jury was well drilled in the funny law which puts technicalities before commonsense.

Identified by Wooden "Fingers."

The Latest in Finger-Print Clues.

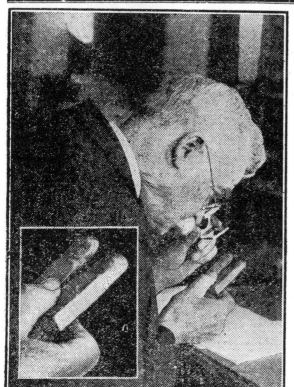

[*Photo: P. & A.*]

READERS of the Detective Supplement are—or should be—by this time well versed in the marvels of finger-print science. The accompanying photograph carries us a step farther. It shows Walter Kaye, the finger-print expert of the U.S. Army, and who is in charge of over 7,000,000 prints, examining skin taken from a dead soldier.

The soldier, with no marks on his body by which he could be identified, and with no papers to give a clue as to who he was or where he come from, was found drowned at Galveston, Texas.

Parts of the flesh from the dead man's fingers were at once removed and preserved in alcohol. The strange relic was then forwarded to the U.S. Army finger-print wizard, who had the flesh mounted on improvised wooden fingers so that prints could be made of them.

In spite of the vast number of prints in Mr. Kaye's keeping, it was the work of a few minutes only after the prints had been made that corresponding prints were found in the files, and the identity of the unfortunate soldier thus established, beyond all possibility of doubt.

Even in death, the flesh reveals its secrets to the scientist who reads the signs that others cannot see, or who, seeing, has not the eerie skill that deep knowledge of the science of finger-prints gives.

This unknown warrior was not to have a nameless grave. It happens to be the fashion in the American Army for all recruits on enlistment to be finger-printed. All such prints are carefully indexed and cross-indexed, so that to turn up a group of prints that bears close resemblance to any sample finger-print that may be submitted for identification is a job not nearly so appalling as it sounds. Attached to each print in that 7,000,000 collection is a list of particulars concerning the owner in question.

The Amazons of New York

By James B. Lindsay.

At first regarded as females whose one desire in life it was to mimic the male and gain notoriety, the New York women who took up policework have builded even better than they knew. They have not only convinced the scoffers and sceptics that women can perform the functions of police better, in some circumstances, than men; but the United States in general and the world at large have copied the example of the New York authorities in encouraging this new arm of the crime repression forces

THE age of the helpless, inefficient woman is past.

In the rush and turmoil of present-day existence there is not room for the sluggard, and women all over the world are realising this, and seizing every opportunity to branch out and do useful work for the community.

Especially may this be said of women in America. One of the organisations which has specially benefited from this phase of the fast-moving period of evolution is the police department, and perhaps the busiest of all the busy women of to-day is Mrs. Mary E. Hamilton, the director of the Women's Police Corps in New York.

To outward appearance an ordinary attractive-looking woman, with thick curly hair and an engaging manner, she possesses a remarkable power for organisation and administration, coupled with a fund of sympathy and tact.

It is the possession of these qualities that has made Mrs. Hamilton such an unqualified success in the work she started some seven or eight years ago. At that time she was New York's one and only policewoman.

To-day she is the presiding genius, the chief in command, and the heart and soul of the women's police department, which has grown so rapidly under her supervision.

When the first policewoman was elected in New York in 1917, the progressive departure from custom thus made caused quite a stir. Until that time policing the streets of the city and the various police-courts had been considered essentially a man's job.

There were desperate gunmen to be subdued, revolver battles, ambushes, rough drunkards to be steered to the police-station, and murderers to be guarded while awaiting trial and punishment.

SUCH things were, of course, beyond the scope of the average woman's physical strength, but there were a hundred and one other duties connected with the prevention and punishment of crime that could be done even better than by men.

This at least was the idea held by Mrs. Hamilton when she took on the uncommon task of founding a women's police corps, and the correctness of her views has been amply proved during the eight years she has been serving in the police department.

It was in 1917 that this first policewoman started her career, and she found her job no easy one. The members of the existing force, while showing her every courtesy and consideration, were nevertheless prejudiced against the innovation, and did not attempt to disguise the fact.

"Police work is not a thing for women," they would say. From all sides Mrs. Hamilton was assailed with this remark, uttered in a tone which obviously admitted the futility of arguing on the matter.

Mrs. Mary E. Hamilton, the first policewoman appointed in New York. She later became head of the policewomen's training school and is now director of the entire women's corps. [*Photos.: G. P. A*]

It took this enterprising woman some years of hard work, in fact, to convince the police chiefs of the importance of the work she was so willing and anxious to undertake.

Possibly she may not even then have been able to convert them to her way of thinking had it not been for the splendid results she was able to achieve right from the start.

Mrs. Hamilton's distinction of being the only policewoman in New York city did not last for long. Very soon she had equipped herself with a small staff of helpers, which she chose with extreme care from the large number of applicants.

Although the job of assistant to New York's policewomen was a number one size job (and Mrs. Hamilton let it be known from the start that it was no sinecure), there was an enormous number of women eager and anxious to join the "force." Young and old were ready to be recruited, some proving themselves eminently suitable, while others were obviously of the wrong type.

One recruit, a young miss in her teens, was extremely eager in her desire to be a policewoman. The earnestness of her letter of recommendation, written by the young aspirant herself, caused no little amusement at the headquarters of the women's corps.

"Although only sixteen years of age," wrote the would-be Sherlock, "I am a keen judge of human nature, an expert in Italian Black Hand and criminal lore, the inventor of twenty lightning-change make-ups, an instinctive senser of crime, and in experience far beyond my years."

The applicant, if not overwhelmingly modest, was at least earnest, but despite the lurid recommendation, Mrs. Hamilton preferred to choose her staff from women, who though perhaps not such "instinctive sensers of crime" were a little older in years as well as in experience.

The qualities and accomplishments demanded by Mrs. Hamilton are legion. Her followers and helpers must first of all be in excellent health. A weakling or semi-invalid would soon come to grief when confronted with an all-night duty or other such tiring task.

They must be fearless, bold, sympathetic, and tactful, with a very generous supply of common-sense, and affection for mankind in general. (This last because Mrs. Hamilton hoped more to win the confidence of criminals and so prevent crime, than to make arrests or punish wrong-doers.)

A course of physical training is necessary, and every would-be policewoman has to possess a capability for disguising herself and acting a part when necessary.

A knowledge of firearms and how to use them is also demanded of these versatile officials, and more than one policewoman has been thankful to have such knowledge and has had occasion to put it to the test.

ONE such was Miss Jean Barnes, a major in the women's police reserves, who was instrumental in pursuing some desperate bandits, and keeping them at bay by the plucky use of her pistol.

As far as her title went, this "major" belied her name, for she was a slender, diminutive woman; but she made up in pluck what she lacked in size.

Two bandits had raided a delicatessen shop in New York, forcing the proprietor into a back room at the pistol's

This uniform has been discarded by the corps of women police, who now work mainly in ordinary attire.

point, while they themselves emptied the till.

Then they fled, but the alarm was soon given, and Major Barnes, who happened to be near at hand in her car, gave chase. Four patrolmen were also soon on the spot, and together these five officials pursued the hold-up men.

Through the crowded streets dashed the cars, and Major Barnes, who was in the van of the pursuing party, had almost overtaken her quarry when the bandits hastily left their car and took refuge behind some huge boulders in a field.

The policemen tried to persuade their fair comrade to back out at this stage and seek safety, but she was deaf to their urgings. Loading and reloading her weapon, she fired shot after shot at the two desperadoes, while the answering bullets zipped round her head and cut up the turf at her feet.

Unfortunately, however, the gunmen eventually got away, although for half an hour the besieged and besiegers fought out their battle, the two bandits behind a boulder and the police officials ensconced in a hedge, with crowds of spectators surging as close as they dared, to watch the uncommon spectacle of a woman taking part in a gun-battle.

And last but not least, the would-be policewoman must have a cool nerve.

No person inclined to hysterics, no sufferer from "nerves," and no woman who got flustered when in a tight corner need apply.

Yet even when demanding such qualities as these Mrs. Hamilton found no lack of material upon which to draw for supporters and assistants as and when she required them. Little by little at first, and later on by leaps and bounds, the policewomen's corps grew, until to-day the one-time solitary policewoman is director over more than a hundred and twenty of her kind.

They include plain-clothes detectives; a "Masher Squad," whose business is to scare away the pests who accost and annoy women; traffic police; patrolwomen; matrons on duty in gaols; and a reserve squad. The latest idea is to establish an aviation corps, to be incorporated with the women's police-corps.

For the training and instruction of her growing staff Mrs. Hamilton has organised a school, where applicants can be taught first-aid, various phases of American law, methods of identification, and other police methods.

A course of psychology is also on the agenda of this training centre, together with various other helpful subjects, not the least interesting of which are the study of firearms, ju-jitsu, and ways of arresting obstreperous persons.

So it will be seen that the potential policewoman has at least a good chance of commencing her career well equipped with useful knowledge to fit her for the task.

The physical culture training is, in Mrs. Hamilton's opinion, one of the most important of subjects to be mastered, and before qualifying as a member of the force the applicant has to be able to register a grip power of 160 pounds with either hand on a special machine which has been installed in the gymnasium, and also to jump at least three feet from the ground over a rope.

But although this policewoman lays such stress on the need for physical strength and adaptability, there is something else that she considers even more potent, and that is personality.

It is in this particular that the capable, lovable woman herself excels. According to statistics there are in New York every year about 17,000 young people who run away from their homes, seventy-five per cent of whom are girls —respectable, morally good girls.

This is where Mrs. Hamilton comes in. Those girls, and boys, too, must if possible be saved from the consequence of their thoughtless action in leaving a good home. In many cases the runaways can, by judicious persuasion, be induced to return, and in nearly every case the young delinquent can be watched, and to a certain extent saved from joining the ranks of the underworld—which was heretofore the usual fate of runaways.

For this purpose a system of supervision of dance-halls, cabarets, cinemas, and other places where the young congregate was established, and the "patrol - women" have done some remarkably good work in weaning these ignorant youngsters away from their criminal companions.

"Prevention is better than cure," is a motto that is applicable to crime more than any other ill, and it is a sentiment often expressed by Mrs. Hamilton. By her work of patrolling the haunts frequented by the young novices in crime, and those who have run away from parental control and are in a fair way of becoming criminals, she has been instrumental in preventing crime to a very large extent.

IT is not hard to understand that a young girl or woman who has done wrong would rather confess her story and her penitence to such a sympathetic listener as Mrs. Hamilton than to a male member of the police force.

The motherly woman is able to gain the confidence of nearly every person with whom she comes in contact. In fact, some of the delinquents who have seen or heard of Mrs. Hamilton are in the habit of forgetting that she is in reality a member of the police force herself. One young girl went so far as to write to her to the effect that she had just run away from home, giving the address of the house in which she had hidden herself. The letter, written in all confidence, concluded with the naive request: "Please don't tell the police."

As Mrs. Hamilton's object is not to make arrests, but to strike at the root of the matter and prevent people becoming criminals, she did not "tell the police" but sought out the misguided young maiden, and, after pointing out to her the pitfalls that beset ignorant youth in the big cities of the world, soon had the satisfaction of returning her to her mother's care.

"This phase of policework is really impossible for men to do," said Mrs. Hamilton, and there are few who will disagree with her in that.

"Frankly," declares the woman police chief, "we don't believe that men have been wholly successful in their methods of dealing with crime. Ever since the time of the first criminal men have been handling wrong-doers by knocking them over the head and putting them away with others of their kind.

"At present our gaols are uncomfortably crowded, our penitentiaries, reformatories, and similar institutions are filled, and we have a steady procession on line waiting for the electric chair. If an employee falls down on a job we give another man a chance. That is why we figure that women should be allowed a chance to show what they can do in the way of halting crime."

Members of the American Women's Motor Corps practise night shooting in the dark with radium sights on their pistols. Thus far do the authorities foster in their women police the art of self-defence.

[Photo: Keystone.]

Another useful work on the part of the women police chief was her assistance in the organisation of the "Missing Persons" Bureau. The results of this collecting together of the various reports of missing persons, which had till then been filled in various sections of the police department, were instantly appreciated.

Hitherto it had been a somewhat lengthy task to dig out the particulars relating to a missing person, but under the new scheme a complete list of the descriptions of all persons reported to the police as missing is kept on file in one department, and can be instantly turned up.

The footprinting of children is also one of Mrs. Hamilton's pet schemes. Babies are constantly being kidnapped in the United States, and babies are, of all people, the most difficult to identify. They change so quickly from day to day that even after only a week or two's absence a mother is often hard put to it to really recognise her own child unless there is some infallible mark upon the little body.

COMPULSORY footprinting would do away with all this trouble, and would supply an absolutely sure and reliable means of identification.

Apart from kidnapping, this procedure would be found extremely useful in infants' hospitals. Where there are a number of young babies in one ward,

piling a list of women who are known to have a strong desire for children, and have none of their own. These are the potential kidnappers.

"We hope, by a system of indexing the names of such women," states this police worker, "to run down many cases of kidnapping."

American policewomen enjoy the same status as do the policemen, their pay, like their male prototypes, being graded according to rank. The minimum rate is about £7 per week, rising in about five years to about £10. It will be realised, of course, as regards these figures, that the cost of living in the United States is high, and wages correspondingly higher than in this country.

For extra qualifications, such as that of a trained nurse, experienced social

the direct supervision of Mrs. Mary E. Hamilton.

The great idea in Mrs. Hamilton's mind is that all women offenders, or women who come within the jurisdiction of the police, should be dealt with exclusively by members of their own sex, and as the first step towards this desired end, the all-women police-station was opened in a very thickly populated part of the city known as "Hell's Kitchen."

A great deal of real detective work is also done by the American policewomen, and it has been found that this work has often been remarkably successful where the male member of the force would have been powerless to glean any information.

ABOVE.—A group of New York policewomen in marching formation. New York has 120 of them. LEFT.—One of the duties assigned to the women police is the regulation of traffic in the vicinity of schools. No accidents have occurred at the busy corner shown here since Major Alice B. Allen took charge.

the nurses find it even more difficult than the parents to distinguish one from another, and cases have been known where a child has been unwittingly substituted.

There are many nationalities in New York, and if a young Italian baby is returned to a mother who left an Irish offspring at the hospital some months previously, she has not much redress unless there is some absolutely infallible mark upon her child's body. Even then the lost one cannot be always traced, especially if it has been released from the hospital some time previously.

All distress of this sort would, of course, be obviated if footprinting were universally carried out. "In fact, there is no reason at all," says Mrs. Hamilton, in a pamphlet on the subject, "why all of us should not be fingerprinted or footprinted, and why these prints should not be put in the Bureau of Records."

Meanwhile, Mrs. Hamilton is doing something herself in the way of collecting records. Her idea is to limit as much as possible the terrible crime of kidnapping. To this end she is com-

worker, or expert detective, the pay is of course more. A detective of the first grade, for instance, earns between £12 and £13 a week, so that the novice has quite a decent salary to start with, and a goal to work for.

The ordinary policewomen work eight hours a day, or night, working in shifts. They are allocated to certain precincts, or "beats," and are responsible to the inspector of that beat.

Their duties are almost innumerable. There is infant welfare work to be done; the adults of to-morrow to be guarded from vice and crime as much as possible, so that they may have a fair chance of becoming respectable citizens; lost children to be cared for and returned to their parents; runaway adolescents to be traced; and would-be suicides, women shoplifters, drug addicts and the like to be weaned from their ways of crime.

New York has the distinction of possessing the first police-station run entirely by women. The officer in charge is Mrs. Isabel Goodwin, an intrepid, energetic policewoman, who works under

In fact, it may be said that the woman detective is indispensable in securing evidence in crimes connected with women and children. She knows so much more of the psychology of the people upon whose emotions she is working than does a man, and can gain confidences and elicit confessions where the tactics of the policeman would fail.

The policewoman's day is usually one of great variety, and especially may this be said of those who are employed on purely detective work, as apart from patrolling or traffic control.

The detective never knows what role she will be called upon to play next, or into what adventure or danger her investigations may lead her.

Various and exciting as her experiences may be, they are at times almost heartbreaking, and the policewoman must have a real love for her job to be a success in any sense of the word.

"Patience is a virtue" is a motto they do well to adopt. Patience and perseverance have made Mrs. Hamilton the undoubted success she is, and many more courageous and sympathetic women are following her close in their attempt to lessen crime in New York, and so relieve some of the awful misery caused by the members of the criminal fraternity.

The Confessions of a Card Sharp.

A Two-Part Article—PART ONE.

Here is no make-believe story of a card sharp's crooked career, no mere figment of the author's imagination. It is open confession, made not in foolish boasting but with genuine sorrow for a wasted life. The writer, who prefers to remain anonymous in order to save the feelings of his relatives, after making gambling a real business for twenty years finds himself bankrupt; with the painful knowledge towards the close of his life that gambling does not and cannot pay.

LUCK is defined as "that which happens by chance, fortune, or lot."

Many persons refuse to believe there is such a jade as Luck; that every happening is guided by immutable laws, and not by any fickle Goddess of Chance. I cannot subscribe to this belief.

Maybe I am superstitious; most gamblers are. But too often have I seen some favoured son of fortune win in a so-called game of chance when the cards were stacked against him; when he was playing against a "sure thing." That is luck, and there is no other name for it.

Mathematically, it can be proved that there are 2,598,960 possible combinations of five cards each in a 52-card standard pack. That means that the chance of drawing a royal flush, of which there can be four in a single deal, is exactly one in 649,740.

Similarly, the odds are 72,193 to one against getting a straight flush; 4,160 to one against four of a kind, and so on down, the odds becoming more favourable as the value of the hand decreases. Do you wonder, then, that I call a man lucky who is able to draw a straight flush against a "sharpshooter" who is "sitting pretty" with a pat four of a kind?

FOR years it was my business to force "luck" to come my way by turning games of chance into games of no chance at all for my victims.

To do this successfully, a man must be possessed of a personality and an address that doesn't smack of the "slicker," for it is infinitely more difficult to trim a slicker who is on the look-out for sharp practices than one who is secure in the thought he is associating with gentlemen.

In the following story I have selected only a few incidents in my crooked career —such incidents as will serve to illustrate the various methods employed by a card sharp to separate his dupes from their money.

For the sake of briefness and in an effort to hold the reader's attention, I have made out of it a continuous narrative, although some of the occurrences were widely separated in point of time. I could multiply these incidents almost interminably; for it must be remembered I garnered a very good living by these devious means for close on twenty years, and in that time have carried on my operations with zest and relish, unmoved by conscience, and without qualm or scruple.

Now, however, when I am nearing the Stygian ferry, I am beginning to be affected by that nameless fear which so often prompts a belated confession. For three months I have been confined in a sanatorium, and during this dreary period I have done more thinking than I have done before in all my life.

Regret over my wasted life, remorse over the lives I have wrecked, alike are useless. I cannot undo what I have done. But I can and will expose such methods as I and my like make use of to swindle honest and unsuspecting persons. This is more than a confession—it is a warning! And it is given in a spirit of sincere though late penitence.

IT was nearly twenty years ago that I quitted Oakland, California, to enter upon a career of gambling and cheating. Even now I am unable to say what caused me to devote my life to dishonesty. The fact remains that I did. I was born of good parents and commanded a decent place in society, but like many another young fellow, I was ambitious to associate with older and more sophisticated men. I admired the "fast" fellow; the flashy dresser and the shallow-pated.

It was in Denver that I made my first big haul. I had been playing a lone hand in the games around the hotels when I met a lawyer whom I knew to be very wealthy. I cultivated him assiduously, and finally received an invitation to dinner. I remember very well how excited I was as I dressed for dinner that night. I was closing in on my prey. I felt like a lion must feel before he springs on the gazelle.

I played cards like a rank amateur that night. I didn't want to win money; I wanted to win the lawyer's confidence. I was content to win a pot now and then to keep me even with the game. And I gained an invitation to his home for the next night.

Early the next morning I went to a drug store near the hotel and made some purchases. They included carbolic acid, a certain kind of dye, and a small quantity of glycerine.

Then, in the privacy of my room, I shaped the weapon with which I hoped to "take" the lawyer and his friends. I first made the ink, which, although not difficult, requires great care. The ink must be of exactly the same shade as the back of the cards. Further, it must be of such consistency that it will not catch the light when placed on the cards.

Beginning with the aces in the pack, which was a duplicate of those I had seen in the lawyer's home, I marked every card. Usually the marks are placed in the upper left hand corner and the lower right hand corner because in playing stud the dealer has to shove back only the top card when he is dealing to see just what cards will fall to the players.

However, because there was no good place on the corners of this particular pack, I was forced to put the marks on the pictured bicycle in the centre of the card.

For the aces I added a spoke to the wheels; for the kings I added a spoke in a different location, and so on, until I had each card marked to my satisfaction. I did not mark the suits as I might have done, because I figured I had plenty of advantage, knowing the denomination of every card in the pack.

And let me add here that it is not necessary for a gambler to mark his own cards any more. There are at least a score of firms in the United States that make a business of marking cards, loading dice, and manufacturing devices which the gamblers use to cheat their victims. The modern gambler does not waste his time making his own "paper." He studies his victim, and then orders by wire the tools he will use.

DINNER over that night and the game started, it was an easy matter for me to switch my pack into the game. I played easily and indifferently for a time, not wanting to scare away the fish. Then came my opportunity. The lawyer, peeved because he was losing as consistently as I was winning, got rattled. He evidently made up his mind that if he couldn't win with the cards he held, he would bluff his way to a pot.

To make a long story short, when the cards had been dealt, he had an ace, king, ten, and nine up. I had an eight, five, trey, and four up. Any card he might have had in the "hole," if it matched one of his "up" cards, had me beaten. But the mark on the back of his "down" card told me that it was an eight-spot. In the "hole" I had a five-spot that paired the one I had "up."

When the betting was finished, the perspiration was rolling down his face in a stream.

"I have only ace-high," he quavered.

"Not high enough," I told him, as I pulled nearly £1,600 to my side of the table, "I have a pair of fives."

The next big winning was in Chicago. There I used a beautiful woman as an assistant, and a good one she made, too. She was called Oakland Annie. She was cultured, and knew how to wear her expensive clothes.

Maintaining an expensive suite in the Hotel Blackstone was one of Chicago's packing magnates. He was yet under forty, had been married and divorced, and was doing the best he could to spend the income from a huge estate. He "fell" for Annie, and fell hard.

Annie soon discovered that the packer was on to faked cards, and that we couldn't get him that way. So I decided to use the "cold deck." After I had ingratiated myself into his confidence, it was easy to start a poker game.

In this particular one were Annie, the packer, a fair friend of the packer's, and myself. We played draw poker. After an hour or so I gave Annie the wink, and she slipped the cold deck into the game.

A "COLD DECK," by the way, is simply a deck of cards the duplicates of which are, of course, being played with. The cold deck has been prepared in advance, so that the gambler will know just what hands will fall to each player, including himself. The deck is usually put in by the assistant, who sits on the right of the victim. When the victim lays down the deck for the person on his right to cut, his attention is called by one of the professionals, and the cold deck is exchanged for the good one. Thus, the victim deals the cards himself, and is not in a position to squawk when he finds himself trimmed.

Our plan worked nicely, and we took £2,600 away from our friend, the packer. But we weren't through with him. He was good for another trimming, I thought.

Several years before, I had given an old toper a few dollars when I was flush with easy money. In return, he had given me a deck of cards with the remark, "Use them with smoked glasses."

I thought at the time he was daft, but one day I tried his plan. Imagine my astonishment when I found that the smoked glasses enabled me to see marks as large as turkey tracks on the back of those cards.

The old drunkard had in some way got hold of a deck of cards marked with invisible dye. That is, it was invisible to the naked eye, but was plainly discernible through smoked glasses.

I knew that such a dye would be worth £200 an ounce to me or any one else of the "profession."

I had no difficulty in conjuring visions of great wealth. But imagine my disappointment when I searched for the

In return he had given me a pack of cards, with the remark, "Use them with smoked glasses." At the time I thought he was daft, but—

old man, and was told he had died two days previously. He took his secret with him, but I kept his weapon intact until I could find big game worthy of it. The packer was the game.

THE packer was clamouring for revenge, but I didn't appear anxious to hazard my winnings.

I wanted him to think that I was a little afraid of him at cards, despite the fact that I had won a small fortune from him. Of course, he fell for my trick—they always do.

Annie was with him constantly, partly to see that he didn't fall into the clutches of another gambler, and partly to wheedle out of him presents of jewels and clothes. When I was all set, I informed Annie, and she arranged another party. She explained the black glasses which I now wore by telling him that I had granulated lids. The packer was so anxious to trim me that he ate very little supper.

After an hour or so of play, the packer had lost £300 to me, and he was nearly frantic. I figured that the time had come to go after all he had. I could get it eventually with my marked cards, but what was the use of sitting up all night if I could get his dough in one hand? I

gave Annie, who was sitting idly by sipping a cocktail, the wink.

It was my deal, and as I picked up the cards, Annie engaged the victim in conversation. It was not easy to do, because his attention was concentrated on the game. But he succumbed to her allurements, and as he looked around at her, I "stacked" the cards. Then, without giving him a chance to cut, I dealt.

I had arranged them so that he would get a pair of aces for his first two cards while I got a pair of sixes. For his fourth card he was to get another ace, while I would get another six. That was all he was to have, but I intended to give myself another six, making four in all. I knew that if I had only a pair of sixes in sight until the last card, he would bet the roof off.

HE bet large amounts on every card, and raised me time and again. His fourth card was an ace, as I knew it would be, while mine was a six. Thus, he had three aces, two of them in sight, while I had three sixes with only two of them in view. Without a second's hesitation, he wrote a cheque for £2,000 (he was out of cash), and put it in the pot.

I, too, had all of my money in the pot, but two could write cheques, even if I didn't have a cent in any bank. I wrote one for £4,000, raising his bet £2,000. Of course, I never would have done this if I hadn't known what the next card would be.

He continued to raise me until the table between us was literally covered with cheques and currency. While he was writing a cheque, I glanced down at the deck, which I held in my hand, and what I saw nearly toppled me over. The six-spot I expected to get was on top of the deck! I had made a mistake, and the six I needed so badly would be dealt first, and thus go to the packer.

"Well, hurry up and deal," he growled.

I did. With a motion so slight as to be imperceptible, I dealt the second to him. That is, with my thumb I slipped back the top card, the six, and dealt him the next card, which was a seven-spot. To myself I gave the six-spot.

In that pot was £12,400 of his money. I gave Annie £2,400, and took the first train for New York.

I SOJOURNED in New York just long enough to lose £8,000 on the stock market. I was a smart gambler, I knew that, and there was no good reason why I couldn't beat the Wall Street gamblers. And, like many a smart gambler, when I played the other man's game, I was in deep water.

I could cite you case after case where gamblers, top-notchers, too, won fortunes at their own games, and then lost it to some one trying to beat an unfamiliar game. When my £8,000 was gone, I decided a trip to Europe would do me good.

I took passage on the Justicia, because I had heard that there were some "high-rolling" games on it. There were, too, but two professionals were monopolising the passengers.

These two, "Short-Card Charlie" and "Three-fingered Dick," they were called, eyed me with suspicion. But I foxed them.

The Hotel Sleuth.
How the Big Hotels Protect Their Guests.

OF late years the London hotels have tightened up their system of protection. This does not mean to say that they spy upon their guests, but that they have made better arrangements to protect them.

In America the house-detective is already a person of some importance, and now all the London hotels have their own sleuth, usually a retired police-officer or an official of the railway police.

Like all business firms, the caravanserais have a trade protection agency which warns them of notoriously bad payers; but in the case of professional criminals and suspects they have to rely on their own police system as well as the help of the official police.

They warn one another against certain undesirable guests, especially the pseudo-nobleman from abroad, or the doubtful officer.

Thus, should Monsieur le Marquis de Carabas have drawn upon himself the suspicions of the manager of the Grand Babylon, he will find that when he drives up to the Imperial Napoleon Hotel the reception clerk will gaze upon him with polite sorrow, and say in dulcet tones: "I am very sorry, sir, we are absolutely full up."

If the marquis argues the point the manager will tell him, quite as politely, that the management prefers him to go elsewhere. A great deal of tact has to be exercised, however, for a mistake might have costly results.

In one large London hotel the lady telephone operator proved so valuable in separating the goats from the sheep that she was unofficially employed as an additional house-detective, and given a free hand.

Curiously enough, she herself was the victim of a robbery, which was an "inside job" committed by a member of the staff who had probably guessed her new vocation.

The hotel detective has many points to watch. Hotel property and "stock" —especially liquid stock—often disappears, and cannot be accounted for. In the majority of cases, this is disposed of by some member of the staff. The firm may not prosecute, as it does not want the doubtful advertisement of the police-courts, but it has no hesitation about weeding out the unfaithful servant.

Then there are little scandals to be hushed up, but this is usually the manager's work.

Scotland Yard notifies the hotels regularly of undesirable guests who may have designs on the property of other guests. Then it is up to the house-detective to take what measures he may think fit.

There was a particularly clever French sleuth employed at the Carlton years ago. He was a little, middle-aged man, who dressed shabbily, but who had ears and eyes which missed nothing. He was an extraordinarily interesting conversationalist, and would have proved a fortune to some of our popular novelists.

On the Continent hotel detective work is not merely of an anti-criminal variety; it also includes political observation.

You may be sure that if the authorities of the country you happen to be visiting wish to know your identity, your room will be visited in your absence and your baggage and papers thoroughly overhauled, and your telephone messages intercepted.

In London, hotel managers wish to avoid scandal or notoriety. It causes them to lose guests and to get into trouble with their directors. Often some hot-tempered lady will sweep majestically into the office and declare that she has been robbed. Investigations will show that she has simply misplaced her jewellery. In one case, a valuable diamond ring was declared to be missing. It was found in the bath!

But there are ladies who regularly lose valuable belongings. Sometimes they are paid compensation "out of court" even when the case is doubtful, but their names are circulated, and they find it difficult to obtain admittance to the best hotels. They are simply professional blackmailers, who play on the management's dislike of a scandal.

To revert to the purely detective side of the business, amusing mistakes are sometimes made. In one case a most worthy bishop of the Church of England was thought to be a notorious confidence man, and was asked to give up his room. He had great difficulty in proving his identity.

He was a good Christian, however, and laughed at the incident, much to the relief of all those concerned, including a C.I.D. man who had been called in and who also thought that the man of peace was a criminal.

Then there are restaurant cases, where guests complain of poisoning. That is why hotels have a regular doctor on whom they can call for immediate advice.

POLICE OF OTHER CLIMES. No. 8.

A Cairo Police-Sergeant.
[Photo: Topical.

Law Talks.—No. 25.

The Law of Naturalisation.

THE alien who wants to become a British subject sends in a written application to the Home Office, setting forth a few required particulars, and with astonishing ease receives a certificate from the Home Secretary which makes of the said alien a subject of King George V., with all the rights and privileges of a natural-born Britisher.

Children and all may be included in the one application. So kindly disposed is this country towards them that the youngsters who have thus been made Britons may, within one year after becoming of age, drop out of citizenship, as it were, by not making the declaration of allegiance—a formality which is required of naturalised alien children when they reach their majority.

A bar to naturalisation is put up to the subjects of countries which were at war with us in August, 1918, the bar to continue until the last day of August, 1928. Exception is made in the case of enemy subjects who fought in the British Army or Navy, or served with the forces of our Allies during the War, and the British-born children of our then enemies.

To get his certificate of naturalisation the alien must satisfy the Home Office at the time of making his application that he has lived for at least five years in British dominions—not necessarily for five consecutive years, but that total must have been reached within eight years of the application being made.

Furthermore, the would-be Briton is required to furnish proof of good character, must know the English tongue, and swear that he is going to make his home in some part of the Empire. The latter condition is waived when the man applying for a naturalisation certificate is in British Government service, or is about to take up such a job.

At any time the certificate may be revoked by the Home Secretary. If it was obtained by misstatement or fraud, if the naturalised alien leaves to take up his residence in any foreign country (unless, of course, he has to go on business for a British firm or on Government service), if he shows by word or deed that he is not a loyal subject, then revocation of his certificate is more or less certain.

But before he is de-naturalised he is informed by the Home Secretary as to what is about to happen, and the man has the privilege of asking that his case might be inquired into. The matter then goes to a High Court of Justice, or is otherwise looked into. The inquiry is conducted with the utmost thoroughness and fairness.

Should the decision go against him he reverts to his former status as an alien, his wife and children also losing their British rights if the Home Secretary decrees so—otherwise, the wife and children retain their conferred British citizenship.

The de-naturalised man's wife is allowed six months in which to think over her position if the Home Secretary's order has not been extended to her. If she wants to remain a British subject she may. If she prefers to revert to her alien nationality she must make a declaration of alienage within the prescribed six months; that step taken, the British flag is no longer a symbol of protection for her and her family.

The CURSE of PENGARTH CASTLE

(*Continued from page 10.*)

"Perhaps you are right—perhaps you are right!" agreed the earl. "Gad, I am feeling better already! I shall be out within a week—out! Eh, Betty? We'll have the old place renovated—tuned up and trimmed! As for you, sir," he added, turning to Waldo. "If I attempt to thank you for what you have done I shall make a mess of it. You're a fine fellow, by gad! And if they call you a crook in my hearing I shall have something to say!"

Waldo chuckled.

"You have no occasion to thank me, Lord Pengarth," he replied. "And please don't think that I go about doing good wherever I can. Quite the opposite! But Slingsby instilled me with fury, and it was purely for my own pleasure that I went to him and obtained his signature to these documents and rifled his safe. Somehow I don't think he'll have the audacity to take any action."

He bowed and moved away.

"And now," he added, "I'll make my departure, if you'll excuse me. I have some other business on hand which cannot wait."

He walked to the door; but Sexton Blake was out in the passage in advance of him, and Tinker came close behind. Tinker closed the door, leaving father and daughter alone.

"What you have done is quite straight?" asked Blake. "I mean those documents are in order?"

"They are, as far as I humanly know," replied the Wonder-Man.

"Of course, you realise that the chief constable is downstairs?" went on Blake. "And you further realise that it is my plain duty to hand you over into his keeping. The fact that you have performed this generous action to Lord Pengarth in no way affects the position."

Waldo smiled.

"Yes, Blake, you're right," he agreed. "And, after all, I stand before you a self-confessed burglar, for I have told you that I rifled Simon Slingsby's safe. But you won't hand me over on that charge, surely?"

"There are many other charges against you, Waldo."

"Really? I'd quite forgotten them," chuckled the Wonder-Man. "But perhaps you are right; I won't argue. And I know for a fact that the police are anxious to see me."

"It would be against all my principles if I gave you permission to walk out," went on Blake sternly. "What you have done for Lord Pengarth is praiseworthy, but I must ask you to accompany me downstairs. My one duty is to hand you over to justice."

Waldo looked surprised for a moment, then his eyes twinkled.

"Why, of course!" he chuckled. "Anything you like, Blake. And I wouldn't dream of keeping you from your duty. Right you are, old man; lead the way. Tinker, stand behind and watch the lamb go to his slaughter!"

. . . .

Colonel Flowerdew was still in the library with Inspector Burgess. They had both worked themselves into a state of sheer despondency by this time. In their own minds they had already seen

Selecting a strong, supple branch, Waldo climbed out, swung, and at the right moment released his grip. He landed perfectly in one clean jump. (*Page 9.*)

the Earl of Pengarth in the dock, they had heard him sentenced, and the unfortunate peer was already hanged.

At this stage Sexton Blake entered to liven things up.

"Colonel, I have a prisoner for you," said Blake crisply. "This man is Waldo. I found him in the deserted west wing, and, very properly, he has submitted to capture. It is your responsibility."

The chief-constable sprang up, startled.

"Waldo!" he ejaculated, looking at the Wonder-Man askance.

"Pray don't disturb yourself!" said Waldo. "I'm quite harmless. I've no intention of smashing up the happy home. Blake says that I must submit to arrest. So what else is to be done? Only do get it over quickly, won't you?"

Inspector Burgess came forward, full of importance.

"What do you know about this murder?" he demanded sternly.

"Nothing!" replied Waldo. "Blake, you might tell the inspector that I'm quite guiltless in that respect. I don't want such a charge——"

"I bring no charge against Waldo whatever," said Blake, turning to the inspector. "I merely know that he is a wanted man, and I formally hand him over. It is for you to deal with him as you think fit. I suggest—— Well, perhaps it is not my province to make suggestions."

The inspector pulled out his handcuffs.

"I arrest you, Rupert Waldo, and you will be taken to Launceston police-station without delay. The full charge will be made against you to-morrow. Colonel Flowerdew, sir, will you be good enough to call the two constables?"

"Yes, yes, to be sure!" ejaculated the

colonel. "You'll need two! This man is dangerous; he's got to be well looked after."

And so, five minutes later, Waldo was marched out of Pengarth Castle in the firm grip of two burly policemen. He had already uttered a cheery good-bye to Sexton Blake, and the chief-constable and Inspector Burgess were in a fine flutter.

"It was the only thing to do, sir; we couldn't keep him here," said the inspector. "Very smart of you, Mr. Blake, to capture the fellow! I can't understand it. I've always understood that he's practically invincible."

Blake smiled.

"Waldo is a peculiar man," he replied. "He will sometimes walk headlong into danger, and he seems quite indifferent to his fate. In the present instance, as you have seen, he has departed in the care of those constables with a light heart."

A few minutes later Blake and Tinker were alone.

"Ten minutes, guv'nor?" asked Tinker carelessly.

"Probably a quarter of an hour, but not longer," replied Blake. "Well, Tinker, we've done our duty, haven't we? If Waldo escapes from the constables, that's their look-out, not ours."

Tinker grinned.

"I can't help it, guv'nor—I like the beggar!" he exclaimed. "And you must say he's acted like a sport over this Slingsby affair. I say, wouldn't it have been worth quids to see that meeting?"

"Yes, I have no doubt that Mr. Slingsby went through a very trying ordeal," agreed Sexton Blake. "But there is one thing that rather puzzles me. Surely Waldo hasn't done all this out of sheer good-heartedness? It was hardly like him to give up jewellery worth thousands of pounds."

"He's taken a liking to Lord Pengarth,' guv'nor—and there's no telling what Waldo will do, anyhow! He's the queerest bird we've ever come across," replied Tinker. "One of these days we shall find him conducting the service at some church or other."

At this moment there was an excited hammering on the great door, and Blake himself went and opened it. As he had expected, the two constables were outside, hot, flustered, and filled with intense alarm.

"He's escaped, sir!" gasped one of them.

"Escaped!" echoed Tinker, aghast.

"What's that?" shouted the inspector, hurrying up. "You dolts! You haven't let him go, have you? Two men like you—and you couldn't keep hold of ——"

"We couldn't help it, sir!" panted one of the men. "We hadn't got to the bottom of the drive before he got out of his handcuffs——"

"Ridiculous!" stormed the inspector. "I put them on myself!"

"I dunno about that, sir; he got out of 'em all right!" said the policeman stolidly. "Fair took us by surprise, too! He caught Joe on the side of the head and knocked him into the ditch! And before I could look round the beggar was gone! Clean gone, sir—there wasn't no sign of him! Vanished like a bloomin' ghost!"

"Bless my soul and body!" ejaculated the chief constable.

Sexton Blake sighed, and shook his head.

"Oh, well, it can't be helped," he said regretfully. "It is not the first time that Waldo has eluded the police. But it is a great pity, seeing that we had him so nicely."

The unfortunate constables were roundly "told off" by the indignant inspector, and Sexton Blake and Tinker walked off in the middle of it. They were both looking duly concerned.

"Well, guv'nor, that's that!" said Tinker softly.

And although Blake didn't exactly wink, Tinker was fairly certain that he saw the flicker of an eyelid.

"Now to work again!" said Sexton Blake. "We have had this interlude, Tinker, and it has been an interruption, but we cannot allow it to interfere with our task. The main thing is to get hold of the murderer of Sir William Brag."

"But the position's altogether better, isn't it, sir?" asked Tinker cheerily, as they went back to the west wing. "I mean, Lord Pengarth is heaps better than he was, and his fortunes have been restored——"

"I'm not quite so sure about that," interrupted Blake thoughtfully. "Those documents must be carefully examined before we can say anything for certain. But Waldo is hardly the man to do anything in a slipshod way."

"In any case, Slingsby won't dare to do anything—he'll be afraid of running his head into a noose," said Tinker. "What about those jewels, sir? They were stolen, and the police know all about it. It won't be very nice for Slingsby if it comes out that they were found in his safe."

"No; I rather fancy he will keep very quiet," replied Blake. "He has evidently been piling up an enormous fortune. A man like that, living in a comparatively small way, is sometimes fabulously rich."

"But what on earth does he want it for?" asked Tinker. "If he only lives in a small way, what good is all that money to him?"

"What good were those jewels in his safe?" retorted Blake. "They have reposed there for seventeen years—untouched, except for an occasional examination, perhaps. Slingsby took them when he took the Cross, and that piece of work was accomplished. I have no doubt, in order that he could afterwards play upon Lord Pengarth's mind regarding the Curse. But the whole evidently proves that Slingsby is a miser—a man who hoards money, and makes money, for the mere sake of gloating over it."

"Well, I'm blessed if I can understand it!" growled Tinker. "Chaps like that don't deserve to live—especially when they swindle other people so that they can add to their rotten store! Fancy! Making Lord Pengarth a pauper, and raking in his income, and doing nothing with it! The man must be mad!"

"He has undoubtedly got a kink," agreed Blake. "But this conversation is not carrying us any further, Tinker. There is still the problem of Sir William Brag's death before us. Until that is cleared up, our host is in a grave position."

"But the police don't still suspect him, guv'nor?"

"Make no mistake, Tinker, both Colonel Flowerdew and Inspector Burgess are convinced that Lord Pengarth is the murderer. They are extremely sorry for him, of course, but they mean to arrest him as soon as he is well enough."

"But you won't let 'em?"

"I shall certainly not; but it doesn't please me to pass on my information just yet," said Blake. "It will be far more satisfactory if I can hand them the murderer myself. And I think I shall be able to do that before the night is out."

Tinker stared.

"Which reminds me, guv'nor," he said. "How the dickens do you know that the murderer has got a ginger beard?"

"It is childishly simple," explained Sexton Blake, as they walked slowly along the deserted corridor. "While examining the body, I found a few hairs clutched in the right hand. It needed no expert to place them as hairs from the human chin—in short, hairs from the beard."

"Oh!" said Tinker slowly. "That's pretty conclusive, isn't it? Lord Pengarth hasn't got a beard, and his moustache is grizzled. Even the old inspector ought to sit up when you tell him that!"

"I have no doubt he will."

"I suppose poor old Sir William saw the blow coming, and made a wild grab at his murderer," continued Tinker thoughtfully. "He didn't get him, but he just managed to clutch a bit of his beard! Is that how you figure it out, sir?"

"Naturally," replied the great detective. "You are singularly adept, Tinker, at stating the obvious. Let us bring our facts into line. We know that the murderer is bare-footed, and that he has a beard. We know that he escaped into this wing of the building. So there is more than a chance that we shall locate him if we search long enough."

"He's probably cleared off by this time, sir."

"That is unlikely," put in Blake. "There has been no such character seen in this district. And a man with bare feet, and splayed toes, to say nothing of a ragged auburn beard, would have been very conspicuous. He is in the castle, concealed somewhere. You must remember that there is sufficient room in these deserted wings to harbour a score, without anybody being a word the wiser."

Tinker went with his master, more eager than ever. Who was this strange, grotesque creature they were after? How long had he lurked in the castle, and why was he there?

As Blake penetrated farther into the deserted wing, he held his hand ready on his revolver, for he had sufficient evidence to know that this bare-footed unknown was a dangerous fellow to come across.

Occasionally they saw a smudgy footprint in the dust, but in the main there was very little trail to follow. The search resolved itself into a careful, diligent examination.

Every barren apartment was searched, every cupboard and recess was examined. It seemed as though they would never succeed. The whole place was dank with age, and there was a smell of dampness and mildew in every hole and corner.

This search, in the middle of the night, was grim and tedious.

Tinker's high spirits left him after the first hour of it. He became jumpy and tense. At any moment he expected to see some misshapen figure leap out at him from the darkness. And he found it impossible to forget how Sir William Brag had been struck down before he could lift a hand to help himself.

And then, at last, Sexton Blake paused upon entering a low, arched doorway. Beyond lay a kind of crypt, grim and mysterious. It was one of the most ancient parts of the castle, and brought up memories of olden times. But it was something else which caused Blake to halt and sniff the air.

THE SEVENTH CHAPTER.
What Sexton Blake Found at Pengarth.

TINKER paused, too, and he caught some of the criminologist's tension. The smell of mildew had so long been in his nostrils that he now hardly noticed it. But, seeing that Blake was sniffing, he did the same.

"Hallo!" he murmured. "Smells a bit queer, sir!"

"Be careful, Tinker! Look out for yourself!" muttered Blake. "There may be no danger, but we must be on our guard."

As they advanced into the crypt there was a distinct change in the atmosphere. Instead of dampness and mildew, they could smell a queer conglomeration of scents—unpleasant, in the main. But, without any doubt, the predominant odour was that of onions.

If this crypt was deserted, as all the other places were deserted, how was it that the fresh smell of raw onions was in the air? Not only that, but other foodstuffs — stale and old. Blake couldn't be sure of it, but he even fancied that he caught an indefinable whiff of stale tobacco.

They advanced cautiously. Tinker still had that feeling that something would leap on him from the shadows. But he steeled himself, and kept his senses fully on the alert.

But at length the crypt was fully examined, and it proved to be as empty as any of the other deserted chambers.

"Well, it's nothing but a swindle!" grunted Tinker. "I thought we were going to find something."

"We have found something," said Sexton Blake. "What do you think of this, Tinker?"

He flashed his light on a portion of the wall. At first glance it seemed like the rest of the old stonework. But then Tinker could see finger-marks—particularly in a certain place. They were of long-standing, and it was clear that hands had been pressed upon this part of the wall countless times. There had been no attempt to keep it secret.

Blake pressed on the spot where the disfigurement was most noticeable, and a section of the wall moved back at once. It was a door. At some remote period it had probably been a secret door, but years of careless handling had rendered the secret visible to all.

Another chamber lay beyond, and now the odour of stale onions was even more distinct. With a sudden movement, Blake strode into the inner chamber, with Tinker at his heels.

From the shadows there was a sudden movement.

Some object leapt, and Tinker gasped.

"Look out!" roared Blake. "Quick, Tinker! Hold him!"

Tinker caught a flash of the figure as it leapt at his master. He saw an unkempt face, with staring eyes. He saw a ragged form, and an upraised arm which held a formidable knotted stick.

With a shout, Tinker threw himself forward. As the stick descended he diverted it, and thus saved Blake from an injury which might have been a broken arm. The next second a fearful fight was in progress.

The stick had been knocked out of the creature's grip. And now, bare-handed, he flung himself at Blake. From the rear, Tinker did everything he could. The torch fell with a clatter and snapped out.

And in the darkness the fight went on.

It was a gruesome, uncanny business. Twice Blake was nearly bitten, and at last he was compelled to place his hands round the throat of the unknown and hold them there. Then, with his knees on the man's chest, he shouted for Tinker to hold the prisoner's lashing feet.

Somehow Tinker succeeded, and, when both he and Blake were nearly exhausted, the fight came to an end. Their captive lay on the floor breathing pantingly, but subdued.

"A light, Tinker!" exclaimed Blake grimly. "I'm afraid my torch is out of action, but you've got one. Switch it on!"

Somehow Tinker managed to pull his torch out. He pressed the switch, and a ray of light fell upon the prisoner. Both Blake and Tinker stared with repulsion.

The figure was evidently a madman—a gibbering idiot. His eyes were staring, he showed his teeth, and almost foamed at the mouth. He had unkempt hair, and a ragged, auburn beard. Altogether, he was an ugly customer.

He was attired in a ragged, tattered suit, and he wore no shoes or stockings. Even now he had plenty of fight left in him, for at the first relaxation of Blake's grip, the creature sought to struggle free.

But he was held, and the next task was to render him incapable of further mischief. Cords were placed round his wrists, and he was rolled face downwards. Further cords were tied round his ankles, and his legs were bent back and secured in this position. Escape was out of the question.

"My goodness!" panted Tinker. "Thank goodness that's over, sir! I thought he was going to kill you that time!"

"Thanks, Tinker, for doing what you did," said Blake quietly. "In spite of all my precautions, the fellow was a shade too quick for me. Any careless action on our part, and one of us would certainly have been brained."

They rose to their feet, feeling the strain of that fight. But one satisfaction filled them both. The murderer of Sir William Brag was laid by the heels, and the shadow over Lord Pengarth was dissipated for ever.

An examination of the chamber proved interesting.

Strictly speaking, there were two—a second inner room leading out of this one. They were furnished in a kind of way. One was a sitting-room, and the other a bed-room. The bed was a small, single iron bedstead, and the blankets and sheets, at least, were scrupulously clean.

And the "living-room," although shockingly untidy, bore traces of having been turned out with a fair amount of regularity. The occupant of these queer apartments was much more dirty and untidy than his living quarters. But how was it that this creature lived here?

"Do you think he's always been mad, sir?" asked Tinker, after a while.

"There can be no question of that," replied Blake. "Just look at his head—the shape of it. Furthermore, he's unable to utter any intelligible sounds. The poor beggar ought to be in proper care—not left to himself in this state of solitude."

"He seems to have been looked after all right, sir," said Tinker. "But whoever would have thought of this explanation?"

Blake had picked up the heavy, knotted stick, and was examining it. He nodded grimly once or twice.

"There is no need to look far here, Tinker," he remarked. "There is enough evidence on this stick to convict the fellow a dozen times. Have a look at it for yourself."

Tinker looked, and shivered slightly.

"It's awful, sir!" he muttered. "That's blood, isn't it? I say, he must have given Sir William a terrible smash. But why? What on earth could have possessed him?"

"I can think of nothing else but a frenzy—a sudden mania," replied Blake. "He can certainly have had no grudge against Sir William, for the latter was practically a stranger. This is the sequence of events, as we now know it. Sir William entered by the window, and this demented creature happened to be in that particular passage."

"And Sir William shrieked out at the sight of him, eh?"

"Undoubtedly," replied Blake. "He was startled and frightened. It may have been his scream, indeed, which precipitated the madman's attack. In his distorted way he thought that he had to silence that noise, so he struck. And one blow was sufficient."

"Then he bunked, and Waldo came along——"

"Am I telling this, Tinker, or are you?" asked Blake tartly.

"Sorry, sir!"

"Then Waldo came along," resumed Blake. "He took in the situation at a glance, picked Sir William's pocket for those documents, and went. Then, all within the space of a single minute, Lord Pengarth arrived on the scene, and stood over the dead man. And that's how we found him."

"It only shows you, guv'nor, that circumstantial evidence is jolly weak," said Tinker, shaking his head. "Why, it looked as black as thunder against Lord Pengarth. I don't wonder the police took it for granted that he was guilty, and made no close examination."

"Nothing should ever be taken for granted, Tinker, particularly by the police," said Blake. "If there had been a smart Scotland Yard man at work here, there would have been nothing taken for granted!"

"We ought to have had old Lennard on the job, sir!" grinned Tinker. "I can just picture him solemnly telling us that Lord Pengarth——"

"Hush! I heard something!"

Tinker glanced at the doorway, and they both stood rigid.

"Put the light out, and step behind here!" murmured Blake, indicating a recess. "I have been half expecting something of the kind, and I rather fancy I know who is coming."

The light was switched off, and they both stood waiting. Faintly the sounds of shuffling footsteps made themselves heard. Then the reflection of a flickering light came gradually into view.

"Tom!" came a quavering voice. "Tom! Are you there? Why don't you come when I call you."

"Jelks!" whispered Tinker, with an inaudible whistle.

Blake said nothing, and a moment later old Jelks came into the inner chamber, holding an old-fashioned storm-lantern. He paused, staring dumbly at the bound figure on the floor. The madman was now uttering all sorts of strange, guttural sounds, mingled with a kind of whimper.

"What's happened to ye, Tom?" gasped Jelks, setting the lantern down, and kneeling. "Who's done——"

He broke off, and staggered to his feet again as Tinker's torchlight flashed out and he caught sight of the pair.

"Mr. Blake!" muttered the old butler, aghast. "Then, then you know?"

"Why didn't you tell me about this at the very beginning, Jelks?" demanded Blake sternly. "Why didn't you tell Inspector Burgess? Don't you realise that you are harbouring a murderer, and that you have laid yourself open to a grave charge?"

Jelks panted for breath.

"I—I didn't know, sir!" he exclaimed. "An' I was that worried an' troubled that I was near off my head."

The old man's distress was so great that Blake could not remain stern.

"This—this unfortunate is your son, Jelks?" he asked.

"How did you know, sir?" moaned Jelks miserably.

"I didn't know—I merely guessed," replied Sexton Blake. "Your attitude has been very significant, too. You could hardly have kept such a secret unless the relationship was a close one. But that is no excuse Jelks; you ought to have told the police the very instant they arrived!"

"But—but I didn't know, sir!" panted Jelks. "Leastways, I wasn't certain, Mr. Blake——"

"Come, Jelks, that won't do!" broke in Blake. "You knew well enough. At all events, your suspicions were so strong that you could have had no real doubt in your mind. As it is, you have placed yourself in an awkward position, and I cannot answer for what attitude the police will take."

Old Jelks was almost a ghost of his usual self. His anxiety and anguish of the past few hours had reduced him to a nervous wreck, and this culminating incident bereft him of all self-control. He sank down upon one of the chairs, and sobbed convulsively.

Blake and Tinker waited, rather uncomfortable.

"Come, come, this won't do!" murmured Blake gently. "You need not be afraid, Jelks; the police won't arrest you. You have done wrong, but your fault was not so very great."

"My son, sir!" muttered Jelks brokenly. "To think that it was he who struck down poor Sir William! It's broke me all up, sir. I'll never be right again—never, as long as I live! My son—a murderer!"

"You are in no way responsible for your son's actions—particularly as he is not responsible for them himself," said Sexton Blake. "The mistake was in keeping the unhappy man in this extraordinary asylum. What does it mean, Jelks? You must give an explanation."

"I will, sir—I will!" panted Jelks, trying to control himself. "I always thought that poor Tom was harmless. He has been, sir, for years—nigh on thirty years now!" he added slowly. "Never harmed a fly, sir; never hit as much as a kitten! Why, Tom was like a baby, sir!"

"He has never caused you any trouble?"

"Never, sir—not one day of it!" said Jelks earnestly "The last thing I thought was that he could harm anybody. And when I guessed it, sir, I was struck all of a heap. Poor Martha is crying her eyes out. She don't know what to do. 'It's all your fault,' she says. An' she swears that the police will take us away to prison, an' that maybe poor Tom will be hanged."

"Your son will not be hanged, and neither you nor your wife will go to prison, Jelks," replied Blake quietly. "If you tell me that your son has always been harmless, then you are not so much to blame, perhaps."

"Harmless ain't the word, sir," said the butler, recovering under Blake's reassuring tone. "Many's the time I've left him alone with the missus' cat, an' he's never done a thing to harm it. An' he's always been shy, too—wouldn't come out and show himself. I can't make it out, sir; it's a mystery to me."

"I am no brain specialist, Jelks, but I can well imagine something snapping in your son's poor, demented brain," said the detective. "And when that moment arrived—perhaps it was caused by Sir William's scream when he caught sight of your son—he hit out blindly. I do not blame the poor fellow. He is more to be pitied than anything else. But again we come to the point, Jelks. What is he doing here?"

"Tom's lived here, sir, for ten years," said Jelks brokenly.

"Ten years!" ejaculated Tinker.

"Ay, sir, all of that—mebbe more," replied Jelks. "I've almost lost count."

"And you and your wife have looked after him?"

"Every day, sir—yes, day and night!" replied the butler. "Looked after him as though he were a child of five or six. He didn't mind this loneliness, and being by himself. Tom liked it, poor wretch! It was what he wanted."

"And does Lord Pengarth know?"

"Bless you, sir, no!" ejaculated Jelks. "Neither does Lady Betty. All this time, sir, an' they've never guessed a thing—never had reason to."

"Has he always been demented?"

"Always, sir, since he was born," replied Jelks, shaking his head sadly. "A rare blow it was to me an' the wife. We never had any other child, sir. Just Tom. He was in an asylum until—until——"

"Until you could no longer afford to keep him there?"

Jelks hung his head.

"In a way, that's right, sir," he admitted. "But Tom escaped the asylum frightened him. He was always afraid of strangers. Poor boy, he only longed to be near mother and me. And when he escaped, and came here one night—he wasn't so mad that he didn't know the way—we took him in, and thought of all these empty rooms."

"Yes, I quite understand!"

"The master wasn't paying us so much wages, then, sir—things was already going bad. And by the looks of it, they were going to get worse—which, as you know, sir, they did. And those asylum fees were terrible, sir; took all we had to spare, and more. So we kept Tom here, thinking that nobody would know, and that no harm would be done. There wasn't nothing wrong in that Mr. Blake, was there?"

"As you saw it at the time, possibly not; but as events have turned out, it is scarcely necessary for me to say what I think, Jelks. The life of Sir William Brag is the penalty for your rashness. But I don't blame you. I understand your position, and sympathise with you."

Jelks rocked himself miserably.

"And to think it was me, sir, that brought you down here!" he muttered. "Not that that makes much difference; the police would have found out."

"Opinions differ," said Tinker. "If the police had been left to themselves, Lord Pengarth would have been accused of the murder, and taken away."

"Never, young sir—never!" vowed Jelks. "I was going to speak. In fact, me and Martha had already decided to tell everything in the morning."

"Well, it makes very little difference," said Sexton Blake. "Tinker, I wish you'd go and fetch Inspector Burgess and those constables. This poor creature must be removed without delay."

THE EIGHTH CHAPTER.
Exit Mister Slingsby.

COLONEL FLOWERDEW puffed his cheeks out, and was staggered.

"The work of a lunatic—Jelks' son!" he repeated blankly. "Bless my soul and body! What an extraordinary affair! And what a relief, Mr. Blake! I thought it was the work of Lord Pengarth himself—may I be forgiven!"

"I am afraid Inspector Burgess took too much for granted," said Sexton Blake. "The circumstances looked ugly, I will admit, but it is always unwise to accept facts at their face value. A little close scrutiny may reveal all sorts of unsuspected flaws."

"You've proved that, Mr. Blake!" declared the chief constable. "By gad, you have! I don't mind admitting, sir, that I was a bit sceptical about your methods. But not now, sir."

They were in the library, and the unhappy murderer had already been carried off in the care of the police, Inspector Burgess himself in charge this time.

For there was no reason for him to remain.

The mystery was solved, and there would be nothing now, except an inquest. Blake, of course, would give his evidence, and it would be a purely formal affair. Sir William had died as the result of an unfortunate meeting with a madman. Lord Pengarth's quarrel with Sir William would never be even mentioned, since it was not relevant to the case.

In was in the small hours of the morning, but nobody in Pengarth Castle had even thought of going to bed. The old earl himself was making extraordinary progress—so much so that the doctor was staggered.

He had declared that the old earl would be in bed for weeks. But by all appearances he would be out again within a few days. Waldo's recent visit had a great deal to do with this rapid change for the better.

For at last Lord Pengarth's mind was at rest.

No longer was he in danger of being turned out of his castle. The Pengarth curse was dead, and it seemed that a time of well-earned happiness lay ahead.

The change in Lady Betty, too, was remarkable.

Her old colour had returned, and the sparkle was once more apparent in her eyes. Her final happiness was assured when she learned that her father was safe from being accused of the murder.

"I am sure that we have to thank you for this, Mr. Blake," she said quietly. "I don't know what we should have done without you. And poor Jelks—he won't get into trouble with the police, will he?"

"Well, I am afraid Colonel Flower-dew is very cross with him, but no doubt the affair will blow over," said Sexton Blake. "But, remarkably enough, it seems to me that you and your father must thank Waldo more than anybody else."

At this moment there came a loud jangling and clanging of the bell. It was so startling and so unexpected, that Lady Betty clutched at Sexton Blake's sleeve.

"Who can that be?" she murmured.

"Slingsby, I'll bet!" murmured Tinker.

"Oh, it can't be—it can't be!" muttered the girl. "He can't come here—he wouldn't dare!"

"Let me answer the bell," said Sexton Blake quietly.

He went to the door, leaving Tinker and Lady Betty standing in the great hall, which was only illuminated in the one corner. It was a place of shadows and great spaces.

Blake passed into the lobby, shot the bolts of the great door, and flung it open. A man came pushing past him—a lean-shouldered individual with sunken eyes, and maddened, feverish expression.

"One moment, sir——" began Blake.

"Out of my way!" snarled the new-comer. "Where's Lord Pengarth? Where is he, I say? By Heaven, I mean to see him! I've been victimised by a rogue—a scoundrel!"

Mr. Simon Slingsby burst right through into the hall, and came to a halt as Lady Betty faced him.

"What do you want, Mr. Slingsby?" she asked defiantly.

"Where's your father?" snarled the lawyer. "I've come here to see him, and I won't be denied. I've been robbed—robbed of tens of thousands! Do you hear me? All my money! Gold—gold! Notes—bundles of them! I've been robbed!"

Slingsby was nearly off his head with rage and anguish.

"Do you expect to find your property here, Mr. Slingsby?" asked Lady Betty coldly. "I am amazed that you should come to Pengarth Castle. And who are you to talk of robbers?"

"I know that the man came here—he told me so!" raved the frenzied lawyer. "I should have come earlier, only I was bound and gagged! My fool of a housekeeper went to bed, and I could make nobody hear!"

"I'm glad you had a nice time of it!" said Tinker bluntly.

"This man—this burgling hound—made me sign some preposterous documents!" went on Slingsby feverishly. "I want them back—I mean to have them back! They are worthless!"

"Not so worthless as you would have me believe, Mr. Slingsby," put in Lady Betty. "And if they are so valueless, why are you so frantic to get them back?"

The lawyer recoiled, shaking with passion.

"That was a nasty one, wasn't it?" asked Tinker. "I don't want to butt in, Mr. Slingsby, but if you take my advice you'll get out of here while you're safe."

But Simon Slingsby had come for trouble, and he was going to get it!

"What's this—what's this?"

Colonel Flowerdew came out of the library, and faced Simon Slingsby with a grim frown. The lawyer recoiled again. He knew, at the first glimpse, that he was facing the chief constable.

"I—I didn't know you were here, sir!" panted Simon Slingsby. "I am glad—very glad! I appeal to you in this matter!"

"Oh, you do?" growled the colonel,

The butler paused, staring dumbly at the bound figure on the floor. The madman was now uttering all sorts of strange guttural sounds, mingled with a kind of whimper. *(Page 22.)*

eyeing him coldly. "What's this you're saying about documents, or something?"

"A man came into my house, held me up and robbed me!" babbled out the lawyer. "He forced me to sign documents, which make over the Pengarth estates to Lord Pengarth—the castle, the park, and tens of thousands of acres, the entire estate! This—this accursed criminal made me sign these documents under threat of death!"

"And are they valid?" demanded the chief constable.

"Yes, of course they are!" raved Slingsby. "I'm a lawyer—I ought to know!"

"Then why did you tell me they were valueless?" put in Lady Betty quietly.

Slingsby started violently.

"I—I was mistaken!" he stuttered. "I must have them back! Unless I get them I will have the whole matter threshed out in court!"

"Indeed, sir!" put in Sexton Blake. "Do you dare to stand there and suggest that you would enter a court of justice and swear that these Pengarth estates are your own property?"

"They are mine—mine!"

"They are my father's, and you know it!" exclaimed Lady Betty. "You robbed them from him, and now that he has got them back, you talk of going to law! You wouldn't dare!"

"I rather fancy you are right, Lady Betty," said Colonel Flowerdew. "Mr. Slingsby, the sooner you leave Pengarth Castle the better! You will get nothing here!"

"But I tell you——"

"One moment, Mr. Slingsby!" interrupted Sexton Blake. "Perhaps you are aware that the Pengarth Cross has been

recovered—to say nothing of some jewellery which has been missing for seventeen years?"

Simon Slingsby turned as pale as chalk. Until that moment he had completely overlooked this seemingly trivial aspect of the case. His mind had been obsessed by the greater loss—a loss which amounted to hundreds of thousands. He had given no thought to the few paltry trinkets which Waldo had taken from his safe—although he seemed to set great store on the bundles of notes and gold which had mysteriously vanished.

But Blake's words hit Slingsby fairly amidships. Blake had suspected that Slingsby had forgotten those jewels, and this little reminder was timely. They had been in his safe! Proof positive that he was a common thief! Even though that burglary had been committed seventeen years before, it made no difference—he was still liable to penal servitude.

"I—I—I——"

The lawyer found coherent speech impossible.

"Don't you think you had better go, Mr. Slingsby?" said Sexton Blake. "There is another little thing I would like to remind you of. About seven years ago there was a rather unpleasant case in Bodmin. A small estate in that town was in the hands of a certain lawyer, and but for a hitch at the last moment that lawyer would have robbed the estate of every penny it possessed——"

"I—I will go!" muttered Slingsby hoarsely.

"If you wish, I will accept Lord Pengarth's commission to look into his financial affairs," continued Sexton

Blake smoothly. "This work is quite in my line, Mr. Slingsby, since it involves a great amount of investigation and detective inquiry. Shall I look into the Pengarth affairs, and find out exactly why his lordship's finances have fallen so lamentably during the past decade? Or do you think it would be better to let matters stand as they are? I leave it entirely to you—you can have your choice."

The lawyer was defeated, and he knew it.

Without a word he stumbled to the door, pulled it open, and passed out into the night. He had received such a shock as he had never anticipated.

One thing was absolutely obvious.

He was afraid—mortally afraid of an investigation!

He would rather let matters stand as they were, with Lord Pengarth in full possession of his property, than lift a finger to make further protest. He had gone—a self-confessed swindler

And soon afterwards, Sexton Blake had a few words with Lady Betty.

"Well, your troubles are now over, I think," smiled the detective. "You need have no further fear of Simon Slingsby. If, by any chance, he does become active, I earnestly request you to call upon me, Lady Betty."

"I will, Mr. Blake, although I don't think it will be necessary," replied the girl. "Without your help, I think we should have given way to despair. And it was owing to you that Slingsby admitted defeat."

"He was compelled to admit defeat," replied Blake. "He knows that a careful inquiry would spell his own ruin. The one fact of those jewels is enough to land him in prison."

"Why didn't you let him go there, sir?" put in Tinker.

"Because his teeth are drawn now and he can do no further harm," said Sexton Blake. "And don't you think that Lord Pengarth has suffered enough, without the trial and worry of a public inquiry? By letting Slingsby go, a beaten man and a physical wreck, all further investigation is rendered unnecessary. It was the simplest way, and I think Lord Pengarth will be the first to admit that it was the best. If the police care to take up the case, that, of course, is their affair. But, somehow, I don't think they will."

"There's one thing I've been puzzling about, sir," said Tinker thoughtfully. "I wonder how much Waldo raked in for himself out of this job?"

"I wonder!" mused Blake.

THE NINTH CHAPTER.
The Monetary Misery of a Miser.

RUPERT WALDO wasn't so far off as many supposed.

In point of fact, he was in Pengarth Castle itself, and for a full hour he had been thoroughly enjoying himself. With his usual audacity he had dodged back after eluding the police, and had calmly entered the castle.

In that great place of deep shadows and endless recesses and passages, he had found hiding in plenty.

And Waldo had been taking an active interest in all the proceedings. He hadn't seen any reason why he should

---

---

be left out at the "death." He had done so much in this affair that he wanted to see it completely through. And so he had been dodging about from place to place, listening.

He knew all about Jelks' unfortunate son: he had heard Slingsby arrive, and had listened to their ensuing conversation. And it had pleased the Wonder-Man beyond measure when Simon had been sent off with his tail between his legs.

There really seemed very little else to wait for.

But before going Waldo performed one last act of audacity. He made his way upstairs, noiselessly entered the sick room, and approached the Earl of Pengarth's bed. His lordship was awake.

"Just popped in to have a last word, Lord Pengarth," said Waldo softly. "In case you don't know it, I've brought you the latest news."

"Gad!" ejaculated the old peer. "What now? They told me you had been arrested, and I called them a lot of dunderheaded fools! Slingsby is the man they ought to arrest—not you!"

"Naturally, I agree," smiled Waldo. "However, it's just as well, perhaps, that Slingsby should slink off. He's lost all his power, and you've nothing further to fear, Lord Pengarth. I don't suppose I shall see you again, so I'll say good-bye. If I've been able to help you at all, I am glad!"

"You're a wonderful fellow!" declared Lord Pengarth firmly.

"Don't have any false impression; I'm only a crook, after all," said Waldo. "But if people think that all crooks are brutes and heartless curs, they're wrong. And now and again I like to prove it. That's all, Lord Pengarth. I must stick up for my profession sometimes, you know."

He slipped out of the room, leaving

---

his lordship staring. And outside, Waldo ran bang into the arms of Sexton Blake and Tinker.

"What, again?" chuckled the Wonder-Man. "We're always meeting, aren't we?"

"Great Scott!" ejaculated Tinker. "He's here again!"

"Can't get rid of me, can you?" grinned Waldo. "That's all right! I'm going for good now. Had to find out the latest news. So long, Blake! We'll meet again one of these fine days."

"I've no doubt we shall," said Sexton Blake.

Waldo was gone before they could follow his movements. He vanished into one of the dark corridors, and any attempt to chase him would be worse than futile.

The Wonder-Man got out of a window, climbed down the face of the building in the most reckless, haphazard fashion, and arrived on the terrace. He was feeling supremely happy.

Through him Pengarth was restored, and he was satisfied. It had been his whim to help the old peer in his trouble, and he had not left until his work was accomplished.

Wonderful Waldo!

A daring, relentless enemy, but a good friend, too. And his supreme happiness was not entirely due to his good work on Lord Pengarth's behalf.

He had not failed to obtain a few pickings for himself.

Reaching the end of the drive, he plunged into the dense bushes, and switched on a small torch. And there, hidden by the bracken, lay two or three small parcels.

But they weren't quite so valueless as they seemed.

Waldo opened the first one, and removed at least a dozen canvas bags. Each one was enormously heavy.

"Gold!" murmured Waldo, with satisfaction. "I am glad that Mr. Slingsby's a miser. This hoarding proclivity of his comes in very useful. It's a foolish thing to keep so much cash about the place. One of these days he'll be sorry for his carelessness. I haven't counted this money, but at a rough estimate, I reckon there's a thousand pounds in each bag."

He opened another parcel, and brought to light some neat, well-packed little bundles. And these proved to be Treasury-notes. They were tightly packed, and represented a big sum. Waldo stuffed them into his pockets, and chuckled while he was doing so.

"Ten thousand, at least," Waldo told himself. "Well, it's Slingsby's loss and my gain. So who cares? Ye gods! Was ever a man such a fool? To stuff his sardine-tin of a safe with bags of gold and bundles of notes! I wonder where I can find a few more misers? You can't get away from it, there's nothing so handy as ready money. It beats every other form of loot that I've ever known. And when you know you're robbing a pretty dirty kind of toad, it makes it all the sweeter!"

Waldo strolled out of the park, contented.

Upon the whole, he hadn't done so badly. He considered that his chance meeting with Lady Betty had borne excellent fruit. Everybody was pleased—everybody, that is, with the sole exception of Simon Slingsby.

But who cares a toss about the monetary misery of misers?

THE END.

WALDO AT WEMBLEY!
COMING SOON—LOOK out for it!

Captain Blood
by Rafael Sabatini

(Continued from page 2.)

Levasseur went back to the adoring lady.

Thither, too, the lady's brother was presently conducted. The captain rose to receive him, bending his stalwart height to avoid striking the cabin roof with his head. Mademoiselle rose, too.

"Why this?" she asked Levasseur, pointing to her brother's pinioned wrists —the remains of Cahusac's precautions.

"I deplore it," said he. "I desire it to end. Let M. d'Ogeron give me his parole——"

"I give you nothing!" flashed the white-faced youth, who did not lack for spirit.

"You see." Levasseur shrugged his deep regret; and Mademoiselle turned, protesting, to her brother.

"Henri, this is foolish! You are not behaving as my friend. You——"

"Little fool!" her brother answered her—and the "little" was out of place; she was the taller of the twain. "Little fool, do you think I should be acting as your friend to make terms with this blackguard pirate?"

"Steady, my young cockerel!" Levasseur laughed. But his laugh was not nice.

"Don't you perceive your wicked folly in the harm it has brought already? Lives have been lost—men have died— that this monster might overtake you. And don't you yet realise where you stand—in the power of this beast, of this cur, born in a kennel and bred in thieving and murder?"

He might have said more but, that Levasseur struck him across the mouth. Levasseur, you see, cared as little as another to hear the truth about himself.

Mademoiselle suppressed a scream, as the youth staggered back under the blow. He came to rest against a bulk-head, and leaned there with bleeding lips. But his spirit was unquenched, and there was a ghastly smile on his white face as his eyes sought his sister's.

"You see," he said simply. "He strikes a man whose hands are bound."

The simple words, and more than the words, their tone of ineffable disdain, aroused the passion that never slumbered deeply in Levasseur.

"And what should you do, puppy, if your hands were unbound?" He took his prisoner by the breast of his doublet and shook him. "Answer me! What should you do? Tchah! You empty windbag! You——" And then came a torrent of words unknown to Mademoiselle, yet of whose foulness her intuitions made her conscious.

With blanched cheeks she stood by the cabin table, and cried out to Levasseur to stop. To obey her, he opened the door, and flung her brother through it.

"Put that rubbish under hatches until I call for it again," he roared, and shut the door.

Composing himself, he turned to the girl again with a deprecatory smile. But no smile answered him from her set face. She had seen her beloved hero's nature in curl-papers, as it were, and she found the spectacle disgusting and terrifying.

It recalled the brutal slaughter of the Dutch captain, and suddenly she realised that what her brother had just said of this man was no more than true. Fear growing to panic was written on her face as she stood there leaning for support against the table.

"Why, sweetheart, what is this?" Levasseur moved towards her. She recoiled before him. There was a smile on his face, a glitter in his eyes that fetched her heart into her throat.

He caught her, as she reached the uttermost limits of the cabin, seized her in his long arms, and pulled her to him.

"No, no!" she panted.

"Yes, yes!" he mocked her, and his mockery was the most terrible thing of all. He crushed her to him brutally, deliberately hurtful because she resisted, and kissed her whilst she writhed in his embrace. Then, his passion mounting, he grew angry and stripped off the last rag of hero's mask that still may have hung upon his face.

"Little fool, did you not hear your brother say that you are in my power? Remember it, and remember that of your own free will you came! I am not the man with whom a woman can play fast and loose. So get sense, my girl, and accept what you have invited."

He kissed her again almost contemptuously, and flung her off.

"No more scowls," he said. "You'll be sorry else."

Someone knocked.

Cursing the interruption, Levasseur strode off to open. Cahusac stood before him. The Breton's face was grave. He came to report that they had sprung a leak between wind and water, the consequence of damage sustained from one of the Dutchman's shots.

In alarm Levasseur went off with him. The leakage was not serious so long as the weather kept fine; but should a storm overtake them it might speedily become so. A man was slung overboard to make a partial stoppage with a sail-cloth, and the pumps were got to work.

Ahead of them a low cloud showed on the horizon, which Cahusac pronounced one of the northernmost of the Virgin Islands.

"We must run for shelter there, and careen her," said Levasseur. "I do not trust this oppressive heat. A storm may catch us before we make land."

"A storm or something else," said Cahusac grimly. "Have you noticed that?" He pointed away to starboard. Levasseur looked, and caught his breath. Two ships that at the distance seemed of considerable burden were heading towards them some five miles away.

"If they follow us what is to happen?" demanded Cahusac.

"We'll fight, whether we're in case to do so or not!" swore Levasseur.

"Counsels of despair." Cahusac was contemptuous. To mark it he spat upon the deck. "This comes of going to sea with a lovesick madman. Now, keep your temper, captain, for the hands will

ANOTHER CONFEDERATION STORY!

Next week's yarn will carry us a stage farther in the exciting events that are taking place in the wilds of Santa Costa and the hinterland of its South American jungle.

Professor Reece's republic of crooks is a thing of the past. Sexton Blake has helped to win it back for the forces of law and order, and Reece himself has been captured and carried off by Fan Too, his Chinese rival for the presidentship of the Criminals' Confederation.

Nevertheless, Blake is after Reece also, and he will not swerve from his quest. Therefore, with his faithful little band he goes after him—

INTO THE UNKNOWN!

What strange adventures befall them there you don't know—yet! What you do know is that these tales of the Confederation mightily appeal to you, so get next week's issue, whatever else you leave undone!

If you're forgetful, cut this out and paste it in your hat!

be at the end of theirs if we have trouble as a result of this Dutchman business."

For the remainder of that day Levasseur's thoughts were of anything but love. He remained on deck, his eyes now upon the land, now upon those two slowly gaining ships.

To run for the open could avail him nothing, and in his leaky condition would provide an additional danger. He must stand at bay and fight. And then, towards evening, when within three miles of shore and when he was about to give the order to strip for battle, he almost fainted from relief to hear a voice from the crow's-nest above announce that the larger of the two ships was the Arabella. Her companion was presumably a prize.

But the pessimism of Cahusac abated nothing.

"That is but the lesser evil," he growled. "What will Blood say about this Dutchman?"

"Let him say what he pleases." Levasseur laughed in the immensity of his relief.

"And what about the children of the Governor of Tortuga?"

"He must not know."

"He'll come to know in the end."

"Ay, but by then, morbleu, the matter will be settled. I shall have made my peace with the governor. I tell you I know the way to compel Ogeron to come to terms."

Presently the four vessels lay to off the northern coast of La Virgen Magra, a narrow little island arid and treeless, some twelve miles by three, uninhabited save by birds and turtles, and unproductive of anything but salt, of which there were considerable ponds to the south.

Levasseur put off in a boat, accompanied by Cahusac and two other officers, and went to visit Captain Blood aboard the Arabella.

"Our brief separation has been mighty profitable," was Captain Blood's greeting. "It's a busy morning we've both had." He was in high good-humour as he led the way to the great cabin for a rendering of accounts.

The tall ship that accompanied the Arabella was a Spanish vessel of twenty-six guns, the Santiago, from Puerto Rico, with a hundred and twenty thousand weight of cacao, forty thousand pieces of eight, and the value of ten thousand more in jewels.

A rich capture, of which two-fifths, under the articles, went to Levasseur and his crew. Of the money and jewels a division was made on the spot. The cacao, it was agreed, should be taken to Tortuga to be sold.

Then it was the turn of Levasseur, and

black grew the brow of Captain Blood as the Frenchman's tale was unfolded. At the end he roundly expressed his disapproval.

The Dutch were a friendly people whom it was a folly to alienate, particularly for so paltry a matter as these hides and tobacco, which at most would fetch a bare twenty thousand pieces.

But Levasseur answered him, as he had answered Cahusac, that a ship was a ship, and it was ships they needed against their projected enterprise. Perhaps because things had gone well with him that day, Blood ended by shrugging the matter aside.

Thereupon Levasseur proposed that the Arabella and her prize should return to Tortuga, there to unload the cacao, and enlist the further adventurers that could now be shipped. Levasseur meanwhile would effect certain necessary repairs, and then, proceeding south, await his admiral at Saltatudos, an island conveniently situated in the latitude 11 deg. 11 min. north—for their enterprise against Maracaybo.

To Levasseur's relief, Captain Blood not only agreed, but pronounced himself ready to set sail at once.

No sooner had the Arabella departed than Levasseur brought his ships into the lagoon, and set his crew to work upon the erection of temporary quarters ashore for himself, his men, and his enforced guests during the careening and repairing of La Foudre.

At sunset that evening the wind freshened; it grew to a gale, and from that to such a hurricane that Levasseur was thankful to find himself ashore and his ships in safe shelter. He wondered

a little how it might be faring with Captain Blood out there at the mercy of that terrific storm; but he did not permit concern to trouble him unduly.

IN the glory of the following morning, sparkling and clear after the storm, with an invigorating briny tang in the air from the salt-ponds on the south of the island, a curious scene was played on the beach of the Virgen Magra, at the foot of a ridge of bleached dunes, beside the spread of sail from which Levasseur had improvised a tent.

The Ransom.

Enthroned upon an empty cask sat the French fili-buster to transact important business: the business of making himself safe with the Governor of Tortuga.

A guard of honour of a half-dozen officers hung about him; five of them were rude boucan-hunters, in stained jerkins and leather breeches; the sixth was Cahusac.

Before him, guarded by two half-naked negroes stood young d'Ogeron, in frilled shirt and satin small-clothes and fine shoes of Cordovan leather. He was stripped of doublet, and his hands were tied behind him.

The young gentleman's comely face was haggard. Near at hand, and also under guard, but unpinioned, Mademoiselle, his sister, sat hunched upon a hillock of sand. She was very pale, and it was in vain that she sought to veil in a mask of arrogance the fears by which she was assailed.

Levasseur addressed himself to M. d'Ogeron. He spoke at long length. In the end:

"I trust, monsieur," said he, with mock suavity, "that I have made myself quite clear. So that there may be no misunderstandings, I will recapitulate. Your ransom is fixed at twenty thousand pieces of eight, and you shall have liberty on parole to go to Tortuga to collect it.

"In fact, I shall provide the means to convey you thither, and you shall have a month in which to come and go. Meanwhile, your sister remains with me as a hostage. Your father should not consider such a sum excessive as the price of his son's liberty and to provide a dowry for his daughter. Indeed, if anything, I am too modest, pardi! M. d'Ogeron is reputed a wealthy man."

M. d'Ogeron the younger raised his head and looked the captain boldly in the face.

"I refuse—utterly and absolutely, do you understand? So do your worst and be hanged for a filthy pirate without decency and without honour."

"But what words!" laughed Levasseur. "What heat and what foolishness! You have not considered the alternative. When you do, you will not persist in your refusal. You will not do that in any case. We have spurs for the reluctant. And I warn you against giving me your parole under stress, and afterwards playing me false. I shall know how to find and punish you. Meanwhile, remember your sister's honour is in

Printed and published every Thursday by the Proprietors, The Amalgamated Press (1922), Ltd., The Fleetway House, Farringdon Street, London, E.C.4. Advertisement offices: The Fleetway House, Farringdon Street, London, E.C.4. Registered for transmission by Canadian Magazine Post. Subscription rates: Inland and Abroad, 11s. per annum; 5s. 6d. for six months. Sole agents for South Africa: The Central News Agency, Ltd. Sole agents for Australia and New Zealand: Messrs. Gordon & Gotch, Ltd.; and for Canada, The Imperial News Co., Ltd. (Canada).—Saturday, June 20th, 1925.

pawn to me. Should you forget to return with the dowry, you will not consider ·it· unreasonable that I forget to marry her."

Levasseur's smiling eyes, intent upon the young man's face, saw the horror that crept into his glance. M. d'Ogeron cast a wild glance at Mademoiselle, and observed the grey despair that had almost stamped the beauty from her face.

Disgust and fury swept ·across his countenance.

"No, you dog! A thousand times, no!"

"You are foolish to persist." Levasseur spoke without anger, with a coldly mocking regret. His fingers had been busy tying knots in a length of whipcord. He held it up.

"You know this? It is a ·rosary of pain that has wrought the conversion of many a stubborn ·heretic. It is capable of screwing the eyes out of a man's head by way of helping him to see reason. As you please."

He flung the length of knotted cord to one of the negroes, who in an instant made it fast about the prisoner's brows. Then between cord and cranium the black inserted a short length of metal, round and slender as a pipe-stem. That done he rolled his eyes towards Levasseur, awaiting the captain's signal.

Levasseur considered his victim, and beheld him tense and braced, his haggard face of a leaden hue, beads of perspiration glinting on his pallid brow just beneath the whipcord.

Mademoiselle cried out, and would have risen; but her guards restrained her, and she sank down again; moaning.

"I beg that you will spare yourself and your sister," said the captain, "by being reasonable. What after all is the sum I have named? To your wealthy father a bagatelle. I repeat, I have been too modest. But since I have said twenty thousand pieces of eight, twenty thousand pieces it shall be."

"And for what, if you please, have you said twenty thousand pieces of eight?"

In execrable French, but in a voice that was crisp and pleasant, seeming to echo some of the mockery that had invested Levasseur's, that question floated over their heads.

Startled, Levasseur and his officers looked up and round.

On the crest of the dunes behind them, in sharp silhouette against the deep cobalt of the sky, they beheld a tall, lean figure, scrupulously dressed in black with silver lace, a crimson ostrich plume curled about the broad brim of his hat affording the only touch of colour. Under that hat was the tawny face of Captain Blood.

Levasseur gathered himself up with an oath of amazement. He had conceived Captain Blood by now well below the horizon, on his way to Tortuga, assuming him to have been so fortunate as to have weathered last night's storm.

Launching himself upon the yielding sand, into which he sank to the level of the calves of his fine boots of Spanish leather, Captain Blood came sliding erect to the beach. He was followed by Wolverstone, and a dozen others. As he came to a standstill, he doffed his hat, with a flourish, to the lady. Then he turned to Levasseur.

"Good-morning, my captain," said he, and proceeded to explain his presence. "It was last night's hurricane compelled our return. We had no choice but to ride before it with stripped poles, and it drove us back the way we had gone. Moreover—as the devil would have it!—the Santiago sprang her mainmast; and

so I was glad to put into a cove on the west of the island a couple of miles away, and we've walked across to stretch our legs, and to give you good-day. But who are these?" And he designated the man and the woman.

Cahusac shrugged his shoulders, and tossed his long arms to heaven.

"Voila!" said he, pregnantly, to the firmament.

Levasseur gnawed his lip, and changed colour. But he controlled himself to answer civilly:

"As you see, two prisoners."

"Ah! Washed ashore in last night's gale, eh?"

"Not so." Levasseur contained himself with difficulty before that irony. "They were in the Dutch brig."

"I don't remember that you mentioned them before."

"I did not. They are prisoners of my own—a personal matter. They are French."

"French!" Captain Blood's light eyes stabbed at Levasseur, then at the prisoners.

M. d'Ogeron stood tense and braced as before, but the grey horror had left his face. Hope had leapt within him at this interruption, obviously as little expected by his tormentor as by himself. His sister, moved by a similar intuition, was leaning forward with parted lips and gaping eyes.

Captain Blood fingered his lip, and frowned thoughtfully upon Levasseur.

"Yesterday you surprised me by making war upon the friendly Dutch. But now it seems that not even your own countrymen are safe from you."

"Have I not said that these—that this is a matter personal to me?"

"Ah! And their names?"

Captain Blood's crisp, authoritative, faintly disdainful manner stirred Levasseur's quick anger. The blood crept slowly back into his blenched face, and his glance grew in insolence, almost in menace. Meanwhile, the prisoner answered for him.

"I am Henri d'Ogeron, and this is my sister."

"D'Ogeron?" Captain Blood stared. "Are you related by chance to my good friend the Governor of Tortuga?"

"He is my father."

Levasseur swung aside with an imprecation. In Captain Blood, amazement for the moment quenched every other emotion.

"The saints preserve us now! Are you quite mad, Levasseur? First, you molest the Dutch, who are our friends; next you take prisoners two persons that are French, your own countrymen; and now, faith, they're no less than the children of the Governor of Tortuga, which is the one safe place of shelter that we enjoy in these islands."

Levasseur broke in angrily.

"Must I tell you again that it is a matter personal to me? I make myself alone responsible to the Governor of Tortuga."

"And the twenty thousand pieces of eight? Is that also a matter personal to you?"

"It is."

"Now I don't agree with you at all." Captain Blood sat down on the cask that Levasseur had lately occupied, and looked up blandly. "I may inform you, to save time, that I heard the entire proposal that you made to this lady and this gentleman, and I'll also remind you that we sail under articles that admit no ambiguities. You have fixed their ransom at twenty thousand pieces of eight. That sum then belongs to your crews and mine in the proportions by the articles established. You'll hardly wish to dispute it. But what is far more

grave is that you have concealed from me this part of the prizes taken on your last cruise, and for such an offence as that the articles provide certain penalties that are something severe in character."

"Ho, ho!" laughed Levasseur unpleasantly. Then added: "If you dislike my conduct we can dissolve the association."

"That is my intention. But we'll dissolve it when and in the manner that I choose, and that will be as soon as you have satisfied the articles under which we sailed upon this cruise."

"What do you mean?"

"I'll be as short as I can," said Captain Blood. "I'll waive for the moment the unseemliness of making war upon the Dutch, of taking French prisoners, and of provoking the anger of the Governor of Tortuga. I'll accept the situation as I find it. Yourself you've fixed the ransom of this couple at twenty thousand pieces, and as I gather, the lady is to be your perquisite. But why should she be your perquisite more than another's, seeing that she belongs by the articles to all of us, as a prize of war?"

Black as thunder grew the brow of Levasseur.

"However," added Captain Blood, "I'll not dispute her to you if you are prepared to buy her."

"Buy her?"

"At the price you have set upon her."

Levasseur contained his rage, that he might reason with the Irishman.

"That is the ransom of the man. It is to be paid for him by the Governor of Tortuga."

"No, no. Ye've parcelled the twain together—very oddly, I confess. Ye've set their value at twenty thousand pieces, and for that sum you may have them, since you desire it; but you'll pay for them the twenty thousand pieces that are ultimately to come to you as the ransom of one and the dowry of the other; and that sum shall be divided among our crews. So that you do that, it is conceivable that our followers may take a lenient view of your breach of the articles we jointly signed."

Levasseur laughed savagely.

"Ah ca! Credieu! The good jest!"

"I quite agree with you," said Captain Blood.

To Levasseur the jest lay in that Captain Blood, with no more than a dozen followers, should come there, attempting to hector him who had a hundred men within easy call. But it seemed that he had left out of his reckoning something which his opponent had counted in. For as, laughing still, Levasseur swung to his officers, he saw that which choked the laughter in his throat.

Captain Blood had shrewdly played upon the cupidity that was the paramount inspiration of those adventurers. And Levasseur now read clearly on their faces how completely they adopted Captain Blood's suggestion that all must participate in the ransom which their leader had thought to appropriate to himself.

It gave the gaudy ruffian pause, and whilst in his heart he cursed those followers of his, who could be faithful only to their greed, he perceived—and only just in time—that he had best tread warily.

"You misunderstand," he said, swallowing his rage. "The ransom is for division, when it comes. The girl, meanwhile, is mine on that understanding."

"Good!" grunted Cahusac. "On that understanding all arranges itself."

"You think so?" said Captain Blood. "But if M. d'Ogeron should refuse to pay the ransom? What then?" He laughed, and got lazily to his feet. "No, no. If Captain Levasseur is meanwhile to keep the girl as he proposes, then let him pay this ransom, and be his the risk if it should afterwards not be forthcoming."

"That's it," cried one of Levasseur's officers.

And Cahusac added:

"It's reasonable, that! Captain Blood is right. It is in the articles."

"What is in the articles, you fools?" Levasseur was in danger of losing his head. "Sacre Dieu! Where do you suppose that I have twenty thousand pieces? My whole share of the prizes of this cruise does not come to half that sum. I'll be your debtor until I've earned it. Will that content you?"

All things considered, there is not a doubt that it would have done so, had not Captain Blood intended otherwise.

"And if you should die before you have earned it? Ours is a calling fraught with risks, my captain."

"Curse you!" Levasseur flung upon him livid with fury. "Will nothing satisfy you?"

"Oh, but yes. Twenty thousand pieces of eight for immediate division."

"I haven't got it."

"Then let someone buy the prisoners who has."

"And who do you suppose has it if I have not?"

"I have," said Captain Blood.

"You have!" Levasseur's mouth fell open. "You—you want the girl?"

"Why not? And I exceed you in gallantry in that I will make sacrifices to obtain her, and in honesty in that I am ready to pay for what I want."

Levasseur stared at him foolishly agape. Behind him pressed his officers, gaping also.

Captain Blood sat down again on the cask, and drew from an inner pocket of his doublet a little leather bag.

"I am glad to be able to resolve a difficulty that at one moment seemed insoluble." And under the bulging eyes of Levasseur and his officers, he untied the mouth of the bag and rolled into his left palm four or five pearls each of the size of a sparrow's egg. There were twenty such in the bag, the very pick of those taken in that raid upon the pearl fleet. "You boast a knowledge of pearls, Cahusac. At what do you value this?"

The Breton took between coarse finger and thumb the proffered lustrous, delicately iridescent sphere, his shrewd eyes appraising it.

"A thousand pieces," he answered shortly.

"It will fetch rather more in Tortuga or Jamaica," said Captain Blood, "and twice as much in Europe. But I'll accept your valuation. They are almost of a size, as you can see. Here are twelve, representing twelve thousand pieces of eight, which is La Foudre's share of three-fifths of the prize, as provided by the articles. For the eight thousand pieces that go to the Arabella, I make myself responsible to my own men. And now, Wolverstone, if you please, will you take my property aboard the Arabella." He stood up again, indicating the prisoners.

"Ah, no!" Levasseur threw wide the floodgates of his fury. "Ah, that no, by example! You shall not take her."

He would have sprung upon Captain Blood, who stood aloof, alert, tightlipped, and watchful. But it was one of Levasseur's own officers who hindered him.

(Next week—The Duel for Mlle d'Ogeron, and its consequences. This story is getting more fascinating every week—don't you think so?)